ENSICKLOPEDIA

A Collection of Horror from Matt Shaw

MATT SHAW

This book contains a selection of Matt Shaw's work previously available on
Kindle:
Tortured
Clown
A House in the Country
Control
Reminiscing
Laughter in the Night
The Cabin
The Cabin: 'Asylum'
The 8TH

The following foreword was written for "Carnage: Extreme Horror":

"The 3 types of terror: The Gross-out: the sight of a severed head tumbling down a flight of stairs, it's when the lights go out and something green and slimy splatters against your arm. The Horror: the unnatural, spiders the size of bears, the dead waking up and walking around, it's when the lights go out and something with claws grabs you by the arm. And the last and worse one: Terror, when you come home and notice everything you own had been taken away and replaced by an exact substitute. It's when the lights go out and you feel something behind you, you hear it, you feel its breath against your ear, but when you turn around, there's nothing there..." - Stephen King

Last year, when I was still working hard to carve myself a name in the over-saturated genre that is horror, I wrote a particular book which not only worried me in terms of its content, but also does not fit in with the three types of terror mentioned by Mr King. And that is the horrors the world is faced with on a day to day basis; people coming home to find an intruder in their home with ill intentions, muggings on the street or even - in the case of my novella The 8TH - a college boy taking a violent and sadistic (some might argue 'justified') revenge on those who have tormented him over the years.

I loved the story and the way it was told - it could be argued that I was biased though -but I was worried about how the public would react to it due to the graphic content and the fact it could be deemed a little 'too real'. In fact

I was so worried that before I released it, I dropped a message asking people on my Facebook page whether there was such a thing as 'too far' when it came to horror. More specifically, I asked whether there was anything that we - as authors of horror - should avoid in terms of what we write.

The answer was pretty unanimous. 90% of the people who replied to such the post said there was no such thing as 'too far' when it came to the horror they read. They further explained that they wanted authors to push boundaries and take things further than they were comfortable with. Even the readers who did state you could go too far agreed that boundaries needed to be pushed, but not in the direction of animals. They were fine with everything else but - under no circumstances - could you kill the kitten. Maiming it was, apparently, fine but…Not allowed to kill them.

Still apprehensive I went ahead and released The 8TH on their say so. I sat back and patiently waited for the first of the reviews to come in and - when they did - I was pleased to see how positive they were.

Moving forward to today, The 8TH remains one of my most highly reviewed books stating that - whilst it was extreme in places - the message was not only positive but also strong. Now, here is where my brain gets weird. Before the reviews came in, I was stressing that people would not enjoy the book and that it would alienate my other works because they would be tarred with the same 'inappropriate' label attached to The 8TH, but when the positive reviews came in, I was a little bit disheartened that my level of 'extreme' horror did not sicken hardcore horror authors.

Whilst my work has always been on the dark side (with the exception of The Missing Years of Thomas Pritchard and Heaven's Calling) it is fair to say that it got that little bit darker after The 8TH. With each successive work I wanted to not only give the readers a story they would enjoy but also present them with scenarios they would not be able to shake from their minds and - for me - the best way of achieving this was to wrap it all up in horror centered around the 'every day' and - more importantly - to make it as extreme as possible.

And so - a few months later - my Extreme Horrors came to be. A mixture of 'gross-out' and 'everyday' horror, I started with a tale of incest and cannibalism in the form of Sick Bastards before moving to Tortured (the story of a man and his family impacted by the recent serial killings of a tor-turer) and my sick revenge story PORN, which takes the gross-out horror found in an everyday situation to a whole new level of grim.

The only Extreme Horror book I released which has any element of Stephen Kings second type of terror (the unnatural) being a pleasant title called Rotting Dead F*cks and - even then - the story follows the survi-vors of a zombie apocalypse as opposed to really focusing on the undead, which has been done a million times in a million other books. Even my next Extreme Horror is focused on the horrors we find in the real world in the form of a psychopath struggling with his obvious mental illness.

I am happy with how these Extreme Horrors are being received and I found myself a little niche market for them. Many reviews are positive and the ones which are not are mainly negative because the reader could not stomach the book, but even that - to me - is a successful review and a sign I have written the book well. Do not get me wrong - there are also some reviews which state my work is tame and badly written but that is fine; I will get those readers with the next story if they ever opt to give my work another go (and I hope they will for I like a challenge).

Going from the reaction to these books, compared to my others, it is fair to say that - so long as there is a good, solid story for the reader to engage in - when it comes to horror - there really is no such thing as 'too far'. I will continue trying to push the boundaries and take the readers to places they may feel uncomfortable but - in the meantime - I would like to present this anthology to you. A book filled with extreme horror stories from some great names in horror - all of whom hoping they can push you to your very limits and haunt your nightmares for years to come.

- Matt Shaw

Tortured

MATT SHAW

CHAPTER 1

I opened my scrapbook up. Pages filled with photographs taken; the different stages of the sessions with my victims - not forgetting the 'before' picture. A photograph of them before I've laid a finger on them. I like the before and after pictures. I like to see the state they end up in. Makes me smile. When I start my sessions, I usually start with the fingernails. A pair of pliers gripped firmly to the end of them - if you pull hard enough they usually rip out with relative ease, but much pain and blood. Better yet, tug upwards when you pull and take skin off too. Of course, the person screams. They all do. The screams fill my heart with a healthy satisfaction as I drop the nails, one by one, onto the concrete floor of the cellar. They can scream as much as they want; no one is coming. No one ever comes. I stand back with a smile on my face and watch the person's reaction. Their eyes are wide with fear and their mouth opens as wide as it can go as the scream continues to echo around the room. I like how wide their eyes go. I like that they don't close them. They keep focused on what is happening to them. And just to make sure they remain so - the eyelids are next. Pliers are swapped for scissors.

⚔

As the sun slowly started to rise in the morning sky, the car backed into the driveway so the boot was facing the garage. Less distance to carry the bags from car to house that way. Ryan shut the engine off and ran his hand through his dark hair before undoing his seat belt and stretching his back. A satisfying click from his spine.

"You okay?" asked his wife, Dee. She wasn't even looking at him. She was resting her head against the top of her seat belt - a makeshift pillow on which to doze whilst Ryan did the driving. She turned to him. Her blue eyes looked red from how tired she was and her blonde hair, a mess from where she'd rested her head.

"I thought you were asleep," he said as he yawned.

"Was trying." She caught his yawn and mirrored it.

"See, some people didn't have much difficulty," he looked in the rear-view mirror towards the back of the car where his daughters were sleeping. Jen (the youngest at ten years old and with her mother's looks and colourings) was sitting behind Dee with her mouth wide open. A small bit of dribble on her chin. "Shame the phone's not charged. Could have taken a picture," Ryan laughed.

Dee turned to see her daughters. "Don't be cruel. Besides you'll be wishing they were still asleep in an hour or two." She looked across to Claire - the oldest at seventeen years. Unlike the blonde hair shared by her sister and mother, Claire was dark like her father. Her eyes too. Neither parent knew where the light freckles on her cheeks came from.

"That's a point. Maybe we could leave them be? I'm pretty tired but I still reckon we could christen the new bedroom." Ryan winked at Dee who just laughed. "It seems morning glory is…"

"Are we there yet?" a small voice piped up from the back of the car. Jen. Ryan looked at her via the rear-view mirror. She was rubbing her eyes, helping to clear her foggy vision.

"Damn," Ryan muttered.

Dee smacked him on the leg, "Stop it!" She paused, "Yes we are, honey." She turned in her seat to see her youngest daughter. She smiled at her, "You ready to see your new bedroom?" she asked.

Jen didn't say anything. She just smiled at her mother. It wasn't a real smile though. It was a smile, which simply said 'if I must'. Claire, who was slowly starting to stir, had the same feelings as her sister. Neither of them wanted to move from their home. More importantly, neither of them wanted to move from their schools and their friends. The prospect of making new friends in a new school, as put forward by their mother when their father explained they had to move home, didn't fill them with confidence. Nor did it answer their questions as to why they had to move in the first place. Both of them liked it there. The reasons why they moved weren't divulged to the children. Not the real reasons at least. That was strictly between mother and father. After all - no child wants to hear their family is broke. Ryan and Dee Knew that, if they didn't move, then it would only be a matter of time before they were bankrupt and they'd lose their house. Moving into a smaller home, slightly further from the middle of the city where prices were higher meant they'd be able to keep their finances in control and stay on top of things in general. Not that their finances were spiralling through any fault of their own. Ryan had taken a pay cut in his job at the bank (it was this or redundancy and he didn't fancy that) and Dee's school-teaching job never paid her a great deal of money. Dee's lower income and Ryan's sudden pay cut meant they were soon living beyond their means.

"What do you think?" Ryan asked Claire. He was referring to the house. The girls had seen pictures of the property but neither had seen it in the flesh (so to speak). The decision of where they should live had been taken away from them. Even Dee didn't have much say as to where they went. This was all down to Ryan - not that she didn't trust him to make the right choice for them. Besides which, he'd said the move was temporary. He promised they'd soon be back to the standards they were used to, and back in another home.

"It's small." Claire said. She undid her seat belt and climbed from the car before anyone could say anything. She slammed the car door shut.

Ryan nervously turned to Dee, "What about you?" he asked. "What do you think?"

"We'll make it our home," she gave him a reassuring smile and followed her daughter from the car. Once Jen had followed her mother, Ryan was sitting in the car alone.

"It's not that bad," he muttered to himself. And it wasn't that bad either. Certainly the best of what was available to them in the price range afforded. He climbed from the car.

CHAPTER 2

I carried on reminiscing as I flicked through the pages. Sometimes they'd pass out whilst I worked on them. My specimens. It frustrated me to begin with, but I soon learnt to control my lack of patience. In the end, I think of it as a blessing - when their head drops forward and they lose consciousness. It means the whole experience lasts longer. I don't work on them whilst they're out cold. I'd miss their screams too much. I'd miss the smell of fear coming from their bodies. So I wait. As long as it takes. And then - when they're awake - I take things slowly. Perhaps start at the toes. The big toe to be more precise. Snap it first. The satisfying crack of bone splintering and the feeling of it of happening in my hands. A simple but effective procedure; you take the large toe in your left hand and grip the rest of the foot with your right hand. And then a sharp tug with the left hand, away from the rest of the foot. Might take a couple of tugs but, they always crack eventually. Satisfaction with more screams ensured. Only once all toes are broken do you go for the garden shears. One at a time, take the little piggies to market. Take a necessary break should the person pass out.

The online shopping, ordered before the Internet was cut off in their last home, arrived before the removal men's promised time of delivery. One company was early and the second was late - typical considering it meant the foods necessary for refrigeration had the potential to spoil and even more frustrating for Dee, who could have sworn she put in the following day for the shopping's delivery. She walked the bags through to the kitchen where she piled them in one of the empty corners - out of the way of the impending delivery men.

"Milk, sugar, tea bags…No kettle. Good start," she muttered to herself as she brought the last bag in - walking past her husband who was pacing the hallway on his mobile phone, waiting for the delivery men to pick up. "Any joy?" she asked as she walked back down the hallway to close the front door.

"It's just ringing - not even going through to an answering machine." It was nine o'clock. The delivery men were supposed to arrive at eight; half an hour after the tired family pulled into the driveway (good timing Ryan initially believed). Dee knew she couldn't say anything to alleviate any of Ryan's stress so she just put her arms around him and gave him a loving hug. He hugged her back with one arm with the phone still pressed to his ear as he hit re-dial on the touch screen. "Shouldn't have paid them upfront. Once they have your money they don't care. Should have done half at the start and the rest on completion," he moaned. Dee hugged him tighter. Before either of them had a chance to break away from their comforting embrace there was a knock at the door. Ryan was first to pull away, "About time!" he said - clearly still irritated they were running late without at least giving the family some notice. After all, moving house was stressful enough. They didn't need poorly run second rate companies adding to their stresses.

"Be nice," Dee warned her husband as he walked to the door. She knew what his temper was like when he was irritated. Fair enough; it took him a while to get to that stage but once he was there - he'd be there for the rest of the day, and would become extremely snappy to anyone and anything. The last thing she wanted was for him to upset the removal men before they offloaded their furniture.

"Oh, sorry, we seemed to have dropped your television along with the box which said fragile," she could hear it now.

"I'm always nice!" said Ryan as he opened the door with the best 'fake' smile he could muster. His smile nearly faded when he realised it wasn't the removal men knocking on the door. Instead, standing before him, was a middle-aged woman and her younger daughter. "Oh, hello, sorry - I thought you were someone else."

"We're not intruding, are we?"

Before Ryan had a chance to answer the woman's question (an answer Dee feared would be inappropriate), Dee stepped into view next to him to take over the conversation, "Hi, what can we do for you?" she asked. Now it was her turn to forge a smile for the strangers. Travelling all night and fretting about where your furniture had gotten to didn't make you very sociable when people came knocking at your door uninvited, but Dee knew first impressions count. She just hoped they were neighbours - as she believed - and not trying to sell something.

"Sorry - we didn't mean to intrude - it's just we saw your car in the driveway and wanted to come and say hello. We live next door, number thirty-six...I'm Jackie and this is my daughter Kara." A nice enough looking mother and daughter. Both had strawberry blonde hair. Jackie was a plump woman in her mid-forties, and her daughter, who looked similar to age as Jen, was starting to shape up the same way.

"Please to meet you," Dee extended her hand and the two mothers shook. Ryan did the same as soon as they'd broken their handshake. "I'm Dee and this is my husband Ryan."

"My husband Mike had to go to work, but he said to say hello. Listen - I'll leave you two to it as you've probably got lots to do, what with moving and all, but I just wanted to see if you fancied coming over to ours for dinner tomorrow?"

"Sure - that would be lovely. Thank you," said Dee - unable to think of a valid excuse not to go.

"That's great. What with modern technology these days, people rarely venture out of their house so we thought we'd make an effort. Shall we say about eight? Shepherd's Pie okay?"

"Sounds perfect," said Dee. She was about to say goodbye and close the door when her neighbour spotted something behind her.

"Oh hello, what's your name then?" she asked.

Dee turned around and saw Jen and Claire standing at the top of the stairs.

"They're my daughters - Jen and Claire."

"Well, bring them too…" Jackie turned to Kara and said, "Don't be rude - say hello."

Kara wasn't as outspoken as her mother and only managed a wave. A wave mirrored by Jen. Claire being Claire simply disappeared around the corner of the landing and back into whatever bedroom she'd chosen for herself - even though she wasn't going to get final say in the bedrooms like she believed she would.

"Sorry about that," Dee was referring to her eldest daughter's lack of manners, "she's still sulking that we took her away from her friends."

"Honestly - it's not a problem. No need to apologise. Listen, if you want, your youngest can come over and play round ours. Be nice for the two girls to get to know each other before school starts in a couple of weeks."

Both Dee and Ryan could sense, from the top of the stairs, their daughter wasn't keen on the idea of being forced to make friends. Especially given the fact the other girl seemed just as uninterested in the idea.

"To be honest we're pretty busy with…"

"That's fine - say no more - we will leave you to it. Don't forget our date tomorrow evening; the whole family! And if you need anything while you're unpacking, you know where we are!"

"Thank you again. It was lovely to meet you."

"See you tomorrow, if not before!" said Jackie as she turned down the driveway with her daughter in tow. "Well they seem nice," she said to her daughter as she reached the end of the drive. Ryan gently pushed his wife to one side and closed the door quickly, before the woman had a chance to turn back around with something else to say.

"She's friendly," Dee laughed. "And dinner tomorrow. Sounds lovely," the sarcasm oozed from her voice.

"What? You couldn't think of an excuse quick enough to get us out of it? Busy? Unpacking? Rather watch paint dry?"

"Don't be like that - she was right, people rarely make the effort any-more. It's nice she is."

"I just can't believe it...Every village has an idiot and we just happened to move next door to it," said Ryan - still grumpy from the lack of delivery men on his doorstep.

"Don't be horrible. She's fine. Probably just nervous." She turned from the door and noticed Jen was still sitting on the top stair. She looked upset, despite there being no tears. "What's wrong?" Dee asked.

"She took my bedroom," Jen moaned. She was referring to Claire who'd decided upon taking the biggest room for herself.

Dee sighed, "Let's sort the bedrooms out, shall we?" she asked her husband. He walked off down the hallway and towards the kitchen.

"That's your area," he laughed, "I'm dealing with the removal men..."

CHAPTER 3

A picture of their face. No lips. I smiled and licked my own lips. I don't take their lips off immediately. Not until toes are broken and cut off, nails removed, eye-lids taken, nose cut off - sometimes that's all I'll do. And sometimes I'll do more. It all really depends on the mood. But I always take the lips. I'm not sure why. Just seems like the right thing to do. The other bits I've removed - I leave those for people to find. Usually in a quiet back road but not so quiet people won't find them. I want them to be found. I need them to be found. Mangled body next to a cardboard box with the bits I cut off. But not the lips. The lips are in another box. Dozens and dozens of them - all mixed up. Can't put them with the owner anymore. Can't even put them in the right pairs. Sometimes I like to open the box. I like to open the box, take a pair of lips out (be they mixed or the correct matchings) and... Well...I love taking the lips off. Scissors are the tools of the trade. Or a sharp knife. Truth be told it doesn't matter which. I pull their lips away - bottom one first because it's not as painful as the top. Blade to one side and slice across in a hacking motion (if using a knife) or - snip - with scissors. Blood. So much blood. And funny screams. Have you ever tried screaming with no lips? The sounds aren't as satisfying as the screams of a person with full lips.

✦

"I just don't see why we need to take something round their house when they invited us," Ryan moaned as he and Dee crossed their garden on the way to their neighbour's house. The kids followed slowly behind - neither of them looking forward to having to eat around a stranger's place Although - in truth - their mum and dad were just as reluctant to go around.

"It's the done thing to do. They invite you and you take a bottle around. It's one bottle." She stopped - causing Ryan to also stop, "Are you going to be miserable all night?"

"We've got so much to do to get the house in shape. We could really do with…"

"And we've done so much already. A night off will be nice." Dee started walking again. Ryan followed.

He shrugged towards his children,' I tried kids."

"And don't encourage them to play up more than they already are," Dee continued to berate Ryan as they got to their neighbour's front door. She gave Ryan a stern look before she knocked.

"We don't have to stay for pudding do we?" Ryan asked as they listened to the footsteps walking towards the front door. Claire tried her best to hide the fact she found her father's comment funny. Dee answered him with a look.

The front door opened inwardly. Jackie was standing there with a smile on her face, which made Ryan think of the Stepford Wives. He tried to shake the image from his mind as she greeted them.

"This is my husband Mike," she said.

"Please to meet you," said Mike as he extended his hand to his new neighbours. "Please come in. Make yourself at home."

"Thank you," said Dee.

"Here - this is for you," said Ryan who'd gone from irritating his wife to a being a polite neighbour. He held out the bottle of wine he'd brought.

"You shouldn't have," said Jackie as she gracefully accepted it. "We'll open it with dinner!" She turned to the girls Claire and Jen, "Dinner's going to be about twenty minutes. The kids are in their bedroom. Just pop on up there and say hello! I did call them down but clearly they'd rather be rude."

Claire went to say something, but was immediately shot down by a stern look from her mother. She rolled her eyes and led Jen towards the stairs. Jackie led her adult visitors through to the lounge.

"So how'd the move go?" asked Mike, "Finished unpacking yet?"

"Lots to do!" said Ryan. "Didn't help that the removal men were late… Three hours in the end with no warning or anything. Didn't even have the decency to answer their mobiles when I tried calling."

"Don't you just hate that?" Mike agreed.

"Oh please don't encourage him," Dee sighed.

"Perhaps it was a mistake getting these two together," Jackie laughed.

"No. If someone says they're going to do something, or be somewhere - if they're suddenly not able to make it…It's common decency to inform the people who are waiting for them," Mike sided with Ryan.

"Exactly!" Ryan agreed.

"I'm going to check on the dinner," said Jackie. She turned to Dee, "Want to come through to the kitchen with me? Leave them to their moaning?"

"Definitely." Dee gave Ryan a little wave as she walked through to the kitchen with Jackie. "You said the girls were upstairs. How many children do you have?"

"Two. One girl and one boy. Kara is eleven years old - the youngest - and her brother Thomas. Thomas is seventeen going on thirty. In fact, I'm surprised he's still here. He told me he was moving out this morning." In the kitchen Jackie put the wine onto the side, next to the cooker and glasses she'd already pulled from the cupboard."

"Sounds like my daughter. Although she hasn't said she's moving out. Not recently anyway. I think the last time we got that line was when we said we were moving from the city," Dee laughed. She laughed now but at the time she remembered it was a stressful argument - one which resulted in tears, tantrums and Claire's bedroom door being slammed shut. "She's probably up there now telling your son what bad parents we are."

☒

Jen and Kara were in Kara's bedroom whilst Claire was in Thomas' room, sitting on his computer desk thumbing through his music collection which sat on the shelf above his large monitor. Thomas, a tall lad with dark scruffy hair, was lying on his bed with a book in his hands.

"So is there anything fun to do around here?" Claire asked.

"Depends on your definition of fun."

"I don't know. What do you do for fun?"

Thomas held his book up. "Read? There's a library. Not the biggest, but it has a good collection."

Claire rolled her eyes. "I was thinking about clubs." She held up a CD, "Somewhere to listen to music? Dance? Get drunk?" She put the CD back on the shelf, "Maybe not to that one though. Did you steal that from your dad?"

Thomas climbed from the bed and walked over to Claire. He leaned across her and looked at the CD she'd just put back. "Pink Floyd?"

"Dated much?"

"Classic." He paused a moment, "Let me guess - you're more into boy bands. Cheesy little pop tunes?"

"Fuck off."

"I'm right, aren't I? Who is it? Westlife? Boyzone? One Direction?" he laughed as he returned to where he was previously lying on the bed.

"You're an idiot," Claire turned back to the rest of the 'dated' music collection. "So basically the only thing you class as decent around here is the library?"

"Yep."

Claire sighed heavily.

"I'm guessing you're not happy about moving here?" Thomas asked. He didn't really care. Truth be told he'd sooner sit and read his book in silence but it was obvious Claire wasn't about to go downstairs and leave him in peace. He figured he might as well make an effort. Besides - she was easy on the eye at least. And the first girl who'd spoken to him without it being part of a bet.

"Yeah. I love being pulled from my school and taken away from my friends, forced to move miles away and then wedged into a tiny room. I'm actually having a blast. You couldn't tell?"

"You like sarcasm, don't you?"

"No. You think?"

Thomas smiled at her, "At least you'll have no trouble making new friends at school." He picked his book up again and thumbed his way through to the page he was previously on. He wasn't being sarcastic with his statement. He knew she'd get on fine at the school. All the girls had a sarcastic streak about them. A nasty one at that. She'd fit in all right.

"Dinner's ready! Get down here!" Mike called up the stairs. His voice started off strongly before fading as he walked through to the dining room where Jackie was dishing up the meals from the large pot she'd cooked the Shepherd's pie in.

Claire stood up and left the bedroom, without waiting for Thomas, "Least it's one step closer to going home…"

Thomas put his book down and called out to Claire as she walked across the landing and towards the stairs, "But seriously - thank you for coming. Made my evening really pleasant. Thanks." He rolled off the bed and followed.

CHAPTER 4

One of my earlier pictures fell from my scrapbook and landed in my lap. Needs more glue. I looked at the photo before sliding it back between the pages. Definitely one of the earlier pieces. No skin. The first time I tortured someone I tried to take their skin off. I wanted to do it in one. I wanted to make a suit. I'd heard of other people - like me - who've made them in the past. Had I managed to make one, I wouldn't have worn it. I wouldn't have dressed up as my victim; a morbid fancy dress costume. I would have displayed it on my wall. A trophy. Just as a hunter may display the head of a recently killed animal, I'd do the same with the skin. Never managed it through. The cuts would start off as good, full pieces of flesh but would get thinner the further down the body I went before eventually tearing off in my hand. Most frustrating. Disappointing. On the fourth person I gave up trying - and that's when I started to take the lips. I closed the scrapbook up and turned in my chair, to the lady behind me. A pretty (untouched) blonde girl, bound to a metal office chair, which had been stripped of any comfort. I smiled at her. Enough reminiscing. Need to get to work.

By the fourth day everything was more or less put in its rightful home. The cupboards were full of food and everything had its place. All that needed to be done was a quick run to the tip to get rid of the many cardboard boxes which had been used in the moving process and that'd now served their purpose (some left in better shapes than others which had clearly been over packed). The tip run would wait until the weekend, though. Dee and Ryan only had the one car between them having been forced to sell the second vehicle in an effort to cut back unnecessary expenses. It wasn't that big an issue - Dee's school was fairly close to the bank where Ryan worked so it just meant she'd drop him off on the way through and then collect him when he'd finish later in the day. She usually finished before him so it gave her a little time to pop to the shops if need be before having to collect him. That being said - today Ryan was driving himself to work. The schools were still shut for the holidays and so there was no need for Dee to go out and about. If she'd needed to venture out she would have done so - it just meant she'd have to get up earlier than she might have planned in order to take Ryan to the bank but at least that meant she had the day free to do as she pleased. Today was all about nesting though. Move the final few bits and pieces, tidy the house up and sit back with a cup of tea in hand whilst she stared at the walls wondering what colour she'd eventually like to paint them in an effort to put her own stamp on the building. Ryan had said the walls were fine as they were, but they weren't and he knew this. He just didn't want to get involved with any of the decorating - a task he hated more than anything else.

"Might start looking at colour charts," said Dee over the breakfast table when Ryan asked what she was planning to do with her day. "Don't worry - I won't ask you to look at them," she continued when she saw his face drop. Despite her words of reassurance Ryan knew, at some point, he'd be forced to look at them. "And before you say it I know we don't have the money to do it yet - just like to look at them."

"I want to paint my bedroom black." Claire piped up. Definitely the family teenager.

"You're not painting your bedroom black," Dee turned to her.

"And I want a pink room like Kara's!" Jen shouted with a mouthful of toast.

"Don't talk with your mouthful."

"I want a pink room," Jen repeated having swallowed the toast.

"No one is changing anything," Ryan put his foot down. He took another sip from his cup of tea. "Everything is fine as it is. Let's just settle in first, yeah? And - besides - as your mother pointed out, we don't have the finances to do any decorating yet."

Claire huffed. "You said I could decorate my room this year!" It was true, Dee had told Claire she could decorate. But that was before the pay cut and before they moved house. That was back when they weren't struggling as much. A time when Ryan simply did his best to hide the financial strains the family was facing in a hope they'd turn around before they'd have an impact on the way he - and his family - lived.

"I like Kara's room. It's pretty."

Ryan stood up and walked his cup over to the sink. He took another mouthful and tipped the remainder down the plug-hole. "I have to go." Dee got up and kissed him on the cheek. She knew he still had another ten minutes before he had to leave but could sense his rising tension. The stress of the move, the stress of money and the worry of what was happening at work was clearly getting to him. He did his best to hide it but she'd been married to him for a while now (and they'd been dating a lot longer before that) and she could tell when he was struggling with his moods. "You sure you don't need the car today?"

"No, it's fine. Try and have a good day. Everything will be fine." He smiled at her. Not because her words hit home with him but more so because he could tell she was trying to cheer him up. "I love you," she said.

"I love you."

"Gross."

They both turned to Claire. She was staring into her breakfast bowl. They ignored her and turned back to each other.

"If you need anything just give me a ring," said Ryan. He gave Dee a kiss and turned from the kitchen and down the hallway. Dee followed him to the front door where he put on his suit jacket.

"Try and have a good day," she repeated. He just smiled at her again. "Girls are you going to say goodbye to your father?" she called into the kitchen.

"Bye!" both girls shouted.

"I'm sure they'll miss you," Dee laughed. Ryan just raised his eyebrows as if to say 'yeah, right'. He opened the front door and stepped into the brilliant sunshine. "Might get in the garden actually," Dee teased, "do a spot of reading in a sun spot."

"Fuck you!" Ryan laughed. He hated having to go to work when she got to stay at home. Sure she had school work to complete during the long summer holidays but working from home was so much better than having to actually go into the school. It was the same every summer too. He'd book a week off to spend it with the family and the girls (including his wife) would have six weeks off! Worse yet (for Ryan) was that Dee insisted they all did their work in the first week in order to get it out of the way so they could all enjoy their holiday before the next term started. Ryan climbed into his car and closed the door. The start of a hot day. No air conditioning in the car and no air conditioning in the bank. He sighed. "One day I'll be rich and I'll get to retire and do nothing," he sighed again. "Yeah and pigs might fly."

"Bye!" Dee waved from the front door.

Ryan waved back, slammed the car in reverse, and backed out of the driveway. Usually he felt good when he'd had any time off work. He felt as though his batteries had been nicely recharged. Not now, though. This time he just felt tired and he was kicking himself for not booking off two weeks to move. At least he could have put his feet up on the second week - enjoyed some quiet time before going back in. Too late to think about that now, he thought, as he set off to the bank hoping that it would, at least, be a quiet day.

CHAPTER 5

It is estimated that presently there are between twenty-five and eighty-six active serial killers in the United States of America. I'm not sure who made the numbers up and I'm not sure whether it's the same in the United Kingdom. Surely it has to be less because the population is smaller. I hope it's less. I don't like the idea of people like me being out there. Not because I live in fear of them but, because I don't like the idea of others trying to outdo what I do. I want to be one of a kind. I want to be the only one. I put the other possible killers from my mind and turn to my latest plaything. A pretty brunette girl I picked up late one night. She was on the way home from a club - walking alone. Staggering from the amount of alcohol she'd consumed. Easy pickings. I smiled at her and bent down to where she was sitting in order to address her. She squirmed against the restraints which kept her bound to the old chair - the same chair I've used for all of my victims. The only piece of furniture in my old cellar.

"I'm going to remove the gag," I told her in a hushed voice. There was no reason for the whisper. I'm not sure why I did it with her - or the other girls I've had down here (always girls). "Do not misunderstand me," I continued, "I'm not inviting a conversation. I'm not going to let you go. You're going to die down here. I just want to hear your screams."

⊁

Ryan knew there was a problem at the bank as soon as he pulled into one of the staff spaces in the car park. The two police cars gave it away. He jumped from his car and walked to the front door of the building. He knocked on the door and waited patiently for someone to come and unlock it. It was his manager who let him in.

"Morning. How'd the move go?" the manager asked - a smile on his face.

Ryan spotted the two officers talking to some of the staff near the front desk. Two more people he didn't recognise were walking into the manager's office - a stack of tapes in their hands.

"What's going on?" Ryan asked.

"Vanessa has been missing nearly a week now. What with everything that's been happening in the press recently - I phoned the police." Vanessa was one of the full-timers who worked on the front line of the bank; helping customers with their various requests such as transferral of funds, deposits, and withdrawals.

"You called the police? Maybe she's just had enough." Ryan knew that was highly unlikely. Vanessa had worked in the bank for two years now and, in that time he could not recall her ever taking a day off sick. Even when she was full of cold, she would still come in with a smile on her face.

"Fiona went around her house. Still has a spare key from when she house-sat for her. They were supposed to meet up but Vanessa never showed up so she let herself in when she failed to get hold of her on the phone…House was empty. No struggles, no mess, no Vanessa…On her file, I had her mum and dad's number but we haven't been able to get through to them. No answer." He took a breath, "Police are going to want a word with you. Nothing to worry about. They just want to know if you noticed anything strange with Vanessa…"

"I've been away…"

"Before you went away. Just standard questions."

Ryan nodded towards the manager's office where he had noted the two men going through the bank's security tapes. "And what about that?" he asked.

"Just going through the footage to see if anything is unusual. Anyway - put your stuff upstairs and come on down. We're going to open a little late today to give the police time to talk to everyone without having to worry about customers."

Ryan left the bank's foyer and headed up the stairs, via the coded staff door. He couldn't help but feel his manager's reaction to Vanessa's disappearance was a bit over the top. A young girl in her twenties who just didn't show up for work? It wouldn't be the first time someone had got bored of their job and walked out. At the same time though - deep down - a part of him worried for her safety. His boss was right; the news had been filled with the most horrific of stories recently. Stories usually contained to eighteen certificate movies from the minds of sick writers. Numerous accounts of dead girls being found. More specifically 'pieces of dead girls being discovered'. Hacked into little, insignificant pieces. Ryan felt a cold tingle run down his spine as though someone walked over his grave. Vanessa was a nice girl. A good solid worker. He hoped his initial thought was correct. He hoped she'd just got bored of her job and walked out - perhaps taken herself on a nice little holiday to reassess her life. It's just a coincidence that her disappearance fell inline with the timings of what the press labeled 'one of the most vicious serial killers of our time'.

Ryan bumped into another of his colleagues as he entered the staff room - a small room with lockers in one corner and a small table in the centre where they could eat their lunches.

"Do you think he's got her?" his colleague asked - another young girl. "Do you think she's dead?" Clearly, she was talking about Vanessa. Ryan shrugged. "You read about it in the papers but you never think it's going to land on your doorstep," she continued. Ryan couldn't help but wonder whether the young woman was worried about her colleague or more concerned about the possibility of also being taken by the person responsible for the missing ladies.

"She's probably just walked out," Ryan said, "could even be on some nice beach somewhere."

"You think?"

Ryan nodded. The more people kept making reference to the serial killer out there - the more he couldn't help but think along the same lines as them. She'd been taken and was most likely dead already.

"I have to talk to the police," she continued, "what do you think they'll ask?"

Ryan shrugged, "Probably just ask about Vanessa. Whether you noticed anything unusual. Or, at a guess, whether you noticed anyone hanging around the bank acting suspiciously. That kind of thing. I'm sure it's nothing to worry about," he said finally.

The young woman smiled at Ryan; comforted by his words. She left the room and walked down the stairs and towards her appointment with the officers. Ryan hung his coat up on one of the wall pegs. A little part of him couldn't help but wonder whether he should phone home and warn his family the serial killer could be moving closer to their lives. He dismissed the idea. Vanessa has probably gone away - just as he told his colleague. She's probably fine. No point worrying Dee - and, besides, Claire and Jen didn't know about the bodies being found. Neither of them had an active interest in the news so it was easy to hide it from them. Definitely no sense worrying them.

CHAPTER 6

"What's your name?" I asked her. She told me it was Stacey. She told me she didn't want to die. She told me other things too but by that point, I had more or less zoned out. I told her, before I removed the gag, I didn't want conversation so my lack of attention should come of no surprise to her. I took a hold of her hand and patted it. A little reassurance, I thought. I took a hold of the pliers, on the floor under her seat with other tools of my trade. "This is going to hurt," I told her as I gripped the end of the nail with the pliers. She begged me not to do it. She begged until she was blue in the face. I didn't listen. I didn't even look her in the face anymore. I just looked at her nail gripped between the tips of the pliers. With my second hand, I gripped her hand before I pulled on the pliers. She screamed. Music to my ears.

⚓

Ryan was greeted by Dee as he stepped into the house at the end of his day's work. She gave him a kiss on the cheek - one which he returned.

"How was your day?" she asked.

He shrugged, "How was your day? I'm guessing by how red your face is - you got some reading done in the garden." He passed her and walked into the kitchen where he started to prepare himself a drink of squash. Dee was talking to him but he didn't hear any of what she was saying. He was transfixed on Jen playing in the back garden. She was with Kara. The pair of them sitting on a blanket - a couple of Barbie-type dolls next to them. Ryan smiled. There was something beautiful about the innocence of children. It was just a shame it faded over the years.

"Kara's staying for dinner. I hope that's okay." Dee said when she noticed Ryan watching the two girls playing. "Are you okay?" Dee asked. She realised he wasn't listening to a word she'd been saying. If he had been listening - he'd have heard her discussing the colour scheme she'd chosen for the house. Ryan put his glass down and turned to her.

"Girl at work," Ryan said, "she's disappeared. We had the police in today asking questions about her."

"Disappeared?"

"Failed to turn up to work. The manager phoned them to report it after he wasn't able to get hold of her family. I thought his reaction was a little over the top but given what the police were saying today - I don't know…"

"What do you mean?"

"They think she's been abducted. There's a chance she may even be one of the unidentified…" he stopped, "…You know…I don't actually want to talk about it."

"They think she's dead?"

"One of those days," Ryan sighed.

"Who's dead?" Claire asked from the kitchen doorway. Her voice made both Ryan and Dee jump; neither of them were aware she was standing there. "Is this to do with the stuff on the news about the missing girls coming back in pieces?" she asked.

"How do you know about that?" Dee asked.

"How could I not know about it? It's in all the papers and all over the news." Claire walked over to the cupboard and pulled out a packet of crisps.

"And you can put those back - dinner isn't far off from being ready," said Dee as she took the crisps from her daughter.

"So come on - who's dead?" she asked again.

Ryan remembered what he thought about the innocence he saw in his youngest daughter. How beautiful it was and yet how quickly it disappeared as evident from his eldest. Seven years between them and yet, as much as he hated to admit it, his eldest daughter's innocence was all but gone.

"No one is dead," said Dee.

"Someone from work has gone missing," said Ryan. "She's not dead."

"They think she's dead though?"

"They're not sure what she is," Ryan said, "other than missing."

"Go and get your sister," Dee interrupted them from their conversation, "I'm about to dish dinner up. And don't say anything to her!" Although dinner wasn't ready right at that moment it wasn't going to be long. Dee was just trying to give Ryan a break from all of the questions. No doubt he'd be tired of them and - even if he wasn't - she was sure he'd be bored of talking about the missing girl after a whole day of having to do it with various people.

Claire muttered something under her breath and walked from the kitchen, via the back door, which she slammed shut behind her.

"They're growing up fast," Ryan said - more or less to himself. He turned to Dee, "Things were different when we were younger," he said, "safer…Do you think - if we knew what a shitty place this world was going to be…Do you think we'd have still had children?"

Dee smiled, "Of course we would have."

"Dangerous place out there," he said.

"It's always been a dangerous place out there. We just weren't as aware of it when we were young. Our parents protected from us just as we're supposed to protect our children from it." She cuddled in close to Ryan, "I'm sure your work colleague is fine. She'll show up."

"I hope so," he said. Ryan wasn't particularly good friends with Vanessa. He liked the girl but not enough to want to socialise with her outside of work, but that was irrelevant. She was a fellow human being and he wouldn't wish any harm upon her. Also - to have a girl taken from his place of work by some demented psychopath - it just made things even more real than the various reports on the news station and in the papers made it. It made it closer to home. If someone from his work was able to be taken then there was nothing to stop one of his daughters being taken - or even his wife. A cold chill ran through him again. Second time that day.

"Come on," said Dee, "go and get washed up. I'll dish up dinner."

He gave her a peck on the cheek and left the room. "Want me to take next door's girl home before you dish up?" Ryan called through.

Dee rolled her eyes.

CHAPTER 7

She was begging me to kill her. She begged me to do it quickly. Begged. I told her - one time only - that I was going to kill her. I'll oblige her on that one. Her second plea; I told her that wasn't going to happen. I whispered in her left ear, moments before I bit it off, that she was going to suffer. I wanted her to suffer. I longed for her to suffer. Just as I did with the other girls. And what I want - I get. I thought she was going to scream the house down, when I bit her ear off. I didn't mind though. No one will hear her. No one ever hears them. I positioned myself until I was face to face with her and then I smiled. Blood trickling from my mouth and down my chin. I flashed her a cheeky wink as I started to chew. It's tough. I won't be swallowing it. Just curious as to the taste and texture of it on my tongue. And curious to see if it's even easy to chew it into smaller pieces. Not the first time I've bitten an ear off someone but it is the first time I've chewed on it. A dirty habit which I won't be repeating. I spat it onto the pretty girl's lap and sat back, a moment, to admire the mess I'd made on her face. I wonder - if I let her go - would she ever want to take another selfie with her phone camera again? That's the problem with girls of today; so vain. If only they knew their vanity made them appear to us men as this girl appears to me now. I laughed. She was looking at me with soulful eyes. She wasn't talking anymore. Just crying in pain. She wasn't talking but her eyes were saying everything. They were doing the talking. They were begging me to release her. They were begging me to let her go or just get it over with. Her eyes. I think I'll take one. Just one. I don't want her being completely blind to what is coming.

⚔

Dinner was finished now and he had been relaxing in the living room with his feet up on the sofa. Claire was lying on the floor. The two girls were upstairs playing in Jen's room and Dee was cleaning away the dishes away in the kitchen. Dee and Ryan usually shared the cleaning duties. One would cook and the other would clean. But whilst she was off from work - she tended to do everything. It was only fair - what with Ryan being out of the house all day working in the stuffy bank. Ryan's heart skipped a beat. The News, playing on the living room television set, started it's bulletins with the announcement that another body had been discovered in the woodlands close to the edge of town - about six miles away from where Ryan now lived with his family. It wasn't the story, as such, which made his heart jump. It was Vanessa. The thought of the dead girl being her.

"Can you take Kara home now?" Ryan asked Claire. She was on the floor, surfing the Internet on her laptop for nothing in-particular.

"It's just next door…" Claire started to put up a fight.

"Now!" Ryan didn't usually raise his voice as it wasn't something he usually needed to do but - when he did raise it - whatever was being asked was done without further argument. Claire sighed under her breath and slammed the lid of her laptop shut before scrambling up to her feet. As she left the room, Ryan leaned forward with the remote control and turned the volume on the News up. His heart beating hard in his chest as he waited for the story of the dead girl to come back around when they'd finished running through the other stories.

A picture of a pretty schoolgirl was shown on the screen. A young red-head with freckles and braces. Light brown eyes. Not Ryan's work colleague. Not Vanessa. He breathed a sigh of relief and - almost instantly - felt a pang of guilt. Just because it wasn't his work colleague, it didn't mean it wasn't someone else's daughter, or friend.

The News lady explained over video footage of woodlands that the dismembered girl was found in a clearing just off the path. No attempt had been made to hide the body - just as there hadn't been any attempts to hide the victims on the previous occasions either. The brazen killer not even trying to cover his tracks. The News anchor stated the police were appealing for any witnesses to come forward and even offered up a confidential line if they were too afraid to go public with potentially seeing something strange taking place. Ryan looked up to the door when it opened without warning. Dee walked in.

"They've found another one," he told her as she looked to the television set to see what had made him set up. "It wasn't the girl from work."

"Well that's good," said Dee. A strange choice of words - she knew it and Ryan knew it but neither of them said anything. They both knew what Dee had meant. Good that it wasn't Vanessa but not good they'd found another body. She took a seat next to her husband. "Do you think they'll catch the person responsible or whether he'll just stop?"

The killings had been going on for weeks now. It wasn't the first time the town had made the news (local, national and international) due to bad things happening. A couple of years ago it had been in the news too. Children had been taken from a shopping centre only to be found with smiles cut into their faces like something straight from a horror story. Reports stated a group of clowns were going around turning unhappy children into happy children - snatching the children from their parents and scarring them for life. Ryan remembered worrying about the state of society then too. The driving force of a group of individuals pushed into doing such atrocities. The latest bout of murders on the television - although not involving young children - were just as horrific as what'd taken place in the shopping centre. This time - a new body being discovered every couple of days or so. Always found in the same woodlands with the exception of one occasion where the pieces of the body were found in a small bag in a shopping centre's car park. On no occasion had anyone stepped forward to state they'd seen something suspicious. For all intents and purposes these dead girls just appeared out of nowhere. Ryan had already considered the possibility of the culprit getting away with it. Perhaps they'd wake up one day and just stop before the police had enough leads to get a trace on them? Part of Ryan hoped that'd be the case and another part of him hoped they'd catch the son of a bitch and bring back the death penalty. Make them suffer just as they made their victims suffer.

"They've said police have stepped up their patrols but that's all they've really said. I wouldn't be surprised if vigilantes don't take to the streets, and woods, soon to see if they can fare better with catching the sick son of a bitch," said Ryan. All the time the story had been playing on the television - his mind had already started playing its own movie in his head; what he'd do to the killer if he caught him. Dee didn't say anything. "The world is a cruel place," Ryan continued. He picked up the remote control and killed the television. The screen went black. They sat in silence for a moment, or two.

⚔

Thomas was standing in the doorway of the neighbour's house with a smile on his face. It wasn't the smile of someone being friendly. It was the smile of someone being sarcastic. "Well thank you very much for bringing her all the way home," he was saying to Claire, "we were all sitting in here worrying that she might have got lost on the way - what with it being so far away."

Kara had already pushed past her older brother and run inside (and straight up the stairs) so Claire didn't feel too bad when she returned Thomas' sarcastic smile and said, "Asshole."

"Now come on, that's not very neighbourly. Okay. I'm sorry. Thank you. I mean it." He hesitated for a moment, just long enough for Claire to maybe think he was being serious, before he finished up with, "We were genuinely concerned something may have happened to her from your front door to our front door…Those forty steps, or so, are pretty treacherous."

"If you want to be a dick about it, my dad made me bring her so - if you want - I'll go and fetch him so you can show him your amazing talent for wit and sarcasm? I'm sure he'll be just as impressed as me."

Thomas laughed at how easy it was to wind Claire up. For someone who didn't have many friends (what with being considered the outsider at school) he had a somewhat unhealthy trait of enjoying being able to rub people up the wrong way.

"What are you doing standing on the doorstep?" Jackie asked. She'd walked through from the living room to see who was at the door. "Did you want to come in? Thomas - why haven't you invited her in?"

"No - no…It's fine," said Claire. Unlike Thomas she tried her best to be pleasant when speaking to Jackie. "I was just bringing Kara home."

"You sure you don't want to come in?" Jackie asked. "It'd be nice for Thomas to actually make a friend…"

"Mum…"

"No really, I can't. But thank you for the invite."

"And thank you for bringing Kara home," Jackie smiled.

"I think my dad was worried that she may have been snatched by that guy on the news if I didn't," said Claire. Thomas' ears pricked up. "One of his work colleagues was taken by this person," Claire continued (even though it wasn't confirmed her father's work colleague was in the hands of the murderer), "and now I think he's worried we could all be taken."

"Well, tell your father I'm sorry to hear that and I hope they find her…" Jackie was cut off mid-sentence.

"…They'll find her okay - in pieces," Thomas interrupted.

"Thomas…"

"No, it's fine. He's probably right…Anyway, I best get back before dad sends out the search party for me."

"Did you want Thomas to walk you back?" Jackie offered.

"Mum…."

"No, it's fine," Claire repeated. "Not exactly far is it." She turned and walked away from the house as Jackie shouted out goodbye to her as well as asking to say 'hello' to Claire's mother for her. Seconds later and they closed the door. Claire stopped at the end of their garden. A strange sensation washed over her - the feeling she was being watched. She turned back to her neighbour's front door. Closed. She shook the feeling from her mind and hurried the last few steps to her own (open) front door. The feeling of unease replaced with a feeling of stupidity for being sucked into her father's own paranoia.

"Get her home safely?" Ryan asked when he heard the front door slam shut.

CHAPTER 8

Reports of my work were on the news last night, which made me happy. The police, lead by a Detective Andrews, appealing for witnesses to my crimes. I'd gone to bed in a good mood. The progress I made on the young woman and the thought of someone finding the other girl - all pleasing to me. I even woke up in a good mood too but that soon changed. My girl, the new one, she'd bled out during the night. She wanted me to let her out of the restraints last night. She wanted me to undo the ropes around her wrists. I told her I wasn't very good at undoing knots. Good at tying them but not so good at removing them. So I took her hands off with an axe which had been hidden under the chair she was sitting on. I should have known that would have caused a lot of blood loss. I should have thought it through more carefully. Carried away by the moment again. Her face, when I slipped the ropes over the bloodied stumps, was priceless. The sight of her dead, knowing I wouldn't hear her screams anymore - that was the start of my bad day and my mood continued to dive further south when there was a bulletin on the television about another missing girl. Some young girl who worked in a bank, close to the city centre. She's nothing to do with me. She's not one of my dolls. She's no one to me. It wasn't the fact she was missing that bothered me. It was the fact she was being linked to my crimes. The police fear for her safety and are asking people to step forward with information, if they have any news on sightings. The main thing, which pissed me off, though, was the fact someone out there might be abducting girls in an effort to do what I do. Someone out there might be copying me, and claiming my work as their own. They say it's a form of flattery when someone copies you, but it's not. It's far from it and if it turns out someone is attempting to carry on with my work - even though I haven't finished yet - I'll spend every waking hour I have in trying to find them. And when I do…They'll find themselves on my red-stained chair before being found, dumped, in the woods. This is my game. These are my rules. I do not play well with others.

Dee drove Ryan to work the following morning so she could be left with the car. Neither of them had really spoken during the thirty-three minute drive. Ryan had hardly spoken since the previous evening - after he'd watched the news. Dee hadn't seen him like this before. It was rare for anything to really bother him - especially the news. She just presumed it was because of his work colleague.

"Maybe she'll show up today," Dee tried to reassure him. He looked at her and smiled. They both knew the chances of her rocking up - as though nothing had happened - were extremely remote. Especially as both of them had seen the news whilst eating their morning cornflakes and toast. Her picture had been all over the channels. People don't get reported as missing, on the news programs, until all possible stones had been un-turned and - in this day and age - by the time they were reported as such it was usually too late for them. They'd already be dead. Dee turned down the final street which took them to the bank's car park. A car park shared by some of the other businesses on the road. She stopped the car before the car park's entrance, "Look." Ryan had already spotted what she was looking at. Numerous police cars all parked in the free spaces with extra cars on the road. Ryan twisted in his chair and looked towards the bank. A hive of activity with police officers going in and out. "What do you think is going on?" Dee asked.

Ryan shrugged. "Wait here."

He removed his seat belt and climbed from the car, closing the door be-hind him with a gentle shove. Dee watched as he ran across the road, towards the bank. As soon as he was near enough, a police officer stretched out his hand as though to stop him from going any further. She watched as they exchanged words. Ryan's boss appeared in the doorway and walked out to greet Ryan. A few other members of staff left the building with him. Some started walking down the road and others crossed over - towards the car park. Dee watched as these ones climbed into their cars. A couple got on their mobile phones whilst the others just drove from the car park and headed down the road - away from the building. By the time Dee turned back to see what was going on with her husband, he was already on his way back to the car. She couldn't tell what he was thinking from the expression on his face.

"Well," he said as he climbed into the car, "I have an unscheduled day off today." He closed the door behind him. "Bank isn't opening today."

"What's going on?"

"The police officer didn't say anything but John said a parcel was delivered. He opened it up and there were two hands in there."

"Hands? Real hands? As in human?" Dee looked disgusted. Ryan nodded. "Your colleague?" He shrugged. She realised the expression on his face. It was one of concern. "So what's happening now?"

"I don't know. I don't know. John said he'd call us all later to let us know what is going on. From what he said - I don't think he even knows what is going on," he said. "Looks pretty shook up. Everyone does."

Dee turned the key in the car's ignition and did a u-turn in the road. Seconds later and they were driving back the way they came. The same silence filling the car, which had accompanied them on the way down. When Ryan had first told Dee his work colleague was missing - she didn't really tie it in with what was happening in the news. Had it been someone in her school who'd gone missing - she may have done so - but it wasn't, and so it was still hard for her to think of something so evil being so close to her little world. After all, the world is a big place. It's pretty bad luck to have something like that happening on your doorstep and - generally - it's not something you believe will creep into your world. It always seems to happen to someone else. With the discovery of the hands, though, it was hard for her to ignore the possibility of the work colleague being taken. It was hard to believe the evil hadn't crept into their comfortable little lives. And it was hard for either of them not to believe the hands believed to Vanessa.

"Did you want me to stay home today?" Dee offered. "I can cancel my plans. I was only going into town with Jackie."

"No. It's fine," he said. It would have been the first time Jackie and Dee would have met up after the meal they shared the other night and Ryan didn't want to stop that. Especially for something like this. He wanted her to go out. He wanted her to make friends.

"I don't mind." Dee reiterated on the off chance he was just being polite so as not to ruin her day. Just as Ryan was fine with her going out, she was fine with changing her plans in order to stay in with him. Especially if he needed her to.

"Really - it's fine. It'll be nice for you to make a new friend. At least one who lives so close anyway."

"As long as you're sure."

"I'm sure."

The rest of the drive home was completed in silence; broken only when Dee couldn't stand it anymore and turned the radio on. When the latest news bulletin started - she switched the radio onto the CD function. Ryan didn't stop her.

⊼

Claire ignored the first knock on the door in the hope Jen would have answered it. After all, more likely than not, it was only going to be Kara enquiring as to whether she wanted to go out and play with her. Kara, or Jackie looking for Dee, or a salesman trying to sell something Claire would have no interest in (and certainly no authority to pay for).

"Jen! Door!" she called out when a second rap was heard against the wooden frame. She heard Jen mutter something from her bedroom before she heard the sound of her sister running down the landing and stairs towards the front door. She smiled to herself. If she'd be forced to move house and then forced to stay in to keep an eye on her younger sister whilst her mother drove her father to work than she'd at least treat her as though she were her own personal slave. Which reminded her, "And fetch me some crisps!" she called out loudly to ensure Jen heard her. Another mutter from down the stairs. Loud enough to know it was her sister moaning but not loud enough to make out what was being said. It didn't matter to Claire though. She'd hit her later regardless. Especially if she didn't bring her the packet of crisps she'd asked for.

Claire was sitting at a small desk in her bedroom drawing in a plain-papered notepad. When she was forced to move home, and taken away from the people she cared about - Claire was surprised when her mother and father left her with the note-pad. She thought (even told them) that they may as well take that from her too - if they're taking everything else from her then they may as well take her main passion (drawing) as well. Dee just told her not to be so melodramatic and that she'd make new friends.

"I don't see why I should have to!" Claire had ranted. "Why do I even have to change schools? It's not as though we're moving country!" and she was right. They weren't moving country. Unfortunately, though, they were moving far enough away to mean Claire, and her sister, were no longer in the right catchment area for their current school. Hence the need to move to a new one and the new to make new friends.

A knock on her bedroom door made her turn around. Jen didn't make a habit of knocking on the door. She'd just burst in and interrupt Claire (something which she often got in trouble for). Claire jumped when she saw Thomas standing in the doorway with a packet of crisps in his hand.

"Hi," he looked to the crisps, "your sister picked out Prawn Cocktail. That good enough?" Before Claire could answer - or even ask why he was in her bedroom - he threw the packet at her. It landed on the desk next to where she was working.

"What did you want?" Claire asked.

"What? Nothing. I just thought I'd pop over and say hello to my new best friend!"

"Best friend?"

"Best friend!"

"Yeah because you've been so friendly from the moment we first met." he walked across the room and sat down on Claire's bed. Claire didn't say anything but he could see his choice in seat annoyed her so he stood up again.

"Sorry," he said, "I can be a bit of a dick sometimes. Nothing was meant by it. Promise. Can we just start again?" He didn't wait for her to answer. He leant forward and extended his hand towards her, "Hi, I'm Thomas. Pleased to meet you."

Claire laughed and took his hand. They shook. "Claire."

"Such a pretty name," he said.

"Really? That's how you make new friends?" she laughed (at him, not with him). "I think I understand why you don't have many friends," she said.

"Who said I didn't have many friends?" He changed the subject, "Is your dad at work today?" he asked.

Claire raised an eyebrow. She didn't expect Thomas to come over but she expected that, as a question, even less. "Why?"

"Just wondered," he said. "That girl show up yet? The one who works with him."

Claire paused a moment as she came to the sudden realisation Thomas hadn't come over to see her, or even make friends with her. "You didn't come to see me did you?"

"What - yes. I said so."

"Uh huh - look, I've got a lot to do today. If you want to see my dad and ask him all these questions, your best bet is to come around this evening." She turned her back on Thomas and started to draw on her pad again.

"No. I came to see you. I was just wondering that's all. Being neighbourly."

"I know who he is, you know."

"Yeah. He's my dad."

"No. I know who the killer is. The one in the papers. I know him."

Chapter 9

felt like a hypocrite sending the girl's hands to the bank. Especially giving them a sign to say she's not with me - the girl missing from the bank I mean. The sign was clear to say I hadn't taken her. I'd taken the girl who the hands were originally attached to. Hopefully they'll be able to run some tests and see it's not the same person. It was never in my plan to send off packages to people. My idol, Art, did when he toyed with the police but - I want to be my own person. I don't want to be perceived as a copycat to him. Especially given my hatred for copycats. Sure, I was inspired by news of his gallery. More so when the photographs of his exhibits were leaked to the Internet (albeit for a short time only before they were pulled). By sending the hands - I just wanted them to know I was innocent of the crime they now believed I was responsible for. Sure I could have taken credit for it - at least until the girl has been found - but that's cheating. I want to be known as the worst (best) serial killer of all time by my own merits. I don't need help from other people. I'm my own person. I'm my own killer. And I can do this by myself. Well, by myself and with my victims anyway. Speaking of which, I need to find a new victim. Someone else to play with. I fancy a brunette.

⋏

Claire was standing next to the desk in Thomas' room. Various handwritten notes were sprawled across the worktop with Thomas sitting in front of them, thumbing through the various snippets of information.

"This is what you do with your free time?" Claire asked. The notes - all handwritten - were various scribblings based on some of the most infamous serial killers of all time; Gacy, Dahmer, Art, Bundy, Sutcliffe and even Gein and Manson were amongst them although - technically speaking - the latter two weren't serial killers. They still had their place in this list though.

"It's interesting to me."

"It's a bit sick."

Thomas found the piece he was looking for, "This is the latest one." He handed it over to Claire. She took it and started reading. Thomas had been writing about the kidnappings and brutal murders in explicit detail. He'd written the dates and times the bodies were found, he'd written how long each of the girls had been missing for and the state in which they'd reappeared - discovered by unfortunate walkers who'd stumbled across them whilst out and about. Claire couldn't hide the fact she found what she was reading disgusting. For some reason, it also made her feel a little nervous. Here was a guy, standing so close to her, who seemed to idolise these monsters. An unhealthy obsession to which she couldn't see a reason. Despite Claire's obvious concerns, Thomas hadn't noticed and carried on excitedly, "I want to write when I'm older. It's the only thing I've ever been good at," he said - bustling with an energy she'd not seen before. "Eventually I want to compile all of these into books. You know, True Crime…Massive market for it and it's fun to write about…"

Claire couldn't contain her nervousness anymore, "Fun?" She held the pages up, "This isn't fun - these are lives. These girls are daughters, sisters - maybe even mothers…"

Thomas shifted uneasily, "I don't think of them as that. I just detach from it…" He realised what he was saying probably wasn't going to make her feel any better about what he'd been spending his time working on and tried to change tact, "True Crime has such a massive market…Can you imagine if I had an interview with your dad in here?"

"What?"

"About his…" he looked at his notes, "…work colleague Vanessa…If he talked about her to me, told me a little about her. It'd make her more real to the reader and…"

"I'm sorry," Claire handed the notes back, "I have to get home."

Thomas blocked her way. "Wait. Don't you want to know who it is?"

"You think you know who the murderer is and yet you haven't gone to the police? Even if I had the slightest of inklings as to who it could be - I'd have reported it on the off chance I was right. And if you were right, if you reported it, that would have made for a more impressive end to your book. Certainly more impressive than a missing girl's work colleague. If I were you, I wouldn't even try talking to my dad about it. He'll just say the same as me."

Claire side-stepped Thomas and walked towards the bedroom door.

"It's your neighbour!" Thomas called out after her.

Claire turned back to him, "You're my neighbour," she said.

"On the other side. It's him."

"I think you need to get out more," Claire said. Clearly, she'd had enough of Thomas. "This…" she pointed to the notes, "…this isn't a healthy hobby. It's just…Weird." She turned and walked from the room, and down the stairs as Thomas called out after her. She didn't hear what he said and she didn't care - no doubt he was just trying to scare her. Some kind of sick prank to make her feel less welcome than she already felt in what was supposed to be her new home.

"Oh hi!" Jackie appeared in the lounge's doorway as Claire reached the bottom of the stairs. "Staying for dinner?" Claire didn't even bother to answer her, she just opened the front door and stormed out. Jackie watched her from the doorway - a perplexed expression on her face.

Ryan and Dee pulled into the driveway of their own home to witness Claire storming from one house to the other. Ryan immediately rolled his eyes - as though he needed any more drama in his life right now.

"Now what?" he sighed.

"It's fine," Dee reassured him, "whatever it is - I'll deal with it."

Ryan paused in the car as Dee opened the door and headed after Claire - calling her name as she did so. Ryan sighed heavily. Whatever it was, he just couldn't be bothered. Not today. Not after what'd happened at the bank.

"Claire!" Dee called out to her daughter who'd already disappeared into the house. She chased after her allowing the front door to close behind her. "Claire, talk to me!" she insisted from the bottom of the stairs. Claire was already halfway up them.

Claire stopped and turned to face her mother, tears rolling down her face. "I didn't even want to move here!" she yelled at her. "I was happy where we were." She shouted again, "I don't want to live here!"

"What brought all this on?" Dee knew Claire wasn't happy with the move. She didn't exactly make her initial feelings hidden from her mother and father. Even so - she thought Claire was at least, starting to come around to the idea of it. Albeit slowly.

"That freak next door!"

"Who?" Dee knew who her daughter was referring to. She knew her daughter and the neighbour's son weren't going to get on from the moment she first met him. He seemed rude when he finally came down to eat dinner with them. In fact - he seemed to be identical to Claire and that was how she knew they wouldn't get on. It was true, the old saying, opposites attract. Claire and Thomas were so similar they were always going to clash.

"You know who!"

"Well what's he done?" Dee asked. If she could understand the outburst, there was a chance she'd be able to fix it before it became more of an issue.

"He came around. He wants to talk to dad…"

"Who wants to talk to me?" Neither Dee nor Claire had heard Ryan walk in through the front door. Dee was the first to look to him. She shrugged. He looked up to his distraught daughter, "Well?"

"Thomas."

"Thomas?" Ryan looked to Dee - clueless as to what was going on and who the hell Thomas was, despite being introduced to him only a couple of days ago.

"The boy next door."

"Ah - the plot thickens."

"No. No plot thickens!" Claire said. "He came around earlier - when you were out - and said he wanted to talk to you."

"Me?" Ryan pointed to himself.

"Yes."

"I don't even know him - why does he want to talk to me?" Ryan asked. Claire sighed heavily. She didn't want her dad to know what Thomas was doing. She knew it wouldn't upset him, so to speak, she just knew he didn't suffer fools gladly. "Will someone please tell me what the hell is going on here?" he snapped. The stress of the move, the stress of money, the stress of work - everything was getting to him and the last thing he needed was his daughter kicking off for whatever reason she deemed necessary this time.

"He wanted to talk to you about your work colleague," Claire blurted out.

"My work colleague? What? Vanessa?"

"Yes."

"How did you even know about her?"

"I might have said something yesterday."

"And why would he want to talk to me?" Ryan was starting to get angry. The fact some jumped up little snot upset his daughter but was also trying to stick his nose into his business too - a step too far from someone who hadn't earned the right to take any steps.

"He's writing about the killer. He's written about lots of them. He thinks he is going to be some big shot True Crime writer…"

Ryan turned to Dee, "Can you believe this? You want to do me a favour and nip this in the bud when you go out with your friend later? Please?"

"I'll get her to talk to him."

"I told him you wouldn't want to talk to him!" Claire shouted to Ryan as he walked off and into the lounge.

"Yeah, you're right!" Ryan shouted back.

Dee turned to Claire. She knew she'd take Ryan's frustrations personally. She was at that age where any form of negativity would be taken the wrong way - as though she were the one to blame for whatever was the cause of upset. Just your average teenager. "Your father's just upset," she told her daughter, "he's not angry with you."

I just want to go home!" Claire yelled before she turned around and ran off towards her bedroom, straight past Jen who'd come to see what the shouting was about. Dee sighed as Claire's bedroom door slammed.

"This is your home!" Dee called out to her.

"What's the shouting for?" Jen asked.

"Nothing," said Dee. Jen didn't need to know what was happening. As far as Dee and Ryan were aware - she knew nothing of what was happening in the news or at her father's workplace. And that was the way it needed to stay. Dee quickly changed the subject, "I'm popping out later with Jackie, did you want to come?" she asked. "See if Kara wants to come as well?"

Jen nodded and smiled. At least one of them was happy.

⋏

It didn't take long for Ryan to calm down. He knew none of what had happened was his daughter's fault. Yes, she probably shouldn't have said anything to their neighbours, about Ryan's work colleague, but she wasn't specifically told not to. And regardless of whether she should, or shouldn't have, at least she put Thomas straight by telling him her dad wouldn't be interested in talking to him. Hell - even if the young lad were a proper qualified journalist, writing an important piece, he still wouldn't talk. Vanessa was someone's daughter and a friend to many people. She shouldn't be the subject of gossip-mongers. Especially whilst she was still presumed missing. If she had been taken - the fact people were talking - it could've pushed whoever took her into doing something stupid. A panicked move to get rid of her before being discovered with her.

Dee had gone out with Jen, Jackie and Kara. She'd offered Claire to go with them too but Claire just ignored the knocking at her bedroom door. She was in no mood to talk to anyone; still sulking about the move and the fact her dad seemed angry at her with regards to what Thomas had asked.

Ryan knocked on Claire's door with his knuckle. A little time-out, in the living room, made him realise he'd probably reacted a little stronger than necessary. Certainly a reaction which had been aimed in the wrong direction. Ryan didn't wait for an answer before opening the door.

"Go away!" Claire said (not quite a shout) as the door creaked open. She hadn't looked up from her drawing pad, where she was furiously scribbling. Had she done so - she probably wouldn't have told her dad to go away. Not because she didn't want to. She just rarely dared speak to him like that. She was fine to bark such orders at her sister, even her mother, but rarely her dad.

"If I went away I wouldn't be able to apologise," he said - a guilty smile on his face. Claire looked up and shot him a look before turning her attention back to the drawing. They both knew she wouldn't stay mad at him forever. She'd have a little sulk and then he'd treat her as though she were eight years old by jabbing her in the side - something which always made her laugh and encouraged play fighting between the two of them. "Just pretty stressed today," Ryan said, "what with the moving and what's happening at work…"

Claire spoke to Ryan but didn't look up from the drawing, "She hasn't shown up then?" She was referring to Vanessa of course.

"No." He wanted to tell her what had happened at work but figured she was still a little too young to hear the grisly details.

"Thomas said he knew who the killer is," said Claire.

"Oh yeah. Who does he think it is then? Jack the Ripper?"

Claire hesitated a second, "He thinks it is our neighbour." She turned to her window and looked out of it. Her window was the one which overlooked the neighbour's garden. Their house was joined to Mike and Jackie's home but there was a small alleyway between their home and this unknown neighbour's own place. Their garden was overgrown and messy. Whoever lived there clearly didn't care about the look of their garden. Obviously they preferred to stay indoors - a statement backed with further proof in that Ryan (nor any of his family) had seen whoever lived there despite a car being in the driveway signifying the chance of someone actually being in.

"Well," said Ryan with a smile on his face, "why don't we go and say hello?"

"What?"

"Come on - about time we started making new friends!" he walked over to the bedroom door and turned back to Claire when he realised she wasn't following. "Come on, I'm not joking. We need to introduce ourselves anyway and it might stop your little friend from trying to force silly ideas onto you again. Let's go."

Claire knew she didn't have a choice. She put her sketching pencil down and followed after her father who started down the landing.

CHAPTER 10

The new girl is sleeping for now. I've used my time to watch the television - news channels in particular - to see if there is any mention of what I'd sent to the bank. Nothing. Now, only now, do I truly understand the frustration of Art when he first set up his pieces of artwork only to have them snubbed by the media. In his case it was probably for the best; it forced him onto the path of making a gallery. It forced him to make something some truly remarkable that no one could ignore it. And, to his credit and my admiration, he succeeded. With regards to my own work - I'm happy my main pieces have made it to the papers and television programs. I think I'm glad the details of the package haven't been leaked, though. The fewer people who know I resorted to such copycat tactics, just to tell the world the missing bank woman isn't with me, the better. I don't want to be remembered as a cheap imitation. I want to be remembered for the people I leave in the woodlands. The pieces of the people at least.

The girl in my basement screamed out loud and I could not help but to smile. The girl is awake now. How exciting. Of course I'll start with the nails as per usual…A knock at the door from upstairs. Funny. Not expecting any guests. I dart towards my new house guest, with fist clenched, and hit her on the side of the temple. Her scream is silenced immediately. I just hope it stays that way. Long enough, at least, until I get rid of the unwanted attention.

I hurried up the stairs towards the front door and my waiting visitors.

Ryan was standing closer to the front door than Claire. She knew, deep down, that Thomas was wrong. Of course the killer wouldn't be their neighbour. And if he was - if it was that simple someone like Thomas could figure it out - then surely the police would have already found him. Even so she couldn't shake the feeling - what if he was right? What if the person, about to open the door, was the killer the police were hunting? Claire felt the butterflies flutter within her stomach. She wanted nothing more than to run home. Not to the house next door. That wasn't her home. She wanted to go back to where she lived before. That was her home.

"Maybe they're busy killing people," Ryan said - a smile on his face.

"Let's go."

"Ssh..." Ryan craned his ear to the door. He could hear footsteps on the other side of it. "Someone's coming."

"I just want to go home!" Claire whined quietly incase the person coming could hear her.

"This is home and we need to make friends with the neighbours. That is what grown-ups do when they move somewhere new. They try and make friends." That was Ryan's excuse but he was more interested in disproving Thomas' theory that the person who lived here was the culprit for all the recent killings. Not just for his own piece of mind but to also help settle his daughter.

The front door opened but not all of the way. Just a little crack. A gaunt looking man with dark hair peered through the gap with only his face. His hand on the door ready to slam it shut if he wasn't in the mood for visitors. His eyes were bloodshot as though he hadn't slept for many nights and his complexion pale.

"Yes?" his voice was quiet. A hint of a shake in the tone.

"Hi," said Ryan. He compensated for the man's deep suspicion by making his own tone more upbeat and his smile wider than it usually would have been when greeting someone new. "Don't worry - we're not selling anything -

we've just moved in next door. Been there nearly a week now and thought it about time we came and introduced ourselves…"

"Okay…"

Ryan shifted on his feet - a little uncomfortable by the standoffish attitude of the strange man standing on the other side of the door. "I'm Ryan." He turned to his daughter, "This is my daughter…Claire."

"Hi," Claire gave a little wave. She was already backing away from the front door. The man's gaze fixed upon her. She thought she saw a little smile spread across his thin lips.

"So - yeah - nice to meet you," Ryan was waiting for the man to open the door and, at the very least, offer his hand for a shake. Usually it would be polite for people to invite neighbours in, maybe offer them a drink or two. A way of building bridges and getting to know each other. Ryan noticed the man was still looking at his daughter. He took a step to the right and blocked his view - instantly feeling that Claire felt a little more comfortable. "We're having a party this weekend. Inviting the neighbours in an effort to get to know everyone - we just wondered if you'd like to come?" Ryan said. A make-believe party in order to try and get something (anything) from this strangle little man.

"I'm sorry. I'm busy."

"Oh - yeah - well of course. It's short notice. Well if you get a minute, a moment off from whatever you are doing, you're more than welcome to pop round. Especially if the volume is too loud…" He was trying everything he could to try and get a response from the man but there was nothing. Other than a vacant look. Still there was nothing. "Well it was good to meet you. And if you ever fancy it - we're only next door." He smiled again at the man. The man just nodded.

"Okay." And he closed the door with a slam.

Ryan turned to Claire. He could see from Claire's face that the visit had not inspired confidence in her. "He seems nice," said Ryan. A second later and he couldn't help but burst into laughter at how surreal the whole experience had been. Another second, or two, later and Claire couldn't help but laugh too. Her laughter being more of a nervous one. "Come on," Ryan lead the way down the driveway - backwards the safety of their own home. He stopped when he got to the end of the drive, though, distracted by an oncoming police car. It slowed to a stop next to where Ryan was standing with his daughter. The passenger police officer jumped out of the car and approached Ryan.

"Mr. Reynolds?"

Ryan shook his head, "No."

"This your house?" the officer asked. He pointed towards the front door Ryan and Claire had just walked away from.

"We live there. We just popped around to introduce ourselves. Is there a problem?" The smile from both Claire and Ryan's face had faded. Replaced with a genuine look of concern.

The officer didn't answer him. He stepped past the two of them and approached the front door. He was closely followed by the second officer who'd been in the car. Ryan recognised the second of the officers from the bank. He'd been one of the men helping with the questioning of the staff on the first day Ryan had gone back to work from his time off moving.

"Come on," Ryan took a hold of Claire's arm and pulled her towards their drive - out of the way of the police and whatever they were about to do. From the safety of their own drive he turned back towards the neighbour's house. The front door opened and he saw the police exchange words with the same gaunt-looking man they'd earlier introduced themselves to. Seconds later and the man stepped from the house, he closed the front door, and followed the police officers back to the car. There were no cuffs. There was no struggle. He simply got into the back of the car before being driven back down the road after a quick u-turn by the officer in charge of the wheel.

"What do you think that was about?" Claire asked.

"I have no idea," said Ryan, "but let's not tell your mother. No need to freak her out when it could be something entirely innocent. Like, maybe, he's a police officer and he needed a lift to the station..." Of all the possible excuses he could think of - as to why his neighbour would have been picked up - this was probably the worst. After all, had he been a police officer, than there is no reason as to why the officers wouldn't have known Ryan wasn't the person they were looking for. They would have simply pulled up, gone to the door, and retrieved their colleague from his house. Ryan opened his front door and Claire stepped in. Ryan hesitated though. Someone was watching. He turned around, slowly, and noticed Thomas was standing at the front of his own house. He was looking in the direction of the police car. He turned around and caught Ryan's own eye. He raised an eyebrow as if to say 'I told you so'. Ryan turned away and stepped into his house, slamming the door behind him.

Claire was standing at the foot of the stairs, "So Thomas was right. It is him?"

"What?" Ryan knew what Claire was talking about. She'd jumped to the conclusion that he'd jumped to when he initially saw the police taking the neighbour away. The only reason he said what he did was to have a little more time to think about what he was going to say to diffuse the situation. Thankfully he didn't need much time. "If they thought it was him, if they really believed it, then they'd have arrived with back-up. And search warrants. For all you know - it could be something completely unrelated that they want to talk to him about." And that was the truth. Just because it was bad timing, on their part, it didn't mean it had anything to do with what Claire and Ryan had been discussing. Just a strange coincidence. One which was made that little bit weirder by Thomas. Ryan knew it had been him who'd phoned the police. That was too much of a coincidence. No doubt boasting of what he supposedly knew before Ryan or Claire got to the police first and told them. Just a little boy trying to claim glory - even if his beliefs were completely misguided (or so Ryan hoped). Claire opened her mouth as though she were about to say something but stopped herself short when the front door swung open and Jackie, Dee and the girls walked in. All laughing. All armed with bags of shopping.

"Now what?" Dee asked as soon as she saw Claire and Ryan and - more importantly - the guilty looks on their faces as though caught red-handed. Surely not another argument?

"Nothing." Ryan was the first to speak. Dee didn't need to know what Thomas had said. It would have only worried her unnecessarily and - again - it was completely unfounded. He turned to Jackie, "Mike home?"

"Not sure what hours he is working today," said Jackie. "I can find out for you?"

"Did you want a cup of tea?" Dee asked - ignoring the fact Jackie and Ryan were talking.

"That's fine," said Ryan, "I'll just pop over there and see." He turned to Dee, "I'll be back in a minute - and yes - I'll have a cup of tea too, please." He flashed her a cheeky grin before leaving the house.

"Go on, girls, go and play upstairs…" Dee told Kara and Jen. They didn't need telling twice and both ran up the stairs past where Claire was standing.

Chapter 11

Ryan hurried across the garden towards his neighbour's house. He didn't care if Mike was home or not. It wasn't him who he really wanted to see. It was Thomas. He wanted to know whether the police had arrived because of Thomas or whether it was because the police had the same feelings as Thomas - albeit without enough proof to really act upon it other than to question him down at the station.

Ryan knocked on the front door. Thomas opened it - just as Ryan had hoped he would.

"Your dad home?"

Thomas shook his head. Ryan stepped into the house, pushing past Thomas. Thomas closed the door behind him and turned to talk to Ryan. "Claire told you?"

"That you wanted to talk to me? Or that you believed our neighbour was the one responsible for what's been going on in the news? Yeah   she told me. Was that you?"

"Was what me?"

"Don't play clever. Did you phone the police?"

Thomas shook his head.

"You didn't phone the police? You didn't tell them about your half-arsed theory about the neighbour?"

"No."

"Why not?"

"What?"

"Why didn't you phone them? You think our neighbour is a murderer and you keep it to yourself?" Ryan was starting to get angry. It wasn't the fact Thomas believed the neighbour to be the killer which made him angry. It was the fact he'd dare to try and upset his daughter by scaring her. Especially when she was already struggling to come to terms with the move. At this point, after all the stress they had with the move, all Ryan wanted was some peace and quiet. Thomas backed up a bit. He could see Ryan was getting angry.

"It's just a theory I have," said Thomas. "I have no proof yet. I couldn't go to the police. They wouldn't take it seriously. Not without proof. I write books..." he went to explain but Ryan cut him off.

"I know - Claire told me. And you want a chat about my work colleague Vanessa. Well here you go. Her name is Vanessa. At least her name was Vanessa. It looks as though the sick son of a bitch, who took her, killed her. He cut her hands off and sent them to the bank," nothing was confirmed. The hands hadn't been identified yet - at least not to Ryan's knowledge - but he knew the chance of the I.D coming back positive was more than likely.

"What? That's great..." Thomas spoke without thinking. He wasn't thinking about it being someone's life. He was thinking about how great the story would be for his new book. Ryan wanted to knock him to his arse with a punch to the face - something to knock some sense into him - but he didn't. He knew better than that. Could have been a different story had Thomas been a little older. He wouldn't have felt bad for hitting him had they been the same age. Even though he couldn't hit him, he still couldn't help but crack a little smile at the thought. He quickly hid it.

"Listen I don't care what you think you know. I don't care. And I don't want to talk to you about your book. Truth be told I think the whole thing is silly. Stupid even. You need to grow up a bit. Find a sensible hobby - at least something you can make some money from. Writing is notoriously hard to do. This is me being a nice neighbour. Pointing you in a better direction..."

"I'm good at writing," Thomas argued.

"…More importantly I'm trying to point you in a direction other than my daughter. She's young - like you - she's impressionable. I don't want you filling her head with silly little ideas which make her feel uncomfortable in her new home. She's already finding this move hard enough without you putting these thoughts in her head. Do you understand what I'm saying?" Thomas nodded. He hesitated for a moment as though he went to say something. Ryan decided to give him the benefit of the doubt, "What is it?"

"I didn't call the police," Thomas said. "I thought Claire did. You know, after I told her. If you're saying it wasn't her and it wasn't you…And I'm telling you it wasn't me." He paused. "Why did the police take him away?" He put two and two together and quickly came to five, "I was fucking right! I told you!"

"No - you weren't. If you were right then they'd have come with a search warrant and an army of police - which is exactly what I told Claire. Look, just stop putting silly ideas in her head and leave her alone. Okay? That's all I ask. Leave all of us alone."

"What's going on?" Mike had walked in from the front door. And once again Ryan was caught having an awkward conversation with someone in the hallway. "There a reason you're asking my boy to leave your family alone? Something I should know about?"

"Your son has been telling my daughter his theories about the recent spout of killings. I'd rather he didn't. She's having enough difficulty in adjusting to her new home without being scared of the neighbour…"

Mike had already turned his attention to his son. When Ryan had finished talking, he half expected Mike to have a go at him but - to his surprise - he wasn't too bothered by his son's revelation, "You told them too?"

"His work colleague was snatched by the guy. I just wanted to get an interview…"

"You and that fucking book," Mike cut in.

"You know about all this? You don't think it might be worth getting him to spend his time doing something a little more…"

Again, Mike cut in, "I won't tell you how to raise your children and you won't tell me how to raise mine. Okay?"

Ryan went quiet almost immediately. He hardly knew Mike and wasn't sure how far he could be pushed before he'd lose his temper. He turned his attention back to Thomas, "I've said what I wanted to say so…Just keep your theories to yourself." He walked over to the front door, which Mike was blocking, "Excuse me, please."

"If it was him," Mike said with a lowered voice, "wouldn't you want to do something about it?"

"What are you talking about?"

"This guy - whoever he is - he's been hacking up girls and leaving them lying around. Could be your daughter. Could be mine. It's already close to our home if it's already reached your place of work…What if it is him? Wouldn't you want him to taste some of his own medicine? See how he likes it?"

"I'd want him to go to prison and serve time."

"Really? A private cell? Meals? Yard time? At the cost of the tax-payer. Scum like this guy - whoever he is - they don't deserve to be alive. Should bring back the death penalty for people like that…"

"Look as lovely as this is - I've said what I came to say…Excuse me please," Ryan said again as he tried to get to the front door.

"And if it is him - do you really want him living so close to your family?"

Ryan snapped, "The police are with him. They came around and collected him. If it is him - he's already in custody so I don't need to worry about it…"

"The police took him?" Mike turned to Thomas. Thomas nodded. "You called them? We spoke about this - we'd get some proof first. Wait for him to leave his house and then get in there…"

"Wait. What? You were planning on breaking into the guy's home? What - you were hoping to find a stack of body parts, or something incriminating? And you're encouraging this? Jesus Christ!"

"He rarely leaves his house since his wife was murdered a few years back. When he does - he enjoys spending time at the woods. I've followed him up there before now. The same paths the dead girls have been found on. Yes, I'll break into house if it helps get evidence of who he is."

"And you think the police will thank you for breaking and entering?"

"The police would never find out."

"Oh - sorry - I forgot. You're the judge, jury and executioner. Should have told me over dinner the other day." He took a deep breath before he slowly let it back out again - trying hard not to let the rage overcome him. "Just let me out of this fucking house and stay away from my family. Your wife too. Stay away from us."

Mike and Ryan held each other's gaze for a moment before Mike took a step to the side, giving Ryan access to the front door. Ryan paused a moment - half expecting another back and forth. Nothing was said. He opened the door and left. As he walked over the garden he didn't bother minding the flowers like he had on previous trips across the grass. He just stepped on them. Squashed flowers symbolising the crushing of neighbourly relationships. He opened the door and stormed through to the lounge where Dee was sitting with Jackie - enjoying their hot drinks and a couple of biscuits.

"Sorry," said Ryan, "Mike was asking after you. I said you'd be right over."

"I'm sure he can wait five minutes," Jackie laughed as she took another sip from her drink.

"Your drink is on the kitchen side," said Dee - not sensing the foul mood Ryan was trying to hide from his neighbour.

"I think it was important," he pushed Jackie. She took the hint.

"Oh, right," she turned to Dee, "well I'd best get back and see what's wrong. He's been acting strange all week so clearly there's something he wants to talk about." She laughed, "As long as he's not having an affair…I think I can handle anything else he throws at me." She stood up. Dee stood up with her and walked her to the front door.

"Thank you for today," she said, "we'll have to do it again sometime soon."

"Of course but I think my credit card needs a little time to heal first," Jackie laughed.

"Tell me about it!" Dee opened the door and Jackie stepped out, calling her daughter as she did so. Kara came running down the stairs and joined her mother on the doorstep. "Got everything?" Kara nodded. "Okay well - take care and chat later." She closed the door after her neighbour also said her goodbyes. When she turned back to the living room she noticed Ryan was standing there - a pissed off expression on his face. She presumed it was to do with the credit card admission. "Don't fret, I didn't spend much!"

"I don't want you seeing her again." Ryan snapped.

"I beg your pardon?"

"I don't want you seeing any of them again. You hear me?" He waited for her to agree to his demands.

"Where did this come from? I thought you liked them?"

"I don't want to go into it. But I don't want you, or the girls, hanging around with them. Okay? They're not right. Trust me…" He turned and walked towards the kitchen where his cup of (now lukewarm) tea was waiting for him. Dee followed him.

"No - you can't just stop me from seeing them without telling me why. What brought this on?" Ryan didn't answer her. He just stopped by the back window and starred out of it - cup of mildly-warm tea in his hand and a blank expression on his face. Unknown to Dee, he was replaying the whole conversation he'd had with Mike and his son back through his head; haunted by how obsessed they both seemed to be with the recent killings. And to think - he said to Dee it was only a matter of time before people set up vigilante groups. Was this the start of it? Had he inadvertently moved into the worst possible area? Vigilantes on one side of his home and a killer on the other side? And what of his other neighbour - the quiet one - why'd the police come for him? Is it all related?

He was still wearing the trousers he'd worn to work for the last two days. He reached into the pocket and pulled out a business card belonging to Detective Andrews - the lead detective in charge of Vanessa's disappearance. Ryan contemplated phoning him. He figured he had a right to know why the neighbour was pulled from his home. He had a family to protect after all.

Dee pulled him back to reality, "Until you tell me what your problem is - I'm going to do as I please." She turned from the room and shut the door, closing him in with his thoughts. The last thing he heard from his wife as she walked down the hallway (back to what he presumed to be the living room) was that he was being ridiculous. He was tempted to call back to her, bring her back in, and explain everything but she'd probably still think he was being silly.

Chapter 12

I looked at the pretty girl. Claire. All this time and she was right on my doorstep. Just goes to show I needed to get out a little more. Met my neighbours. Had it not been for them coming around my house, I might never have noticed her. The fear in her eyes was evident. And for good reason. The news programs had done a really good job of sensationalising what I do. Not saying that the reality of the situation will be better than what's reported - it's just nice that it gives my ladies something to expect. Something to look forward to. Something to dread. I smiled at her as I pressed the knife against her cheek. She tried to pull away but I stopped her with a strong grip of the back of her head with my other hand. She whimpered. I smiled. I like it when they whimper. Their pain, their fear, their sense of dread - it's all music to my ears. I love it. With no warning (for her) I threw the knife into the floor of the cellar. The blade pierced the floor and stuck the knife in. She screamed out with fear. Don't blame her. It was quite close to her foot. Such a pretty foot. I'd already taken her shoes and socks off so that I could see her feet. Her prettily painted toenails…Her toes…A shudder of excitement ran through me as I thought about what I was going to do to those pretty little toes. Not yet though. As always I start with the finger nails…I reached under the chair on which she sat and pulled out the pliers. I held them up to her face so she could get a good look at them. Rusty gold pliers tainted with the dried blood of the other ladies who'd had the displeasure of meeting them. I moved them down to her hand and gripped the nail of her index finger with them, applying enough pressure as to make them go white. I wonder - does she have any idea as to how much this is going to hurt? I do hope so. Still, I suppose it doesn't matter if she doesn't realise for it won't be long before the pain does make itself known.

"Please don't. Whatever you want. I'll get it for you. Anything. Please." The voice didn't belong to my pretty neighbour. It belonged to her father. The idiot who introduced me to his daughter. The idiot who introduced me to my new play-thing. "Please," he said again.

"Ssh."

He went to open his mouth again so I yanked on the nail. It split away from the girl's hand with ease leaving a little bloody slice of skin gaping behind. She screamed. He screamed. We all screamed together.

⋏

Ryan woke with a start and bolted upright in his bed. The moonlight spilled in through the window illuminating his room as though it were day as opposed to night. Ryan's heart was beating ten to the dozen. Beads of sweat were running across his forehead as though he'd recently run a marathon.

"You alright?" Dee asked from her pillow on the bed next to where he lay. He looked around to her. The sleepy look in her glazed eyes told him he'd disturbed her sleep.

"Bad dream," he said, "it's fine. Sorry for waking you. Go back to sleep." Dee didn't need telling twice. Before he'd even finished his sentence she was practically asleep already. Ryan carefully crawled from the bed so as not to disturb her again. He looked out of the window and noticed a taxi sitting in the road just outside of his house. The driver of the cab reached up and turned the interior light on illuminating both himself and his fare. The neighbour. What had the police officer called him? Mr. Reynolds was it? Mr. Reynolds leaned forward to the driver and handed him what must have been some money before he opened the car and slid from the seat. He slammed the door and watched as the taxi drove off. And then he froze. What was he doing? Ryan squinted into the night to try and see. The tall man slowly turned around until he was staring right up at Ryan's window. Ryan panicked and ducked down. He couldn't have seen him watching him. He couldn't have. It's not as though they had any lights on in the room. Maybe he just sensed he was being watched? Slowly Ryan positioned himself next to the window so he could move himself up in order to see over the ledge and outside once more. Mr Reynolds was still standing there - staring straight back into the room. What was he doing? Ryan continued to watch as the man slid his left hand into his left trouser pocket. Seconds later he pulled out some keys and a few more seconds after that - he finally turned his attention towards his own home (his front door in particular). Without looking back, he continued down his own drive and out of Ryan's vision. Ryan didn't dare move from where he was still crouched next to the window even though he knew he was being stupid. If the man had been released from questioning - surely the police didn't consider him to be dangerous. Clearly he wasn't the man they were looking for. He'd helped them and they'd let him go. Everything was fine. Mike and his son, Thomas, were wrong. He wasn't the threat they believed. He was just a quiet man who preferred to keep himself to himself. Ryan didn't understand how he wasn't able to move then. If he really believed that - surely he had nothing to fear from him?

⟑

The rest of the night dragged. It was hot and sticky, but Ryan wasn't comfortable in opening the window to let some air in. His imagination got the better of him. So, the neighbour looked to be innocent of whatever the police wanted to talk to him about. So what? It didn't detract from the fact that somewhere - out there - a killer was lurking and there was nothing stopping said killer (in Ryan's imagination anyway) from climbing in through the open bedroom window and killing everyone in the household whilst they slept.

By the time Dee stirred from her sleep, Ryan was already dressed in a fresh suit ready for a day at the bank.

"You're going to work then?" Dee asked.

"I haven't heard anything so I guess we'll be open today." Unless another package was sent to them - a thought which passed through his mind but remained unspoken. There was no point in saying anything like that to Dee. She'd only worry that whoever took Vanessa could come back and hurt her husband. Ryan internally told himself off. There's still no proof Vanessa didn't just walk out. Just because they can't get hold of her, or her parents, it doesn't mean she's been taken. Chances are she's just been taken on holiday by her mum and dad. Somewhere nice and hot, Ryan hoped. Besides - there was no evidence that suggested the person in the news took old people; like Vanessa's mum and dad. If he did take them all then it meant he'd changed his pattern and Ryan knew - admittedly from the films he watched - that it was rare for serial killers to act in such a manner. "Did you need the car?" he asked Dee. She shook her head and snuggled back down into the bed as though telling him she planned to stay there all day. Bitch. Not long left now before the school holidays were over and she'd be getting out of bed at the same time. Not long at all. She should just enjoy it whilst she could. Part of Ryan wished he still had more holiday to take at the bank. If so - he'd be sure to time it with Dee's first few days back in the classroom. She'd have to get up and he could snuggle down in the comfort of their bed. See how she liked it.

Dee stretched and reached over to her phone, which rested on the bedside cabinet, "Look at the time. Why didn't my alarm go off?"

"You looked peaceful. I was up so I turned it off. Thought you might have wanted to sleep in."

"I could have made you breakfast."

"I'm sure I can work a toaster."

"So I get breakfast in bed?" she asked with a cheeky grin.

He smiled at her, "If only I'd got dressed a little quicker. Now I just have to grab my toast and run. Sure one of the kids will sort you out though," he smiled again. Not because he knew one of the girls would look after their mother but more because the thought of one of them actually doing anything to help around the house tickled him. He opened his cupboard and reached for his tie before putting it around his neck, "What are your plans for the day?" he asked.

Dee shrugged. "Not sure."

"I meant what I said yesterday," he continued, "I don't want you seeing the neighbours."

"What did they do to piss you off so much? I happen to like Jackie."

"Just trust me, okay. They're not good people."

"They're fine."

"I'm not going to argue about it with you, Dee. Just, for once, listen to me…" he shot her a stern look. A look he didn't often give her but one which always made her feel like one of her naughty school children.

"Fine. But you'll have to tell me sooner or later. In the meantime - what do I do if Jackie comes over? I'm not just about to be rude to her without knowing the reasons." Dee knew she would still see her neighbour. They were friends after all. In her eyes it was Ryan who was being stupid. Maybe he did have reasons for his family to keep their distance from the people next door but, if he wasn't prepared to share his them - she had no reason to listen.

"Just make an excuse. Same goes for the kids." Ryan turned to Dee. He finished putting his tie on and straightened it. "How's that?"

"Fine."

Dee didn't continue the conversation about the neighbours. She could see it would only escalate to an argument she couldn't be bothered for and Ryan didn't continue it either (for much the same reasons).

"Are you sure you don't need the car today?" he asked.

"No. It's fine. I'm going to stay home. Thank you."

Ryan walked over to Dee and gave her a kiss on the forehead. Every morning when one of them had to get up (and the other didn't) it was the same. Never kiss on the mouth. Not first thing. Not with the morning breath given off by the one who'd only just stirred from their slumber.

"Coming downstairs?" he asked. "I literally have time to brown some toast and I'm gone."

"Do you mind if I stay in bed?" she asked. She snuggled down again.

"I hate you sometimes," Ryan smiled at her. "I'll text you at lunch." He walked from the room after giving her another kiss on the forehead. As he made his way across the landing, towards the stairs, he stopped by Claire's bedroom. The door was shut. He went to knock on the door but stopped himself. He wanted to tell her he'd seen the neighbour come home during the night - just to put her mind at ease that he couldn't have been that bad if the police let him go again. It wasn't important though. At least not enough to wake her. He'd tell her in the evening when he returned from the bank. He continued across the landing.

CHAPTER 13

My visitors annoyed me. Of all the times for them to come around - uninvited I hasten to add - they had to choose then; the moment I'd chosen to introduce myself to my new play-thing. I was standing in front of her. She was still unconscious. I had tried slapping her in the face, gently, to try and bring her back to consciousness but there was nothing. The lights were well and truly out. I was so frustrated my hands were visibly shaking. I shouldn't have hit her so hard but I didn't have a choice. Had I not silenced her, she would have alerted them to her presence and the game would have been over. Looking at her now, I wonder whether she'll even wake up. She's breathing funnily. Unless..A fleeting thought passing through my mind… maybe she is pretending. Maybe she's playing dead in the hope I'll leave her alone. I couldn't help but smile. One way to find out. You know, just to be sure. I reached under the chair she was still sitting on (and bound to) and pulled out the pliers again. As always, I start with the fingernails.

Ryan pulled up into the car park - across the road from the bank - with his thoughts still stuck on his broken dreams. His imagination working overtime questioning what he'd do if the serial killer did manage to get his hands on his daughter. His thoughts were so poisoned with dark scenarios - he barely remembered the actual drive to work. They called it driving amnesia. He pulled the key from the ignition and sat back in the seat.

"Come on, pull yourself together, pull yourself together…" He took a few deep breaths in an effort to calm his thoughts. When he realised they weren't going anywhere any time soon - he threw his seat belt off and climbed from the car. He slammed the door shut. Already he could tell today was going to be a bad day.

When he was out of the car he surveyed the car park. Only one police car today - parked in the far corner of the car park as though it had been there, tucked away, all night. Ryan wanted everything to be over now. He wanted Vanessa back to work - where she belonged - or at least word she was alive. He wanted the murderer caught so he could relax and he wanted his family to be happy. Better yet - he wanted them back in their own house. The one they had before the financial difficulties. The one they had before moving to where they were now. He couldn't help but feel this whole mess started when they moved. He knew Vanessa's absence was nothing to do with changing house. But the paranoia he felt, that the murderer was close to his own life, was no doubt brought about by the stress of the moving. Stress, lack of sleep and the fact he didn't feel comfortable in the new home yet. He felt out of place - a feeling he knew would have passed had he had the opportunity to relax in the new accommodation. Instead of the chance for relaxation, though, he just found more stress. The argument with his neighbours hadn't helped but - after last night's dreams - he couldn't help but think about what they'd said.

"Scum like that doesn't deserve to be alive."

All the time they're alive they're a burden to the society they once plagued. They cost the tax-payer money and they live their life in what some prisoners have called 'luxury' (despite others saying to the contrary). It would just be society's luck that, if they did find the killer, they'd realise he was one of the ones who relished living within the prison walls. And if that were the case - clearly the justice system would have failed the victims' families. Ryan felt himself getting worked up and immediately felt stupid for doing so. They hadn't even caught the man (or woman) responsible for the killings and yet here he was getting worked up at the prospect of the person enjoying his life in prison. He shook the irritating thoughts from his mind and hurried towards the bank's main entrance where he knocked on the door. A brief pause before the manager opened it - as per usual.

"Good morning!"

"Morning," said Ryan. It had been the first time since coming back to work he'd seen his manager remotely jovial. He couldn't help but wonder whether he knew something Ryan didn't. He stepped over the threshold and instantly noticed two officers monitoring camera footage in the manager's office. "Have they found anything yet?" he asked. He knew the answer. Had they found anything he was sure they wouldn't still be sitting in the office reviewing footage of the customers who frequented the building.

"Still reviewing footage," he replied. "It's strange - we see the customers come and go on a daily basis but…Well I was watching some of the footage. I didn't realise some of the customers came in more than once a day. And some of them only wanted to be served by Vanessa. You can see it in the footage. They purposefully let other people go in front of them just to ensure they're served by her."

"Really?" Ryan hadn't noticed this before either. As his manager stated - they're busy working and rarely notice little things like that. It was definitely odd though. Most of their customers they'd only see once (maybe twice) a week.

"Mr. Jenkins and Mr. Reynolds in particular. Both of them came in multiple times on the last day Vanessa was in."

"Mr. Jenkins? As in Peter?" Ryan knew Peter. A man in his early thirties. Tall with dark hair. There was no denying the man had a soft spot for Vanessa. Even if he wasn't served by her - he still couldn't keep his eyes from wandering over to where she was serving her customers. He certainly wasn't a murderer though. At least - not that Ryan believed. He was a quiet spoken, but polite man. Multiple trips to the bank as he was trying to get his affairs in order. Something he said in passing - he was leaving soon. He didn't say where he was going but - at one point - he'd thanked Ryan for all his help over the months.

"From what I understand the police are talking to them both - and a few others from the tapes - in the hope of ruling them out from anything suspicious." He shook his head, "The whole thing seems silly to me but I guess they daren't leave any stone unturned."

"Did they say anything about the," Ryan hesitated, "package which was delivered?"

"No. Nothing."

"Wait a minute - did you say Mr. Reynolds?"

"Yes."

"He's my new next door neighbour!"

The manager laughed, "Best hope it's not him they're looking for them!"

Ryan didn't laugh. He turned and ran from the building. The manager called out after him but he ignored his voice and continued across the road and back towards his car. In his mind all he could think about was the possibility of Mr. Reynolds being in on what was happening. Yes, the police took him in for a few questions which related to the disappearance of Vanessa but what if he was clever enough to appear innocent despite being anything but. And the dream - the dream of the man cutting his daughter - was plaguing his thoughts too. What if this was nothing more than a premonition? He quickened his pace until he was at the car. A quick twist of the key, in the car's lock, and he was in, guiding the same key into the car's ignition. If Ryan stopped, for a moment, and listened - he'd have heard a quieter part of his consciousness screaming at him that he was being ridiculous. But he didn't stop for a moment. He just wheel-span from the car parking area and sped off down the road - back towards home.

Claire was sitting at her desk. She'd not long been out of bed and was back to doodling in her pad again. There was not a lot else to do in a place you didn't know and where you'd not had the chance to make new friends - other than the weirdo next door who seemed a little too-obsessed with serial killers. She stopped sketching as a coldness rushed through her. That feeling again. The sensation of being watched. She turned to her bedroom door. It was still shut. Just being stupid. She glanced out of the window and froze. Out there - standing in his garden - was the next-door neighbour she'd met (briefly) the day before. He was standing in one of the only clearings of his garden and staring right up at her window. He saw Claire had noticed him and smiled. She couldn't help but smile back. A smile of nervousness. He waved. Slowly Claire moved back away from the window and - more importantly - his line of vision. What the hell was he doing out there? Just standing there waiting for her to appear at the window? And when did he even get home?

She crossed the room to where her mobile phone was charging on the bedside cabinet. She knew her father was at work but it didn't mean she couldn't text him. He wouldn't get the message immediately - what with being stuck with customers - but he'd see it on his break at least. And with any luck, she thought, he wouldn't have had his first break yet. She opened up a new text and quickly tapped out a new message asked for him to give her a call. Little did she know - he was only five minutes away now.

Ryan couldn't help but wonder whether Mr. Reynolds (what was his first name?!) had recognised him when he went to introduce himself. Maybe that is why he didn't open the front door to him? Maybe he didn't want to be recognised by the bank worker? Why? Did he have something to hide? Why else would you hide away? Ryan pressed his foot down harder on the accelerator. Fuck the possible speeding fines, he just wanted to get home in a timely fashion.

His mobile phone signalled the arrival of a new text message. Despite knowing better, he reached into his pocket and read it. His daughter's text message made his heart skip a beat. She rarely text him asking for him to call her and he couldn't help but over think the situation until he'd settled upon the worst possible scenario. It was now he wished he had a faster car.

CHAPTER 14

The smell of desperation emulating from the play-things turns me on greatly. The only time I've ever really noticed scents. Growing up - my friends used to say they loved the smell of a hot meal cooking (usually a roast) on a cold, rainy day. Other friends said they liked the smell of fresh cut grass and others were awakened by the smell of rain after a hot spell. Not that we get a lot of hot spells in this dirty country. I guess, growing up, they went abroad a lot. Those smells never did anything for me, though. Sure I could smell them but they never made me feel alive. Or maybe they did but only now do I realise it wasn't as much as I'd first believed - now I finally knew a scent which really got my juices flowing. The girl was awake now. Finally. And the fear and desperation coming from every pore of her skin - most arousing. I ripped the final nail from her right hand and relished in the sound of her scream. I dropped the pliers onto the floor - along with the nail - where they landed with a bloodied thump.

"Please stop!" she kept screaming again and again. Not sure why. Just as I tell all my play-things, I won't stop no matter how much they beg or what they offer.

I reached under the chair and onto the tray, which rested there. My little tray of tricks. I opted for the knife. I'm not sure why but I kind of fancy having another go at slicing skin from bone. Another attempt at making myself a suit from my play-thing. Who knows, maybe one day I'll manage it and venture out of the house dressed as them. See if I can continue living their lives as they did before I stole them away. I laughed at the idea. I know it's crazy. I know it's stupid. But it's still funny. Imagine going to see her parents. Imagine if they don't see through the mask. Imagine spending a whole Sunday with them, perhaps sharing lunch, and finding out more about who I'd be pretending to be. Maybe - at the end of the evening - I'd pull the mask away and show them who I really am. Reveal The Evil Lurking Within.

I nicked the top of her forehead with the knife. Just enough to be able to get a good grip on the skin. Something to hold onto as I pull it away whilst making further incisions with the sharpened blade. I just hope she sits still. Such a delicate procedure.

I stopped what I was doing and looked her in the eye, "Are you ready?" I asked.

"Please don't."

"You may wish to brace yourself." I gave her a comforting smile.

⅄

Ryan was standing in Claire's bedroom. He was looking out of her window, straight into the neighbour's garden.

"And he was just standing there?"

"Yes!"

"Well what was he doing?"

"Nothing. He was just staring up at my window."

Ryan stepped away from the window and turned to his daughter. He rested a comforting hand on her shoulder, "He's just a bit strange. Just ignore him. If he were dangerous - or if there was even a chance of him being the man they were looking for - the police wouldn't have let him go. Just think of that. They picked him up. They released him…"

"Yeah because they never make mistakes do they!" the sarcasm was thick in her tone of voice. Ryan chose to ignore it as Dee walked into the room.

"What are you doing here? I didn't hear you come in," she said.

"The bank was shut again," Ryan lied. He shot Claire a look - a look which told her to keep her mouth shut and not to say anything to her mother.

"Really? What - no one was there?"

"Only the manager and a few police officers again. They're still review-ing the footage…"

"Anything?"

"Not yet."

"You'd think they could open though. Must be losing money…"

Claire looked uncomfortable. Almost as uncomfortable as how Ryan was feeling. They both just wished Dee would drop it. Better yet - leave them alone again so they could continue their conversation.

"Maybe they'll open tomorrow," he said.

Dee nodded. "Well I'll leave you two to it." She turned back to the door, "Oh - just so you know though - your manager phoned. He was wondering if everything was okay and asked that you call him when you get in." She didn't wait to hear Ryan's reaction (which was only to mutter the word 'shit'), she simply walked from the room and closed the door behind her.

Claire looked at her father's (now anxious) face. "Why don't you just tell her?" she asked.

"Because it's something else to stress about, isn't it? You hate it here, our neighbours on both sides are weird, everything is just weird at the bank…" he felt himself off-load to Claire. He hadn't meant to but it was only a matter of time. He could only keep everything buried, within, for x amount of time. And this - the fact he'd been caught lying to the woman he'd promised never to lie to - was the final straw. The one which broke the camel's back. "Fuck!" He realised his language, "And don't let me hear you say that either."

"Just tell her, dad. She needs to know."

Ryan sighed. Claire was right. Even if he didn't want to tell Dee - he didn't have a choice now anyway. Not now he'd been caught out lying. "You're right," he said. "Okay - keep your sister out of the way, yeah?"

Claire nodded. "And then we can move back home."

"This is home."

Dee was washing up in the kitchen. She didn't need to. They had a dishwasher. Ryan had bought it with a month's bonus a few years ago because he hated the deal the married couple had; Dee did the cooking and he did the washing up. Now it became - Dee did the cooking and he put the dishes in the dishwasher. Sometimes he even made the girls do it. When he did, Dee didn't moan. It wasn't as though they did anything else to help around the house and it still meant she didn't have to do it herself. Ryan walked in behind her and closed the door in so no small ears could hear their conversation. Dee knew he was there, behind her, but she didn't turn to him. She just continued washing up the dishes from breakfast.

"We have a dishwasher," Ryan pointed out, "you don't need to do that." Dee didn't answer him. Just carried on washing up. "I'm sorry I lied to you." Those were the magic words. She stopped washing up and turned around.

"Why did you?"

"Didn't want to worry you."

"What's going on? You've been acting strange for days now. What is it?"

"This whole thing at the bank."

"Vanessa?"

"Not just her but the girls in general - the ones in the newspapers."

"The dead ones?"

"If Vanessa's been taken by the serial killer - that's right on the doorstep. That's practically in our home. It might as well be for how it's affected me." Ryan shifted on his feet. Dee could see that just talking about it was getting him stressed again. "Could have been Claire. Or Jen. Imagine if they'd been taken?"

"But they haven't." She paused a moment, "So what's the story with our neighbours then? Why am I not allowed to see them?" Ryan shifted on his feet again. "Ryan…" Dee pressed him.

"Their son…"

"Thomas."

"He started telling Claire that our other neighbour is the killer."

"What?"

"You came in yesterday with Jackie and the kids. I went next door to tell him not to put silly ideas in her head. She doesn't need them. You know, as much as I do, she is struggling with this move. And that little prick isn't helping her settle, you know?" He took a breath. "Well I went there to tell him to keep his ideas to himself and Mike walked in. He thinks the same. He agrees with his fucking son. More than that - they're talking about breaking into the man's house to get proof. Something about him going mad after the death of his partner, or something like that…"

"They want to break into his house?"

"Yes. Find proof that he is the murderer."

"They'd find the killer and then get arrested for breaking and entering? It doesn't matter what the circumstances are - I'm pretty sure there isn't some get out of jail free card you can use. What does Jackie think?"

"I don't know - she was here with you. For all I know, though, she feels the same as them. And that's why I just want us to keep our distance from them. Oh - with regards to the police - the way they were talking; they weren't discussing taking the matter to the law. They were talking of taking the law into their own hands."

"What?"

"A taste of his own medicine."

"A taste of his own medicine? What's that even supposed to mean? What - they want to torture them? They think that's acceptable?"

"That's what I'm talking about, Dee. This is what I've been trying to tell you! These people think it's okay to break into someone's house and they think it's okay to take justice into their own hands. They're trouble."

"I don't think Jackie…"

"Please don't argue with me on this," Ryan cut in. "I mean it. They're trouble. And I don't need them upsetting Claire anymore. Or accidentally saying something in front of Jen." He leant back against the kitchen work-top. "The move was hard enough," he whined, "we don't need this too."

Dee hesitated. She wanted to say something to make him feel better but could only think of one thing to say, "What about the neighbour? The other one? The one they believe to be a murderer. People don't just decide someone is a murderer without something prompting them to do so. So why would they say it?"

Ryan shrugged. "I went round there yesterday to introduce myself," he explained, "the guy is quiet, yes, maybe even a little weird but I don't think he's a killer. A hermit perhaps. Besides - if the police thought he was a risk they'd have kept him in."

"Kept him in?"

"They picked him up yesterday," Ryan said. "But they let him go. So clearly the guy isn't who they're looking for."

"Well they must have had reason to think he could have been responsible or else they wouldn't have taken him in."

"They just needed to rule him out. Hell, the only reason he was picked up is because he's a one of the bank's customers. It just so happened he was caught on camera frequenting the bank more than once a day and that he'd always insist on being served by Vanessa…"

"What and you still think he is innocent?"

"What?"

Dee sighed, "Your colleague is missing. He has been stalking her…"

"I wouldn't say he was stalking her…"

"He went in - more than once a day - and only got served by her? And now she is missing? Ryan, alarm bells are ringing!"

"The police let him go!"

"A lack of evidence to keep him in doesn't mean he isn't guilty. Maybe the neighbours are right about him. Maybe we should be talking to them and telling them why he was taken in."

"What are you talking about? What you think their way of dealing with it is right?"

"You'd rather live in ignorance when there is the slightest chance we could be living next door to a…."

"Why is everyone shouting?" Jen asked as she walked into the room. Claire was with her. She mouthed, to her father, she was sorry for interrupting them. Ryan didn't react. Neither he nor Dee even realised they'd been shouting in the first place. Their voices must have gradually been creeping up the more they spoke about the situation. "I'm hungry." Jen whined.

"Well you're in luck," Dee said with a false smile on her face, "your father has offered to take us out for food…Exciting, huh? Go and get your coat."

Jen hurried from the room with an excited bounce in her steps.

"We're going out?" Claire asked, confused as to how that came about.

"Sure. Be nice to get out of the house, don't you think?" Dee asked.

"I guess."

"Then go and get your coat."

Claire followed her sister. Dee turned back to her husband, "You need to talk to Mike and his son. Find out their exact reasoning as to why they feel he may be dangerous. There's no smoke without fire and the fact he has been seen - often - in your bank should be enough for you to realise there's more to him than what you believe. I mean it. Apologise to the neighbours and find out what's what."

"And then what? You want me to break into the man's house and sneak around with them too? Maybe I could keep a look out for them?"

"If he's dangerous, we have a right to know. I just want my family to be safe." She stormed from the room leaving Ryan to his thoughts. He'd rushed home because he was worried about his family. It was an instant reaction to the situation he was presented with. He was worried about the neighbour - yes - but he was also worried about the attitudes of Mike and Thomas (and maybe even Jackie). On the drive home, he envisioned packing his family up and running away - back to the house where they once lived. But as soon as he pulled up in his driveway, he had no idea what he was supposed to do next. All he knew was that his head was absolutely pounding. Stress, anxiety, a lack of sleep and a the horrible feeling they were all in this position because of him. He had forced the move, he had chosen the property. If they had gone anywhere else Vanessa would have still been missing but at least they may have had normal neighbours.

Chapter 15

Her face was off now and she was unconscious. I couldn't do it in one piece dammit! Her head was tilted back. A bloodied mess. Still, disappointing though. And speaking of mess - I looked down to the piles of gore I'd hacked off with the knife. Need to sharpen the knife again. The more I cut off, the harder it became to slice the skin. That's probably why I failed to hack it off in a single satisfying cut. I tilted her head back by a handful of hair and moved my own face closer to get a good look at the mess I'd left behind. It's beautiful. I reached under the chair and pulled another of my tools from underneath where she sat. A little trick I found to wake them up - a bottle of vinegar.

"Time to wake up," I whispered to her. We have much to do and I'm worried it has been too long since I'd left a present for someone to find out in the woods. Need to speed this up and get something out there before I'm forgotten or no longer the leading story on the news programs. If you're not the top of the news - there's little point in even being mentioned. No one remembers the little stories. I don't want to be one of them. Jesus - starting to sound more and more like my idol, Art. I'm not him. I'm not him. I'm my own person. I'm something worse (better) than him. I'm better. Bigger and better. And to prove it - I tipped the vinegar over the play-thing's face. She screamed herself awake. I continued to pour the vinegar.

Ryan and his family were sitting around the table of their local Harvester restaurant in silence. With the exception of Jen, all of them were thinking about the situation with the neighbours.

"Why is no one talking?" Jen asked. She was young, but fairly astute as to what is going on around her (with the exception of things which are hidden from her - such as horrific stories in the local papers).

"What would you like to talk about?" Dee asked her. Jen responded by shrugging. "We're all just thinking about what to choose for dinner - that's why everyone is quiet."

"Well I know what I want," Jen replied. "I'm having the chocolate fudge brownie."

"And for your main meal?"

"Same."

"Chocolate fudge brownie for your main and your pudding? Yeah - I don't think so, kiddo. Nice try though." Dee handed her the menu again, "Now why don't you see if there's anything you'd rather have for your main meal."

"What are you having?" Jen asked her sister. Claire shrugged. Anyone at another table could easily spot they were sisters despite the different looks about them. They used exactly the same mannerisms.

"Gammon and egg, I think." Ryan had chosen his meal. He closed the menu and placed it on front of the table in front of him. "Or ribs." He tried to lighten the obvious mood at the table, "Maybe I'll have both. Two plates. I'm a growing lad, after all…"

"Growing outward, fatty!" Dee seized the chance to join him in lightning the mood. Ryan shot her a look. He knew what she was trying to do (the same as him). Her comment was a little mis-judged though given the frosty atmosphere between them.

"I'd like a burger," Claire placed her menu on the table on top of the one her father had used.

"That's what I want!" Jen said.

"Well you can both have burgers!" Ryan snapped. He immediately regretted snapping at them. He leant back in his seat and rubbed his neck in an effort to try and ease some of the tension from it.

"This is nice," Dee continued - ignoring Ryan's comment. "We should do this more often."

Claire looked at her. She knew something was up between her mother and father and - more importantly - she knew exactly what it was.

"Can I go and play round Kara's when we get home?" Jen asked.

"No!" Ryan said.

"Yes. Of course you can," said Dee. She shot Ryan a look. "I'll take you around there when I go and see Jackie," Dee said. She knew her comments would annoy Ryan but she didn't care. She wanted the whole mess sorted out and the sooner the better as far as she was concerned. After all, if the neighbour was as innocent as the police believed him to be then he (and they as his neighbours) had nothing to worry about from him. If anything, they might even get to know him a little better. And it meant that it didn't matter what Mike and his family felt towards him - the man would be innocent so they'd obviously leave him alone. Everyone would go about their lives just as they did before everything kicked off. On the flip side of the coin - if the man was a danger to their family then Mike and his son should be allowed to act accordingly. Besides - despite what Ryan told her - she didn't actually believe they'd do anything other than hand him over to the police if they did discover something off which proved his guilt. Just because they said they'd like to give him a taste of his own medicine it didn't mean they'd actually go ahead with it. It wouldn't have been the first time someone had mouthed off about 'sorting' something.

A waitress came over with her plain note-pad in hand, ready to scribble down the family's order, "Good afternoon…Have you guys had a chance to decide what you'd like to order yet?"

"You know what - can we just get the bill?" Ryan asked her. The waitress looked surprised but nodded anyway. She went off to fetch the bill for the four drinks they had ordered when they first took their seats at the table.

"What are you doing?" Dee asked. She felt her face redden from embarrassment. It wasn't every day someone would come into the restaurant just to order four drinks before leaving again.

"You heard Jen. She wants to see Kara," Ryan said in a shitty tone of voice, "and you want to go and see Jackie…So…Let's go! I didn't want to come out anywhere. This was your idea and now you've clearly changed your mind. Well let's save some money and go home. Jen can play with Kara, you can see Jackie and I'm sure Claire and I will find something else to do."

Dee went to say something back but fell silent when the waitress returned with the bill in hand, "Here you go. Do you need the card machine?"

"That's fine, thank you." Ryan took the bill from her and opened his wallet, revealing a handful of small notes. "Sorry to mess you around. My wife thinks she knows better." He threw some money onto the table (more than enough to cover the bill) and slid out from his seat before heading towards the exit. The waitress just stood there with a dumbfounded expression on her face. She may have seen someone come in and order a round of drinks before leaving but she'd rarely encountered an outburst like that.

"I'm so sorry!" said Dee. She kept her face low to try and hide her embarrassment. The waitress told her not to worry as Dee ushered her family out of the door.

人

"Girls cover your ears!" Dee called back to the rear of the car as she climbed in next to Ryan who'd already started the engine up with the key. "You're an asshole!" she said to Dee.

"Fuck you!" Ryan snapped straight back at her.

Claire reached across to Jen, in the back, and gave her hand a gentle squeeze. When Jen looked across to her sister, to see what she wanted, Claire gave her a little wink and a smile. Her way of letting her sister know, without saying anything, that she was there for her and - despite appearances - everything was okay. Jen smiled back but her face clearly showed she wasn't convinced everything was alright. In fact - her expression revealed she was extremely nervous about the situation. Probably more so because Ryan and Dee usually tried their best not to argue in front of the children.

"Just take me home!" Dee demanded despite the fact Ryan was already driving out of the multi-story and heading back towards their new home.

"And for the record, when we get home, I'm going to see Jackie and Jen is going to play with Kara."

"So you keep telling me."

"I don't want to go round," Jen piped up from the back seat. Her mind had been changed after the arguments started - not because she didn't want to go - because she thought her request had been the root cause of the sudden hostility between her mum and dad.

"You're going!" Dee accidentally snapped at Jen. She was so wound up by Ryan that she hadn't even noticed. Nor had Ryan. Claire noticed though and gave her sister's hand another squeeze.

"I'll come with you," Claire whispered to her. Jen smiled at her.

The rest of the drive was completed in silence - more or less. A few sniffles from an upset Jen in the back of the car and the quiet seething of both parents in the front, which was only drowned out when Dee leaned forward and turned the radio on.

Chapter 16

The girl has no eye-lids, most of her facial skin missing or pealed back at the very least. Her breathing has become shallow; raspy even. Her finger-nails have been removed, fingers individually broken along with her toes. Her pleas for release have stopped now. I know she'd be calling out if she could. I know that. But she's dying. We're getting to the end of our time together. A pity. I've enjoyed myself. Good stress release; an added benefit of my sexy little hobby. Anyway no time to think about that. Each moment which passes, she gets weaker. If I want to have one last bit of fun - I need to act quickly.

I kicked her chair over. It slammed back, with her on it, onto the concrete floor of my cellar. She's barely conscious; didn't even groan from the force of the slam. I need to be really quick if I want to feel pleasure from what's coming. It's not fun if they're dead or they don't feel what's coming...

I walked over to the corner of the room with a newfound sense of urgency and took a hold of the sledgehammer, which rested up against the battered brickwork of the corner wall. It's rare they're usually still alive at this stage of our relationship so - when they are - I like to really enjoy it. I took the sledgehammer back across to my plaything and lined it up with her kneecap. I raised the tool high up in the air and held it there - for a moment - with a tingling sensation running through my body. Not only is this fun but it also makes it easier to cut the limbs with the hacksaw, when I'm gearing up to drop their body's into the woodlands. The sledgehammer makes such a mess of the bone…So much easier to cut through it. A final smile and I brought the sledgehammer down hard and fast. Not only did her leg crack, her kneecap smash, but so did the chair. Foolish mistake. I should have taken her off the chair first. I should have laid her down on the cool concrete of the floor. Especially given the fact she isn't in a position to make a run for it. One more kneecap to go and then the same for the arms - right about at the elbow joint. She isn't screaming. Still breathing but not screaming. Pretty sure she's out for the count again. She will not wake up again.

Ryan sat in his living room, alone. He'd closed the curtains blocking out the outside world. Dee and the girls had gone around to Jackie and Mike's despite Ryan's protests. Dee didn't listen to him and the girls didn't have a choice either way. Dee just wanted them all away from Ryan. Two reasons; she was angry at him and didn't want to be around him and because she hoped the time alone would give him some time to think about what was going on in his life. He couldn't keep letting the stress get to him. And - more to the point from Dee's perspective - he couldn't keep taking it out on his family. He'd been shitty ever since he found out his colleague was missing from her work place. But Dee didn't know the whole truth. She couldn't. Ryan wanted to tell her - on more than one occasion - but he knew it could spell the end of his marriage. The end of his family. His wife would hate him. His daughters would hate him. He'd be the bad guy.

He leant forward in his seat and reached for his mobile phone, which he'd stuffed in the back pocket of his trousers. A quick search of the contacts until he came to the number he was looking for. Her number. Vanessa's number. Of course it hadn't been stored under her name. The number was stored under John. Ever since he found out she was missing he wanted nothing more than to give her a ring but he was sure she wouldn't answer. Especially if she wasn't answering the calls of people she actually classed as true friends. What Ryan and Vanessa had - it was one night. Not even a full night. A drunken fling a few months ago, at the Christmas Party. Drunken kissing lead to drunken fumbling and that lead to a drunken fuck.

An encounter which temporarily confused Ryan as to what he wanted with his life and an encounter which lead Vanessa to believe she had a chance with him - a married man.

"I can't," Ryan had told her, "I'm married. I'm sorry. That," he had paused a moment to think about what he was going to say so as not to cause more upset than necessary, "was a mistake."

He sat there, on the couch, and cursed himself for the choice of words he'd used when talking to Vanessa, the next time he'd seen her at the bank. He threw his mobile phone down onto the coffee table in the middle of the room. He can't call her. He can't. If the police check her phone records (which they will) and see he's been calling then they'd get in touch with him. They'd want to find out why he was so desperate to speak to her. Obviously he'd tell them it was because he was concerned for her - just like everyone else at the bank - but he wasn't sure whether they'd know he'd had that encounter with her. Vanessa said she wouldn't tell anyone but what if she'd told one of her girlfriends? And what if one of those had told the police. Ryan regretted that night more now than he'd ever regretted it before. It was months ago and he'd thought he'd got away with it but now it was more than possible for it to come back and bite him on the arse. He knew, if people had been talking, it would have been easy for them to add two and two together and come up with five. And when people come up with five - it meant he'd be a prime suspect in why she vanished.

Part of him wondered whether he should just tell the police, on the quiet, what'd happened between him and Vanessa. Let them have the full facts before they came to him with half of the facts and a handle of half-truths. He worried though that, even doing it on the quiet, word would still come out and find its way back to his family. His family - who were currently playing happy neighbours with the psychopaths next door. The folk who seem to think they're allowed to take the law into their own hands and act as they want. He stood up and started to pace the living room as he wondered when everything went so wrong for him. He regretted not taking the redundancy the bank had offered. Sure it could have lead them to more problems - what with not having a job - but at least he wouldn't have ended up moving to this house. And if he had taken redundancy when it was offered - he wouldn't have been at the Christmas party either. His sordid little rendezvous with Vanessa would never have happened. He probably wouldn't even be aware of the fact she was missing - although, chances were, he'd still have seen the reports on the news between the programs he actually gave a shit about.

He picked up his now-cold cup of tea and took a swig from it. He spat the liquid back out and threw the cup against the wall where it shattered into tiny pieces.

"FUCK!" he screamed. He dropped to his knees, onto the carpet and stared into space with his mind wondering in different directions before settling down upon his neighbour, Mr. Reynolds. What if Mike and Thomas are right with their conclusions? If they were then it meant Mr. Reynolds was the man responsible for taking Vanessa; snatching her away from her quiet life. Ryan still presumed the hands, posted to the bank, belonged to Vanessa and understood it meant the chances of her being alive were slim. But, what if she was still alive? What if the sick son of a bitch had kept her alive and was just teasing the other bank employees and the police department? What if there was still time to find her? He shook his head. It didn't matter. Mr. Reynolds had been questioned by the police, and they found no reason to keep him in or go back to his property. As far as they were concerned he had been ruled out completely and was free to do as he pleased. If she were still alive and he was the killer - it wouldn't be long until the rest of her happened to show up either at the bank or in the same woods where the other girls had been discovered dotted around the place. "Shit!" Ryan's brain was trying to convince him that Mr. Reynolds was the murderer now and that he'd got away with his crimes. His brain was even trying to tell him, despite knowing the likelihood, that Vanessa was still alive next door. No hands but still with breath in her lungs. The more he thought about it - despite fighting with the various options running through his mind - the more he started to worry that Mike and Thomas were actually correct with their assumptions and that they did need to get into the house to see what they could uncover. If they did it - as in Mike and Thomas…If they were the ones to break into the house then nothing could come back to Ryan or his family. It would be down to them. They'd be the one in trouble with the law. If they didn't find anything then - so be it - the man is innocent but if they did then Ryan could convince them to get the authorities involved. They'd arrest him, he'd go through the justice system and - more importantly - the police questioning Ryan about that night with Vanessa would never come into play meaning his marriage wouldn't collapse. The mess it was in now, after the arguing, that was fixable with an apology or two. Definitely fixable. Dee finding out her husband had fucked a girl a good few years younger than him - even with alcohol to blame - that probably wouldn't be fixable.

Ryan clambered to his feet and walked over to the mirror. He stared at the reflection of the man who risked his married for a drunken fuck and hated what he saw. There's no need for his marriage to fall apart. There's no need for this dirty little secret to come out into the open. No need at all. If Mike and Thomas are right - and Ryan got the police involved before they could take justice into their own hands - then everything could be fixed without any secrets being spilled.

"And if they're wrong?" Ryan asked himself. "They won't be wrong. It's him. Think about it. The man was picked up by the police. He only ever let Vanessa serve him in the bank. He saw her multiple times during the day. Clearly, the guy was infatuated with her. Maybe he asked her out and she said no and so he did to her what he did to other girls who refused his advances?" The more Ryan stood there, in front of the mirror, thinking about it - the more he convinced himself that Mr. Reynolds was the man the police were looking for and that, somehow, he'd managed to throw them off his scent. What Claire said - in the bedroom earlier - was right; it wouldn't be the first time someone had fooled the authorities into believing they were innocent.

Ryan hurried from the room and out of the front door, slamming it shut behind him. A desperate hope in finding Vanessa alive with Mr. Reynolds, and catching the killer red-handed clouded his judgement.

CHAPTER 17

Her kneecaps were unrecognisable now. Nothing more than smashed up mush. I envisioned the bone being but a chalky powder under the ripped skin. She'd long since stopped breathing, the shock of everything I'd put her through finally taking her to what people believe to be a better place. Part of my cruel torture being to tell them - before I start -that there is nothing better for them when they do die. There is simply nothing. Just as we remember nothing from when we're in the womb, when we're dead we also remember and experience nothing. We simply stop being part of the human rat race. We are simply no more.

I lifted the sledgehammer again. I don't need to hit her joints anymore. My work on those is well and truly done. I am, however, curious as to see what would happen if I were to bring it down upon her head with as much force as I could possibly muster. How many hits before her already bloodied face is completely flat? I'm not sure but I'm willing to find out. I brought the heavy tool down the flat of her face. The loudest crack I'd ever heard in all of my life; a sound which seemed to echo around the room along with my uncontrollable laughter. I pulled the hammer away from her face and noticed her nose had completely caved with the force of the blow. Some of her teeth had shattered whilst other teeth had ended up pointing back into her open mouth. Her jaw was also at a funny angle with the bone from the top of the jaw line poking through the bloodied mush of her face. I couldn't help but drop the sledgehammer and fall to my knees with the fits of the giggles. I'm glad I took a photograph of her before I started. I've already forgotten how pretty she was when we first began our time together and it'll be good to compare the before and after shots. I only wished I'd taken it a step further and videoed the blow.

⚔

Jackie opened the door to Ryan. She was usually a friendly, bubbly woman (bordering on irritating with how happy she appeared to be) but this time Ryan was confronted by a completely different woman; a hostile one who looked displeased to see him.

"May I come in?" Ryan asked. He felt sheepish. He wasn't sure who'd spoken to Jackie about what he'd been saying about her family - whether it was Mike, Thomas or even his own wife - but clearly someone had been saying something to her.

Jackie held the door open, letting him walk in. She couldn't very well say 'no' when his wife was sitting at their dining room table clutching a cup of tea in her hands.

"She's through there," Jackie pointed the way before she closed the door.

"Thank you." Ryan walked through, kicking his shoes off before he did so, and stopped in the dining room's doorway. Dee was sitting with Thomas, Claire and Mike. Another placemat, with another hot drink, showed where Jackie had been sitting before Ryan disturbed them. Scattered on the table were Thomas' many handwritten notes. All in the room looked up to Ryan when they noticed him. "I, er, I owe you all an apology," he admitted. "I'm sorry for how I've been behaving and I'm sorry with what I said about your family," the latter part of the apology being aimed at Mike.

"What brought this about?" Mike asked. He wasn't expecting an apology. He wasn't even expecting to see Ryan again after their last conversation. God knows he was surprised to see Dee and the girls standing in the doorstep when they first knocked as he was under the impression the whole family was banned from speaking to him (and his family).

"The police are at work," he continued, "I know why they came to see Mr. Reynolds - our neighbour. It's because he is a customer of the bank. Well, we have footage of him being served by my colleague - the lady who went missing…" he didn't want to say her name again as he didn't want to sound as he was that friendly with her. He thought if he kept mentioning her by her name - at some point Dee might have started to become suspicious. He thought incorrectly. The thought hadn't even crossed her mind. But then - his thoughts were most likely down to the guilt he felt. He continued, "They wanted to talk to him because on more than one occasion he visited the bank to see my colleague…As in - more than once a day. The tapes showed he would let others go before him if another of my colleagues called him over. He'd let as many people in front of him, each time, until she was ready to serve him. And then, he'd go over and see her. It's a bit strange and enough of a lead to make the police want a chat with him."

"So he did take your colleague then?" Mike asked.

"I don't know," Ryan admitted, "but it's odd. I was thinking about what you and your boy were saying. You know, about wanting to look around his house…See if you can find anything…"

"You said the police let him go again," Claire piped up.

"You said it yourself," he reminded her, "it wouldn't be the first time they'd got it wrong and let a guilty person go free." Ryan took a seat at the dining room table. "Look I'm not saying it is him. I'm not saying he is a murderer. I'm just saying that maybe it would be worth taking a look around his place, when he is out. Hopefully you'll find nothing," Ryan was careful to use the words 'you will' as he had no intention of breaking into the man's house, "and we can just forget this whole thing…Maybe even laugh about it."

Mike looked him dead in the eye, "And if we find out he is the man they're looking for?"

Ryan locked eyes, "We let the authorities know. The families who've lost their children to his crimes will get some closure and your son gets some great bits for his first novel. Everyone is a winner," he finished. It felt wrong saying 'everyone was a winner' but it helped him get his point across. The group sat in silence around the table - each thinking about what had been said.

Dee was the first to break the silence, "You owe an apology to your other daughter," she said. She was referring to Jen who was busy playing upstairs - well away from the adult nature of this conversation. "And you owe us a meal out."

"Fine and, yes, you're right. I'm sorry. I've just had a lot on my plate what with one thing and another. The sooner this is dealt with - one way or the other - the better." Ryan's brain had almost stopped telling him there was a chance the neighbour was innocent completely now. In his mind he was guilty as sin, just as he was in the minds' of everyone else sat in the room.

Mike turned to Jackie, "Why don't you go and start dinner?" he suggested. "I take it you and your family would like to stay for something to eat?" he asked Dee.

"We wouldn't want to be any trouble."

"It's no trouble. Right, honey?" Mike looked to his wife for back up. She shook her head as if to agree with him; it would be no trouble.

"Then that's sorted. Perhaps you and Claire would like to help Jackie? Or at least keep her company in the kitchen so she doesn't get lonely." Mike finished. Ryan looked at him. Not only was the guy a possible psychopath but he was also starting to come across as a male chauvinist with how he spoke to the girls. It wasn't without reason though. He wanted the girls out of the room so he could converse with Ryan about what they needed to do next. Specifically it would be a conversation about breaking into the neighbour's house to see if they could find anything and the less the girls knew about that, Mike thought, the better. Especially if anything went wrong - at least this way the girls could deny knowing anything. Jackie lead the way through to the kitchen with Dee and Claire following. None of them protested to the orders as they all read between the lines. Mike turned to Thomas, "Want to give them a hand?" he asked.

Thomas shook his head. He knew his father was looking out for him. He wanted what was best for him plain and simple but - at the end of the day - Thomas was the reason they were all sitting around the table. He'd got Claire involved and - subsequently - Ryan and, even before that, it was his discussions with his father which made Mike realise all was not right with their seemingly quiet neighbour. Although, in fairness, Mike didn't need much encouragement to take a dislike to his neighbour. From the moment they first met, back when Mr Reynolds wife was around, he thought he was 'odd'.

"I want to be a part of this," Thomas said. He was smiling. The idea of breaking into someone's house - who may or may not have been a killer - clearly turned him on and fired his senses.

"So when are you going to do it?" Ryan asked.

"We."

"I'm sorry?"

"We're going to do it. You're a part of this now too…"

"I can't," Ryan protested, "he knows me. He comes to where I work…"

"He knows all of us," Thomas pointed out, "we live next to him!"

"We're not doing this without you. You're as much to do with this as we are now," Mike said. The tone in his voice was enough for Ryan to know he wasn't joking around. "Besides it'll be quicker if there are three of us. In and out."

"I don't know anything about breaking and entering!" Ryan said. The panic clearly written all over his face - never mind the fact his voice was shaky.

"And you think we do? We just put gloves on and go in via the back where no one will be likely to notice us. We'll go down the alleyway next to your house and over his fence…If need be, break a window to unlock the door…"

Ryan shifted uncomfortably in his seat. Already things were going wrong. The idea was to get Thomas and Mike to do the donkey work. They go in, he sits back from the safety of his own home. Anything goes wrong - he could deny everything. "I'm not happy about this," he pointed out.

"It's the only way it's going to happen," Mike said. "Unless you're happy to sit back and pretend everything is okay and we'll just drop the whole thing. Hopefully, he's innocent anyway. As you said, the police let him go so there's a good chance all is good with him…And even if he isn't - I'm sure he wouldn't shit on his own doorstep…" Mike sat back and watched Ryan's reaction. His words hit home just as he knew they would. By shitting on his own doorstep he was referring to snatching girls from where he lived. Specifically Claire who was closest to the age bracket of girls being taken. Any age between seventeen and thirty-two so far. Again, Ryan shifted in his seat - his mind imagining the look on the man's face when he was looking up to Claire's bedroom window. In reality the look was that of a curious man looking into the window of a pretty girl - which wasn't ideal - but in Ryan's head he could picture Mr. Reynolds rubbing his hands together at the prospect of getting Claire into whatever room he liked to torture girls in. There was a long pause.

"So when do we do it?" Ryan asked. Ideally they'd get it done as soon as possible, in his mind. Especially if there was a chance Vanessa was still alive - a stupid thought which his brain struggled to let go of even though he knew it'd be easier (safer for his marriage) if she were dead. What happened to her now wasn't really a priority for Ryan. Saving his marriage and family were and if that meant breaking into someone's house to do so then so be it. Especially as he knew there could be a strong chance of the police knocking on his own door again - with the additional information, to hand, of the affair. Ryan shouted at himself internally. It wasn't an affair. It was one night. Not even the whole night. It didn't matter, though. When people spoke of it - if they were to speak of it - they'd blow it out of proportion.

"As soon as he is out," Mike said. A smile spread across his thin lips. Ryan wasn't sure whether this was because he was planning to do something to frame him (just as Ryan planned to use Mike and Thomas as the fall guys) or whether it was because Ryan was finally on side with him; driven there by sheer desperation.

"Right and when do we know when he is out?" Ryan asked. His mind already told him they'd need to be setting up some sort of surveillance on the property.

"The easiest way is to knock!" Thomas pointed out. The two grown men looked at him. It was simple, yes, but it was also effective. If he answers - clearly he is in. If he doesn't answer than the coast is clear. Mike smiled at his boy as though it were all something to be proud of. Ryan bit his tongue. There was nothing proud about this moment. If anything this was what was wrong with society.

"Well," Mike stood to his feet, "no time like the present."

CHAPTER 18

I always fall into a little depression when I've finished with my play-things. My relationship with them is over and I find myself alone again. It has always been this way. Before I started taking people - things weren't much better but my solitude wasn't the driving force behind my choices. I couldn't tell you what the driving forces were. I don't know where the urges initially came from. I know I was inspired by people but that didn't mean they were what made me actually do it. I didn't wake up and decide to be them, or like them. It just happened. And now it has - I want to be the best I can. A strange compulsion but one I've grown accustomed to.

I leant back, on the cellar's wall, and looked at the mess that laid across the floor before me. The blood, the mush, the various bits I'd cut off. I miss her already. Once again my time with her was far too short for what I had planned - not that I've finished with her completely. Not yet. I need to bag her up, later. I need to take her out. I need to dump her for someone to find. Then - and only then - will I be done with her and, once again, on the lookout for someone else to play my games.

Another knock at the door, upstairs, pulled me back to reality. My heart skipped a beat. I don't get people visiting me. Never. This is the second person within the space of a couple of days. Another knock. Harder this time. Ignore it. They'll leave. Another knock.

✦

Ryan was hoping the door was going to open but it was looking less and less likely to be the case. Mike knocked on the door again; three hard hits with the side of his clenched fist. Thomas watched on, smiling. Unlike Ryan, Thomas was hoping the neighbour was out. A teenager on the verge of breaking into someone's house knowing they couldn't get in trouble for it. Not when he had his father's permission to be there.

They'd left the girls in the kitchen of Mike and Jackie's. When asked where they were going they didn't try and hide the truth from them. They told them they were going around to knock on Mr. Reynolds' front door. They didn't tell them - though - that they were going to break in if he was out. That was their little secret and would stay that way until the task was done and - more importantly - they'd gotten the facts they needed whilst also getting away with their crime.

"I think it's fair to say he's out," Mike said. "We ready to do this?" Now he was the one who was looking unsure Ryan noticed. Perhaps he wasn't as bad as Ryan first believed him to be.

"Fuck, yeah!" Thomas piped up. Mike turned to him and gave him a look. Not because of his enthusiasm as to what they were going to do but because of his son's rather colourful language. Mike's look was enough. Thomas sheepishly looked to the side of the house, "So - that way, yeah?" He walked past his father and Ryan - leading the way down the alleyway towards the back gardens. Mike followed him as did Ryan - although Ryan did have the sense to have a quick look up and down the road to see if anyone was there, or watching them. Sadly there was no one there. No one to see what they were about to do. No one to stop them…

Ryan took a deep breath and disappeared down the alleyway.

Dee and Jackie weren't really talking. They weren't stupid. They knew what was going on. They knew where the men had disappeared to and why. It's not as though they'd been really secretive talking about breaking into the house to have a snoop around. The only sense they had was to not discuss it in front of the younger children. The two mothers just got on with preparing the meal. Chili Con Carne tonight - mainly because it was easy to cook and Jackie had the bits in the house. It's not as though she was expecting to cook for Dee's family. Earlier in the day she thought she wouldn't be seeing any of them again - after Mike had told her what'd happened with Ryan. She thought that was it. Another neighbour living next to them that they'd know nothing about.

Jackie was browning off the mince whilst Dee was preparing the kidney beans and onions. Claire was just standing there - watching the two of them. She felt nervous of the situation still. The neighbour, in his garden, watching her had spooked her even though her father said he was most likely innocent. If he really believed that she couldn't help but wonder why he was going around there now. If he was innocent there'd be no reason to go. They could just leave him be…Not that she wanted him to leave him. She wanted him to at least have a word with him. Tell him not to look into his daughter's bedroom. Warn him off. She nervously took a sip from her summer fruit drink Jackie had earlier made for her. She swallowed it so noisily that her mother couldn't help but to turn and look at her. Claire seized the opportunity to say what was on her mind, "Do you think they're talking to him?" she asked.

Jackie stopped what she was doing. Claire asked exactly the question which had been on all of their minds. She slowly turned around to Claire. Jackie had an expression on her face which neither Dee nor Claire had seen before. It wasn't that she didn't look as friendly as she had done so before. She just appeared to be more in charge than before. Whereas Mike appeared to be the man of the relationship and Jackie seemed to be the one who simply towed the line - when Dee and her family first met them - now she appeared to be the one in charge of the situation. She was the one leading the way.

"I think you need to put the whole thing out of your mind." Jackie said. Her voice suddenly stern. She turned to Dee, "You too. All of us. We just need to forget about the whole thing. We didn't hear any of the conversation."

"Why?" Claire asked.

"Do as she says," Dee butt in. She knew exactly why Jackie said what she said. She wasn't trying to lay the law down. She wasn't trying to dictate what they should or shouldn't do. She was trying to protect them if things went South. A wave of uncertainty washed through Dee all of a sudden and a sickness hit her stomach. "Have you ever done anything like this before?" she asked Jackie. Jackie looked at her. She didn't answer her vocally but her face said everything Dee needed to know. "Claire - why don't you go and watch the television," Dee said to her. "Nothing else to do and we'll be through soon." In truth Dee didn't want Claire out of her sight - not with everything that was going on but, at the same time, she didn't want Claire to be part of the following conversation. Not just that, she also worried that Jackie might not open up to her if Claire was there listening too. She hoped that, with the two of them talking woman to woman, she'd be more inclined to open up to her.

"It's fine," Jackie said, giving Claire permission to go on through to the living room to watch the television. Claire didn't put up any protest; she took a hold of her half-empty glass and walked through to the living room. Jackie followed her to the edge of the kitchen and pushed the door shut. She turned back to the kitchen worktop where she added the beans and onion to the mince. From the other room - they heard the television buzz into life.

"How many times have you found yourself in this position?" Dee asked her.

"Cooking dinner?" Jackie asked. She smiled at her. Playing dumb.

"How many times have you found yourself covering for your husband while he runs off to break into people's homes?" she pressed her further. "This isn't the first time you've been in this position, is it? I can see it in your eyes."

"We live in a bad world and sometimes the only way to feel safe is to take a really good look at your neighbours. And to do that...We do what we need to do." Jackie said it in such a matter-of-fact way it was clear she didn't think there was anything wrong with their actions. "You want to keep your family safe, don't you?"

Dee didn't answer her. She didn't say anything. The two of them just stood in silence for a moment. The drone of the television humming still in the background of the house. The noise of two young girls happily playing upstairs. A few more minutes went by before Dee broke the silence between the two women, "You invited me out. And the girls. Claire stayed home but ended up here, with Thomas…You knew Ryan was at work," she hesitated a moment unsure as to whether she really wanted to hear the answer, "…Did you break into our house?"

"I was with you."

"Your husband wasn't. Mike wasn't. Did Mike break into our house?"

"Of course not!" Jackie acted as though she were offended. "We're friends!" She didn't act well enough though and Dee saw straight through her. She had broken into their house. Not her admittedly. Her husband. He'd seized the opportunity to sneak in when they were all out. No doubt annoyed that Claire had stayed behind - Thomas had gone round and pulled her from her room, dragged her back to his place to show the many pages he'd written detailing serial killers; nothing but a rouse to get her out of the house and give Mike the necessary time to snoop around to see if they were 'suitable' neighbours.

The two women stood in silence again. Jackie quietly hoping she'd thrown Dee off with her lie. Dee quietly regretting that her husband had gone off with Mike and Thomas. She wanted him back by her side. More than that - she wanted them all back in their own home with the front doors locked. She wanted to move away - a completely feeling of violation at what her neighbours had done.

"Just think," Jackie said, "if they find anything - they'll put a stop to it. They'll be able to make the neighbourhood a safer place."

"By breaking and entering into everyone's house?"

"A necessary crime. Think about the bigger picture. It's for the best." She looked up to the clock mounted on the wall behind where Dee was standing. "They shouldn't be that much longer. Normally he's in and out." She smiled at Dee. "Did you want another drink while we wait? Could crack open a nice red wine?"

Ryan's earlier words went through Dee's head. His stark warning that not all was right with their neighbours. His order to leave them alone. She smiled at Jackie, "Sounds nice," she said. She watched as Jackie pulled a red wine from a wine rack over by the microwave and couldn't help but wish she'd listened to her husband.

CHAPTER 19

heard a door from somewhere upstairs splinter as someone used force to come through it. Did someone really just break into my house? For once did my play-thing has come to me? I won't pretend to be a little disappointed. I do enjoy the hunt - looking for new prey - but it'd be rude not to play with whoever has dared breach my property. Especially as they're uninvited. Despite the fact someone had just broken in - I couldn't help but smile. Most people would have been angry. Some people would have even been scared. Not me, though. I'm actually finding it a little funny. Of all the houses they chose to broke into...Boy did they choose the wrong house...I quietly reached down for the knife I'd earlier used to slice my play-thing's skin. The trick will be to maim them enough that they can't get away but not so much that they bleed out before I've gone through the motions with them. It's a fine art. I walked to the stairs of the cellar and paused. I listened intently. A voice. Someone is calling out up there.

⊼

"Hello?!" Ryan called out into the darkness of the house.

"What the fuck do you think you're doing?" Mike asked.

"Making sure he's out."

"He's out. We knocked. Remember?" Mike snapped.

"I guess. And if he didn't hear the knocking - I'm sure he would have heard the door breaking, right?" Ryan had had enough of Mike's shit; the way he went around thinking he was the one in charge. He wasn't. No one was in charge of the situation as far as Ryan was concerned. The whole thing was a train wreck. A point proven when Thomas broke the back door. So much for sneaking in and out without being noticed. There was no way Mr. Reynolds wouldn't notice a broken back door when he did get home.

"Just shut the fuck up!" Mike snapped. His earlier disapproving look at Thomas, for his use of bad language, seemed somewhat hypocritical now but no one picked him up on it as he started looking through the various cupboards in the kitchen. Thomas started at the other end of the cupboards - pulling each one open, having a quick root around before closing it again.

"What exactly are we looking for?" Ryan asked.

Mike didn't even look at him when he spoke, "Anything that's out of place...Suspicious..."

"I'm sorry - I've never done this kind of thing before," Ryan snapped back having sensed a tone in Mike's voice. After tonight, no matter what they found, he wouldn't be speaking to him again even if Dee did want to stay friends with them. He wanted nothing to do with them. More so, a tiny part of him just wanted to cut his losses and move out. Find somewhere else to live. Perhaps rent for a while - somewhere in the countryside (they couldn't afford to move there). A nice quiet house in the middle of nowhere with no neighbours. The sound of a plate crashing to the floor, smashing into a dozen small pieces, pulled him back to his current situation. He turned around, in the direction of the noise. Thomas was looking sheepish and Mike was looking angry.

"It was an accident," Thomas said quietly.

Mike looked at me, "There's nothing in here. We need to check the rest of the house." Mike walked out of the kitchen, pushing past Ryan in the process.

"What about the broken plate?" Ryan asked.

"What about it? As you already pointed out - door's broken anyway... No fixing that in the little time we have," Mike walked into the living room. Thomas joined his father in the living room and started going through everything. Ryan followed but stopped in the doorway. Now he was in the house and snooping around, he couldn't help but think he had been wrong. Especially with Mike's erratic behaviour. The more he opened his mouth, the more Ryan felt he'd made a mistake - something he'd always known deep down. His judgement blinded by his need to keep his sordid secret and desperation in keeping his family safe.

"Maybe we're wrong," Ryan said. Thomas stopped what he was doing and looked at him. A disappointed look in his face. Just as Ryan had made a mistake - he was starting to think he too had made an error in judgement. He shouldn't have trusted Ryan was capable of doing this. He wasn't a potential part of the unofficial neighbourhood watch. "There's nothing here," he continued.

"We've checked one room. You think we were ever going to find anything in the kitchen? We never find anything in the kitchen!" Mike stopped. He realised, all too late, what he'd said. Ryan had picked up on it too.

"You never find anything in the kitchen?"

"A slip of the tongue. Who'd hide anything in the kitchen? Nobody with any sense."

"Look we should just go. This was a mistake. There's nothing in here."

"What about this?" Thomas was sitting on the floor by an open bookcase. He had a shoebox in his lap. Both of the adults turned to see what he was talking about and what he'd found. He held the box up. "Look."

Mike shot Ryan a look and walked over to his son. He took the box from him and started filtering through it. He took it over to where Ryan was seemingly rooted to the spot. He thrust it towards his gut and Ryan caught it before looking down to the contents.

"Still think he's innocent?" Mike asked.

Ryan reached into the box and pulled out a handful of photographs. Seemingly hundreds of photos - all of which of young women who appeared to be completely unaware they were having their photo taken and all of them captured, in the polaroid, going about their daily lives.

"What the hell?" Ryan wasn't talking to anyone in particular.

"If he wasn't guilty - why'd he have this? This isn't the behaviour of someone normal."

Ryan threw the box of photos on the sofa and reached into his trouser pocket. He pulled his mobile phone out and unlocked the screen.

"What the fuck are you doing?" Mike asked.

"What do you think? I'm phoning the police…"

"The police?"

"They need to come down here. They need to look around for themselves. What if we contaminate the evidence? What if we…?"

"We're not getting the police involved. You do realise we've broken into this house…"

"….And found this." Ryan went to dial the number. Mike stopped him by swatting the phone from his hand. It landed - screen side down - on the floor. "What the hell, Mike? We need to call them. If we touch anything we could ruin the whole investigation."

"There isn't going to be an investigation. You really want the police to come here? We get in trouble for breaking and entering. He somehow talks his way out of it again…Do you want that? Keep going through the pictures," Mike picked the box up and started to thumb through the photographs again, "have you checked to see if there is one of Claire in here? Or even Jen? People like this - they don't deserve justice. We, the people, deserve it…"

Ryan reached forward and grabbed Mike's arm - stopping him from thumbing through the pictures anymore. "Wait!" He snatched the photographs from Mike and went back a couple. There, in the middle of the photographs, was a picture of Vanessa. She was outside of the bank, unaware she was caught in the framing of a photo just as the other girls had been. Dressed to impress at work. "That's my work colleague…"

"Well - damn - I guess we best phone the police…" Mike taunted Ryan. He turned around to his son who'd just been watching the two of them arguing, "What else is there?"

"I haven't been looking."

"Well don't stop. There must be more." Mike joined his son in the search.

Ryan hesitated for a moment and then helped - turning the place over in the hope of finding more than just photographs. Ryan figured he'd argue about calling the police after they found more evidence despite knowing, for sure, he had found the man the police (and media) were looking for.

"What are you doing in my house?" a meek voice asked from the living room's doorway. All three stopped their search and turned to see Mr. Reynolds standing there, in the doorway, watching them. A large kitchen knife in his left hand.

Chapter 20

Ryan shifted uneasily; embarrassed at being caught in Mr. Reynolds' house and nervous as to his next move (and the fact the man was standing a few feet away from him with a knife in his hand).

Mr. Reynolds asked again, "What are you doing in my house?" Mike noticed the man's hand was shaking as though he wasn't comfortable with the blade in his hand.

"What are you doing with these?" Mike countered his question with another question and pointed towards the box of photographs. He didn't take his eyes off the man although he did slightly step in front of his son. Mike didn't think his neighbour would use the knife. He didn't think he had the balls. The fact he was shaking suggested as much. The knife was there not for violence but rather to defend himself if the need arouse. It didn't matter though. Mike still blocked the path to his son. After all - it was better to be safe than sorry. Mr. Reynolds looked across to the photographs. His face reddened at the sight of them. He knew he'd been caught out. His hand tightened its grip on the blade's black, plastic handle. Mike noticed that too. "I asked you a question."

"You don't have any right to be in here," Mr. Reynolds said. His voice was shaking as much as his hand but it didn't make Thomas, Ryan or Mike any less nervous about the situation they found themselves in. Mike had broken into other homes, to snoop around, but - until today - he'd never actually been caught. Not like this.

"You're right," said Ryan. He saw a potential way out of the mess. If he thought about it in depth, a little bit more, he might have realised it wasn't a way out. It was a way of escalating the situation. "Maybe you should phone the police. Let them know we're here," he continued. Mr. Reynolds turned to him. The first time he'd properly looked him in the eye. These weren't the eyes of a killer. These were the eyes of something else. Something Ryan couldn't put his finger on. Not a killer though.

"And then we can show them these pictures too," Mike jumped into the conversation.

"They're not mine," Mr. Reynolds snapped his gaze back to Mike and Thomas.

"So the police won't find your prints on them, or anything else in the house which shouldn't be here?" Mike asked.

"We'll go," Ryan pressed, "and forget the whole thing. You can go about your business and we can go about ours." He moved - slightly - towards the door but Mr. Reynolds didn't budge out of his way. He didn't even make a hint as to move out of the way.

"Like hell we will!" Mike raised his voice. His gaze was fixed upon Mr. Reynolds. He tried to back him -verbally - into a corner, "What are you doing with these photographs? What? Are they pictures of your the girls you killed? What's the betting we go through here and find a picture of your wife?" he continued. He moved slightly towards Mr. Reynolds. Mr. Reynolds responded by backing away slightly.

"They're not mine!" he continued.

"Then why are they in your house?" Mike asked - taking the lead in the showdown.

"You put them here."

"We put them here?"

"Yes."

"Now we both know that's not the case."

"Mike, let's just go. Now isn't the time." Ryan said.

"Then when would be the right time? We leave and - before we know it - he's moved out. Disappeared into the city, perhaps another city…Gone without a trace to carry on whatever the fuck it is he does."

"I work the night shift in a supermarket," Mr. Reynolds said - his voice still shaky and meek. If he was the killer the press had reported about, he was doing an excellent job of keeping it hidden from them. The quietness in his voice, the shaking - he wasn't coming across a killer. He was coming across as weak. Pathetic almost. Ryan couldn't help but think how he'd have reacted if he were in this man's shoes; standing in his home confronting people who'd broken in.

Ryan turned back to Mike, "I'm telling you - this isn't right. Something feels wrong. We've made a mistake…"

"Then how do you explain the pictures?" Mike snapped at him.

"They're not mine."

"Shut the fuck up."

"Yeah shut the fuck up!" Thomas chimed in, peering around from behind his father's back.

Ryan turned back to Mr. Reynolds, "There are intruders in your house. You need to phone the police," he said. "The police can deal with this." The perfect outcome for Ryan. He'd say he was coerced into helping Mike and Thomas - for fear of his family - and the police could investigate the nature of the photos along with anything else which may have been in the house. No one would get hurt though. At this stage, with the knife pointing towards him, that was the important thing.

"He won't phone the police," Mike shouted, "because he knows he is in the wrong. He knows what he is. He invites the police into his home and he's shut down. Finished. No more. Prison for him."

"I haven't done anything…"

"No - of course you haven't." Mike laughed.

"Then you have nothing to fear by calling the police. Call them. It's okay." Unlike Mike's voice, Ryan's voice was calming. Mr. Reynolds looked between the three men standing in his living room. The telephone was sitting on a small coffee table to the side of the settee. It was evident to see he wanted to use it. He wanted to phone for the police. He nudged, slightly, towards it. Mike seized the opportunity to make a dash for him - helped by the fact Mr. Reynolds was still looking at the telephone and there was only a few steps between the two of them. He hit him with his whole body and the two of them crashed down to the floor. The impact caused Mr. Reynolds to drop the knife. Thomas cheered as he too dashed over to help his father. Ryan just stood there, on the spot, frozen. Part of him wanted to make a dash for the back door, part of him wanted to make a move for the phone and the other part of him was curious to see how this played out; the latter being out of morbid curiosity. Was this really the man the authorities had been hunting? He did have the photographs after all.

Jackie, Claire and Dee were sitting in the living room unaware of what was taking place a few houses away from them. The three of them sitting in silence as the end of a soap opera played out on the television set. All of them were watching the screen but none of them really paying it any attention. Claire was thinking about where she used to live, and the friends she missed. Jackie was thinking about what the men were doing and Dee was wondering whether any of them would get away with what was happening. She knew it had always been the plan, on their part, to break into the house but now it was happening - and now she knew it was something they did regularly, she couldn't help but wish she'd never become a part of it. Too late now, though. She knew she couldn't turn back the clock.

Kara and Jen came into the lounge.

"Mum, I'm hungry," Kara whined.

"Dinner won't be long," Jackie reassured her. Her tone had no emotion. Dee couldn't help but think she'd turned off from everything - including her daughter. Perhaps that was the way she dealt with what was going on? She simply switched off. The friendly woman, Dee met when Jackie first came around to the house, making up for the times she'd turned her emotions off. Overly happy to compensate from the times she'd switched off to the world around her when times called for her to be more subdued. It was a theory.

"Where's dad?" Jen asked.

"Just popped next door with Mike and Thomas," Dee said. She knew she wouldn't think of 'next door' as being the neighbour's house. She'd just think they had nipped to their own home.

"Why?"

"Because they did."

"Can I go and see them?"

"Not yet - they're busy," Dee told her.

"Can we have a biscuit?" Kara asked her mother.

"No, you'll ruin your dinner."

"But I'm hungry."

"Well, I said, dinner won't be long!"

"Well how long?"

"When your father gets back."

"When is he getting back?"

"Why don't you and Jen go and play upstairs," Jackie said. Her patience clearly running out. She shot her own daughter such a look, Kara wasted no time in going back upstairs to the solitude of her bedroom with Jen right behind her.

"We didn't get a biscuit though," Jen moaned before the door was closed.

CHAPTER 21

"**T**his is fucking crazy!" Ryan protested. "We can't do this!" He was pacing the living room where they'd pulled the curtains shut - blocking out the outside world from what was happening within the now-darkened room. Mike was standing in front of Mr. Reynolds who was sitting on the corner arm chair. Mike had hold of the knife now and - unlike Mr. Reynolds who was whimpering - he didn't look out of place with it in his hand.

"We're already doing it," Mike hissed. "Now you're either part of the problem or you're part of the solution. Which is it? Time to pick a team."

"The photos…They're not mine…" Mr. Reynolds kept saying over and over again.

"Shut up!" Mike shouted. He put the knife against Mr. Reynolds' cheek. "Shut, the hell, up!"

"Mike, think what you're doing. This takes it way out of breaking and entering territory into something much worse…We need to phone the police. We need to let them deal with it."

"We'll see what's what when the boy comes back."

Mike was referring to Thomas. Whilst Mike and Ryan watched their neighbour, Thomas had been instructed to search the rest of the house for more evidence pointing to the crimes Mr. Reynolds was responsible for - not that, in Mike's eyes, any further proof were really necessary. He had everything he needed, hidden in the shoebox, as far as he was concerned. The man was guilty and punishment needed to be issued.

"I'm sorry," Ryan told Mr. Reynolds. He didn't know why he said the words. Perhaps to try and appease his own guilty conscience for what the man was having to go through.

"You're sorry? You think he's sorry for the women he cut up? You read all the reports? You read what he did to them before he let them die? Did you? I did. Let me tell you - it made for some horrific fucking reading, you know?" Mike was ranting. Any chance of a sensible conversation with him was long gone. It was clear he only had one thing on his mind. Revenge.

"We don't know that he…"

"The pictures! What more proof do you want?"

"They're not my pictures!"

"Shut the fuck up!" Mike turned around hit Mr. Reynolds in the face with the back of his hand, splitting his lip in the process. Mr. Reynolds winced in pain. "You know what - that felt good." He hit him again; a clenched fist this time. The bridge of Mr. Reynolds' nose split open to the sound of a satisfying (or horrifying) crack. Again, Mr. Reynolds cried out; a cry drowned out by the cheer of Mike and the voice of Ryan telling him to stop. Thomas walked back into the room. He was empty handed. He froze when he saw what his father had done. A sadistic smile on his face showed Ryan's hope of the son talking the father down were out of the window. Mike turned to him, shaking the sting from his fist, "Well - what did you find?" he asked. Thomas shook his head. "Nothing?"

"No."

Ryan didn't feel any relief. If anything he felt worse. So far all they'd found were pictures which was suspicious but hardly enough to condemn the man. If anything Ryan would have felt better had Thomas come back with reports of dead girls stashed in the rooms upstairs. At least then he wouldn't have felt as guilty about what was happening. Guilt? So many mixed feelings ricocheting around his soul.

The three of them stood in silence. Only the whimpering sounds of their now-hostage were audible. Mike slowly turned around to him, "You're a piece of shit and you're going to hell!" he said. "We know what you did to those girls. We all know. The fucking world knows. Been enough reports about it in the press. But you have a real chance to help yourself now. A chance to cleanse some of your twisted soul. And if I were you…if I were in your position - about to meet my maker - I'd take that chance of redemption. Confess…"

Mr. Reynolds stuttered over his words, "I didn't do anything." His protests of innocence were met with a clenched fist directly to the same spot as the previous punch. He let out a wail of pain as his head jarred backwards from the force. Thomas laughed. Ryan couldn't do anything. Stuck to the same spot. People like him - they weren't built for scenarios like this. It wasn't in their programming. His place was sitting behind the desk at the bank or in his home (wherever that may be) with his family.

"What's with the pictures. And, God help me, if you say they aren't yours…"

"They're pretty…." he screamed.

"What?" Mike wasn't expecting that as an answer.

"The girls. They're pretty. I liked them…"

"So much that you killed them?"

"I didn't kill them."

"You did. You cut them into tiny pieces and left them for people to find. You're sick."

"No. I didn't." He was crying now. "I just took their picture. I wanted to ask them out. I wanted to see if they'd like me but I never could. I just took their picture…"

"Are we going to find pictures of your wife in the box too?"

"My wife left me. She said she didn't love me anymore. She said she'd met someone else from her work…"

"So you killed her!"

"I didn't kill her! She left me!" he wept. "I loved her."

"You killed her and you killed the girls in these pictures. Like his colleague at work." Mike turned to Ryan, "What was her name?"

"Vanessa," Ryan said quietly.

"I didn't kill her. I didn't touch her. I liked going there. I liked talking to her. I asked her out once but she said no…"

"You're lying!" Mike shouted.

"I'm not! I just wanted someone to like me again. I just…" his words cut short by another punch to the face and another cheer from Thomas.

"Stop it!" Ryan shouted.

"He's lying to us. Don't you want to hear the truth from him?"

"What if he's not lying?" Ryan asked. His tone full of desperation.

"He is!"

"I'm not!"

"Well…" Mike stood back a moment. "We'll see…" He walked from the room.

"What are you doing?" Ryan called out after him. He wanted to follow, to keep trying to talk him down, but he didn't dare leave Thomas and Mr. Reynolds alone. The possibility of one hurting the other being too great and - at this stage - he wasn't sure who'd be the one dishing out the hurt.

A

Jackie was making fresh drinks for her guests who were waiting in the living room - still not talking whilst the television played whatever program was on in the background. Jackie was so lost in what she was doing, she jumped when the back door opened and Mike walked in.

"How's it going?" she asked. "You've been longer than usual."

Mike smiled. He put his arms around his wife and gave her a hug before kissing her on the lips, "We found him, baby. We found the sick son of a bitch. All this time, right there. Just as Thomas said…"

"You've found him?" She smiled.

Mike released her from his grip and walked to the cupboard in the corner of the kitchen. "That's right, baby. He has pictures of the girls collected together in a shoebox. Sick, son of a bitch had the box in his living room - in plain sight of anyone who'd come by." He reached into the cupboard and pulled out a bag. Sticking from the top of it was a hammer.

"What are you doing round there?" Jackie asked when she noticed the bag.

Mike flashed her another smile, "Getting a confession before passing sentence!"

Jackie didn't know what to say and Mike didn't wait to hear what it would be. He simply walked out of the door, closing it behind him, as though what he was doing was perfectly normal and acceptable. It hadn't been the first time he'd broken into a house - to snoop around - but it was the first time he'd pass out punishment to the individual. The strange thing was Jackie didn't have the words to say to him. She didn't know what to say. Yet she didn't seem to mind what he was doing. In fact, she took the news as though it were something as every-day as her husband going off to fix something around the house. She guessed this was because he was fixing a fault with the house. Not their house admittedly. But the fact a killer was living a few hundred yards away from where they lived - definitely a fault to be dealt with. A few more seconds as his news sunk in before she smiled to herself. She didn't run into the other room to tell Claire and Dee though. She thought it best to keep it to herself until the task was done. She returned to making the drinks, proud of her husband. He was keeping the family safe and also saving a drop in properly value. After all - if people found out this was the neighbourhood where all the murders took place - property prices would plummet.

By the time Mike got back to Mr. Reynolds' house all hell was break-ing loose. He heard the shouting as he crossed the back garden, from the fence to the broken door. The voices belonging to his own son and Ryan. Of course one of the voices would belong to Ryan. As for the sound of Thomas' screeching - Mike couldn't help but feel embarrassed. This must be what their other neighbours hear when Mike and Thomas are having one of the arguments.

He hurried through to the living room where Thomas was blocking the doorway - stopping both Ryan and Mr. Reynolds from leaving.

"What the fuck is going on?!" Mike barked.

"They're trying to leave, dad!" Thomas backed up, letting his dad through. The very act of Mike walking through pushed Ryan and Mr. Reynolds back into the living room.

"What is it with you?" Mike asked Ryan.

"Me? Look at what you're doing!" Ryan shouted.

"Keep your fucking voice down. We don't want anyone coming round." He looked at Mr. Reynolds, "Sit!" Mr. Reynolds did as he was told without hesitation.

"I don't deny he's not strange, I'll give you that, but he isn't the man being hunted for the murders. He isn't. Come on, look at him. He has made absolutely no move to try and get away or fight us...Nothing. He's just... Fucking weird!"

"I told your wife we caught him," Mike lied. His voice was calmer now. He hoped the words would offer some form of comfort to Ryan. A little sign that what he was doing was okay. Acceptable even. "You know what she said? She said good."

"What?"

"She was happy. I told her what we were doing. You think she was upset? You think she reacted like you did? No. Still happy. She thought we were doing the right thing. For the sake of the neighbourhood and our own families. More than that though - we're making things better for society. We're getting rid..."

"Getting rid...What the hell are you talking about?"

Mike put the bag of tools onto the table, next to where he'd dumped the knife earlier, and opened it up. He took the hammer out and handed it out to Ryan who didn't take it, "We're getting rid of the trash. One way or the other - this is how it plays out. He confesses and we deal with him fast. He drags it out...Well we drag it out too. We do as he did to his victims."

"What?"

"We torture him."

"Are you messing with me? Is this some kind of sick joke?" Ryan turned to Mr. Reynolds, "Are you in on this? Some kind of sick welcome to the neighbourhood prank...Something to see the type of family we are?" He could tell by Mr. Reynolds' expression that he had no idea what was happening or what was going to happen. He turned back to Mike, "Very funny. You got me. I believed you. You tricked me. Boy - don't I feel stupid now." He laughed but it was more out of nervousness as opposed to finally getting the 'joke'.

Mike smiled at him. Ryan smiled back - he foolishly thought this was the end of it now. Mike proved to him it wasn't. It was just the start. He smashed Mr. Reynolds in the kneecap with the hammer. Mr. Reynolds screamed out in pain and reached for his leg. Thomas laughed, as did Mike. Ryan screamed out too having also felt the pain despite not actually receiving the blow himself.

CHAPTER 22

Mr. Reynolds was weeping, still clutching at his knee. Mike was still standing next to him with the hammer in his hand. Thomas and Ryan were standing close to the living room's door - neither one of them knowing what was going to happen next. In fact no one did. Other than Mike. This was his show now.

"Why did you kill the girls?" Mike asked Mr. Reynolds. "Is it because they turned you down? You asked them out, they said no and so you killed them brutally…Made sure you did it in an ugly fashion? You take away their beauty with violent acts? Make sure no one will want them? Am I close?"

"I didn't kill them."

"Nope. Not the right answer." Mike made a sudden move forward and grabbed Mr. Reynolds' still shaking hand. He forced it down onto the small coffee table and kept it held there. Mr. Reynolds was screaming already - the knowledge of what was coming nearly as painful as the act itself. Mike raised the hammer high in the air and brought it down hard into the middle of the sweaty hand. A crack signalled that it was broken. The force of the hammer broke the skin and blood trickled out. The area, around the rip in the skin, already purple. Mr. Reynolds screamed again. "I can keep doing this all day. Just tell us why you did it."

"I didn't!"

Mike hit the man's hand with the hammer again. This time straight onto the fingertips, which also broke upon impact. Another scream.

"You're going to have to tell us the truth if you want this to stop!"

"I just took pictures of the girls. I liked them. I took their picture. I didn't do anything else."

"Liar!" Mike hit him again. Another hard blow, which sounded off with another satisfying crack. Another scream from Mr. Reynolds.

"Just tell him for God's sake!" Ryan yelled at Mr. Reynolds.

"I didn't hurt anyone. They hurt me!" he screamed. Mike let go of his hand and Mr. Reynolds snatched it back. He held it against his chest with his good hand. "I didn't hurt anyone," he said again, "they hurt me. She walked out. She left me. The others, they didn't want me either. No one does."

"So you kill them!" Mike shouted.

"No I didn't! I'm not a murderer!"

Mike slammed the hammer down on the man's second kneecap. He screamed out in pain once more. Tears streamed down his face as the pain was almost too much to bear.

"Please stop!"

"Is that what they said?" Mike him hit again. Another scream.

"Just fucking tell him!" Ryan said again - if only to make the pain stop for the man he wanted him to say something, anything. Even if it were a lie. "Just tell him! Something! Anything!" The amount of pain he was taking, without spilling anything, it was easy to see how he'd have managed to fool the police.

"I'm not a killer!"

Mike stepped back and dropped the hammer to the floor. Ryan audibly breathed a sigh of relief. "Son," Mike said, "fetch me out the hacksaw."

"What are you doing?" Ryan asked. He still couldn't move from where he was rooted to the spot. Everything being too much for him to take in. That wasn't the case for Thomas though. He was relishing the whole experience. As per his father's request, he hurried across to the tool bag and pulled out the hacksaw. He handed it to his father who took it with a friendly wink - a little sign, to his son, that he was proud of him.

"Make things easier for yourself," Mike told Mr. Reynolds, "just tell us why you did it. Tell us why you killed the girls."

"Please - I didn't - I didn't kill anyone," he stuttered. He was starting to look pale. Ryan wasn't sure how much more pain the man could take yet he knew there was going to be a lot more issued before he was released (one way or the other).

"You expect us to believe you're just some fucking pervert going about taking pictures of girls he fancies? Collecting little mementos of girls who'd knocked him back? We don't buy it. The police wouldn't either, if we called them. Not that you'll ever know what they think. They'll never know of this. They'll never know of what happened to you…" Mike reached forward and grabbed Mr. Reynolds' battered hand from the grip of his good hand. He placed it on the table and held it there with his own hand whilst he lined up the teeth of the hacksaw blade - right where the fingers connected to the hand. Ryan wanted to call out. He wanted to tell him to stop but he didn't. He didn't say anything. He knew there was no point. He turned his back on him and closed his eyes. "Last chance. Tell us why you did it. Help us understand. Maybe we'll understand. Maybe we'll carry on your fine work. Convince us. Why did you do it?"

"I'm just a dirty pervert," he stammered his words out, "I just take pictures of girls. I take the pictures and I keep them in a shoebox," he started to cry again, "and then - occasionally - I'll masturbate over them…"

"You're fucking disgusting…" Mike pushed down with the hacksaw. He pulled back with his arm. The teeth tore straight through the flesh and into the bone. A sound, reminiscent of cutting wood, echoed through the room. Mr. Reynolds screamed the house down. "Shut him up!" Mike ordered anyone else in the room. He didn't care who it was. Thomas stepped forward and clamped his neighbour's mouth shut with his hand quietening his scream. Mike continued sawing. It didn't take more than a few seconds before the fingers dropped to the floor with splashes of blood. It was only now Ryan gave any thought to D.N.A evidence and the worry of what they were going to do with the body if they followed this through to the end as Mike had suggested. "You can make all of this stop," Mike said, "just tell us why you did it!" He suddenly started slapping his neighbour in the face, "Oh no…Wake up…Don't pass out…You're not allowed to pass out…Tell us why you did it and I'll let you sleep…"

Ryan turned back to face the carnage. He nearly threw up at the sight of the bloodied hand missing its fingers. "Mike - it's one thing to break into someone's house but this…How the fuck do you think we're going to get away with this? You're taking things too far. Please stop. Stop whilst we can still put things right…" He knew there was no putting things right. Things had gone too far the moment they'd broken in the house. As far as Ryan was concerned - they were already heading for a prison sentence (a thought which made him feel sick to the stomach knowing he'd be leaving his family behind), the question was now how long they were going to spend there. At this rate - most of their lives.

"All he needs to do to make this stop is tell us. Don't you want to know what happened to your colleague? Don't you want to know what happened to her and where she is? I do believe they haven't found her yet. What was her name again? Vanessa. Was that it? Don't you think her friends and family deserve to know what happened to Vanessa? This motherfucker - this cunt - he's the one who knows what happened. He's the one with the information." He turned back to his son, "Hold his mouth shut again." Thomas did as he was told. Mike took a hold of his good hand and forced it onto the table despite a brief struggle from his neighbour. He lined up the hacksaw again. He laughed as he started to saw away - he didn't care about the prospect of prison. He knew there was plenty of time to worry about that (and fix it) after the event. For now, he just wanted to enjoy what he was doing. All the time his thoughts telling him he was in the right despite the atrocities he was committing. He was protecting the neighbourhood, his family and society. He was in the right no matter what anyone else thought.

"Stop it!" Ryan grabbed the knife from the table and dashed forward with it. Thomas jumped back, as did Mike but Ryan didn't go for either of them. He plunged the knife into Mr. Reynolds' throat. If the man was going to die - he'd rather it was over and done with quickly. He couldn't let Mike and his son continue torturing him. They didn't care why he did what he did. At least, Mike didn't. He was just looking for an excuse to torture the man himself. Was that why he broke into people's homes? Some dark desire to find someone bad enough to warrant hurting? It didn't matter. Ryan couldn't allow it to continue. With the knife in Mr. Reynolds' throat, he fell backwards onto the sofa. His eyes transfixed on his neighbour as he struggled to breath around the knife poking from his throat. Bubbles of blood spilling from his mouth as he gasped. Mike and Thomas were just as transfixed with the final death throes of Mr. Reynolds. Unlike Ryan, the pair of them were smiling. A sick satisfaction at witnessing his death. A death which came fairly quickly as he breathed his last.

"What the fuck did you do?" Mike snapped. Now the man was dead, he was angry at Ryan's interference. He had denied him of his pleasure and denied Mr. Reynolds of what was deserved.

"I put him out of his fucking misery!" Ryan snapped back. He didn't move though. He was fixed to the sofa, unable to take his eyes off the dead body. In Ryan's eyes - they were all just as bad as Mr. Reynolds. They'd become what he was perceived to be. A torturer. A murderer. But what they had become was worse and the truth of the situation was played, on the television set, in the house two doors down.

⚔

Dee had gone through to the kitchen to help Jackie who seemed to be taking her time with the drinks. She'd left Claire in the living room with the television playing. It was the News. Breaking News no less. Reports were coming in stating they'd found the murderer. Claire hadn't paid much attention to the start of the report and only managed to pick it up halfway through. Something about DNA evidence found on a parcel the killer had sent to the bank. Prints which lead the detectives directly to the culprit. They'd gone around his house and kicked the door down. They'd found him red-handed, literally. Standing with the corpse of another dead girl. Claire screamed for her mum to come and see what was on the television. Both Dee and Jackie ran through and were both left, dumbstruck, by what they saw; video footage of the guilty man (some unknown man with only one minor prior) being lead to a police car.

He was smiling directly at the camera and boasting he'd killed more than Art. Boasting he was Britain's most prolific serial killer. The report ended and all three women just sat there. No one knew what to say. No one knew how to break it to the men who were busy going through the neighbour's house (so Dee and Claire thought). Jackie was panicking slightly more. She knew the full extent of what was happening in the next house. And she knew there was very little she could do about it now. Her husband (even herself) wanted their neighbourhood and family to be a safe place to live and yet - unwittingly - they were the problem.

"We need to tell Mike!" she said. A slight crack in her voice. Before either mother could do anything to stop her, Claire jumped to her feet and ran from the room exclaiming that she'd go and tell them. When she realised what was happening - Dee chased after her daughter, followed by Jackie who knew what the girls were about to run into.

"No! Wait!" Jackie called out as she ran after them.

EPILOGUE

A neighbour from across the road had phoned the police. They'd driven home from work and pulled into their drive, just as they did every day, and had heard the screams of a man coming from across the road. Unusual not just because the man was screaming so loudly but also because he was usually so quiet. He kept himself to himself and most days people would often forget anyone lived there at all. Especially since his wife had left him. When the sounds first started the neighbour didn't think much of it until the screams continued. By the time they had walked across the road, to investigate, they realised all was not right in the house. The screams were loud originally but, by the time they reached the front door, they could hear they were being muffled - as though something held over the screaming person's mouth. They didn't even wait to get home before they phoned the police. They pulled their phone out immediately and dialled the number.

The police didn't take long to get there and - when they did - they were confronted with a horrific sight. Three men and three women - all in a panicked, excitable state - standing in the same room as the homeowner. Mr. Graeme Reynolds. A knife sticking out of his throat. The fingers on both (bruised) hands cut off. Two bloody patches on his knee-caps. A bloodied hacksaw on the floor next to a hammer and the back door hanging on its hinges from where they'd seemingly forced entry.

As the police lead the six of them out of the house in handcuffs they stepped over a mobile phone with a cracked screen. A message flashed up on the screen. A message Ryan would have received earlier had he phoned his boss back as his wife instructed him too.

"Hi Ryan, just wanted to inform you…Detective Andrews phoned. They ran some tests on the parcel. The hands didn't belong to her. They belonged to another girl who's been missing for a couple of days now. I mean, I know it's not good news but at least it's not Vanessa, right? Gives us some hope. Not just that - they think they've found the man too. They said there were another set of prints on the box. Someone who's known to them. That's all they said but - could well be over now, hey! Anyway, call me. I need to know if you're coming in tomorrow. We'll just put today down as a holiday day, if you want?"

A crime scene investigator scooped the mobile up, from the floor, and dropped it into a clear bag. He sealed it shut.

T H E E N D

Discover what happened to Vanessa in 'Happy Ever After Volume 1 and Volume 2'

Discover the inspiration to The Torturer in 'ART'

Discover other hidden Easter Eggs in further reading of Matt Shaw's work

www.facebook.com/mattshawpublications

www.mattshawpublications.co.uk

Keep reading for notes from the author:

Clown

MATT SHAW'S

CHAPTER 1

The children's screams were music to my ears. If my life had a soundtrack - such a sound would surely be the first track in the collection. Children screaming, followed by the sounds of canned laughter. I raised my white-gloved finger to my lips again and shushed them silent. The screams took a while to fade to a slight murmur. This was my favourite bit. The bit which got the biggest scream before everything finally finished. My very own encore.

I looked around the group of children sitting in front of me and reached into a large bag that I had brought with me. Their young, innocent eyes fixed upon it as they wondered what could possibly be contained within. What else had I got up my sleeve? I flashed them the biggest smile my mouth could stretch to - accentuated by the heavy red lipstick around my mouth - as I pulled out a paper plate. Keeping the smile from fading from my powdered face, I clamped my teeth around the prop before reaching back into the overly large bag. I pulled out a rubber chicken and gave it a puzzled look. I shrugged to the audience as I threw it over my shoulder. A ripple of laughter from the young crowd. I reached back into the bag and ferreted around some more. Seconds later and I pulled out an old bicycle horn. Another puzzled look in the prop's direction. It was one of those old style hooters; a trumpet with a black inflatable ball attached to the other end of it. I held it up to the face of the child I had sitting next to me on a stool we'd pulled from his mother's kitchen. Not that he could see what I was doing; his eyes were covered by my stripy scarf. I gestured to the watching children whether

I should give the hooter a squeeze or not, and they all nodded frantically. Gleeful expressions on their faces. I gave them a farcical wink and went to squeeze the hooter only to stop at the last second. I turned back to my young crowd and gave them a disapproving look before sending the hooter over my shoulder and in the same direction as the rubber chicken. Back in the bag and, after another ferret around, I pulled out a can of whipped cream. This is what I had wanted. I dropped the bag onto the floor - next to my huge clown slippers - and took the plate from my mouth. I held it out and pressed the can of cream's trigger, causing a frothy mess of cream to splatter onto the plate. I kept spraying as the children watched on with amusement. They knew what was coming. At least, they thought they did. As soon as there was a mountain of fresh cream piled high enough on the paper plate, I threw the can over my shoulder in the same direction as the previously used props. I flashed them another smile as I made a gesture as though to splat the blind-folded boy in the face. They all nodded enthusiastically. Of course they did. They always did. The chance to see their friend splattered in the face with whipping cream was too good an opportunity to miss out on.

The boy in front of me was ten years old yesterday. His name was Johnny. Yesterday being a school night meant the boy's party was pushed until this afternoon. Probably for the best. Yesterday, it rained heavily for most of the day and yet today it was bright and sunny with temperatures soaring to a near-uncomfortable degree - at least uncomfortable when standing in this get-up - and the parents have decided to move the party to the garden. An act - on their part - which turns me to a smiling-on-the-inside-crying-on-the-outside kind of clown. Of course I do not say anything to them. To do so would be rude and unprofessional of me. Rude entertainers, or those who lack professionalism, do not get repeat bookings.

I waved the plate of cream in front of Johnny's face once more and - again - the audience nodded with an unrivalled enthusiasm. Their keenness at seeing their friend hit in the face with cream made me wonder whether they were really his friends at all or whether they were here for the free party bags and cake. I suppose kids will be kids. They just want to laugh.

I held up three of my gloved fingers and mouthed 'In three' at the kids.

I lowered my fingers.

I held up one finger and mouthed 'One'.

I held up a second finger and mouthed 'Two'.

I held up my third finger and mouthed 'Three'.

I raised the plate high in the air above Johnny's face and then - as planned - had it snatched from my loose grip from the boy's father. It had all been arranged at the time of booking. He wanted to be seen as The Hero of The Day, the man who stopped his son from wearing a face full of cream. The idea had come to him when he saw one of the children - at another party - get upset when he was on the receiving end of the cream splat. Johnny's father wanted to book me on the strength of that show but was worried his son would have the same reaction. To be fair, most of the children enjoyed the cream ending I lined up for them. Most of them found it funny. I'd say there were only two out of ten who didn't see the funny side. Regardless - Johnny's father wanted to spare him and asked whether he could snatch the plate from me and hit me with it instead. I didn't mind. Why would I? Still getting paid at the end of the gig. And so the plan was formulated that he'd grab the plate and splat it into my face. I'd fall over on the floor in shock whilst he took the blindfold off his son. He would then encourage his son to give me a kick up the bum as I struggled to get up, blinded by the cream. The kick was to be the final act of revenge. At that stage of the plan, I'd run from the garden - into the house - doing a comical scream; a scream I practised throughout the previous evening, much to my neighbour's annoyance.

I acted surprised when the plate was snatched from me. The look upon the children's face suggested my over-the-top melodramatic acting was absolutely spot on once again but then that's to be expected with the rate I charge. Not too expensive, but not selling myself short either. I want to entertain the children, I want them to remember their parties but, at the same time, I do have bills to pay and the cost of the various storage units is not exactly cheap.

"What are you doing?!" I asked Johnny's dad as the audience gasped. Johnny himself pulled the blindfold from his vision so he could see what was happening. Even his eyes went wide with amazement when he saw his father lean forward and slam the cream pie straight into my face. "You're ruining my show!" I shouted in an eerily high-pitched voice as I stumbled back onto my bum. I was surprised by the lack of laughter from the audience.

"It's not nice, is it?" Johnny's dad shouted at me. Again - still no laughter. I rolled around on the floor with my arms and legs flailing about. I must have looked pathetic. "Well you're not doing it to my son!" His voice changed. He initially sounded as though he were being serious, as though he were genuinely upset that I was about to playfully hit his son with a cream pie. The second line he shouted though, the bit where he said I wasn't going to do it to his boy - that was better - much more over the top. More…What was it…Cheesy. Fake. A small ripple of laughter ran through the crowd. Johnny's father noticed this too. "You're a big, fat bully!" he said. Another ripple of laughter. Louder this time. I took the opportunity to go on all fours - my big padded arse pointed to the party-goers. "And we don't like big, fat bullies, do we?" he asked the children.

"No!" they all screamed.

"Let's teach him a lesson!" Johnny's dad - the Hero of The Day - shouted. He ran up behind me and gave me a gentle kick on the bottom. I playfully screamed. "Who else wants a go?" he asked.

"ME!" several children shouted out - Johnny being one of them.

As I pretended to struggle to get up, each of the children lined up behind me and gave me a kick on the bum, their infectious laughter getting louder by the second. The perfect end to the perfect party and another satisfied customer.

"Thank you for that," Johnny's dad said as he stepped into where I was hiding in the family living room. His name was Colin. He was a tall man, fairly well built. Not the biggest of men but - even so - I'm glad he pulled the kick just a little bit. I had a feeling that had he not done so, it would have left a bruise, even with all the padding on the suit I wore. "I was worried, for a moment, that they weren't going to like the alternative ending," he said as he reached into his pocket and pulled out a white envelope. That would be my payment. What's inside, not the envelope. He handed it over to me and I slid it into the zipper pocket on the side of my yellow suit. "Think they started off thinking I was being serious," he continued. To me, this was the awkward part of the events I attended. I always found them a struggle; having to be polite to someone when all I wanted to do was put my feet up and rest a little. I'm fifty in a couple of weeks, slightly overweight (not overly so) and pretty unfit. I loved this gig. It meant the world to me but that didn't stop it from tiring me out. Can't be rude though. Need to think of repeat business. His son is ten years old. There's a chance he could want a clown at his party for at least a couple more years yet.

"I think they loved it," I forced out. "My bum - not so much," I laughed. Had Colin known me, he might have known the laugh wasn't a genuine one. Again, laughing on the outside and crying on the inside.

"Well, thank you again. I've slipped a little extra something into the envelope for you as an additional thank you," he smiled and winked at me. It was always good when they felt the necessity to tip and - thankfully - most of them did. But then, I did always give one hundred and ten percent to the shows I put on. For a reasonable rate they got balloon animals, dancing, silly walk competitions, animal impressions and anything else I could think of. Most of my routines were the same for each party; I tended to keep the same order of events too. Why change a winning formula? Even the cream pie ending. The kids would sit there on their chairs, blindfolded, but they knew what was coming. I think the anticipation was half of the fun for them. Well - usually. Like I said - two out of ten kids weren't as keen on the act but you can't win them all and I tended to try and make amends with them by letting them get me back with their very own cream pie. Fair is fair after all and I hated to leave on a sour note.

"Thank you, but you didn't have to," I said.

"Listen - if you want - you can use one of the rooms upstairs to get changed in? Must be boiling in that get-up."

"It's fine, thank you. Used to it now," I laughed. "Right. Unless there's anything else I can do for you, I'll slip out now."

"They're just cutting the cake up now and then I think we're more or less finished for another year. Unless you wanted some cake?"

I struggled to get out of the seat. Had to stand up. If I'd stayed there much longer, chances are I'd have fallen asleep. The effort taken to perform such a show, especially in this heat, sure does take it out of you. "I'm good, thank you. But - listen - it's been fun."

Colin extended his hand to me and I took it in my own. We shook and I picked up my bag of props; pretty sure I have it all.

"It was great. I can't thank you enough…"

"Well if you know of anyone in need of a clown…"

"…I'll be sure to recommend."

"That's all I ask," I replied as he walked me through to the front door. He opened it and I carefully stepped out. There was only one step down to the driveway but - in these shoes - that's sometimes enough to send me flying to the floor in a crumpled heap. Been doing this gig for so many years and still get caught out from time to time. And the problem is - when you do fall - people think you're joking around, what with being dressed as a clown. They just clap and cheer. A free laugh at my unplanned expense.

I made my way down the drive and onto the road where my van was parked up. A white van with my working name etched down the side of it along with a generic picture of a clown. Nothing fancy. It gets me from A to B and that's all I care about. People don't hire me for my van - just my prat falls and silly antics. I kicked the over-sized shoes off my feet so I was barefoot and jumped into the van. I threw my bag of props across to the passenger seat, along with the shoes. They slumped off and landed in the footwell. I leaned back in the comfortable seat and sighed. A quick moment to catch my breath before I slid my white gloves off and tossed them to the side too. Sweaty hands wiped down the front of the already dirty clown outfit. Guess I'll have to wash that when I get in. A shame, considering how tired I am. Sometimes I go home full of energy and other times I go home with the distinct feeling of being too old for this, part of me contemplating finding something else to do for the remaining years of 'work' I have left. But what does a retired clown do once he hangs up the big, red nose? I guess I could always work in a joke shop, or something similar. Maybe a fancy dress store? I shuddered at the prospect of getting a steady nine to five job as I slid the van's key into the well-scratched ignition. A quick twist and the old girl spluttered into life, coughing a thick plume of black smoke from the rear exhaust. Had I charged a little more for the services I provided, I may have been able to get her fixed or replaced depending on costs.

I crunched my way into first gear and pressed my foot on the accelerator. At least I'll be home soon with an evening to myself before tomorrow's appointment. Funny how it goes. You can go for ages without a single hint of a booking, using more and more of your savings with each passing day and then - suddenly - they all come along at once. Johnny was my third booking this month. Tomorrow's booking makes four and - more importantly - the least amount of money needed to ensure all bills are paid. Well, all bills are paid so long as I have a bit of a fiddle on the taxes. As I approach sixty, I guess it's fair to say I'll never be a rich man unless I win on a lottery ticket but to do that I might have to start buying them. It was a good thing I didn't do this job for the money.

It was never about making money.

It was only about bringing joy to the lives of the children I met.

II

My house was as quiet as it always was. Sometimes this was a blessing and sometimes it felt as though it were a curse. Just me bouncing off the walls of the modestly-sized building that was only mine due to a generous last will and testament. I threw the clown shoes and bag of mixed props into the corner of the hallway. One perk of living alone is the fact I do not have anyone due to come home who'll moan at me for not putting things away properly. I unzipped the front of the clown suit via a small, concealed zipper which ran from neck line down to belly and slipped it off my shoulders down to my waist, instantly refreshed by the cool breeze blowing in through the house due to the windows left open. In this day and age not many people are comfortable leaving their windows open but I have nothing to lose. Not a lot in here for anyone to steal. At least - nothing that's of any worth. Hell, I don't even have a flat screen television, just some old, dated set that can't even receive the signal for digital transmissions. Not that there is anything worth watching upon the channels missing. Just depressing news stories about crimes; murders, government conspiracies, missing children - always the same.

I pulled the green wig from my head and felt instant relief. All these years wearing the damned thing, you'd have thought I would be used to it by now but it still itches like crazy. Had I had more hair, I'd have just dyed that green. I threw the wig onto the stairs so I knew where to find it the following day. By the time I walked down the hallway and into the kitchen, I had more or less stepped out of my outfit completely. Just the make-up on and the red nose (which surprisingly isn't as uncomfortable as you'd imagine). I pulled the nose off and threw it over my shoulder, back down the hallway, and walked over to the washing machine. Supposed to hand wash this but I have to be honest - I can't be bothered and the washing machine hasn't done any damage to it after all these years so…Why stop? I slammed the door shut and set it up for a quick wash. Not enough time for a full wash; not if I wanted it to be dry in time for tomorrow's booking.

And now - now I could take the time to relax. I walked through to the living room and dropped down onto the sofa. My reflection stared back at me in the television screen. I was still wearing the white powder upon my face. I rarely take that off. I don't like the face underneath. I don't like the person underneath. I find him hard to control. I find him hard to talk to. I find him hard to keep quiet. The make-up I wear keeps him hidden. The make-up keeps him at bay and that's the way I like him. I reached for the television controller and hit the little red button. The screen buzzed into life. A second later and sound came from the small speakers. A button press on a second controller, next to where I sat, and my small DVD unit spun into life. I'm not really a film person. I do not like the violence and unnecessary bad language. The only disks in my collection are old movies featuring Laurel and Hardy - the best comedy double act of all time in my humble opinion. They don't make them like this anymore. The film's production company blurred its way onto the screen and was soon replaced with the main title of the film. I settled back in my chair and reached for a lever tucked between my sofa's padding and its arm. A quick pull and it activated the foot rest. That's better. I knew I wouldn't see the whole movie. My eyes were already feeling heavy but it didn't matter. I had seen it more times than I could remember.

"Wake up."

I opened my eyes. I hadn't even been asleep. I was merely resting my eyes for a moment.

"Look at you. You look a state. You let Laurel and Hardy see you like this? You're a fucking disgrace."

"Shut up. You aren't here."

"Yes, I am. Doesn't matter how many layers of fake you bury me under. I'm always here."

"No. You're not."

"This out-of-sight-out-of-mind bullshit you're running with…It doesn't work. You know it doesn't work. Stand up."

"I don't want to."

"Stand the fuck up, cunt!"

I can't afford to anger him so I pulled myself to my feet.

"Go to the bathroom."

"Please…I just want to relax. I just want to watch my programmes."

"We have work to do. Go to the bathroom. You need to see this."

"I don't want to."

"I will hurt you."

I walked through to the downstairs bathroom, a small room to the side of the front door - a room I purposefully kept shut.

"Please, I don't want to go in there."

"Quit being a little bitch and get in there!"

I opened the door with my hand shaking. A slight hesitation and I stepped into the room.

"Look in the mirror."

"I don't want…"

"Look in that fucking mirror."

I turned to the wall adjacent to the door. Hanging on the wall was a small mirror. I caught sight of my reflection within its tiny frame: five foot nine - fairly stocky (sadly not muscle), balding, hardly an oil-painting despite the layers of powder and paint upon my face, slight facial hair - not quite stubble and yet not quite a beard (currently covered by white). I smiled at myself.

"See. Doesn't matter how much shit you put on me, I'm still here. I'm always here and you need to get that in your goddamned head once and for all. You understand me? We have work to do."

Another flash of my pearly whites and a wink.

CHAPTER 2

I smiled as the front door opened. The shock on the lady's face suggested she wasn't the one who had booked me.

"One for you," I said as I handed her one of the balloons in my hand. I always turned up to parties with a large bunch of balloons. I always found it a good ice-breaker: turn up, enter the room where the party was happening, hand out the balloons to the children (and sometimes the parents). From there I'd go onto making balloon animals. I say animals plural but there were only ever a couple of choices and - even then - I tended to opt for the simple choices such as 'dog'.

The lady took the balloon from me, a confused look upon her face. I started to worry that I had the wrong house. I'd never done this before - gotten the wrong house - but I guess there is a first for everything. And after the poor night's sleep I had last night, it wouldn't surprise me if today was the 'first'.

"I'm sorry..." the lady said...

Here we go...I have the wrong house. How embarrassing.

"...I think there has been some kind of unfortunate mix-up."

Okay. Wasn't expecting that.

A man appeared behind her.

"Oh shit," he said. He looked sheepish. I could already tell I wasn't going to like where this was headed. "You didn't get my message?"

"What message?" I asked. I never switch my mobile off. I never have it more than a few feet from where I am. When you're self-employed, such as I am, you know the importance of keeping it close by as you do not want to miss any potential business opportunities.

"Our son changed his mind…"

"Changed his mind? What? He doesn't want a birthday party?" I could hear children laughing and screeching in the background. Clearly there was a party taking place within the suburban home. I peered around the front porch and in through the living room window. There are about twenty children in there.

"He didn't want a clown," the man said. I forget his name but I'm pretty sure we spoke before on the telephone; when he was booking the party. He didn't cancel it. He hadn't tried calling me. Even if he had, there would have been a missed call on my phone, something to suggest he'd attempted to contact me. But there was nothing. I wanted to stand here and argue with the (I presume) father but it wouldn't serve any purpose. He didn't want me there. There was nothing else to it. Arguing on the doorstep wasn't going to change that. "Here," the man held out a ten pound note, "for your troubles…"

The temptation was to take the money but I didn't. I didn't think it would give a good message to prospective customers. After all, mix-ups happen. "Keep it," I said. I turned away from him and started off down the drive. I stopped and turned back to the man and woman, "Just one thing… What did he choose?" There weren't many more people in this small town who offered entertainment at children's parties, so it sounded as though there was some more competition to contend with, not that competition is necessarily a bad thing.

"Iron Man," the man said.

Iron Man? I had another look in through the living room window. Standing in front of the children, in what appeared to be a second-rate outfit, was a knock-off Iron Man. Going by the screams from the house - doesn't look as though the kids cared.

"Did you want your balloon back?" the lady asked from the doorway.

I turned away from the window. "No, you can keep it," I said as I walked back to my tired, old van, a distinct feeling of 'hurt' running through me. It wasn't the fact that I had been ousted from a job; after all, there was no sense being there if the child yearned for something else. It was more to do with the fact I wasn't even worth a phone call. Sure, he said he had phoned but he didn't. He couldn't have. Could he? Maybe my phone was broken.

Back in the van (shoes off), I pulled my mobile from my pocket and dialled through for any possible voice messages. Just as I suspected there weren't any new or saved.

"What did you expect?"

"Please leave me alone, I'm not in the mood."

He was staring at me in the rear-view mirror of the car. What he had said the previous night, he was right; he was always there, despite trying to hide me underneath the make-up. He was always there waiting to taunt me, waiting to upset me, waiting to make me do those things he kept whispering to me during the night.

"You pride yourself in being a professional."

"There's nothing wrong with that."

"Not necessarily. In any other job. But do you honestly expect people to take you - us - seriously wearing that? Look at yourself. Look at what you've become throughout the years. A laughing stock."

"I'm supposed to be, it's my job."

"You know what I mean. No one takes you seriously. They treat you like the fool that you are."

"What does it matter to you?"

"Because they do the same to me."

I shifted in my seat uncomfortably. He hated the fact I did this for a living. He believed children should be seen and not heard. Or - better yet - neither seen nor heard. I argued with him for many years before I turned to this; my argument being that there is no better sound in the world than the sound of children screaming with delight. Joyous laughing is infectious and you can't help but feel it with them. The smell lingering in the van from a late night drive last night reminded me of his stance on the subject. I tried to stop him - of course I did - but he didn't listen. He never did. Just called me a pussy and made me take a hold the knife.

He continued, "Walking around the town pretending to be everyone's friend. Volunteering to help out at charity events - these people are laughing at you and not in a way you're trying for," he hissed.

"You're wrong."

"I'm not. And you know it. You can see it in their eyes, just as you think you can see the evil in mine. But of course you won't listen to me. You'll just try and bury me under any layer of shit. Fucking pathetic."

"You're wrong," I repeated once more.

"Of course I am. I am always wrong. You're right. I'm wrong."

"Please. Why can't you just leave me alone?"

"What are you going to do with the rest of your day then?" he asked, clearly ignoring my pleas. "What else have you planned now this gig has fallen through?" He was sneering at me, his top lip curled up. "Hey! I know, why don't we go to the park and put a free show on for the darling little children?" He was mocking me.

On the warmer weekends - such as this - I did go down to the town's park, a large grassy area with a playground and small cafe area. It was always so busy down there with the families making the most of the sunlight. I didn't mind working for free, going around and making them laugh with various antics but it was a good place to network. The amount of business I had got from working the park. So - in answer to his question - yes I probably would go to the park and work the crowds. After all, I was already dressed up. And it meant the delay in taking the mask off. Keep this mask on for as long as I can.

He laughed, "You realise the mask doesn't make a difference. I'm still here…"

"It does."

I punched the rear-view mirror knocking it off-centre. Can't see my reflection here. I breathed a sigh of relief as I fired the van up. Another splutter of smoke hacked from out the back. Had the gig not been cancelled this month, I might have had enough left over from paying the bills to get the van seen to. I guess that's out of the window now. A quick check over my right shoulder to check the road for oncoming traffic. The road was clear and I pulled out.

"So - are we going to the park?"

II

By the time I got to the park, and found a space for the van in the over-crowded car park, he had gone quiet. Thankfully so. His incessant talking was getting to me. Over the last few days, maybe even weeks, he had been getting louder. It wasn't just his voice which disturbed me. I knew he had been going out at night too, whilst I slept, taking the opportunity whilst I rested to take the van and head to wherever he chose to go during the twilight hours. I don't want to know where he goes and so I've never asked him. What I don't know can't kill me.

I swung my bare feet from the van and sat there for a moment, perched on the edge of the driver's seat, looking out at the rolling fields of the park before me. Just as had been suspected, the fields were littered with people of varied ages. From the comfort of the van, I could see some of them were merely walking hand in hand, others were walking with their pet dogs on long leads, some were kicking a ball around, whilst others were watching their children play in the park's playground (behind a fence near the park's entrance).

The sun on my heavily made-up face feels nice. Would give anything to rest up now and just sunbathe along with everyone else but that doesn't get the bills paid. Being self-employed, you find you need to keep working. You need to keep yourself visible to potential customers. You need to keep networking. People think my job is easy - the amount of people who've made such comments at the end of one of my gigs. I'd love to see them slip the shoes on, and the outfit - especially on hot days - just to see how they fare. My shows usually last for about an hour. I reckon - these people - they wouldn't last twenty minutes. And even if they did, I'll wager they're incapable of raising a laugh from the crowds watching.

I shut my eyes a second, enjoying the sun beating down upon me. Could stay here all day but it won't do. I opened my eyes and leaned back into my van towards the passenger side where I'd earlier thrown the over-sized shoes. I pulled them out and dropped them onto the floor, next to where I was perched in the van. Before I slid into them (and it really is a question of sliding into them), I reached back to the passenger side and grabbed the large fabric bag of props. To be honest, I'll probably not need this today. A day like this, an audience who can freely come and come…I'll most likely end up just doing balloon animals. Balloon tricks always pull in the crowds. And - when the kids leave the impromptu show with a new 'toy' - it means they're more likely to remember me when they get home. The balloon gimmicks are quickly forgotten by the parents but the smiles on their kids' faces aren't as easy to forget and before you know it, I'll have a booking (or two).

I stepped into the shoes and bent down to do them up. As I was tying the laces, I could already hear people had spotted me: a buzz of excitement bouncing from the corners of the car park from the children who'd spotted me; a feeling of 'money slipping through finger tips' at the thought of having to spend money on whatever they believe I am offering. The fact I'll charge for nothing will come as a nice surprise to them.

I closed the door of the van and locked it up before sliding the key into my pocket.

Here we go.

Show time.

III

It wasn't a complete waste of my Sunday. The odd balloon animal here and the odd balloon animal there. Smiles on the faces of the few people who did stop to watch me, which was nice, but a feeling I'd earlier felt at the lost gig as more and more families walked on by me without so much of a backward glance; the desperate feeling of losing my audience. First they're stolen away by a fake Iron Man and then they're stolen away by the lure of…What…

Kicking a ball around a park or swinging backwards and forwards on a swing? Both things they could do at anytime. How often did they get to see someone such as myself perform for them?

Usually, a day of performing in the park - or even the town centre - would see me give out more than a dozen business cards; nothing fancy, just a card with a picture of balloons and my phone number. I always meant to get the cards updated, so they looked a little more appealing, but it just never seemed to happen. After a day like this, I'm not even sure if it is worth getting them updated. Maybe I should re-think what I do? Invest the money in fake Iron Man suits, or something similar. When I started, there were superheroes around but they never seemed to be popular for children's parties. Clowns, though, were in great demand. But as the years have gone on, that demand has dwindled. It kind of makes me wish I had purchased superhero outfits before they became popular and the price trebled.

Shoes thrown in the corner of the hallway, green wig dropped on the stairs. I was lying on the bed staring at the ceiling, fully dressed because I couldn't be bothered to change from my clothes. I'm so very tired. Felt tired all day. Rough night I guess, although I don't remember stirring. I remember talking to him and going up to bed. Soon as my head hit the pillow, I was out like a light. I don't know, maybe I'm coming down with something? Either that, or age is squeezing the energy from my body as the years continue to slip on past me at a rate faster than I'd like to acknowledge. It probably doesn't help that I've not eaten anything today other than an ice cream I bought from the van parked up in the middle of the park. Can't be bothered to cook now, just want to sleep forever. So tired. Don't even remember leaving the park.

Chapter 3

I hate him. Whiny, pathetic, little runt. A cunt. Always bleating on about his love for the children. Oh it's their screams of delight that drive me. The sound of their laughter is like music to my ears. He's in his fifties; deaf cunt wouldn't know music if a monkey hit him over the head with a frying pan all the time a tune was belting out at maximum speed. He makes me sick. Ashamed to think of him as my housemate. How he even made it this far in life is beyond me. He should have just been drowned at birth by his whore mother and alcoholic father.

"Don't worry, honey, we'll get it right the next time," the drunk father could have been heard to say as he held what he perceived to be the bastard child under the shallow water of the bathtub. Drink it, you little fucker, drink it until you breathe no more. Although if that were the way his life started I'm not sure where that would have left me. I don't know - maybe I would have found a home with someone else? Thinking about it now and that doesn't sound as though it would have been bad. Certainly couldn't have been any worse than where I am now. Stuck in here, with him. The cunt. His drive to do what he does - despite the knowledge it cannot and will not last forever - annoys me more than words can say. If the overly large shoe were on the other foot, I'm sure he'd be saying the same about me. But would he? The pussy rarely speaks out. He does all he can to avoid confrontation. He believes it isn't professional. He believes it will harm his business. Someone queue jumps him in a queue for groceries, he tells them not to worry about it and the next thing we know, he is letting more people past him because he 'has all day'. Someone pushes past you in a queue, you should take that position back. I've told him this. Not just once but on many occasions. He doesn't listen though. Never does. He either pretends he hasn't heard me or he argues the toss with me. By the time we have finished having a back and forth, the person who needs to be moved back to the rear of the queue has not only left the shop but also loaded their transport and driven from the store's car park.

I stand by what I've told him before - he is the laughing stock of the town but not in the way he hopes, or argues, for. It isn't because of the outfit he wears or the acts he performs. He raises a smile, and a laugh, because of his pathetic nature.

And that's why I need to restore the balance whenever the opportunity presents itself.

Like tonight.

II

I borrowed his van. I never ask for permission and I presume he doesn't mind. He never says anything to stop me so if he does have a problem, until he is man enough to deal with it face to face with me I'll continue to take it. He should just be thankful that I at least replace the fuel that I use so it's not all coming out of his tiny wage.

I do not enjoy driving around in his clapped out banger of a vehicle. The bad paint job, the stuttering engine hacking out plumes of black smoke upon start up - it's an embarrassment but still better than walking. We've had the conversation about changing vehicles in the past but it always ends the same way; he needs it for his work. I can't exactly go out and trade it in against a new model - more's the pity. I think if I were to do that, it could well be the final straw for us. A fragile friendship pushed to breaking point. Loves this fucking van as much as he loves children.

I don't know - part of me thinks I'm going to wake up one day and find his name on some kind of sex register, not that I get to see the news very often. He doesn't like reading or watching TV, so that means I don't get to read or watch, either.

"Well, officer, he told me he loved children but I never thought he meant like that…" Of course I'd plead ignorance. No way I want to go down with him. I know what they do to perverts in prison and that's definitely not for me.

I turned down a quiet alleyway which was only just wide enough to fit the van down, as made evident by the fact I clipped the wing mirror turning in. I'm sure he won't mind. State of the fucking van, I'm sure he won't even realise.

My mind keeps coming back to his cancelled party and the poor show he had in the park; if this carries on, I wonder if it means he will start to see the world the way I see it or whether he'll just throw himself into denial even more? It would be great if he didn't feel the need to hide himself behind make-up. Great if he'd grow a pair of balls and quit being such a fucking pussy. I don't know. Knowing my luck he will most likely ruin it for the pair of us and end up doing something stupid like blowing his brains out or hanging himself from one of the rafters in our home. Mind you, if he gets down that route, he'll have to lose some weight first. Fat cunt will most likely snap the fucking rafter. But then maybe that's what he needs? A close call with death to show him how much he wants to actually live? Perhaps I could set something up for him? No. I can't. Knowing my luck he won't stop me and I'll end up killing him. Major backfire.

I think half the problem with him is because he enjoys dressing up as a clown. He pretends he doesn't do - I don't know - I think he does. After all, why else would you continue doing it, especially when no one really respects you? He pretends it is all about the parties and the entertaining but that's a thinly-veiled lie. He enjoys dressing up because it gives him a chance to hide who he is. He thinks I do not know this but I do. I think that, if he were not able to wear such an outfit anymore, he might just start to realise who he really is and what is really important to him. He'll come to terms with all of that and what he really wants to do with his life. This would be great for me because - if he were to do that - well, we both want the same thing.

A check in the rear-view mirror, straightened up after his earlier pathetic outburst, and I was clear from people following me. I killed the van's lights, plunging us into near darkness thanks to the lack of street lamps down this particular alley, an alley chosen for this very reason along with the fact it was pretty isolated from the main part of the town where the nightclub boys and girls may still be milling about. I opened the door and jumped on down from the driver's seat. I left the engine running so as not to have to endure the loud backfire when the time comes to start it back up again.

I walked to the back of the van and opened it up. The smell hit me more or less straight away. Leaving this in here during the hot day clearly had not done anything for its freshness. I reached in and took a hold of the black bin liner with a white gloved hand (courtesy of borrowing part of his uniform). As I pulled the bag from the van, a little liquid leaked from a small hole in the bottom of it. My fault. I should have double bagged it. It was obvious the weight was going to be too much for the one bag. I dropped it to the floor with a dull thud and looked back to a dumpster I had seen as I drove down the alley - a large metal can with a lid tucked into the back doorway of what looked to be a Chinese restaurant. I walked over to the dumpster and lifted the not-so-heavy lid. Fucking smell of rotten chicken and other meats hit me. Jesus. Should have brought a fucking nose-peg with me. I lifted the first few bags from the top and put them on the floor before walking back for my own bag. I lifted it and reached under to hold it from beneath. Don't need the bag splitting all the way.

I staggered it over to the dumpster and lifted it to the edge of the opening. A second later, to catch my breath, and I pushed it in. Easier than I imagined. I picked the bags up from the floor and buried my own bag with them. The fucking smell of this dumpster, I couldn't have picked a better place to dump my bag. The sheer stink of this dumpster - no one is going to go ferreting around in it. I slammed the lid shut and returned to my van. Despite the problems I'm having at home - with him - I'm feeling good. I always am when I dump the bags off. It's like a heavy weight lifted from my shoulders.

I leaned down to the radio and turned the dial. Music crackled through the damaged speakers. I half-expected it to be some kind of carnival music, given the look of the van and my 'sometimes' friend's like for all things 'clown'. Thankfully, it was a standard radio channel - some presenters talking about this and that. Sure I'll pick it up the more I listen and - until then - I do not care. Homeward bound.

III

I stepped into the shared home and quietly closed the door so as not to wake him up. I don't want the hassle of having to explain where I've been this evening. He's always so paranoid that I've been up to no good and it doesn't matter what I say to try and appease him; he never believes anything I have to say. I can't say I blame him, given the fact we both know what I've been doing all night. I say we 'both' know but he never admits it to me; never lets on he knows what I get up to when the sun goes down and the cover of the night hides my movements.

I crept through to the kitchen and dropped the white gloves on top of the rest of the outfit. He'd come in from the park and thrown it in front of the washing machine. Not sure why he didn't just put it in the washing machine. Probably testing me. Probably wanting to know how long it will be before I put it in there for him. Well - he has a long wait. I'm not his bitch. If anyone is the bitch - he is mine. I froze as I noticed a tiny speck of red on the white fabric of the glove. It's not massive but I noticed it and that meant there was a good chance he would too. I can almost hear the conversation now, quizzing me over what I'd been using his gloves for. Of course I'd deny touching them at all and try and make him believe it was him who had tainted them. What's the point? It would only cause an argument.

I bent down and scooped the outfit up before throwing it into the washing machine.

He'd best not get used to it.

I slammed the washing machine's door shut and turned the machine on.

"What are you doing?"

My heart skipped a beat. Didn't even hear the bastard coming. Rare for him to make me jump. Usually it is the other way round.

"I'm doing you a favour. Would it hurt you to say thank you?"

"You? Doing me a favour? Why am I suddenly suspicious?"

"If you want, I can turn it off and let you do it yourself?"

"No. It's fine. Just you don't usually…"

"Next time I won't bother. That suit you better?"

"I'm sorry. Didn't know you were down here anyway. I only came down for a glass of water."

I didn't respond. He'd fucked me off. Regardless of why I really put the stuff in the washing machine, the fact is I put it in the washing machine. I saved him from having to do it. He should have just said thank you but - no - he has to question my intentions. He has to be suspicious as to my motives. I'm sick of him looking down his nose at me as though he's the better person. How he can believe anyone to be better than him - knowing he dresses as a fucking clown for the living - is beyond me. He is the bottom of the food chain. He just doesn't realise it.

I watched as he poured himself a glass of water. He thinks I am the selfish one and yet he didn't even bother to offer me one. No that's fine, mate, you just do whatever you want. Never mind what I may or may not want. Still waiting for my thank you.

"What have you been doing?" he asked me. There he goes again, being suspicious. I watched him take a sip from his cool glass of water.

"Wouldn't you rather know what I am doing?"

"Do I want to know?"

"Try me."

"Okay - what are you doing?"

"Oh, nothing, just standing around here waiting for some fucking thanks."

I leaned down and turned the washing machine back off again. If he can't even say thank you to me, he can do the fucking thing himself. Before he had the chance to say anything I stormed off, leaving him to it. Even if he did say a thank you now, it would only be because I brought it up. I don't want some afterthought thank you. A pathetic token gesture of thanks. No. I'm better than that. I'm worth more than that.

Fuck him.

IV

The reaction was typical of him. To be fair, I'm so tired still that saying thank you didn't even cross my mind. Definitely have the feeling I am coming down with something. It's like I've been running around all night even though I've been up there sleeping in the comfort of my bed. Glad I don't have any bookings this week. At least, glad in so much as I don't have to get up in the morning. Can stay in bed and try and sleep this bug off.

I leaned down and flicked the washing machine back on. It started through with its spin cycle as I walked back over to the kitchen sink. A twist of the cold tap and I re-filled the glass. I walked back up the stairs towards my bedroom. I put the cup of water on the side and collapsed onto the already ruffled duvet. Can't believe it's so cold already. I've only just gone downstairs and yet it feels like I've never been in here. I pulled the cover over myself and shut my eyes.

I'm tired and yet my brain feels more awake than it has felt for these past few months. What was he doing up at night? What was he doing in the kitchen? Usually he doesn't disturb me. I very rarely hear him moving around at night even when I know for definite he has been up and about. I come downstairs and things have been moved from where I had left them. Never really know for sure what he does at night and pretty sure I wouldn't want to know. Not going by some of the things he whispers to me when we're at the parties. He's a monster.

I twisted and turned as I struggled to get comfortable, troubled by thoughts of what he had done, or had been doing. For all I knew, I was making a mountain out of a molehill but I didn't know for sure and it was impossible to ask him outright after he stormed off leaving me on my own. Funny - normally I want nothing more than for him to leave me be. The one time I want him here, he isn't around.

"I am here."

"I thought you'd left?"

"Where would I go?"

To Hell.

"What were you doing tonight?" I asked him.

"A favour for you."

"Before that," I continued to push him.

"Why don't you let me show you?"

"Just tell me."

"No. I want to show you."

"I'm not sure I want to see."

"You're ready to see it."

"Not sure that I am."

"Let me show you. I'll even walk you through it - step by step. It'll be a good chance for us to bond."

"I'm not…"

"Stop being a fucking pussy, you snivelling piece of shit. Get out of bed and come with me."

My heart skipped a beat at the sudden aggression. I should have known it was coming. It didn't matter how a conversation started with him it always ended with the same amount of aggression. The anger and hostility coming - usually - from him not getting his own way.

I threw the covers off and slowly climbed out of bed.

"Yes, that's it," he sneered. "Grow a pair of balls." He laughed. "You need to put your shoes on. We're going out," he continued.

"Where are we going?"

"Hurry up. We don't have much time left before the sun will start to come up."

"Just tell me where we're going."

"I can't. You need to see for yourself. Trust me; I think it will be good for you."

I felt uncomfortable. I was the one who usually kept the control. I was the one who decided what we did and didn't do together and yet here he was, dictating to me what was to be done. It didn't feel right. I didn't like the feeling of not being in control. Just to get to the end of the evening though - and find out what he did - I walked from the bedroom, down the stairs and to where I'd kicked my shoes off earlier. I slid them on and tied the laces as he watched. I could hear him breathing. He sounded excited. A feeling of dread washed through me. Where were we going?

CHAPTER 4

I watched as he drove my van. He seemed at ease behind the wheel which didn't surprise me. Had he not driven it before, he'd have probably been a little nervous about driving it. It was, after all, quite a bit bigger than a car - the sort he'd possibly be used to driving. He'd driven it before, though, despite his protests. I'd get in after a good night's sleep and the driving position would have changed. Or I'd go to get the keys from where I'd left them and they wouldn't be hanging there - or they wouldn't be hanging on the exact peg I'd left them on. It was the little things, the little details he thought I didn't notice but I did. I always noticed.

"Where are we going?" I asked him again.

"You'll see," he said.

"Can't you just tell me?"

"Even if I did, you wouldn't be any the wiser. You need to see for yourself."

I looked out of the window and didn't recognise where we were and yet there was a strange feeling that I should have known. I was sure I hadn't been there before, yet…A nagging doubt in the back of my mind that I had. It was weird. We turned down another unknown-to-me road. I wasn't sure where he was taking me and yet I already knew I wasn't going to like it. The fact he wasn't telling me where we were going - keeping it secret - just made me feel that little more uneasy about it all.

"How far is it?" I asked him.

"We're nearly there," he said. His eye caught mine via the rear-view mirror. There was a glint there which cemented my feeling of uneasiness.

"How'd you even find this place?" I asked him as he turned the van down another quiet road.

"Exploration."

"What were you even doing out here?" I asked.

He turned the van down a tight alleyway, clipping the wing-mirror in the process. I stared at the rear-view mirror in the hope he'd see my disapproving look. He didn't.

"Well," he said. He pulled the van to a stop with a judder.

"What? We're here? There's nothing here.'

"You wanted to know where I went this evening - get out."

"Is this where you drive off?"

"Don't tempt me."

I opened the van door, as did he, and climbed out. I closed the door.

"This way," he said. He walked us to a dumpster.

"What is this?"

"This is a dumpster," he said.

"I don't understand."

"Of course you don't. Open it."

I looked at the dumpster. Even from here - a few feet away - I could smell it. The contents, whatever they were, were clearly rotting. Hardly surprising given the daytime temperatures recently.

"Open it," he repeated, his voice showing a brewing irritation.

I hesitated. "Not sure I want to," I told him.

He sighed. "Are you ever going to grow any fucking balls?" he hissed.

"It's a bin. You want me to go rooting around in the bin?"

"Sooner rather than later, if you could. Day is coming."

"Look - it's not my business what you do in the evening. If you're happy - it's fine…I'm sorry, I shouldn't have stuck my nose in…"

"Open the fucking dumpster. You need to see this. It will do you some good. It'll make you realise what you need to do with your own life."

"I just…"

"Get the fuck out of the way."

II

I pushed him out of the way. He didn't take much to move. He was just standing there, watching, as I stormed over to the dumpster. Fucking stinks. I lifted the lid and pulled out the first few bags - the ones I'd used to bury the bag I had thrown in there. I dropped them at his feet and couldn't help but laugh as a little (I guess) chicken juice splashed him.

"Is this entirely necessary?" he asked.

"Yes."

"Honestly, it's fine if you don't want to tell me…"

"Shut up and give me a hand."

We both reached into the dumpster and pulled out the heavy black bag, carefully placing it on the floor.

"What is it?"

"It's a fucking bag, what do you think it is? Open it."

III

He wasn't going to let me not open it. Not after dragging me out here and fishing it out of the bin. I was nervous. I guess because I already knew what was in there. He'd whispered it enough to me during times when he thought I was asleep. He told me of the things he yearned to do. My hand was shaking like a leaf as I tugged at the knot.

"Hurry up," he rushed me.

"Just…Shut up!" I hissed back at him. I didn't need him getting in my face right about now. I didn't need him pressuring me into this. More to the point - I just didn't want to hear his voice right now as I continued to struggle with the knot. I just wanted silence. I needed silence. Needed to mentally prepare myself for what I was going to find.

The knot came apart in my shaking hands. This is it. Slowly, I pulled the two parts of bag away from each other and peered in. The contents were hard to see, not helped by the fact that the moon was hidden behind a multitude of clouds. Didn't keep the smell away from me though and I couldn't help but gag.

"What is it?" I asked, scared of the answer.

"Put your hand in."

"I don't want to."

"Put your fucking hand in. You wanted to know what I do. This is what I do."

I slowly put my hand in the bag and fumbled around. I felt something. What is that? Hair? Hair. I moved my hand further into the bag. Skin? Wet. What is this? I pulled my hand out of the bag and stood away from it.

"What the hell is this?" I asked. "What the hell is in that bag? What have you done?"

"So many questions, so many questions. Where would you like me to start?"

"What have you done?"

"A wasted question - you know what I've done."

"I need you to say it."

"I killed him."

"Who?"

"The boy."

"Stop fucking about with me!" I shouted. "What boy?!"

"Ooh - raising your voice at me, I'm impressed."

"I swear to God…"

"Shut up! This macho bullshit - it's not you. It doesn't suit you. You're just coming across as desperate."

"Desperate?! I am desperate! I'm desperate to know what you've done and why!"

"Tie the bag up and put it back in the dumpster. The sun will be up soon and we really don't want to get caught standing here. I promise that once you've done that you can go back to being macho and the big man…But for now - think with your fucking head."

"Put it back in the dumpster? You want it back in the bin? You put it back in the fucking bin!"

I turned away from him. I was done being his pawn. And I refused to tidy up what he had done. I wanted no part of it. I sat there - pissed - and watched as he lifted the bag back into the dumpster. Once again, just as he had done before, he buried it under the other bags we'd taken out. He slammed the lid down and walked back to the van. He jumped in the driver's seat. Guess I'm the passenger then. The van coughed into life as he turned the key in the ignition.

"What boy?" I asked him as he reversed us out of the alley. We hit the main road and he slammed the van into first gear before heading off in the direction we'd previously come from.

"The one from the park. The one who was crying constantly. His mum was shouting at him. She stormed off saying she'd go home without him. A common ploy put into play by desperate mothers. They think their threat of leaving without their child is supposed to scare them into running after them. Might work in some cases, but not in this instance. Mummy might have come back for him but it was too late. He wasn't there.."

"You snatched a child from the park? What if someone saw you…Where the fuck was I?"

"I don't know where you were. For all I know you stropped off because your day wasn't going as you'd hope it would. Quite frankly, I didn't give a fuck. I wanted to have some fun. I think I deserve that much…"

"By snatching a child from the park? Again - what if someone saw you? You put him in my fucking van."

"Where else was I going to put him?"

"Did someone see you? Oh shit, I don't even want to know."

"What the fuck do you take me for? No one saw me."

"We're going to jail. You know that, right?"

He didn't say anything. He just frowned as though his mind was going elsewhere. I don't even want to know where it went. If he was capable of… What…He killed a boy? If he could think of that - what the fuck else could he do? Don't question it. I don't want to know.

"We needed to do this," he said finally, breaking the silence between us.

"I'm a children's entertainer - why the fuck would I want to hurt a child?"

"It wasn't one of your children - one of your precious little darlings who enjoys laughing at your pathetic bullshit." His voice irritated me. It sounded like he was taunting me, trying to get a reaction from me, but what sort of reaction was I supposed to give after seeing what he had just done to a child? "The child was a cunt…"

"The child was just that…A child."

"A noisy, spoilt little shit cunt."

"Someone's son."

"Demon Seed."

"What the fuck is wrong with you?"

"Me? What's wrong with you? Hiding behind your day job. What happened tonight, what happened with the child - that is who we are. That is what we're about."

"No it isn't."

"Yes it is and the sooner you realise that - the better."

"Just don't even talk to me. I need to think about what we're going to do."

"What we're going to do? There's nothing to do."

"You think hiding a body in a dumpster is enough to keep us safe? You think they won't be able to trace the murder back to you? Back to us? And you say I'm an idiot? Jesus fucking Christ…"

"You need to calm down. You'll give yourself a brain aneurysm."

"Just - please - shut the fuck up."

"By morning, when you have had time to think about this properly, you'll come crawling to me. You'll realise this was the right thing to do. Is the right thing to do. So I killed an unhappy child. Big deal. They deserved it and - you know - they're probably up there in some fucking Heaven thanking me for what I did to them. Clearly they weren't happy with their mummy and daddy. I did them a favour…"

"SHUT UP!" I screamed at him. He stared at me via the rear-view mirror. There was an anger in his eyes I'd seen on more than one occasion. I shifted in my seat. I don't want to annoy him, not knowing what he was capable of, but I can't hear his voice right now. The man is poison. Pure poison. Sure - at times children could be irritating when they weren't happy but only because it's hard to get them to change their attitude when they're having a sulk. People like me, I just want to make the world smile. Children like that? If they were having a sulk about whatever - children like that are hard to make smile. It doesn't mean I'd want them to die. Especially at the hands of a psychopath.

We drove the remainder of the journey in silence. My mind focused on whether we were going to be caught for his crimes. My mind wondered whether there was a way out of it for me. Not him. He can go down for the crime. He deserves it. I don't though. This was all him. It was nothing to do with me. I'm fuming that he could even bring me into it without first checking with me. I angled myself in my seat so I could see him in the side mirror of the van; he looked like he was as fuming as I was. Well stuff him. I don't owe him anything. I'll wait until morning and then I'll turn him in. The authorities might go easy on me if I turn him in. It would go a long way to show I'm not a part of what he did. It was all him.

I don't owe him anything.

CHAPTER 5

I hadn't slept all night. I had lain awake, tossing and turning. Occasionally, I heard him trying to talk to me - trying to say something - but I ignored him. Whatever he had to say, I didn't want to hear it. My mind was too caught up with getting taken in by the police when the crime is discovered.

The sun shone through the cracks in the curtains reminding me that it was a new day. All night I had been wrestling with what would be the best course of action in my mind and - only now - had I finally come to a decision. The thought I had whilst he drove us home was the best way to go. For me at least. Phone the police.

I rolled off the bed and reached across to where my mobile phone was charging on the bedside cabinet. I unlocked the touch-screen and went through to the keypad function. I pressed the first nine. My finger wavered over the nine when I heard him speak to me.

"What are you fucking doing?"

"What I have to do."

"Jesus. Have you heard yourself? You think you're so fucking high and mighty. Well - fine - phone them then, if that's what you think is the right thing to do."

"Of course it is. You're a murderer!"

"So are you. Your prints are on his face just as mine are."

"I'll tell them you took me there to show me what you did and that I reached into the bag because it was too dark to see. That's the truth."

He laughed, "And you think they'll believe you? You're even more fucking pathetic than I first thought."

"Me? I'm not the one killing children."

"Call them then. They'll take us both down but if that's what you want to do, I won't stand in your way. Here, fuck it, I'll even help." He called my bluff by pressing the second nine. "Come on, just one more press and both of our lives are over."

"Only yours."

"You're sure about that? They'll somehow take me away and leave you behind? The innocent party in all of this?"

"I am innocent."

"From where I stand, you have as much blood on your hands as I do. Anyway - sorry - I didn't mean to distract you. I believe you were in the middle of making a phone call? Please. Don't let me stop you."

"Fuck you!" I threw the phone onto the bed.

"No balls. You lack conviction in everything you do."

"Don't push me," I hissed.

"Why ever not? The worst you're going to do is shout and whinge at me. Although, to be fair, that is irritating. Gives me a headache whenever you talk…"

"You give me a headache."

"Well isn't this the most childish of conversations! You spend too much time with kiddies. Surprised you're not dating one of them."

"Fuck off."

"Unless that's why you're upset I killed the boy? You think it's a waste of prime meat? Maybe next time I should have given you some alone time first…You know - let you fuck the virgin ass before I stuck a knife through his eye."

"Is that how you did it?" His words made me feel cold to the core.

"Fuck his ass?"

"Stuck a knife through his eye."

"You want the details?"

I hesitated. I wasn't sure if I wanted them or not. I wasn't sure if I wanted to hear how he killed an innocent child. Part of me wanted to know (I guess that much was obvious) and part of me wanted to bury any knowledge of what he'd done. I felt a sickness brewing within the pit of my stomach.

"You're not going to be sick, are you?" he asked. "Maybe you want a little time in the bathroom first?"

"Just tell me. What did you do?"

"You going to tell the police?"

"I'm not sure."

"Because if you are, I'd rather you just listened in on the conversation with them. Not sure I want to be repeating myself all day long, you know?"

"Just tell me!" I shouted. My voice echoed through the room.

He sat on the edge of the bed and picked the phone up before clearing the screen from the previous dialled numbers. He set the phone to one side, back on the bedside cabinet. He hesitated a moment as he cast his mind back to the previous day.

"Like I said," he started, "you disappeared - not sure where. I figured you were just in a mood because your day hadn't gone as you planned. You know, what with the cancelled party and then the poor reaction in the park...So I was waiting by the van so I could catch a lift home and I heard all this commotion. This woman was screaming at her child for some reason or other. She ended up getting in her car and wheel-spinning from the car park as though abandoning him there. He didn't seem to care. Just stood there screaming his head off, you know - a proper fucking rant. God only knows what it was about. It was embarrassing."

"Children play up from time to time."

"Yes - and should be shot for it. You want me to fucking finish?" I didn't say anything. I waited patiently for him to continue his story. He took another deep breath and continued, "So this bastard thing was screaming and screaming. I looked around and the mother wasn't coming back. Fuck knows where she had disappeared too, and there wasn't anyone else coming to his aid. No one else was even around, to be honest. Seems most of the park was empty at that time but then - you did decide to leave it really late. Why was that?"

"I was touting for business."

"You sure about that? Or were you waiting for the perfect opportunity to snatch a child?"

I ignored him. I knew what he was trying to do. He was trying to bait me into an argument with him. He was trying to get me to say what he did was right, the decent thing to do. But I wouldn't admit it. I'd never admit it. You can't go around killing children. It wasn't right. Murder is bad but it's worse when children are involved. I tried to get him to continue the story, "So you snatched him?"

He nodded, "Threw him in the back of your van."

"How did I not hear him?"

"That would be the punch to his head. Knocked him clean out. I tell you what, too, the blissful silence of the day when he stopped screaming. Heaven."

"You're sick."

"Because I like peace and quiet? Whatever."

"The mum - she would have come back."

"She did come back."

"What?!"

"Asked me if I'd seen her son. I asked her if she meant the one who was screaming in the middle of the car park and she just looked embarrassed. Can you imagine that? Embarrassed by your own child. I wonder how many parents feel like that? You make them - you should stand by them no matter what; whether they're making a scene in the car park or whether you find them a weak disappointment of a child...You should stand by them. The fact she didn't - clearly she didn't want him..."

"Or she was trying to..."

"Don't try and justify it. You weren't there."

"What did she say?" I changed the subject back to the story to save another argument.

"When I told her I had seen him, she asked where he went. Of course I pointed her out in a completely different direction. Said he headed to the park."

"She believed you?"

He shrugged. "I even offered to help her find him. Because that's the nice sort of fella that I am."

"You're sick." I wanted to grab for the mobile phone but knew I wouldn't be able to phone the police, no matter how much I wanted to. He'd always stop me. "When did you kill him?" I asked.

"I brought us home. Couldn't very well kill him in the van, could I?"

"Where did you do it?"

"It's not important."

"It is to me..."

My mobile phone started to buzz on the bedside cabinet signifying an incoming call. With each buzz it danced a little further across the wooden top. I looked in its direction.

"You going to get that?" he asked.

I wanted to but, at the same time, I didn't want to stop this conversation. I wanted to know all the details. For some reason I thought it might have made me feel a little better to know what had happened. That, maybe, I'd be able to come to terms with it. Was that even possible? A child had died because of us. Was there any coming back from that or had we crossed a line which could never be taken back?

Without any warning he reached across to the phone and took a hold of it. He accepted the call and pressed the phone to my ear. Didn't really give me much of a choice but to talk to the person on the other end of it.

"Hello?" I asked, trying my best to sound normal. Trying my best to sound as though I wasn't in the middle of a discussion detailing how a child had died the night before. Does guilt even come across in the tone of someone's voice?

I listened to the man (Mr. Cartwright) introduce himself on the other end of the telephone. He explained that he'd seen me at a party a couple of weeks ago and his own son's birthday was fast approaching. Apparently, his son couldn't stop talking about me since he'd seen me and so Mr. Cartwright wanted to hire me. I felt my mind screaming at me not to accept the booking. I heard the voices say I should just hang the phone up and then other voices say I should go; if I suddenly disappeared now, without word, it would just look more suspicious. Mr. Cartwright was unaware of my internal debating and proceeded to ask me for my rates.

He answered for me. I wanted to scream at him to shut the fuck up but I knew Mr. Cartwright would hear and - more importantly - that he wouldn't understand. Before I knew it, he had gone one step further to accept the booking. I wanted to ask him what he was playing at but - again - I knew I couldn't. I could only sit there as he reached for the diary which was always kept close to my mobile phone. This coming Saturday was clear until he started to pencil in Mr. Cartwright's address. Please stop. Tell him we're busy. Tell him we have a booking. He doesn't need to know we're not accepting them at the moment because we killed someone last night. He doesn't need to know any of that. Just that we're busy. Tell him.

My heart sank as Mr. Cartwright thanked me for my time. He responded on my behalf once again before putting the phone down. He threw it to one side, with the diary, and lay back on the bed with a self-satisfied smug look on his face.

"We make quite the team," he said.

"We can't go to that booking. You need to call him back," I said.

"Forgot to get his number. Sorry. This is why you take your own bookings. I've never been one for this side of the business."

"This side of the business? What other sides are there?"

"We provide a service. That's what I wanted to show you last night."

"What are you talking about?"

"You entertain the good children. I punish the bad. It's quite simple."

My heart skipped a beat.

"You can't do that again," I hissed. "What you did last night - that was it - you can't do it anymore."

He smiled, "If you watched the news - you'd know I can do it again. And I have done it again…"

"What? What are you talking about?" Had he killed more than one child? If so, how many? What were the numbers and where was I when he was doing it? The sickness brewed within my twisting gut once more. He didn't answer me though. I screamed at him to tell me what he meant. I screamed at him to answer my questions but he didn't. He just sat there, smiling. And then, without a word, he disappeared from my sight. "Talk to me!" I screamed at him but he was gone. I jumped up from the bed and ran through to the landing. I called out for him to come back and talk but he ignored me. I screamed and dropped to my knees, surprised tears streaming down my face as I felt both the weight of what he'd just told me and the weight of what we'd been a part of the previous night.

II

I was going from room to room. I was out of breath, I was moving so fast. Not sure exactly what I was looking for. Just something, I guess, to let me know whether he'd brought the boy into the house. After all if he didn't do it here, where else would he have done it? There was nowhere else I knew of which would have given him the privacy to carry out such an atrocity.

At first I thought he'd done it in the van but the rear was completely clear of any evidence and yet was still messy from where I hadn't cleaned it for ages. Impossible to clean up the evidence without showing some trace that a cleaning operation had recently taken place.

In the house I had a good look around the living room and nothing was out of place. At least, nothing which hadn't been left out of place by myself. The study - a small room - was seemingly undisturbed too; the layers of dust again suggesting no clean up had taken place. The room was dusty as I rarely went in there. Only went in once every couple of months to try and get a head start on my accounts and, during those times, I never thought to give it a clean. Upstairs only had a modest sized bathroom and a couple of bedrooms and those too looked as though they hadn't played a part in what he had done.

The final room to check was the kitchen. I walked in, wondering why I hadn't checked here first. After all, this was the room I had seen him in that night, acting suspiciously. I cast my mind back to what he was doing - ah yes, the washing machine. I opened the door and pulled my work uniform out. I gave it a shake and examined it. Seemed to be okay. He wouldn't have worn this anyway, would he? He hates me wearing it. Unless he'd put it on that night in order to frame me should he have been discovered? Would he have done that? I wasn't sure but I couldn't put it past him. It's not as though the two of us are close.

I dropped the uniform in a crumpled pile by my feet and continued to scan the room for evidence of foul play. Nothing. The place was spotless. Well - as spotless as things got in my house. I froze. My eyes were fixed upon a door in the corner of the room. One which I tended to keep shut. To people visiting, they'd have presumed it led to nothing but a cupboard but that wasn't the case; it was the door to what was originally intended, I presume, to be a wine cellar. I had never used it. Only been down there once and that was when I first moved in and I was exploring the home. There was something about the room - some energy - something down there…It made me feel uncomfortable. I got out of there as fast as I could and I vowed never to go back down there. Soon, I didn't even see the door when I went into the kitchen. I was blind to it. With this feeling running through the pit of my stomach, I wished I was still blind to it. I can't be though. I need to go down there. I need to see. Already know what's down there…Need to go down. Shit.

I walked across the kitchen floor and reached out for the handle. What are the chances of getting down there without him knowing? Does it even matter if he finds me, or knows I've been down there? I reached out and took a hold of the handle. I paused a moment, unsure as to whether he was going to come running in to try and stop me from seeing anything I shouldn't have. Nothing. Silence in fact. I paused a moment longer; not to give him further chance, but to enjoy the silence. It had been too long since I'd had pure silence in my life. It's blissful. A child screaming in the back of my mind snapped me back to reality. What? I'm supposed to hear the child screaming now too as though I'd been present for his murder?! I wasn't there. It was nothing to do with me. Fucking guilt consuming me.

For my own peace of mind, I turned the door handle and leaned into the cellar. Hanging by the side of the wall, before the first of twelve steps down, was a piece of string connected to the light-switch. I gave it a tug, half-expecting the bulb to be dead. It slowly flickered into life, illuminating the room below me. Shadows cast from the over-hanging light revealed the room wasn't empty. Proof he had been down there. I remember the room as being empty.

III

"Where do you think you're going?" I hissed in his ear as I stopped him from venturing further down the stairs.

"Get out of my way."

"You have no business down there."

"It's my house. I can go where I want."

"You never wanted this room. You left it for me. You have no right…"

"I never said I didn't want this room!"

"You're scared to be in here. Because you're a fucking pussy."

"I'm going down there."

"You're not."

IV

I pushed past him and made my way down the stairs, each step creaking underneath my weight. My mouth fell upon when I reached the bottom step and saw into the cellar.

"What the fuck is this?" I asked.

He didn't need to answer. It was obvious as to what it was. The question I should have asked was what the hell was all of this doing in the cellar.

"What does it fucking look like?" he hissed.

"It looks like you've been hiding a lot from me."

I stepped off the last of the steps, onto the cold concrete of the cellar floor - unsure of where to look first, my mind temporarily distracted from the real reason I was down here.

Chapter 6

There were different shaped easels set up around the room. Canvases were perched on top of them - some blank and some already stained with oil paint. The floor was littered with painting instruments, different sized brushes thrown here and there with no rhyme nor reason. He's been coming down painting? What the hell? I understood why he kept what he did with the child a secret from me but why hide this? If anything, this was the sort of thing we should have been sharing...I froze on the spot as my eyes fixed upon a pile of canvases leaning against the wall. Considering the front canvas is finished - I'm guessing all of these have been completed. I just hoped that they didn't all have the same picture painted upon them - more specifically the same subject matter. I walked over to the pile and lifted the front one up to get a closer look.

"A work of art, don't you think?" he whispered in my ear.

The picture was a close-up portrait of a small boy from the torso upwards. He was naked. His eyes stared out of the painting. It didn't matter which way I tilted the picture, they seemed to stay fixed on me. A haunting, dead expression. The boy's mouth was slightly agape, his tongue visibly lulling to one side There was a wide cut across his throat and you could clearly see the inner workings of his throat through the rip. Was this real? A portrait of the boy he killed? I didn't see his face when I felt into the bag. I just touched his face. I don't know what he looked like. This could be him. Is it?

"Who is this?" I needed to know.

He smiled, "You know who."

"The child you took me to?"

He nodded.

"You killed him and painted him?"

He nodded again.

That could only mean that…I lowered the picture and noticed, for the first time, a small bed in the corner of the room. Chains either end of it. A mattress stained with red, brown and yellow. I gagged. So they lie there, dead, and he stands here watching over them, painting them as though no crime has been committed? I looked down at the pictures. The second one was of a different figure. What were the chances he just had a good imagination and it was the same dead child but with a different face painted? I looked to him. He was standing there, shaking his head as though he knew what I was thinking.

"They're all dead?" I asked.

He nodded. I gagged again as I suppressed the need to vomit. How long had he been doing this, killing innocent children? How hadn't he been stopped already? I wanted to tear him apart limb from limb but I knew I couldn't. I looked down at the pictures and reached for another, throwing the one of the boy with the slit throat to one side.

"Be careful with that. Might be worth something one day," he said.

I pulled a second painting out from the middle of the pile and was immediately horrified: the image of what appeared to be a young girl's body. Her legs had been cut off at the top of her thigh, her arms cut off from the elbows and her head cut off at the neck. All pieces which had been removed were missing from the picture. It was literally just her torso. Where the limbs had been removed there were harsh red brushstrokes, with a similar brushstroke over where her genitals would have been.

"A personal favourite," he said, glee in his voice.

I threw the picture across the room as I reached for another. I could hear him huffing and puffing at me – irritated, no doubt, by my lack of care. Well sorry, but I didn't care. If I could have, I would have thrown him across the room. A third picture was primarily of an eyeball. It was balanced in a hand and sliced down the middle. In the background of the painting was what appeared to be a young boy crying. He was huddled up into a ball, a harsh red brushstroke coming from a black hole where his left eye should have been.

"How his screaming didn't wake you up, I don't know."

I dropped the picture and looked at the remaining pile. I had seen enough of them, but was giving them a quick count where they rested on the floor. Over twenty of them.

"They're all finished paintings?" I asked.

He nodded.

We both just stood there a moment. I didn't have a clue as to what to say. I think, going by the buzz in my head, he had plenty to say but was giving me the time needed to process it. Well, silly really, there wasn't enough time in the world to process what he'd shown me already and now this on top of that? I could never understand what would drive a person to do such a thing.

I lunged forward and knocked one of the easels over. A second later and I knocked over the second and third until they were all on the floor. He didn't say anything. He just watched. I guess he knew I needed to vent my initial feelings of anger from my body or else there'd never be any hope of us moving on from this. Moving on from this? Why am I thinking like that? There's no way we can move on from this. As far as I am concerned, we're done.

I gave a final look around the room and hurried up the stairs before I accidentally saw something else which I wouldn't like. Can't take anymore. Back in the kitchen, I slammed the door shut before struggling to move the kitchen table across the floor in an effort to block it. That door never needs to be opened again. He still remained silent. He just stood there, watching what I was doing. With the table in place, I dropped to my knees and started to weep for the children.

II

I'm loath to call it a make-up table because it sounds so feminine but I guess that's what it is. A table, against my bedroom wall, a few feet away from my bed, with a small oval shaped mirror. It may look strange to people looking in, a single man of my age with a set up like this. I suppose, thinking into it a little more, it could be perceived that I'm a widower with the table and mirror - the whole set-up - belonging to my dead partner. Not the case though. There is a perfectly valid reason as to why it is here though, and that's because I need to apply my 'work' make-up somewhere. Sure, I could do it in the bathroom but it's easier to put it on whilst sitting comfortably.

I was sitting at the table now. My eyes were red raw from crying. My skin was so pale. I haven't looked as though I'm in the best shape for as long as I can remember but - even so - I feel as though I've aged dramatically over the weekend.

I had all my work get-up out, spread across the table: a children's face-painting set. I could have bought professional make-up to get the look but I found this to be more than adequate. It also happened to be a lot cheaper.

"You can't ignore what you've seen."

I took the lid off the white colour and dipped the sponge into it. I looked into the mirror one last time before applying make-up and smiled. The first time I'd seen this particular face and smiled. I'm not smiling because I am happy with it. I'm smiling at it because it's soon to disappear.

"I'll still be here."

I pressed the sponge onto my forehead and wiped over my brow. Every piece of visible skin (neck, face, ears) was to be coloured in this pasty white colour; a good foundation for the other colours needed - such as the purple rings around the eyes and the overly large smile drawn on.

"You can't bury me."

The whole face takes approximately ten to twenty minutes to complete, closer to the latter if I want it to look really professional. Right now, I'm not too worried. I just want to hide him from my sight. Help silence him.

"You're being a fucking retard!"

III

I was standing in front of the full-size mirror I had stashed in the second bedroom. I was in my full get-up. The face was finished; I'd put the yellow wig on this time around and slid into the red jump-suit - my oldest one and - to look at it - you could tell. Definitely seen better days and, truth be told, I should have potentially thrown it out a long time ago. Not sure why I haven't; a difficulty in letting go of the past? Not sure why that is - wasn't exactly the best. Despite not planning to leave the house I had also stepped into the large clown shoes. Also red. I smiled as broadly as I could - accentuated by the use of the make-up. Not sure if I actually look very kiddy-friendly today or whether I look sinister.

I waved at myself, a gentle side by side with my hand.

Definitely sinister.

Was that how I always looked? Had I just not noticed it before? Or is this just because of him? He has tainted how I feel about myself in either guise. I'm not sure. Hopefully I've always looked like this - rather that than know he has managed to change me within the space of a night. Maybe it's the smile? Maybe I need to tone it down a little bit? I changed the smile to a less dramatic one. I still feel as though I look evil. Please let me have always looked like this. Please. Please let it be that I'm just feeling paranoid about it now he's made me part of his little hobby. Please. Don't let him have changed me.

"I haven't changed you," he hissed in my ear, "you're the one who changed. If anyone changed anyone, it was you changing me."

I saw him in the mirror's reflection. He looked expressionless as he stared back at me with cold, dead eyes. I flinched and lashed forward with my right fist, smashing the mirror in the process.

He laughed, "Whoops. That's seven years bad luck for you then."

IV

I was sitting in front of the television (in full make-up) with the volume turned as loud as it could go in an effort to drown out his grating voice.

One of my DVDs was playing on the screen in an effort to bury the horrors I had discovered over the last few hours, not that the film was doing a very good job of it. In the background of every scene, I couldn't help but see the images of dead children mingling with the other onscreen extras as though they'd always been there, part of the film, and I was only just seeing it. At one point - twenty minutes into the film - I momentarily believed they had always been there and that he had simply opened my eyes to it.

They couldn't have been real, the pictures in the basement. Surely. They couldn't have been real pictures of real people he had killed. They couldn't have been. A mumbled, distorted voice told me they were real but I ignored it. They were most likely fake pictures. Scenarios he imagined in his troubled mind. Yes, that was it. They were the work of a sick individual and not the product of a genuine crime. There's a big market for sick and disturbing images like that - clearly he is just trying to tap into it a little? Maybe, if I were to look around on auction sites on the Internet, I'd find links to where they're being sold? Of course. All makes sense when you think about it. A mumbled voice asked me about the body I saw.

"I didn't see the body," I said, despite meaning to ignore him. "For all I know, you're just messing with me. You're trying to make me think we killed someone. That's all. A sick game to try and mess with my head. Although I don't understand why."

The voice mumbled something under the shouting of the film playing on the screen. I reached for the controller and killed the volume in the hope he would admit the truth to me; it was just a sick prank to try and teach me some kind of lesson, whatever that could be.

"What about the bed in the corner of the room? The stained mattress?" he asked.

Maybe that was there from a previous occupant and he'd just left it there as moving it was too much hassle. That would make sense. It's not as though I go into the room so he knew I probably wouldn't have helped him dispose of it.

"If you're that sure it is all a prank, you'll be happy to watch the news," he sneered. "Look at the time. It's coming up to twelve now, the lunchtime bulletins." He showed me his watch and it was indeed coming up to the lunch-time news program. "If you're that sure it's a prank, change the channel."

"I can't," I told him, "and you know I can't. It's an old set. Won't receive digital transmissions."

He laughed.

"What's so funny?"

"The television accepts digital transmissions. What do you think that box is?" He pointed down to a small black box which sat next to the DVD unit. I'd never noticed it before. How long had it been there? "Television just needed an upgrade and that was easy enough to sort." He picked the television controller up and switched the channel. Adverts came onto screen, the first time I had seen any for as long as I could remember.

"You never told me."

"You never seemed bothered. Every time you watched the television it was always one of your silly films."

"They're not silly."

"Whatever." He pointed to the screen, "Here you go."

The news' opening credits rang through the living room. The pro-gramme opened with a story about a children's entertainer who'd been ar-rested after a number of people stepped forward to make child molestation accusations against him, dating back thirty years.

"There's some sick people out there," he whispered.

There was a second story about some affairs happening overseas. I didn't listen to what was said as I knew it was most likely to be scaremon-gering. Most stories about foreign affairs seemed to be designed just for that - a way of making us feel at ease about the government's latest plan to push forward with stepping in and getting involved. Why they couldn't just keep their noses out of business which didn't directly concern them I do not know. It's not as though they need to…I stopped mid-thought. My eyes were transfixed to the screen: a picture of a smiling child that had been taken on a bright, sunny day in what appeared to be a back garden. He was sitting on a swing, a padding pool to the side of the photo and fences behind him.

"He didn't look like that at the park," he said.

"Shut up!" I hissed.

The story ran through. The boy had disappeared from the park yesterday afternoon. Jack, aged nine. His parents were said to be distraught. Any information and you were invited to phone through, with a number provided.

"You really did it?"

He nodded, "I did say so."

"The pictures are all real?"

"Good, aren't they?"

"They're not just what you imagined?"

"No. They're real. Just as I told you." He hesitated, "So what do you think? It feels right, doesn't it?"

"What are you talking about? They're fucking looking for him!"

"They're not looking for him. Relax."

"Did you not just watch that?! His picture was on the news. It's probably in the papers too. They want their son back!" I shouted.

"Calm down!" he shouted back. He waited until I was calmer before continuing, "They're not looking for him. They don't give a shit about him. And I can't say I blame them - the whiney little cunt."

"He was on the news."

"A picture which did not represent the boy I took was on the news. People will be looking for the kid shown in the pictures, not the one I disposed of."

"Are you fucking insane? They're the same person."

"Are they? Are they really?" He stood up and walked us through to the bathroom. He looked into the mirror. "What do you see?" He was staring at me, his eyes almost rabid with excitement. He screamed at me, "What do you fucking see?!"

"I see you."

"And I see you. Are we not one and the same?"

"I am nothing like you."

"You are me!"

"I'm not!"

"When people see me, they see you."

"No. When people see you, they see a monster. When they see me, they see an entertainer."

"Then - by your own argument - the boy in the picture is not the same as the boy I took...They are two different people and if that's the case... They will never find him." I stormed from the bathroom and slammed the door shut. "Admit it - we got away with it. Just as we always get away with it."

"Why can't you leave me alone?" I begged him. I hurried through back to the living room and slammed that door shut too. I just wanted some peace and quiet. I sat myself down on the sofa and flicked the television channel back over to Laurel and Hardy.

"Why do you keep denying who you really are?" he whispered in my ear. He didn't sound annoyed, as he had done so before. In fact, if anything, this was the kindest I had ever heard his voice. Almost compassionate. Had it been the first time I'd ever spoken to him, I may have believed him to be sincere. But it wasn't the first time I'd met him. And I knew who he really was. A murderer. "You could be so much happier if you just stopped lying to yourself..." I reached for the controller and went to turn the television back up to its maximum level. "You want space?" he asked. "Fine. But just so you know, I'm going out tonight and I'd very much like for you to join me."

"Where are you going?"

"If you want to know - you'll come with me," he said with a broad smile on his face. "You know where to find me."

CHAPTER 7

The rest of the day was filled with thoughts of the dead children. I couldn't help but picture how frantic their parents must have been, desperate for their safe return. He seemed to relish the pain he caused the children, the fact he killed them. He couldn't seem to understand that they were someone's child. Someone out there loved them no matter what he thought of them, whether they were being too loud with their screaming or tantrums or whatever. He didn't have the right to end their lives. No one had the right to do so.

In the brief moments where I wasn't thinking about the dead, I found myself growing concerned about what he had planned for the night. Maybe I should go with him? Perhaps, if I did so, I could stop him from doing whatever he wanted to do. But then what if I couldn't stop him? What if I had to witness it first hand? The atrocious acts he was capable of carrying out sickened me, yes, but they also frightened the hell out of me. It's one thing to see painted pictures of what he once did but it's another thing altogether to witness the act itself. It didn't matter how many times he tried to tell me I needed to join him, I needed to be a part of it - I didn't want to. I couldn't see it. I couldn't be a part of it.

When I went upstairs, I carefully moved all of the furniture against the bedroom door. I wasn't being careful so as not to damage it though. I was being careful so as not to disturb him. Had he caught me moving the bits and pieces, he would have easily stopped me - far more easily than I could have stopped him when it came to carrying out his heinous acts anyway.

I knew the blockade wouldn't stop him but I hoped, regardless, that it would at least put him off from trying to go out. Perhaps a laziness stopping him from bothering to start moving things back to where they belonged? I hoped so.

I sat on the edge of the bed and stared ahead at the blockade, unblinking. It was getting late now and I knew it would only be a matter of time before he sees what I've done. May as well use the last bit of quiet time to mentally prepare myself for an argument. I kept asking myself why I was putting myself through this and delaying the inevitable. The man was sick. He didn't need locking in his bedroom like a reprimanded teenager, he needed proper psychiatric help; help that I was unable to offer him even if he were prepared to listen. I should just phone the police. I should just warn them of him and let them deal with him, whether that be putting him in jail or a mental health facility; he needed to be removed from the streets before he hurt anyone else. But where would that leave me? We weren't the same person. I didn't deserve the same treatment and yet that's exactly what I would get. They'd tar me with the same brush. Not just the authorities but everyone else too; all those who'd get to learn of what he did to those poor children. Even if they'd go easy on me - the courts and professionals - the stigma the crimes would carry with them…That's the sort of thing that would never leave you.

I reached down to the small make-up mirror on the floor and picked it up. It had toppled off from the table when I was dragging the whole thing across to the doorway. I hadn't bothered to pick it up as the additional weight wouldn't have done anything to help with the blockade. I looked at my reflection in the shattered mirror. Due to the various cracks, there were lots of my made-up face looking back at myself. I couldn't help but wonder which was the real one. So many faces, so many potential personalities. Was there a 'real one' or were they all necessary to form the bigger picture? I threw the mirror back to the floor and was relieved when it broke a little more until it was at the point of now being completely useless to use. I wished I could curl up into a little ball and just wither away into nothing. More than that, I wished I'd not been born at all as thoughts turned to my mother and father.

They divorced when I was young. Mother moved away and I found myself left with my father, a stern man who liked a drink. His demons mostly came at night where he then found the need to take them out on me. By morning, he'd always come into my cramped bedroom apologising and hungover, but I could never trust him. Even when he promised me it would never happen again, I could never take him at his word. There was always a part of me which waited for the night-time monster to come crawling into the bedroom - that look on his face. I shook the image from my mind. I don't need to be thinking about that now - not whilst I am feeling vulnerable.

I lay back on the bed and shut my eyes. The blackness provided by my closed eyelids was nice. It made me feel at peace with the world, despite knowing there was no such joy to be experienced. I wished it could last forever. Who knows, with a little encouragement like - say - the tip of a blade against my wrist, maybe it could?

II

I woke with a jump to the sound of his irate voice. I must have fallen asleep. Hardly surprising, considering the fact it's quite late now and I hadn't slept much the previous night when we got home, despite feeling as though I were absolutely shattered. He was standing up and staring at the blockade I had prepared for him in front of the bedroom doorway.

"What is this? This some kind of fucking joke?"

"No joke."

"This is supposed to stop me how exactly? I'll just move it."

"Look - whatever you're planning tonight - just stay in. Stay in with me and we can talk."

"Talk? You're having a fucking joke. Very good. Funny. Nearly had me there. Come on - give me a hand moving this shit out of the way. I have things to do, places to be…"

"I'm not moving anything. I mean it. Don't go out. Stay home. Talk to me. We need to know what we're going to do from here on in."

"What the fuck are you talking about? Seriously? I know what I'm going to do. I'm going to go to a bar and I'm going to get some fucking drinks inside of me and see where the night takes me. You're more than welcome to join me. Who knows - maybe we can pick up some skank and have ourselves a little three-way. In fact, fuck it, you want to bond? That's what we'll do. We'll have ourselves a three-way. See if we can meet in the middle. What say you?"

"No."

"No?"

"No."

"No. What? That's it? Just no."

"I'm not going out with you. I don't want you to go out. I want us to stay in and talk things through like adults."

"Adults? You're dressed as a fucking clown and you want to talk things through like adults? Fuck, man, you should be a standup comic. You're coming out with some funny shit tonight." His voice changed and became even more hostile in what seemed to be a blink of an eye, "Now help me move this fucking shit out of my fucking way before I do you some fucking damage. Understand?"

I sat on the bed. He can threaten me all he likes but I won't help him. I want no part in this. Just as I want no part in going out with him to try and bond over the back of some drunken whore.

He waited for me to help and then realised I wasn't going to, "Fine. Fuck you too."

He hopped to the blockade and started throwing the items across the room in an effort to get out.

III

He's a fucking child if he thinks this is going to stop me. What? A few bits of furniture thrown in front of the fucking door and - bam - just like that he thinks he has me trapped? Absolutely pathetic. I grabbed his precious make-up table and lifted it clean off the floor.

"Please be careful with that."

"What? This?" I threw it across the room and watched with glee as it splintered into pieces over the bedroom floor. Had he really given a shit about it, he wouldn't have used it to try and block my path. He should expect everything in my way to get broken because I aim to smash it all. Teach him - maybe - that he has absolutely fuck all control over me. I heard him cry out when the table broke. A possible lesson learned. I picked up the next item in my way - the chair that went with the make-up table - and launched it at the window as hard as I could. It smashed through, sending glass flying to the floor outside.

"Okay. Wait. Let me get it for you."

"No - seriously - it's fine. You just fucking stand there and watch. I've got it."

I grabbed at the chest of drawers, the last item in my way, and toppled it over with a hard shove to the side. It crashed to the floor, sending the items within spilling out all over the place. At least we know what he'll be doing tomorrow whilst I'm getting over my hangover. He'll be cleaning. I reached forward and grabbed the door handle. I twisted it and pulled it open.

"Wait. Please. Come on. We need to talk."

I stood there in the doorway for a moment. I could stay and talk to him but what was the point? He'd only carry on with the same bullshit about how I am wrong for doing what I do. The same crap I'd heard time and time before. I wished I could believe him about wanting to actually talk. Not what he wanted to talk about but what we needed to talk about. I shook my head and headed off down the stairs. It won't be a discussion about what needs to be discussed. No sense wasting my time. At the bottom of the stairs, I threw my Chuck Taylors on, trying my best to keep my back to him to avoid anymore pathetic conversations. With my shoes on, I walked over to the front door and reached out for the handle. I paused. I'll give him one more chance. I slowly turned back to him.

"One more chance," I said.

"For what?"

"To come with me."

I could see he wanted to come. He was tempted. But it wasn't because of the reasons I wanted him to accompany me. I could see it was because he thought it gave him more chances to turn me away from the path I was set upon.

"Forget it," I told him. I reached over to the side where the keys to his van were hanging. "I'm borrowing your van," I said. I didn't wait for him to argue with me. I turned back to the front door and let myself out, slamming the door behind me.

I walked over to the van and climbed in. I slid the key into the ignition and leaned back, catching a sight of myself in the rear-view mirror. Fuck me. Still dressed like a fucking clown. That's just fucking brilliant. I put my hands on the steering wheel and screamed out in a blind fit of rage. That fucking cunt is starting to get to me. Well I can't go back in. I can't go and get changed - not with him in there. It will just invite the possibility of more conversation. Fuck it. It doesn't matter. At least if anyone sees me, they won't actually see the real me. They'll see him. I get to have the fun, he gets to take the fall. Sure I'll go down with him, but they'll know it was him. They might go easy on me. I fired the engine up and slammed the van into reverse. Sooner I get out of here, the better.

IV

I like these calmer moments. He isn't around. He isn't whining in my ear; pathetic little cunt that he is. It's peaceful. Even when I have company and they're screaming. To me - it's still a calm moment.

I don't have company with me tonight though, as I drive around in his holly-jolly fucking van. Shame there aren't any garages open where I can part exchange this heap of shit - not that people would be happy to take it off my hands. I'd probably end up owing them money.

With the house out of sight, in the rear-view mirror, I pulled the van over to the side of the road and reached across to the glove compartment where he stored his satellite navigation system. I pulled it out, along with the plug in cable, and plugged it into the cigarette lighter. The screen shone to life as I waited a few seconds for the menu screen to become available.

"Come on, come on," I said - could my words hurry it up? The menu screen appeared on the small display offering up various options. The one I wanted was the choice for 'most recent'. I pressed into it and selected the top postcode.

A message flashed up a second later, informing me it was calculating the route.

"Thank you, modern technology."

I never paid attention when he did the driving. If you told me I had to go to where he'd be only a couple of hours earlier, I would never have been able to get there. Not without stopping and asking for directions anyway. Thanks to wonderful tools such as this, all I had to do was press a few buttons. A couple of buttons and - just like that - I am guided there via the quickest possible route.

"Where possible, perform a u-turn," the machine ordered me.

I selected the first gear and did a clumsy three-point turn (actually a four-point turn) in the road before heading back in the direction I had just come from, a beaming smile on my face as I drove. He should have come with me tonight. He may be on the fence about what I do in my spare time but - I think - this could have changed his opinion. This could have made him see the light. Maybe I'll take a little project home. Keep it downstairs until he is ready to watch; ready to lend a helping hand so he can understand - and see - how much pleasure there is to be gained from it.

I drove for about twenty minutes or so, following the route offered to me via the satnav, and eventually pulled into the road I was looking for. He hadn't entered a house number when he'd previously put in the postcode for the property but that was fine - I didn't need an exact number. I wasn't good at remembering directions but I was when it came to remembering what the properties looked like. I drove to the end of the road, away from where I actually wanted to be, and let the van roll to a stop.

It has gone midnight now. All of the houses have their lights off with the exception of one at the far end of the street. Night owls I guess. Bad news for people like me as it increases the chance of someone seeing me - and it's hard enough to remain inconspicuous whilst driving around in this clapped out heap of shit.

I leaned to the key, sticking from the ignition, and turned it counter-clockwise, killing the engine in the process. As I sat back in my seat, pulling they key out in the process, I turned my attention to the house I had come to visit.

"Iron Man is cool," I mumbled, "even if it is a dodgy outfit. There's no escaping that." I hesitated a moment, "Why couldn't we dress up like Iron Man? Instead I get to be Bobo the fucking clown. So queer." I jumped out of the van and walked towards the house, avoiding the street lamps as I did so. The trick about doing this is to remain in the shadows as much as possible so there's less chance of detection. "Regardless of how we dress up though, that doesn't detract from the fact it's just fucking rude to cancel at the last minute - or, worse yet, pretend you've cancelled. What if we'd turned down other bookings just to attend this one? It doesn't matter what I think of the job; at the end of the day it is a job and it puts food in both of our mouths."

I pushed my way through the bush and stomped my way up the garden to the front door.

"If he apologises, I'll let him off."

I reached up with my gloved finger and pressed the doorbell.

"A sorry and - I don't know - half of the fee. Yes. That would go down very well."

V

As quickly as I could, I dragged him from the front porch and threw him into the bush before hiding myself. I put my hand over his mouth to stop him from shouting out - and just in time too as the front door opened.

I recognised the man before I recognised the property. He had been the one to cancel the party he'd booked for his child. He's the man who set me down this dark path of discovery. After all, had it not been for him I might still be none the wiser about the children rotting in various dumpsters. Mind you, I think there's a part of me which would have preferred not to know.

I watched, with my heart in the back of my throat, as the man looked from side to side - clearly looking for who dared pressed his doorbell in the middle of the night. Earlier he looked as though he were just arrogant but now he looked as though he were seriously angry, a face on him which suggested you'd be unwise to mess with him. He stepped back into his house and quietly closed the door so as not to wake the rest of the household (had they been fortunate enough to sleep through the initial door ringing).

"What the hell are you doing?" I hissed.

"What do you think? He's in there laughing at you and you're doing nothing about it."

"He's in there laughing at me? He's in there trying to get some fucking sleep before he has to - no doubt - get up for work in the morning!"

I climbed from the bush and started to walk back towards the van.

"What are you even doing here anyway?" he called after me.

"What do you think? You think I was going to let you out by yourself after knowing what you get up to? You're even more screwed in the head than I first believed - and, trust me, that is saying something."

I reached the van and pulled on the door handle only to find it was locked.

"Give me the keys," I told him.

"You want people laughing at you? You want people walking all over you? If you walk away now it will never stop. They'll continue treating you like the pathetic piece of shit that you are," he hissed.

"I said - give me the fucking keys."

"No. I'm not done here."

He started back towards the house. I didn't have a choice but to follow.

"What are you doing? You're messing with my life!"

He stopped a minute. "Have you ever stopped to consider you're messing with my life? You're the one who likes to dress like a fucking retard. You see me wanting to wear this shit when I leave the house? I don't fucking think so. You're making the pair of us a laughing stock and I'm not having it anymore. You understand me?" I didn't answer him. I didn't know what to say. Who could really tell who was right and who was wrong? In my mind, I was right but in his own mind - even though it was clearly fucked - he believed he was right. He headed towards the house again.

"Just wait a minute," I begged him but he didn't listen; he just kept walking back towards the house. I physically stopped him just before he stepped onto the drive. "So what - you're going to do what here, exactly?"

"Actions speak louder than words. You're here…Come and watch."

"You know you can't get away with it forever, right? Whatever you're doing and however you go about doing it - you won't get away with it forever. They'll catch up with you."

He laughed, "With me?"

"Yes."

"I don't fucking think so," he snarled, "they'll catch up with you. You're a bad, bad man." He started to laugh and - only then - did I realise he was dressed up to look exactly like me. "I keep telling you - I'm the normal one. You're the sick one. You need help but don't you worry…When they catch up with you - and they will - I'll be there for you."

He shrugged me off and started up the drive towards the house.

I called out after him, "Please don't do this."

"I'm not. You are."

Chapter 8

I could but only watch in horror as he kicked the front door down. Two heavy kicks and it broke, allowing him the entry he desired. I looked around to see if anyone had heard the commotion. From the quick glance, it didn't look as though they had. Lights in properties nearby remained off and there was no one on the street out for a late night walk. I hurried in after him, calling out for him.

"Don't do this!" I screamed.

He didn't listen to me as he stormed through the house, charging up the stairs to the second level. I followed close by, always close by, and tried in vain to stop him but I knew now that there was no stopping him - not in this mood. I'd never seen him like this before and it was fair to say it scared the hell out of me.

"What are you doing in here?"

The father was standing by a bedroom door. I could hear his partner screaming from within the room. His earlier angry look had all but vanished from his face, replaced by a look of nervousness no doubt caused by the stranger stomping down his landing towards him.

"Call the police!" he called out to whoever was in the bedroom.

A boy - young - was screaming from another doorway across the other side of the landing. I felt sorry for him. No child should have to see this. This is the kind of thing which stays with you for life.

"Let's just go! They're calling the police!" I screamed out to him, one last-ditch attempt to stop him from doing whatever it was he planned to do. One last-ditch attempt and then I'll leave him to his own devices and get myself out of here.

"Shut the fuck up!" he screamed back to me as he swung his heavy right fist towards the father. The punch connected with a ferocity I'd never seen before, one which knocked the man down to his backside. Another punch was thrown before he started stamping his foot on the man's face. The woman in the bedroom continued to scream, frozen to the spot with fear. On the plus side, she wasn't making any emergency phone calls but I couldn't say the same for the neighbours. Within the blink of an eye, the flurry of kicks and punches were being aimed at the woman - knocking her off the bed and onto the floor in the process. Again, it didn't take long until her screams and cries fell silent leaving only the sound of the sobbing boy on the landing.

I looked to both the man and the woman - the boy's parents, their faces covered in blood and barely recognisable as human. Meanwhile, he was turning his attention to the boy.

"You know what they say about children?" he asked the petrified boy.

The boy shook his head as tears flowed freely down his face.

"Please don't do this. Come on. Let's just go before anyone phones the police. Come on…"

"If you want to go, fuck off!" he hissed. There was so much venom in his voice. I knew he wasn't going anywhere - not without doing what he came to do, whatever that was.

I looked at the boy, "I'm sorry." I couldn't be a part of this and left the two of them. Whatever he wanted to do, I couldn't stop him. I couldn't stand in his way. There was no point putting myself through it too.

II

"I think we're alone now," I spat at the boy - this fucking child who'd sooner have Iron Man at his party over a clown. In truth, I didn't give a good fuck what he had at his party. I was just using it as an excuse to hurt him. Usually

I'd had to find vulnerable children to take, those who were lost or - in the case of the child at the park - abandoned as part of a 'harsh lesson' to them when they're misbehaving. Picking this kid though, this little cunt-fuck, it just made the whole process so much easier. Took out a lot of wasted time hunting around for someone suitable. "I asked you a question," I said.

"Please don't hurt me."

"I asked you a question. Allow me to repeat it. Do you know what they say about children?"

He shook his head. It was hard to know whether this was the truth or whether he was too scared to answer me. I thought 'children should be seen and not heard' was a popular saying? I could be wrong though so I won't hold it against him. Not that it makes a difference either way.

"They say children should be seen and not heard. I disagree with that. Don't think it is right. You want to know what I think the saying should be?" I asked him.

He stood there and didn't say anything. He just kept weeping like the annoying little shit that he is. He shrugged.

"I think children should not be heard. That part of the saying I agree with…But you know what else?"

"No," he whimpered.

Whiney, little, irritating shit.

"I think children should not be seen either. And you know what…"

"What?"

"You're never going to be seen again."

I dashed forward and grabbed him. He screamed a final, short scream.

III

Not for the first time I found myself pacing the lounge wearing nothing but my boxer shorts. Pretty sure - at this rate - I was going to wear a hole in my carpet. I felt sick. What he did to their faces. There was no remorse there. There was no control. He was like an animal. A rabid animal. I have to turn him in or else there'll be no stopping him. Besides, even if I don't turn him in, they'll come for him. They'll come and they'll arrest him. And me. If I don't turn him in, they'll think I am a part of what he does. I can see it now. They'll think I am just as responsible. And who could blame them? If I am innocent of it all, why would I sit back and just watch? I wouldn't. No one would.

"The washing machine would have finished by now," he said. His voice made me jump. I'd been so lost in my own thoughts I didn't realise he was there watching me. "I only put it on for a quick wash."

"What do you want? A medal?"

"I was hoping you could hang it up for us?"

"Yeah, okay."

"Really?"

"Sure - put your feet up…Tell you what - I'll get you a pedicure whilst you're at it. Maybe a nice neck massage? You've had a busy night, after all, and must be tired."

"Sarcasm doesn't suit you."

"Murdering people doesn't suit me."

"Yet you seem to have mastered it."

"I haven't killed anyone. It's all you."

"No. It's you. You're the clown. I'm the serious one. You're the one stalking the streets, you're the one snatching unhappy children. It's all you. To be fair, I hardly get out these days. Not since you keep continuing to hide me."

"Why are you doing this?"

"Which bit? Washing your outfit? Killing people?"

"Why are you trying to ruin my life?"

"You're trying to ruin mine. You're denying who I am. You're denying who you are. You need professional help, my friend."

"You're ruining my life!" I screamed back at him.

"Really? You seem to be the one who does whatever he wants. I'm just the passenger. So I get to go out and play from time to time - it's not nearly as much as I'd like to."

"Last night - all that screaming…"

"Yes - there was a fair amount…"

"Someone would have seen you."

"No, someone would have seen you. They'd have seen a clown running from the house. They'd have seen a clown backing the clown van up to the house and they'd have seen a clown running back into the house before coming back out, loading the clown van up and jumping into the front seat and speeding off…They'll have seen you."

"So you're trying to frame me?"

"You're not too bright, are you? You go down and I go down. I'm trying to survive. I'm making it so you can't go out dressed as a fucking clown anymore. The day job - it's over. Now we can go out as we're supposed to be seen. Maybe a nice suit…Maybe jeans and tee shirt. I don't know. Anything but a fucking clown outfit. Oh, and for the record if you choose to start wearing a dress to avoid me…We're having words, you understand me?" He continued, "I'm sick of you trying to hide me all of the time. Like you're better than me? Seriously? I'm the alpha here. You're the one who tags along like a pathetic, friendless little cunt."

"I won't let you get away with this," I warned him.

"You can't stop me, just as I can't stop you. All I can do is make it harder for you to be who you want to be. The fact you enjoy dressing up – well, that just makes my job that much easier, you know?"

"You're a piece of shit."

"Which technically means you're a piece of shit."

All this time hiding him under the heavy make-up of a clown, I had forgotten what he was really like. I'd forgotten the monster waiting beneath the face paint. Would people really believe I was the one responsible for his crimes?

"Your little hobby - have you been doing that just to stop me from hiding you?"

"Dear God, man, no. I've been doing that because I enjoy it. As I keep telling you, it's a great pastime. I've only just thought - these past few occasions - to use your outfit to shift the blame to you instead of me…You know - on the off-chance I do make a mistake. Like last night. I won't lie. That was sloppy."

"You're unbelievable."

"Thank you. I'll take that as a compliment."

I didn't know what to say to him. He was off the hinge. Completely mad. And now he was pulling me into his games but using my guise to his advantage and my disadvantage. Once again, I felt a sickness brewing within me. All this time I thought I was in control. Now I doubt I was ever in the driving seat. Was I always his passenger?

"Come on - stop sulking," he said. "I've got you a present. Something to say no hard feelings."

"What are you talking about?"

"Come with me. You'll like this."

The sickness brewing within me bubbled away furiously. I followed him from the living room, into the hallway and towards the kitchen. The house was silent apart from the sound of my heartbeat pumping away furiously. We stopped in the kitchen.

"Down there," he said.

The cellar door was wide open. I didn't want to go down there. I didn't want to see what he had supposedly done for me. Not after seeing what he'd previously done down there - something I wished I could forget but knew I couldn't.

"What have you done?"

He laughed. "Come on now," he said, "I think you already know what's down there, don't you?"

He wouldn't have. Would he? I tentatively walked towards the door. I cranked my head to one side in an effort to hear any kind of movement down there. Nothing. Silence, other than the sound of my own breathing.

"Come on," he said, "trust me." He gave me a nudge towards the door and suddenly stopped me, "Wait a minute…Might want to pop some clothes on. Probably best not to go down there dressed in just your boxers. First impressions and all that…"

It was then I knew for definite that we weren't alone in the house. Someone else was down there and it didn't take a genius to know who. I hurried through the downstairs of the house, to the stairs, and up to my bedroom where I quickly threw on some jeans and a tee shirt. I returned to the kitchen nervously.

"Are you ready for this?" he asked me as I stopped by the cellar door.

"No."

"Come on, you have to admit, it's all pretty exciting."

I walked through the open door and stepped down onto the first step.

"Hello?" I called out. No one answered. I flicked the basement light on and walked down the flight of rickety stairs. At the bottom, my eyes were instantly drawn to the bed in the corner of the room. More particularly - the boy lying on it. He was stripped to his underwear with a dirty gag around his mouth. Set up just in front of him was a blank canvas on one of the easels. The boy looked petrified. I ran back up the stairs and out of the room - back into the kitchen.

"What's wrong? You don't like your present?" he asked me.

"What the fuck is wrong with you? Take him back."

"No can do. Doesn't come with a receipt. No returns permitted."

"You have to let him go. If you don't, I will…"

"Not your smartest move. You let him go, he goes to the police and we both get arrested."

"I'll tell them you took him."

"And he'll tell them he saw a clown kill his mummy and daddy. All very heartbreaking…"

"We can't keep him here; we need to get rid of him."

"And that's what you're going to do. That's why I brought him back to you."

He wanted me to kill him. That much was obvious. I don't know why though. I don't know what he was trying to prove. What? Maybe that we were one and the same? We're not. I'm not a killer. I won't kill a person - let alone a child.

"Get him out of here!" I snapped at him.

He laughed, "I'm going to leave the two of you alone for a while, okay? Give you time to come to terms with the situation."

"What? Don't you fucking leave us…Hello?"

Silence.

I called out again, "Hello?"

He was gone.

I turned back to the cellar. The thought of the boy down there. What must have been going through his head? What must he have been thinking? Not just because he was down there; snatched from his home…But what he saw in his house before he was taken. He saw his mum and dad murdered before his very eyes. Is there any come back from that for him - even if I can get him out of the house?

Slowly, nervously, I made my way back to the cellar's stairs.

IV

I hesitated at the foot of the stairs. The little boy was looking at me, his eyes wide with fear - not that I expecting anything different. I smiled at him but remembered how I looked in the mirror's reflection when I was testing my grin and quickly changed my expression to a more neutral look.

"Hi," I said coyly. He didn't reply. I'm not sure whether that was because he was scared or whether it was because of the gag. I walked over to him and he flinched. "It's okay," I reassured him, "I'm not going to hurt you." Slowly, I reached down to him and removed his gag. He didn't say anything but he seemed grateful; it was in his eyes. "Is that better?" I asked him. He nodded.

"Is the clown here?" he asked.

"No. Why?"

"I don't like him," the boy said. His voice was shaking. "He scares me."

Of course the clown get-up scared him. Under the circumstances they met each other, it would have scared anyone. I felt bad for him but I also felt disappointment at his misguided fear. It wasn't the clown he should be scared of. The clown is the entertainer. The clown is the fun one.

"He's not here," I reassured him again.

"Can I go home?" he asked.

I didn't know what to say. I wanted the boy to be able to go home. Of course I did. But I knew he couldn't. For one, his parents were dead, and for another, he'd tell the police of us, and our home. I knew there was no chance of his safe return.

"Please?" he continued.

"I'll be right back." I turned away from him and hurried from the cellar, back up to the kitchen. I slammed the door shut behind me. Out of sight, out of mind.

"I wouldn't get too friendly with him," he was back, speaking in my ear. "It will only make it harder when you kill him," he continued.

"Please. I can't do it. I can't. I'm not like you…"

"…You are. You just don't know it yet."

"No. I'm not like you. I can't do it."

"Well you're going to have to."

"I can't. I won't."

"You will."

"Please. I need you to do it."

He shrugged, "I'm not going to do it for you."

"I can't do it!" I yelled.

"Then you'd better find out what he likes to eat for dinner because you've got yourself another mouth to feed." He laughed, "Good luck with that."

Chapter 9

I was hiding in my bedroom, the broken furniture still lying around from where he'd thrown it last night. I was trying to pretend none of it had happened - last night, what he did whilst wearing my outfit and the boy. I was trying and failing. Hard really - even with the door shut and him in the cellar - I could still hear him crying for his parents. I wonder if he realises they're dead? He must. He must know there is nowhere for him to go. Even if I didn't care about the police taking me - taking us - and I did let him go…Where would he run to? His life is over in more ways than one.

"You going to hide up here all day?"

"I can't just kill someone. I'm not like you."

"You like this boy?"

"I don't know him."

"Then what's the problem?"

"Just because I don't know him, it doesn't mean I want to kill him. He's a person. A human."

"He's human? Of course he is. So you're aware that - in time - he's going to die anyway. What's the problem with bringing that time forward a little?" he sneered.

"It's not my place to do so."

"Listen to him," he said. He paused long enough for me to hear the young boy crying. "He's upset. He's in pain - mentally and physically…You kill him - you're just putting him out of his misery. Keeping him alive, you're just prolonging the inevitable." He stopped talking. All I could hear was the boy's wailing. It dawned on me - what he said about a child crying - that it was annoying. Perhaps children should be seen and not heard after all. The constant screams were driving me mad. "If anything," he said, "keeping him down there, as you are, is actually crueller than killing him."

Was it crueller? Was I just delaying the inevitable? Would it be nicer just to go down there and put him out of his misery? I hated him for making me doubt my own beliefs. I hated him more than words could describe.

"Would you rather I did it?" he said finally.

"Yes."

"Well - okay. I'll do it for you."

"Thank you." It was strange to say that I felt relief for his offer yet that was exactly the feeling I had. Relief. Relief that I didn't have to kill the boy and relief that - soon - the boy would be with his mother and father, hopefully in a better place.

II

I walked over to the cupboard and pulled out one of the clown outfits hanging there. This one was red with big yellow buttons and a large white frilly collar. How the fuck he spent so much time in these things is beyond me! How did he not feel like a fucking retard?

"What are you doing?" he asked me. Jesus! Even knowing I'm the one who is going to go down and kill the boy for him, he is still talking to me in that irritating, snivelling tone of voice. I wish I could beat it out of him. Man up, for fuck's sake, you pussy.

"What do you think I'm doing? I'm getting myself dressed to go and do your dirty work."

"My dirty work? This is all down to you. If it weren't for you, he wouldn't even be here. If it weren't for you, his parents would…"

"Shut the fuck up. You're like a broken record. Take some fucking responsibility in your life once in a while." I stepped into the clown suit and zipped myself in. There. I look like a fucking dick.

"Why the outfit?"

"You'd rather I go down and kill him without it? It's no skin off my nose. I'm wearing this for you. You think I want to be wearing it? Because I don't."

"You're wearing it for me?"

"This look is tainted - the whole clown outfit…After what happened last night. You know it is. You think you'll ever be able to dress in it again? You know - without thinking of what happened? Because I don't think you will. This way, the killings are confined to the clown outfit as far as you're concerned and the look you have when you're not dressed like a pillock… Well…That's the good look, the safe look - the look where you haven't actually witnessed anyone die. You see what I mean?" He looked confused - as though he didn't understand how the 'normal' look (without all of the make-up) was suddenly the look which felt safe, and the one he'd hidden behind for all these years was the one he associated with murder and mayhem. I smiled. He'll never be able to put this suit on again. He'll never be able to hide me again. I have stolen his identity. I looked to the floor where I'd thrown the make-up table. Various make-up products and face paints were scattered around next to it. I walked over to them and picked it up. "You going to at least help me put this shit on so it looks the part?"

III

We were standing in the upstairs bathroom, looking into the dirty mirror (part of the medicine cabinet hanging on the wall). I was applying the white face paint with one of the sponges he'd picked up for me. I was on auto-pilot, not really listening to what he was saying, a feeling of sadness that the outfit I had been hiding behind had forever been marred with what he'd done last night in his fit of rage or revenge, whatever the hell it was that drove him to do that.

"When you were a kid - did you ever have the tendency to wear make-up? I only ask because you're pretty good at putting it on."

When I was a 'kid' as he put it, I was living in relative peace. He hadn't been a part of my life. Not when I was young. He only came to live with me when I hit my teens. He was relatively quiet to start off with. The occasional whisper in my ear after my pa had visited me in one of his many drunken (horny) states.

"You going to let him get away with that?" he'd ask me as I wept into my pillow, a trickle of father's so-called love running down between my legs. "I wouldn't. I'd fucking kill him. We can - if you want. We can do it together. I'll take your hand, I'll show you how."

He only got louder when I ignored him. His hatred towards my dad turned to hatred towards me;, especially when I cried. He'd call me pathetic and worthless. He'd say I deserved everything I got. I tried to block him from my mind. I tried to make sure I didn't hear any of his words but they only got louder. By the time I was in my late teens he was practically impossible to ignore - and soon it wasn't just me that he was talking to.

"You fucking touch him again and I'll kill you," I heard him say to Dad once. Dad responded by hitting him. I screamed for Dad to stop but he carried on until his hands were too sore. Soon after, I moved out of the house I shared with Dad. I never spoke to him again. Soon after, he was dead - beaten in the back alley of a pub with no witnesses. I wasn't alone. He went with me. At first I was glad for the company. He kept telling me that everything was going to be okay if I stuck with him. He said he'd look after the pair of us but he was always quick to temper.

I stopped applying the make-up and stared into the mirror. He stared back.

"What?"

"Did you kill him?"

"Who?"

"Did you kill Dad?"

He smiled at me. That was his answer. Words weren't needed.

"Did he suffer?"

He gave me a wink, "It was about as uncomfortable as things were made for you when you were growing up."

"What happened?"

"I hit him with a brick." He said it so matter-of-fact that it made me nervous. There was no emotion there. No empathy, no guilt, nothing. Which is exactly what I felt too. He smiled at me. "He begged for his life as he lay there on the floor, shell-shocked. He stopped begging by the fourth hit."

I realised then - when he was talking to me - that it wasn't him who was smiling at me but, for the first time ever, I was smiling at him.

"Thank you," I said. I went back to applying the various face paints. He didn't say anything. I think the both of us were shocked at my gratitude. I know I was, but to know he did that for me - killed my dad, the man who made me suffer as I grew up behind locked doors…Maybe he had my back after all?

"I'm going to cut him," he said after a few more minutes of blissful peace.

"What? Who?"

"The boy downstairs. That's how I'm going to do it."

I swallowed hard. I wasn't sure whether I wanted to hear the details. I wasn't going to go in the room with him; I was going to leave him to it.

"I want to know how long it will take for someone to bleed out from their asshole."

"What?"

"That's where I'm putting the blade. Never done it before but always been curious about it."

"You can't. That's cruel."

"You think I'm nice to the people I've had down there?"

"Can't you make it quick for him?" I begged.

"For all we know, it might be quick."

"I meant - suffocate him or something? Something, I don't know, a little more humane?"

He smiled at me and leaned in close to the mirror until we were practically touching, "You're welcome to do it yourself?"

Any thanks I felt towards him - for what he did to my father - soon disappeared. I was backed into a corner. I didn't have a choice but to do it myself. Not if I wanted the boy to die without unnecessarily suffering.

"I'll do it," I sighed.

"Attaboy!"

IV

I was standing in the kitchen staring ahead at the cellar door. The wig was in place, the outfit was on and I knew what had to be done, yet I wasn't thinking about it. My mind was on how we had got to this stage. Everything had happened so fast. I was a children's entertainer. I was doing okay with my job. I enjoyed it. No, I loved it. And now - I'm an accomplice to murders (God knows how many exactly), and I feel as though my personality has been pulled in the direction of his own. A darker and more uncomfortable path - one I wish I could turn away from but...Like I said, I don't know how I have ended up here.

"You're going to make it harder for yourself," he said to me. His voice wasn't snappy. If anything, he sounded as though he were trying to be genuinely helpful. Was he? Or was this another trick? Had he even been tricking me? Had he been pulling me in this direction or was I heading there anyway? "The longer you wait," he continued, "the harder it will be to follow through with."

"I'm not sure I can do this," I told him. "I need to think about it."

"Making it harder. Not just for you. For him too."

"I..."

"You just need to get down there and do it. Trust me."

I reached out for the handle and stopped myself from grabbing it. I pulled my hand away.

"Five minutes and it will all be over," he pushed.

"I don't want you to come down there with me," I said. "I need to do this by myself." By going down alone, it still left me the possibility to leave without hurting the boy. At least, not hurting him anymore than I'd already done so. Why am I blaming myself? It wasn't me. It was him. Just because he was dressed like me. Wait...That's it...I'll explain to the boy what happened and then...I can let him go and if he does go to the police (and I'm sure he will), he'll explain I'm the innocent one.

"I'll give you your time," he said.

"Thank you." Another 'thanks'? It was beginning to become a habit.

"Any ideas how you're going to do it?" he asked.

I shook my head. He had spoken of cutting him but I knew I wouldn't be able to do that. I didn't have it in me to push a knife through someone's skin, hard enough to penetrate organs. The mere thought of doing so repulsed me.

"I'll think of something," I said.

I waited by the stairs as he made himself scarce. When I was sure he'd gone, I stepped onto the first step and slowly made my way down. The kid screamed when he saw me; I'd made it halfway down the stairs before he did so. I continued down the stairs until I was on the same level with him. I turned to him and put my hands up to show I wasn't carrying anything, "It's okay," I told him. "I don't want to hurt you." The boy burst into tears. I slowly walked over to where he was lay. He fidgeted on the mattress, straining to get away from me. "Please don't," I asked him. I was trying to keep my voice quiet, calm - soothing almost - but I don't think the tone mattered. I don't think he heard the tone. Looking at his panicked expression, I'm not sure if he is hearing the words either. "I don't want to hurt you," I told him. "I won't hurt you. I just want to talk to you."

To try and relax him a little, I stepped a little further back from him. Maybe my proximity was causing him more distress. I noticed some of the paintings would have been visible from where he was lying on the bed. No wonder he was so upset; they probably scared the hell out of him. I turned them around so he couldn't see them anymore.

"They're not mine," I told him as I turned the last of the paintings around. "They're his."

There was a chair standing in the corner of the room. I walked over to it and perched myself on it. The pair of us fell into an uncomfortable silence, neither of us knowing what to say for the best. For a brief moment I contemplated putting on a show for him. Not sure what exactly. According to his dad, he didn't want a clown at his party. He wanted Iron Man. Did that mean he hated clowns and what we do? Or was it more to do with just preferring Iron Man? Maybe he loves clowns? Yes. He loves them but opted for Iron Man because he thought his friends would prefer that. An unselfish act on his part. He doesn't deserve to die. I ran through the performance possibilities in my head wondering what he'd prefer: a balloon animal or a card trick? Maybe a few jokes? Jesus. I don't know. I don't know anything about this kid. Other than the fact he saw his mum and dad stamped to death.

I broke the silence and cut straight to the chase, "Do you recognise me?" I asked.

He nodded.

"That's good." He realised I was the man who'd previously spoken to him down here, before going away and putting this costume on. That might mean he realises it wasn't me standing in his house. It wasn't me and - more importantly - that it was him pretending to be me.

"You were in my house."

My heart sank.

"You hurt my mum and dad," he started to cry again.

"No - you see - that's what I wanted to talk to you about. It wasn't me. It was him. He was dressed as me."

"No, it was you."

"It wasn't. I promise. I wouldn't want to hurt you. I wouldn't want to hurt anyone."

"You hurt my mum and dad," he said again, tears streaming down his face.

"No. You're not listening. It was him. He dressed up like me so I would get the blame for it but - and I promise - it wasn't me at all. It wasn't. I'm not like that. I'm on your side…"

"What the hell are you doing?" a harsh voice cut in making me jump.

"I told you not to come down here," I hissed.

"I asked you a question. What the fuck do you think you're doing? What are you saying?"

"Nothing. I wasn't saying anything."

The boy looked both confused and scared. I tried to give him a look - a quick glance to let him know I'm here and I'm on his side - just as I had promised to him only seconds earlier.

"Why are you trying to make fucking friends with the little cunt? You're down here to kill him. Why the fuck are you making things complicated for yourself? No. Not just yourself…Complicated for both of us. What? You a selfish cunt, is that it?

"You're being over the top. You've got the wrong end of the stick…"

"Have I fuck. I was here, listening. I heard it all. You're trying to tell him you're the innocent one…"

"No. I wasn't saying…"

"Don't you fucking lie to me."

"I'm not!"

"Please stop it!" the boy cried out as he pulled against his restraints.

"I swear to God I'm not!" I said, ignoring the boy.

"Then prove it! Finish him!"

There was no way the boy was getting out of there alive. I should have just stormed over to him and done what was required but I couldn't move. My feet were rooted to the spot. I couldn't help but think of the boy as a life. It wasn't mine to take, no matter what it meant if he got away. So what if I go to prison? Perhaps I deserve it? I should have just turned the pair of us in as soon as I realised what he was doing in his own time. Jesus - how could I have been so blind to it? All this time, right under my own nose - a fucking murderer!

"You're fucking weak! You're a disgrace. A fucking coward!" he screamed at me, a rage in his voice I'd not heard before. I could only watch as he stormed towards the boy. "If you want a job done…"

V

"…Do it yourself!" I yelled. The child screamed as I approached him. Quite right too; I'm not a pussy like that prick. I pulled the pillow out from under his head and promptly muffled his scream by placing it over his squirming face.

"Get off him!"

"Why? Are you going to finish this fucking thing?"

"Just get off him."

I tried to pull him away but he shook me off.

"I will kill you!" he hissed. "As soon as I'm done with him, I will fucking kill you if you touch me again. Do you understand me?"

VI

The boy's limbs were flailing around underneath his weight. I could only watch in horror as I became witness to another death. I started to gag. Soon, the boy's limbs went limp and yet he still didn't climb off from him. He waited there, on top of him, with the pillow over the boy's face as though making sure he was definitely gone.

"Get off him," I begged.

"Fine."

He got off the boy and dropped the pillow to the floor. I saw the boy's face - pale with lifeless eyes - and couldn't hold in the sick anymore. I ran to the corner of the room and threw up on the floor.

"I know I keep saying it but - really - you are a fucking joke. An absolute joke."

I started to weep; not because of what he was saying, but because there - in the corner of the room - was another dead boy.

"Get the fuck out of my sight whilst I finish up down here!"

I didn't need him to ask me twice and promptly left.

CHAPTER 10

I kicked the clown outfit off and threw it towards the washing machine where the other one was already soaking, post-service. With the outfit off, I leaned into the sink and threw up again. I'm glad he was preoccupied so he didn't witness that. He already thought badly of me. Badly? That was a joke. The way he was talking to me, I thought he was going to kill me as soon as the boy was disposed of. I'm still worried he may try.

I ran the tap water into the sink to wash the vomit down the plughole; whilst doing so, I looked towards the cellar. I'm not sure how to fix this. I'm not sure how to make all of this go away. All I know is that he's tainted my way of living beyond repair. I feel as though he has destroyed me. Another bubble from my stomach. Hold it in. Hold it in. Don't be a pussy. Am I being sick because of what I've witnessed these past few days or because of stress - worry about what he's going to say (or do) to me? He might not be able to kill me but he has already proven he can make things awkward for me. And what if he does figure out a way to kill me? Would he? I know - if I could - I'd end his life.

"I think we need to talk!"

His voice made me jump. I caught sight of him in the kitchen window's reflection, a look of pure hatred in his eyes. Wait. No. Is that hatred? It's not. It's not the same look I've seen on him before. It's something else. What is that? That's it. I know it. Disappointment. My dad used to look at me like that on nights I failed to please him.

"I thought we had reached an understanding?"

It didn't matter if his tone did match his expression (definitely disappointment), I still found myself feeling nervous of him. For the first time ever, I realised I was actually scared of him. You can't blame me; I had witnessed him murder people and I know there are more that he has killed.

"What? You not talking to me now? The silent treatment?" he pressed me further.

"I can't understand you."

"You can't understand me? Why ever not? I'm probably the easiest person to understand…"

"No. I can't understand how you can kill people."

"It's easy. Think about it."

"I have thought about it. Ever since you showed me that bag…I can't get my head around it. I can't. It's not the right thing to do."

"Says who?"

"Society."

"What if society is wrong and I am right? Have you ever thought of that?" He took a breath, "I want to show you something."

"I don't want to see it." I had seen enough of what he wanted to show me. Whatever it was he had for me to see this time, I didn't want to know.

"It's not really an option," he whispered.

Before I could answer, he dragged me back down to the cellar. I fought with him as he pulled me towards the bed where the small boy still lay. When we were close enough, he forced me to look upon it. The poor boy staring dead ahead - was he looking at me?

"Please let me go," I begged him. I didn't want to be seeing this. I wanted nothing to do with it. He knew this, so why was he forcing me to see it? He knows I'm not the same as him. I don't have it in me.

"Look at him," he whispered in my ear. He no longer sounded as though he was disappointed, nor angry. He sounded very 'matter-of-fact'. "You remember how much pain he was in?" he asked. "You remember how upset he was?"

"Of course I do," I said.

"Do you remember the pain in his eyes?"

"Yes."

"How much pain was there?" he asked.

"A lot."

"A lot. Yes. Now look."

Again, he forced me to look the boy in his eyes.

"What do you see now?" he continued.

I tried to relax a little. I realised I wasn't going to get away with not looking. I had to go along with whatever it was he was trying to show me. Besides, the sooner I went along with it, the sooner he might let me go about my own business (which was anything other than this). I looked at the boy more closely but I wasn't sure what I was supposed to be looking at.

"Do you see it?" he pushed me for an answer.

"I don't know what I'm supposed to be seeing," I said.

"In his eyes."

I shrugged, "I…don't…."

"Peace. He looks peaceful."

I looked in the boy's eyes again. There was no pain, there was no fear, there was nothing - in that respect, I guess there was peace.

"He's not crying anymore," he said. "There's no stress, there's no worry, there's nothing - just absolute peace. Now, do you remember a time when you've ever seen that much peace in someone's eyes?"

I shook my head, "No."

"That's right. No." He continued, "It's nice, isn't it?"

I wondered whether he believed any of what he was actually saying or whether it was just for my benefit. He walked over to one of the easels and slid a blank canvas onto it. Once in place, he reached for a small paint brush from a pot of various painting implements. I watched in silence as he started to outline what looked to be the boy.

"Don't you wish you could feel peace like this?" he asked, with a nod of his head towards the boy.

"Yes."

"Yes. Do you think any of us will ever feel peace like that?"

I shook my head.

"I can't hear you."

"No."

"No," he agreed. "You see those pictures over in the corner of the room as souvenirs from lives I have taken, but I see it differently. I see it as children I have given peace to."

I didn't say anything as he continued to paint the dead child. I just stood with him, in silence, as I contemplated what he had said, wondering whether he believed it or whether he was simply trying to turn me into his way of thinking - and the 'peace' theory just so happened to work in his favour.

He stopped painting, "Sorry - did you want to give this a go?" he asked. "It's very therapeutic."

"No. No, thank you."

"Suit yourself," he said as he resumed what he was doing.

I looked at the painting. At first, I thought he was going to draw everything in front of us but - with each little stroke of the brush - it was becoming apparent that this particular picture was going to be of the young boy's eyes only.

II

The same thought kept racing through my mind as I sat in the living room, leaving him to whatever else he wanted to do; he is killing people because he believes he is giving them the peace they deserve, the peace they long for. I knew it was still wrong, regardless of how you dressed it up but - when you looked at it like that - it wasn't as bad as I first believed it to be. I mean, he isn't necessarily a cold-hearted murderer. He is a man on a mission of mercy. I wonder, would the police go easy on him if they knew the truth? What if I phoned them up and told them? Would they go easy on both of us? I looked across to the telephone which sat on a small coffee table next to the sofa. Whilst he's busy, I should phone them. It's the right thing to do. Surely he'll see that when they come for him? Wait a minute, no. They won't see it like that. They can't. The boy is at peace now but they'll argue he was at peace before he was taken from his home. He was at peace before he saw his mum and dad killed. Shit. What a tangled web we weave. As my mind raced with various thoughts it stuck on one in particular, something he'd said to me when he first showed me what he had done. Something about children being bastards, or cunts. I can't remember the exact words he used. There was more. Something about children being seen and not heard...The child in the park - he said he was doing the mum a favour by getting rid of the kid. There was no mention of giving the child the peace he yearned for. Everything he'd said to me, in the cellar, was just bullshit and - again - I'd been suckered in by it. Fuck.

I reached my hand out but went past the phone. I grabbed the controller instead. Thoughts of the child in the park - I'd been so busy with what happened last night...Had they found the boy yet? Did they have any leads on what happened?

I flicked the television on via the controller and started hopping through the channels. So many channels. I'm sure the last time I paid any attention to the TV there were only four. When did there become so many? And, more to the point, why can't I find what I'm looking for on any of them? Chat show, chat show, chat show (how many chat shows?), soap, some shitty made-for-television film with piss poor acting and a distinct lack of any serious direction...No news.

The clock on the front of my DVD player showed it to be coming up to midday. There must be something coming on the channels soon. I'll just sit and wait. Ignoring the child in the park for a moment, I need to know if the bodies from last night have been discovered and, more to the point, whether there were any witnesses or not.

"Regardless," his voice made me jump again. I wished he would stop jumping out on me. "You might want to hide the van, just to be safe..." A feeling of panic rushed through me. I hadn't given much thought to the van. It was hardly the most inconspicuous vehicle out there. It wouldn't have been hard for someone to spot it at the crime scene. Either crime scene.

"You realise they probably already know about us?" I said. My voice was quiet. Downbeat. "Someone would have seen the van. It'll only be a matter of time before the police come knocking on the door, asking all sorts of questions."

"Then you'd better think of an alibi," he said, "but if I were you, I wouldn't say you were with me."

"What if they come here with search warrants?" I asked as I started to panic. Before the investigation for what happened last night was possibly even open, my brain was telling me it was already over for us. If they came here, with papers, they'd find the cellar (no hiding it) and they'd find not only the boy's body but also the paintings of the other children. Even if I told them they weren't real - just the product of a diseased mind - I doubt they'd believe me.

"You think I haven't already thought about that?" he asked. "Do you take me for an amateur?"

"Look, I'm sorry, but all of this is kind of new to me."

"Go back down to the cellar."

"I don't want to. I've seen the fucking cellar," I snapped at him. Snapping was a mistake. It served no other purpose than to anger him and he barked - once again - for me to go down to the cellar before dragging me down there against my own will.

I couldn't believe what I saw when we made it to the bottom of the stairs. The room was a mess, yes, but…There were no signs of anything untoward happening down here. The bed was leaning on its side against the far wall as though it had been abandoned by previous owners of the home - certainly easier than disposing of it themselves and certainly nothing to raise any suspicions. The cellar was clearly a dumping ground for junk just as attics were used for similar. I continued to look around. The paintings were missing too. Where they'd previously been leaning in a neat mile, there was nothing but dust on the floor. Even the damned easels were missing. Had they ever been here? Was it all just a figment of my imagination when I'd earlier seen it down here?

"What the fuck are you talking about?" he laughed.

"Am I losing my mind?" I asked him. If I were to drive to the boy's house and knock on the door, would his mum and dad answer? The pair of them perfectly unharmed? Would the boy come to the top of the stairs to see who was calling on them? Maybe hopeful it was his one of his friends coming around to invite him out? Was everything that happened recently all in my damaged mind? I felt a piece of hope flow through me. That was, at least, until he opened his trap again.

"Look in the other corner," he laughed. He turned my head towards the darkest corner of the room. "Look at the floor."

There was a freshly dug (and re-covered) hole.

"The boy?"

"The boy."

"And the pictures?"

"Of course not. You know what the rotting flesh will do to the paint? I need them hidden, not completely ruined." He turned my head towards the wall opposite to where the bed leaned. Bricks. I looked closely in the dim light. They'd been disturbed too. Not all of them. Just enough of them. Enough of them to make a small hiding hole for, I'm guessing, the pictures.

"You've been busy," I said. I'd so wished my mind was damaged beyond all boundaries of sanity. I'd rather that, if it meant the boy and his family (and the other children) were alive. My mind is damaged beyond all repair but not in a way which allowed me any peace. They were dead and he was very much in control as to what happened between us. All these years, I thought I was in the driving seat but no, it's him. It has always been him.

"Like I said," he continued, "you need to think about what you're going to say should the police come. And, more importantly, you need to get rid of that van...I've done my bit. You do your bit. For once. Understand?"

He left me standing there in the cellar, so he could go and rest up, with so many thoughts buzzing through my head, only one really loud one though: the nagging doubt that I'll have it in me to throw anyone off the scent of what we have done here. I'm not a good liar. I always go red. I squirm. It's uncomfortable and I hate it. Even now I'm starting to feel my face burn up at the prospect of having to lie to someone, let alone someone as important as a police officer. I know I can't. I'll let us down. I'll let him down. He'll be angry with me. Again. He'll never let me live it down if I ruin things for us. He'll continue to plague me with his beliefs about what is right and what is wrong, always ignoring my own thoughts.

Something he'd said when forcing me to look the dead boy in the eyes popped into my thoughts, specifically a question he'd asked. He asked whether either of us would feel the peace the boy felt in his death. I'd said no. I didn't feel we could feel the same level of peace he felt and it tore me apart inside. The knowledge that I'll never be as happy as other people I bump into in my life. I'll never have that feeling of satisfaction they have with their lives. I tried to think what I had done to deserve such a life. Why had I deserved such misery and pain and suffering? What had I done that was so bad? Even at a young age, when I was living with Dad, I was being seemingly punished and for what? Why? I was just a normal kid trying to live my life. I didn't ask for what happened. And then he showed up in my life. I didn't ask for him to come by and I certainly didn't ask for him to get involved with Dad. He simply took it upon himself to do so and now he expected me to be grateful for it? It was unfair.

I left the cellar via the stairs and entered the kitchen. I'm never going to be happy. I know that. Why should I keep trying to live a life like this? It's not good for either of us. And now his murderous impulses are out in the open, it's clearly not good enough for other people either. I don't want to live like this. Not with him. Especially when we're taken into custody. A lifetime spent rotting in a cell with only his hostile company? No. That's not for me…

I stormed over to the kitchen worktop and pulled a knife from one of the drawers. I held it firmly in my right hand and pressed the tip of the blade against my shaking wrist. It will hurt. I know that. But it will only do so for a moment. A moment of pain for the same blissful feeling the children were rewarded with. I want that. I want what they found in their death. I want what he gave them. I pushed down a little harder. A small trickle of blood appeared where the tip of the blade had pierced my skin. It stung but not in a bad way. If anything, with all my pent-up feelings, I felt a bit of a release.

He pulled the knife away from me and threw it across the room. I watched on, helplessly, as it penetrated the cellar door and stuck in the wood.

"What the fuck are you doing?" he hissed at me.

"I thought you'd gone. I thought I was alone!"

"You're trying to kill yourself? Is that it? What - you want to fucking die?"

"I don't want to live. I want the peace."

"You're a coward."

"No I'm not."

"Yes you are. You won't face your responsibilities. You're a fucking coward. You think there is a peace to be found by taking your own life? There's not. Eternal damnation waits for those who die by their own hand."

"We're damned anyway, thanks to you."

"I won't let you kill yourself. I won't let you kill us."

"Please…"

I tried to cross the kitchen to where the knife was stuck in the door but he stopped me. For the first time ever, I realised he was actually stronger than me. It never used to be like that. We used to be equal but these last couple of days were really starting to take it out of me.

"No."

"I don't want to live like this," I begged him.

"You don't have a choice."

"I can't live like this."

"I'll make you."

"Please…" I tried again to lunge for the knife but - again - he stopped me. With the feeling of despair at how weak I felt, I wanted to scream.

"Not got much fight in you, have you? Fucking pussy."

I watched helplessly as he sauntered over to the knife and pulled it from the door. He laughed as he waved in front of my face, "Is this the knife you wanted? It's nice. I can see why you picked this one. Fucking sharp. Do some damage with this."

"Fuck you."

"Fuck me? No. Fuck you. You tried to kill us both because you're too much of a pussy to carry on? Fucking selfish, not forgetting weak and pathetic."

I tried again to take the knife from him but he kept it from my reach, even laughing at my attempts to regain control. He slammed the knife down into the worktop so that it was sticking out from the wooden top, a cheap version of the sword in the stone.

"You want to play with knives?" he hissed. "Fine - let's play with knives."

He reached down to the washing machine and yanked the door open.

"What are you doing?" I asked as he pulled the now clean, but still damp, clown outfit from within.

"We're going out."

"No. Okay. I'm sorry. You're right. I'm pathetic. I'm a pussy. Let's just stay in. We can work something out…" I begged as he started kicking his clothes off.

"Every time I've talked to you, you've ignored me or tried to go behind me back. And to think, you believe I am the evil one. You need your head examining."

"Well you haven't exactly been upfront with me. You don't want to offer the children a peace they're missing from life - you just want them dead."

"Well…True…But - hey - it was a white lie to make you feel better about yourself. You, on the other hand, are just destructive," he sneered. He slid the cold, damp clown outfit on. "How do I look?"

"Take it off. Put your normal clothes back on. Let's go and have a conversation."

"I would but…So many people to kill. I just don't have the time."

He reached out, grabbed the knife and stormed from the kitchen. I followed, knowing I was powerless to stop him from doing whatever it was he had planned. He grabbed a pair of trainers from a cupboard under the stairs and stepped into them before grabbing the wig from the stairs - where it was always abandoned. He got to the door and reached for the handle.

"Please…" I tried one last-ditch attempt to stop him.

"Do you really want to die?" he asked. His voice seemed to have less hatred in it.

"It was a mistake. A moment of weakness."

He smiled, "You're lying. Again. You want to talk and yet you always lie. You can't help yourself."

"Fine. I want to die. I want peace. I want what the children have. You know, the ones you killed…"

"I won't be able to watch you all the time," he said.

He was right. No matter how strong he believed he was, there was no way he'd be able to watch me all the time. There'd be times where he wouldn't be with me and - as soon as that time came - I'd do what needed to be done. I would end my life and find the peace I sought.

He smiled again. I felt unnerved.

"I'm not ready to die," he said, his voice cold and low. "And so, we have a problem."

"It appears so."

"That's all I needed to know. Thank you."

He reached out for the door handle, twisted it, pulled the door open and stepped out of the house. He slammed the door shut. My mind was panicking as to what was going through his own mind. He was up to something.

Chapter 11

I opened the van's door and jumped in, throwing the knife onto the passenger seat. This fucking vehicle.

"Where are you going? What are you planning? Tell me!" he was still bleating in my ear like the little bitch that he was. I wanted to tell him to shut the fuck up but I didn't. I managed to restrain myself as I fired up the engine; another cloud of black smoke spewed from the back of the van.

I leaned across to the satnav system and starting going through the recent additions to various postcodes he has visited as part of his job. The one at the top of the list was where I'd taken the boy from. The one underneath - that boy whose father wanted to play the hero -he'll do.

"What are you fucking doing?" he screeched like a wild banshee when he saw I had selected the postcode. I ignored him as I sat back in the seat and reached for the seat belt. "Whatever you're planning…Please don't. Please. I'm begging you. Whatever you want, I'll do it."

I glared at him via the rear-view mirror, "I can't ever leave you without fearing you're going to do something stupid so, really, you haven't left me much choice."

"I won't do anything. I won't. I promise. Let's just go home."

"I don't think so."

I selected reverse gear and backed out of the driveway, onto the main road. The gearstick slipped through to first and I slammed on the accelerator, not that this van was particularly quick at pulling away but still…

"What are you going to do?"

I looked to the knife and smiled. Did he really need me to spell it out? Out of the corner of my eye I could see that he wanted to snatch the knife from the chair so I reached across and took a hold of it. I put it on my lap, just to reiterate it's my knife. Not his.

"You won't get away with it!" He sounded desperate now.

"I don't plan to."

"Then why are you doing it?"

"Because I don't want to die. I can't trust you not to do anything stupid so you've left me one option...Get all of my killing out of my system today, tonight, and then turn us in."

"They'll throw away the key..."

"That's right so I'd better really make an impact tonight," I laughed.

"But what's the point? They'll never let us out..."

"Exactly. And when I tell them of your suicidal tendencies, they'll never let you out of their sight either. You won't be able to wipe your arse without them watching, let alone kill yourself."

"You're throwing away your freedom."

"Freedom, yes. But I am saving my own life."

"This is fucking ridiculous!"

"Said the man who wanted to take his own life. Just shut the fuck up and enjoy the ride," I snapped. I leaned down to the radio and turned it up to its full volume to drown out his whining voice. He wanted to die, I wanted to live. The way I saw it, this was the only option I had: have one great day and night - a time to really build some strong memories - and then spend the rest of my time in a small cell replaying those memories whilst ignoring his pathetic bleating. It may not sound ideal but I'd sooner live a life like that than not live a life at all.

He screamed over the sound of The Animals' tune "House of the Rising Sun" blasting from the van's crackling speakers, "You won't even get to your destination! The police will see the van and they'll pull you over! You said yourself last night was sloppy!"

He was getting desperate now. Yes, there was a chance that he was right - the police could pull us over before we got to where we needed to be but I figured it was a slim chance. Certainly worth risking, considering what was bubbling away in my dark thought processes.

I turned down another road. Despite the time, traffic was relatively sparse. I was quite thankful about that. The last thing I wanted to do was find myself sitting in a jam with this whining son of a bitch.

"You're being a fucking idiot," he screamed.

I always found it funny when he swore and couldn't help but laugh. For some reason, it just didn't suit his tone of voice and, instead of sounding threatening, he sounded like he was desperately trying to be one of the cool kids. Well - whatever - as long as he is ranting and raving instead of trying to get in my way, he can do whatever the fuck he wants. I don't need to listen.

We continued to drive for about twenty minutes until I eventually pulled up outside of the house I'd been aiming for. I can't remember the name of the kid and I can't remember the name of the dad who so desperately wanted to be seen as a hero in front of his son. I had been pretty excited ever since leaving the house because of what I had planned to do but now we were sitting outside of the guy's actual house, I was fucking buzzing: a grin stretching from ear to ear, a pleasant tingling sensation rushing through my very being. I killed the engine and - in doing so - the radio. The sound of (near) silence. My ears were ringing. Not sure whether that was because of the radio's previous volume or whether he'd been constantly panicking and flapping in them.

He tried one last time, "Please, I'm begging you, don't do this."

"Hush now." I snatched the knife from my lap and kicked open the driver's door. I hopped down and looked around. Relatively quiet. Not that I would have given a fuck if it hadn't been. I stomped my way from van to house and knocked heavily on the door. Little pig, little pig - let me in…

"I don't want to see this," he said, his voice audibly quivering.

"And yet you stay here with me."

We could hear footsteps from the other side of the door. I slid the knife into the oversized pocket of his suit. A second later and the door opened. A woman was standing there with a bemused look upon her face. What? She never seen a clown before?

"Can I help you?" she asked.

"I'm here to see the birthday boy!" I said. I tried to sound jolly but I think I came across as loud. Need to try and camp it up a bit so I can sound a little more like him, the pathetic faggot. He was trying to talk, trying to warn her, but I managed to keep him quiet with a little concentration on my part.

"Johnny?" she asked.

Johnny, that was the fucker! And his dad's name was Colin. Cunty Colin. I remember now. Not that I'd bothered to speak to either of them when we were last here. Fuck getting involved with that shit. I let him do all the talking back then.

"Oh it's you! You did his party!" she said, a look of sudden realisation on her face as though she'd solved the world's greatest mystery. I wanted to deny it - tell her it wasn't me who'd performed at the party - but I couldn't. I knew that would just cause problems by confusing her. "What can I do for you?" she asked, seemingly more at ease now.

"Is Johnny in?" I asked, trying to keep it light. "I have a present for him that I forgot to give to him at his party?"

"Really? Oh wow! He'll be so excited to see you. He was talking about you for days," she said. She stepped back a bit and opened the door wider for me. Does she really think I'm that fat? Cheeky whore. Can't say she'll live to regret that moment of rudeness. I thanked her (because I'm polite) and stepped into the house. She closed the door behind me.

"Johnny?" she called up the stairs, "You have a visitor!"

"Who is it?" came the squeaky voice of a runt.

Kids aren't just annoying because they're whiney and selfish, throwing temper tantrums when they don't get what they believe they deserve… A lot of the reasons they're generally annoying is down to their voices. Slightly higher pitched than they need to be - one octave away from being audible to nearby dogs only. They just kind of squeak at you when they speak. And some of them have the need to touch you when they're talking too, probably because they know you're not really listening. They come up to you and just tap you whilst saying what they think they need to say. You, in turn, stand there and listen to them - even if you were in the middle of a conversation with a friend or partner - because you know it's the quickest way to get them to fuck off. Oops. Footsteps at the top of the landing. Happy face on.

Johnny's face beamed when he saw me. My face beamed too, despite wanting to kick his fucking head in right there and then. Him and his rude mother. A quiet voice was yelling at me in my head to tell me to behave, ordering me to get out of the house. Not going to happen.

"Hi, kiddo!" I yelled enthusiastically.

I turned to his mother, "Colin due home?"

"He'll be home in a couple of hours," she said. She looked just as thrilled as her son. I somehow think that was more to do with his reaction at seeing me than seeing me for herself, especially going by the look on her face when she first opened the front door to me.

"That's a shame," I said, "he'll miss your death…"

"I'm sorry?" she turned to me, a sudden look of terror in her eyes. Before she could react further, or even have the time to scream, I pulled the knife from my pocket and stuck it into her throat. Her eyes bulged in both pain and fear as a smile spread across my thin lips and a scream burst from dear little Johnny. I pulled the knife from her throat to a satisfying spray of blood and an audible gargle. She dropped to her knees, clutching frantically at the wound as her son about-turned and charged back up the stairs. Silly little Johnny. The front door would have been a safer option for him. less chance of me catching him before he finds sanctuary with an alarmed neighbour.

I stepped over his mother's body as she continued to writhe around in pain. She wouldn't last much longer, going by the blood pumping from her scrawny throat. At the bottom of the stairs I shouted up to my new best friend, "Johnny! Where are you going? We have two hours of playtime before Daddy is home…Don't you want to make the most of it?" I laughed as I started my way up the stairs.

II

I was desperate to do something to help them but was powerless. What was wrong with me? Why couldn't I regain control and take charge of the situation? Why am I letting him control me like this?

"You've had some fun, I get it. You're in control…" I tried telling him. I wasn't sure whether he wasn't hearing me or whether he was ignoring me. It didn't even matter if I was shouting at him.

"Johnny!" He was walking up the stairs, calling out the boy's name in a low voice. "Johhhhhhhhnny…..Johhhhhhhhnnnnnnnnnnnnyyyyyyyyyy….. Got a little pressie for ya!" He stopped at the top of the stairs and looked down the landing for any sign of movement. "Come here, Johhhhhhhnny, time to play a little game…" I watched, desperate to reach out and stop him, as he tapped the bloodied knife on the side of his face as he weighed up his options with regards to which room to try first.

"You can't do this, please…"

"Oh, hush your mouth," he hissed at me, the first time he has responded to me in what seems to be an age. I seized the opportunity to keep him talking - maybe long enough for help to come (Colin returning home, perhaps?) – just to keep the boy alive.

"We have to go home. Let's go home and talk things through. I promise - I won't try and kill myself again. I'll do whatever you want. I'll even let you keep control, at all times. I won't interfere. Please. I promise. You have to believe me. Just let the boy live.

There was a mirror hanging from the longest wall of the landing. He looked into it - at my reflection - and slowly raised his finger to his lips.

"Ssh!"

III

I turned my attention back to where little Johnny could possibly be hiding. No way out from up here - at least not without jumping from the window or running back down the stairs and I can't see him doing either.

What I like about little children is that it's easy enough to scare them from their hiding place before you've even found it. Just one little sentence to force them into the light. Three. Two. One.

"Ah ha!" I shouted. "I SEE YOU!"

It didn't matter that I had no idea where he was. All that mattered was he believed I could see him. From across the landing - the bedroom at the far end - Johnny screamed and ran from one room to the other (the bathroom) where he slammed the door shut. I heard the lock bolt across. Silly boy. He's only making this harder on himself.

"Fe-Fi-Fo-Fum…I smell the blood of a soon-to-be-screamin- in-agony little shit-faced cunt!" Not quite the words known, but good enough. I stomped loudly down the landing all the way to the door and tried the handle, despite knowing he had it locked. It didn't move. I rattled it backwards and forwards as he screamed from within. "Little shit, little shit, let me in…" I threw my weight against the door (he screamed again), shoulder first, in the hope I'd fall straight through. No such luck but there was definite movement. It won't take too much before it gives. I threw myself again the wooden door again, to the sound of yet another shriek from beyond. Scream all you want, kiddo; help isn't coming. A third slam against the wall, a four and fifth. On the sixth hit, the door finally gave in and I fell through, landing on the floor with a hard bang. Had it not been for the adrenaline - and the reward of getting in - that could have hurt. I looked up from the floor and saw the boy standing in the empty bath, clutching onto the shower curtain as though it were enough to stop me. Damn it. Foiled by a shower curtain. I don't fucking think so. I stood up to my full height and smiled at the boy. "Did you not hear me knocking?" I asked. I held the knife up and he screamed. I do wish he'd stop screaming. Little children should be seen and not heard. To his credit, he didn't try and run past me. He remained rooted to the spot, shaking like a leaf. I squeezed the handle of the knife tighter in my grip and took a deep breath in before…

These are the moments I live for.

These are the moments which make me feel alive.

The build-up.

The anticipation.

I thrust forward and penetrated the child's stomach with the knife to the accompaniment of the loudest scream I think I've ever heard. I'm unsure whether it is the boy or…whether it is him, crying into my ear. I twisted the knife deep in his intestines. No way that's going to seal itself back up again when I pull the knife out. No way he will survive the attack. Another scream from he who must be ignored as I stabbed the boy again, slightly to the side of the last hit.

IV

I looked away from the scene as he pulled the knife from Johnny's gut and thrust forward again. The poor child sounded as though he was in so much pain as he fell back against the wall. Out of the corner of my eye, I saw him slowly slide down into a sitting position, clutching his wounds as blood poured out from the gaping holes. I can't watch. I won't watch.

"What are you doing?" He sounded surprised that I was able to look away without much resistance. To be honest, I too was surprised. "Don't you fucking look away!" he yelled.

V

I snapped his head back to the boy, who was pale and gasping for air. It's my favourite bit, getting to see the life slowly slip away from the children. They make their parents suffer with their whining and constant demands - now it is my turn to make them suffer for as long as they're able to stand it (which is never usually that long). I thrust into his stomach with my white gloved hand - my fingers closed together and palm flat as though in a karate chop position. He's so near death now that he barely registered what I was doing. My hand was in his stomach. I opened my fingers up, stretching him wide, and took a hold of intestine. I smiled as I took a handful and slowly started pulling them from his gut. His body shook as I did so and his eyes rolled to the back of his head. A final gasp, like a fish out of water, and he stopped moving - at least stopping moving on his own accord. His body was still twitching due to my continued pulling out of his insides.

I've never done this before. They slipped to the floor with a watery slosh sound. Not sure why I've never thought to do it before. I have to say, that was pretty satisfying.

"You're a monster!" he was weeping in my ear. He tried to look away from my handiwork but I wouldn't let him. I wanted him to watch. I wanted him to see. This is me. This is us. And it's only going to get worse as the day and night progress.

I'm excited.

Chapter 12

I should have done this at night for maximum impact for the father - the hero - Colin. I wanted him to walk into the living room illuminated with candlelight but it was too bright outside. Even with their curtains shut, daylight still managed to leak into the room. I had dragged both bodies into the living room - the mother and the boy. I'd sprawled them out on the floor by the unlit fireplace.

In my head, everything was so much better. Daddikins would come home, call out for them and there'd be no answer. He'd walk into the living room, eventually, and there he'd see them, propped up with their lifeless eyes staring straight into his own soul. The reality was much different and - compared to how it should have worked out - a little disappointing. The bodies wouldn't sit up properly. Every time I tried to make them, they'd just topple over. Worse yet, I had managed to spill so much blood from each body when I dragged them through to the living room that I had left a long trail of gore, enough of a mess for him to spot it as soon as he walked through the front door. Total lack of surprise, gone.

"You're a fucking monster."

He was still sulking with me. Had barely said anything to me whilst I was dragging the bodies around. Just the odd whimper here and there as he tried to hold his shit together. Fucking pathetic.

"I thought you'd left me," I sneered at him.

"I wish I could."

"As do I. At least we agree on that, hey."

"Fuck you."

"Don't worry," I told him, "the night will soon be over and all of this will be nothing but a distant memory…Unless, of course, it haunts you every night whilst you're locked in your little cell…Ooh, I can't imagine that will be too good for your precious little conscience."

I expected him to snap back at me but - to his credit - he remained silent. Probably saving his strength for the moment he is faced with the police so he can protest his innocence loudly enough to be heard. Little does he know, I won't let him. We're both going down for this. We're both going to prison. I won't let doctors psychoanalyse either of us. I won't let them take him off the sharp hook I have so skill-fully impaled him on. Fuck that.

With the bodies in place and the curtains shut, I took a hold of the knife again. The blade was filthy so I wiped it upon my suit until it was once again glistening. There. As good as new.

"Do you think he'll still love his wife?" I asked, as I looked at the pale body of a once mediocre-looking woman. "Or do you think he'll find her ugly now that she's dead? I've often wondered that. If you go through your whole life loving someone, if they die…Do they suddenly become ugly…"

"You're fucking insane."

"Of the two of us, my friend, I'd say that was you." I paused a moment, "But what do you think? Do you think he will still love her or…Did that love fade with her last breath?"

"I don't fucking know."

"You see - I only ask because - I was wondering whether you'd like one last fuck with her whilst she is still kind of warm. Get it in one final time before joining her in the bowels of Hell…"

"What makes you think they're in Hell?"

"Why wouldn't they be in Hell?" I asked.

Silence. "I might give him the choice. Maybe it's your influence but…I have to say…I'm feeling a little generous."

"Then let him go. Take us home. We can pack a bag and just disappear. Talk things through. Work things out between us…"

"Shut the fuck up. You're like a broken record."

We both froze when we heard a key slide into the front door's lock.

"Please don't," he whispered, "we can still get away…"

"I'm home!" a male voice called from the hallway. It sounded like Colin - which was to be expected. "Honey? What the hell has happened here?" he shouted. And there goes the element of surprise. He's spotted the pooling of the blood from where his wife's body was slumped. "Susie?" he called out.

I didn't bother hiding myself. I just stood there, a proud look on my face, waiting by the bodies of his family members. One dead wife and one dead son to go, please.

"Susie?"

I took a step back to the mantlepiece above the fire and purposefully knocked one of the many pictures from it. It crashed to the floor. Only did it because I'm fucking bored of waiting for the cunt to come in here.

"Susie?"

Colin stepped into the room. He immediately spotted me. Second up - he saw his wife and child. His expression. He didn't know what to make of it. He was just standing there with his mouth agape. Say something. Show me some kind of reaction. He fidgeted on his feet. I could tell he didn't know what direction to go - whether to charge me or whether to run from the house.

"If you want to say goodbye to her body before you join her soul, she's still a little warm. But only if you fancy it," I offered. A kind offer. Generous. Is…he…turning me into a fucking faggot all of a sudden? Next up I'll be offering mercy. I laughed. Will I fuck.

"Wh-what…What is this?" Colin backed up slightly.

"Home invasion I guess. Nothing better to do." I raised the knife up so he could see it, "So what's it to be? Fancy having a good goodbye session with your wife or…Shall we just get on with this?"

Colin - the Hero of the Hour - started to cry like a baby. He dropped to his knees and wept. Well, I have to be honest, I expected a little more of a fight than this. Nearly as much of a pussy as he is.

"What the fuck are you doing?" I shouted at him. "What, you're not even going to try and fight? Not even going to try and get revenge? You're just going to kneel there like a fucking pussy?"

II

He was blinded by his own rage. I seized the opportunity and chucked the knife towards Colin. It landed to the side of him.

"Please!" I shouted. "KILL ME!"

Colin looked at the knife and then looked at me. Yes. That's it. Do it.

"What the FUCK are you doing?" he screamed in my ear as he took a step forward in an effort to take back the blade. I stopped him and we stumbled onto our knees. Colin reached over and grabbed a hold of the knife but still didn't rush us. Please. Come on. You have to do it. Quickly.

"I can't hold him back much longer!" I cried out. "Please! Kill me!"

Colin dragged himself up but still didn't rush forward. What the hell was his problem?

"Put that fucking knife down, you cunt!" he shouted at Colin.

"Shut up!" I shouted him down. "We deserve this."

"You do. I don't."

I turned to Colin, "We killed your family! KILL US!"

Colin screamed and rushed towards us with the blade held out in front of him. Yes. That's it. Come on. Do it. Stick that blade in me! Put me out of my fucking misery and end his life. Please!"

III

As Colin neared, I took control of the situation and jumped up. In the blink of an eye, I managed to grab Colin's hands and turn the knife back onto The Hero of the Hour. Using his own weight and momentum from his sudden rush towards me against him, I shoved it right into his gut. His eyes widened just as his wife's eyes did. Colin put his hands up to my throat and started to squeeze as I continued to twist the knife in his stomach. His grip didn't hurt.

He was already starting to weaken. I laughed as I twisted the blade again. Not just because his efforts to hurt me were extremely amusing but - also - because of how we ended in this position.

"That's fucking team work, right?" I laughed.

He wasn't laughing though. He was screaming in my ear. He was scream-ing - calling me a 'murderer', a 'monster' - all the names under the sun. Some temper he has there but the name calling didn't bother me. For the first time in as long as I could remember, I felt as though we had bonded. Properly. And, more importantly, I'd shown him how easy it is to kill. The shouting was just for show. I bet - deep down - he fucking loved helping me put the blade in. Fucking loved it as much as I did. Maybe he'd get a taste for it? One thing seeing it, quite another doing it yourself (or at least having a helping hand in it). Maybe we could still run from here and live a life killing who and what we wanted? My mind was flowing with various plans on how we could get away with living a life like this…The two of us…

IV

I grabbed for the knife and pulled it from the father's stomach. With no hesitation I turned it back on myself and rammed it straight back into my chest until it was up to its handle. Surprisingly, I felt no pain. I felt nothing. It wasn't my chest. It was his chest. We dropped to our knees, the pair of us gasping for breath. He took a hold of the handle and pulled the blade from our chest and dropped it to the floor. I sensed he was trying to say some-thing to me. No doubt trying to call me a fucking idiot or words to that ef-fect but I didn't care. Didn't give a shit. I just watched the blood flow freely from the hole he'd left behind by removing the blade.

Our legs feel cold.

I feel sleepy.

Not sure where I managed to find the strength to do this but…I'm glad.

We slumped forward, face first, onto the family's cream carpet. The blood was soaking in. Not sure whether it's the family's blood or my own blood…Doesn't matter.

Really sleepy.

I smiled.

It's peaceful here.

V

I snorted. Too weak to laugh. Didn't see it coming. Have to admit.

I couldn't keep my eyes open. My eyelids slowly closed. Can't open them again.

I can't believe he killed us.

What…

…A

…Cunt.

T H E E N D

A House in the Country

MATT SHAW'S

Broken Dreams

A curvy brunette with green eyes, Jess first caught Dean's eye when they were in their early twenties. Dean had ended up in the hospital where - at the time - Jess was training to be a nurse. He'd tripped down a flight of stairs and twisted his ankle awkwardly when leaving the home he still (embarrassingly) shared with his mother and father. He walked home many hours later with the news that his ankle was only bruised. He also managed to leave Accident and Emergency with a phone number for Jess who had been observing the nurse seeing to the potential break. They had hit it off immediately and had dated for two years before moving into their first property together; a small house on the outskirts of the city. A year later, with the last of their savings, they were married and - not long after that - found that they were expecting their first child; although this came as a surprise to both of them. Two years after that (and a little more planned) their second child was born. Now both Dean and Jess were in their mid-thirties.

Today…

The house was a mess. Boxes were piled up in every corner of every room - not that there were many rooms. The lack of space being the main reason for Jess and Dean's decision to move. The property had served them well; a two bedroom terraced house on the outskirts of the city. The first home they had purchased together after they got married almost nine years ago now (they'd rented previously). With two daughters, Sophie who was six and Caroline who was eight, the second bedroom was no longer big enough for the two of them to share. Combined with the fact that work was going well for both Jess and Dean - they decided it was the right time to move to a bigger property. A house where Sophie and Caroline could have their own rooms and a home where they could all continue building happy memories to look back on when they were grey and old.

"Damn!" Dean leaned against the landing wall and rubbed his toe. His youngest daughter Sophie had pulled him from his slumber. She was screaming out - another nightmare probably - and he'd run from his bedroom, forgetting the boxes lining the way. As a result; box meet toe, toe meet box. A quick rub until he had taken the sting off enough to be able to continue walking on it. He put his foot down and winced in pain, thankful at least that no one else had witnessed his stupidity. He hobbled through to the bedroom where Sophie was sitting up, crying. As he made his way across the empty looking room (other than the piled up boxes of toys and clothes waiting for the removal men to collect them) he cast a quick eye towards Caroline. She was fast asleep, her headphones still in place where she'd fallen asleep listening to her music again. Both Dean and Jess had told her not to go to sleep listening to music; both of them fearful she'd one day strangle herself as she twisted and turned throughout the night. He'd deal with her second. First he would deal with the daughter who was actually awake and calling for him. Always calling for him. He often wondered why she never called for Jess.

"Your daughter is calling for you!" Jess had told him when she also stirred from her sleep.

"She's your daughter too!" Dean reminded her, annoyed at the prospect of having to get out of his warm bed. Their daughter was no stranger to nightmares and it was always Dean who was the one she wanted to comfort her. He didn't mind but - at the same time - he could not help but think it would be good if Jess also went once in a while.

"Yeah but she is calling for you!" Jess would tell him as she rolled back over, snuggling back down onto the soft mattress.

"Hey, what's up sleepy-head?" he sat down on Sophie's bed, next to her. Immediately she threw her arms around him and gave him a tight squeeze.

He gave her a squeeze back. "Another nightmare?" he asked. "It was just a dream."

"I don't want you to die!" Sophie sobbed.

Always the same dream.

Moving Day

"Have you been teasing your sister again?" The family were sitting around the breakfast table in the near-empty kitchen (again, other than the packed boxes). Dean was looking at Caroline whilst he ate the last slice of his toast.

"No!" Caroline answered him, looking him directly in the eye. Dean and Jess knew she was telling the truth. She was only eight years old and hadn't learned to lie properly yet - not without giving many a tell-tale sign at least.

"She didn't say anything!" Sophie stuck up for her - just as she always did when her mother or father accused her of something she hadn't done.

Dean turned his attention to his youngest daughter, "Must be some reason you keep having that dream, honey." Sophie had been having the same recurring nightmare for over a year now. It had gotten to the point where neither Jess nor Dean needed her to explain what the 'bad dream' was about when it woke her up; they instantly knew. Instead they'd just put their arms around her until she stopped sobbing and then tried their best to settle her back down again whilst reassuring her that it was just a dream. Nothing more, nothing less. Sophie heard what they said and understood it was nothing more than a bad dream but it never made it any less upsetting.

"What about what we spoke about?" Jess asked Dean. They had stayed up a while, after Dean got back to bed the previous night, discussing Sophie's bad dreams. Both of them were concerned but neither of them knew what they could do about it. It had been Jess' suggestion to get a specialist involved; someone who may be able to help Sophie understand where the dreams were coming from or, even better, someone who could help her stop having them at all. Dean looked at Jess. He hadn't wanted to approach the subject with Sophie yet - not until they'd investigated the cost implications at least. And even if they already knew the costs, moving day wasn't the best time to bring up such discussions. They had enough on their plates. Too late now though. Sophie was staring at him, waiting to see what her mum and dad had been talking about.

"How would you feel about talking to someone?" Dean asked. "About your dreams," he clarified. Sophie shrugged. "Might be good," he pushed her, "they might be able to stop you from having them? That would be good, wouldn't it?" Sophie nodded.

"What about me?" Caroline asked. She was at the age where she liked to tease her younger sister from time to time, or blame Sophie for things she had done but she was also at the age where she always felt as though her sister was getting special treatment over her (not that she was). "I want to talk to someone too!"

Jess smiled at her, "You can talk to me!" Caroline turned to her younger sister and poked her tongue out at her. "Er - that's enough thank you!" Jess quickly stopped an argument from escalating. Dean ignored it and continued talking to Sophie.

"Well - when we've settled into our new home - we'll see if we can find someone nice and friendly for you to talk to!" He tried to say it with enthusiasm; hopefully making it sound more exciting and appealing than it was likely to be. He turned to Caroline, "Oh and while we're talking about last night - both your mother and I have already told you about listening to your music when you go to bed. If you do it again we'll take your iPod away from you!" a threat previously agreed with his wife. They knew Caroline would sulk if they took her iPod away but they'd rather that then have her hang herself by getting tangled up during the night.

"You'll take it away? Forever?"

"Forever!" Jess backed Dean up.

Caroline wasn't sure whether her mum and dad were being serious with their threat but - at the same time - she didn't really want to find out. She just sat there, a wide-eyed expression on her face as though the mere thought of being without her beloved music player was the most daunting one in the world. Sophie leaned across to Caroline and stuck her tongue out.

"Don't you start!" Jess warned her.

Dean changed the subject, "So who is excited about seeing their new room today?" he asked. Both girls cheered. They'd all loved the house from the moment they first saw it; a large white-bricked house in the middle of nowhere with four double bedrooms (one with an en-suite bathroom), two family bathrooms, a study, dining room, living room, large kitchen with breakfast bar, cloakroom and a double garage - all surrounded by luscious green fields and forests. A huge difference to the house they were currently living in. Dean stood up and took his plate over to the sink where he proceeded to run it under the tap - rinsing the toasted breadcrumbs down the plug-hole. Jess walked up behind him and put her arms around him. She gave him a kiss on the neck.

"I know I am," she smiled. "I'll miss this place though," she continued, "so many happy memories."

Dean turned around - still in her arms - so that he was facing her. He embraced his loving wife with his own arms, "Memories which we will take to the new house," he said, "and - once there - we'll build upon them with even better ones." He gave her a kiss as the two girls laughed from the table. "Shut up, you little monkeys!" Dean laughed. "Come and give your old man a hug!" They didn't need asking twice as they jumped from the table and ran towards their mum and dad - throwing their arms around them. "Enjoy the calm," Dean told Jess, "for it all goes out of the window as soon as the removal men get here!"

Dean watched on as the removal men loaded the first of the boxes into the back of the first lorry. Their lives - all four of them - packed into various shaped cardboard boxes. Their lives - enough to fill two medium sized lorries. Looked at it like that, it was fairly depressing.

Jess was standing in the doorway to the house; a tray of hot drinks in her hands as she waited for the removal men to come back. Dean walked over to her, "Imagine if they just vanished," he said.

"What? Who? The removal men?"

"No. Well - yes. The lorries. Imagine if they just disappeared. You know never to be seen again."

"What are you talking about?" Jess asked. She was already stressed despite it being the beginning of the moving process and - other than packing - she hadn't really done that much. Packing and tea making. Dean went to reply but stopped himself from saying anything as the removal men came back to the house. As they went by Jess, they each took a cup of tea - thanking her in the process.

"That's our lives," he told her. "That is everything about us and our family. If those lorries vanished then so do all of our memories." Dean continued when the coast was clear to do so.

Jess looked at him. She didn't look amused by his thoughts. "Well thank you for that," she said, "as if I didn't have enough to worry about what with getting our precious belongings from point a to point b without breaking in the first place. Now I get to imagine a world where our belongings just disappear into thin air. So - yes - thank you for that."

Dean couldn't help but to laugh. He leaned close to her and gave her a kiss before reassuring her, "Everything will be fine. These guys are professional." His words were badly timed as - from inside the house - a smashing noise was clearly audible. He sighed. "Wait here…" he said as he disappeared into the house to see what had happened.

Day One

By the end of the first day both of the lorries had been completely cleared of their contents. Much to Jess' delight this was done without the lorries disappearing without a trace, as Dean had joked, and without any more of the boxes being dropped. In fairness to the removal men, it hadn't been their fault the first box had been broken anyway. It was an overly large cardboard box stuffed with way too many of the girls' toys and the bottom had simply fallen through - but they should have expected that; that's what you get when you ask two young girls to help pack up their toys - everything gets crammed into the one box with the lid slammed shut (or folded shut in this instance).

The two lorries turned around in one of the fields, as permitted by Dean who was now the proud owner of the land, and headed off back out of the drive and down the narrow street they had originally travelled down. Dean watched as they disappeared round the corner before stepping back into his new home. He closed the door and surveyed the mess; cardboard boxes stashed in every visible corner and their furniture literally just dumped in the rooms they belonged in. He looked at Jess who was trying to move the larger of the sitting rooms sofas back against the wall.

"Not quite sure where to start!" he told her. He was knackered before he had even started.

Jess stopped dragging the sofa and stood up straight - her eyes fixed on her husband, "You could start with grabbing the other end of this sofa," she told him.

"Shit! Sorry!" he realised he'd just been watching her struggle. He grabbed the other end of the sofa and helped his struggling wife move it back against the longest of walls. They had chosen where the furniture was going before they had got to the house. They had looked around the house three times before putting in an offer and - on the third visit - they had decided which room was going to be used for which purpose. The only rooms they had not decided upon were where their daughters were going to sleep. They had chosen the front room, overlooking the drive, for themselves as it was the biggest room (with the en-suite) and that was as far as they had got. They knew, before they even pulled up into the property with the convoy of moving lorries, that there were going to be arguments over the remaining rooms.

"MUM!" Caroline was shouting from the top of the stairs. Before Jess or Dean went to investigate the shouting - they knew what it was going to be about. Dean was first to the bottom of the stairs. He looked up at his eldest daughter who had a face like thunder.

"What is it?" he asked.

"She won't get out of my room!" Caroline whined.

"Your room? But your mother and I haven't decided who is getting which room yet."

Jess joined her husband, "What's the matter?" she asked him.

"The room issue."

"Ah."

"I told her which room I wanted but now she won't get out. She says it is her room."

Dean turned to Jess, "She called for you. You can deal with this. I can't be bothered with it," he shrugged, "I'd sooner be doing the important bits like unpacking…"

Jess knew Dean was tired. They'd all been doing their bit to help with the packing but Dean had also been working full-time in the office to ensure everything was up together in order to give him the luxury of time off with which to move. "I'll sort it out," she whispered to Dean. Dean nodded at her and walked back through to the room with the sofas (soon to be their lounge) and Jess headed up the stairs to deal with the girls. "Right," she said using her best voice of 'authority', "what's going on up here?"

"I want this room!" Sophie called out from the third biggest room on the second floor of the house. Her voice, just as whiney as her sister's.

"I said first!" Caroline moaned. She ran through to the room. Sophie was sitting on the floor, having surrounded herself with boxes. Jess was actually surprised. Both her and Dean thought the girls were going to argue over the second biggest room (across the landing), not this one.

Jess turned to Caroline, "Well - as the eldest - don't you want to have the other room? The bigger one?" she asked.

Caroline shook her head and started to whimper, "I want this one. I don't like the other room."

Jess frowned, "You don't like the other room? But it's bigger! And the views over the back garden are much better than the view from this room…" In truth the views from both rooms were similar - overlooking the fields out the back of the house which seemingly stretched on for miles - but the size of the rooms were definitely different.

"I want this room!" Caroline stamped her feet.

Jess turned to Sophie, "And you don't want the bigger room?"

Sophie moaned, "It smells funny in there."

Jess frowned as though her daughter's words surprised her. She turned from the room and walked across the landing to the room that neither girl wanted. As soon as she walked in, the smell hit her; a heavy musk hanging in the air. Of all the rooms to stink of damp it had to be this one. She walked over to the window and opened it. She walked back across to the other bedroom where the girls were still arguing over whose room it was, "It's just damp in there," she said. "I've opened the window so - by morning - the smell will be completely gone."

"I want this room!" Caroline whined again. "I said it first!"

"No you didn't. I did!" Sophie shouted back.

"Have you even looked at the third room?" Jess asked - trying her best to keep from shouting at the two of them. They had gone from sharing a room to having one of their own. You'd have thought they would have been happy with either of the rooms. They both shook their heads. "So you've decided you both want this room without even seeing all of the rooms on offer?" Jess shook her head, irritated at the stubbornness of her own children.

Dean's voice made her jump, "Sorted it?" he asked from the doorway.

Jess turned to him, "They're being stupid. They both want this room."

"Really?" Dean was surprised. He had also prepared himself for the girls to be arguing over the second biggest room available. "What's wrong with the other room?" he asked Jess. He turned his question to the girls and repeated it so he could hear it straight from them, "What's wrong with the other room?"

"It smells funny in there!" they both said in unison.

"So you both want this room then?" he asked. Jess immediately knew where he was headed by the tone in his voice. The tone which suggested he wasn't in the mood for silly arguments. "You're sure about that?"

"I saw it first!" Caroline whined.

Dean turned to Jess and shrugged, "Then they can share it. Half each." He turned from the room and headed back down the stairs, smirking at the girls protests coming from the room about how they didn't want to share and that they wanted a room of their own.

Caroline was the first to ask to see the last bedroom on offer. Jess walked her through to the other room, down the end of the landing at the front of the house and - surprise, surprise - Caroline fell in love with it more or less straight away.

"I'm glad that's settled then." Jess walked back down the landing towards the stairs. "And remember - don't go emptying all of your clothes and toys everywhere until your father has had a chance to move your furniture around!"

The bedrooms were to be the easiest of the rooms to sort out. With the exception of what was to be Dean and Jess' bedroom, they all had built in wardrobes - other than that - they only needed a bed to be built; something Dean had planned to do before the end of the day having left the girls' bunk beds in their last house. No sense dragging that around with them when they'd be able to afford the space for their own beds, he thought. It was just a bind that it meant he had to build two beds before they could really unpack anything.

Before Jess went back down the stairs - to start unpacking the kitchen in order to fix something for everyone to eat - she couldn't help but look towards the second bedroom. Her eye caught by a slight movement of the open door. She dismissed it as being caused by a gentle breeze from the open window. Of all the rooms to smell rotten - it had to be that one. She shook the thoughts from her mind and hurried down the stairs with only the slightest of chills running down her spine as though being watched by someone. Or something.

⋏

Dean collapsed onto the clean sheets of the Queen-size bed he shared with Jess. The day had been full on and they were still nowhere near being done yet with many boxes still waiting to be unpacked - and a stack of boxes which needed to be put up into the attic until they were needed again (if they ever were to be needed again). The living room furniture was placed where they intended it to stay, as was the furniture in the dining room. Both rooms had the relevant boxes stashed there - some of which they had even started unpacking. Everything was out of the boxes in the kitchen - and spread across the work-tops ensuring there was very little space with which to actually prepare food - ready to be put into the cupboards once Jess had decided where she wanted everything stored (a very important decision when arranging a kitchen). The two beds, in the girls' rooms, had been built with very little shouting from Dean who'd always hated Do-It-Yourself tasks and the girls' boxes had now been emptied across all available space in their rooms, which was their contribution to unpacking.

"I'm absolutely knackered," Dean huffed as he settled down onto the soft mattress.

"At least we made good progress. At this rate we might not have to use our whole week unpacking. We might get some time to actually sit back and relax!" Jess pointed out - ever the optimistic. Dean looked at her. He didn't want to think about everything they had left to do. He just wanted to switch off for the night and enjoy the peace and quiet. It had been a long, long day and he had been fit for bed for the past three hours but every time he thought he was going to go up - he found himself starting another job. "What?" Jess saw the way he was looking at her.

"Oh nothing but if I die tonight - in my sleep - you know, from exhaustion, just know that I loved you very much," he smiled at her.

"That reminds me," Jess said, "did you go into the bedroom."

"We have four bedrooms now, honey, you'll have to be a little more specific."

"The bedroom," said Jess, putting more emphasis on the word 'the' than entirely necessary. Dean knew what she was talking about, he just didn't want to talk about it. They had spoken about it - at great lengths - before deciding to put the offer in. Both of them had agreed it wouldn't be a problem for them, what had happened in that room, and that they just wouldn't talk about it. Yet here they were on night one and Jess was trying to bring it up.

"We said we wouldn't talk about it," he reminded her.

"There's a funny smell in there," said Jess. "Smells like…"

"…The house has been empty. There's bound to be a few smells lingering. That's what happens. Especially in buildings this old. Did you open the window?"

"Yes."

"Then by morning it will be aired. Nothing to worry about." Dean leaned across and gave Jess a kiss on the cheek - hoping such an act would put her mind at ease. Clearly, by the look on her face, it hadn't done as he'd hoped for.

Thanks to full disclosure on the property, when Dean had asked the estate agent why the house was going for such a low price, considering the size and location of it, they were informed about the previous owners. A man named Stuart Keane who'd lived there for many years with his wife, Cathy. Stuart was a hard-working man who traveled a lot for business. He knew his wife struggled when he was away. She'd always been prone to bouts of depression and the solitude she faced, when alone, always forced the ill-feeling to the forefront of her mind. And then, one day, when Stuart came home from a week away - he was greeted at the front door by a foul stench hanging in the air. He called out to his wife but there was no answer, despite her car being in the driveway. She wasn't downstairs so he investigated up-stairs. There, at the top of the stairs, he was struck dumb by the sight of his wife hanging by a tight noose wrapped around her neck; her skin blue, eyes closed, swollen tongue hanging from her mouth. The house had been put on the market within the fortnight, Stuart being unable to stay there. Upon learning the sad story Jess and Dean had discussed at great length their feel-ings towards the property (that room in particular). Neither of them liked the fact someone had died there but, at the same time, neither of them felt it was enough to stop them from moving in - especially at such a low asking price. They agreed that, if they went for it, they just wouldn't discuss it again. And here they were - night one - already discussing it.

"Are you okay?" Dean asked when he realised it was clear that Jess wasn't.

"It just feels strange knowing that - you know - someone killed them-selves in the next room," she continued, "and I know we said we wouldn't talk about it but…I don't know…I'm just being stupid…Earlier the door moved and I know it was just a breeze coming from the window I had opened but I felt as though I was being watched."

Dean sighed. This was exactly what he didn't want to happen. They get the property of their dreams. They move in. And then Jess freaks out be-cause of the history in the house. This is why they had talked about it before even putting in an offer. To avoid this very situation. "We spoke about this," he reminded her once more.

"I know we did and I'll be fine - it's just…It's the first night. I'm al-lowed to feel a little off sorts on the first night, right? I promise I'll be fine by morning. And - when everything is unpacked and where it should be - all of this will be nothing but a distant memory."

"Promise?"

"Promise."

"I just want this to go smoothly. We've had great memories from the last house and I want more from this one. I don't want anything tainting it. I want the kids to grow up and remember the fun they had here, you know? I want them striving to achieve the same with their own families some day."

"And I want the same. I promise - it's just first night nerves."

"Okay."

Jess changed the subject. She could see Dean was tired and that usually meant he was quick to anger. He wouldn't do anything when angry other than have a bit of a shout and a sulk but she didn't want that - not for their first night together in their new home. She moved closer and reached down with her hand, a smile on her face. "So how tired are you?" she asked. She started to stroke the inside of his leg before moving her fingers to the shaft of his (temporarily) flaccid penis. His look of concern soon disappeared - replaced by a smile. Jess leaned forward and kissed him on the mouth before she moved down, under the duvet. Dean gasped as he felt first her breath and then her lips against his skin. He smiled.

Night One

Dean woke with a start at the sound of his youngest daughter's scream ripping through the night. Two nights on the trot. He sat up trying to remember if there had ever been an occasion where she'd had the same dream on two consecutive nights. The dream was recurrent but usually a couple of times a month - not daily. He rubbed his eyes and looked over to the clock on the bedside cabinet. 3:30am.

"She's calling for you!" Jess pointed out. He looked down to where she was lying. She hadn't even opened her eyes. Clearly she wasn't going to be getting up. Dean shook his head. Why was it always his name his daughter called out? He threw the duvet back and swung his feet from the bed. "Could you get me a drink as you're up?" Dean turned back around to his sleeping beauty. She still hadn't opened her eyes. He shook his head and stood up - every joint in his body aching from the moving of the furniture and general D.I.Y he'd been doing throughout the day.

"Jesus I ache," he moaned as he staggered his way to the doorway. He flipped the hallway light on via the switch on the wall just beyond where he was standing and reached for his dressing gown which was hanging on the back of the door. "Fucking freezing," he moaned to Jess - even though he could tell by her breathing that she was already asleep again. "I'm coming!" he called out to Sophie in the hope that his voice would soothe her enough to calm her crying. He walked down the hallway to his youngest daughter's room and leaned in, flicking the light switch on. Sophie was sitting up in bed, tears streaming down her face. Dean wished he could stop her night terrors. He wished he could take away the fear she felt during the nights. He guessed the sooner the better with regards to finding a professional. He walked over to the bed and sat on the edge of it. Sophie threw herself into his arms and held him tightly. She was shaking like a leaf - more so than he'd ever felt her shake before. In fact to his knowledge, she usually woke up screaming and that was it. She didn't usually shake. If she had – it certainly hadn't been enough for him to notice or remember. He gave her a squeeze, "Did you have the dream again?" he asked. She shook her head and moved away from her dad before looking towards the door. She was pale. Dean frowned and followed her gaze - unsure of what had got her attention. "What is it?" he asked.

"Someone was standing in the doorway. They woke me up."

"Your sister?"

Sophie shook her head.

"Are you sure? Your mum and I were asleep and there's no one else here."

"I thought it was you."

"Me? Not unless I sleep walk." Sophie wouldn't look away from the doorway. Perhaps she was scared that, if she did, the thing she saw would sneak up on her? "It was probably just a shadow," he tried to comfort her.

"It spoke to me!" she looked at her dad. Still shaking.

"It spoke to you? What did it say?"

She looked back to the clear doorway, "I thought it was you," she said. Her voice quivering. It shook its head and said no…" Dean could see how that would scare someone. If he woke up to such a sight, he was pretty sure he'd be just as freaked out. "And then it moved from the doorway."

"It did? Where did it go? Back towards your sister's room?" he couldn't help but feel the likely culprit was going to be Caroline. It wouldn't be the first time she'd played a prank on her sister. Admittedly it would have been the first time she had done such a thing during the night - especially at this time. He'd check on Caroline when he had settled Sophie. She shook her head. "Not towards your sister's room?" she shook her head again.

"That way!" she pointed out of the door. Dean followed her finger towards the empty bedroom across the landing. He felt a chill run through his body but did his best to hide it.

He turned back to her, "You were probably still asleep. Still dreaming... Just thought you were awake. There's no one else in the house. Just us. It probably just felt more real because the house feels strange to you at the moment but that will pass. First nights are always scary," he smiled at her; an act of reassurance. "When I first moved into our old house, with your mum...Do you want to hear something funny?" Sophie nodded. "I went to the toilet in a cupboard. I woke up during the night and thought I was in the bathroom. You know - your mummy teased me for a long time after that! And you know why I did it?" Sophie shook her head. "Because my brain was confused. Just as your brain is confused now."

"Can I sleep in your bed tonight?" she asked.

Dean nodded, "Just for tonight." He stood up, bent down and scooped her up in his arms before carrying her through to his own bedroom - getting her to shut the lights off as they passed the relevant switches. As he pushed his bedroom door shut - the door to the empty room closed too.

DAY TWO

Dean woke up and stretched his aching joints. With so much work to do he had hoped the aches would have gone by morning. No such luck. He rolled onto his side and noticed that both Jess and Sophie had already woken up and left the room - no doubt on quiet purposely to ensure they let Dean rest before he had to face what was to be another busy day. He rolled from the bed and had another stretch; a satisfying click from his back. He made his way through to the en-suite bathroom and caught a sight of himself in the mirror. He jumped.

"Christ. Looking old." He reached for his toothbrush and a near-empty tube of toothpaste. A gentle squeeze of the tube onto the brush and he began brushing his teeth - all the time looking at his reflection, haunted by how tired he looked. He couldn't help but feel that he should have left all the mirrors wrapped up in their blankets until after the move was finished. At least that way he'd have had a chance to make himself look a little better - with a bit of a rest - before having to see his aged reflection staring back at him. Might have taken the sting off a bit. He spat the toothpaste froth from his mouth to the sink and rinsed both his mouth and toothbrush off before putting the latter back in the glass holder. Back in the bedroom he put his dressing gown on and stepped onto the landing; any luck Jess still had some bacon left over from the other day. A nice sandwich to fix himself up for the day. "What are you doing?" he asked. No sooner had he stepped onto landing then he had spotted both Sophie and Caroline. They were standing at the other end of the landing. Both of them were staring into the empty bedroom. Neither of them were saying anything. "I said what are you doing?" Dean repeated himself.

They both jumped at the sound of Dean's voice. "Nothing!" said Caroline. She dragged her sister back towards her own room, "Come on!" Dean frowned and watched as they disappeared into Caroline's room. Caroline closed the door after a final glance back towards the empty bedroom. Dean hesitated a moment and then walked down the landing towards the second bedroom where he stopped in the doorway. He peered in and noticed that the contents of several cardboard boxes had been emptied onto the floor as though someone had been searching for something. He sighed and walked into the bedroom to get a closer look at what had been emptied on the floor; various compact discs - certainly nothing the girls should have been going through. He bent down and picked them up before dropping them into the open box, sighing as he did so. The empty boxes weren't the only thing he noticed either. The smell, which Jess had mentioned, hit him too. He looked towards the window and noticed it had been closed. "Thought she said she opened this," he muttered under his breath before opening it back up - as wide as it would permit. Satisfied, he walked back down the landing, towards Caroline's room, and opened the door after giving it a gentle knock. "What were you looking for?" he asked.

"Nothing," Caroline piped up from where she was playing on the floor with her sister. Both had small dolls in their hands.

"So why did you empty the box out? You must have been looking for something."

"It wasn't us."

"I saw you standing there."

"We didn't touch the box!" Caroline argued.

"Then who did?" Dean guessed it could have been Jess but - had it been so - why were the girls standing there acting suspiciously? More likely he had walked out of his room and caught them doing something they knew they shouldn't have been doing in the first place.

"Maybe it was the person from last night!" Sophie suggested.

"Honey - we spoke about this - there wasn't anyone standing in your doorway last night. You were dreaming."

"No I wasn't. I watched them go into that room. Maybe they went through the box?"

Dean sighed. Obviously neither of them were going to tell him the truth he sought. "Look - just stay out of the room, okay?"

"Okay daddy," they both agreed.

"Good," he said - if only because he couldn't think of anything else to say to them. He pulled the door shut and headed off down the stairs, to the kitchen, where he could hear Jess banging around as she put various pots and pans in their new homes. "Did you go through the CDs this morning?" he asked.

"Oh. Good morning. How are you? Yes. I'm well thank you…." Jess said sarcastically.

"Sorry. Good morning. How are you?" he asked. He leant in and gave her a kiss on the cheek.

"What CDs?" Jess asked.

"There's a box in the spare room - been emptied out onto the floor. The girls were standing in the doorway, looking in, so I thought it was them but neither one admitted to it. Did you go in there?"

Jess shook her head as she put a saucepan into the cupboard, "I've been sorting out the kitchen," she said as she put a frying pan up into the same cupboard. "Nearly done too!" she pointed out.

"Well if it wasn't you and it wasn't them…"

"It probably was one of them. You know they'll say anything to get themselves out of trouble."

"I guess."

Jess sensed her husband seemed a little apprehensive about something, "What's the matter?" she asked.

"Last night…Never mind." Dean stopped talking. After the conversation they had had, before going to sleep, he thought it best not to mention anything to do with what Sophie thought she saw during the night.

"No. You don't do that," Jess told him. "Last night - what?"

"It doesn't matter!"

"Tell me!"

He sighed when he realised Jess wasn't going to let it go, "Sophie said she saw someone standing in her doorway. Said they disappeared into the spare room. That's why she was crying during the night - it scared her."

"What?" Jess seemed alarmed. The funny smell in the room had reminded her of what'd happened in the room and she was already on edge about it. The thought of her daughter seeing things - especially things disappearing into the same room - just made her that little bit more nervous.

"It's fine," Dean reassured her, "I told her she was probably still dreaming. It's just a coincidence."

"That's a hell of a coincidence, don't you think?"

"Honey, it's fine. I promise. Have you never woken up before now and been in a confused state between awake and dreaming?"

"Funnily enough - no."

Dean sighed again. "It's fine."

"Stop saying it's fine. Our daughter saw someone in the house last night. Someone who supposedly died here when they took their own life."

"No. Our daughter thought she saw a person here. She didn't say whether it was male or female because she couldn't see them properly. Besides - for all we know it could have been Caroline looking for the toilet. Got up in the middle of the night, got confused and wandered into the spare room. Remember that time, in our last flat, when I..."

"Did you ask Caroline?" Jess interrupted him. "Did you ask her whether she got up during the night?"

Dean felt a temptation to lie; a little white lie to rest his wife's nervous mind. He resisted, "No. I haven't spoken to her."

"Maybe we should get someone to come by and give the house a blessing," Jess' mind drifted.

"I'm sorry - what? Someone to give the house a blessing? Seriously?"

"You know, like an exorcist."

"An exorcist? Do they even really exist?"

"Our daughter thinks she is seeing ghosts - what harm will it do?"

"A lot when we have to explain to the children why we have some fucking nut walking around chanting whatever they chant in each of our rooms. Look - it was a dream. She thought she was awake but she was clearly still dreaming. You know what she's like with her dreams. And the smell - I was just in the room - it's damp. Nothing more and nothing less. It will go. I opened the window again…"

"The window was open. I opened it last night." Jess looked alarmed again.

Dean was quick to stop that conversation from spiralling into anything more to do with restless spirits, "Then one of the girls must have closed it when they were going through the boxes…Jesus - I wish I had never said anything about any of it. This is ridiculous."

"Oh so now I'm being ridiculous?" Jess snapped at her suffering husband. Clearly she was still tired from the previous day's move and unpacking. They both were.

Dean looked at her, "I didn't say you were ridiculous. I said THIS was ridiculous. We're supposed to be enjoying our new home together - you know, making happy memories - and instead we're talking about the possibility of ghosts and calling in the ghostbusters. It's stupid. We're both tired, both irritable - let's just…Let's just start the morning again." To emphasise his point he walked from the room before turning back in again, "Good morning, sexy lady…How did you sleep last night?" he gave her a cheeky wink and a smile.

"Funny you should ask, darling, but I had a somewhat restless night. What with the ghosts and all…"

Dean sighed.

⅄

Jess had been unpacking the kitchen for the whole morning - more specifically putting the things away in their new homes dotted throughout the various cupboards, having done the actual unpacking the previous day. Dean had left her to it and concentrated on making the living room more of a 'homely' environment by clearing the boxes away - giving them all somewhere pleasant to rest at the end of another day of clearing up; it was hard to rest in a room when you were surrounded by boxes of all shapes and sizes which you knew needed to be put away at some point. At least this way they could come into the room and put their feet up after closing the door to the rest of the mess. Out of sight out of mind - which is exactly what the children were. They had come downstairs and started playing amongst the boxes, after breakfast, but Dean sent them up to their bedrooms to play out of the way. All the time he was trying to move around them, he couldn't help but think they'd missed a trick by moving with the girls still quite young. Had he waited a few more years until they were grumpy teenagers he could have trusted them to help unpack the boxes without damaging any of the contents.

Jess walked into the living room, "How are you doing in here?" she asked. She looked around the room. Nearly all of the boxes were gone - but she expected as much considering a fair few of them had been stacked outside of the living room, in the hallway. Most things were sitting around on the shelving units.

"Nearly done," he said.

"You're actually putting things up on display already?" Jess asked. Dean fired her a look. He was tired and irritable from the second night's broken sleep in a row and already knew where she was going with her sentences. "I hadn't cleaned them yet," she reminded him. And there it was. Just as he expected.

"There's no point in cleaning before we unpack everything," he told her.

"Everything is dusty though," and it was. The shelves had a thin layer of dust on them which matched the cupboards in the kitchen - which she was disinfecting prior to loading up with various appliances.

"And the more we unpack, the more mess we will make. We can blitz everywhere when everything is in its rightful place," he told her. "Otherwise we'll spend loads of time cleaning now and then more time cleaning when we're done." What Dean suggested made sense to him but he knew it would annoy the hell out of Jess who liked everything to be just so. He was more interested in unpacking as quickly as possible, though, to ensure he had at least a couple of days in which to relax before going back to the office. Jess was just looking at him. They both knew, as soon as his back was turned, she was going to dust the shelves down and give the carpet a hoover.

Jess changed the subject, "What's going on with the boxes out here?" she asked.

"More old records. We never listen to them so I was going to put them in the loft until we do a car boot sale, or something."

"A car boot sale? You?"

"Okay - until we eBay them," he admitted. Neither of them knew of a time where they'd ever done, or visited, a car boot sale. "I just don't think we need them cluttering the room." To his surprise, Jess nodded in agreement. The way the day was shaping up - he was sure she was going to argue with him about that too. When people say moving was stressful they were wrong, Dean realised that now. It wasn't the move that was stressful but rather the frayed tempers of the tired individuals clashing over the silly little things (such as dusting before you have completely finished unpacking). "I'm more or less done in here," he said, "so I'll take them upstairs now to get them out of the way. Probably stick them in the loft tomorrow, or something."

Jess nodded again, "In that case - I'll probably just give this room a quick clean…"

Dean rolled his eyes.

Night Two

Despite the moving boxes and general mess, the house had a different vibe about it during the lighter hours. It seemed homely, warm and welcoming. But by nightfall it seemed to change. Everything became darker and not just in general lighting conditions but (and it's hard to explain) the feeling of the home. The mood seemed to blacken as the shadows slowly crept across the rooms with the sinking sun, both Dean and Jess had noticed it though neither would admit it to the other. They both snuggled down under the thick duvet. Both shattered from another hard day of unpacking and lugging furniture around. On the plus side most of the unpacking had been completed now and the house was - slowly - starting to look like a proper home to be proud of. The spare room still needed to be set up and the boxes, filled with the goods not needed, had been moved to the top of the landing, just underneath the hatchway to the loft, ready to be put amongst the rafters the following morning.

"Can we never move house again?" Jess breathed heavily as she laid her head back on the soft pillow. "I'm so tired." She closed her eyes. "So tired." She didn't need to say as much. Dean knew she was tired from the way she had snapped at him throughout the day. She fidgeted onto her side and cuddled up against Dean who was lying on his back - staring at the ceiling. "I'm sorry if I was horrible to you today."

"You were fine," Dean lied. There was no sense in starting a fight with her when he wanted to go to sleep. He knew she wasn't snapping at him because she didn't love him or because she was angry with him. She was just exhausted - emphasised by the fact she was already breathing heavily; a sign she was about to fall asleep, if not already dreaming. Dean couldn't help but think of Sophie in the other room though, wondering whether he'd have another disturbed night's sleep. He hoped not. Just one night of unbroken sleep. That's all he wanted. One night. He felt his eyelids grow heavy.

Despite the family sleeping off their busy day, the house didn't fall silent. Water pipes from the attic space banged together; caused by a worn seal on a faucet valve. The television, recently unwrapped from a bundle of blankets in the living room, occasionally creaked for no reason. A dripping noise constantly tapped the sink in the kitchen - another issue with a faulty seal which would be easily fixed when the family had the time to do so. Worst of the noises though was the one which started half way through the night when the family was in a deep sleep. The sound of the floorboards creaking underfoot and then…

3:30am

The sound of the door to the spare room closing and - finally - the sound of deafening silence.

DAY THREE

J ess opened her eyes and blinked the early morning fog from her vision. A loud banging, which seemed to come in threes, had awoken her. She sat up; at first unsure whether she had even heard it or whether she'd imagined it. When the banging echoed through the house another three times she jumped from the bed and hurried to the door to see what on earth was going on. Dean was standing on a two-step ladder underneath the loft hatch - a broom in his hands. He reached up and used the end of the broom to hit the loft hatch another three times. His two daughters standing next to him, watching intently.

"What the hell are you doing?" Jess asked. It hadn't been the best way to wake up in all honesty.

Dean stopped what he was doing and looked across to where she was standing, "I'm sorry. Did I wake you?" he asked.

"Did you wake me? It's echoing through the whole house!" Jess said. She didn't believe Dean didn't realise the noise he was making and didn't wait for another apology. She turned back into the bedroom and slammed the door shut.

"Whoops! Looks like daddy is in trouble, girls!" Dean laughed.

They didn't care. Both of them were completely fixated by the hatch to the attic. "Hurry up and open it, daddy!" Caroline moaned, eager to see what was in the attic even though Dean had told her it was most likely empty and - more importantly - she wasn't going up there regardless. Dean gave the hatch another three, solid hits with the broom.

"It won't open," he told her, "it's stuck fast." He jumped down from the steps and threw the broom onto the floor. "Shit!" he said under his breath.

"Daddy!" Sophie berated him for his bad language but he didn't pay any attention. He was frustrated by the stuck hatch.

He walked through to the bedroom where Jess had climbed back into bed. He stood at the foot of the bed until she looked at him, "Thanks for waking me up," she told him again.

"I'm sorry. I didn't mean to. It was an accident." He hesitated. "I'm trying to get the stuff put away. So we can relax..."

"I was relaxing. I was asleep!"

Dean continued, "Damned thing won't budge. Should have asked the estate agent to let us see up there before signing anything."

"It's stuck?"

"I've been hitting the hatch..."

"I heard."

"...and it won't even give a little. It's either stuck or something has fallen on top of it. Something heavy. God only knows how I'm going to get up there," he sat on the edge of the bed. "Fucking annoying."

Jess sat up. Clearly she wasn't going back to sleep. "What are you going to do?"

"Have to buy a ladder."

"I thought the estate agent said there was a ladder in the loft - one which came down when you opened the hatch?"

"Yep. But how do you propose I get to it if I can't open the hatch? Need to get up there so I can try and put more weight against it and - to do that - I need a longer ladder. Those steps are good for changing lightbulbs and that's about it," he moaned. "Means I can't put the boxes away just yet. Probably be a couple of days."

"It's fine but promise me one thing?"

"What's that?"

"When you do put the boxes up there, can you at least wait until I am awake?"

Dean smiled at her, "Can't make any promises. And - I know you won't believe me - I was trying to be quiet. I wanted it all done before you woke up. Clearly I'm a failure."

"Hmmm, I still love you though."

"Yeah but I love you more. Hence I was trying to do something nice for you."

"No, you don't."

"What you think you love me more?" he asked, a cheeky grin on his face. "Prove it!"

Jess raised an eyebrow and smiled at him. She knew what he was hinting towards. "You'd better shut the door then," she nodded towards the bedroom door, "don't want the kids coming in."

"Well I'm not sure what you're thinking but," he laughed, "I was after a bacon sandwich." Jess opened her mouth - an over exaggerated gesture to show her shock at having her advances turned down. Dean laughed again as she gave him a playful hit on the arm. "And can you make it crispy, please?"

"You're such an asshole!" she laughed.

Sophie called from the doorway, "Mummy! You're not allowed to swear!"

"Yeah, mummy, you're not allowed to swear!" Dean laughed again. "No wonder we're raising little monkeys. Practically dragging them up!" He jumped back when Jess took another playful swing at his arm.

"I'm sorry," she said to her daughter, despite the smile on her face showing she wasn't actually sorry at all. "Anyway he called you a monkey! Doesn't he get in trouble?"

"I'm hungry!" Sophie changed the subject; her voice having gone from stern to whiney within the blink of an eye.

"Yeah, mummy, she's hungry. She wants bacon too, don't you sweetie?" Dean adopted the same tone of whiney voice as his daughter. He looked at her, having asked the question, and she nodded.

"I swear I'm going to beat you black and blue," Jess laughed.

"Did you hear that? Your mummy wants to hurt me!" Dean tried to get Sophie on side.

"Can you do it after you've made me breakfast?" Sophie asked. Jess laughed. Clearly breakfast was more important than her father's health.

A bang from the landing made all of them jump. Dean was first out of the bedroom (despite Sophie being closest). Caroline was standing on the small step ladder and attempting to copy what her father had been doing.

"What the hell are you doing?" he shouted. "Get down from there!" She wasn't that high up - where she was standing on the step - but, by the time you factored in the fact it was more than possible to fall over the bannister from where she was, it was enough to panic a parent. Caroline got down from the step ladder.

"I was trying to help!" she argued - she started to cry; the sound of her father's harsh voice startled her.

Dean picked the step ladder up and walked through to the spare room with it where he dumped it against the far wall. Jess walked in after him. "She was trying to help, you can't be angry with her for copying what you were doing." She paused, "Jesus - it still stinks in here. You still think that's just damp?"

Dean sighed. "How's about we go for a walk?" he suggested.

"What?"

He called out to the girls, on the landing, "Who wants to grab some breakfast and then go exploring outside?"

Sophie cheered at the suggestion - as did her sister, albeit a little quieter.

Dean turned to Jess, "Let's take a break today. We're doing well with the unpacking. Let's just go for a walk and take a look around the place. I'll pop to town tomorrow and get a ladder. We've worked hard these past couple of days, I think a few hours off will do us good." They'd seen the front of the house when they came to look around it, before making their purchase, but they'd never actually taken the time to look around out back; certainly no further than seeing that it backed onto fields and trees anyway. Jess nodded - happy to go along with his plan. He smiled. Not only did he get out of doing some more work but he also successfully avoided any further conversation about the lingering stench in the room.

Dean and Jess were walking through a small wooded area just behind the house. The pair of them holding hands as though they didn't have a care in the world. The two girls running ahead of them, laughing and smiling. A picture perfect happy family out enjoying the early morning hazy sunshine. On the surface at least. Dean and Jess were both aware the other had been silent for a while now; both aware they were lost in their own thoughts.

"Pretty, isn't it?" Jess was the first to break the silence between the two. She was looking back at their house not too far in the distance, the fields around it - lush green grass (some patches in need of a cut already) and tall, tall trees which seemingly reached to the few white clouds above.

Dean followed her gaze and nodded, "That it is." He turned around to her and smiled, "And it's ours." To his surprise, Jess didn't smile back at him. "What's wrong?" he asked. He already knew. She was thinking about the room. In particular she was thinking about what had happened in the room; the lonely wife who'd taken her own life.

"Do you think we've made a mistake?" she asked, after a couple of seconds hesitation.

"A mistake?"

"Moving here. Do you think it was a mistake." She was looking back towards the house. Dean paid more attention to her eyes. She was looking at the back upstairs window; the spare room.

"Turn around," he told her. "Look." He pointed towards the girls who were picking wild flowers just beyond a row of trees. Both of them were smiling. "See that? That's the start of happy memories in our new family home…Do I think we made a mistake? No. Not a chance. I think we made the best decision of recent years and we need to forget about what happened in that house, just as we spoke about the other night and just as we talked about before we even put in an offer. If we keep dwelling on the past - their past - it will drag us down. Don't know about you but I don't want that. Do you?"

Jess shook her head. "I'm just having trouble settling in," she said in a hushed tone.

"It will become easier - especially when all the moving boxes are disposed of." He gave her a reassuring smile, "Trust me - it will be good. No. It will be great." He pulled her close and gave her a hug.

The sound of Sophie approaching made them pull apart. They half expected her to join in but she didn't. She pointed back to the house. "Who's that?" she asked. Her mum and dad turned back to the house quickly, in the direction Sophie was pointing.

"Who?" Dean asked. He was scanning the back of the house but couldn't see anything.

"They were in the window," Sophie said, "but they've gone now."

Dean called Caroline over from the wild flowers she was still picking from, "Caroline, come on, we're going home now!" She went to say something in protest but Dean had already turned his back and started to hastily walk back to the house. The girls followed - although Jess purposefully hung back a little; not because she was scared (although a part of her was) at the prospect of someone being the house but more so because she wanted to protect her children from whoever it could have been.

"Wait here," Dean told his ladies when he got to the back door. He stepped in, purposefully leaving the door open, "I'll go and take a look around." As he walked past the kitchen work-top he grabbed a knife from the draining board and took it with him. He hadn't seen anyone in the house, only Sophie had, but that didn't mean he did not want to be prepared for bumping into a possible intruder.

"Why do we have to wait here?" Sophie asked her mother.

"Because your father asked you to," was the easiest answer for Jess. The girls rarely argued with their father. In part this annoyed Jess a little as they tended to be argumentative with her but, flip side of the coin, it meant she was able to turn around and use the threat of telling their father if they were up to no good. It certainly tended to do the job of keeping them in line.

"I need the loo," Caroline whined. She didn't need the toilet, Jess knew this, she just didn't want to stand around outside when she believed something far more exciting was happening in the house. Had Jess let her go in, to use the bathroom, Caroline would have run straight past it and headed to her dad.

"Well you'll have to wait a minute," Jess told her. Her voice clearly told both daughters that she wasn't in the mood for any nonsense. Caroline tutted but - other than that - didn't say anything.

After what seemed like an eternity Dean re-appeared at the bottom of the stairs. Jess watched as he walked down the hallway and into the kitchen. He put the knife back on the side and shrugged - a sign to Jess that the house was empty. She didn't breathe a sigh of relief though. The fact of the matter remained that someone had hanged themselves in the property and, on two occasions now, Sophie had thought she'd seen someone that shouldn't have been there.

Night Three

Jess and Dean were lying in bed together. The room was illuminated by two lamps on the bedside cabinets which sat either side of the bed. Neither of them had been able to sleep despite their obvious exhaustion; both of them pre-occupied with thoughts of the house and their youngest daughter.

"I'm worried about Sophie," Jess said, "I think we need to take her to a specialist." It hadn't been the first time they had discussed the prospect of taking her to see someone. Dean had admitted it would be a good idea, once they were settled into the new home, to try and find her some help with regards to the dreams she was having. Now Sophie was seeing things when she was awake, Dean felt the same as Jess; waiting may no longer be an option. Especially given the things she was supposedly seeing was fuelling the paranoia both parents were feeling about living in a property where someone had taken their own life for whatever reason. Jess was aware Dean hadn't responded to her so asked him directly, "What do you think?"

He hesitated - not because he didn't agree but because he felt as though he was failing his youngest daughter. If she was having issues, whether they be bad dreams or the belief she was seeing things, as her father he felt he should have been able to make things better for her. He should have been able to fix her. "I think we might need to," he reluctantly agreed. It would have been easier to ignore it had Caroline, or even Jess and Dean, seen a figure in the house too but they hadn't. It was only ever Sophie and that, on top of the bad dreams she regularly had, suggested she clearly needed a little help. Jess felt relieved. She thought he'd have been too proud to go along with it. Too afraid to put his hand up and admit he (they) needed help. "The Internet is being set up in a couple of days," he continued, "we can search around for someone as soon as it's plugged in."

Jess started to cry. "I'm sorry. Ignore me. I'm being stupid. Just tired."

"It's fine." Dean moved over and pulled Jess towards him. He held her tightly against his body. "Give it a few months and we'll both look back at this and laugh." Jess didn't reply. She snuggled in close to her husband. Dean was glad she moved closer to him as it helped to hide his face; the doubtful expression. He wanted everything to be okay and - deep down - he was sure that would be the case. At the moment he was struggling to see the light. They both fell into a comfortable silence as their brains continued to work scenarios through whilst they waited for sleep to take hold of them.

⅄

3:30am

Caroline stirred from her sleep and jumped when she opened her eyes and saw Sophie standing at the foot of her bed, "What are you doing?" she asked.

"I can't sleep," she moaned. "Can I come in with you?"

"What? No. Go away."

"Please! I'm scared!"

"Go away!" Caroline hissed. Sophie didn't move. She was standing there - a look on her face which gave all signs that she was about to cry. Caroline realised she wasn't going anywhere and sat up, "Go back to your room."

"I want to sleep in your bed!"

"There's no room! Go away!"

"Please?"

"No!"

Sophie reluctantly walked from the bedroom before her sister started shouting at her. She didn't go back to her own room though. She just stopped there, outside her sister's bedroom door, staring ahead towards the other end of the landing; towards the spare bedroom's door in particular.

"Leave me alone," a voice hissed at her from within the darkened room. Slowly, the door closed. Sophie ran back to her own bedroom and dove underneath the covers.

Day Four

Dean dressed himself after his warm shower and left the bedroom. Immediately he noticed Jess across the landing in Sophie's bedroom. She was ripping the sheets from her bed. Sophie was standing nearby - a sheepish look on her face. When Dean walked into the room he noticed Sophie had been crying. Jess looked angry.

"What's going on?" he asked.

"We had a little accident during the night," Jess said. Dean looked at Sophie who - in turn - did all she could to avoid his gaze. "Didn't we?" Jess turned to Sophie. Again, Sophie avoided her eye line.

"What happened?" Dean asked Sophie directly. She hadn't had an accident for as long as he could remember - certainly more than a few years anyway. Sophie didn't look at him; still too embarrassed. "Hey!" he gave her a playful nudge. He wasn't angry that she'd wet the bed (unlike Jess apparently), after all accidents happen. "What happened?" he asked her again when she finally looked at him.

Jess butted in, "She got scared during the night and didn't want to get out of bed." Jess threw the last of the sheets onto the pile on the floor.

"You were scared?" Dean asked. "What were you scared of?"

"I had a bad dream," Sophie lied. Sophie was a sensitive girl and could pick up on moods in the house. The mood she'd recently picked up on was one of stress and frustration from her parents and she felt that she'd only be making it worse if she told them she didn't like the house; how the house scared her.

"Another one?" Dean asked. "What happened?"

"I don't want to talk about it!" Sophie said.

"Okay, that's okay, you don't have to if you don't want to. That's fine." Dean turned to Jess as she scooped up the dirty laundry. "Where's Caroline?"

"Well she's in her room," Jess hissed as she walked out of the room and started down the stairs.

Dean frowned and followed her (to the top of the stairs at least). "Why did you say it like that?" he asked. "What's she done?"

"Your youngest daughter went into Caroline's room during the night because she was scared and your eldest daughter turned her away." Jess disappeared down the hallway and towards the kitchen.

Dean sighed. It was always 'his' daughter when one of them had done something wrong. When they were good - it was 'their' daughter. Something bad - 'his' daughter. He turned back to Sophie who was still standing next to her stripped bed looking sorry for herself. "What was your dream about last night?" Dean pressed her once more.

"I don't want to talk about it!" Sophie repeated herself.

Dean nodded, "Okay. Well. Not sure if I ever told you this but - did you know dreams often work in reverse; so you think something bad is going to happen but - in reality - something good actually happens." Sophie looked at him as though she knew he was lying. Truth be told, Dean didn't know if he was lying or not. It was something his mother had told him when he was growing up; not that he had many bad dreams as a youngster. "As for the bed," he changed the subject before she questioned his logic, "don't be embarrassed. At least you just had an accident. Remember what I told you? I actually went to the toilet in a cupboard by mistake! That was something to be embarrassed about."

Sophie laughed.

"Right - get dressed - you can help me in the spare room today," Dean gave Sophie a pat on the head and turned back to the door.

"No!" Sophie screamed out.

Dean turned back to her - shocked by her outburst, "I beg your pardon?"

"I don't want to go in there!" she started to cry. "We're not allowed in there!" she shouted. Dean closed the bedroom door so they wouldn't be interrupted by Jess, or Caroline if she dared leave her own room.

"Who said you aren't allowed in there?" Dean asked. He knelt down so he was level with Sophie. "Your sister?" Sophie shook her head. "Then who?" He realised Sophie wasn't going to tell him. "This is your house," he said, "and there are no rooms which are off limits to you or your sister. Come on," he took her hand, "come with me." He walked with her out of the bedroom and towards the spare room. Sophie pulled herself from his grip and ran back towards the door of her own room. Dean just stood there a moment, confused by her reaction. "Sophie - really, it's fine... Look!" he turned back to the spare room and opened the door. The first thing that hit him was the smell in the room. The second was that - once again - various boxes had been unpacked and their contents spread across the floor. "What the hell?" A door slammed behind him and made him jump. He turned around and saw Sophie had hidden in her room again, closing the door behind her. He looked back to the mess in the spare room (one of the last rooms to unpack) and wondered whether she had taken everything from the box. She knew she had been naughty (because of the mess) and then had the accident during the night whilst she lay awake fretting about it, instead of actually putting the stuff back where she originally found it. Certainly a better thought than thinking she was too scared to go to the bathroom and so wet herself. And most definitely a better thought than the belief the house was being haunted by a lonely woman. He walked into the bedroom to see what had been moved this time and noticed the window had - again - been shut. Makes sense, if it was her moving all these bits and pieces around, it's a fair assumption to say she could have been cold, what with it being the middle of the night (or later). He reached across and opened the window once more.

"What's all the commotion?" on edge, the sound of Jess' voice made Dean jump. He turned to her and noticed she was standing in the doorway. She had heard the slamming of the door.

Dean pointed towards the mess, "This. I think I know why our daughter was scared to go to the bathroom last night. I reckon she was up, rooting around in here, and then started to worry what we'd say when we woke up."

"That doesn't make any sense," Jess said.

"Do you have another suggestion as to how these things got emptied onto the floor and the window closed then?" Dean asked.

"Maybe…"

"Don't say it." He knew what she was going to suggest; perhaps the window was closed, and boxes emptied, by a wandering spirit.

"It would make sense! Sophie thought she saw someone in the house, woke up the other night to the sight of someone, it's not the first time the boxes have been emptied in here and we already know that someone hung themselves in this very room!"

"Okay - yes - we know someone killed themselves but, come on, a ghost? Have you heard yourself? And putting that to one side - the common denominator in everything you just said is 'Sophie'. Sophie saw this, Sophie saw that…I think she is going through a difficult time at the moment and she needs help. Professional help that we're unable to offer her."

"And what if they say she is fine? What then? Will you even consider the possibility that there could be something left behind in this house?"

Dean didn't answer her immediately. He didn't know what to say. If the girls hadn't emptied the boxes - and it wasn't Jess or him - it didn't really leave a lot of other scenarios to explain it as much as he hated the thought of something more sinister. "I'm going to finish this room today. And when I go to town to pick up a decent ladder, I'm going to buy a load of plug-in air fresheners. By the end of the week - latest - what happened in this room will be nothing but a distant memory and even that will come to fade." He started picking their scattered belongings up before dropping them back into the boxes (in no particular order). Jess stood there a moment without knowing what to do or say for the best. She could see Dean was getting stressed with the whole situation; his tormented daughter, and what had happened in the room.

"I'm sorry," she said eventually, "I didn't mean to upset you."

Dean stopped what he was doing and straightened his back. He turned back to his wife and forced a smile, "I'm not angry with you I just wanted everything to go smoothly. This was supposed to be a great step for our family, the start of more adventures together and instead it's…Well…It's shit, isn't it? Our daughter could be nuts…"

"Don't say that."

"…And if she isn't nuts then we're most likely getting haunted by a fucking ghost. I'm not being funny but neither scenario is exactly an example of what one would call smooth running." He felt himself getting worked up again and stopped. He took a few deep breaths, "Shit."

It was Jess' turn to reassure him. She didn't think anything was going smoothly at all, in fact she wished the sale had fallen through and they'd been forced to look elsewhere for their new home but - seeing Dean's level of stress - she knew she couldn't agree with him or else it would just keep escalating and, from there, it wouldn't be long before they'd both be shouting at each other. "It'll be fine," she told him. "You said as soon as the Internet is installed we can start looking for some help for Sophie. And last night, I'm sure the bed wetting was just a one off. It was an accident. These things happen from time to time. She just needs time to adjust to the new environment. It's strange for adults. Imagine what it is like for children! And - as you said again - once this room has been set up into how we want it…The memories of what happened here will fade." She walked over to him and put her arms around him. It took a couple of seconds until he gave in and put his arms around her too. "As you said - it'll be good here. A nice family home." She smiled at Dean, hoping her words had made him feel a little better about the situation. He smiled back but each passing day, the more they experienced strange things, the less he believed the words she had said (and the words he'd previously said too).

He broke her grip and pulled away. "I don't even know where to start in here!" he said - trying his best to act 'normal'. There were boxes all around the room with very little with regards to built in storage space; just a single, narrow cupboard in the corner of the room. Dean walked over to the cupboard and opened it; empty. Plenty of room. "Probably just dump what I can in here," he said.

Jess knew he was trying to act as normal as he could; a way of distracting himself from the various frustrations. She played along. "Do you have to?" she asked.

"Yeah look…" Dean started shifting the boxes from the room and into the cupboard - stacking them as high as he could, "Look at that, much better in here already," he teased her. If anything, teasing Jess was the best way of making things appear more normal. Previously - before the move - there hadn't been a day go past without a gentle bit of teasing here and there. Jess didn't mind. She knew it was his way of showing he loved her. Jess had a thing for cluttered cupboards and wardrobes. Nothing annoyed her more than opening a door just to have the contents spill out across the floor because someone was too lazy to put them in place properly and Dean knew this - hence the gentle teasing. He wasn't going to leave the boxes in the cupboard, he was going to empty them and find proper homes for the contents. But, for now, it gave him room to move about a bit without constantly bumping into things. When the cupboard was full, he closed the door. "See - perfect!" he said. There were still a few boxes on the floor but not nearly as many as there had been. "Now - we just need to never open this cupboard again, okay?"

"You're funny."

He smiled at her. Already he was starting to feel better. They both were.

"So what do you want to use this room for?" he asked. "Study? Playroom for the girls? Generic spare room what posh folk, like you and me are, tend to have?"

"Generic spare room what posh folk tend to have? Not the best use of English right there, honey. How about a nursery?"

Dean coughed, "Now who's being funny?" He changed the subject, "Right - I best get to town and see about getting a ladder. If you have any serious thoughts about what you'd like to do in this room - you can let me know when I get back…" He started to make his way out of the room and towards the top of the stairs.

Jess followed, "I was being serious actually. What about it?"

Dean stopped at the top of the stairs and turned to her, "You're serious? You want…" he looked around to see if the children were within ear shot before whispering, "another baby?"

Before Jess could answer a loud bang and crash came from the spare room. Loud enough to make them both jump. Dean frowned and walked back into the room, passing by Jess in the process. Again, she followed a few steps behind. The cupboard door in the spare room had opened and the boxes had toppled out across the floor.

"Shit!" Dean muttered.

"So who do we blame for this? The ghost or your dodgy stacking skills?"

Dean gave her a look; a simple look which seemed to simply say 'fuck you'. He smiled and walked from the room, "I'm going to town," he said.

Jess hurried after him, "And when you get back we can continue our conversation," she said, smiling. Dean looked at her from the bottom of the stairs. A look of disbelief on his face. Of all the things Jess could have said, that was probably the last thing he expected to hear. "What are you looking at me like that for?" she asked.

Dean smiled, "You never fail to surprise me," he said. He crossed to the front door stepping into his shoes on the way.

"Surely that can't be a bad thing," Jess said as she followed him towards the front door. Dean opened the door, turned around and kissed Jess goodbye.

"We'll talk," he said - still unsure whether she was even being serious.

Sophie slowly opened the door to her room, soothed by the voices of her mother and father. Her eyes were drawn to the spare room. The open cupboard. She watched, wide-eyed, as a hand reached out of the cupboard and shut the door. Sophie slammed her door again and dove back onto her bed, hiding under the duvet.

Day Five

When Dean pulled into the driveway, the car was crammed with bits he hadn't actually intended to buy. He had the ladder, which was an intended purchase, laid out across the back seats of the vehicle (only just fitting) but the boot was also full of goods; paint in particular. A shade of magnolia with which to decorate the spare bedroom. It was not something that had previously been discussed between himself and Jess - he just bought it on a whim when he walked down the aisle in his quest for the ladder. The house was fairly neutral with its colourings and it looked as though it must have had a fresh coat in recent months. Perhaps after the original owner decided to sell up? Dean certainly didn't feel as though the house actually needed decorating at this stage but, at the same time, he figured it might be a good idea to put their own stamp on the spare room at least. Make the room their own. Help eradicate the past memories from the house. He figured it would help bring the girls closer together too. Since moving into the home they seemed to be growing further and further apart. He figured that maybe it was something to do with them no longer sharing a bedroom. Give the girls a paint brush and let them paint on the walls - the only time in their young lives when he'd make such an offer - before he and Jess went over it properly. He knew it would also encourage Sophie into the room; help her see that she was allowed in there and that whoever had told her to stay out was wrong to do so. That comment had irritated him for most of the day. He couldn't understand who would have told her she wasn't allowed in the room. Jess wouldn't have cared if she was in there or not, he certainly didn't and - no matter how hard he tried - he couldn't picture Caroline saying she wasn't allowed to venture in either. In the end he put it down to being in her head. She was a sensitive girl so maybe she was picking up on the bad vibes both he and Jess had about the room. He'd made a mental note to himself to have a word with his wife when he got home. They would both need to be more careful with regards to what they said in front of their daughters.

Jess had come out of the house and helped him unpack the car when she heard him pull into the driveway. They'd carried the ladder up to the top of the stairs, where they laid it flat across the landing floor (and told the girls not to touch it) and they'd carried the paint through to the spare room where they'd stacked it up against the wall - Jess very much in control of the stacking after the incident with Dean's packing of the boxes into the cupboard earlier in the morning.

Jess smiled when she initially saw the paint. She knew Dean hated decorating - which in turn meant she knew she'd be doing most of it - but it was the fact he had bought it which made her happy. Clearly he was thinking of the family when he did so; an effort to try and make them feel more at home. She also liked the idea of disguising what had happened in the room by putting her own mark on it. She just wished she had been consulted as to the colours purchased. Magnolia was safe. Magnolia was boring. She would have liked to paint it a funky lilac colour, or something similar - which Dean would never have bought without being told to do so. Men just don't choose colours very well - it needs a woman's keen eye. She did not mention this to Dean when she saw the colour of the paint. She just smiled and thanked him. No sense rocking the boat. He was obviously quick to temper at the moment and that would have only annoyed him; the fact he'd tried to do something nice just to have her moan at him for his colour choices. Magnolia for now and then - in a year or two when they came to decorate the rest of the room - she'd choose something a little…brighter.

With the ladder on the landing and the paint neatly stacked in the corner of the spare room - Jess had asked Dean where he wanted to start. He had told her he wanted to start on the sofa with his favourite ladies and a hot cup of tea - perhaps, even, a chocolate digestive biscuit or two to dunk into his drink. She knew - at that point - he had no intention of doing more work that day. Not that she minded. They'd all had a crappy morning so it was probably a good idea to bring the family together and relax for what remained of the afternoon. Especially given the fact the girls had both been in their own rooms not speaking to each other and playing on their own.

By the time Dean had returned home on the previous day it had gotten so late that he wanted nothing more than to crash in front of the television with his wife and children - a Disney cartoon playing through on the blu-ray player. It was moments like this he cherished; all of them together and the sounds of the girls laughing at the antics of some cartoon character they had grown to love. In this instance the character in question was Olaf from 'Frozen' - one of the few cartoons Dean didn't actually mind watching repeatedly although he did wish he could skip through the songs. He wished, even more, that his daughters didn't feel the need to keep singing them out loud for the following week. By the time they had stopped singing them, they were ready to watch the film again and so the process repeated itself.

The rest of the day and early evening had very much been what some would consider as a lazy day. They watched 'Frozen' (Sophie wanted to put it on for a second time), they'd had dinner, they'd played a game or two of Operation - a kids' game which featured the picture of a man on an operating table. On various points of the picture there were holes and - in those holes - there were different shaped pieces which represented the man's internal organs. The game was simple enough - you had a pair of tweezers and each player took it in turn to remove one of the man's organs. If you weren't careful the man would make a buzzing noise and his nose would light up. When Dean first played the game, when they bought it for the girls last Christmas, he'd said it would have been a better game if the had tweezers emitted an electric shock if you weren't careful enough. A point Jess disagreed with.

At the end of the day the girls were bathed and sent to bed whilst the adults settled down on the sofa, snuggling in close together, with something more age appropriate on the television. A glass of red wine each in their hands. A peaceful evening to what had started out as a shitty day.

The following morning did not start as the previous night had ended and - within five minutes of waking up - tempers were already high.

"Someone must have done it!" Dean shouted. He was standing in the spare room with Jess. Both Sophie and Caroline were standing in the doorway - nervous looks on their little faces. The paint, which had carefully been stacked up, had been spilt across the room. Not in a way which suggested they had, somehow, toppled over just as the boxes had but a way which suggested it had been done on purpose. Some of the paint had splashed up the walls, most of it on the carpets. Some of it had even managed to find its way across to the other side of the room - marking both wall and carpet there too - and that was what really bothered Dean. There was no way it could have made it across there by accident. Someone had to have done it on purpose. Dean (and Jess to some extent) had woken up and both been happy. They'd had a great day and evening together and managed to get through the whole night without being disturbed by anything or anyone. Dean had even turned round to Jess and pointed out that things were already starting to get better and they hadn't even painted the room yet. Jess - helpfully - told him not to jinx it. And yet here they were standing in a mess of spilt paint. Dean looked at his two daughters but neither of them would admit to it. Both were looking down at the floor. Dean turned to Jess. "Anything to say? Any suggestions?"

Jess turned to the girls and went down to their level - a less intimidating approach than the outburst Dean was currently experiencing. "Did either of you come in here last night?" she asked. They shook their heads. Even if they had - they wouldn't have admitted it to their parents now. Not after seeing Dean's reaction.

Dean turned back to the room to survey the damage done and to try and formulate a plan on how best to deal with it. By doing so, he accidentally kicked one of the half full tins over, causing more of the magnolia paint to spill across the room. "Shit!" he shouted. Had his foot not connected with the tin he might have seen the hand print on the carpet, behind one of the boxes; a hand print that was clearly too big to belong to either of the young girls.

"It's fine," said Jess, "this is why we have house insurance." She turned to the girls, "Why don't you two go downstairs and I'll be down in a minute to prepare your breakfast."

"Sorry, daddy!" Caroline said before she turned and ran from his sight. He wondered whether that was an admission of guilt, and that she'd spilt the paint, or whether she was just sorry because he was upset about it. Dean went to call her back but Jess stopped him.

"You said we could have a fresh start in this room," she reminded him, "shouting at the girls now, before we decorate, probably won't help with the happy memories in this house." Jess was upset about the spillage - of course she was - but she also knew that there was nothing they could do about it now, even if they did know who was responsible. What was done was done. All they could do now was fix it.

"Not sure whether the house insurance would cover this. Not sure how it works - what with moving house and everything. I mean I told them, I'm sure I did, but…" he sighed, "…guess it's complicated."

"Worst case we phone them and ask the question. If you want - I'll do it."

"The boxes splashed with paint, we're going to need to go through them and make sure it hasn't gone through. Might have damaged whatever was in the boxes."

"And there's no sense fretting about that until you've actually seen…"

"Well - whatever - the paint was clearly a waste of money."

"I'm sure there is enough in here to at least do a corner of the room," she laughed. Dean didn't laugh. His nice gesture, at sorting the room and making it their own, was now dripping down the walls and staining the carpet. In his eyes - there was nothing to laugh about in this room and probably wouldn't be anything to laugh about for a long time.

"Do you think Caroline did it?" he asked. "Maybe upset because you told her off yesterday morning for not looking out for her sister? This is her way of dealing with it?"

Jess shook her head, "She's never done anything like this before. Fine she can be…hard work sometimes….But she'd never do this. Even if she did - she won't admit it. Neither of them will. They're not stupid." Jess looked around at the mess in the room, "Least we have an excuse to pull up the hideous carpet," she said. "Come on - smile - no one got hurt, we're probably covered under the house insurance…It's fine. In the great scheme of things it is fine." Dean knew she was right but it still didn't take the immediate sting off. Yes the room would be sorted and yes no one got hurt but it just meant more stress and more hard work to fix it all. "Come on, I'll go and get us all something to eat. We can just shut the door on this room for now and deal with it later. It's not going anywhere." She took Dean by the hand and pulled him from the room. She closed the door behind them. "See - gone!" She smiled at him. He still didn't smile back.

"I'm going to go for a walk," he said, "just need to cool off a little."

"Okay." Jess knew it was probably for the best; when Dean was angry the best thing you could do was give him the time to calm down. They rarely argued but when they did - it was usually because she didn't give him this necessary space. A few arguments later (and it was a few) and she'd learned the lesson - a lesson she also shared with her daughters when she found herself, from time to time, telling them to leave daddy alone for a while. "I'll get you something to eat when you're back," she told him. "If you're good, I might even make you a bacon sandwich. I think we have some left." Dean smiled at her and headed off to get ready for his walk.

Dean's walk took him to the edge of the large garden. He didn't plan on going much further - he just needed time away from his family and, specifically, that room. The whole business of what had happened there, and what was happening with his youngest daughter, was starting to get to him despite his best intentions not to let it. The girls hadn't put their hands up to the incident with the paint (not that he really expected them to) and, if they didn't do it, not many other scenarios were left to explain it. At least - not many scenarios which didn't point towards the home's tragic past. He didn't believe in spirits. That was one of the many reasons why he found himself able to move into the house in the first place. So a woman had killed herself there, so what? It didn't mean a vengeful spirit would be left behind to harm all those who dared move in. This wasn't the movies. This was real life and - in real life - things like that didn't happen.

Dean found himself thinking about the woman who had lived there previously. After the estate agent had told him about what had happened, he had gone home and Googled the story. Good old Internet has everything hidden away on there somewhere and the suicide was no different. He remembered how he felt when he read about it; the feelings the owner must have felt when he found his wife hanging by her neck. He put himself in his shoes and wasn't sure how he'd have gone on living had he found himself in the same position. Seeing your wife dead, knowing she had killed herself because she felt so desperate, so lonely. Had that been Dean, he knew he wouldn't have been able to go on living - at least, if he were in the exact same position as the previous owner. They didn't have children together, unlike Jess and Dean. With the children to look after he knew he'd have found the strength, from somewhere, to stay alive and ensure they were okay. But, definitely, if Jess and Dean were living in the same conditions as the previous owners - he wouldn't have wanted to go on. He might not have killed himself immediately but he knew it would have only been a matter of time before he gave up. He wondered whether the man had found any sort of happiness by moving out. Part of him feared the previous owner had managed to steal a part of his family's own happiness and that they, in turn, had inherited some of his sadness. Previously, he had never been a pessimistic person but - recently - he felt as though that was all he was and it consumed him despite his best efforts to remain positive. The trouble is it was hard being upbeat about everything when you were surrounded by so much stress and anxiety. He cast his mind back to the weeks leading up to the move, when he was at work, and how he wanted nothing more than to be at home with his family; helping to prepare for the next stage of their lives. Now he was at home he found he wanted nothing more than to be back in the office. The amount of time he 'wasted' there when he should have been at home with his family, he hated himself for wishing to be back behind the desk. And thinking of his family, he knew he had to get back to them soon. Let them know that he'd calmed down and that everything was fine. After all

Jess was right - it could all be fixed with a little time, patience and - unfortunately - more money.

He slowly started walking back down the long stretch of grass and towards the house. His eyes were drawn to the top window on the right hand side; the spare room. His heart skipped a beat when he noticed a shadow in the window. He quickened his pace until it turned into a run. Once at the back door he burst in and charged up the stairs, calling out for Jess all the way.

She walked out of the spare room with an alarmed expression on her face, "What is it?" she asked. Dean's panicked shouts had - in turn - set her on edge.

"What are you doing?" he asked. He immediately knew that the shadow he'd seen, at the window, had been his wife's.

"We thought we'd start clearing up. We were hoping to get the worst of it done by the time you got back," she moved to the side so Dean could see into the bedroom. The girls were in there, with wet cloths, wiping the walls as best they could (not that it was making much difference) and the boxes had all been moved to the side of the room to give them a clearer idea of the actual damage caused. "You know - it's not actually as bad as we first thought. Sure the carpet will need replacing but the walls were going to be painted anyway so…Nothing ruined there. I've had a look in the boxes too and everything inside seems okay. I think we were lucky - all things considered." She stopped talking as she noticed how exhausted Dean appeared to be, "Are you okay?"

He laughed, "Yes. I'm just being stupid. And thank you for this," he said, referring to the cleaning operation taking place in the bedroom. "I'll just take my coat and shoes off and then I'll come and help." He went to go back down the stairs but was stopped by the sound of Sophie's voice.

"Daddy?" Sophie asked.

"Yes, honey?"

"Is this the room where the lady died?"

Night Six

Dean walked into the bedroom and collapsed on the bed next to Jess. It had turned out to be a long day (and evening).

"They're finally asleep," he said. The pair of them had spent the majority of the day explaining what had happened in the house in the most kiddy-friendly way they could think of. The problem was - whenever you were speaking about death, there was never a way that was really suitable to discuss with children. They never understood it no matter how hard you tried to make it easy for them. Out of the two girls, Caroline had been the one who was more freaked out than her sister; which surprised both Dean and Jess. They figured that because she was a little older, she would understand more. She had surprised them by reacting badly saying that she wanted to move out and go back home. They told her that this was her home now and that nothing bad could happen in her own home but she didn't believe them. Jess had put Sophie to bed and she seemed to go to sleep fairly quickly; perhaps because she'd had more time to come to terms with what had happened (having already known about it) but Caroline, who Dean put to bed, was a different story and - for the first time since she was about five years old - she'd demanded that the light be left on. "How'd she know?" Dean asked.

Jess shrugged, "I don't know. Maybe she heard us talking about it?"

"But we've been careful not to say anything in front of the girls."

"I know but you know what they've like. They have a tendency to hear most of what they're not supposed to. They pick up on things."

"Well I can't wait to hear what the counsellor says about it when Sophie brings it up with them - if we ever find a suitable one. We're probably going to be labeled with the bad parent sticker...You know that, right?" Dean got up and started to remove his clothes - ready to climb into bed. "If it's not one thing it's another," he groaned.

"By tomorrow they'll probably both have forgotten about it," Jess told him, "you know what children are like."

"I know children have active imaginations. No wonder she thinks she has been seeing things. She must have heard us talking and now her mind has put two and two together to come up with...Whatever is going on in that mind of hers. You know we've probably broken our daughter, right?"

"Don't say that. She'll be fine. Tomorrow we'll phone around some specialists and see if we can get her an appointment with one of them. Let's just...Let's just get to tomorrow, shall we?"

Before he'd even finished talking to the girls about the tragedy in the spare room, Dean had already decided to utilise tomorrow for finding a counsellor for Sophie to talk to. The girl already had bad dreams even before she had found out that someone had killed themselves in the house, and this probably wasn't going to do those any good. If anything he felt they were likely to get worse. Now it was all about damage control as quickly and efficiently as possible. It didn't even bother him that the Internet might not be working by morning, if it still hadn't been connected, he was happy to use his mobile phone and a copy of the Yellow pages they had found by the front door when they first moved in; much to his surprise. He was sure they'd stop producing that since the Internet took off. It didn't matter what he thought. Now he was just grateful it had been left for them. He stood there for a moment, at the end of the bed, with his mind racing overtime. Jess noticed he'd stopped getting ready for bed.

"What's the matter?" she asked.

He walked from the room and down the stairs, towards the front door. They'd casually tossed the book in the corner when they'd started bringing their boxes in. It was still there. He grabbed it and walked on through to the living room with it tucked under his arm. He knew he wasn't going to sleep this evening - his brain was working overtime with concerns for his children (and stress). Why bother waiting for the morning to go through the section detailing various counsellors? Using his time productively now - by morning he could have a list the length of his arm of telephone numbers to try. Lying in bed, tossing and turning all night, was nothing but a waste of time. At least doing it this way, he felt as though he was doing something useful.

Jess walked into the room, confused as to why he had suddenly walked from the room, "What are you doing?" she asked.

"I'm not tired, I figured I'd get a head start on looking for a counsellor."

Jess didn't move from the doorway, "Did you want me to help?" she asked.

"Only have one book," he pointed out. "Besides - there's no sense both of us sitting up. You might as well go on up to bed." Truth be told he wanted some alone time anyway; a little peace to clear his head as he thumbed the booklet for telephone numbers.

"Okay. Well. If you're sure." She walked over to where he had crashed onto the sofa and leaned down for a kiss. He didn't look up, too busy looking down at the book. She hesitated a moment - and then kissed him on the forehead when she realised that he was already caught up in the book. "Well. Good night." She walked from the room.

"Good night," Dean replied, still without so much as looking up at her.

3:30am.

The house was mostly quiet with the exception of the dripping tap in the kitchen. Both Caroline and Sophie were sleeping soundly in their bedrooms. Dean was still downstairs, lying on the sofa. His mouth was wide open as a small trail of drool seeped out onto the open page of the telephone directory resting on his chest where he'd dropped it before resting his eyes 'for a minute'. On the floor, next to where he dreamt, was a piece of paper and a pen; the paper had ten numbers scrawled across it. His snoring suggested he was in a deep sleep.

The living room door quietly clicked shut before a pair of footsteps made their way up the stairs - hardly making a sound as they did; almost as if they weren't quite touching the floor.

Jess was sleeping soundly in her bed. She stirred slightly as the door opened slowly.

"What time is it?" she asked. She didn't open her eyes. She didn't even move. In reality - she didn't even need an answer. She was already asleep again.

"Ssh," whispered a voice which was not her husband.

She stirred again as the bed creaked on Dean's side. The duvet moved as someone climbed in behind her.

"Mmmm, that's nice," she sighed as she felt someone push up behind her. "I love you," she said before falling back into a deep, deep sleep. Her visitor didn't reply.

DAY SEVEN

W hen Jess woke up she noticed Dean's side of the bed was empty. She rolled over onto it - half expecting to feel the warmth left from his body and smell his natural scent - but was surprised at how cold the mattress and (that side of) the duvet were. Almost as though no one had actually slept there. She buried her face in the pillow and suddenly pulled it away - retching as she did. A dank, musty smell stuck to the pillow as though it hadn't been washed for many years.

"Jesus!" she moaned, "Guess I know what I'm doing today!" A day of stripping the bed linen off and giving everything a good wash. She presumed it must have got dirty in the move - even though they were all bagged up neatly. She threw the duvet off and climbed from the bed before sticking her head into the en-suite bathroom. She frowned when she noticed it was empty. Figured Dean may have been in there - perhaps washing himself ready for a busy day of whatever he'd planned to do. Realising he wasn't in there, she threw her dressing gown on and stepped from the bedroom and onto the landing. "Dean?" she called out. Nothing. She poked her head in on the girls - both of them were still sleeping. Hardly surprising given the late night they'd had. At least neither of them appeared to have had nightmares. Jess walked down the stairs towards the living room where she'd last seen Dean. He was still in there, fast asleep. The book on his chest, his neck at an extremely un-comfortable angle. "Honey?" she whispered loud enough to wake him but not loud enough to startle him. Nothing worse than being woken up with a jump. "Honey?" she whispered again when he didn't stir. This time he did.

"What time is it?" he asked as he pushed the heavy book onto the floor.

"It's early. Just gone seven."

The book landed with a thud. "My fucking neck!" Dean moaned as tried to rub the ache away. "I tell you - this is not a comfortable couch to fall asleep on…"

"Why'd you come back down here?" Jess asked.

"I told you - I didn't think I'd be able to sleep so thought I'd try and find a number for a counsellor. Need to get this sorted," he said.

"I presumed you'd found one when you crawled into bed during the night."

"I found a few…Wait…What? I didn't come to bed last night. I fell asleep here," he said.

Jess' face went white, "You woke me up getting into bed."

"Jess, I've been down here all night. I swear."

"No, you didn't."

"Yes, I did. You just woke me up."

"Then who crawled into bed with me?" she asked. Panic all over her face.

"One of the girls? It wouldn't exactly be surprising if one of them couldn't sleep after yesterday!"

"I've just checked on them. They're both asleep in their own beds. They don't go back to their own bed after coming in with us, you know that. They stay until morning."

"Well - Jesus, Jess - I don't know what you want me to say. I've been down here all night."

"You promise?"

"Why would I lie about something like that? I've been down here all night." He sat up. He expected Jess to come over and sit with him but she didn't move from where she was standing in the doorway.

"Look - I think we should seriously consider our options here…"

"Our options? Our options to what?" he asked before giving her a chance to explain.

"This place. This house."

Dean didn't like where this was heading, "What are you talking about?"

"I don't feel safe here. Something is very wrong with this house."

"Jess…"

"No, I mean it, I don't feel safe here. I haven't since the first night. I'm not comfortable."

Dean tried his best to keep his temper under control despite feeling it build up inside him. They'd spoken - at length - about what had happened in the house to avoid this very situation and yet, here it was, rearing its ugly head. "I'm pretty sure we can't back out of a signed contract. The deal was done. This is our house now. We chose it. Together. We can't just pack up and move out….Hell we…" he cut himself off and fell silent. Jess started to cry. Dean didn't get up to offer her any form of comfort or reassurance. He sighed heavily - as though he'd lost all patience and will to even continue with the conversation but did so regardless, "This was supposed to be the start of the next chapter in our lives. You know, what we discussed, a place to continue raising the children. A place to make more happy memories…"

"We need help!" Jess went to argue. "Something is happening with our family and we need help to deal with it…"

"Oh now we need help?" That was the final straw. Dean raised his voice, "The other day it was Sophie who needed the help. We were fine. It was our daughter who was fucking insane but now it's all of us? Brilliant. Nice one. Well…" he stopped. He noticed a shadow behind where Jess was standing. He peered around her and noticed Sophie and Caroline were standing there - both of them appeared upset. "Shit," he muttered under his breath. Judging by their expressions it was obvious they'd heard more than enough. "Sophie, daddy's sorry…I didn't mean it…" he got up and walked towards the girls. Jess, in the meantime, turned to face them. Despite the outburst from Dean - it appeared the girls' minds were elsewhere.

"I don't want you to die," Caroline whispered. Her voice was quivering as she addressed her father. She burst into tears as though she'd been containing them for months upon months and was no longer able to hold them. Dean sighed again. That was all he needed, Sophie had been telling Caroline of her dreams. They had worked so hard to keep them from their eldest daughter just because they didn't want her to start to have them either; a little seed planted by Sophie which would grow into a huge oak tree of problems.

Jess knelt down to her daughter's level and put her arms around her, "Your father's not going anywhere," she reassured her.

"But he is though," Caroline whimpered. Sophie started to cry too.

Dean turned to his youngest, "Did you have that dream again?"

She shook her head. He couldn't help but wish they had never mentioned the possibility of her seeing someone - a specialist - to try and help with the bad dreams (and other issues). Ever since they had dropped it into a conversation, to see what she had thought, she had clammed up and refused to admit to anything to either her mum or her dad. This time she must have woken up, in a panic, and shared her sad thoughts with her sister - and her sister clearly listened and took it straight to heart.

"What makes you say that?" Jess continued talking to Caroline.

"Because he is going to die! He dies in his sleep!" she started to become more distressed. Jess held her tighter than before - a gesture to show she was there for her.

Dean muttered, "At least it's peaceful," he said.

Jess glared at him, "You think this is funny? Look at what is happening to our family. We can't do this, Dean. We're falling apart."

Dean walked back into the living room and picked up the piece of paper he'd been working on during the night before he had dozed off, "Look - telephone numbers for counsellors - a whole list of them. I'll phone them this morning and try and get an appointment for the whole family. We can all speak to someone and let them decide how best to proceed; whether it be one on one or group sessions for all of us. If that's what you want - we'll do it - but we can't move out of this house. It's nothing to do with the house…"

"But it started when we moved in!"

"The dreams were occurring well before we moved here," Dean reminded Jess. "Remember? How many times have I lost out on a good night's sleep because I've had to go and comfort her? In case you've forgotten - loads of times." He reiterated, "It has nothing to do with this house and what happened here and you need to put that out of your mind. You're making it a problem and you need to stop!" Dean realised he was saying too much in front of the girls but he couldn't stop himself. Just as Caroline's floodgates had been opened, so had his - and his emotions came out in a more hostile way than Caroline's. Jess just looked at him - her arms still offering comfort to her weeping daughter - a look of hatred in her face.

"You're an asshole," she said - her voice was low.

"Well - that's a maybe but I'm the only sane one here right now."

Jess stood up and walked from the room, leading both daughters away. Dean stormed over to the door and slammed it shut. He returned to the couch and sat down heavily on it. This was supposed to be the next stage of their content family life and yet the whole thing was going to shit. And to think - it wasn't long ago that Jess was hinting at wanting another child. He sat there, desperately trying to figure out where it had started to go wrong and - more importantly - how to fix it. He couldn't put the house on the market. The ink wasn't even dry on the contracts yet. He couldn't just sell up and move out again. Besides, these problems were nothing to do with the house. Maybe they'd flared up from the moving and general stress involved with that but it wasn't the house. There's no such thing as ghosts and houses don't hold into past memories. They're just brick and mortar. They don't store karma - whether it's good or bad. It doesn't work like that. He looked down at the piece of paper and the numbers listed upon it. His mind was telling him there'd be no shame in seeking help for all of them, though. An outsider who could listen to their problems and help guide them back to the happy family they once were. He felt a little embarrassed at not being able to fix the issues himself but clearly things were getting out of hand. Despite the harsh words he sometimes used when he spoke to Jess - he didn't want to lose her. He didn't want to lose any of them. If they needed to speak to a stranger then so be it.

He reached across to the telephone and started to dial the telephone number situated at the top of the list. Whatever it takes - he was determined to keep both his family and their new home.

With the number dialled, he pressed the handset to his ear and listened as it began to ring.

⅄

"I'm sorry," Dean was the first to apologise as he walked into the spare bedroom where Jess was still tidying up from the previous day. Her eyes looked as though she'd been crying all morning. "Where are the girls?" Dean asked when Jess didn't acknowledge his apology.

"Outside."

Dean walked over to the window and looked out. The girls were playing in the garden; running around and laughing. Dean smiled. The image below was what he'd imaged it to be like before they moved in; the girls running around with room to play, the pair of them smiling and laughing as they enjoyed themselves.

"Look at them," he pointed out of the window for Jess' benefit. She didn't move from her spot near the corner of the room, "Please?" he begged. Reluctantly she stood up and joined Dean at the window. "Look at them out there. They look happy, don't they?" Jess didn't answer. "You know - this is what I imagined it to be like when we were waiting to move in. No arguments, just joy. Happiness." Jess didn't say anything. She wiped a remaining tear from her cheek. "Isn't this what you wanted?" he pressed her, trying to get her to talk. She nodded. "I am sorry for earlier," he continued. "It's just - I wanted this to work out so badly for us, you know? I wanted us to be happy here. I thought we would be. Never imagined we'd be arguing the way we are right now anyway…"

"Me neither."

"Pretty stupid," he said. "I'll try and fix things. I'll try and make things better but this is our home now. We need to make the house work. I know you said you don't feel safe here but everything is just getting blown out of proportion; no doubt because of the stress of moving and what's going on with Sophie. But - this room - what happened; we spoke about it. We were both fine with it and I don't understand the sudden turn around you're having."

"I just feel like we're always being watched," Jess admitted. "I don't feel comfortable here. I know it's silly but I can't shake the feeling that - everywhere we go - there are eyes on us."

"Look, hows about we unpack, we decorate this room and make it our own, we see the counsellor - as a family - and then, if you're still not satisfied that there's nothing wrong with the house...Then we'll look at putting it back on the market and finding somewhere else to live. Is that fair?" Jess didn't answer. "Come on, please, I'm trying really hard to make this work here. You need to work with me, please. What do you say? I promise, after speaking to the counsellor and sorting this room out, if you're not happy we'll move...Yeah?" Jess nodded. She didn't look as though she was entirely convinced but Dean didn't care. She still nodded and that was better than nothing. "And I think I've found us a counsellor," he explained. "It only took most of the morning but there's one - not too far from here - who is able to see us in the morning if you're interested? I took the appointment just in case you said yes but - if you don't want to - I can always call them and cancel?"

"We should go," Jess said.

Dean nodded, "Fine - whatever you want." Nearly whatever she wanted anyway. She wanted to move out. She wanted to go back to their old home, even though it belonged to someone else now, but she couldn't have that. "So," he hesitated, "am I forgiven? Could I get a hug?" Jess looked at him. She knew they'd both been stupid about the situation. They'd both over reacted. Dean continued, "And - maybe - as the kids are outside...Maybe I could get a blow job?" Jess laughed.

"You're such an asshole!" she said. Her outburst didn't matter this time - not all the time she was smiling about it. Her words didn't come with the venom presented earlier. Dean smiled and leant in for a sneaky kiss of her cheek. A second later and he put his arms around her, holding her close to his body with their two children playing in the garden beyond the window.

A happy family.

"Come on," he said as they continued their hug, "let's go outside."

"What about the room?" Jess asked.

"What about it? It's not going anywhere. Just leave the window open to try and air the smell of paint and leave it. Family time is more important. These days won't last forever," he reminded her. One minute your child is your baby, the next they're running around as teenagers and then - before you know it - they've moved out and are starting a family of their own. Dean didn't want to miss any of it. He took Jess by the hand and walked her from the bedroom and down the stairs.

NIGHT SEVEN

The rest of the day had been spent playing in the sunny garden - running around playing tag and kicking one of the plastic footballs - and was concluded with a nice barbecue; although it had to be cooked in the kitchen as they didn't actually possess a proper outdoors barbecue due to the lack of room in their last home. Despite the rocky start to the morning, the day was filled with laughter and smiles. At least - it was until it came for the girls to go to bed. Neither of them wanted to go up, despite being allowed to stay up half an hour later than their usual bedtime.

The usual routine of putting them to bed went along the lines of telling them to go to the bathroom (making sure they went to the toilet) to brush their teeth and then to say goodnight to each other (and their parents) before heading off to their own rooms. Sometimes, rarely, Sophie would ask for a bedtime story. Tonight - for the first time in as long as Dean could remember - both girls requested a story. Jess offered to read for Caroline after Dean said he'd read for Sophie first and then Caroline but their eldest daughter refused her mother's offer. She wanted her dad to read it to her and became teary at the possibility of him not doing so.

"It's fine. I'll do it," Dean had told Jess.

It upset Jess, from time to time, when the girls always requested their father. Sophie called out for him when she cried - it was always her father she wanted and now Jess wasn't even good enough to read a story to her eldest child. When she had mentioned it a while back to Dean - he had told her it was because he was always stuck at work so - in their eyes - wasn't around as much. His words made sense but - occasionally - it still bothered Jess. She cooked for them, she cleaned for them - would it really have hurt to be asked to read for them from time to time too? Tonight was one of those nights she felt unappreciated.

"You can make me feel loved when you're done," she had told Dean with a cheeky smile on her face. He knew what she'd meant and couldn't help but smile too. As he climbed the stairs, to where his girls waited in their bedrooms, he wondered how fast he could get the individual readings done. Hopefully in record breaking speed, he thought, so he could venture off to satisfy his wife's needs.

Dean closed the book and put it on the floor next to Caroline's bed.

"I think that's enough for tonight," he told her. She'd chosen Swallows and Amazons and there was no way he was about to read the whole thing to her in one night, despite her pleas for him to continue. "We'll read some more tomorrow," he told her. "In fact - you can read it to me," he suggested. Not just because it saved his voice and saved him the embarrassment of doing the various voices but because it happened to be good practice for her too. He leaned across to her and gave her a kiss on the forehead, "Nighty-night!" She didn't respond. Dean stood up and walked to the door. He reached for the light-switch.

"Please don't die, daddy."

Dean froze. He didn't quite know how to respond. It was clear that Caroline was upset and immediately he realised why she'd wanted him to read to her as opposed to Jess. She wanted to cram in as much time with her dad as humanly possible. Clearly Sophie's conversation had upset Caroline more than she had let on. Dean walked back across the bedroom and sat on the edge of the bed.

"Promise me," Caroline continued.

"Honey - we all go up to Heaven I'm afraid so I can't promise you that. But what I can promise you is that it won't be for a really, really long time, okay?" Caroline had tears in her eyes - clearly on the verge of crying.

"So not tonight then, okay?"

Her words alarmed Dean but he tried his best not to show it and tried to comfort her some more, "You know - as I told your sister - if you have a bad dream...They tend to work in reverse. So all the bad stuff you dream about actually turns out to be good things. If you dreamt of me dying tonight - I'm actually going to die in years to come."

"But what if I didn't dream it?" she asked. Fear on her face.

"Then it's all in your head and you're being silly for no reason," Dean smiled at her.

"It's not in my head though. I was told you were going to die tonight," Caroline started to cry.

"By whom? Your sister?"

Caroline shook her head.

"Who?"

"I'm not allowed to say. If I tell anyone then mummy will die too..."

"What? You're being stupid. Who has been saying all this?"

Caroline stopped crying. Her eyes went wide with fear. Something over Dean's shoulder had caught her attention. She pointed, "He told me!"

Dean frowned. Slowly he turned around to face the direction Caroline was pointing. There, just a few feet behind him, a man stood with a knife in his hand. Before Dean could say anything the man took a step forward and swiped at his throat with the tip of the blade. The blade cut through Dean's skin as though it were a hot knife through butter. Blood sprayed across the room as a major artery was cut right through. Dean grabbed his throat and fell off the bed, onto the floor where he started to try and crawl towards the door, away from his attacker. Caroline wanted to scream out loud but didn't dare. She remembered the man's threat and - more importantly - the conversation they'd had the previous night. He was going to look after her. He was going to be her new daddy. They'd be one happy family. Him, the two girls and Jess. But if they dared to tell anyone about his nightly visits, then both their current daddy and their mummy would have to die. The man stepped over Dean's body and shut the bedroom door to stop any unwanted attention coming their way. He raised his finger to his mouth and shushed Caroline quiet.

"Ssh, it's okay..." He walked over to her and sat on the bed. Caroline didn't move. She was rooted to the spot. The man leaned forward and kissed her on the forehead. "Daddy's here now," the man whispered.

⚓

Jess walked up the stairs towards her bedroom to prepare herself for Dean; a quick shower and the opportunity to slip into something a little less uncomfortable. As she walked past the spare room she couldn't help but notice the strong smell of paint. She peered into the room and noticed the window was closed. She walked in - to open it - and stopped dead when she realised the cupboard was open. Not just that but a light too - coming from the ceiling in there. She walked across the room to investigate, stepping around the (now dry) puddles of paint and opened the cupboard wider. Her heart skipped a beat. Inside the cupboard, there was no ceiling. Just a hole where it should have been. A hole which lead straight through to the attic space. A light shone down from the space.

"What the hell?"

She used the shelving unit on the back wall of the cupboard to clamber up high enough to see into the attic. Her heart skipped another beat when she realised what she was looking at in the far corner of the room; some kind of shrine built up around pictures of a woman. Next to that, she saw there was a mattress - surrounded by food wrappers. Two buckets in the corner of the room. She pulled herself up into the loft to get a closer look. As she walked across to what appeared to be a 'living space' she noticed several heavy weights had been left on top of the loft hatch. No wonder Dean hadn't been able to open it. She didn't look into the buckets. She didn't need to. As she approached, the smell hit her hard. They were full of waste. She gagged. A closer look at the shrine and she noticed random scribblings on post-it notes stuck to various different pictures of the woman. Notes which spelt out how sorry someone was, how much he loved her. She knew instantly it belonged to the previous owner. He'd been living in the attic all this time?

She ran back towards the hole in the cupboard ceiling and carefully dropped down the various shelves until she was back in the spare room again.

"Dean!" she called out.

She ran through, across the landing, to Sophie's room and stopped dead. Her daughters were standing at the other end of the landing, next to Caroline's room. They both look petrified. A strange man - the previous owner? - was standing between them with his arms around them. In his hand was a bloody knife.

"Hi, honey!" he said. He smiled. "I hope you don't mind but I thought the kids could stay up a little later tonight. Was thinking about putting on a midnight snack or something. Don't know about you but I am absolutely starving." He turned to the girls. "By the way - we've been talking and I'm not sure their names suit them. I think we should call them Beth and Gloria…" He turned to the girls, "What do you think? You like those names?" They didn't say anything. They just stood there, trapped in his embrace, with tears running down their faces. He turned to Jess, "And - I hope you don't mind - I was hoping I could call you Cathy?"

Jess screamed.

T H E   E N D

Control

MATT SHAW

Now

DAY SEVEN

All twelve applicants were sitting around the long dining room table enjoying breakfast. Various conversations between them, all seemingly centred on the evening's coming eviction, a nervous energy filled the room as no one wanted to be the first out of the house, not that any of them were admitting it they were all there to win.

"Who do you think will go?" Paul asked Jack between mouthfuls of his cornflakes. At forty-two years of age, Paul was the eldest of the group and had already taken the father role. When the others got too drunk - when they were allowed alcohol, he would be the one to put them to bed. When the others argued over - apparently - nothing of any great importance, he was the one to step in and break it up. A shoulder to cry on when the younger members of the group started to miss their families despite only being a few days into the eight week show.

Jack looked around the group. You could tell by his face he was judging each character on an individual basis in order to try and answer Paul's question. Truth be told though it was an impossible question to answer. They had barely gotten to know each other in the short first week they had been in there, let alone get an idea how the public would be reacting to them as they watched each day's forty-five minute show.

"Okay," Paul rephrased the question, "who would you want to go tonight?"

Both Paul and Jack turned to look at Morgan as he filled his cereal bowl for the third time since sitting down to breakfast. Another over-filled bowl once again filled to the very brim with milk.

"That's pretty unanimous then," Paul laughed.

"I don't know - he just irritates me and even if he didn't, look at how much he eats!"

Morgan was in his thirties, tall with dark hair and was pretty much the clown of the group. Thirty-five years old, going on five. If there was an in-nuendo to be made, he would make it. If there was someone to scare, he'd be the one jumping out. If there was someone to wind up, he'd be the one pulling the ropes. At first the group thought he was overcompensating to offset against his shyness but by day three they realised he wasn't - this was just his personality and it was fucking annoying.

Morgan realised Paul and Jack were looking at him, "What?" he asked, a mouthful of milk spilling from mouth to bowl. He returned to the table and sat next to Paul, in his original seat. "What you guys talking about?" he asked.

"Just wondering who is going tonight."

"So you thought me?" he asked. The tone in his voice suggested he did not find much to joke about in this instance. He almost sounded as though their speculations had hurt his feelings. Morgan was the house clown but that didn't mean he was stupid. Having caught both Jack and Paul staring at him, it didn't take a genius to put two and two together; they were talking about who was leaving and they were looking at him. And there you have it.

It was the seventh day though and already Morgan had been involved in more than a handful of arguments. It was never Morgan who was doing the arguing, or shouting, but it was always him who had managed to wind the others up to such an extent that something kicked off.

"So does anyone else think I'm going tonight?" Morgan raised his voice so the rest of the table would stop their individual conversations and turn their attention to him. "Well?" he asked when he knew he had everyone's undivided attention. "Anyone?"

"We don't know who is going tonight," Jordy said. Twenty years old and mad as a box of frogs but in a good way. A fun way. Unlike Morgan she knew there was a time for fun and a time to be serious. She'd caught Morgan's abrupt tone and judged now as being a time to be serious.

"Well these two seem to know," he snapped. He scooped another spoonful of cornflakes up and shoved them into his mouth.

"I'm sure they didn't mean anything," Jordy tried to play peacekeeper. Jordy was fun, that you couldn't deny. Clearly she had been chosen to go on the show because the producers thought she might liven the place up a little, just as they had chosen Paul to go in because he seemed like a nice man who would be able to keep the housemates in line, to stop things from really becoming silly, but what Jordy was not - was a peacekeeper; a role she tried to fulfil but often failed.

"How could they not mean anything by stating I'd be the first out? I think it is pretty obvious what they meant - either they both hate me out of everyone here and want me gone or they think the public will hate me and want me gone. You can't get any more fucking obvious than that!" he started to cough on his cornflakes.

Jordy didn't have anything to say to that. She turned to Paul in the hope that the real peacekeeper of the house would be able to say something to justify the conversation he had been having with Jack; Jordy's favourite of the house's 'talent' as seen in a drunken conversation between Kate and herself in the episode showing what happened on Day Four in the house.

"Maybe you should go tonight?" Morgan pointed at Paul as he continued to cough.

"Maybe I will," Paul said. "No one knows who is going tonight. It was just a conversation about who we think could be in danger. You can't deny you have caused quite a storm in here these past few days with your practical jokes and scare tactics and…" his voice was drowned out by Morgan's coughing.

Fiona, thirty-eight, walked to the kitchen of the open-plan house and fetched a glass of water. She brought it back to the table and went to hand it to Morgan. "You're bleeding!" she said. Morgan was holding his throat as a burning sensation ripped through it, a small trickle of blood leaked from the corner of his mouth. A look of panic on his face as his coughing got harder. Fiona turned to the group, "What do we do?"

Stuart, sitting next to Morgan, jumped up and started to pat his back in an effort to dislodge whatever was causing the choking, unaware something more sinister was afoot. "It's not working!" he said, as he continued to hit Morgan's back.

Georgia, a pretty blonde twenty-four year old, who'd been put in the house for her looks as opposed to any personality she may bring with her, had run over to the Control Room - a room where, at any time, the house-mates could talk to The Controller; The Controller being one of the many producers who helped to run the newly televised show. She pressed the doorbell in the hope that the lights surrounding the door would go from red to green - an action they did meaning you were permitted to go in. The lights didn't change as Morgan continued hacking in the background, "Come on, come on! Why aren't you helping?!" she said as she looked up to one of the cameras just above the door.

"Maybe it's at the back of his throat," Paul said. He leaned across the table and forcefully opened Morgan's mouth in an effort to see if he could see anything lodged there. Morgan coughed dramatically and covered Paul's face in a sludge of deep red blood and mucus and then - just like that - he stopped coughing.

"Are you feeling better now?" Stuart asked. He twisted Morgan round to face him and went pale instantly. Morgan was as white as a sheet. His eyes fixed upon Stuart for what seemed to be a split second and then rolled to the back of his head. He slumped backwards, off the chair, and landed on the floor with a bang. Stuart dropped to his knees next to Morgan and felt for a pulse. Nothing. He looked up, "He's dead."

"This is The Controller," a loud dominant voice boomed over the speaker, "all Housemates go to the bedroom immediately!"

"He's fucking dead!" Stuart repeated, panic slowly starting to set in just as it was with the rest of the group too.

"Why didn't they help?!" Georgia screamed from the door of the Control Room –which was still illuminated in a red light. "Why didn't someone come and help us?!" she screamed again.

"This is The Controller! All Housemates go to the bedroom immediately!"

"Come on," Paul lead the group through to the bedroom. The door shut automatically when the last of the weeping group walked through the door. A red light illuminated the door surrounds as the blinds started to come down, sealing off the rest of the house and - more specifically - the twitching body of Morgan.

"What the hell was that about?" Chris screamed. "Why didn't they come and help us?" Like Jack and Paul - Chris was just your average twenty-five year old. His head was screwed on, he had a good job in the outside world and had signed up to the show for experience rather than a shot at the prize fund.

"You're sure there wasn't a pulse?" Paul asked Stuart. He knew the answer. From the moment they had first arrived in the house, Stuart had been very vocal about his First Aid training. He had boasted about it as though it were something to be proud about, something that no other person could have achieved by the age of twenty-six - despite courses being readily available for people of all ages who expressed an interest. Stuart didn't answer, he was pacing the room backwards and forwards with a panicked look on his face. "Stuart!" Paul called out, the father taking control of the situation.

"What?" Stuart stopped pacing and turned to him.

"Are you sure there wasn't a pulse?"

"I'm positive! There was no pulse!"

"Fuck! Fuck! Fuck!" Philip started shouting out over the girls' crying. Eighteen years old and still trying to find a way of expressing himself in a way which did not involve vulgar language. "What the fuck?!"

"Every one just calm down!" Paul shouted above all of them. "It's shocking but we need to stay calm…"

"What's going on out there?" Georgia asked.

"I'm sure they will let us know what is going on as soon as they have an idea themselves. For now though, we just need to get a grip and calm down. Getting hysterical about it isn't going to help anyone." Paul sat on the edge of his bed.

Jack muttered, "Do you think what happened to Richard was real?"

The group fell silent with the exception of a few occasional sobs from Karen - the youngest, and most sensitive, of the group at only eighteen years old.

Up until now Philip had been fairly quiet in the group. From Day One he seemed to have more of an issue fitting in despite being of a similar age (mid-twenties). The group was surprised when he turned around and casually muttered, "Do you think the eviction will go ahead tonight?"

Before

JACKLETTS

The queue snaked round the interior rooms and corridors and out of the main front doors of the building where it continued to circle the exterior. Thousands of desperate hopefuls all clamouring for their five minutes of fame and their shot at winning the one hundred thousand pounds being offered up to whoever survived the twelve weeks in the house. Some had come dressed to impress in their finest of clothes, some had come in fancy dress in an effort to steal away the producers' eyes from people they were competing against and some - the better looking ones of the crowd - came dressed in little to nothing.

Jack Letts, twenty-three years old from the South East of England, skipped this queue. Like a few hundred others, he was invited in through another set of doors, away from the impatient rumblings of the main queue, on the strength of his ninety-second video audition he'd sent in more than three months prior to this day. His queue was much, much shorter and he soon found himself sitting in a large waiting area lined with various vending machines along with the other successful video applicants who'd gotten through to the second stage.

He was nervously sitting, watching the other hopefuls. All of them had stickered name badges stuck to their tops. He seemed to be the most nervous there. At least, he was the one who appeared as though they were struggling with hiding their nerves compared to the rest of the group. Some had made friends with the people sat around them and were quietly chatting whilst others did as Jack did and just sat there - isolated in the crowd - looking around with a look on their faces which could only be described as 'rabbit in the headlights'.

A three-man television crew were milling around the room. A long-haired, loud mouthed presenter Jack recognised from the television, a sound man and a camera operator. Jack did his best to avoid eye contact with them as they continued to negotiate their way around the crowded room pouncing on those who appeared to be more nervous or easy to pick on. The presenter fired questions at them mercilessly as the cameraman and sound man tried their best not to laugh. Sometimes the presenter wouldn't even wait for an answer before shouting out his next question. Jack could only cringe as he watched those picked upon go red in the face and stutter their way through the impromptu grilling.

"What makes you think you'd be a good contestant?"

"..."

"You look boring to me. BORING. Are you boring?"

"..."

"Do you speak English? Would you like a translator?"

"Er..."

"I'm sure we've got someone on the staff who can speak idiot..."

And - with that - he'd venture on to the next victim. Of course not everyone felt for those being picked on. Jack was in the minority there. Most just laughed as the wannabe applicant was brought down a peg, or two. Jack guessed they enjoyed it because it meant the person's confidence was severely knocked more or less forcing them out of the running before they'd even started the race for real. Of course - smiles soon faded from faces when they were chosen next for the over-the-top roasting.

"You're ugly! We don't want you on the show! People will see your face and be forced to change the channel!"

Jack looked out of the window and caught sight of his appearance. He looked tired. His blonde hair was all over the place - and in dire need of a cut - there were bags under his eyes from where he'd been forced to get up early to get to the auditions in time and there was an unsightly stain down the front of his shirt, caused by an early morning commuter spilling his coffee over him when the train jolted to a stop at London Waterloo.

"Come far?"

Jack snapped back to reality and turned to his right. A large male teenager in what looked to be women's clothes was sitting next to him - a look of desperation Jack had seen on the faces of many other people patiently waiting to be called through. Jack couldn't help but notice the boy's sticker had him labeled as Jo-Jo.

"Southampton. About an hour and a half on the train. Not too bad, I guess."

"What kind of people do you think they're looking for?" he asked.

Jack shrugged, "Not sure." He shifted in his seat nervously. On the one hand it was good someone was talking to him because it made him less of a target for the roaming television crew but - on the other hand - this guy was irritating.

"I dreamt last night that I won," he continued. "Such an amazing dream. I ended up in a room with the one hundred grand rolling around naked. I was rubbing the notes over myself. What do you think it meant?" he asked.

Jack raised an eyebrow and turned to look at him. He wasn't sure whether Jo-Jo was being serious or whether he was on the wind-up, just to get a reaction from him. Jack shrugged again, "Honestly I have no idea," he said.

"It means you're a freak!" a male voice shouted.

Both Jack and Jo-Jo jumped at the sudden outburst. They both turned round and were confronted by the television presenter looming over them with a sadistic grin on his face. The presenter turned to the camera and sound man, "Tell me you got that?" They both nodded. Jo-Jo was glowing red. Even Jack felt his own face heat up from embarrassment as the presenter turned his attention to him, "You've got weird friends, mate, if I were you I'd dump them. At the bottom of a sea. With a rock tied around their ankles."

"He isn't my friend. I don't know him!" Jack protested.

"That's the spirit! Ooh…Mercenary! You'll go far!" the presenter laughed. "But how far will you go? If I offered you one hundred grand right here and right now, would you drop him into the bottom of the ocean?"

"Er…I…"

"I'm just joking with you!" the presenter laughed and skipped off to his next 'victim'.

N O W

Jack was sitting on the bed he had been sharing with Morgan. Not everyone shared a bed. Some of them were singles so some of the group had a bed to themselves whilst others were forced to double up, unless they wanted to sleep on the uncomfortable floor. He looked stressed, as did the other housemates too, but he seemed more so.

Paul went over and sat next to him, "Penny for them?" he asked - referring to the thoughts Jack was clearly struggling with.

"I was just thinking about Richard," he said. "We all laughed. Remember?"

"I do."

On opening night the housemates had walked into the house, one by one, after a quick introduction to a baying crowd by a female presenter who none of them had recognised. The housemates would come through some double doors, walk down a small gangway to where the female presenter was waiting, they'd have a quick interview and then be instructed to enter the house via a set of spiral stairs leading to a door. On the other side of the door was a narrow corridor which lead the way to another set of doors - the final set to go through before getting into the house for real.

Richard had been the last housemate to walk in but - unlike those who went before him - he did not make it into the main house, only the corridor. The first door locked behind him and the second door remained shut; the now familiar red illumination around it.

"We thought it was a joke, a twisted little set-up to make us feel uncomfortable from the get go. The producers said things would be twisted…They warned us before we signed on the dotted line to become official housemates."

"I know."

"So what if it was real? And what if what happened out there - to Morgan - what if that was real too?"

"He just choked on his cereal and - as you said - what happened on Day One was just to rattle us a bit. Probably increase viewing figures. It wouldn't surprise me if we have to go through the same thing when we are evicted. Think about it - we didn't see him get crushed did we - the cameras cut to black and sound effects were played through the speakers of bones being crushed. Easily staged."

"Why are we locked in here?" Kate was standing at the door, rattling it despite knowing it wouldn't encourage the producers to open it any sooner. "What are they doing out there?"

Paul looked over to Kate and called out to her that, "They need to help him, don't they? These things take time. I'm sure they'll let us out and tell us what is happening as soon as they know themselves."

Kate was a fiery redhead. At twenty-three years old she thought the world revolved around her and - as a result - had a temper on her which was quick to flare up over the silliest of things. The last thing Paul needed now, both on a personal level and thinking about the other housemates too, was Kate kicking off for whatever reason.

"This is bullshit! Why waste time locking us in here when they could have just come in and helped right from the get go? They might have been able to save him," what Kate was saying was true but the way she said it - the tone she used - wasn't helping. If anything it would simply rile up the other housemates until they were all kicking off again.

"Shut up for fuck sake!" Philip shouted out from the corner of the room. He was on his way back to his bed, having come from the en-suite bathroom.

"I can't believe he's dead," Karen was on the bed next to him being comforted by Jordy who was also struggling to hold back the tears. Neither girl particularly liked Morgan, mutual feelings shared by the other house-mates, but none of them had wanted to see him dead. They wanted to watch him die even less. That's the kind of thing you do not get over.

"Seriously - you two can shut the fuck up too. He's dead. Big fucking deal. Get over it. None of you liked him. If you had - he wouldn't have been up for nomination this week. You got what you wanted, albeit in a round-about way, he's out of the fucking house." Philip continued. He wasn't raising his voice, he wasn't getting irritated. If anything - he seemed to be the calmest of the group.

Jordy hissed, "Who are you?" It took a lot to annoy Jordy but Philip was managing it with ease. Philip had been quiet all week and now, twice within a short period of time, he had said something which shocked his fellow housemates. Two uncalled for outbursts.

"Who am I? I'm the one being practical. None of you liked him. He was irritating. We all wanted him gone today. Well - guess what - he's gone! And good riddance too. One less going for the one hundred grand."

"Just stop talking!" Jordy said. She turned her attention back to consoling Karen.

Jack was still talking to Paul, "When I went for the audition process - the presenter guy they had there, running around being a dick to the applicants, he joked about giving me the prize money if I offed the guy sitting beside me."

"What did you say?"

"I didn't. He said he was joking and left us. But it's been a week and so far two of us are dead."

"One of us is dead. The other was staged. It's just poor timing, that's all. You saw, Morgan was getting himself wound up. He choked on the food he was cramming down his throat…"

"He was coughing up blood. I've never seen someone choking do that before now."

"Seen a lot of people choke?"

"I just have a bad feeling about this."

"It'll be fine. We just need to sit tight and wait to hear from The Controller, or the producers. That's it. Nothing else we can do."

"Guys, can I have some help, please?" Jordy called over from the bed where she was still comforting Karen. Paul and Jack glanced over at the sound of urgency in her tone of voice. "I can't calm her down, she's hyperventilating."

Paul hurried over to the bed where Karen was having a panic attack.

Stuart jumped up and joined him, "Have we got a carrier bag or something?" he asked. His First Aid training coming into play.

Before

KAREN REEVES

Karen was standing in front of a small group of people, all of them wearing stickers on their tops introducing themselves to everyone else in the room. The group itself was a mixed bag of people of varied ethnic backgrounds and ages. In front of the group was a desk where three official people were sitting and - to the side of them - a fourth person operating a large camera sitting on a tripod.

Each person had been instructed to talk about themselves for no more than three minutes. There was no clock in the room, they just had to keep going until they thought the time was up. The rest of the group were told to listen so they could ask questions at the end of the three minutes; a simple process where they simply raised their hands in the air until invited to speak by one of the three people sitting at the front of the room.

So far the process had proven to be fairly brutal. It was hard enough talking about yourself for three minutes, if you weren't expecting to do so, but the hardest part were the questions. Everyone in the room wanted to make themselves look good and stand out from the others. To do so they all tried to run the 'speakers' down by pulling apart what they had said.

Karen had finished introducing herself. She touched upon the fact she was at college, she touched upon what she wanted to do with her life, she told the group that she was a lesbian and that she had been adopted at an early age after her mother and father were killed in a car crash; the final snippet of information she had had no intention of saying when she had first stood up. It had just slipped out of her mouth as her panicked brain ran out of things to say.

"Any questions?" she asked.

Her heart was beating so hard she thought she was going to vomit right onto the floor.

"Don't you think eighteen is a little young to decide you're a lesbian?" one large man asked.

"No." Karen squirmed, uncomfortable at the question. She didn't know what else to say.

"Maybe you just haven't had the right man," the man continued. A young lad, late teens, sitting on the man's right started to snigger as he realised where this was going. "If you want to try again - with a real man - I'd be happy to oblige you. I mean, for a fee of course." The young lad laughed harder. A few others in the small group raised a smile too.

Karen's face suddenly lit up as though possessed for a moment, "I'm pretty sure - you're the reason lesbians exist in the first place," she said. The group, with the exception of the man who had challenged her, laughed.

He continued, "And what's with the sob story about your folks?" he pushed. "You going for the sympathy vote?" No laughter from the group. Even that was a question too far for them.

"The same way you're going for the Special Needs vote with your dress sense?" Karen turned to the youth sitting next to the man, "As his Carer, I think it might be a good idea if you keep him under control a little better," she said.

One of the three at the front stepped in, "Okay, thank you, if you'd like to take a seat."

Karen didn't wait for a rebuttal from the man, or the lad sitting with him, and took her seat back amongst the group. The next person stood up and took centre stage. Karen settled in her chair and breathed a sigh of relief. Her comebacks surprised even her but she found it hard to put the man's comments from her mind. She glanced over to the man and the expression on his face revealed his annoyance at being made to look stupid. The faint smile on the face of one of the three, at the front, suggested they enjoyed the back and forth between Karen and the man. She smiled and started to relax into it. This wasn't her - the girl who answered back - but if it's what the producers wanted then she'd give them exactly that.

NOW

Karen was sitting on the bed. Jordy was by her side still. Stuart had a paper bag in his hands and was encouraging Karen to breathe deeply and slowly into it in an effort to calm her down.

"And in, and out…" Stuart instructed her.

Jordy was rubbing her back - more so out of offering comfort than really doing anything else to help. By now the other housemates had crowded around her too, despite Paul telling them to give her some space. The only housemate to listen to his order was Philip. It wasn't so much he was listening to what Paul was saying, but more to do with the fact he had yet to move from his bed as though he were completely unfazed by what was going on around him.

"This is ridiculous. Why are we locked in here? They should just cancel the whole show," Kate suggested.

Philip laughed, "This is the show. Why would they cancel it? This is the best footage they've had for ages. Imagine the viewing numbers. They'll be through the roof when this gets aired."

"That's just sick. They won't show this. They can't."

"Did you read your contracts? You are aware you basically signed away the rights to your soul for this, right? Trust me - they'll be showing all of this."

"Feeling better?" Stuart pulled the bag away from Karen who nodded in response to his question. "Good."

"I want to go home," she whimpered.

"Well you can always ask them," Stuart said.

"Please...There's only one way we leave here." Philip spat, under his breath.

"This is The Controller! Can all housemates gather on the sofas!" the voice boomed over the intercom system throughout the house. Before the voice had finished giving it's instruction, the red light illuminating the locked door switched to a light shade of green to signal the door had been unlocked. The voice repeated itself before anyone had a chance to move, "This is The Controller! Can all housemates gather on the sofas!"

"Now what?" Fiona walked through to the sitting room and sat on one of the sofas - three long sofas laid out in a U shape with a small coffee table in the centre. The rest of the group joined her.

Georgia nodded towards the dining table, "They've moved him."

The group all looked in the direction of where they had left Morgan's body. He was gone, along with any trace of what had happened.

"Look!" Chris pointed to the wall behind one of the sofas. The wall had thirteen screens across it laid out as two rows of six with a larger plasma screen above the two rows. Each screen had a picture of one of the members of the group and all had a green hue about them except for both Richard's screen and Morgan's. They had a red hue and, under their faces, the words ELIMINATED. The larger of the screens - the one above the two rows - flickered into life revealing Philip sitting in The Control Room; a small room with a single chair in it which pointed towards a camera to ensure the occupant was always facing (and talking to) the screen.

"What is this?" Philip asked. He shifted in his seat, uncomfortable in the knowledge of what was coming. The rest of the group glanced at him. Under other circumstances they would have - perhaps - been smiling at his embarrassment as they wondered what he was about to do on screen which would result in it getting shown to the rest of the house. With recent events though, none of them found themselves grinning and all were suspicious.

"Housemates, tonight is a double elimination!"

"What the hell is going on?" Jack asked.

Before

DAY SIX

Philip made himself comfortable in the large chair, facing the camera. He looked suspicious immediately. His sixth day in the house and first time called into The Control Room with no reason he could see.

In front of him - between the chair and the camera - was a small table just in the shot of the camera. A small vial, filled with some kind of clear liquid, caught his eye.

"Hello, Philip."

"Hi," Philip turned his attention away from the vial and looked up to the camera as though trying to form a connection with whoever was talking to him.

"As you are aware tomorrow is the day of the first Elimination."

"Yes."

"How are you feeling?"

"I'm okay," he replied. "I mean - obviously - I don't want to go yet. It's only been a week. I wouldn't mind staying a little longer to see how crazy things are going to get but…Yeah…I know things happen for a reason so… I'm ready."

"How would you like to potentially save yourself for one more week?"

"Go on…"

"In front of you is a small vial…"

"Yes…"

"If you can slip the contents of that vial - unnoticed - to either Morgan, Paul, Stuart or Fiona…You will be safe from the first elimination."

Philip smiled, "Okay."

There was brief moment of silence. Philip laughed nervously.

"Who would you like to drink the vial?" asked The Controller.

Without hesitation Philip nominated, "Morgan." He took a moment to reflect before putting forward his reasons, "The guy is annoying. I mean - I know he is supposed to rile people up but, even so, he's doing my head in. The sooner he goes out the better. It's him or me. Hell, if I can't get him to drink the contents - I'll drink them myself…" he laughed and picked the vial up off the table.

"Thank you, Philip, and - remember - none of your other housemates are to know about this or there will be serious repercussions."

Philip nodded and slipped the vial into his trouser pocket before leaving the room. He walked down the stairs, back towards the main part of the house, aware that the cameras were following him.

N O W

The group were stunned into silence. The television screen went blank before switching off completely. Slowly every one turned their attention to Philip who was squirming uncomfortably on his sofa. Those who were sitting near him seemed to slowly edge a little further away from him.

"Housemates, thanks to Philip, Morgan has been eliminated but as you are aware - tonight is a double elimination…"

A small panel on the coffee table slid open to reveal a small hole. Slowly a perplex box rose up out of it; a handgun sitting on a stand within the box.

"…And who goes is up to you…"

"What the fuck is going on?" Kate shouted.

"You killed him?!" Paul's attention was firmly fixed on Philip.

"It was a task! I didn't know what was in the vial!"

"When? When did you do it?" Paul carried on.

"I want to go home! Please! Let me go home!" Karen was staring up to one of the many cameras on the ceiling.

Jack was muttering under his breath, "I was right... They want us to eliminate each other for real!" Jack stood up and addressed the group, "It's okay - they want us to eliminate each other so all we have to do is not play their game. Go on a strike until they let us out. It's fine! We are in control here, not them. We just need to..."

The Controller's voice boomed out of the purpose-built home's intercom system, "Housemates, you need to make your nomination within the next two minutes or severe punishments will be issued!"

Karen was crying whilst the other girls just looked nervous and confused. Paul had not taken his attention off Philip who was staring at the gun, the finger of his left hand twitching as though he wanted to make a move for it.

"This is ridiculous! They can't get away with this! They'll be shut down!" Chris was looking at the camera - his mind wondering what sort of sick son of a bitch would be running a show like this. More to the point, what kind of sick fuck would be watching - an answer to which he found depressing when he realised thousands of people would watch this, if only out of morbid curiosity.

"We just need to stay calm and stick together," Jack continued, "they're not in charge. They may think they are but we're the ones who have the power. We're the ones..."

Paul grabbed the lid of the box and threw it off. By the time it crashed to the floor, he had the handgun in his hands. The girls screamed whilst Stuart and Chris dove for cover. Before anyone else had a chance to react, Paul pulled the trigger six times - the barrel aimed directly at Philip. Each bullet tore a hole through Philip's chest. By the time Paul had finished firing, Philip was dead. His body slumped to the side before slipping off the sofa.

"What the fuck are you doing?!" Stuart yelled from behind the sofa.

The picture of Philip on the wall of photographs switched to red. The words ELIMINATED appeared underneath.

"All housemates must return to the bedroom immediately."

"If I hadn't killed him, he would have killed us. You saw the footage. He killed Morgan," Paul started to defend his actions. "I did it for all of us. Can you honestly say you trusted him? Even before what we saw on the tape…"

"All housemates must return to the bedroom immediately."

Paul continued, "What you said is right - we need to stick together. We can't when we have someone like that in the group…No one was safe…"

"I just want to go home," Karen was whining again and - once again - Jordy was comforting her.

"All housemates must return to the bedroom immediately."

"So basically whoever gets the one hundred thousand pounds is the one who has to be prepared to kill everyone else in the house…" Chris and Fiona were looking at Philip's body. He continued, "I don't know about you but I don't need the money that much…"

"Neither do I," said Fiona, "but - at the same time - I don't want to die either."

Chris looked at Fiona. All trust that may or may not have been there - in that split second - was gone for good.

Georgia said, "This was supposed to be fun. A good way of spending the summer vacation. Something to help my career…How did we end up here?!"

"All housemates must return to the bedroom immediately or face the consequences!"

Georgia screamed, "How did we end up here?!"

BEFORE

GEORGIA SANGSTER

DAY ONE

After an initial chat to the camera (and, therefore, the viewers) whereby the show's concept was explained, the female presenter - a pretty girl in her early thirties who'd not been seen on television too much before this - lead the way through the house showing off the various rooms it had to offer and where the housemates would be spending the next eight weeks of their lives - unless, of course, they were eliminated.

One of the highlights in the house included a jacuzzi hidden underneath a small canopy in the garden ensuring they could enjoy a dip no matter the weather. The garden itself was a good size with plenty of room for the housemates to have their own space if it were required - and the producers knew that it would be. Inside the house - everything was open plan with the exception of the bedroom. There was only one bedroom. A room filled with double beds and single beds. To the casual observer the bedroom would look like a place of sanctuary for the housemates to rest in - without fear of being disturbed by anyone still milling around the rest of the house. In reality - it was the perfect place to lock them in whilst the production team set the other rooms up for whatever 'games' they had in mind for their guests.

The presenter - Emily - sat in The Control Room's large chair and spoke directly to the room's one camera.

"And there you have it - a very impressive looking house… But there's just one thing missing." She leaned forward to the camera, "We need some housemates!"

One of the show's producers spoke into the ear-piece in Emily's ear informing her they had gone to an ad break. She had two and a half minutes to get out of the house and into position on the main stage, by the front door of the house, ready to greet the applicants who'd successfully made it to this stage of the show.

Emily slipped through the side door of The Control Room, which was meant as a fire escape, and negotiated the winding corridors, around the exterior of the main part of the house, until she got to a large set of double doors. She pushed them open and stepped out onto the metal walkway which paved her way towards the main stage, surrounded by a cheering crowd - all of whom were waving signs around with various messages saying "Hi" to their friends watching at home.

Emily took her position in front of one of the cameras - centre stage. She watched as a couple of crane-mounted cameras swept over the cheering audience. The people frantically waving their homemade signs in an effort to be noticed by the people at home. A producer - once again in Emily's ear - warning her to be ready - the cameras were about to roll once more.

"Welcome back!" she chirpily said to the camera (audience at home). "So - who wants some housemates in there?" she asked. The audience cheered. "Let's bring on Housemate Number One!"

Emily turned her back to the camera and faced a large plasma screen which hung on the wall of the main house. The screen was showing the show's logo. A split second later and it was replaced with the image of Georgia. She was sitting on a stool, in front of the camera, talking to someone off-shot. Her name flashed up on the bottom left of the screen.

"What would I do to win? Absolutely anything," she laughed. The video cut to various shots of Georgia acting the fool; cartwheels in her garden, messily cooking a cake in the kitchen, laughing with friends all sitting around a dining room table eating the cake she'd been baking. Her voice played over all of the scenes, "My name is Georgia, I'm twenty-four years old and I'm just your typical fun-loving crazy girl! When I'm not out partying with my friends, there is nothing more I like than baking. One day I hope to open my own cake shop! What kind of housemate would I make? I'll be the fun one! I'll definitely be dragging the others up from their seats to dance and party! And if they don't - well…I'll let them know how boring I actually find them!" The video cut to her sitting in front of the camera again, "I don't suffer fools gladly and boring people can just do one!" A close up shot of her face as she repeated her video's opener, "What would I do to win? Absolutely anything!" she laughed and the video cut back to the show's logo.

Emily turned to the camera, "Let's bring out the first housemate!"

The crowd cheered as a black limousine drove down the road towards the red carpet which lead the way to the stage where Emily was waiting, microphone in hand. Her blue eyes were fixed upon the limo as it rolled to a stop - turning at the last minute to ensure the back door was in line with the carpet. A security man stepped forward, and opened the door. Georgia stepped out to the sound of cheers from the waving crowd. She had a huge grin on her face - like all of her Christmases had come at once - as she ran down the red carpet, slapping hands with all those who held their palms out for her.

She stopped at the end of the carpet, before the few stairs to the stage, and struck poses for the handful of camera crew. When Emily felt as though the press had taken enough shots - she urged Georgia to join her on the stage.

"So what can we expect from you?" Emily asked.

"Fun!"

The crowd reacted positively.

"Well then get yourself in there!" Emily ushered her towards the stairs. Georgia wasted no time. She ran up the metal stairs to the platform leading towards the entrance to the house. She turned to the crowd and gave them a wave before the door opened and she stepped in. The door slammed shut behind her and the screen - hanging on the exterior wall for the crowds - showed her walk down a narrow corridor towards the next set of doors.

Emily turned to the camera, "Well it's not going to be much fun with only one housemate…Who wants another?" her voice rose at the end of the sentence in order to encourage more screams from the waiting crowds.

N O W

Georgia was sitting in the corner of the bedroom. It wasn't her bed but she didn't care. The bed belonged to Philip but it was fairly clear he wasn't going to be using it anymore. She wiped a tear from her eye - a tear spilt because of her situation as opposed to worry about another life lost.

All of the housemates had been locked in the bedroom once more. At least this time they knew why. The production team was out there clearing away the body and blood spilt. No one was really talking. Karen was on the bed she shared with Jordy, neither speaking nor crying. Jack was on the double bed he once shared with Morgan. Stuart was on his bed in the other corner of the room - the one he was supposed to share with Paul. Kate and Fiona were on theirs and Chris was sitting on the edge of his. Only Paul was up and about. He was standing in the bathroom, next to the sink, frantically scrubbing the blood from his face. By now he couldn't tell whether it was the remnants of Morgan's blood, spat at him earlier, or whether it was splatter from Philip's corpse. It didn't matter - whosever blood it was, he wanted it off.

"Congratulations housemates!" The Controller's eerily jovial voice boomed over the intercom system making some of the housemates jump. "You have all survived the first week! Eliminations will continue next Friday! Who has what it takes to win one hundred thousand pounds?" The voice crackled off and the intercom went silent. No one seemed happy.

Stuart called over to Jack, "Hey." Jack looked at him but didn't answer him, "You mind if I bunk up with you?" he asked.

Jack had lost his bed fellow earlier that day so it was fair to assume he wouldn't have minded sharing the bed with someone else - especially someone who was seemingly uncomfortable about sharing a bed with a murderer - but, even so, he just wanted to be alone. Given half the chance, he would have walked out the front door there and then and returned to his own home - the quiet sanctuary he had left behind. Sure the money would have been nice, welcomed even, but it wasn't worth this. Had it not been for Karen's desperate pleas to go home being unheard earlier, he would have tried the same. He rolled onto his side - away from Stuart. Stuart took the hint and looked at the others in the room in the hope someone would offer him some space. Every one avoided eye contact.

The bathroom door opened and Paul stepped into the room. The door slammed behind him. No one turned to him. If anything, they seemed keen to avoid eye contact.

"Are we not even going to talk about it?" he asked.

Silence.

"No one?"

"What's there to talk about?" Jack stood up. He didn't step towards him though. He stayed rooted on the spot right where he was. "You killed him. You shot him. Not just once."

"I had to. We had to eliminate someone else," Paul argued, "you heard The Controller."

"The Controller? Some sicko sitting behind a monitor controlling us like puppets?! All we had to do was sit there and do nothing. If we don't listen to them then they have no show. No show, they have to let us all go."

"Do you really believe that?" Paul's voice raised by a slight notch.

"You think the authorities will allow them to air a show where contestants kill each other? They're probably on their way now. All we had to was sit tight and wait but now," he paused, "now you've put yourself in the firing line. Just like Philip. The man you killed."

Paul visibly calmed himself down and took a moment to collect his thoughts, "And what if the show doesn't go out until the series is over?" he said. The room fell silent. They presumed it would have been airing on a day to day basis from the moment they went into the house with the crowd cheering them. It wasn't until Paul mentioned it now that the thought of the show not airing immediately sunk in. Paul continued, "For all we know the show won't end until all but one of us is dead."

"If we don't play the game, they'll have to let us go!" Chris took Jack's side.

"Three of our group are dead. One of them was the result of The Controller himself but the other two are dead because of the actions of the people in this house, do you really think they'll just let us all leave peacefully when there's a strong possibility of us going straight to the police? Or do you think there's a good chance they'll clean their mess up and just do away with all of us?" Paul argued.

"They can't just kill us. Our friends, our families... They all know where we are."

"Because we signed a contract and said where we were going?" asked Paul.

"I didn't tell anyone," Kate piped up from next to Fiona.

Fiona shook her head, "I didn't."

"None of us were supposed to tell anyone. We signed stating we wouldn't. All housemates need to remain anonymous until the show begins. Remember that clause in the contract? You did read it right? Who else didn't say anything to their family or friends?" Jordy, Chris, Stuart put their hands in the air along with Kate and Fiona. "I didn't say anything either."

"Well that's fine. I did. And I'm glad I did," said Jack. He turned to Karen and Georgia, "Who did you tell?"

"I told my mum," said Karen.

"My friends. It just slipped out," Georgia looked sheepish.

"That's fine. My family, Karen's family and your friends - they all know where we are."

"No!" Paul raised his voice again. "They know what the production team wanted us to know and nothing more than that. X amount of weeks, one winner, one hundred grand prize... Do you honestly believe they'd have information on that contract which could lead people right to where we are? You really think these people - the ones who are playing us off each other - are stupid enough to not cover their tracks one hundred percent of the way?" he hesitated, "Well I'm glad you're confident because I'm not. The way I see it - we're here for the duration." The room fell silent again. Paul made his way back to the bed he was supposed to share with Stuart. As soon as he was close, Stuart turned away and looked in the opposite direction. Paul stood on the spot. "We aren't bed partners anymore?" Paul turned back to the group, "Okay so we do as you say and we don't play their games anymore... Can you honestly say you trust everyone in this house?"

Before

DAY TWO

Paul and Jack were sitting in the comfortable outdoor chairs in the garden. They were watching the rest of the group, through the window, socialising in the living area. Paul took a drag on his cigarette as he watched Morgan jump up from the sofa only to start bouncing around the room in what appeared to be a high state of excitement. "I'm not sure about Morgan. I mean - what is he doing now? That - that's not normal behaviour."

"He is a little…" Jack hesitated. Unlike Paul he wasn't smoking. He was simply there to keep his new friend company since they had become close from the moment they met.

"Say it," Paul pushed him.

"Over the top."

"Over the top? The guy is a fucking moron. He's not over the top. Just a fucking moron."

They both laughed as Paul took another drag on his cigarette.

He puffed the smoke out, "I don't know - I just don't trust him."

"I wouldn't say that," Jack argued, "he seems…"

"He seems like he is over-compensating for something. He seems like he is hiding his true character. The Morgan we're seeing is just a show to try and make us like him."

"Well he's not doing a very good job then," Jack laughed.

"Too right. I just want to bash his brains in."

"Bit aggressive…" Jack laughed again.

NOW

Paul asked the question again, "Well? Can you honestly say you trust everyone here in this house?"

Jack argued back, "Well I don't know - if you asked me the other day… Say back on the second day where you yourself were telling me you didn't trust someone… Then I would have said I did. I may not have liked some individuals as much as others but…"

"So you trust everyone enough to say they won't take your life given half the chance?" Paul cut him short. Jack didn't say anything. He looked from face to face as each looked back at him waiting for a response.

"I don't know. I thought I could. But then I thought you were a decent person too so - I don't know - maybe my sense of judgement is completely out of the window." Jack sat back on the edge of the bed. Clearly he'd had enough of arguing. Especially as he knew it wasn't going to get him out of the situation.

Georgia piped up, "I don't want to kill anyone."

"No one wants to kill anyone," Paul told her.

Chris butt in, "Really? Because - from where I was sitting - you seemed pretty eager to put a bullet in Philip."

"If I hadn't - who is to say he wouldn't have picked the gun up and shot you. Or anyone else here for that matter? He had already killed one person and he didn't seem too fussed about that - sitting here, on the bed, acting as though butter wouldn't melt in his mouth…"

"To be fair, he is right…" Jordy was the only housemate to stand up for Paul.

"Going by your logic," Jack argued, "that means you're fair game. After all - you killed someone so what's to say you haven't got a taste for it and want to kill more?"

"You're being stupid."

"Is he?" Chris said. "You killed Philip because you were worried he might have killed someone else - maybe yourself or maybe one of us. But what's to say he killed Morgan because of the very same reasoning? Kill or be killed? You're saying it is okay for you to protect yourself but not for him to do the same?"

"He drew first blood…"

"Because he was told to by The Controller. He probably thought - if he said no - then someone else would be given the poison to use."

"We should just tell them we don't want to partake anymore," Karen interjected. "They might let us leave voluntarily."

"We've already established that isn't very likely," Stuart told her. "Paul's right, they're not going to let us walk out of here. They can't afford to. If we want to survive - we're going to have to play their sick games."

"We're going to have to kill each other?" Karen whimpered.

"No one is killing anyone," said Jack.

"Okay so we don't play along - what is your great plan? Because, from where I am sitting, there aren't many options."

Chris pointed to the far wall, "What about that?" he suggested.

The group turned to where he was pointing, towards a fire exit door.

"You want to walk out?" Stuart asked.

"Why not?"

"Well - for one - we don't know what is on the other side of the door. They may take an attempt to walk out as a sign we aren't playing their game anymore giving them all the excuses they need to terminate the programme - and, more specifically, us."

"Then why have the emergency door there?" Stuart asked.

"Keeping up appearances," Paul stepped in again.

"So what the hell are we supposed to do?" Chris yelled.

"Let's just wait and see what happens in the morning. You heard The Controller - we've all survived the first week. Eliminations will continue next Friday. Maybe one of us can talk to them tomorrow and - I don't know - try and figure out what is going on."

"I don't care about what is going on. I just want out." Kate spat.

"Whatever you want - we need to talk to them. I'll go in, in the morning, when we're allowed out of this fucking room," Paul took charge.

"And what - we're supposed to trust what you tell us?" Chris asked.

"We'll all go and see them tomorrow. All of us," Jack suggested. No one disagreed with him.

Paul turned back to Stuart, "So…Are we bed buddies still or do I need to make up a space on the floor?"

Stuart moved to his side of the bed and smiled. He wasn't happy about the situation but he didn't disagree with what Paul was saying; the reasons he killed had Philip. Paul climbed onto the bed next to Stuart.

"So what now?" Kate asked.

The production team answered her question by shutting off the bedroom lights despite knowing that none of the housemates would be sleeping that night.

Before

DAY ONE

There was a free for all more or less as soon as the bedroom doors opened - signalled by the red light around the door switching to a green colour and the sound of a 'click' coming from the remote control lock. The excitement was obvious and not just because of the bedroom being unlocked but also because they were finally in the house after months of waiting after having passed through the audition process. Philip lead the way as he was closest to the door when it unlocked but was closely followed by the rest of the group with everyone splitting off in their own direction as soon as they'd got through the narrow door.

"It's gorgeous!" Jordy said as she cast her eyes around the room for the first time. "I could get used to this kind of luxury." And it was luxury. The double beds and single beds had the best mattresses on them and were covered in thick duvets. The pillows, filled with feather, were thick enough that, no matter your preference, you would only need one for a good night's sleep and everything was nicely decorated with space being utilised to the max with additional clothes space in drawers underneath the beds. Jordy sat on one of the large double beds.

Karen approached her, "Do you mind if I share with you?" she asked.

"No - not at all." She jumped up, "Which side would you prefer?"

Paul and Stuart were standing at one of the other double beds. Paul turned to Stuart and said, "What about it? Bed buddies? I sleep like the dead…"

"So long as you don't fart during the night!"

"Can't make any promises," Paul laughed.

"If you boys need to do that - you can go to the bathroom," Georgia pointed out.

Philip put his jumper down on the corner bed as though to claim it as his own. He turned to the other housemates who were busy claiming their beds too - some with no fuss and some with lots of fuss as they believed they should have had their own bed; Kate being one of the most 'put out' at the thought of having to share with a stranger.

"Well I'd swap but pretty sure…" Philip turned to the older lady Kate had been paired with, who was preparing her side of the bed, "…Sorry what was your name again?"

"Fiona."

"Ah yes - sorry, I'm rubbish with names. Anyway, as I was saying, I'd swap but pretty sure Fiona wouldn't be happy about sharing with a man. And - on another note - I'm sorry to announce to the room that I do snore."

The room groaned in unison. Stuart jokingly looked up to one of the cameras hanging from the ceiling and asked, "Can we have permission to set Philip up his own bed in the garden?"

"Just throw something at me, it's fine!" Philip suggested.

"Can't we just smother you with a pillow?" Paul asked.

NOW

The room was near enough pitch-black to encourage the group to sleep and yet no one had drifted off. All of them lying there, lost in their own personal thoughts. Jack was lying in his single bed staring up at the ceiling whilst Chris was doing the same in the single bed near to him.

Paul's comment, on the first night in the house, kept playing through Jack's exhausted (and confused) mind along with the comment he'd said in the garden a couple of days later about bashing Morgan's brains in. Both comments - at the time - that Jack had found quite funny. He presumed Paul had a dark sense of humour, much like his own. But now - lying in the black of the night - he wondered whether Paul had ever really been joking or whether the murderous comments were part of his somewhat darker psyche.

Had Paul been called to The Control Room and offered the poison, instead of Philip, would he have used it as freely his now 'ex' housemate had? He rolled onto his side and looked in the general direction of the bed Paul shared with Stuart. Two outlines lying on the mattress; one seemingly on his side and the second - sitting bolt-upright. Jack couldn't help but wonder which was which. Was Paul trying to get to sleep whilst Stuart was sitting up or was it the other way around? Stuart desperately trying to get to sleep whilst Paul was sitting up surveying the room. Perhaps - in his mind - wondering who would be the best to eliminate next for 'the good of the house'.

"Maybe none of it is real?" Chris whispered.

Jack didn't say anything. He wasn't sure if Chris was talking to him. Hard to tell with little to no light in the room.

"What do you think?" Chris continued.

"You talking to me?" Jack whispered back.

"Yes. Maybe everything is a trick? Some kind of sick game to see how we would react if we were forced to bump each other off?" he continued - sure to keep his voice low. "The ultimate test of how far you'd go for the prize money?"

Jack thought about it for a while. When they first went into the house and had watched the walls close in on Richard, they'd all laughed as though it were some sick illusion set up to unsettle them - had Chris and he been having this conversation back then, he'd have been inclined to agree but... Morgan was coughing up blood as he choked and Philip... The way his body moved as each slug penetrated him, the way the blood splattered the scene. It was all too real. Jack didn't think it was a trick. He didn't think it was fake. But, even so, he didn't have the right to take away someone's hope. "Maybe," he said.

"If it's not," Chris continued, "who do you think we need to be wary of? You think Paul is one to watch after what happened earlier?" Chris' voice was low but that didn't stop Jack from worrying Paul could hear every word being spoken. "What he said earlier - if you think about it - it kind of made sense, didn't it?"

"We should try and get some sleep," Jack whispered. "It's going to be a tough day tomorrow."

He turned his back on Chris and closed his eyes. He half-expected Chris to keep talking, keep asking questions, but was relieved when he didn't continue with his train of thoughts - at least, not out loud. Like many of the other housemates, he laid there in silence, unsure of what to say for the best.

"I can't sleep!" Jordy said out loud, breaking the uncomfortable silence filling the room.

Before

JORDY HINTON

DAY FOUR

K ate and Jordy were sitting in the corner of the garden. A heater between the two kept them outside despite the sun having gone down and the temperature dropping. The other housemates were indoors where they continued to enjoy a party thrown for no other reason than generosity. Music was pumping through the house and alcohol was free flowing. At least the alcohol had been free flowing - now it was very much drying up.

"I would say… I don't know," Jordy giggled.

"Yes, you do!"

The pair of them were discussing which of the housemates they found attractive. Kate managed to worm her way out of giving her own answer by playing the 'boyfriend outside' card.

"I don't. I haven't really thought about it!" Jordy laughed.

"Of course you have! I've noticed you looking at them."

"Jack. I'd say I fancied Jack!"

"I knew it!" Kate laughed. "And…Really? What about Morgan?"

Both girls laughed.

"And speak of the devil," Kate continued. The smile instantly faded from her face as she watched the french doors slide open and Morgan step out.

"Oi, oi! You two look like you're having fun…" he called out, a drunken slur very evident in his voice.

"We were," Kate muttered under her breath. She looked at Jordy and rolled her eyes.

"How much has he had to drink?" Jordy whispered.

"Can't say I blame him - not like he has had the warmest of receptions from everyone. Although - only has himself to blame. The guy is a prick."

Morgan sat next to Jordy and put his arm around her. It was clear from her expression, even in her drunken state, this wasn't welcome.

"So what are we talking about then?"

Neither of the girls was quick to answer him. Kate was trying very hard not to just tell him to fuck off and Jordy was doing some subtle squirming in the hope Morgan would remove his arm. Kate was the first to break the awkward silence.

"We were having a private conversation."

"Okay. What about?"

Kate rolled her eyes again and stood up before walking from the garden after telling Jordy, "I'm going to get another drink."

Morgan and Jordy watched as Kate disappeared into the living area of the house. She slid the door shut so Morgan didn't follow - not that he was planning to. He turned to Jordy with a smile on his face, "So…How about it then?"

"How about what?"

"You and me. I think we'd make a cute couple. I mean - obviously - I'd be the cuter one but I reckon we would look good together." he gave her a cheesy wink. Jordy looked at him. She couldn't tell whether he was joking or not.

"How drunk do you think I am?" Jordy asked.

"I'm hoping drunk enough?" Morgan flashed her another smile.

A shiver ran down her back.

"Besides," he continued, "Georgia wasn't interested and Fiona isn't my cup of tea."

"How old are you again?" Jordy laughed.

"Don't think of it as 'old'. Think of it as 'experienced'." Another smile from the alcohol-fuelled sex pest.

Jordy laughed, "Here's me thinking I couldn't handle my drink very well!"

"So come on," he continued, "what will it take for a bit of fucky-fuck?"

"Money," Jordy laughed. "A lot of money. Possibly more than you'd be able to afford!"

"I'll hold you to that," Morgan leaned down to the ground and picked up one of the wine glasses previously left there by another of the housemates before they retired indoors. "We'll continue this conversation after I've won the money!" He downed his drink.

"I can hardly wait."

The french doors opened and the rest of the housemates spilled into the garden. The music - in the house - had stopped now and they'd decided to continue their party in the fresh air.

"What's going on out here then? You two look cozy," Paul shouted out as he stepped onto the perfectly cut grass.

"We're talking sex," Morgan slurred.

"Always a good conversation to be had," Stuart laughed.

Jack sat next to Jordy.

"So what about the sex then?" Stuart asked, keen to join in with a bit of filth.

"It will cost me money but…She hasn't said no."

"Well - that's good…Isn't it?" Stuart looked to Chris with an eyebrow raised. Chris shrugged.

Jordy leaned over to Jack and whispered, "You wouldn't have to pay. You could have it for free." She laughed as Jack blushed.

Now

DAY EIGHT

The green light had illuminated the bedroom door over an hour ago. Most of the housemates had spilled into the main section of the house - each finding their own space. Jordy was standing in the kitchen looking at the bowls stacked on the side - ready to be used for breakfast.

Jack walked up to her, "You okay?"

"I was horrible to him," she said.

"Morgan?"

She nodded. Jack didn't say anything to her. There was nothing he could say. None of them had been particularly nice to Morgan when he had been alive. Most were irritated by him and had hoped he was the one who was leaving in the first elimination. Jordy nodded towards the cereal, "You think that's even safe to eat?"

Again, Jack didn't say anything. Jordy looked at him and wondered what he was thinking about. From the moment he'd walked into her life (the house) he seemed to be more of a 'thinker' than a 'sayer' - not that she thought there was anything wrong with that.

Paul stepped over from the dining area, up into the kitchen. He waited for Jack to turn around and face him before he spoke. "Well - are we going upstairs then?" he asked. "No sense putting it off." He was - of course - referring to the necessary conversation with The Controller; the voice behind the people running the show.

"We should wait for the others," Jack said.

"There's no need," said Paul, "you and I can do it. I think it's safe to say - after last night - that we aren't exactly in bed together figuratively speaking. Unless, after a good night's sleep, you can see where I am coming from now?"

"A good night's sleep? I don't think anyone had a good night's sleep. Let's just get this over and done with, yeah?" Jack started towards the stairs which lead the way to The Control Room.

Paul followed, with Jordy - who'd decided to tag along. By the time they caught up with Jack - the red illumination around The Control Room door had turned to the welcoming green light, signalling the door was ready for them to venture through. Jack went through first and the door slammed shut behind the last one through. The green light switched to red.

In the Control Room, Jack was standing next to the chair. Paul and Jordy a few feet behind him as though uncomfortable to take a seat without Jack taking one first.

"Please unlock the doors," Jack blurted out - still standing. "We wish to leave."

"Hello, Jack." The voice of The Controller boomed through the room; a strict voice of authority - not that Jack cared. Currently, all he wanted to do was get out of the house once and for all.

He repeated himself, "Please unlock the doors. We wish to leave."

"Who wishes to leave?"

"What do you mean who wishes to go? Everyone does. We don't know what kind of sick game you're playing but we don't want to be a part of it."

"Jack, when you came into the house you knew that only one person could leave with the one hundred thousand pound prize."

"What? We don't want the prize money. We just want to go home."

The Controller didn't answer and the room filled with an awkward silence.

"Hello? Anyone?" Jack pushed them.

"Was there anything else we can help with?" the voice boomed.

Jack looked back to Paul, "This is a joke, right?" Paul shrugged. "Just unlock the doors - we wish to leave," Jack continued.

"Jack, during the audition process, housemates were told they would have a number of tough decisions to make during their stay in the house if they were to leave with one hundred thousand pounds."

"We don't want the fucking money. How hard is that to understand? We just want to go back to our lives. We want out of the show."

"Morgan and Philip were two such decisions."

"What? How was that a decision? It's not as though anyone really had a choice!"

"Everyone always has a choice," The Controller's voice echoed through the room.

Jack turned to Paul, "Are you hearing this?"

He nodded but still had nothing to say.

"Housemates were also informed how they'd leave the show and that was via elimination."

"And by elimination you meant death…" Jack raised his voice.

"All housemates must be eliminated in order for one to leave the show."

"We're not just going to kill each other because you demand it," Jack continued, "you're out of your fucking minds…" the words came from his mouth despite the truth of the matter being; two housemates had already been murdered by people living in the house with him. A third housemate, Richard, being the only one who'd died at the direct hands of The Controller.

"To not partake in the tasks and missions set forth by The Controller would be deemed a serious breach of the rules and - as such - will be met with serious consequences."

It was now Jack realised why Richard had been killed before he even got into the house; it was a performance by the production team to show all housemates that they could take a life without losing any sleep. It was a sign that the people living in the house were nothing to the production team but little monkeys ready to dance for them at their beck and call. The small Control Room was filled with an uncomfortable silence again.

"Was there anything else The Controller can help you with?" the voice boomed.

Jack pushed past Paul and Jordy and reached for the door. He pulled on it but it didn't budge. The red light around the frame saying why.

"Open the fucking door!" Jack shouted. Both Paul and Jordy stepped to the side, to give Jack more room. There was a lengthy delay, as Jack continued to pull on the door, before the red light flicked to green and the door unlocked. Jack stormed from the room. A second, maybe two, later and Paul and Jordy followed.

"What did they say?" Chris called up to them.

The rest of the housemates, Chris included, were standing at the foot of the stairs with hopeful looks for freedom on their faces. They didn't need to ask though - they could tell, immediately, from Jack's glum expression that the news wasn't what they had hoped.

Chris asked again, "What did they say?"

BEFORE

DAY FOUR

"They said we're having a party!" Paul came down the stairs with a basket of alcohol under his arm and a smile on his face. The group, sitting in the living area of the house, cheered as Paul approached them, putting the bottles of alcohol on the coffee table between the sofas.

As soon as the last bottle went down, loud pop music pumped into the household to another burst of cheers.

"Of course we should make the most of it," Chris suggested, "because you know it will only be a matter of time before they turn the tables on us!" he laughed.

Jordy reached forward and grabbed one of the bottles of wine from the table, "Rude not to," she said.

Kate sidled up next to her, "It's only right that I help you with that," she laughed. Meanwhile Karen and Georgia took to the clear space of the living area where they began to dance - completely carefree.

Chris sat back with a grin on his face as he watched the two girls dancing together.

"No need to ask what you're thinking about!" Morgan laughed.

Philip was the only one who didn't seem to care about the alcohol or the music. He stood up and walked from the room, choosing - instead - to be alone. Paul noticed and followed him.

"You're not in the mood for a party?" he asked as he entered the bedroom. "It's a good chance to get to know each other," he suggested.

"What's the point?" Philip asked as he made himself comfortable on his bed.

"It'll be good."

"I'm not much of a drinker."

"Come on, it'll be fun."

"I just don't see the point in getting to know the very people we're going to have to eliminate over the coming weeks. You don't want your emotions clouding the issues, do you? I know I don't. I just want to do what is necessary and – get it done - that's it. Nothing more and nothing less. So - yeah - forgive me if I don't want to go drinking with any of you."

"Anyone ever tell you you're a real asshole?" Paul asked.

"Not often but - when they do - I don't dispute it."

Paul shook his head and walked from the room muttering under his breath, "It's only a fucking game."

Now

DAY NINE

Day eight had been a wash-out with regards to being 'good' television for the production team. The housemates hadn't spoken to each other since Jack informed them of what had been said in The Control Room. Most hadn't even sat with one another. If what The Controller had said was true - they would potentially have to turn on each other at some point. With that playing through in the backs of their minds - none of them really felt like socialising. It was different now, though. They were all sitting together at the request of The Controller.

He had selected Paul, Stuart, Fiona and Jordy to all sit at a table whilst the rest of the group - Karen, Georgia, Jack, Chris and Kate - were all instructed to sit on the nearby sofas. The housemates on the sofa didn't need asking twice to sit on the sofa - out of the way - and, to Jack's surprise, neither did the housemates at the table need asking twice.

"Why are you listening to them?" Jack asked.

"You heard what was said in The Control Room yesterday. If we don't - it's a breach of the rules and consequences will be severe," Paul reminded him, not that he needed reminding.

"Yeah well you just seem a little keen," Jack pushed.

"Do you want to swap places? More than fucking welcome!" Paul spat back. "Eliminations are every Friday...Whatever this is...It'll be fine."

"I'm glad you trust the murderous people who stuck us in here," Jack hissed.

"Guys! Please, just shut up… I'm sure they'll tell us what is going on in a second - just as soon as you two stop bickering."

"Least it's bringing out the real you. Kept that well hidden from us when you first came in."

"What do you think this is?" Fiona asked. She was looking at the metal helmets on the table. Each one joined to the table with a series of wires attached. Next to them were hand-held devices with a single red button on them. There was an envelope at the end of the table.

"Please put the head gear on and strap it into place," The Controller's voice made some of the housemates jump. Paul, and the rest of the housemates at the table, looked nervous as they did as they were instructed by putting the headsets on. They each took it in turn to strap the gear to their heads, using the chin straps.

"I don't like this," Jordy said. "Do we have to do this?"

"You heard what they said in The Control Room yesterday," Paul reminded her. "Just remember what I said - eliminations are every Friday. We'll be fine."

It was clear from the expressions of the others, sitting alongside her at the table, that none of the housemates were particularly keen about putting the head-gear on. They were simply going through the motions because they had to.

"Housemates!" The voice boomed through the house again. "In front of you are controllers. Please take hold of these now." The four at the table leaned forward and took hold of the buttons.

"Why are we wearing these things?" Fiona asked. She had panic written all over her face.

"There is a sealed envelope on the table. One of the housemates on the sofa should take this envelope. They are not permitted to open it."

Chris stood up and walked to the table. He picked the envelope up and walked back to where he had been sitting.

"Housemates at the table are to take it in turns to press the red button. Each time they do, the person to the left of them will get an electric shock.

Every round they make, the shocks will get stronger until the housemates are no longer able to withstand it. If they complete more rounds of the table, than written on the piece of paper in the envelope, they will win the house a luxury meal for this evening…" The Controller's voice echoed off.

"What the fuck?" Jordy said - more or less under her breath.

Fiona thought she didn't understand what was being asked of them so re-explained it for her, "We have to shock each other until we can't take it anymore. We do more shocks than the number written in that envelope - we get a meal tonight."

"I hate electric shocks," Stuart whined.

"This is fucking ridiculous," Jack called out from the sofa.

"Just be thankful it's not you sitting here," Paul reminded him. "Let's just get on with it, shall we?"

"I don't want electric…" Jordy's sentence was cut off mid-way through as Paul pressed his red button. "Ow!" she complained. "This is stupid. Can't we just give up and forgo the meal?"

"We can't do that," said Paul, "it would be the same as not taking part. Severe consequences. You saw what they did to the housemate who didn't get in. They crushed him. You saw what they masterminded with Philip and Morgan… You want to risk this or you want to just get on with it?"

"Just press your button," Stuart told Jordy. He had every right to tell her to do so as he was the one sitting to the left of her it would be him on the receiving end of it. "It's just electric shocks. We'll do one round and then we'll stop. That way they can't say we didn't try."

"You're sure?" Jordy asked him.

He nodded. "Let's just get it over and done with. As Paul said - it's not like it's an elimination." He flinched as Jordy pressed her button. A second later and he pressed his - giving Fiona a mild electric shock. She didn't bat an eyelid and immediately pressed her button with little to no hesitation. Paul jumped.

"There," Jordy quickly spoke up, "we tried." She turned to the five housemates watching the proceedings, "Help me get this off," she said referring to the helmet as she fiddled with the strap. She suddenly let out a little squeal of pain and turned to Paul, "What the fuck?!"

"It wasn't that bad, admit it. The first round...It was bearable."

"We said one round and that would be it," Jordy protested.

"There's no way one round will win us the luxury meal..."

"I don't care!" Jordy said. "We said one round..."

"I don't think they'd have put the number of rounds that high. The number in the envelope. I think it will be low to give us some sense of hope. Especially after last night. We might as well keep going until it's too painful." Paul turned to the rest of the group. "What do you think?"

The housemates viewing the proceedings didn't say anything. They just sat there as the participating housemates argued amongst themselves. They knew it wasn't up to them how far they pushed themselves. After all - they just had to watch.

"I don't want to," said Jordy.

"Just press it," Stuart told her. "Otherwise your electric shock was for nothing."

Jordy paused a moment. Stuart was right. She'd had her turn and if it stopped there than the shock she just felt would have been for nothing. Also - although unpleasant - it wasn't that bad. "You're sure?" she turned to Fiona and Stuart. Both nodded - Stuart a little more reluctantly than Fiona. Jordy pressed her button and shocked Stuart who - in turn - shocked Fiona who circled it back to Paul.

"Right, fine, there. We're done," Jordy said. Paul had other ideas and zapped her again. "Seriously - what the fuck is up with you?" she screamed.

"I actually heard that one," Chris whispered to Jack. Jack was just sitting there, a concerned look on his face as to how far this was going to go.

"We can do one more at least," Paul told her. "Again - you've had your shock. You can relax."

"Paul - this is bullshit, man. We agreed..." Stuart protested.

"I don't know about you but I want a decent meal tonight. Who knows what is contaminated in the kitchen from whatever shit Philip was playing around with."

"He poured that into Morgan's food bowl," Fiona pointed out.

"Did he though? Did you actually see him do it? Was it the whole vial or did he put some anywhere else? I can't be sure and if any of you are saying you are sure - well, you're lying to yourselves." Paul looked towards the housemates sitting on the sidelines, waiting for one of them to chip in with their thoughts.

"He is right," Kate said - spurred on by his look.

Paul turned back to Jordy, "You've had your shock. Just press the button."

She looked to Stuart, "I'm sorry."

"Just fucking press it," he hissed - his eyes fixed on Paul.

Jordy pressed her button quickly as though it would lessen the shock given. It didn't. The power had increased significantly since the first round.

"Fuck!" Stuart shouted. He turned to Fiona, "Ready?"

She nodded and braced herself. She barely flinched as she was shocked. Within a split second, she too pressed her button. Paul visibly jumped at the shock.

"Go again," Fiona barked; a look of sheer determination on her face.

Everyone looked at her - surprised by her order.

BEFORE

FIONAPEDDLE

Fiona was sitting opposite a table which had been set up as though it were some kind of judging panel. Unlike the room Karen had found herself in - talking about herself in front of three people and a person operating a camera - there were only two people sitting at the table. There was no camera present. In front of the two people sitting at the table were two clipboards. One, in front of the person on the left, was a page of handwritten notes. The second - had a blank piece of paper where one of them could make further notes if required.

"…And I'll take things as far as they need to go to achieve the desired results," Fiona said. Her eyes were fixed dead ahead at the two people sitting behind the table. They were both nodding as though she'd just given a great speech. The person, an older official looking woman, sitting on the right scribbled some notes down. She turned to the second person - a man of equal age - and nodded as though completely satisfied.

"In which way do you think you could convince the other housemates to go along with your actions? There will be some strong characters in there," the male interviewer asked. The female poised herself to make notes.

"The trick is to be quiet and nice. Soft-spoken. That way, when you want something, people are more inclined to do it for you because they think you're a good person. You start shouting the odds at them, ordering them around - well, they're less likely to do anything for you and you'll find yourself arguing more. Nice is definitely the way forward."

The room fell silent as the lady finished writing her notes. Again, she gave a nod to her colleague.

"Well, thank you, no further questions," he said.

Fiona relaxed, "Thank you for the opportunity. Do you know when you'll be letting people know?"

The man didn't answer her. He simply asked, "Can you send the next one in please?"

Fiona waited a moment, on the off chance the man was about to answer her. When it was clear he wasn't, she nodded, stood up and left the room. A second, or two, later and Jordy walked in clutching a piece of paper.

"Please take a seat," the man said without looking up. He pulled the top sheet from the clipboard and tossed it to one side. As Jordy took a seat, where Fiona had been sitting moments earlier, the man gave the next sheet of paper a quick scan. He looked up, "Do you have the necessary paper-work?" he asked.

"Yes." Jordy leaned forward and slid the certificate onto the table. The female took hold of it and gave it a read. She looked to the man and nodded. He ticked something on the sheet in front of him.

Now

DAY NINE

LUXURY

The housemates were sitting around the dining room table; the first time since witnessing Morgan choking to death. There wasn't a trace of the blood he had coughed up though. Everything was meticulously clean (thanks to the production team working through the night). And instead of Morgan's corpse, the table was littered with various bowls of food - roast potatoes, peas, carrots and a plate of perfectly sliced meat in the middle of it all. No one was eating. They were all looking at the food suspiciously.

"It smells so good," Georgia pointed out.

The food did smell good. And why wouldn't it? It was their reward for completing the electric shock task. They needed to do two rounds according to what was written in the envelope. They managed eight before they couldn't continue.

"By all means," Karen said, "help yourself."

Jack turned to Paul, "You said it yourself - there are no more eliminations until Friday. Why aren't you tucking in?"

Paul looked at Jack, and then at Chris who was also staring at him expecting him to make a move for the food. He smiled and reached for his fork. With his fork in his hand he started stabbing at the potatoes, moving them from bowl to plate. Next up he attacked the meat and did the same. The vegetables he dished up last - enough of each sort to be labeled a 'token gesture' as though it were programmed into him, from an early age, that - even if he didn't like them - he should at least put some on his plate. The housemates watched as he forked one of the potatoes into his mouth. He hesitated a moment and then started to chew down on it - slowly at first and then, when he realised it actually tasted quite nice, with a little more haste. "It's good," he said.

The other housemates started to help themselves. Jack was the last to dish his plate up. Despite the good food, none of the housemates settled into the relationships they had made since before the first murder. All of them sat in a stony silence, unsure of what to do or how to behave.

The Controller countered the awkward silence by playing soft, classical music into the house.

Fiona piped up as she continued to eat, "Well this is nice."

"Look this is silly," Paul said after the room sunk into another uncomfortable silence, "we have to live together. We can't do this if we're not going to talk to each other - let alone trust one another."

"The only way we're going to get out of this house is if we eliminate one another. You heard The Controller. How are we supposed to trust each other when we don't know anyone properly?" Jack said. "It's impossible."

"We're just going to have to try," said Paul.

"Easier said than done, don't you think? Earlier you said you'd just go around the table once in that task and yet you instigated a second time round. Not forgetting, of course, that you blew someone away with a fucking hand cannon!" Chris said.

"You know why I killed him. I had to. I wasn't given an option. And the task - the first shocks didn't hurt. I made the right call to continue. By the way, you don't have to thank me. You just sit there and enjoy your meal."

"We're going round in circles," Georgia said, "clearly everyone is going to disagree about what has already happened but we really need to get a plan together as to how we can all survive this."

"You want to survive? Fine. Kill everyone in this room. That's what they were saying yesterday. That's the only way to get out of this," Paul said.

"There must be another way," Jack argued.

"Look at the trouble they have gone to for this. You really think they'll have an exit plan we can use? I'm glad you're confident because - as I keep saying - I'm really not," even Kate was getting involved.

"Please can everyone just stop arguing?!" Karen said.

The room fell silent.

"This is such bullshit," Kate muttered. She threw her knife and fork down on her unfinished plate. "I'm not even hungry."

"You have to eat," Paul said quietly as he shovelled more food into his own mouth.

"Oh? Really? Why's that then?" Kate snapped. "In case I starve to death?"

"Because - whatever they have planned - we're going to need our strength," Paul said - still keeping his voice relatively low.

Stuart nodded along with Paul, "He is right."

Kate grabbed a piece of meat and shoved it in her mouth before giving them a look as though to say 'fuck you'. She chewed frantically and swallowed it down. "Well, I am stuffed," she said. She got up and walked from the dining room table towards the lounge area. The group didn't try and stop her. Most of them kept their heads down. Only Paul watched her cross the living space to the sofa, shaking his head as he did so.

Unseen by Kate, the wall-mounted camera turned to look at her. It focused in for a split second before the plasma television hanging on the wall flickered into life.

"Something's on the television!" she called over to the others.

They got up and hurried over to see what was being shown.

"What is it?" Fiona asked, the only one of the housemates to carry her plate of food through to the sofa area.

On screen revealed an immaculate kitchen area. Nothing happening. Before anyone had a chance to question what was happening on screen, a man in white overalls stepped into the shot.

"I know him!" Fiona spoke up.

"Who is he?" Jordy asked.

"Hello, Housemates," the man said with a thick accent.

"He's this chef. Used to have his own show. Cooks all these weird and wonderful dishes. Well, I say wonderful… I wouldn't want to eat them. The ingredients he uses are… Well… Pretty disgusting."

"I hope you are enjoying your meal that I lovingly prepared for you at The Controller's request… A big thank you to the housemates who participated in the task to earn everyone the luxury meal this evening! I had a great time making it for you and wish you all the best of luck for the days to come!"

Fiona continued, "Oh God! He made it?!"

"And remember - if you fancy seconds… There is plenty left!" He points to the side. The camera pans around and focuses on the corner of the room; red gore spread up the white walls, and the mangled corpse of Philip - with chunks cut out - resting on the work top.

The screen switched off as some of the group screamed whilst others vomited onto the floor.

"It's a joke, right?" Jack was the only one to speak. He jumped up and climbed onto the sofa so that he could get his face as close to the camera as possible; his brain telling him that, if he made himself appear bigger, The Controller would take him more seriously and confess to the whole thing being nothing more than a sick joke. "Tell me it's a fucking joke! I just ate that shit!" he yelled as he looked up to the camera filming them. He jumped down from the sofa and punched the wall. His fist didn't even make a dent. "You're fucking animals!" he screamed. "FUCK YOU!"

BEFORE

CHRIS GLENN

Chris was standing in a large group of about twenty or so people - all of whom were spaced out in a long line. He was supposed to be watching the young girl, in the black tee shirt and black jeans, standing in front of the line but his eyes were fixed on a much smaller group of individuals who were walking straight through the back doors.

He whispered to the person to his left, one of the only people he'd managed to bond with before getting pulled into the line, "Where do you think they're going?"

The person to his left was a pretty girl called Andrea. If Chris had to guess, he would have put her age at around seventeen years old. By far, she was one of the younger ones in this particular group. "I wouldn't worry about it," she said, "They're the ones who have been fast-tracked."

"Fast-tracked?"

"Yep. Was talking to someone who had a golden ticket earlier. Gets them out of doing all this shit."

"Well how'd they get fast-tracked?"

"I'm presuming it's on the strength of the video applications they put in. I wish I could see what they had sent, though, because - honestly - I thought I had nailed it," she said.

"I didn't do a video application," Chris said.

"And that would be why you're standing here ready to make an idiot of yourself in the hope you manage to get the attention of someone who can put you through to round two."

"What do you think we'll have to do?" Chris asked. His nerves were starting to get the better of him now. The old familiar feeling of 'trouble' starting to bubble away in his stomach just as it always did when nerves set up home.

"Okay," the girl in the black top was shouting so all could hear, "we want you to go around the hall - don't be afraid to use the whole area - pretending you're an animal!" she shouted.

"An animal?" Chris asked Andrea. He felt his face redden at the mere thought of it. He thought he'd come down, have a chat with someone and that would be it. He didn't think he'd have to prance around a hall pretending to be some kind of animal. "What are you doing?" he asked her.

Now

"**W**hat are you doing?" Chris whispered from his bed.
He was trying to get Jack's attention. He could see the outline of him in the darkness. He'd watched him leave his bed and dart to the other side of the room where he'd been doing something up against the wall. It was too dark for Chris to see properly since The Controller had once again turned all of the lights out in order to encourage the housemates to sleep.

"Jack, I know that's you over there. What are you doing?" he asked again.

"Shut up, you fucking idiot!" Jack hissed back.

"What's going on?" Fiona stirred from her sleep.

"Nothing!" Jack tried to shush her quiet again. The lights flickered on revealing exactly what he was doing to the housemates and - more worryingly - The Controller. He was toying with the fire escape door, trying to get it open.

"What the fuck are you doing?" Paul was the first to jump from his bed. He tried to pull Jack away from the wall but he slipped from his grip and continued trying to open the door.

"All Housemates are to return to their beds immediately!" The Controller's voice boomed through the house's intercom system.

"You realise you're going to get us all killed, yeah?" Paul shouted.

"We stay here, we're dead anyway!" Jack argued. "I'll take my chances."

"All Housemates are to return to their beds immediately!"

"FUCK YOU!" Jack screamed up at the camera.

"He's right!" Chris jumped from his bed and started kicking the doorway.

"They will kill us all. Think about it!" Paul turned to the others to try and rally up some support in getting Jack and Chris to stop what they were doing but Georgia, Karen and Kate all looked keen for the pair of them to break through the doorway too. Only Jordy, Fiona and Stuart were in agreement with Paul.

"All Housemates are to return to their beds immediately."

"Stop kicking!" Jack screamed. He had managed to get his fingers between door and frame. "Help me!" Chris pushed his fingers through the gap too and got a grip on the doorway. "Pull!" Jack yelled.

"All Housemates are to return to their beds immediately or else face severe consequences!"

"FUCK YOU!" Jack screamed again as he tugged on the door, matching the rhythm used by Chris. The wooden door started to splinter. Georgia leapt from her bed and gave help too. Something cracked from behind the door. "One more tug!" Jack yelled.

"Think about it! Think about what you're doing!" Paul shouted.

"All Housemates are to return to their beds immediately or else face severe consequences!"

Jack, Georgia and Chris gave another hard tug and the door cracked open.

"What the hell?!"

Behind the door was nothing but a solid wall of bricks.

"What the hell is this?!" Jack shouted.

"All Housemates are to return to their beds immediately or else face severe consequences!"

"You're a fucking idiot," Paul said to Jack. "You really thought it was going to be that easy? Do yourself a favour - do us all a favour - and get back into your bed."

"Back to bed? Are you mental? Why would I get back into bed?"

"Because they're telling you to. You've pissed them off. They're giving you a way out. I suggest you take it for all of our sakes."

Georgia took a few steps back and slumped down on one of the beds, "Maybe he's right. We're not going out that way."

"You think they'll punish us?" Karen asked Paul.

"What are you asking him for? He doesn't know anything. He just likes to think he does. He's in as much of the dark as us." Jack spat back as he walked over to his bed.

"All Housemates are to go to the garden immediately!"

"Well I don't know about you guys but I, for one, won't be ignoring them." Paul walked over to the bedroom door. The red light changed to green as the door unlocked. He yanked on the handle and walked out followed by Jordy, Stuart and Fiona. Karen hesitated a second but soon gave chase to the others, along with Chris.

Kate, Georgia and Jack were left in the bedroom.

"What are you thinking?" Georgia asked - her eyes fixed on Jack.

He suddenly ran towards the garden, "The garden!"

Georgia and Kate followed. The bedroom door slammed shut behind them and immediately locked; signified by the red light. Neither girl cared as they followed Jack through to the garden. He stopped in the centre of it - away from the other housemates who were congregating at the seating area. The two girls stopped by Jack. He was staring at the walls surrounding the complex. Not only were they too tall to climb but - even if he were able to scale them - the top was covered with razor-sharp barbed wire. Jack didn't need to say anything - his disappointment was clearly written on his face. He turned around and noticed Paul was watching him like a hawk.

"You got a problem?" Jack barked.

"Just leave him," Georgia tried to pull Jack away, towards the other side of the garden.

Paul called out, "You realise we're all likely to be punished for that stunt of yours?"

"At least we tried something! What did you do? Just stood there acting all high and mighty!" Chris shouted. He turned his back on him and stepped between him and Jack to stop it from escalating further. "I don't want to panic you or anything but - he killed a man he thought was going to hurt the rest of the group. He didn't really give it much thought, either. If he thinks you're a danger to him, or the rest of the group... He wouldn't need much of an excuse to eliminate you this coming Friday. You know what I'm saying?"

Jack didn't say anything but knew exactly what Chris was saying; he'd put himself directly in the firing line.

"We don't really know anything in here - as you quite rightly pointed out. The last thing any of us should do is put our necks on the block, you know?"

Jack nodded and changed the subject, "What do you think they'll do? About the door I mean."

"Honestly, I have no idea. All I know is - I wouldn't put anything past them." Chris walked over to the side of the garden and slumped down with his back to the wall. By doing so he allowed Paul right back into Jack's line of sight. Paul was staring at Jack.

B E F O R E

D A Y T W O

P A U L K E L L Y

Paul was sitting in The Control Room. A content look upon his face.

"Hello, Paul." The Controller sounded informal.

"What can I do for you?" Paul asked.

The Controller had put an announcement through the house - asking Paul to come to The Control Room. Paul was in the dark as to the reason.

"The Controller just fancied a conversation to see how you were fitting into the house," the voice echoed around the room.

Paul visibly breathed a sigh of relief. "I'm good."

"And how are you getting on with the Housemates?"

"They seem nice. I think I'm probably closest to Jack. He seems cool. Friendly."

"The Controller reminds you not to get too close to your fellow Housemates," the voice said, "some tough choices are due to be made."

Paul nodded. "You don't need to tell me."

"Do you think there are any housemates who will cause you any problems?"

Paul shook his head, "I've been in this game for a long time," he said. "I'm pretty sure I can handle them."

"Who do you think has it in them to go all the way?" the voice asked.

Paul hesitated for a moment, "I quite like Jack but I'm not sure if he has it in him to be able to go all the way. Maybe. Maybe Georgia. She has a fire in her. As has Kate. Fiery. In fact - you know what - at this stage I couldn't possibly call it. There's a few of them who may have it in them."

"The Controller would like to thank you for your cooperation and hopes that he can count on you in the future," the voice said.

"I've got your back, just say the word!" Paul gave the camera a knowing wink.

"Thank you, Paul. The door is unlocked." The red light turned green backing up The Controller's statement. Paul jumped up and left the room. The door shut behind him and the light switched back to red.

Now

DAY TEN

The housemates spent the whole night locked in the garden. By the time morning came, they were all freezing and tired. The main door, to the house, opened giving them the access they craved. Jordy was the first through the door - bursting for the toilet. The others went through to the bedroom and noticed that the fire escape door had been fixed and was - once again - shut.

"Why didn't they just leave it open?" Georgia asked. "Not like we can leave that way - what with all the bricks."

"I don't know - could have used Paul's thick head to knock through," Jack whispered to her.

"What was that? Something to say?" Paul barked from next to his bed.

"Guys - can we just have one day where you're not at each others' throats? Please!" Fiona begged. "Look, I've been thinking, we just need to take one day at a time. Okay? That's the best way forward and you know it. But we can't do that all the time you're going at each other."

"That's the first sensible thing I've heard since this whole thing turned sour!" Kate chipped in.

"Can all Housemates please gather at the sofas," The Controller's voice made them all jump.

"Shit, here we go." Paul turned to Jack, "This is down to you."

"We don't know that," Fiona said, desperate to try and keep the peace a little while longer than two minutes, "let's just go and see what they want."

They solemnly walked through to the sofa area and each took a seat.

"Can Jack please come up to The Control Room," the Housemates voice boomed.

Jack's face went pale. He didn't know what they wanted but he knew it couldn't have been good. Not after what he had done the previous night; not after the escape attempt.

"Well," he said quietly, "wish me luck!"

Georgia got up from her seat and gave him a hug. She rubbed his back despite it being of little comfort. The others could barely look at Jack; couldn't look a dead man in the eyes for fear of being haunted by what they saw in the depths of his soul for the rest of what little time they may or may not have had left. Jack took a breath and walked towards the stairs. He grabbed a hold of the bannister and forced himself to go up towards The Control Room door - which was already illuminated green - giving him the access The Controller demanded.

"What do you think they want with him?" Karen asked.

"They need to set an example," said Kate, "he tried to break out. If they don't do anything, what's to stop him - or any of us - trying again? They need to punish him." She believed what she was saying but she didn't look comfortable about it.

"You don't seem very sad," said Karen.

Kate looked at her and kept her voice low, so as to keep her conversation private, "I don't want him dead but... If all but one needs to be eliminated for someone to get out of here... Well - it's one less we need to worry about."

"You think they'll eliminate him?" Karen looked panicked.

Chris had overheard the conversation and butted in, "Can't we just say it how it is? Do you think they will kill him just as they killed Richard?"

The room went silent.

"Wait a minute, where's Jordy?" Paul asked.

Jack nervously stepped into The Control Room and took a seat in front of the camera. On a small table between Jack and the camera was a small saucer with two small blue pills on it. He sat there for a while in silence, unsure of how best to proceed - curious as to what the pills were for. As the silence continued, part of him wanted to apologise for the previous night but the other part of him wanted to stay strong and defiant. He broke a door - yes - but they were instrumental in the death of three people - so far. The way he saw it - they owed him an apology. And a way out.

"The Controller has noticed you like to play the Hero," the voice echoed through the room once more. Jack nervously shifted in his seat. "How would you like to play the Hero now?" it asked.

"Go on," Jack urged him.

"Thanks to your antics last night," the voice continued, "today - we are to have a surprise Elimination."

The housemates on the sofas downstairs were watching everything as it was being broadcast direct to the plasma screen.

"I fucking knew it," Paul sighed.

"However," The Controller's voice continued, "this is not a definite elimination. You have a chance to save her."

"Her?" Jack asked. "Who?"

"Jordy," Stuart pointed out to the rest of the housemates, "it has to be Jordy. She's the only one not here."

"What have you done?" Jack hissed. "Who is up for elimination?"

"If you wish to save her, you are permitted to utilise the two blue pills in front of you," The Controller continued. "Or you may feel you don't need them. So - Jack - the question remains: Are you a Hero or are you one to stand by and let someone else perish? In five minutes, you will be called back to The Control Room where your answer will be expected."

"You haven't told me what I'd need to do."

"To save your fellow Housemate, you will have to give them the chance for life."

"What is that supposed to mean?"

"Your time starts now."

The red light around the door illuminated green, allowing Jack to exit The Control Room.

"What is that it? That's all you're going to tell me? I need to know what you expect me to do. What? Do I have to change places with them? Is that it?"

There was no answer. He waited a moment longer than entirely necessary, reached forward, grabbed the two pills and left The Control Room.

"What the fuck was that about? Is everyone okay?" he asked as he hurried down the stairs and back towards the living area where the Housemates were still gathered.

"You need to see this," said Chris.

Jack realised they were all still transfixed by the plasma screen hanging on the wall.

"What is it?" he asked. He pushed past so he could see. There, on the screen, was Jordy. She was in a different room, one that none of the housemates recognised. She was strapped to a cross, naked. Above her head, hanging from the ceiling, was a large drill-piece. She was blind-folded. Her screams and pleads for help revealed she was also scared. "What the fuck?" The drill span into life. A loud buzzing noise but not a lot else. It wasn't moving. It wasn't coming down. It was just there, spinning, as though to tell her - this is what will happen to you if Jack doesn't save you; this is how you will die. Jordy screamed. "What the hell is this?" Jack shouted. He turned to the camera hanging from the corner of the room, "Let her out of there, you sick fucks!" He turned to the rest of the group, "Did you guys hear what was said in The Control Room?" he asked. "Did they stream it through to the television?"

"Yes. Yes they did," Kate said. She couldn't take her eyes from the screen. "They said you will have to give her the chance for life if you want to save her."

"The chance for life? What the hell is that even supposed to mean?" Jack frantically asked.

"Show me those pills," Chris snatched them from Jack. "Mate, they're viagra."

"What?"

"To save your fellow housemate, you have to give her the chance for life," Paul said. "Don't you get it? It's quite clear - either you fuck her or The

Controller does. The chance for life is a metaphor; they want you to cum inside of her."

"What?! They want me to have sex with her? With a fucking drill above her head? They want me rape her in order to save her?"

Paul shrugged, "You fucked with their fixtures and fittings. They're making you fuck something else. This should be easy for someone like you."

"I can't do this."

"She'll die!" Karen said.

"Jack, just swallow the pills. It's a bitter pill to swallow, I agree but… You need to do this or she will die."

"So what?" said Paul. "From what they were saying - we're all going to die anyway. Well, nearly all of us. One will live. Let her die, it's one less to be eliminated further down the line, right?"

Jack snatched the pills back from Chris and necked them, "I'm not like you," he hissed at Paul when they were swallowed down. He turned and ran towards the stairs and back up to The Control Room. Paul almost looked sad.

"Where is she?" Jack shouted at the camera as soon as he was able to gain access to The Control Room. With no words, a door on the opposite wall clicked open. He walked through and into a room with a black ceiling, black walls and the horizontal cross in the centre of the floor space.

"Who's there?" Jordy called out over the sound of the drill bit above her head. Her voice was shaking, as were her limbs on closer inspection.

Jack hurried over to where she lay. Her wrists and ankles were cuffed to the cross. Metal cuffs. There was no way these were getting undone without a key. Jack looked up to the spinning drill. He realised that - slowly but surely - it was coming down.

"Who's there?" Jordy called out again. "Please. Get me out of here. I don't want to die."

Jack looked around the room to see if there was anything he could use to try and get to the drill bit in order to rip it from the wall but there was nothing. Just him, the spinning drill bit, a camera in each corner of the room and the bound and naked girl.

His racing heart stepped it up a notch when a loud clanking noise echoed throughout the room and the drill bit dropped a fraction - never once letting up with the spinning motion.

Jordy screamed, "Get me out of here!"

BEFORE

Jack laughed as his partner of three years tied his wrists to the headboard of her bed.

"What are you doing?" he asked. They had been fooling around together in bed, their last night before he was to disappear into The Controller's home for a while, when Natalie had pulled a scarf from underneath her mattress.

"I've seen reality television shows," she said. "They always put pretty girls in there!"

"You're jealous?" he asked.

"Not at all…"

"You're tying me up so I can't leave you?"

"No, it's a good opportunity for you." She finished typing the final knot and leaned in close to his ear, "What I'm doing is ensuring you don't forget about me out here in the real world…"

He interrupted her, "I'm not going to forget about you!"

She ignored him, "…by giving you a night to remember."

"Oh in that case - ignore me, I'll shut up." He laughed as she kissed her way down his naked body, starting at his neck. He sighed as he felt her lips engulf his swollen penis. "I should go away more often," he said as he strained against the restraints holding him in place. "Fuck."

NOW

The housemates were watching the plasma screen. Jack had his back to Jordy and his hand down his trousers. He was furiously tugging backwards and forwards. His eyes were closed while he tried taking himself to a 'happy place' to try and achieve the desired results with regards to getting (and maintaining) an erection in order to complete the task forced upon him.

"What's he doing?" Karen asked.

Chris looked at her. The expression on his face said it all. Was she really that stupid? He played along regardless, "Guessing the pills haven't taken effect yet," he told her. "That's quite a lot of stress to perform under. Can't believe he is even trying to be honest."

"Because she'll die if he doesn't," Kate fired him a stern look.

"At some point she's going to die anyway. Unless of course she has it in her to kill each and every last one of us," Chris retorted. "Personally I think it would be doing her a favour - to let her die. Least it's over with for her. I mean, do you know what else they have up their sleeves for us? They've crushed someone, had someone poisoned, had someone shot and served up as ex-housemate."

"You wouldn't kill her yourself but you'd let her die?" Paul asked.

"I guess."

"Letting her die and killing her yourself - aren't they, on a basic level, the same thing?"

The screen went blank.

"What's going on?" Fiona asked. She walked over to the television and reached up, giving it a tap on the side as though it would - by magic - turn it back on again.

"I guess we've seen all we're supposed to see," said Paul. He turned away from the television and walked back towards the kitchen where he started to make himself a drink, "Anyone else want a cup of tea?"

"You're pretty calm about all this," Georgia spat at him.

"Do I have any control over what is happening in there?" Paul asked. He answered too, "No, no I don't. What is the point in getting myself worked up over it. If she lives, great. If she dies - too bad but - there's a lot more death to happen yet."

Karen turned to Kate, "Do you think he is saving her?"

"Depends what you mean by the term saving."

Before

KATE EVANS

Kate was sitting in a room at the conference centre where auditions were being held. In front of her was a camera - pointed directly at her. Behind the camera was a black curtain which blocked off the other half of the room. The curtain - more importantly - blocked off the two people interviewing her. A cheap, easy to construct Control Room and a good way to see how the contestants would come across in the real control room if they were to make it all the way through the audition process. This was the third round. Kate looked nervous as she waited for the questions. She fiddled with her long red hair, twirling it round and round between her fingers.

Only one of the interviewers spoke. The second person made notes as a back-up in case the camera stopped recording for any reason - not that it ever did.

"Hello Kate," the interviewer (male) spoke in an authoritative tone. Hostile, almost.

Kate nervously giggled, "Hello."

"Well done for getting this far."

"Thank you. I think."

"What would it mean for you to get into the compound?" the question was asked before Kate had even finished her previous sentence.

"It would be amazing…"

Kate hadn't told the producers that she had a son waiting for her at home; six year old Callum. He was the reason she was trying to get onto the show. She was desperate to make it as an actress but worked in a dead-end job due to lack of acting opportunities out in the sticks where she lived. The job paid the bills but didn't leave much room for travelling to the city for auditions. Certainly not as many as she'd like to go to anyway. She thought the show would give her some much needed exposure and that she'd come out to a flood of offers. She also thought the fact that she had a son would dampen her chances of being selected.

"And what would it mean for you to win?" the interview asked.

Being selected to go in the house would definitely be the best experience of her life. One that would give her opportunities which would - in turn - lead to a better life for her son. Winning it, though, would be the icing on the cake. The fast track to the good life for the both of them.

Kate smiled at the thought of walking away with the one hundred thousand pound prize fund. In her mind she had already spent the cash; deposit on a nicer home closer to civilisation, clear some debt and - just as important - Callum's first holiday. She didn't know where - she just knew it would be somewhere hot. Not just Callum's first holiday abroad either, but also hers.

"It would mean the world. To know people are voting for me to stay there above other people in the house… Well, let's be honest, it is just a popularity contest at the end of the day, isn't it? Who wouldn't want to win that!" she said. She was clever to keep all mention of her son and change of lifestyle out of her answer. She smiled, looking directly into the camera.

NOW

DAY TEN

As far as Jack was concerned, the only positive to his current situation was the fact the drill bit was moving slowly. The pills were yet to work their magic and he was still unsure of what he was going to do. He didn't want Jordy to die. He didn't want anyone to die, even the ones he didn't necessarily gel with but - at the same time - did he really have it in him to rape someone for that was what he felt he was being asked to do. Here was a girl - naked - tied to a horizontal cross who hadn't asked to be put in this position. She hadn't asked to be killed nor had she asked to have sex with a stranger.

"Please! Who's there?" she asked. "What's going on? What's that noise? Please talk to me!" the noise she was referring to was the ongoing scream of the drill.

Jack walked over to Jordy and crouched down to her so his face was close to her own face, saving him the hassle of having to shout out over the sound of the drill. He wasn't sure whether he was allowed to talk to her, to tell her what was going on but - considering they hadn't told him he couldn't - he figured it was his best course of action, "It's me, Jack…" he said. He kept his voice low in the hope that The Controller wouldn't be able to hear due to the sound of the drill. He knew it wasn't likely to be the case, considering the state of the art microphones they were all forced to wear since being in the house, but even so - nothing to lose.

"Jack? What's going on? Where am I?"

"You're in a room away from the main house…"

"What's that noise…"

Jack realised there was no easy way of explaining things to her, "There's a drill above your head. You have been chosen for elimination…"

"I don't want to die," she started to cry.

"… And I have been given a chance to save you," he said.

"Please save me…"

"To save you, they want me to have sex with you. That's why you're naked."

"What? I don't understand…"

"We don't have much time. They called me into The Control Room. Said that - as I liked to fuck things - they're giving me the chance to fuck something else. I'm so sorry this is my fault. I don't know what to do," he said, "I don't want you to die but…" he hesitated.

Jordy was crying, "Please - just do what you have to do. Don't let me die."

It was exactly what Jack needed to hear. Permission - of sorts. She didn't want to die so was happy for him to take any necessary course to save her.

"I'm really sorry for this," he said.

"Just stop talking. Stop wasting time. Get me off of this thing, please!" the desperation in her voice broke Jack's heart. He hated them for what he was forced to do but, right now, he didn't have time to think about what he would like to do to them given half the chance. He had to think about her. Not just the thought of saving her. He had to think of her as an attractive girl. A sexy girl. He had to think of her wet, tight pussy. Anything to help give the pills the kick start they needed. How long did these damned things take to work anyway? He looked up at the drill. It was moving slowly but it was still moving.

He walked around the cross and positioned himself between Jordy's split legs, as close to her vagina as he could stand. A quick cursing look towards the camera. He looked away. He knew he had to put them out of his mind; the people watching. He tentatively reached to her genitals with his shaking hand. He ran his thumb up the lips and gently pushed into them until he was able to move his thumb to her clitoris. She was still crying but he couldn't focus on that. He started moving his thumb over her clit in small circular motions - careful not to press too hard. He hoped the process would help her juices flow despite the circumstances not being the most romantic of situations to be in. Jack looked up to her face. The blindfold was still covering her eyes - he thought it best to leave it there; couldn't bear the sight of her looking at him whilst he was doing what needed to be done. Despite not being able to see the tears - he was sure she was still crying. He tried his best to put the emotions from his mind as he crouched down until he was mouth to vagina. He gently lapped at it with his tongue as he continued to stroke her clit - not only to make the process less painful for her, by adding spit, but also because it was one of his favourite sexual activities and if anything would help him get in the mood for sex; this would be it. He wondered whether it was wrong for him to like the taste and whether it was wrong for him to find any satisfaction in what he was doing - two thoughts he, once again, tried to ignore.

As he continued licking her, probing his tongue in further each time, he fumbled at his jeans and undid the buttons helping to keep them up.

Once undone, he pushed them halfway down. They didn't need to come off completely. It would have just been wasting time. They just needed to be low enough to be out of the way.

With his spare hand he started stroking his cock. It was semi-erect and not much good for anything. Another glance up to Jordy's face. She was sighing now. Didn't appear as though she was crying. He hoped it was down to what he was doing and that his actions were enough of a distraction for her.

"I'm sorry," he repeated as he pushed into her as best as his semi-erect penis would permit. He closed his eyes, took himself back to a happier time with his girlfriend in the outside world, and started to move his hips back and forth. With the feeling of her wet cunt against his own skin it didn't take long for him to stiffen. At least he presumed it was down to that. For all he knew - the pills could have now been starting to take effect.

As he started to thrust harder, the drill slipped down another notch.

Before

STUART RILEY

The power drill tore through the living room wall with ease until it hit something a little harder causing the drill bill to stop dead and the machine's motor to scream for help. Stuart cursed as he took his finger off the trigger, killing it within a split second, "Shit."

"You hear me calling?" a female was standing in the doorway. It was his girlfriend, Claire.

"What? No. I'm sorry." He continued, "I don't know what the hell is under here but whatever drill bit I use - I just can't get through it. Might have to pop to the shop and get some other bits I could try…"

"I was calling because there's a phone call for you," said Claire - ignoring what Stuart was saying.

"For me?"

"Yes. It's Pauline. She tried calling your mobile number but couldn't get through."

"She did?" Stuart set the drill to one side and reached into his pocket. He pulled his mobile phone out and noticed four missed calls on the screen. "Shit."

"You coming then?" Claire was getting impatient. Clearly the call was stopping her from doing something important.

"Sorry. Yes." Stuart dropped the phone back into his pocket and headed towards the hallway, where the telephone was waiting on a small table at the foot of the stairs. "She might have some work for me," he said optimistically. "Might be able to pay some bills!"

"That would be good."

Claire walked down the hallway and disappeared into the kitchen. She closed the door behind her to give Stuart some privacy - not that he asked for it.

"Might be able to get some people in to put these damned shelves up for you. Save me the hassle," he called after her as he picked up the telephone. "Hello? Sorry to keep you waiting."

"Hello, Stuart. That job we spoke about last week. I've heard back and they're interested in taking things further with you," Pauline's voice crackled through on the other end of the line.

"They are? That's awesome!"

"Before they proceed, they need to check up on your first aid certificate. You said you had one."

"That's right."

"Future reference, that's the kind of thing that would be good to have on your file."

"Sorry, I didn't think."

"Well, if you could scan a copy through to me, I'll get it emailed over to them. Hopefully we'll be able to get something signed off over the next couple of days. I know they're keen."

"Brilliant. Thank you. I'll get that done for you now."

"Okay. I'll keep you posted," Pauline said before she hung up. Stuart replaced the phone back into its cradle and run up to his office. The sooner he got the relevant documents over - the sooner he got the job. The shelves could wait. Any excuse.

NOW

DAY TEN

Jordy was lying in her bed. All of the girls were comforting her. She wasn't crying. She was just lying there, staring at the ceiling. Her complexion pale. Black rings around her eyes where her make-up had run earlier.

Paul was standing in the bedroom doorway. He was looking at the girls - Jordy in particular. Jack was in the living area of the house. He was sitting on the sofa looking at the housemates' pictures on the wall next to the plasma screen. Just as the girls had rallied around Jordy, the boys had rallied around him.

"You okay?" Chris asked.

Jack didn't respond.

"I know it doesn't feel like it but you did a good thing," Stuart piped in. "Because of you she is alive. That's good. That's a good thing you did."

"Is it?" Jack asked. It had been the first thing he had said since coming down from the secret room with Jordy. The others rushed over to see them both but neither said a word. Jordy went through to the bedroom, and Jack went to the living area.

"Can Jack please come to The Control Room," The Controller's voice made Jack jump.

"Don't go," Chris said. "Fuck them."

"Can Jack please come to The Control Room."

"And then what?" Jack asked. "Another punishment?"

He stood up and walked towards the stairs. Stuart and Chris walked with him.

"Well - good luck," said Chris. He stopped at the bottom of the stairs. Jack continued up them towards the green lit door.

Stuart turned away and headed towards the bedroom where the others were.

"She did well," Paul whispered as Stuart walked past him.

"I knew things were going to be extreme but," he hesitated, "well - I never expected this. This just seems sick."

"It was necessary," Paul said. "Besides - she does worse in the outside world."

"Well is it going to stop?" Stuart asked.

"Pretty sure we're getting to the end."

"Thank God for that. I've had enough of this. I didn't sign up for this."

"We all did."

"What happened to you?" Stuart asked. "One minute you're the father figure of the house and the next you're doing whatever it is you're trying to do…"

"What I'm trying to do? I'm trying to end this bullshit as quickly as possible so I can get back to my own life. We've all been paid, right? I just want to go home."

"So you're being an asshole on purpose?"

"I'm doing what I'm supposed to. I think you're forgetting the way things happen around here. They say jump, we ask how high. It's simple. And like I said, the sooner we're done, the sooner we go home and everything can go back to normal."

Stuart looked towards Jordy, "How is she doing?" he asked.

"How do you think? She's fine. She's playing her part well."

Stuart shook his head, "You don't have to be an asshole to everyone. She does have feelings you know." He pushed past and approached the bed. "You okay?" he asked Jordy.

Karen turned to Stuart, "She hasn't said anything. She's just staring at the ceiling. Do you think it could be shock?"

Stuart turned to her, "Can you do me a favour and get a sugary cup of tea?" he asked.

Karen nodded and hurried from the room towards the kitchen area. Stuart turned to Georgia, "Shit. Meant to ask - can you get some biscuits too? Again - the ones with the sugary tops probably best."

"I'll be right back," Georgia said to Jordy. She gave her hand a gentle squeeze and followed Karen out of the room.

Stuart turned to Fiona and caught her eye. He nodded towards Kate.

"Kate, why don't you help me in the kitchen? We need to think about food and people are more likely to trust eating it if two of us are preparing it."

"I'm not hungry," said Kate.

"Even so - others might be. Let's let Stuart check Jordy out. Clearly The Controller isn't sending anyone." She didn't wait for Kate to answer her back. She took her hand and walked her from the room leaving Stuart and Jordy alone.

Stuart sat on the edge of the bed and leaned in close to Jordy, "They've gone."

She blinked and looked at him, "They've called Jack into The Control Room."

"I know."

"I'm scared."

"It'll be fine."

"What if they can't stop him?"

"There's enough of us here to stop him…"

BEFORE

PAPER WORK

Jordy walked into the interviewer's room clutching a piece of paper.

"Please take a seat," the man said without looking up. He pulled the top sheet from the clipboard and tossed it to one side. As Jordy took a seat, where Fiona had been sitting moments earlier, the man gave the next sheet of paper a quick scan. He looked up, "Do you have the necessary paperwork?" he asked.

"Yes." Jordy leaned forward and slid the certificate onto the table. The female took hold of it and read it. She looked at the man and nodded. He ticked something on the sheet in front of him.

"And would you be available in the month of August? You will be required for the period of two weeks maximum."

Jordy considered it for a moment and nodded with a smile, "Yes. That's fine."

The man nodded - satisfied with her answer. The lady ticked something else off on the piece of paper in front of her. He pointed towards the piece of paper Jordy had handed over, "And we're going to need to take a copy of that document for our file."

"You can take that one," she said.

The female slipped the piece of paper between the others attached to the clipboard. She then pulled some papers out from the middle of her collection of paperwork and passed them over to Jordy who gratefully received it. The document was attached as one with a strong staple in the top left hand corner.

"This is a copy of the terms and conditions and states your fee, plus an additional amount we hadn't discussed. If you'd like to give it a read," the man said.

"Okay. Now?"

"Now would be good. We're keen to get this signed off…"

"Should I go to the other room?" Jordy asked.

"Here is fine."

The man continued to watch Jordy as she settled back to read the paperwork through as per his request. He then picked a pen up from the table, took the lid off, and slid it across the desk towards Jordy.

NOW

Jack was sitting in The Control Room. A piece of paper rested on the small table between him and the curtain.

"Hello, Jack."

He didn't answer.

"Congratulations on saving your fellow Housemate. How do you feel?" The Controller asked in such a way that anyone listening in would have thought the conversation was about something entirely innocent.

Jack didn't answer.

The Controller continued, "Did you enjoy fucking your fellow Housemate?"

Jack didn't answer.

"It appears you're not the only one who likes to fuck things," The Controller said. "Have a look at the piece of paper in front of you," he said.

Jack looked down at the paper. Some kind of official looking paperwork, "What is it?" he asked.

"Pick it up, don't be shy."

Jack sighed and reached down to the paperwork. He picked it up and started reading. His face went pale as he read the contents, "Is this a joke?"

"The Controller can assure you it is no joke," the voice was stern. Serious.

Jack scrunched the piece of paper up and threw it towards the camera, "Fuck you!" he hissed.

"Jack, behind the chair you are sitting on is a box. Inside that box is a handgun. You are now presented with another chance to eliminate your fellow housemate. As always - the choice is yours."

Jack didn't say anything. He just sat there, visibly shaking. His eyes had darkened changing his whole look. He stood up and hesitated a moment - torn between heading for the door or fetching the box from behind the chair. He took a deep breath of air in and walked to the door.

"Jack, if you leave the room, you will not be permitted to come back for the handgun. Would you like to take it in case you change your mind?" The Controller asked.

"Please let me out," Jack said. He kept his voice calm. He knew there was no point in getting upset with them. They had the power. If he got upset, they'd only make his life more unpleasant.

"Last chance, Jack. What if you have been infected now?" The Controller asked.

Jack tried to shake his words off, just as he was trying to shake off what he had read on the paperwork he had been shown. The only reason he was in this position was because of them; the production team. It wasn't his fault. It wasn't Jordy's fault. They had both been forced into this. The facts clearly spelt out on the paperwork were just by the by. Besides - if he had been infected with what she had - it didn't matter all the time he was in the house. Only one person would walk away from this and - if it was Jack - he'd worry about it then.

He repeated, "Please just let me out."

The door lock clicked and the light changed to green. He pulled the door open and stormed from the room and back down the stairs.

"What did they say?" Chris asked. He noticed Jack's expression, "Are you okay?"

"I'm going to lay down for a while," he said as he stormed past Chris, towards the bedroom.

Chris followed and waved the girls back to the kitchen when they started to walk towards Jack to see how he was. He shook his head to emphasise not to say anything. He didn't know what had been said in The Control room but he could tell by Jack's expression that it wasn't particularly good.

"So there's nothing to worry about if you think about it. It's the best possible outcome!" Paul was talking to Jordy. Stuart standing next to him, nodded in agreement. He shut up as soon as Jack entered the room. Jordy, Stuart and Paul all looked towards Jack expecting trouble. All were equally surprised when he walked directly to his bed and slumped down onto it. Without any words he pulled the duvet over himself until he was completely covered.

"You okay, bud?" Stuart called over to him.

Jordy looked at Paul, confused. He shrugged.

"Jack?" Stuart called over again.

"I'm fine," he replied. His voice muffled by the bedding he was buried beneath.

Paul whispered to Jordy, "You need to go over there. Talk to him."

"What? What am I supposed to say?" she asked. She also kept her voice low.

"Just talk about what happened. You both need to clear the air," Paul pushed her. He turned to Stuart and whispered, "Let's leave them to it."

"You can't go!" Jordy said.

Paul put his finger up to his lips to shush her. He pointed out of the bedroom and whispered reassurance that they'd both be standing outside the door if they were needed. "It'll be fine."

Neither Paul nor Stuart waited for Jordy to argue further with them. Paul lead the way out of the bedroom, "Just leave them alone for a while, let them talk," he said to Karen as she approached with the previously requested cup of tea for Jordy.

Jordy climbed from her bed and cautiously walked over to Jack's bed. She sat on the edge of it without waiting to be asked to do so. Nervously she put her hand out and placed it on Jack's covered leg - an act to let him know she was there.

"Are you okay?" she stuttered over her words but forced them out.

"Is it true?" he asked.

Jordy swallowed hard, she knew part of what was coming. She knew what he was going to say. She just didn't know how he was going to react. From the moment she had gone in - she knew there was a chance of early elimination but, even so, she wasn't comfortable with it. She didn't know what to say. She wanted to say it wasn't true just to avoid the hostility.

"Well?" Jack pulled the duvet away from his face. His eyes were watery as he struggled to hold back the tears. Jordy nodded. A tear escaped from the corner of his eye.

"I'm sorry," said Jordy.

"I saved you."

"I know."

"HIV?"

She nodded again.

"Technically you're already dead. Why didn't you say something? Why did you let me go ahead and do it…"

"I thought they'd have given you protection."

"They want us to kill each other. You think they're going to worry about something little like that?" he asked. He wiped his eyes.

"I'm sorry."

"So am I."

Both of them fell silent.

"It doesn't mean you have contracted it," she continued. "There's a chance, yes, but it isn't definite." Her words were supposed to offer him some comfort but there was little comfort to be had.

"What does it matter, hey? Chances are we're all going to die in here, right? So what if I do have HIV? I doubt it will be that which ends up killing me." Jack turned his back on her, "I just want to be left alone, please."

She hesitated a moment, "Okay." She stood up. "I am sorry," she said again. "Really."

She walked from the room.

BEFORE

"You're sorry?" Kate hissed.

Kate was standing in front of her ex-boyfriend, Michael. The two of them had never been one hundred percent serious. When they got together they were drunk, they were young and - more specifically - they were stupid. But their stupidity resulted in a little boy whom they both loved dearly.

Callum lived with Kate but Michael had access to see him whenever he wanted and - as the years went on - even took him for the whole night from time to time. Kate had never asked Michael for anything despite her own mother telling her (when she was alive) to at least get maintenance from him. Today was the first time she had asked him for help.

"He's your son!" she continued.

"And he's your son too and - what - you want to drop him off to me so you can go off gallivanting around on some television show? I have a life. I have a job. I can't just put it on hold to turn babysitter for however long you're away. I haven't even been in this job for a month yet. Even if they did permit me some time off they won't pay me so what the hell are we supposed to do for money?"

"Your mum could help babysit," Kate argued.

"And she also works full time. You're being ridiculous."

"Do you know what this could mean for us? It would raise my profile as an actress. I could get spotted…"

"And then what? You're going to be disappearing on film shoots or into the West End? You have a son!"

"So do you!" Kate shouted. "I have never asked you for anything. This is the first time."

"And it's not practical."

"Imagine if I won."

"More time away for interviews and magazine shoots? Before you know it your son will be bullied at school as his friends show him topless photographs of his mum in some grotty magazine? Brilliant. What are we waiting for?"

"One hundred thousand pounds. Yes, I might get work from the exposure. No, I won't be doing topless photographs. But think about that money - it could make a massive difference to his life. To our life. You want your son growing up on the poverty line? Oh wait - you pick and choose when you see him so you probably won't give a shit," she hissed.

"That's not fair."

"When I told you I was pregnant you said you would be there. I told you I wasn't sure if I was going to keep it and you begged me not to abort it. You begged me. We agreed we would raise him together and wherever possible you would help me out yet I never asked you for anything."

"I can't take the time off work," he protested. "It's the school holidays. What am I supposed to do with him? Look, if I could, I would take him. You know I would.."

"No. I don't. I've asked you this one favour and straight away you've said no."

Michael sighed and ran his hand through his hair. "Look, I'll talk to mum. Maybe she has some holiday she is owed… She might be able to help…"

NOW

DAY TEN

Kate was in the kitchen. She was staring down at the sink which was filling with soapy hot water ready for her to do the washing up. Ten days in the house and the first time she had volunteered to wash up - an act, on this occasion, used to try and distract herself from her thoughts and current situation. An act, on this occasion, which wasn't working.

Chris approached her and turned the taps off when he realised she wasn't going to and that the water was close to over-flowing. "You okay?" he asked.

She smiled at him. The smile didn't hide the truth, though. She wasn't okay. Her thoughts firmly fixed on the boy she had left behind. The wasted wish of wanting to turn the clock back and take Michael's first refusal at looking after their son as the end of the conversation. She would be at home now, still struggling, but she'd be alive. She'd be able to watch her son grow up and live his life. Now she wasn't even sure she would see him again. Not unless she killed a house full of people.

"How did we end up here?" she asked.

Chris shrugged, "Desperation? A longing for adventure? I don't know."

"I don't understand how a show like this can even exist. What television channel would even air it? It's ridiculous."

"You really think it's part of a television show?" Chris pointed out. "It's just a sick game. This isn't going on television. No way. It's just a sick game devised by people who have the money to carry it through."

"You think there's even a prize for the last person standing?" she asked. She already knew the answer, she just wanted him to say it.

He shook his head solemnly. "I don't think anyone will be left standing."

Kate changed the subject before she got even more upset, "How's Jack and Jordy?"

Chris shrugged again. "I don't know. Not good. I'm not sure what The Controller called Jack into The Control Room for but - whatever it was - I'm pretty sure it was bad. And Jordy hasn't been herself since coming down from the other room. But can you blame either of them?"

"No." Kate sighed, "Jesus. What's next? I just wish they'd fucking get it over with."

A female scream from the bathroom made both Chris and Kate jump.

"That sounds like Karen…"

In a couple of seconds all the housemates rushed over to investigate. Karen came running out of the room, her hands covering her face and visibly shaking. Paul stopped her and cradled her in his arms as Stuart disappeared into the bathroom.

Kate and Chris ran over to the door. Chris opened it so they could both see what had caused Karen's reaction. Fiona was hanging from the rafters, her dressing gown cord wrapped round her neck, her head drooping down - eyes fixed on the floor.

"Here," Paul gently pushed Karen over to Chris who took her in his arms, "look after her." He hurried into the bathroom and helped Stuart get Fiona down from where she was hanging.

Chris, Kate - and by now - the other housemates watched from the doorway as Stuart started performing mouth to mouth.

"I just went in there and she was there," Karen was crying. Chris kept her tight against his own body, offering comfort as best as he could given the circumstances. "She was just hanging there…"

"It's okay," Chris tried to reassure her despite it being the stupidest thing he could have said. Nothing was going to be okay. Nothing. This was further proof of that. Another dead body. Four dead, eight left.

"She's dead. You're wasting your time," Paul stopped Stuart from performing the CPR. They both knelt there a moment, next to her body, unsure of what to say. Chris pulled Karen away from the doorway to hide her from the body. She didn't struggle. The others - Jack, Jordy, Georgia and Kate - followed; all seemingly sick of seeing death.

"All Housemates are to go to the bedroom immediately," The Controller's voice barked through the intercom system. The order didn't need repeating. They knew the procedure now; someone dies, they go to the room so the production crew could clean away the corpse.

Paul and Stuart were the last into the bedroom. The door clicked shut behind them as the light switched from green to red.

"Did she seem strange to anyone?" Kate asked.

"Is anyone themselves at the moment? I know I'm not," Georgia said.

"I can't believe she hung herself," Kate continued, more or less ignoring what Georgia said.

"Look on the plus side - one less person one of us has to murder," Paul said.

"What did you just say?" Chris spat at him. He was still holding onto Karen who was still crying. It didn't matter how many times they'd seen a dead body - it never got any easier.

"Just what everyone else was thinking," Paul retorted.

"Just shut your fucking mouth," Jack hissed.

"Fuck you!"

"Please don't start this again!" Kate moaned. "We have enough to deal with without everyone going for each other."

"She was upset when I came downstairs," Jordy said. "She was worried that she might have been put in the same position I was…"

Jack shifted uncomfortably where he was standing.

"Don't think she would have had anything to worry about. I wouldn't have touched her with someone else's," Paul muttered under his breath - suggesting she wasn't good enough to lie with.

"Are you purposefully trying to wind us up? Are you playing some sort of fucking game?" Jack snapped. He clenched his right hand into a tight little ball as though wanting to hit Paul in the face.

"Just ignore him," Chris stepped between the two of them.

"Yeah - it's not like you're going to do anything about it anyway."

Jack pushed Chris out of the way and faced up to Paul, "Fuck you!" With no warning he swung a punch at Paul who easily side stepped it whilst laughing at his efforts. Using Jack's own weight against him, he gave him a shove - toppling him to the floor in a crumpled heap.

"Stop it!" Karen shouted, to everyone's surprise she started hitting Paul. Paul responded by putting her in a vice-like grip until she had calmed down.

"Calm it!" he shouted at her. She struggled for a while before she gave up. As soon as she did, Paul released his grip. She pulled away. "Considering no one wants to play the games we're expected to play," he said with a calmer tone, "you should all be thankful she took her own life. One less person to worry about."

"You're so cold," Kate muttered. She was watching Paul. He had changed so much since coming into the house. The nice warm-hearted father figure had been replaced with someone a lot more hostile, someone a lot more dangerous and it wasn't just Kate who'd spotted it.

"It's called survival," Paul replied. They held eye contact for a while before Kate broke off her gaze.

Before

Fiona was sitting on a sofa in her comfortable looking home. The living room, to be precise. A large sofa, an armchair, coffee table and sensibly sized television. Nothing out of the ordinary. She was going through pages and pages of paperwork; a smile on her face as she read what was listed. A man walked into the room and sat opposite her; her husband, Pete. He sat there a while waiting to see if she was going to acknowledge him but she didn't say a word. It was always the same when she had stuff to go through; she got completely absorbed in it so that there was no one else in her world.

He coughed, "Is it good?" he asked. Fiona didn't look up. She had a shocked expression on her face as she nervously turned the paper over. Pete raised his voice slightly to try and get her attention, "Honey?"

She looked up, "Sorry… What is it?"

"Just wondered if it was any good? You've been going through it for hours," he said. "I wondered if I was going to see my wife tonight at all."

"Sorry I lost track of time." She put the paperwork down on the coffee table. "What did you want to do?"

He hesitated a moment before leaning forward. He put his hand on the paperwork, "Can I?"

Fiona didn't look sure, "I'm not supposed to show anyone."

"Come on, I'm your husband, who am I going to tell?" he asked.

"Okay, fine, but you can't say a word."

"I won't." He lifted the paperwork and started to read it. Within a couple of paragraphs he was frowning. He flipped the page and his eyes went wide, "Jesus - what the hell is this?"

"Rent."

NOW

DAYELEVEN

The house once again awoke to a subdued atmosphere. Paul was sitting in the garden by himself whilst the other housemates were congregating in the living area. They kept looking out of the window towards Paul. Conversations were about how much he had changed in the house and his attitude towards Fiona's death - a conversation lead by Jack.

"You realise it's getting close to Friday again? I think we need to watch him - and I mean watch him closely. He's cracking up," Jack was saying.

"Aren't we all?" Georgia asked. She nodded towards Karen who was staring out of the window at Paul. Her complexion hadn't gone back to its proper colour since she had seen Fiona hanging by her neck and her eyes were red raw from where she'd spent a restless night crying.

"What he was saying yesterday, I honestly think he might try something on Friday. Not just Friday - I think he might try and win," said Jack.

"I think he's right," Chris agreed, "he was just sitting up in his bed last night - after the lights went out. Just sitting up and - I guess - watching the rest of us. Made me nervous."

"So what are we supposed to do about it?" Jordy drove the conversation forward.

"It's what he said about Philip all over again - kill be or killed," Jack continued. He didn't say anything else, he waited to see the reaction from his statement. This was a popularity contest and - before the killings started - Jack would have put good money on Paul being able to walk away with the prize but not anymore, not since the killings. He only hoped the others thought the same.

"But where do we go from there?" Stuart asked. He wasn't disagreeing what with Jack was saying but he did raise a valid point. He continued, "He did what he thought was right at the time. Had he not done so - Philip might have killed one of us. But now we're turning on him because we know he has it in him to kill someone. Won't that make us as bad as he is?"

"It's called survival," Jack argued.

"Which is exactly what Paul called it back when he shot Philip - and then again when we spoke about what happened to Fiona."

There was silence in the room as Stuart's words sunk in.

"What's he doing?" Kate asked.

Paul was looking directly into the room. He waited for the rest of the group to look at him. Once he had their undivided attention he raised his hand and gave them a little wave with a smile on his face.

Stuart turned back to Jack, "And who is going to kill him, if that's what everyone agrees, are you going to do it seeing as it's your idea or you going to expect someone else to do your dirty work?"

"My dirty work? It's not my dirty work. It's for the good of all of us."

"You sound like him," Stuart pointed out.

"I'm not doing this for the money," Jack argued.

"Neither was he," Stuart said.

"This is bullshit," Chris muttered, "I don't even need the money. I'm not here for that. I'm here for the experience. That's what I wanted. The experience." He started to laugh as he turned to the rest of the group, "I wanted this. This."

Jack hadn't taken his eyes off Stuart. His words had annoyed him; comparing him to Paul. He was nothing like Paul. At least, in his head, he was nothing like him. To the rest of the group, it was easy to see the resemblance between the two. Other than their age - right from day one they had always been similar, which is why they'd managed to strike such an early bond before the first killing destroyed it. "So what do you suggest we all do come Friday's elimination then? It's obvious they won't let us get away with not having someone eliminated so - yeah - who do you think we should eliminate? Go for one of the weaker of the group? Eliminate one of them?"

Stuart didn't know what to say.

"Maybe every week you'd have us draw straws? The person with the shortest straw gets eliminated? Is that fair? Or maybe you'd have us all state our case for why we deserve the one hundred thousand pounds more than the others? Eliminate in the order of those who deserve it the least?"

"I have a son," Kate said. "That's why I am here..."

Jack turned to Chris, "You don't need the money. You said it yourself. So - sorry - you're dead on Friday. Don't blame me, not my fault. All down to him," he pointed to Stuart.

"Maybe we should play the game out the way it is supposed to be played out?" Paul was standing in the doorway staring at the group; a crazed look in his eyes. "People are clearly not prepared to kill for the money but maybe it'll be a different story if people are killing for their own lives? Fuck it - why wait until Friday? We could just all grab a knife from the kitchen and just got for it right now..."

"You really think they're going to let anyone leave this house? And even if they do - you really think they're going to reward them with money? They're going to kill us all. We were talking about it the other day - it's just the games of a sick fuck curious to see what would happen in these circumstances. Nothing more and nothing less," Chris said. There was an anger in his voice - driven by Jack's suggestion that he should be eliminated on Friday.

"And for the record," Paul continued ignoring him completely, "I'm pretty sure it is against the rules to talk about eliminations. You want to be careful, Jack, or you're going to get the house punished again. Good way to make enemies," he finished.

Before

J ack was sitting in front of the camera in the make-shift Control Room. The black sheet behind the camera hiding the people interviewing him just as had been the case with Kate when she reached this stage of the audition process.

"Do you think you'll make friends in the house?" the interviewer asked; the same man who had been asking Kate her questions.

"I think so," said Jack. "I'm pretty easy to live with. It's a fair assumption that not everyone will get on in the house but it's pretty unlikely that they'll all turn against me." He laughed. "That being said, though, if people are quick to start a fight with me then I'm not the sort to forgive and forget very easily. I tend to hold grudges quite easily. I've been told it's a serious flaw in my character but I like to think it keeps me protected from assholes." He grabbed his mouth, "Sorry, can I say that?" he asked.

"Jack, at this stage The Controller doesn't mind foul language," the interviewer said.

Jack laughed again, "Well I'll try not to," he said.

"If there was to be conflict how would you resolve it?" the interviewer asked.

NOW

DAY ELEVEN

"Kill him," said Jack.

He was sitting in the bedroom with Chris. The two of them had gone in there to get away from the rest of the house for a little peace and quiet and the conversation had soon turned to who they'd kill and in which order. The first person he decided to kill being Paul.

"That was the easy one," Chris replied. "But who would you get rid of next?" he asked. "And what would your reasons be?"

"I think I'd kill Stuart next," said Jack.

"Yeah, I'm not sure about him."

"The guy is an asshole. You hear what he was saying earlier?"

"Who next?"

"Jordy."

"Jordy? After you saved her?"

"They called me into The Control Room. You know we did those medicals before we came in? She is HIV positive. They made me fuck her. You realise I might have it now too?"

"Fuck. And you didn't kill her?"

"No sense worrying about it. Not like I'm going to get out of here, is it? But - knowing she has that - makes little sense to let her out of the house to carry on living. Sure there is medication to prolong her life but - even so - she's a time-bomb. If I have it, so am I."

"I would have throttled her to death as soon as I found out..."

"She didn't ask for what happened to her. It's not Jordy who needs to be punished. It's the fucks who put me in the same room as her for that to happen."

Chris shuddered at the thought of it and changed the subject back to what they had been discussing, "Okay. That leaves Georgia, Karen, Kate, me and you."

"Here's where it gets hard. I like all of them. I mean - if you took the reward thing as gospel - if the winner gets the pay day and their freedom when they're the last man standing… You said yourself, you don't need the money. Kate is a mother. She needs the money and her son needs her. Karen has her whole life ahead of her…"

"You can't say that," Chris butt in. "She isn't that much younger than us."

"I suppose."

"Georgia seems like a nice person. I wouldn't begrudge her winning. But, same as with Jordy, there's little point in me living over someone such as Kate. Not if I am infected."

"But you might not be."

"There's a chance."

"Twice you've mentioned her name though."

"Who?"

"Kate. I take it she is your winner?"

Jack nodded. "As long as she can kill me by suffocation," he laughed. "Sit that pretty ass on my face until I'm dead." He laughed again, as did Chris. The smiles faded from their faces as they realised there really was nothing to laugh about. After all, what they were talking about was killing people. "I need to get a drink."

Jack left the bedroom and walked to the kitchen. Chris watched his movements for a while before turning his attention to Kate. He could see her clearly from the bedroom window which gave full access to the rest of the house. She was sitting in the living room with the others. None of them were talking. They were just sitting there lost in their own thoughts. All of them simply waiting for the next torturous task or waiting to die. Chris couldn't help but think about what Jack had said about Kate deserving to win because she had a child in the outside world and needed the money. Well they all had someone waiting for them outside, whether it was partners or family or even both, so that wasn't a good enough reason. And what, she deserved to live because the money would come in handy? Chris might not have needed the cash but he was pretty sure there were others in the house who could have benefited from it too. The thought of Kate getting a pass to the end of the game because of those two factors rubbed Chris up the wrong way. In his mind - if he were to play the game - he'd start with Kate.

"Could Chris please report to The Control Room," the Controller's voice made Chris jump as it boomed from the intercom system. Chris' heart skipped a beat. Since the killings started it was the first time he had been called to The Control Room. He stood up and noticed all of the other housemates were looking at him. Some of them looked nervous whilst others looked suspicious as to why he was called and they hadn't been.

Chris walked from the room and into the main living area of the house. He ignored the eyes staring at him as he made the lonely walk to the stairs leading to The Control Room.

"What do you think they want?" Georgia asked as he paused at the bottom of the stairs.

He shrugged.

"Well - good luck," she said.

Chris wondered whether she really meant that or whether she was saying it to sound as though she were being nice. If they gave him a task to hurt someone, or eliminate them, chances of picking Georgia - that nice girl downstairs, the only one who seemed to care - would be slim. Was that her game? Get friendly with everyone in order to save herself and then, when it is down to the last two, she'd show her true colours? Chris dismissed the thought and continued up the stairs.

The door was already illuminated with green. Chris pushed the door and stepped in. The other housemates watched as the door slammed shut behind him.

"Well we know it's not going to be an elimination," Paul - as usual - was the first to speak; the first to try and offer some misguided reassurance.

"Because it's not Friday?" Jordy asked. "That didn't seem to matter when they put me in that room." Jack couldn't help but look up and stare at Jordy when she mentioned being in the room. The nagging thought bouncing around his stressed mind that she wasn't the nice girl he thought she was when he first met her. Not because of her infection but rather the fact she had let him fuck her to save her own life knowing full well there was a chance she could have passed it on to him. Had the shoe been on the other foot - he would have chosen death rather than let someone else be infected.

His mind drifted to putting his hands around her throat and squeezing until she breathed no more - the thought placed there by Chris. He shook it from his mind. It wasn't his place to take a life.

BEFORE

CHRIS - AGED EIGHT

A young Chris was standing over the body of a dead frog. The frog was crushed almost beyond recognition. A baseball bat, gore on the end of it, was in Chris' shaking hand. Tears were streaming down his cheeks as he sobbed uncontrollably.

His father, a strict man, was approaching from the large house which Chris shared with his father, his mother and two siblings, who were slightly older than he was. His father had a sterner look on his face than usual as he strode towards where Chris was standing. Chis dropped the bat to the floor as soon as he noticed his father approaching.

"What the hell do you think you're doing?" his father's voice was deep and petrified Chris at the best of times but none more so than now. Chris knew that what he had done was wrong. He didn't know why he had even done it. One minute he was playing baseball with his brothers and the next he had stormed off with the bat when they struck him out from his go at batting. He had started hitting things around the garden with the bat, to work out his frustrations at being beaten by his brothers just as he always did, when he had seen the frog nestled deep in the long grass near to the pond. Without a second thought, picturing his brothers, he had raised the bat high in the air and brought it crashing down upon the frog. Not just once but more than a dozen times. Unbeknownst to Chris - his father had witnessed the whole thing from the living room window where he had been standing, sipping on his hot drink trying to decide whether today would be a good day to cut the grass or not. His father picked the bat up from the grass, "You won't be needing this again. Gone. Mine now. Too bad." He looked at the frog and then to his son, "What have I told you about hurting animals before?"

The frog wasn't the first animal Chris had killed but it was certainly the biggest. He usually just killed insects as most boys his age tended to do. Whether it was pulling the legs off daddy longlegs or burning ants with the heat of the sun magnified through a magnifying glass he had stolen from his brother's bedroom - his father always said the same thing, "If you can't make it, don't break it."

Chris didn't say anything. He just stood there sobbing. His father looked at him and realised he wasn't happy with what he had done and he knew that shouting at him wouldn't turn the clock back and bring life back to the frog. He shook his head at the boy, "Just go to your room. I don't want to see you," he said.

Chris turned and ran from the garden and into the house. The back door slammed shut behind him. His father looked back down at the mangled mess of a frog and shook his head again. He couldn't help but wonder where his son's nasty streak had come from. He didn't understand it and, more to the point, he didn't like it. Neither did his wife. She'd said to him that - if things continued - it might be worth seeking some kind of professional help for their son. Someone who could point him in the right direction where, with certain things, they were clearly failing.

NOW

DAY ELEVEN

Chris was sitting in The Control Room's chair - a look of apprehension on his face as to why he had been called into the room, especially given what had happened when Jack was called in.

"Chris, as you are aware it is against the rules to discuss who you would put up for elimination…"

He didn't say anything but you could see the contempt on his face.

The Controller continued, "Chris - The Controller thinks the Housemates have been through enough this week so we are not going to punish you as initially intended."

Chris looked at the camera, "What do you mean?"

"The Controller would like to reward you."

"I don't understand."

"The Controller would like to offer you a taste of Power."

Chris waited for them to explain more.

"As you like discussing eliminations with your colleagues, The Controller would like to give you the chance to discuss eliminations with him right now. The Controller would like you to choose three of your fellow Housemates to face elimination on Friday."

"I won't kill anyone."

"Chris, you are not being asked to eliminate anyone. You are being asked to nominate three of your Housemates for elimination."

"You want me to name three people I would put up for elimination?" he asked. His question was met by silence. "I don't need to kill anyone. We're just talking about who I would put up?"

"That is correct, Chris."

"Well - okay then. I'd put Kate, Paul and Stuart up for elimination," he said without giving it much more thought. It made sense to put Paul and Stuart up, despite it being Jack's suggestion to do so. They were the stronger of the Housemates; the ones who could possibly hurt Chris if push came to shove. And Kate - if Jack thought she deserved to win then it meant Jack would choose to save Kate over Chris. If she were already dead then there'd be one less reason for Jack not to save Chris over the other Housemates. A tactical nomination.

"Thank you, Chris."

"Is that it?" he asked.

"Chris, you may leave The Control Room."

Chris sat there a moment - bemused as to why he was being chosen for this out of all other available housemates. He was expecting them to say something else; expecting them to put a sting in the tail but there was nothing. He stood up and the red light around the door switched to the familiar green.

He pulled the door and stepped out, letting it close behind him.

"What did they say?" Stuart asked.

All of the housemates, even Jack, were standing at the bottom of the stairs waiting for Chris to re-appear from The Control Room. Chris stopped in his steps. The last thing he wanted was to be questioned by the household. He certainly wasn't about to tell them what had been discussed.

"Well?" Paul pushed him, "What did they want?"

Chris hesitated, "They - er - just wanted to talk about Friday."

"Friday? What about it?" Georgia asked.

"The eliminations?" Kate pushed.

"Yes. They wanted to know how I felt about it."

"How you felt about it?" Kate asked. "How are you supposed to feel about it? How are any of us supposed to feel about it? They're asking us to bump each other off…" She hesitated a moment, "What did you tell them?"

Chris went to open his mouth but was stopped by the sound of his own voice, "You want me to name three people I would put up for elimination?" The playback was coming from the plasma screen in the living area. All of the housemates turned at the sound of it.

"What is this?" Chris ran down the stairs and pushed past all of his colleagues. He ran over to the plasma screen and looked for a way to turn it off as the other housemates followed him, "No, no… This wasn't part of the deal. This was a private conversation."

"What's going on?" Kate asked. "What is this?"

"Well - okay then. I'd put Kate, Paul and Stuart up for elimination," Chris said on the screen. The screen paused. Chris slowly turned around. All eyes were on him.

"What the hell was that about?" Paul asked.

"Pretty obvious, isn't it? He's put us up for elimination," Stuart said.

"Is that right? What have I done to you?" Kate asked. She genuinely looked hurt by what was revealed on the screen. Chris didn't say anything. His face reddened - both out of embarrassment and anger (the latter towards The Controller). Kate rushed towards him and slapped him in the face, several times. With each hit she called him a, "Piece of shit."

Jack pulled her away from Chris, "Just leave it…"

"What have I done to you?!" she screamed again at Chris. "Fuck you! I have a son! I have a son at home! Fuck you!"

"I'm sorry!" Chris shouted back as Georgia pushed him back towards the bedroom where he could be kept separate from the ones he had put up for elimination. "What choice did I have? We all have to do this. All of us!" He wasn't sorry for putting Kate up though. He wanted her gone for reasons already explained. She was competition. She needed to be gone. He was sorry because The Controller had played the conversation into the house for the others to see. An action which had immediately put him up as a target to the others; although, in truth, he was only worried about Paul.

Jack led Kate through to the garden away from the other housemates, "Come on," he kept saying over and over again as he pushed her through. She was sobbing.

"What did I do to him? He knows I have a child," she said.

"I don't know why he did it. That could have been anyone called up there though. We're all in the same boat."

"But what the fuck have I done to him? I thought we were friends…"

"There's no such thing as friends in here. Not anymore. You've seen what this place is doing to us."

"They might give one of us a chance of being saved though, right? Like they did with Jordy?"

"I don't know. I'm sorry. I don't have any answers for you."

"We need to kill him," Paul spat as he too came into the garden - accompanied by Stuart and Jordy. "We kill him before he has us killed. That's what we need to do."

"Shit," Jack muttered under his breath when he heard the conversation the two of them were having as they stepped into the garden. It was only a matter of time before the housemates turned on each other but he wanted to keep it 'civil' for as long as possible. Once they started turning on each other, he knew it would snowball so fast with no control. It would literally be a free-for-all until there was only one left standing.

"You think they'll let us off if we kill him first?"

"Unless it's a double elimination, I reckon so - yes," Paul said. The two of them looked at Kate. A look on their faces which suggested she'd also have to go - on the off-chance it was a double elimination. Paul looked at Jack, "Although I'm guessing they won't give a shit who is eliminated as long as someone goes."

"What, you threatening me again? This is getting really old. If you think you can take me, by all means make a move," Jack stood up, ready to defend himself. In his head he'd already played the scenario through; Paul would rush him, Jack would hit him on the head with one of the garden chairs. Simple.

"I can't do this," Kate continued to cry, "I just want to go home. I just want to hold my son."

Jack turned away from Paul and Stuart and went back to offering comfort to her, "They're right - as much as I hate to say it - if Chris goes, they may not make anyone else leave. Think about it, they'll have the show scheduled for x amount of time. They've already lost Fiona this week. One more is probably all they're looking to eliminate. One more. And if it's Chris... Well, he put himself in the firing line." Jack didn't like talking like this but he liked the idea of Kate's son growing up without a mother even less. Paul looked at Stuart and gave him a wink.

Stuart smiled.

BEFORE

DAY SIX

"**W**ho would you like to drink the vial?" asked The Controller.

Without hesitation Philip nominated, "Morgan." He took a moment to reflect before putting forward his reasons, "The guy is annoying. I mean - I know he is supposed to rile people up but, even so, he's doing my head in. The sooner he goes out the better. It's him or me. Hell, if I can't get him to drink the contents - I'll drink them myself..." he laughed and picked the vial up off the table.

"Thank you, Philip, and - remember - none of your other housemates are to know about this or there will be serious repercussions."

Philip nodded and slipped the vial into his trouser pocket before leaving the room. He walked down the stairs, back towards the main part of the house, aware that the cameras were following him.

"Did you want a drink?" Karen called over to him from the kitchen where she was busy making a round of hot beverages for her fellow housemates. Karen didn't really have a game-plan as such but was very much of the opinion that, if you were nice to people, they'd have very little reason to nominate you. Six days, so far, of making tea for people she barely knew.

The Controller's voice came through the intercom system again, "Can Morgan please come to The Control Room."

Morgan looked puzzled and got up from the living room sofa where he had been chilling with Jordy and Kate - much to their annoyance. "Try not to miss me too much, girls," he said. Kate wondered whether the ever watching camera picked up on her eye-roll. "Any idea what they want?" he asked Philip as he started walking towards the stairs.

"Just asking how people are and how they feel about tomorrow," Philip said. Morgan's face immediately dropped.

"Oh. Right. Okay."

"I'm not worried about tomorrow," Kate continued the conversation with Philip as Morgan disappeared up the stairs and towards the waiting interview with The Controller, "I mean no one wants to go on week one, do they? But I do miss my son. I didn't realise how much I'd miss him!"

Morgan took his seat in The Control Room. There was a small box in front of him, the size of a matchstick box. He looked at it suspiciously before speaking, "Hello."

"Morgan. You have been chosen for elimination tomorrow."

"But I'm not ready to go yet. Can't someone else go?"

"Morgan, you are aware that your time in the house was limited. We will not be eliminating anyone instead of you."

"But…"

"Morgan, in front of you is a small box. Inside that box are three blood capsules."

"Blood capsules? It doesn't sound as though it's going to be the most memorable of exits."

"Tomorrow, Philip will be pouring a small vial into your morning breakfast so please be sure to eat something which involves liquid."

"I eat cornflakes," Morgan said - a sulky tone.

"Philip will let you know when he has done this. You will then have to slip the capsules into your mouth and bite down on them when you're ready to do so."

"Okay, yes, thank you - I get the idea…"

"Morgan, do you have any questions?"

"You mean like - what if they check my pulse?"

"A Housemate will be checking for a pulse," The Controller continued, "they will give confirmation you are no longer breathing."

"And why does Philip need a vial?"

"Morgan, The Controller needs this to look as authentic as possible. If Philip is seen to be using the vial, it will give more weight to the game," The Controller said.

"You're not going to poison me for real, are you?"

The Controller didn't answer.

"And can't someone else do it? Philip is a prick. I don't want him having the satisfaction."

"Morgan, no one else will be carrying out the task."

"And what about Jordy? Can't we get her to try and give me mouth to mouth resuscitation?"

"Morgan, no one will be attempting to bring you back to life."

He sat there a moment in silence.

"Morgan, The Controller would like to thank you for your services."

"Yeah, brilliant, thanks for killing me first. I appreciate it," he said sarcastically. "Here's me thinking this was going to be good for my career." He paused a moment, "What screen time do I even have? You've been filming for six days now - do I at least get a decent amount of exposure that was promised to me?"

"Morgan, The Controller would like to reassure you that you will have the exposure you were promised and - once again - would like to thank you for your hard work on bringing this to life."

"Yeah, fuck you."

He reached forward, grabbed the small box and pocketed it before leaving the room.

Now

DAY ELEVEN

"**Why would they** play it into the house?" Chris asked. He was shaking from both the stress of the situation and the apprehension towards the freshly opened can of worms the playback had caused. Georgia was sitting with him, as was Karen.

"Because they want us to kill each other," Georgia said.

Karen wasn't saying anything. She too was shaking despite none of the attention being on her. Even if there was a chance to feel normal in the house, it was never long before things took a turn again and something cropped up to remind them of the danger they all faced.

"Should I go out and explain why I said what I did?" Chris asked.

"I'd just stay away from them for a while. Give people a chance to calm down."

"If someone else was called into The Control Room, someone else would have had to nominate people. I did what I had to do."

"I know you did," said Georgia. "It's a shitty situation to be in for everyone."

"Did Fiona do the right thing?" Karen asked. Her voice startled the others. They had grown accustomed to her silence. They turned to her. "Would it be easier if we all just killed ourselves?"

None of the group knew what to say. Although unspoken it had been a thought which had crossed most of their minds at some point or other. The bedroom door opened and Paul walked in with Stuart, Jordy, Kate and Jack. The only one who had any kind of expression on their face was Jack and it didn't fill Chris with any comfort.

"Look," Chris didn't wait for anyone to speak, "I didn't have a choice. I had to…"

Stuart cut him off, "No, it's fine. We understand."

Kate sat on the edge of her bed and shuffled back until she was leaning against the headboard. She was staring at Chris, a look of hatred on her face that he hadn't seen before. He shifted where he was sitting.

"What would you have had me do?" Chris asked her. "Eliminate myself? Hang myself like Fiona?"

Paul laughed, "Well this is tense, isn't it? I do wonder how it will end."

"Are you threatening me?" Chris got up from where he was sitting, despite Georgia trying to stop him from doing so.

"So what if I am? What are you going to do about it? Eliminate me?" Paul sneered.

Chris looked around. Paul, Stuart and Kate were staring at him with a look of hatred - detest - in their eyes. Karen was weeping, Georgia was looking apprehensive and Jack had a look on his face as though he knew what was coming.

"I'm not living like this," Chris hissed.

"So what are you going to do about it? Bitch and whine about it?" Paul spat. He stood up too - ready for confrontation.

"We have to kill each other? Why are we delaying it? What's the point if we're all dead anyway? Let's just get it over with, yeah?" Chris stormed from the room. Jack followed.

"Chris!" he called after him.

"What's he doing?" Georgia jumped up too.

"He doesn't have it in him to eliminate anyone. Has to do it behind closed doors by nominating three of us. Probably going to do a Fiona and top himself. Well - good fucking riddance," Paul shouted out so Chris could hear him.

BEFORE

"What are you doing?" Pete called up the stairs in the family home he shared with Fiona where she was lugging her suitcase. "I didn't think you were leaving yet?"

"I just wanted to get everything ready so we could relax for a couple of hours."

"You should have called me."

Pete ran up the stairs and took the suitcase from Fiona. She moved to one side to make it easier for him to get it past her as he took it down the rest of the stairs for her.

"Thank you," she said when he reached the bottom.

"Heavy. How much you got in here? I thought you were only going for about ten days."

"Well things might change. They might want me in there longer."

"I don't know - the script seemed pretty dead-ended. What with you having a noose around your neck," he laughed.

"Ssh! You're not supposed to know that."

"There's only us here. I think we're quite safe from people overhearing. Unless..." he looked around, "... you don't think the place is bugged, do you?"

"I just don't want you accidentally saying it in front of someone. I could get sacked."

"What are they going to do? Write you out of the series?" he teased again.

"It's not like that. Anyway - nothing is definite. The pages were just a guide line to what they're going to be looking for."

"Seemed pretty sure about themselves," he said.

"It all depends how the others react," Fiona said.

"See - I really don't understand this…"

NOW

DAY ELEVEN

Chris stormed through the living area to the kitchen. The others followed; some concerned, some bemused and some finding the whole thing funny. Chris grabbed a handful of sharp knives from the cutlery drawer and headed back to where the housemates were watching. He threw the knives on the floor, with the exception of one which he kept hold of for himself.

"Chris, what are you doing?"

Chris' eyes were fixed on Paul, "Pick one up."

"You're going to kill me?"

"Chris, put the knife down…"

Both Kate and Karen reached down and grabbed a knife of their own. They didn't point it at anyone but kept it close to their bodies as though ready to defend themselves should the need arise.

"Well? Are you going to kill me?" Paul asked again. "For one hundred thousand pounds - can you take a life?" he continued.

"They can keep the money!" Chris shouted. He went to lunge towards Paul but stopped in his tracks as a loud siren played into the house. The siren stopped as the plasma screen switched on - it's volume turned up to maximum output.

On screen was the main interviewer from the audition process, "Housemates stop what you're doing," the man said, "the experiment is over."

Paul, Stuart and Jordy cheered. Georgia, Chris, Jack, Kate and Karen just looked puzzled.

"What's going on?" Chris asked. He kept his knife raised towards Paul - unsure of what to believe anymore.

The man onscreen continued, "You were selected to take part in a televised experiment to see what would drive a normal person to commit murder; whether it be for financial reward or their own survival…"

"What the fuck is going on?!" Chris asked again.

Jack sat on one of the living room sofas - also unsure of what to make of everything.

"Everything you have been subjected to has been elaborately staged."

Jack looked over to Jordy. He was wondering how that had been elaborately staged. He had been forced to fuck her. Had he not fucked her - what would have been the outcome for her? This so-called experiment - would it have been over, their bluff called? And the meat they had eaten. They had seen Morgan's body cut up. Was that too fake?

"Housemates, sit tight - we're coming to get you," the man said before the screen went black.

"Congratulations!" Paul said.

"I don't understand," Chris dropped the knife. "I don't get it."

"The whole thing was a televised experiment to see what would drive someone to commit murder - myself, Jordy, Stuart, Fiona, Morgan, Richard, Philip - we're all actors brought in to drive the experiment forward… Make it seem real. I had you fooled, right? Honestly thought you were going to kill me," he laughed.

Chris sat down next to Jack who was looking at Jordy, "You're not HIV?"

She shook her head, "No - I had to do blood tests to prove it. I'm clean of everything."

"They made us…"

She shook her head again, "No." She hesitated, "I guess I can tell you now but… I got to choose you out of a handful of candidates…"

BEFORE

Jordy was sitting opposite the two people interviewing her.

"This is a copy of the terms and conditions and states your fee, plus an additional amount we hadn't discussed. If you'd like to give it a read," the man said.

"Okay. Now?"

"Now would be good. We're keen to get this signed off…"

"Should I go to the other room?" Jordy asked.

"Here is fine."

The man continued to watch Jordy as she settled back to read the paperwork through as per his request. The man picked a pen up from the table, took the lid off, and slid it across the desk towards Jordy's. After a few minutes, Jordy stretched across and took hold of the pen. She signed the paperwork off and passed both pen and paper to the two officials.

The man reached down to a case, by his feet, and pulled out a handful of files.

"If you could just choose the candidate you'd like to have in the house with you," he said as he handed the files across the table.

Jordy laughed, "It's weird - I don't usually get a choice in what my punters look like."

NOW

DAY ELEVEN

Jordy was explaining, "I knew the part I had to play, I got to choose someone I liked the look of to play it through with me," she said. "That's why they took your blood too in a medical - make sure you were clean."

"All this for a fucking television show?!" Jack couldn't believe it and he wasn't the only one.

Karen screamed and ran forward, blade in hand. Before anyone could do anything to react she stuck the tip of the blade into Paul's chest. The girls screamed out as Paul dropped to his knees. Stuart ran to his aid as Jack and Chris wrestled the knife from Karen.

"It's a trick!" she was screaming. "It's just another trick. They're playing with us. They're going to kill us all!"

The door to The Control Room opened and Morgan, Philip, Fiona and Richard came running into the house cheering as they did so. Their cheers stopped when they saw what had unfolded in the living room. Paul was gasping for air with the blade sticking from his chest, Stuart and the girls were trying to comfort him and Jack and Chris were holding Karen to the floor where she continued to scream and writhe around. The sight of the ex-housemates, once thought dead, caused Jack and Chris to loosen their grip on Karen. She took the opportunity to lunge forward with the knife again - this time catching Chris in the throat. He gargled up a mouthful of blood as he fell backwards onto the floor, his eyes wide with fear. Before Jack had a chance to react, Karen slashed him across the face and he too fell back clutching his now bleeding face.

"Only one of us can leave!" she kept screaming again and again. The Control Room door opened and security came running out to take control of the situation and help those who needed it - at least give aid to those who were still able to be helped. Paul and Chris' eyes were fixed forward, unblinking - chests unmoving.

Across the nation in several million homes - people watching the events unfold over their late night snacks had their screens suddenly cut off. Eleven days of viewing only to have their pictures replaced with static as the experiment came to an end. Despite the static - enough of the experiment had been seen by millions. People will do anything they need to do in order to survive and - when push comes to shove - societies will crumble.

THE END

REMINISCING

MATT SHAW

✦

I had been my birthday party. I hadn't wanted one. My friends insisted though.

"Valerie, you're having a party and that's that."

"I don't want one."

"Well... We do. Take one for the team."

And that was that. It was taken out of my hands and my friends threw me a party, not because they cared (although I'm sure they do on some level) but because they wanted an excuse to let their hair down. There was little point in arguing. I can't remember what I wore to the party. For all I know it could have been one of my many Hello Kitty tee-shirts; the ones my friends always joke about. No doubt matched perfectly with jeans and converse trainers. Hardly surprising I can't remember all of the little details. This party was about four and a half years ago. I do remember the party being better than I expected though. My friends got suitably drunk. I got some nice gifts but more importantly it was the night I met him.

My Sparkle.

My Brian.

I couldn't help but laugh as I remembered what I did to him that night. He was saying something, I can't remember what exactly, and I just shoved a cup cake up his nose. He laughed. I laughed. We ended up spending the whole party together. We spent the whole night talking and laughing, happily joking around. I remember thinking - as I looked at him from above the rim of my drink - my friends had brought me a good present...

And then - as time went on - one thing lead to another and about a year later he became my husband. I was happy. I *am* happy. We were happy. We *are* happy. Nothing has changed on that front. Nothing will ever change on that front. Nothing. We got married and then shortly after he became my husband, he also became a father to my son - Tyler - who I'd had in a previous relationship. He loved Tyler as though he were his own child and I'll never forget that. I had met the perfect man; even if he did like to dye his hair various colours all the time. I'd go out in the morning and come back hours later and he'd look different.

Pink.

That's what colour it is at the moment; pink.

A pink mohawk.

I can't recall the colour it was before then. There have been so many. And why? Well -because he says he likes to look different and who am I to argue? If it makes him happy, it's fine with me. It's not as though it hurts anyone and - besides - it's fun. I just hope he doesn't go bald in the future or else he'll have to find something else to dye.

I once thought about colouring my own hair various colours too. And why not? If it is good enough for him, it's good enough for me. But he wouldn't let me. Well - it's not that he didn't let me... He just says he likes it as it is. He fancies me as I am; long brown hair with blonde highlights. Matches my brown eyes nicely. That and - apparently - it is his 'thing'. I need to find my own 'thing'. It's comments like that which make me worry about him...

My mind jumped to where we were living. At the time we had an apartment. I say 'we' had an apartment but it wasn't ours as such. We were renting it. We stayed there for a while before finally deciding to move out. We talked about it for a short while and then packed up our belongings to move to pastures greener; a trailer of all places.

It might have looked strange to people looking into our lives from the outside but - to us - it made perfect sense. Here we were throwing money away on rent when we could have been saving the money to buy our own property. At the time we could only afford a trailer but in a few years from where we are now it will be fully paid off and we can upgrade to a new home; a bigger one.

This is merely the stepping stone to something bigger and better.

I wiped a tear from my cheek as it rolled from my right eye.

I guess that plan has changed now.

Don't think about it. Don't stress about it. It will only make things harder. Just keep reminiscing; just keep casting your mind back to happier times. Keep things light. Try and relax...

The trailer.

Our home.

Okay. Our home. Our stepping stone. It is a good size for our family. There are three bedrooms and two bathrooms. Hardwood floor throughout with the exception of the master bedroom which is carpeted. It's big enough that we can have our own space if necessary and Tyler - now nine years old - spends most of his time in his room anyway; playing on his Playstation 3. Sometimes he'd be playing games with the biggest smile on his face, clearly enjoying the experience he was being presented with, and other times he'd be sitting there with a look of sheer frustration on his face from something which was causing him some grief, be it a puzzle or boss at the end of an unnecessarily difficult level. I found both scenarios good to watch. On the one hand it was nice to see him enjoying something and having fun and - on the other - it was funny to see him getting wound up by what was - at the end of the day - just a game.

My mind drifted from the happy images of seeing him getting frustrated at various games to seeing him standing above a broken games console; upset that he'll never be able to play it again.

No.

Come on.

Don't let the bad thoughts in. Don't let them take over. Stay in control. Stay positive. Everything is going to be okay. Everything is going to be more than okay. Things are going to be amazing again - just as soon as we're over this little speed bump. For that is all this is; a little speed bump. Something that - together - we will overcome. I felt sick as the bad thoughts continued trying to find their way in, despite my best efforts to keep them at bay. And they were good efforts. For all intents and purposes, considering what I was going through - they were extremely good efforts. With that in mind don't lose track of them. Come on... Get the good thoughts back on track.

Okay.

Brian, Tyler and myself.

We also have three cats.

I wiped another tear from my cheek.

We had three cats.

No.

We *have* three cats. Come on - stop letting the negativity in. Talk about the cats, not as though they're dead but as though they're still here - breathing, meowing and purring. Talk about them like that.

There's Sparky. He's the boy. Sweet enough. I'm not sure whether he is Brian's favourite or whether Brian is Sparky's favourite. Squeak - Sparky's sister - is Tyler's cat. If he is in his room playing his console, she's in there asleep. When he goes to bed, she goes with him. And that leaves the third cat - Zazzy. A full grown cat who looks like a kitten. Absolutely gorgeous and possibly my favourite and not just because she's so damned cute but because she likes to spend all of her time lying on me.

Another tear hit my cheek. They're becoming more frequent now despite my best efforts to keep them at bay. It didn't help remembering the cats. Are they around or are they somewhere safe? Please let them be somewhere safe. But then - so what if they are? - that just means they're out there scared and (soon) homeless. I'm not sure which is the worse fate for them. Please let them be together at least. Please let them stick together. Remain hopeful that a neighbour has seen what is happening. Remain hopeful that a neighbour has called for help and also taken the cats in to keep them away from danger. Please let that be the case. I feel myself starting to panic again...

Stop it, Valerie.

Stop it.

I don't want to panic.

I want to remain calm.

I want to remain hopeful.

Hope is all I have right now. I turned my mind back to the positive thoughts that I could presently remember...

My son performing in his taekwondo classes. Watching him sparring with his friends as he works his way through the various belts. The look of intense concentration as he works through the different moves - and techniques - he is being taught. I can but only hope he has that same look when sitting in classes at school...

I'm sure he has.

He's a good lad.

In his martial arts, he's currently a brown belt but I know it won't be long before he moves up to the next colour. He's certainly determined to keep on moving up. I think he pictures himself starring in all these action films. I think he can see himself as being one of these actors.

Another tear.

Will I see him achieve the next level? Who'll be there cheering him on? It won't be me. It can't be... No! Stop it! Come on! What is wrong with you? You're not doing yourself any favours. Stop dragging yourself down. Keep positive. Keep hopeful. Everything is going to be okay. Keep telling yourself. Everything is going to be okay. I took a few deep breaths in the hope they'd help me calm myself; help me focus back upon the good in my life.

Cinema trips!

We don't go as often as we like but... We like to go to the cinema as a family. We also collect Brian's daughter Haley. She lives with her mum and grandmother and we try and see her as much as possible but it's not easy. She's eighteen years old now. She has a life and is always seemingly busy. Even more so now she has her first job and a steady boyfriend. But - as much as we can - we drive the hour to her house and take her out to the cinema. Cinema. Cinema… What was the last film we watched? What was it? Come on. Think about it. What the hell was it?

Damn memory.

Can't remember it.

That's okay. You can ask her tomorrow. You can call her up and ask her what the film was and then - whilst you're at it - you can arrange to go and see another one too. Maybe not just a film? Maybe go for something to eat too? And if she can't live without the boyfriend - well, he seems nice enough - bring him too. Just arrange something. We don't have unlimited time here. We need to make the most of it. I'm going to make the most of it. I swear…

I wiped another tear away…

… I swear - if tomorrow comes, I'm going to make the most of it.

Tomorrow I will phone Haley up and arrange a time to see her. Arrange a movie to watch. And then I'll go to the shops with Brian. Pick him some nice new colour hair-dye. A new hair colour for the fresh start that tomorrow will bring. Make a day of it - why not - and go to the computer game shop with Tyler. It has been a while since he has had a new game. I'm sure there'll be something out there that he'd want. I'll find it with him and I'll buy it. My treat. I won't stop there either. I'll get some treats for the cat; something for them to eat and something for them to play with. Maybe a toy mouse, or something? I don't know. I don't know. I'll find something though.

Another tear.

I heard Brian scream my name, "Valerie!"

He sounded distant. Is he not in here? Is he outside?

"Brian!" I screamed back. I coughed.

"Valerie!"

Is he coming to get me? Please say he is coming to get me. He's coming to make everything better.

"Brian! I'm in the bathroom!" I screamed unsure if he knew where I was - or even if he could hear me.

"Valerie?"

"Yes! I'm here!" I burst into tears. "I'm here."

"I can hear you!" he shouted back. "I can hear you! Are you okay?"

"Is Tyler with you?" I yelled. I coughed.

"Are you okay?" he called out again.

I screamed louder on the off-chance he didn't hear me the first time I had asked, "Is Tyler with you?" There's a few things in my life that scare me. One of those things is the thought of not being able to protect my son. I would die for him yet here I am - about to die - and I'm not sure if he is okay. No. Stop it. You're not going to die. Brian knows you're in here. Brian knows where you are. He's coming for you. He's going to get you out of this. He's going to save you. But what about Tyler? "Is Tyler with you?" I yelled again.

"He's with me!" Brian shouted back.

I breathed a heavy sigh of relief and coughed. I wasn't sure if I heard it right but it sounded as though there were a crack in Brian's voice; a crack of emotion. Why did he sound as though this was the last time we were going to talk? Why? Don't. Don't panic. You'll only make matters worse.

Positive thoughts.

Positive thoughts only.

We've been married for about three and a half years now. I started to wonder whether it was too early to renew our wedding vows. We could invite the whole family, we could use some of our savings for our new home... We could throw the best party anyone had seen before. And at the centre of it - us - our love. We could have champagne reception, we could have the finest food, everyone could get a free pair of converse. I laughed as my mind got carried away as the plans became more and more elaborate in my mind.

I coughed.

I was pulled back to reality with a second cough as the severity of my situation became more and more obvious. The smoke was coming through the gap between door and floor. I was lying on the bathroom floor trying to avoid the heavy plumes of smoke but there was no doubting the room was getting heavier. Getting hard to breath. And the heat. So damned hot.

Putting the back of my hand against the door, I can feel that the fire is close. Lying on the floor and looking under the gap - I could see the flames licking away close to where I was; I could feel their heat. I coughed again. My heart was beating so damned fast I thought it were going to just give up the ghost right there and then. Part of me wished it would. Has to be an easier way to go than choking, or burning, to death.

No. Stop it, Valerie. You're not going to die. He's coming for you. Your Sparkle is coming for you. He's going to get you out of this and he is going to take you away from it all. And tomorrow will be the first day of the rest of your life. This is not the last day. This isn't. You're not going to die here. You're not.

The flames were closer. I moved back away from the door - keeping as low as I could - as the flames started licking underneath the door. I couldn't contain the tears anymore as they fell freely. I didn't try and stop them. I didn't try and contain them. Let them flow. Let them.

In the corner of the bathroom, I noticed a spider on the wall next to where my face was pressed. Normally I'd freak at this. I'd run from the room and demand Brian get rid of it, or I'd crush it with whatever was close to hand. Now though, now I didn't care. If anything I was almost grateful that this little spider was here with me.

I wasn't alone.

I nervously reached up with my hand and put it next to the spider. Pretty sure this is the first time I've ever attempted to do this. With my other hand, I nudge the back of the spider so that it moved across onto my hand. Funny how circumstances change the way we look at things. Had this been yesterday, I'd have killed the spider or - at least - had it thrown from the house. It's feet tickling the palm of my hand as the spider took a few steps across. I hated it but…

I wasn't alone.

Bottom of the door was on fire now. Flames eating away from the bottom and working their way up. The damage the flames were causing, I couldn't believe how quiet it was. I could hear things breaking in other rooms of the trailer. I could hear cracking from the wood. I could hear parts of the trailer collapsing. Couldn't hear the flames though.

"Valerie! They're coming! Help is coming!" Brian called.

I didn't shout back. I tried to keep my mouth shut. So much smoke in here now. If I open my mouth the smoke will just fill it. I held the spider close to me, cupped in my hand - wondering whether I was protecting it from what I was about to endure. I wondered whether it was as scared as I was. I wondered if it were grateful for me as I was for it.

It was not alone.

We were not alone.

I could hear sirens coming. They sounded distant but they were definitely coming. Help was coming. Flames licking the ceiling of the trailer and spreading across them. Everything they touched turned black before catching fire too. Flames coming across the floor too. Flames close to me.

I moved my legs as far back as I could but there really is no room to move now. There really is no where for me to go.

"Over here!" Brian was screaming.

I could picture him in my mind, waving down the approaching fire truck. Sirens practically on top of us now. They didn't completely drown out the sound of the trailer falling part around me, though. I didn't want this to be the last thing I heard. I wanted it to be either Brian or Tyler. I wanted their voices to be the ones which sent me to Heaven. I wanted them. I flinched my leg as a searing pain shot through me. I looked down. Flames licking at my jeans and converse. Tiny bathroom with nowhere to hide. If help is coming, they need to be quick.

I screamed out loud.

Brian screamed back - calling out my name.

Another voice calling out. I could tell it belonged to Tyler despite not being able to hear it clearly. I could hear the fear in his voice. I could hear the panic. I wished I could tell him everything was going to be okay. I wished I could tell him mummy was coming right out but I couldn't say anything. Face pressed against the floor, trying to get the last of the air available but all I can see now is smoke. Not sure what's going to get me first; the smoke of the flames. I prey it's the first. I'd rather choke to death than burn to death. Burn me when I'm dead.

Please not before.

I screamed as the flames reached my feet. No where else to move them. No where else for me to run to, or hide. All I could do was sit here as they burned jean to flesh. All I could do was hope and prey that help would put them out in time.

As the searing pain burned through me I couldn't stop myself from screaming out loud again. In response, I could hear Brian screaming too - as though he could feel my pain. I wanted to tell him to take our son away. I wanted to tell him but I couldn't. Thick smoke filling my lungs as flames burned. I was choking now. I kept trying to stop myself but I couldn't. The more I fought against it, the more I seemed to suck in. Stop it. Please stop it. My head is thumping. The worst pain I've ever experienced from a head-ache. Please make it go away. Tops of my legs are burning now. Doesn't help with the pain.

I tried rolling onto my front to try and extinguish the flames but there isn't enough room and I don't have the energy to try and even make it work. Need oxygen. Can't stop hacking... And the pain.

That pain.

Ignore the pain.

Take yourself back to a happy place.

Take yourself back to a better place; my wedding.

Exchanging the vows, the smiles on our faces, the tears of happiness in my eyes. The happiest day of my life.

The happiest day of my life.

Everything fades to black.

FIN

LAUGHTER IN THE NIGHT

MATT SHAW

The house was a mess. Three months they'd been living there and yet there were still boxes lying around half filled with random bits neither Elizabeth (Beth to her friends) nor her girlfriend Tracy had bothered to put away. Most of the stuff belonged to Beth. Tracy had already been living there when she asked her to move in. She occasionally asked if Beth was going to find a proper home for the belongings which remained out of the box but the answer was always the same.

"What's the point? We'll only be packing it all back up again in a couple of months."

Tracy never argued. Beth was right. In a few months (September to be exact) they were going to be packing once more, ready to move back to Beth's hometown of Liverpool.

It had been a long day. Beth worked for the cat rescue centre close by and a few new cats had been brought in which she needed to deal with. People often spoke of their jealousy with regards to the job itself. They envisioned Beth sitting down all day, with a hot black coffee in hand, stroking cats whilst enjoying her favourite past-time; reading random horror novels from unknown authors she stumbled across on Amazon and Goodreads. If only her job was like that though. Her friends - or strangers who came in to find themselves a new pet - annoyed her when they mentioned how easy the job be as it was anything but easy. They come in for five minutes at a time and see the cats sleeping in their holding areas. What they don't see is the cleaning (both on the scene and behind the scenes) and constant food preparation, the paperwork, ensuring the animals are up to date with whatever treatment they may have been having. The hardest part, for Beth, though was having to leave the animals there at the end of the shift. She'd have a final look around to ensure everything was done and - occasionally - she'd catch the eye of one of the animals. They'd just be looking at her with a sadness in their eyes; a feeling of abandonment. If she could, Beth would have taken them all home with her. She was sure they'd fit in with the rest of the animals; Harley and Morgan (the two chihuahuas), Rooney (the cat), Spyro the always-randy Bearded Dragon who spent most of his time trying to get to the females Cynder and Isla and - of course - not forgetting Aragog and Rory the whites tree frogs. What harm would one more cat be?

"Even if we had the room, do you really think Indigo would be happy with another cat brought into the family?" Tracy was often heard to be said when Beth returned from work full of enthusiasm for adopting yet another feline. Indigo (sometimes called Indy) was a young kitten of just a few months but was already on his way to earning the reputation of the naughtiest cat in the world. If he wasn't supposed to have something, he'd have it. If he wasn't supposed to be somewhere, that place would be his new sleeping area. He was a bastard all right yet they still loved him.

Beth didn't collapse on the sofa when she got home. She simply hesitated by the living room's doorway as though stuck on what to do for the best. Tracy was already home. She was sitting there, a book to her side, with a hot drink in her hand.

"How was work?" Tracy asked. She looked up and noticed her girlfriend seemed a little 'off sorts'. "What's wrong?"

"Rough day," Beth said. She walked over to the front window and looked out into the road beyond. A few cars went by but - other than that - it was pretty quiet.

"Can I get you a drink?" Tracy asked. She got up from the sofa.

"Love a coffee. Even more if it comes with a cigarette."

"For you? Sure." She walked over to Beth and gave her a sweet kiss on the cheek. Beth smiled but still seemed distracted. Tracy didn't notice - at least, if she did, she didn't say anything. She left the room and headed for the kitchen as Beth turned back to the window. Still quiet out there. She started to ease up a little and turned her back to the window as she made her way to the sofa where she collapsed. The day hadn't just been busy. It had been traumatic. Someone brought a cat in - an older, tabby cat with a sweet face. They'd hit it in their car and the poor feline was in a dire state. Its back legs were broken, possibly the front one too and it was bleeding profusely from somewhere underneath its fur on his side. The man was in a state too; distraught that he'd hit the animal. He'd brought it to the rescue centre because it was the closest place where he knew the animal could get the attention it was in desperate need of.

Tracy walked back into the room and handed Beth a freshly made coffee, "I was thinking about ordering take-away," she said as she took the seat next to her. "Don't know about you but I'm not really in the mood for cooking."

"Take-away sounds good."

"So. Tell me about your day. You look tired."

"Gee. Thanks."

"In a nice way."

"Anyway I don't really want to talk about it. Rather leave it all at work." Beth didn't want to tell Tracy about the cat's owner. They managed to track him down through the cat's microchip. The man - Steve Bullins - was at work when they called and said he'd be there as soon as he could. It was over an hour later when the front door opened and a concerned clown rushed over to the reception desk. At first the receptionist thought it was a joke and started to laugh. She only managed to regain her professionalism when she realised the man wasn't there acting out some kind of prank.

"I had a phone call," he told her. His voice was shaky. An older man who attended birthday parties dressed as a clown in order to pay his bills - his cat was his only company when he went home after a busy day entertaining people. Within the next five minutes - he'd learn the harsh news he was too late. The on-site vet couldn't wait for him to arrive and had to put the cat out of its misery with the aid of an injection. Beth had been the one who had to tell Mr Bullins. The grown man, still in clown outfit, wept.

"I still fancy you even though you look tired and haggard," Tracy laughed. She cuddled up to Beth. She was surprised by the lack of response from Beth. She looked at her; her eyes fixed upon the window. Tracy moved away from her, "Okay - look - something's clearly bothering you…What is it?"

"I said, I don't want to talk about it."

"No secrets. We always said - we'd never have secrets between us. Come on, tell me, I might be able to help."

"It was just a rough day. We had to put a cat to sleep. It was brought in to us by some guy who accidentally hit it with his car. The vet didn't have a choice but to put it out of its misery."

"I'm sorry," Tracy cuddled back into her.

Beth didn't tell her what else happened. Mr Bullins wept at first but then his temperament changed as a vile anger took a hold of him. Harsh words from his mouth blaming Beth of all people for the death of his pet and yet it hadn't been her who was behind the wheel and it hadn't been her who pierced its skin with the needle. The only thing Beth had done was to be present when the euthanasia took place (and even that wasn't where she wanted to be).

"Do you have pets?" he had asked her.

"Yes."

"Maybe someone should take them away from you?"

"I beg your pardon?"

"I bet you do."

"I'm sorry, I don't understand."

"I'm saying they should confiscate them before you kill them."

Beth had tried to explain to Mr Bullins that they did what was best for his cat but he didn't listen. He just shouted over her. He wished her pets the same fate as his own; their death. The receptionist called for security to come through as Mr Bullins' voice continued to rise. The anger and hostility started was already upsetting Beth as he continued to vent his grief upon her. "By the end of the night - everything you hold dear will be fucking dead, you cunt!"

Beth ran from the room, tears streaming down her face. She was a strong woman the majority of the time but the stranger's outburst caught her by surprise. That on top of the fact she never enjoyed having to see an animal get put to sleep - she had to get out of his presence.

Beth knew he was just grieving and venting but she couldn't help but keep replaying what he said through in her head. The harsh words promising death upon her animals. Her colleague at work suggested she spoke to the police about it but she didn't. She just wanted to put it from her mind and get on with her day. The nice thing about the job was that it was continuously busy meaning she had plenty to distract herself from it. But on the way home - what he said came back to the forefront of her tired mind. She wasn't sure whether it was his tone which scared her or the fact he was dressed as a clown - a figure which just so happened to be one of her greatest phobias.

Beth moved away from Tracy.

"What's up? Am I digging in?" Tracy asked.

Beth shook her head, "No. Look. I'm sorry. I'm just really tired. Might go to bed."

"Bed? It's only just gone seven…"

"I'm sorry, I just don't feel too good."

"Well do you want me to come up?"

"No. That's fine. You stay up. Order yourself a take-away, use my card."

"You're sure?"

Beth nodded, "I'm sure." She leaned across to Tracy and gave her a kiss before standing up. She walked to the doorway, and stole a final look out of the window. Still quiet out there. As she made her way up the stairs, she couldn't help but wish she was already asleep. By morning everything would be better.

The sounds of a dog barking woke Beth with a start. It sounded like Harley, the male chihuahua. Didn't sound as though he was in the need of the toilet. It was more of a distressed barking.

"Your dog needs you," she whispered to Tracy, her voice clearly struggling to wake up. It was always the same when the pets were up to no good - they were Tracy's - and when they were being cute and affectionate, that were Beth's. She rolled over and was surprised to see Tracy's side of the bed was already empty. "Tracy?" She didn't answer. For a split second Beth presumed she'd already got up to see what was wrong with Harley but then she realised the other side of the bed had not been slept in. The cover wasn't creased and the mattress was cold to the touch. Beth looked round to the clock. 3am in the morning. She imagined Tracy had fallen asleep on the sofa. No doubt overate on the take-away food and dozed off feeling comfortably full with a glass of wine in her hands.

Beth flung the duvet off and threw her dressing gown on. Harley yelped and stopped barking. "What the hell is going on down there?" she called out as she got to the top of the stairs. She hesitated a moment, before venturing further down the stairs, half expecting Tracy to appear at the bottom of them with an irritated expression on her face from where the dog woke her up. She even thought she may have heard Tracy scolding the dog for waking her up in the first place. But there was nothing. Just an eerie silence. "Tracy?" she called out again. Another pause and still no reply.

Slowly she crept down the stairs. She held her breath as she half-expected Tracy to suddenly leap out and scare the living crap out of her - not that she made a habit of such childish antics (even though is was often fun to do such a thing when aimed towards their friend Lizzi who was scared of pretty much everything).

"Yeah, I'm the weird one," Lizzi once said after being made to jump by something stupid. "At least I'm not scared of green olives." Beth couldn't help but smile at the conversation's memory. Lizzi always threw that in her face; Beth's own silly little phobia for olives. The smile faded from her face as she neared the bottom of the stairs and still there were no sounds from around the house. Even Indy was quiet and he'd usually wait until the middle of the night to go completely scatty.

Beth reached the bottom of the stairs and walked into the living room. Tracy wasn't in there. The television was on but the volume was muted. The controller was on the floor as though it had been dropped or, more likely, the damned cat knocked it off the coffee table again.

"Tracy?"

She left the room and walked towards the kitchen. The door was shut. No wonder the dog had been barking - probably got themselves locked in there by mistake. She reached out and opened the door.

"Hello again."

Beth screamed.

Mr Bullins was standing in front of her, at the other end of the kitchen. In front of him was Tracy. She was sitting on one of the kitchen chairs. Her wrists and ankles bound to the furniture's frame and her mouth gagged with a red-stained rag of some description. Her eyes wide with fear and he auburn hair dishevelled. Next to her neck was the tip of a rusty looking chainsaw. The whole visual imagery made worse by the fact Mr Bullins was standing there in his clown outfit; his face painted up to make him look like an insanely happy clown.

Before either of them could speak again the microwave pinged.

"That'll be for you," he said. His voice was low and menacing; complete contrast to how the make-up was supposed to make him look. He gestured towards the microwave which rested on the kitchen's side.

"Please…What are you doing? Let her go…"

"I said…That'll be for you…" he gestured towards the microwave again.

Beth slowly turned to it. The interior light had gone out making it hard to see what was on the other side of the microwave's door. She could just see a shape. Slowly, with a shaking hand, she reached out and opened the door. She screamed again at the sight of her two beloved pet dogs. Cooked from the inside out; their remains a bubbling mess of intestine and fur from where they'd exploded. Beth fell backwards, away from the microwave, giving Tracy the opportunity to see the contents. Through the gag, she also screamed.

"Now I know it doesn't look nice but you'll have to trust me on the taste. Go on…Dip a finger in and give it a whirl," Mr Bullins tormented her. Beth shook her head. "Maybe you didn't hear me." He started the chainsaw up which roared loudly into life. Tracy screamed again through the gag as the blade whirred precariously close to her neck. "I said give it a taste!" Mr Bullins screamed over the sound of the machine.

Beth reached out and put her finger in the bubbling mess. She pulled it out again - a thick, sticky mess lingering upon her flesh, burning her in the process. Mr Bullins watched on with a gleeful expression as Beth slowly raised her finger to her mouth. A quick hesitation before she slipped it between her lips. The strong taste of iron made her gag as Mr Bullins killed the power to the chainsaw.

"See - that's gourmet that is."

"Fuck you!" Beth spat.

"Ooh - you have a fire in you, that's good."

"Please just leave us alone…"

"I told you, at at the cat centre, I told you that by the end of the day the ones you hold dear will be dead. I'm a man of my word."

"Please. Just leave us alone. Please."

"Can't do that." He paused a moment. "Did you think I was kidding? Did you think I was joking around?" He had a dead pan expression on his face. Combined with the fact he was in a clown outfit, it just made it that little bit more creepy.

Beth was crying as everything hit her at once; her dogs were dead and her and her partner were soon to follow. Steve smiled at her. Again, there was nothing reassuring about this smile.

"Don't worry," he said, "you will survive this night. You'll live another day yet." It was as though he read her mind; her fear of dying.

"I don't understand."

"You killed all that I held dear. I am going to do the same to you. Eye for an eye."

"Please…"

"Your dogs were for starters and this…." he fired up the chainsaw again. Both Beth and Tracy screamed (albeit Tracy's scream was through the dirty rag). "…This is the piece de resistance." Beth wanted to run towards him and push the chainsaw from his hands but was rooted to the spot with fear. She screamed as loud as she could that it wasn't her fault, the cat was in such a bad state they did what they had to in order to put it out of its misery but her words were lost underneath the roar of the chainsaw screaming through the night. She hoped a neighbour had heard the initial roar of the machine where he turned it on a few minutes previously and that they'd called for help. Even as they stood there, the police were on their way. She hoped.

She screamed (pointlessly) again, "PLEASE DON'T."

The clown with the creepy smile didn't hear her though. Even if had he - he did't register her words. A glint appeared in his eye as he stuck the edge of the chainsaw into Tracy's shoulder. She screamed through the rag, as did Beth. Blood splattered across the room in a jet spray arc of beautiful red as her body rocked backwards and forwards with the motion of the chainsaw and backwards and forwards motion Mr Bullins made. He continued to saw through the top layers of skin, then muscle and eventually bone. The whole thing over in seconds. He pulled the chainsaw out from the side of Tracy's body and the top quarter of her body slumped to the floor in a pooling puddle of gore and gut. Steve killed the power to the chainsaw not long after he killed Beth's love. He dropped it and smiled to Beth as though he'd done no wrong. He took a step back, towards the back door, as Beth ran to Tracy's twitching corpse; a final spew of blood from her mouth. She hadn't stopped screaming since first starting when Steve first dug the chainsaw into Tracy. She dropped to her knees and continued to weep as she held close to her the piece he'd cut off.

"We're even now," Mr Bullins said. He turned to the back door and opened it. He stopped himself from leaving as a thought crept into his mind. He slowly turned back to Beth, "I'm going to need a new pet…Can I come see what cats you have in the cattery?" he asked.

Beth screamed.

T H E E N D

Welcome To Brattleboro

WE HOPE YOU ENJOY YOUR STAY!

Prologue

"Dad, I'm bored!" my youngest daughter, Ava, yelled from the backseat of my Dodge Ram. I winced in pain as I bit my tongue. How can she be bored? She has everything she could possibly need back there. She has a television screen built into the back of my seat playing her favorite cartoon movie, the pink Nintendo DS she got for her sixth birthday last week after begging and pleading with us for several months prior, a stack of games to play on; most of which were also on her extensive present list she deemed fit to drop on our laps at the start of her birthday month. She even has the magazines she begged Susan for at the last gas station we visited. And yet she's bored? She should try sitting in this traffic. She'd soon understand boredom then.

I looked in the rearview mirror at Jamie, my eldest daughter, who was staring out of the window blissfully unaware of her sister's boredom thanks to the headset of her MP3 player replacing Ava's whining voice with Heavy Metal. What happened to my sweet little girl? As soon as she turned seventeen years of age her pale complexion was made even paler with thick, white foundation and her dark brown eyes were suddenly surrounded by black eye-shadow and eye-liner. When she first started wearing it I teased her saying that she looked like a panda bear but she paid no attention; just grunted at me. The grunts being another side effect brought on by her seventeenth birthday. I'm just waiting for the day she comes home with tattoos and piercings all over her body. Susan, my snoring, open-mouthed wife in the passenger seat next to me, promised it was a phase. To her everything is a 'phase'.

"Dad! I'm bored!" Ava yelled again.

I wonder whether Susan is even asleep or just pretending so as not to have to deal with Ava's constant moaning. I swear, when I get home I'm selling Ava's toys. Wonder if I can sell Susan too...

"Dad!"

It's a shame I can't get away with pretending to be asleep. I twisted the rear-view mirror to make it easier to see her, "Play your game," I said. I tried my best to sound 'friendly' despite my tired mood wavering towards *psychotic*.

"It's boring," she moaned.

"Well play another one."

"I don't want to. I don't like them."

I am definitely selling her toys, "Then watch the film!"

"I don't like it!" she moaned. I hate it when she moans. Thankfully it isn't very often. Nine times out of ten she's a good kid. I guess she stayed up too late last night. No doubt, when Susan wakes up, that will be my fault.

"How about a game of I-Spy?" I suggested if only to keep the peace. I-Spy with my little eye - back to back fucking traffic.

"Noooo..." she whined.

I want to meet the person who put the rule in place which states you can't hit children. I'd like them to borrow Ava for the day. Make that a week.

"How much furtheeeer?" she asked. I hate it when she moans. She seems to add extra vowels to the last word of the sentence to make it even longer and more whiney than if she had just said it normally.

"Stop whining," I snapped. I don't dare tell her we're hours away yet. It'll only set her off. Hopefully she'll fall asleep when the truck starts moving, once we're out of this God-awful traffic.

"Where are we? Are we there yet?" asked Susan as she stirred from her unexpected slumber. I shot her a look. I can see the headlines now, *Local author guns down family out of frustration*. "What?" she asked.

"We're not even out of the city yet," I replied.

"What? How come?" She looked out of the windscreen to see what the hold up was. "Traffic?"

I really wanted to say something like 'No, I just thought I'd pull up to the sidewalk for a few hours but, instead, opted to go with, "Must have been an accident."

"Mum, I'm boreeeed..." moaned Ava from the backseat.

"Play your game then," said Susan.

"I don't like them, they're boring!"

"Then watch your film - it's your favorite..."

It's going to be a long trip. I reached across to the radio and turned the volume up.

The Cabin

Chapter 1

"The kids are getting hungry," Susan pretended to observe.

"They've got food," I said.

"Chocolate isn't food," Susan argued.

"Try telling them that. If you let them, they'd live off it."

"Okay, *I'm* getting hungry," she corrected me, "and I don't want to live off chocolate."

"Oh, well, darling why didn't you say so? Of course I'd love to stop off to get some food for you, and our delightful children, just as the traffic has all cleared and we've finally managed to make some fucking progress..."

"Watch your language. It's not my fault the traffic was bad."

"I'm hungry too," Ava piped up from the back.

"I know, baby, we're stopping off soon," said Susan even though, technically, I had made no such promise. I didn't argue with her and took the next available turning off from the highway. I could already feel my temper was frayed and it would only lead onto a shouting match had I started an argument; neither of us like to back down once we get going. My temper because of everyday stress and her temper because she's from Brooklyn. I had hoped leaving the city would have helped me calm down more or less straight away but then my temper probably wasn't helped by the traffic. There's something about New York, something in the air maybe? Something, that is, other than smog and pollution. I always feel so stressed which is why I like to escape the city life when the pressures are too much and, with my agent breathing down my neck for a new book, the pressures are definitely too high at the moment.

"Are you okay?" Susan asked. The first time she had asked for as long as I can remember. I must really look like I'm close to cracking.

"I'm fine," I lied, "I just can't wait to get to Brattleboro."

"You have looked more stressed than usual," she pointed out the obvious, "the break will do you some good."

"Yeah, I know." Another lie to keep the peace.

I love how she thinks this is a break. The whole point of escaping to the family cabin, in Brattleboro, was to try and get my head down to do some serious writing. Instead, she decided to turn it into a family weekend away. It's not even as though the kids wanted to come. She made them. She said it would do us some good to get away, as a family, and they'll enjoy it when they get there. Ava will be wanting whichever toys we didn't pack for the trip and Jamie will be missing her boyfriend Zak. I have a feeling I won't be getting any writing done.

"Fresh air, long walks, peace and quiet - it'll be perfect. Romantic."

I smiled at her but desperately wanted to weep.

"Sounds great but I do need to get some writing done too," I said. I tried my best to stress the importance of the writing without making it sound as though her own plans weren't important too.

"I know," she said. I felt myself breathe a sigh of relief. "But it won't take all weekend." And, just like that, the relief I had just felt had completely disappeared and been replaced with dread once more. I suppose it's my own fault as I tend to only write when she's out of the house otherwise I can't get anything done because she's normally too busy fussing around me, or making noise, for me to be able to concentrate. Because she's not normally present when I'm writing, the first she knows about my new book is when I tell her I've finished it; when I sit back with a cigar in one hand a glass of champagne in the other. My little rewards. The 'speed' in which these new books pop up probably makes her think they're easy to write but they're not. They're incredibly draining. People don't seem to understand that, as an author, you tend to experience all the emotions your character experiences too. What happens to them also happens to you and, if like me the authors write in the horror genre, well sometimes we can go through a lot of different emotions in any one given day of writing. Another good reason to ensure you're home alone when you're working. That way you don't take your moods out on anyone else.

I turned into the car park for McDonalds, "This'll do."

"MCDONALDS!" screamed Ava with excitement. Finally something to break the sound of whining.

"You're joking, right?" said Susan.

"What?" I asked.

"McDonalds? I think we can do something slightly better than McDonalds."

"Are you hungry?" I asked. She nodded. "Good," I said, "then you'll eat it."

I turned the engine off, undid my seatbelt, and climbed from the truck. Ah, fresh air. Immediately I felt my building headache begin to subside. We'd only been on the road for just over an hour and it had done me in. Perhaps stopping for food, if only for hour an hour, was the best thing to do for all concerned. Everyone can eat and I can unwind a little before setting off again. Definitely a good idea to unwind before we drive through Massachusetts regardless. If they still haven't done anything to help the traffic flow there, other than to open the breakdown lane, I could end up getting stressed again as we go bumper to bumper once more. Maybe I should let Susan drive the rest of the way. Actually no, forget that. We'll never get there whilst it's still daylight.

Susan climbed from the truck still moaning about my choice of restaurant, "I just think we could go somewhere a little better than McDonalds. A nice steak house or something."

"And I heard you but, right now, all I want to do is get to Brattleboro. We can get a proper meal there this evening. Whatever you fancy, I promise. Besides which," I pointed towards Ava who was excitedly bouncing around in the back of the Ram, "the kids are happy. In fact, if I were you, I'd take a picture; this is probably going to be the happiest you'll see them all weekend. Well Ava at least. I think Jamie's forgotten how to smile."

"I heard that," said Jamie as she climbed from the backseat.

"Did I hear that right?" I asked. "Did you really just speak to me in something other than a grunt? You did, didn't you? Honey, did you hear that? We communicated!"

"Stop winding your daughter up," said Susan as she helped Ava down from the truck. Meanwhile Jamie just shot me a dirty look.

I simply smiled back. "I have such a happy family."

⅄

Susan reluctantly agreed to get our dinners on the understanding I looked after Jamie and Ava at the table in the far corner of the fast food restaurant. Given the choice between standing in what has to be one of the longest queues I've ever seen or looking after our children I'd always choose the latter of the two. Well, not always. Today, though, I think I've had my fair share of queuing.

"One happy meal with nuggets for Ava, one Big Mac for daddy, a chicken wrap for mummy and a box of nuggets for Jamie," she said when she finally came back to the table. She sat on the opposite side to me, next to Ava who was more interested in the toy which came with her meal than she was in actually eating the food. "Put that away until you've finished your meal please, baby," Susan took the toy from her and dropped it in her handbag. Oh good, more junk for the house. Had she let her play with it now Ava would have probably been bored with it by the time we came to leave and we could have just dropped it into the bin with the rest of the rubbish, or given it to another family to be stuck with until their next yard sale at the very least. I didn't say anything. No point.

I looked at my miserable looking burger and laughed, "Have you ever noticed how these things look nothing like the pictures on the wall?" I picked it up and held it in perfect line with the poster which advertised it. "Look at that, the burger in the picture is all plump and juicy - tasty looking - but this…"

"It's flat!" laughed Ava.

"See," I said, "she gets it." I peered into the box which hid her food, "What do you have? A box of chicken heads?"

"No, daddy, nuggets!"

"Nuggets? You best let daddy try one of those! Just to make sure, of course." I leaned into the box and grabbed a nugget before I popped it into my mouth.

"Daddy, their mine!" she shouted.

"Oh, I'm sorry," I said, "did you want it back?"

I opened my mouth wide enough for her to see the mushed up state of the nugget within and she laughed. Even Susan, the ice maiden, laughed.

"You're so disgusting!" moaned Jamie. There was a time when she would have laughed too. I turned my head to make sure Jamie had a good look too.

A step too far for Susan, "Stop being disgusting!"

"Yes, mum!" I said. Ava and I laughed.

"What's wrong with your burger?" Susan asked Jamie. Whilst the rest of us were tucking into our food she hadn't touched any of hers other than her milkshake.

"I'm vegetarian," she said before taking another sip from her milkshake.

"Since when?" asked Susan.

"Since seeing the state of this burger probably," I said as I took another bite.

"You chose to come here so stop your complaining!" she said. She turned back to Jamie, "Why didn't you say something when I went to get the food?"

"You didn't ask," Jamie answered back. This was typical Jamie. I had learnt to ignore it long ago but Susan always rose to the bait. Jamie would soon decide she wasn't a vegetarian when the hunger kicked in. "Zak told me how the animals are treated right up until the time they die…Did you know sometimes…"

"I don't want to hear it," snapped Susan. "If you…"

I interrupted to save a full blown argument kicking off, "Do you honestly think they'll stop killing them just because Jamie Hopkins of New York City decided to jump on the vegetarian bandwagon?"

"I don't care…"

"What's a vegetarian?" asked Ava.

"Someone who only eats vegetables," said Jamie.

"Vegetables are yucky!"

"Do you know how they make what you're eating right now?" said Jamie.

I had a feeling it was more of a rhetorical question and jumped in with, "They make it in the kitchen. Duh! Everyone knows that!"

"Yeah, everyone knows that!" shouted Ava. She mimicked my 'duh' sound too. A good effort. Jamie turned away. She'd already lost interest in the conversation.

Right from when I could first remember, Ava had been fussy with her food, the last thing we needed was for her to be scared off meat just because her sister was trying to impress some lad she had only just met in class.

"Did you want to get something else?" I reached into my pocket and pulled my wallet out. Jamie shook her head and started to eat her fries. I'm not entirely sure whether the fries are suitable for vegetarians but considering this is most likely, as Susan would put it, a phase - I'll keep quiet. "How's the chicken wrap?" I asked Susan. I don't know why I asked her, I could tell by the expression on her face she wasn't enjoying it.

"It's good," she lied. "Thank you for insisting we stopped here. I can't believe I nearly missed out on experiencing this."

Ooh, she nearly has the sarcasm as pinned down as I have. A little more practice and she might even be just as good as me.

"See I take you to all the best places," I said. I flashed her a smile after ensuring my teeth were suitably coated in the various sauces found in my burger.

"Daddy!" laughed Ava.

"What?"

Susan gave me a playful slap on the arm and laughed, "You're a dick!"

"Language!" I whispered. I have to confess it felt good to tell her off as opposed to the other way round. I wonder if she gets as much joy when she has a go at me for my occasional foul-mouthed slip up.

"Well at least your mood has improved," Susan pointed out.

Jamie stood up and moved out from behind the table.

"Where are you going?" asked Susan.

"The bathroom. That okay?"

"Take your sister, please." Susan ignored Jamie's rolling of the eyes expression and turned to Ava, "Go with your sister." She slid herself away from the table's bench, so Ava could get out, and sat back down again.

Just the two of us.

"I'm glad your daughter has stopped whining," I said.

"Ava?"

I nodded. "I'm not sure I could have taken that all day."

"Last I checked she was our daughter..."

"No, she's our daughter when she's being good and your daughter when she's being bad. She falls into the latter of the categories when she's whining."

"She was just hungry. She didn't eat much for breakfast. You seem better now," Susan pointed out.

"Was just the traffic. Wound me up. Listen, I'm sorry if I've been a dick recently. It's just I've had a lot on my plate. My agent is rushing me to get this novel to them and...Well...I'm struggling to be honest. That's why I wanted a quiet weekend down the cabin."

"It'll do us all good to get out of the house for the weekend," she said. She still didn't take the subtle hint I wanted a quiet weekend down the cabin. "Is there anything I can do to help?" she asked.

A sweet gesture but an empty one as there was nothing she could do. Well nothing other than stay at home and that ship had sailed already.

"It's fine," I said. "I'll figure it out. I have a good feeling about this weekend."

Susan smiled and took another bite of her chicken wrap. Her smile faded when she noticed a hair sticking out of the wrap's salad.

"See," I said, "that could have been in my burger. I definitely have a good feeling about this weekend," I laughed. Susan flashed me one of her speciality 'angry' looks as she hooked the hair from between the lettuce leaves and placed it on the side of the tray. I pushed Jamie's nuggets towards her, "I don't think Jamie's going to be eating them," I said, "not now she's a vegetarian..."

Susan pushed the nuggets away from her, clearly put off by the stray hair nestled in her wrap, "It's just a phase..."

CHAPTER 2

"**T**his is your fault," Susan helpfully pointed out. She was referring to the bumper to bumper traffic we were sat in. "You jinxed us when you said you had a good feeling about this weekend.

"Are we nearly there yet?" asked Ava.

"I can't even see why you want to come up here anyway, we could have gone to the coast. What's so special about this cabin anyway?" Great, even Jamie was starting too.

"The coast? I thought you people burn up in direct sunlight?" I snapped back. In the rear-view mirror I saw Jamie pull a face.

"You've got such a lovely face," Susan turned to talk to Jamie, "why do you have to hide it behind all that make-up?"

"I'm in mourning for my lost childhood," retorted Jamie. Credit where credit was due, that was a good comeback; quick, witty and remarkably inoffensive by her usual standards although I'm not entirely sure whether it's from a film or not.

Susan ignored her and turned back to me, "Why don't you come off the highway? It might be easier taking the other route."

"Did you want to drive?" I snapped. The traffic was getting to me again and the damned air conditioning was broken. Too much pollution and noise, outside, to want to have a window open.

"I'll drive!" said Jamie with a flash of the excitable girl she used to be.

"I don't think so," I said. Might as well kill off the excitable little girl once more, I've grown fond of my truck and don't need her crashing it! Besides which, I'm getting used to the black 'mourning' make-up she seems to favor. I'd probably die of shock now if she were to come downstairs with normal make-up on.

"When are you getting to let me drive?" she moaned. "You're so unfair!"

Ah, I wondered when we'd get the 'so unfair' whinge from her. I had my money on actually being in Brattleboro before we heard it. I guess I just lost that bet. Thankfully she didn't continue with listing the ways in which her mother and I were so cruel to her, like she normally does, instead she just sat back and continued staring out of the window at all the lucky people who have been allowed to drive.

"Are we nearly there yet?" asked Ava once more.

"Soon, baby," said Susan.

Why does she always insist on calling her 'baby'? It's no wonder she seems to be maturing slower than the rest of the kids in her class; the poor kid is probably confused. Mum calls her a baby so she continues to act like one.

"I'm boreeeeed!" she whinged.

"Shut up moaning!" Jamie snapped.

"You shut up!"

"You!"

"BOTH OF YOU SHUT UP!" I snapped.

"Honey..." said Susan with her typical disapproving tone.

"What is up with this fucking traffic today? It's not even rush hour yet! If we hadn't stopped for McDonalds..."

"...We'd be sat in traffic somewhere else. I'm sure it will start moving soon."

"Well I'm glad you're so sure," I said.

True enough we did start moving. Not to a speed which could be considered 'decent' but I'd take what was offered. At least we were moving.

"We still could have gone to the beach. We would have been there by now."

"Your father wants to visit his cabin," said Susan.

"I just don't see what's so special about a cabin."

"Tell them," Susan urged.

"They'll just think it's stupid."

"What's stupid?" asked Jamie.

"His dad used to take him to this cabin every summer. It just used to be the two of them for the whole weekend..."

I cut her short, "It was nice."

I used to love the trips away with my father. Whenever he was at home he was always highly strung fretting about the state of the business and finances; worrying I had what I needed for my education and that mum was able to keep the cupboards stocked with decent food. When I was younger I never understood why he was always in a bad mood. I remember constantly feeling the need to tread on egg shells around him; tip-toe so as not to cause him to get angry. It was different when he took me away. It was almost as though our father and son holidays were his way of apologizing to me for his moods. Just him and me. For those three days, sometimes four, he left all of his worries and stresses at home or in his office.

I hadn't been to the cabin for years. In fact I think I had only managed to get there once since Jamie was born, and that was when I needed to finish my first horror novel, 'The Spider's Web'. The first piece of many works I had written which was picked up by a literary agent; the book which finally got me a decent publishing deal and afforded us the luxury of moving to a better neighborhood. Every year I promised myself a trip out there to make sure everything was okay but every year there was another reason why I couldn't go. It's stupid, really, considering it's only four hours away from my home.

"Does it at least have a shower?" asked Jamie.

"Yes, Jamie, it has a shower," I said. At least it did the last time I was there. God only knows what state the place is in now. For all I know, we could end up checking into a bed and breakfast. I hope not. That won't exactly help my writing; the real reason I'm even going to the cabin in the first place!

"Is there a play area?" asked Ava.

"There's a nice Princess Tower you can visit," I said.

"Craig! Don't!" Susan barked.

"What? I didn't do anything!'"

"You know what," she said with a stern look on her face.

"Jamie would love it there...I bet you anything."

"Love what?" she asked from the back of the car still trying to sound uninterested.

"The cabin is a short walk away from a large, stone tower. It was built by patients of the Vermont Asylum in the late eighteen hundreds..."

"So?"

"Craig, they don't need to hear this."

"At the time doctors believed hard labor could help patients regain some of their stability so some of them were made to build it as a nice, scenic over-look of the Asylum grounds. Rumor has it that, in the years following it's con-struction, a number of patients threw themselves off of the top of the tower onto the rocks below. But, you know, you get those kind of stories at most der-elict constructions. The thing, with this one, is that hundreds of people have reported seeing an airborne human-like form at the top of the tower which just suddenly disappeared into thin air and other people have come forward to speak of seeing ghostly shadows in the woods...All pretty creepy."

"Bullshit!"

"Jamie!" Susan snapped.

"What? That's bullshit! Clearly!"

I gave Jamie a quick look in the rear-view mirror and her expression gave a different story to the false bravado in her outburst. She looked nervous.

"It's fine," I said to Susan. I looked back to Jamie in the rear-view mirror again, "I said the same thing to my dad when he told me the story but then... ah, forget it. You'd just think I was stupid."

"No. What?" she asked. A clear look of nervousness on her face.

"Well...It's just that...When we were at the cabin..I'd hear strange noises during the night...Like someone was walking around outside. I remember waking my dad up, to tell him, but he didn't believe me. Not until he heard it too; footsteps walking along the wooden porch which lined the front of the building. They passed right by his bedroom window and stopped at the front door. We both heard them, clear as day. I remember there was the briefest of pauses before a loud knocking on the front door..." I knocked on the truck's dash four times for added drama. "Dad told me to wait in his room whilst he went and opened the door, to see who it was, but he said there was no-one there. He just heard the loudest, most blood-curdling scream he had ever heard. He said it was as though whoever was doing it was stood directly in front of him yet there was no one. Scared the life out of him - and me when he told me. The next day he asked in town if anyone had experienced this and people got pretty nervous. Eventually we found out that, anyone who had heard the scream...A year later they were dead. And, as you know, a year later my dad had a massive heart attack and died."

"Is that what really happened?" asked Jamie.

"Of course it is! I'm hardly likely to make something up about my dad, am I? Actually that tower I told you about...There's a nice walk we can do which let's us see it. Can head out there in the morning, if you want. See if we can see any shapes falling from the top."

Jamie didn't say anything unlike Susan who, unsurprisingly, wasn't impressed with my story, "That's really nice! When the girls have nightmares tonight, you can go and sit with them and I'll be the one staying in bed."

"And good news, kids, we're now officially in Vermont! Not too much longer now!" I said as we passed a road sign for Windham County.

"Can we see the Princess Tower too, daddy?"

"Sure, sweetie," I said.

$$\lambda$$

I nudged Susan awake after I had stopped the truck, on the side of the road, next to the store. I've never known a passenger to fall asleep as much as her.

"Are we there?" she asked; her voice still sleepy.

"Hey! No. Not yet. Nearly." I whispered, "I'm getting some supplies. Did you need anything?"

"What are you getting?"

"I don't know yet. Probably just bread, milk, juice, potato chips, toilet paper...That kind of thing. Anything you can think of?"

"Not off the top of my head," she said. "Can always pop down in the morning?"

"Okay. Sure there's nothing you can think of now?"

She shook her head again and closed her eyes, keen to get back to whatever dream she must have been enjoying. "Don't be too long, okay?"

I nodded, not that she saw, "The girls are with me," I said. Had Susan paid attention, when I woke her up, she would have noticed they were already waiting for me outside. Susan didn't answer back.

I climbed from the car and noticed Jamie and Ava were chatting to some kids to the side of the store. Kids? Not kids. They look older than Jamie. Six of them in total, five lads and a girl. The eldest looking one standing uncomfortably close to Jamie. I couldn't hear what they were talking about and I'm pretty sure I wouldn't want to even if I could.

"Jamie! Ava!" I called out. "Come on." Ava came running over to me. She was excited to go into the store, no doubt, because she wanted to choose a chocolate bar. "Jamie!" I called again. I stopped by the store's entrance and waited for her.

"Dad, I'm chatting to some friends! I'll be in a minute!"

"Come on, Jamie, you don't even know them!"

"Be cool, dad, we go to the same school!" shouted the eldest of the group. "We're in the same class."

"Oh, really, and what school is it you all go to?" I asked.

"Dad, you're embarrassing me!"

I shook my head disapprovingly and walked into the store with Ava, who was practically dragging me in by my jacket anyway. Jamie's big enough to make her own mistakes and it's not as though I'm going to be very long.

"Hi." I greeted the shopkeeper, a podgy old man with white hair and a bushy white beard, as I walked past him towards the first aisle. It was quite weird seeing him, the last time I saw him he had jet black hair. He looked a lot slimmer back then too. The years have been unkind. Probably best if I don't mention it. He looked at me the same way most small town shopkeepers look at strangers - a look of suspicion on his face. Obviously he doesn't recognize me.

"Help you with anything?" he asked.

"I'm good thanks," I replied as I continued into the first aisle where Ava was waiting, "just getting some supplies..."

"Supplies?"

"Staying at my old man's cabin down the road from here," I called back. "Just for a weekend with the family."

"Well the weather's on your side," he said.

Ava ran over to me with a packet of toilet roll, "That one?"

"It'll do...Now see if you can find us some bread." Ava smiled and ran off down the aisle before disappearing around the corner.

"You can put everything on the counter if you want; I'll ring it through and bag it," offered the old man. I wish I could remember his name. My dad used to chat to him for ages whilst I waited outside, kicking stones around impatiently. Although, when I was growing up, there weren't as many idiots hanging around out there.

"Thank you," I said. I put the toilet roll on the counter and, just as he said he would, he rung it through before placing it in a brown paper bag.

"Got the bread!" shouted Ava from somewhere in the store.

"Milk! We're going to need milk!"

"The milk's down the last aisle," offered the old man.

"Ssh!" I said. "Trying to tire her out before we get to the cabin. It'll be dark by the time we're there so it would be useful if she just wanted to go to sleep!"

The old man laughed, "Not a lot to do in the woods at night for a young 'un."

"Exactly."

"So what brings you down these neck of the woods? Just a vacation?"

"I was hoping for some peace and quiet," I said. "Trying to make some progress on a book I'm working on."

"Reading or writing?"

"Writing," I laughed.

"You're a writer?" he asked. "We used to have another writer come stay this way...Not seen him for a while...Wonder what happened to him..."

I smiled, "He died." The old man looked at me. "He was my dad."

"Well I'm sorry to hear that," said the old man. "He used to spend hours in here talking about his work."

I laughed, "And I used to stand outside kicking stones around whilst he did."

"That was you?" the old man seemed surprised that I had grown up over the years.

"Taller and uglier!" I said.

"Decided to follow in your pa's footsteps, huh?"

"I got the milk!" shouted Ava.

"I'm sorry," I said to the old man. I called out to Ava, "Bring it all here then."

I was sorry too. I'd have loved to carry on chatting with him. Who knows I probably would have had it not been for the group outside. Not too comfortable at the thought of leaving Jamie out there any longer than necessary and I'm pretty sure my dad would have felt the same had it been me out there with them. Ava appeared from the far side of the store and handed over the milk and bread.

"Anything else you can think we need?" I asked her.

"Chocolate?"

"Quickly then."

She smiled a broad smile and ran towards the rack of different chocolates.

"You written anything I would have read?" the old man asked as he seized the opportunity to engage in conversation again.

"My most popular book is 'The Spider's Web'."

"No. Not read it. Don't much like spiders."

"Well it's not actually about spiders..."

"Bit of a strange title then really, if you ask me..."

There was no sense arguing with the man. I don't think he meant to be rude.

"Daddy..." Ava came bounding over with a bar of chocolate in her hand.

"Okay," I said, "pass it to the nice man..."

Ava held it out for the man but he didn't take it, "That's okay," he said, "you can have that on me."

Ava looked at me, unsure of what to do.

"What do you say?" I said. She carried on staring at me. All those years of teaching her not to talk to strangers or accept anything from them - she's probably confused.

"Thank you?"

"Not to me..."

She turned to the old man, "Thank you."

"My pleasure," he turned back to me, "will that be everything?"

"For now. Sure there'll be some other bits and pieces."

He pressed a few buttons on the cash register, "That'll be three dollars twenty-five..."

I fished around in my pocket and handed him the money I pulled out. He, in turn, handed me the change.

"Thank you," I said.

"You be sure to come again."

I thanked him again and left the shop with the bag of shopping tucked under my right arm, my left hand on top of Ava's head who was already tucking into her chocolate bar.

Outside and Jamie was still chatting to the youths. Her mobile phone was in her hand. Don't get mad. She'll never see the kids again even if she does have their number. Another good reason not to let her drive yet. I walked over to the car and threw the groceries in the back, after Ava jumped in, before opening the front door.

"Jamie, say goodbye to your friends, we're on our way."

She slipped her phone back into her jacket's pocket and walked over to the truck. "I'll call you later," she called out to them. I can rest easy. The woods are so thick, I doubt she'll have phone signal.

"You see who your daughter has been hanging out with?" I asked Susan who had just woken up due to the noise Ava and I had made climbing back into the truck.

"My daughter?"

"Yep, I've told you before...When they're bad...Your daughter...When they're good...Our daughter..."

"Who were they?" asked Susan.

Jamie jumped into the truck and slammed the door shut, after giving her new friends a final wave goodbye. "His name's Josh. He plays for the school football team."

"Of course he does," I said as I turned the truck's engine on.

"Are we nearly there yet?" asked Ava with chocolate smeared around her mouth.

"Did you get me some chocolate?" asked Jamie.

I ignored them both as I pulled out from the side of the road with a little spin of the wheels...Not a lot...Just enough to give Josh and his friends a coating of dust and dirt.

Chapter 3

"**W**e're not staying here!" said Jamie.

I killed the truck's engine and just sat there, staring at the front of the cabin.

"Honey I'm sorry," Susan said quietly in my ear.

"What? No. No. It's fine. It's cool," I said. It wasn't cool and it was far from fine.

I opened the door and climbed from the truck to get a better look at the cabin; the place which held so many happy memories between my father and I. A better look at the graffiti which decorated the front of it. I called back to the truck where the girls were waiting, "It's probably just some bored kids, right? Probably Jamie's new friends. You know what it's like around here, there's nothing to do so they make their own entertainment..." Their own destructive entertainment. "It's probably purely cosmetic," I said. "Inside will be fine."

I walked towards the front door with the keys in my hand, not that I needed them as I noticed the door had been kicked open. I should have known I couldn't just leave the cabin vacant for a number of years and expect to come back to find everything as I left it. No sense stressing about it, just go in and assess the damage. See if it's fit for us to stay here. So much for a peaceful weekend writing.

I heard Susan open the truck door behind me, "How is it?"

I pointed to the various colors of spray-paint plastering the outside wall, "Colorful? It's probably fine inside. Wait there," I said. I pushed the door open further and stepped inside.

First impressions it isn't that bad. They've been good enough to leave the windows intact. Just looks as though someone has been using it as a little hideout. Somewhere to take shelter...I spotted some beer cans on the living room floor...Somewhere to drink....Potato chip packets scattered around the place with various empty sweet wrappers...Somewhere to snack between meals...I walked into the first of the two bedrooms. A dirty sheet was on the bed with condom packets scattered around the floor. Somewhere to fuck. Nice. A quick look in the second bedroom where the kids would be sleeping showed nothing that different in there; more of the same empty wrappers and evidence of kids having a good time. Nothing which can't be scrubbed down and cleaned up. I should, at least, be grateful for that much.

"Well?" Susan was stood behind me. The sound of her voice made me jump, I didn't even hear her come in.

"I told you to wait in the truck."

"How bad is it?"

"Nothing which can't be fixed. I should have expected something like this; a cabin in the woods...Asking for vandalism really. We should be thankful the place isn't torched to the floor," I said.

"Not from the want of trying by the looks of it."

"What do you mean?"

She led me back through to the living room, which led onto the porch, and pointed to the middle of the carpet where there was a large black scorch mark. "Looks like they tried to start a fire."

"No, I don't think so. It would have been easy enough to set this place alight if they really wanted to. Probably just trying to keep warm."

Susan looked around the room, "I don't suppose you have some cleaning products here?"

I shrugged and walked through to the small kitchen. On first appearance everything looked as though it was still in it's rightful place. The oven even looked as though it had been used. The cupboards were open, though. Open and bare.

"That'll be a no then," said Susan as she followed behind.

"I'll pop back to the store and grab some bits," I said. "You want to come with me?"

She shook her head, "If you want to stay here tonight it'll probably be a good idea to start clearing this place out."

"Thank you," I said. I leant forward and gave her a kiss on the forehead. "We'll start our holiday tomorrow, yeah?"

"Looks like it! What if they come back?" she asked.

"I doubt they will. Look at the place. Doesn't look as though anyone has stopped by here for a while. Probably just used it as a shelter last winter."

"You think?"

I nodded.

"I'll take Ava with me. Don't need her picking anything up which she shouldn't. Jamie can give you a hand," I said, "I'll go and get her."

"Sure she'll love that."

"It won't kill her," I replied. I gave Susan another kiss on the forehead and walked out of the kitchen, through the living room and out of the cabin towards the truck.

"Tell me we're not staying here," said Jamie when I opened the truck door.

"Come on. Out! Go and help your mother, please."

"You have got to be joking. I'm not cleaning that shit up!"

"Come on!" I repeated. "I'm taking Ava back to the store with me to get more supplies. Looks like we're going to need them."

"Why can't I come with you?"

"You really want me to leave your mother here by herself?" I asked.

Jamie didn't say anything, at first. She knew I had a point but the silence couldn't last forever. "So unfair!" she moaned. She undid her seatbelt and jumped from the truck. "And what if whoever did this comes back when you're not here?"

"Can't you just text him and ask him to stay away?" I joked as I slammed her door and climbed into the driver's seat. "I mean you are best friends for life now, right?"

"Josh didn't do this..."

"Because you know him so well." I closed the door and fired the engine up once more. In the process I drowned out more of Jamie's moaning. I'll call that a success. Ava, bless her soul, didn't say a word.

⚓

I pulled up by the side of the road, opposite the store, once more. Thankfully it was open. Sadly the youths were still hanging around to the side of the building; the same place I had hit them with a dust cloud earlier.

"It'll probably be easier if you wait in here this time, Ava."

"Can't I come in and see the man again?"

I shook my head. I knew exactly what she meant by that. She was hoping he'd give her another bar of chocolate. "Not this time, daddy's in a rush." I pulled the key from the ignition and jumped from the truck. "If you wait here, like a good girl, and promise not to tell your mum...Might even get you another bar of chocolate." A huge smile spread across her face. "Do we have a deal?"

"Yes!" she nodded with the grin securely fixed into place.

"That's my girl! Now wait here and I'll be right back!" I closed the door and pressed a button, on the key-fob, to lock the door behind me.

"Hey, man! That was uncool what you did earlier!" said, I presume, Josh as I approached the store's entrance.

"I honestly have no idea what you're talking about..."

"You know," he said. He positioned himself between the entrance and me. I looked at him. If he was Jamie's age, he was big. Even if she hadn't told me he was on the football team, I would have guessed. Looking at him now, up close, I doubt he's her age, though. If anything, he has to be a couple of years older. Older than the rest of the group for sure. "I think you need to say sorry, man."

"Yeah...Not going to happen. But speaking of apologies, do you guys owe me one?"

"Fuck you talking about?"

"You lot been hiding out in the woods at all?"

The youths looked at each other. Josh was the first one to speak again, "What the fuck are you talking about? I just want a fucking apology for the shit you covered us in."

"And I want a fucking apology for the state you left my cabin in."

"Ey! Yo! Just hit dis motherfucker, Josh!" said one of the other lads. The rest of the youths closed in around me. Part of me started to wish I had left Ava back at the cabin with Susan and Jamie. Josh, spurred on by the cheering of his friends, squared up to me.

"Step off. I won't tell you again," I warned him. I didn't want to hit an embryo but, if it came down to it...

"What's going on out here?" asked the old man. Over Josh's shoulder, I saw that the old man was standing in the doorway of his store; an angry expression on his face.

"Go back inside, old-timer," said Josh.

"I said what's going on out here?" the old man repeated. This time he pumped a semi-automatic shotgun that must have been in his hands. I couldn't see the gun, from the middle of the youths, I just recognized the sound of the pump-action being primed. A sound, for some reason, the youths were also familiar with. The group separated and turned to see the old man. He was aiming the gun directly at Josh.

"Nothing's going on. We were just having a conversation." Josh turned to me, "Ain't that right?"

"Cabin's been vandalized," I said ignoring Josh, "just come by to get some cleaning products."

"Well," said the old man, "come on in then." He stepped to one side to allow me entrance to his store but kept the gun aimed at Josh. "You lot got a home to go to?"

"Sure, we were just leaving."

"I thought so." The old man stood and watched as the youths slowly dispersed. They went so slowly it was almost as though none of them were worried about having the gun aimed at them. Had that been me as a teenager, I would have run and not looked back. When they were away from the store, the old man lowered the gun and came back into the store.

"Thank you for that," I said.

"I saw what you did earlier...wheel-spinning off like that. Had no business covering them in dirt...Asking for trouble. Inviting it in."

"It was an accident."

"Bullshit. Look I don't want any trouble. Business is quiet enough without having trouble from that lot to worry about. Just get what you came for and leave."

I nodded. There was no point in arguing about who was right and who was wrong. "Can you point me in the direction of the cleaning products?" The old man pointed towards the middle aisles. "Thank you." I walked down the aisle, as directed, whilst the old man returned to behind his counter. As I picked up the floor cleaner, I heard him put the shotgun down on the wooden flooring. I tried changing the subject to try and get him back on speaking terms, "We got to the cabin and it looks as though kids have been using it as a den; littered with all kinds of rubbish." No answer. "I left my wife there to make a head start on the clean-up operation but I'm not sure we'll be able to stay there tonight. You know of a good place with a couple of beds for the night?" No answer. "Or a locksmith? They kicked the door open to get in, busted up the lock real good." Still no answer. Jesus. He had his say, how long's he going to sulk for? Had it not been for the fact we spoke earlier, I'd have thought he was one of the inmates from the asylum. Or simple. "No matter," I said, "the wife's mum and dad live a couple of hours away, I suppose we could go and stay there for the night. Head back to the city tomorrow. So much for our family holiday, hey?" Again there was no answer. I've made enough effort, I feel. I continued to get the cleaning supplies trying my best to ignore the uncomfortable silence.

Maybe I should have brought Ava in with me too. I doubt he would manage to ignore her as well - not without coming across as really rude anyway. Mind you, he probably doesn't care and I, for the sake of a conversation, I don't think I'd want a shotgun waved around in Ava's face!

I took the last item, a roll of black sacks, from the shelf and staggered across to the counter with the rest of the goods I wanted to buy. The old man didn't even look in my direction when I dropped everything on the counter. He just stood there, staring out the front of his store. He didn't even bat an eyelid when the roll of black sacks rolled off the counter and onto the floor by his feet.

This is ridiculous. "Look, I'm sorry," I said. "I didn't like the way they were talking to my daughter. I just thought I'd have a little fun that's all. No harm, no foul."

The old man turned to me, "You live in New York?" I nodded. "Thought so. You big city folk are all the same...You come through here thinking you're better than everyone..."

"No. That's not true. Come on, man, let's not do this. Can I just buy the stuff? I'll get right out of your hair and, if you'd rather, I won't even come back."

The old man went to say reply but stopped short when he noticed some-one enter the store behind me, "Now look, I don't want no trouble..."

I span around to see who had him spooked; Josh. He looked angry; an-grier than he had appeared earlier, outside of the shop during our confronta-tion. I didn't say anything. I didn't feel I needed to, not with the knowledge of the old man's shotgun waiting behind the counter for times like these. Josh didn't say anything.

"What the hell you want, boy?" the old man suddenly blurted out.

Josh reached inside his jacket and pulled a handgun from within. Both the old man and I jumped back in shock, neither of us having expected that.

"Not nice is it," said Josh as he waved the gun between the old man and I, "having a gun shoved in your fucking face. How'd you like it?"

"Now look, son," said the old man, "we don't want any trouble..."

"Come on, Josh...That is your name, yeah? Come on...I've got a daughter waiting for me outside."

"Fuck you!"

Out of the corner of my eye I saw the old man slowly try to reach for his own gun. "Look," I said, "let's all calm down..." I cautiously edged myself between the old man and Josh. Whilst I was nervous of Josh's trigger finger, I knew for certain the old man would shoot without hesitation. No one needed to die. "I've got money," I said. "Whatever you want, you can have it...Just name it." At this point I'd offer anything to get him to lower the gun. "Come on, I have a little girl in the car. You don't want to do this. What'll it take?"

"An apology," said Josh. He aimed the gun directly at my forehead.

"What?"

"You heard me!" he shouted.

"I'm sorry. I'm sorry for covering you with dirt earlier," I said. I knew an apology wouldn't be enough to make him lower the gun. He was just playing the power card; showing me he was the one in charge. He is the one in charge too. For now. If I side-step to the left, or the right, and the old man has the shotgun in his hands...Josh won't be in charge of shit. "Come on, I've said sorry."

"Beg."

"What?"

"Beg for your fucking life."

I couldn't be sure he wouldn't pull the trigger. I didn't know him; didn't know what sort of person he was. I knew nothing about him. Not even his family background. For all I knew he was on day release from the asylum, or the retreat as they prefer to call it these days...No, he couldn't be from there. He'd have never got his hands on a gun so quickly.

"Step aside," the old man urged me.

"I can't do that," I said. A statement aimed at both Josh and the old man behind the counter. If I did step aside, Josh would be dead; just another statistic. Maybe he'd get a shot off as he gets hit and the old man would die too? And I don't want to beg for my life. I've given him the apology he most likely deserves but I'm not begging. Not even with a gun in my face.

"Step aside," the old man said once more with a tone, in his voice, which suggested he wasn't messing around.

"Ava!" I suddenly turned to the door. Josh turned too which was just what I wanted him to do. Ava wasn't stood there but it gave me the distraction I needed. With a sudden surge of adrenalin, I lunged forward and grabbed the barrel of the gun. A bit of a scuffle as Josh tried to maintain control of his weapon and a loud, ear shattering bang as he accidentally released a bullet from the chamber. A hard punch to his face was all that was needed, after that, to make him release the gun completely.

"Don't shoot!" he screamed, putting his hands in the air, as I turned the gun on him.

"Call the sheriff!" I urged the old man. He didn't answer. I turned to address him face to face, in case he didn't hear me due to his ears ringing from the gunshot. As soon as I saw him stood there, I felt my life stop. He was looking down at his chest. Blood was seeping through his shirt's material. He looked up at me and tried to say something but couldn't. Before I knew what was happening, he dropped to his knees before falling to the floor behind the counter.

"You shot him!" screamed Josh.

I didn't do it. Did I? No. Josh pulled the trigger. He did it. That doesn't matter now, though...The smoking gun is in my hand. My prints all over it. "No, that's not what happened," I said. "That's not what happened...You did it," I said, "you had control over the gun...It was your finger which squeezed the trigger..."

"Fuck you! You did it!" Josh moved towards me.

"Don't fucking move!" I screamed. Josh hesitated for a moment before he called my bluff and moved closer still. I need to get out of here. "We'll call the sheriff...We'll tell him what happened..." I reached into the right hand pocket of my black pants and pulled my cellphone out.

"What are you doing?"

"We need to call the sheriff..."

"I can't let you do that!" Josh suddenly ran towards the counter. I knew exactly what he was doing. He was going for the old man's gun. "You're not calling the sheriff! I can't go back..."

No time to second guess what he meant by that, as he dove to the floor behind the counter. I turned and ran from the store, keeping the gun in my hand. I can call the sheriff from the cabin. Let him know what happened. Explain it. As I hastily approached the truck I hid Josh's gun beneath my jacket - tucked neatly into the top of my pants. Ava's innocent face was looking at me through the slightly tinted window.

"What was that noise?" she asked as I climbed into the driver's seat. I didn't answer her. I couldn't. Didn't know what to say. I had just killed someone...No...We...Josh and I had just killed someone.

Quickly I turned the key in the truck's ignition, firing up the engine, and sped from the scene - Josh, in the rear-view mirror, was standing in the road with the old man's shotgun. I kept watch of him, not caring what was in front of the truck, as he raised the gun in our direction. Please don't fire. Please don't fire. Please don't fire...Not with Ava here with me. Please don't fire.

No shot came.

"Daddy you forgot my chocolate!" Ava noticed.

CHAPTER 4

By the time I came to stop the truck, outside of the cabin, my hands were still shaking and my ears were still ringing. I can't believe he's dead. Had I not left the youths in a dust cloud...Had I not answered them back, outside the store...Had I begged for my life...Had I not tried to wrestle the gun from Josh...The old man might still be alive. He might still be running his store. He might have sold me the cleaning products I needed...The group of teenagers might still have loitering outside, by the road...Teenagers...Teenager... Josh is a fucking teenager...Why'd he have a gun?! I swear to God this country has gone to shit.

"Craig?!"

I looked up from the steering wheel and saw Susan standing in the cabin's broken doorway. No doubt she was waiting for the cleaning products.

"What are you doing?" she asked. I didn't answer her. I just kept on staring. Truth be told, I'm not sure what to say. "Did you get the cleaning products?" I shook my head.

"Daddy, what are you doing?" asked Ava. I only registered I needed to answer after she shouted, "Daddy!"

I turned around to talk to her, "Wait here, baby." I climbed from the truck and called out, "Jamie!"

"She's inside. What's wrong? You look upset..."

"Can you get Jamie, please."

"Honey, what is it? You're scaring me..."

"NOW!"

Susan leaned into the cabin and called out, "Jamie, your father wants you..."

Seconds later and Jamie appeared at the doorway. Susan stepped to one side so Jamie could talk to me. "What is it?" she asked.

"Get in the car, please, it's time to go."

"What? I'm in the middle of cleaning..." she started to say. I gave her a look to shut her up. Honestly, I ask her to clean and she starts an argument with me. I ask her to stop and she starts an argument...

Susan knew something was wrong and backed me up, "Get in the truck, Jamie."

"Fine. Whatever." Jamie pushed past Susan and stormed over to the truck.

I waited until I heard the obligatory door slam before I stepped up into the cabin so the girls couldn't hear me. It was bad enough Ava heard the bang, I didn't need her catching wind that someone had died...I didn't need either of them hearing. Susan followed me in, "What's the matter? Why were you gone for so long?" I didn't know what to say. I didn't know how to break it to her that I had just witnessed someone die and, more than likely, was to blame for it. "Craig! You're scaring me! Say something!"

I tried my best to hold back the tears, "It was an accident."

"What was?"

I need to tell her. I have to. "There's been an accident." I pulled the gun from under my jacket.

"What have you done? Who's fucking gun is that? Craig?!"

"There was an argument at the store. Josh and the rest of the group blocked my path from getting into the shop...The old man came out with a shotgun and chased them off..."

"Who's gun is that, Craig?"

"Josh. He came back, whilst I was shopping for supplies...He had this with him..."

"Then how come you've got it?" she asked. Her face had gone as white as mine felt.

"I wrestled it from Josh but it went off...The clerk was hit in the chest..."
I couldn't hold the tears in anymore, "I think he's fucking dead, Susan..."

"What?"

"We killed him!"

"Where's the boy gone?"

"I went to phone the sheriff...Josh went for the shotgun..."

"What?"

"He didn't want me calling anyone...said something about not wanting to go back...You don't understand, I thought he was going to shoot me. I ran..."

"My baby!" Susan screamed as though she suddenly remembered Ava had been with me.

"She didn't see anything. She was in the truck. She only asked what the noise was when I got back...I didn't tell her. Of course I didn't. She's fine. She didn't see anything..." and that was a relief. A girl so young, I couldn't stand to have her innocence destroyed at such a young age. I know I do a bad job of it but I even try and protect Jamie from the badness which oozes from the world. I'd do anything for my girls.

"What are we going to do?" asked Susan. I had been wondering the very same thing myself. All I know is, this is my mess. It's nothing to do with them and I don't want them caught up in it. "Craig? What are we going to do?"

"You need to leave."

"What?"

"You have to go. Now," I said.

"I'm not leaving you here."

"I've just witnessed a murder, Susan...Just saw an old man gunned down before my eyes. I need to stay and fix this."

"Fix this? What are you talking about? How are you going to fix this?"

"I need to tell the sheriff what happened..."

"What if they try and blame you? What if they say you shot the clerk?"

"I don't know, Susan, I don't know! I can't just leave it. I can't just drive off. You realize how bad that would look if they did trace anything back to me?!" I felt myself getting wound up by the stress of the situation and tried to reel it in a bit. After all, there was no sense shouting at Susan.

"You left the scene anyway. That won't look good!"

"He was going for the other gun! Josh...The boy...He ran for the store clerk's shotgun...Had I stayed...I didn't want to have to shoot him and I sure as Hell didn't want to get shot! What was I supposed to do?!" She didn't answer me. She knew I was right. What was I meant to do? It wasn't a situation I had ever found myself in before. "Take the girls up to your mum and dad's house...Stay there until you get a call from me. I'll call the sheriff and ask him to meet me here..."

"I can take you to the station..."

"No! I just want you out of here...I don't want the girls getting wind of this. None of you need to get in the middle of this. I'll call you just as soon as everything is sorted. I promise. I could even get a cab up to you...We'll take a completely different route home so as not to have to pass through this town again...It'll be fine. It will all be fine. I promise."

"What do I tell the girls? Jamie'll know something is up."

I paused for a moment before hatching an idea, "You can just tell her I'm staying here to make sure this place is secure and sorted and I'm joining you all later on. A couple of hours. Worst case, I'll be with you by morning. Just tell her this place isn't fit enough to stay in. She's seen it in here! It's not exactly a lie!" I cast my eyes, briefly, around the living room - the lack of cleaning products had certainly slowed down their progress with regards to sorting the mess out. Not that the mess is really an issue anymore. It's taken a back seat along with my novel.

"I don't like this," said Susan.

"I don't either but it's for the best. The girls don't need to know. Everything will be fine. The sheriff will know it was an accident. It's not as though I have a record to worry about. What's the betting the same can't be said for the lad? He said he didn't want to go back...Want to bet he's been on the wrong side of prison bars before?" Susan didn't say anything. "Look, go to your mum and dad's, don't tell them anything other than I've stayed on to sort this place out..."

"They'll want to know why we didn't stay to help. You know they will," she said. Her voice was shaking.

"I really need you to hold it together Susan. It's fine. Everything is fine. This is my mess and I'll put it right. I promise. Look at me..." she looked me in the eyes, "I swear I'll put it all right. I'll sort it. Tell your parents you went on to their place without me because I told you to. I didn't want the first day of the girls' holiday to be spent cleaning...Okay?" She didn't answer. "Okay?" I repeated.

"Okay."

"Good. Now, give me a hug."

I put the gun down on the side cupboard. She moved in close and put her arms around me. I put my arms around her and rested my chin against the top of her head. I'm not sure whether the hug was more to calm her nerves or mine. I pulled her closer.

"I love you," I said.

"I love you too."

I pulled back slightly and kissed her on the forehead. "Everything will be fine." I stepped back and wiped a rogue tear from my eye, "come on," I said, "put your happy face on...The kids will be wondering what's taking so long."

"Okay," she said. She too stepped back, wiped her eyes, and then - together - we both took a deep breath and stepped out of the living room and out of the cabin, towards the truck where the girls were patiently waiting.

As we neared the truck, I passed her the key.

"Call me when you get to your mum and dad's," I said, "let me know you've got there okay."

"Okay," she opened the truck's door and sat down in the driver's seat. "You sure you'll be okay?"

I nodded, "Of course...It's only a bit of mess to clean up," I said. I tried to act cheerful although I'm not entirely sure if I managed to pull it off. Neither of the kids said anything so I guess all was good. "Soon as I'm sorted I'll give you a ring."

"What's going on?" asked Jamie.

"We can't stay here," I said saving Susan from having to tell a lie as I know she hates them. "I'm going to stay behind, clean up a bit and fix the door and then come and meet you guys..."

"Well where are we going?" Jamie asked again.

"I'm taking you to your grandma and grandpa's. We'll spend the weekend there...Be grateful," said Susan, "at least they're close to the beach." Susan did well. Had I not been part of the conversation in the cabin, I'd have believed everything was fine. I certainly wouldn't have believed someone had been killed. She turned to me, "You have got your cellphone, haven't you?"

I nodded, "Actually, that reminded me...Jamie, can I see your cell?"

"Why?" she asked from the backseat.

"Jamie...Your cell!" I held my hand out. I'm fed up with having to justify everything to her. She moaned under her breath and passed me the handset.

"What are you doing?" she asked.

I didn't tell her. I just opened up her contacts and found Josh's number. As soon as I had it highlighted, I deleted it. Goodbye Josh.

"Thank you," I passed her phone back. "You best get going," I said to Susan. "Drive carefully, won't you."

"You sure you aren't coming now?"

"I need to fix this," I said. "I'll be with you as soon as I can, okay?"

Susan looked as though she was going to cry but managed to hold it back. She looked like she wanted to tell me how scared she was, how she was worried about what was going to happen but she couldn't. Just as I couldn't tell her all the things I wanted to.

"Love you," I said once more as I closed the truck's door.

She fired the engine up and, after a beat, started to reverse down the dirt track towards the main road. I stood there, in the clearing, watching them go. Susan did a three-point turn when the track presented an opportunity. I could see Ava, she had turned her head to see out the back window - her little hand waving frantically. I gave her a wave back. In the panic to get them out of here, I forgot to say goodbye. I forgot to say how much I loved both of them dearly, just as I loved their mother....Even if I could be temperamental from time to time. I'll just have to remember to say it when I see them both next. Hopefully it won't be long before we're together again...And away from here.

Chapter 5

The sheriff, and his partner, didn't take long to get to the cabin. I gave them a minute to get out of their car before I walked over, having stepped down from the porch when I saw their car coming down the dirt track.

"Thanks for coming," I said. I was unsure of what to say given the circumstances.

"Well that's what we do when someone phones up to report a murder," said the Sheriff; an older, stern looking man who looked as though he had lost every ounce of whatever patience he had. "Now care to explain why my partner and I are way out here instead of sitting down to supper with our respective other halves?"

I looked over to his partner. He also looked as though he had little to no patience in him. I guess it must have been a tough day for law enforcement in the little town of Brattleboro...

"There's been an accident..." I went onto explain.

The Sheriff cut me short, "Accident? We're here for a murder. Which is it, son?"

"Accident...Well...Murder...."

The two officers looked at each other wearily before turning their attention back to me. "Why don't we take it from the top?"

I wasn't sure what to say. I wasn't sure whether to own up to spraying dirt and crap over Josh earlier or whether I should just keep that to myself. Was it relevant? Would I be seen as provoking what happened in the shop?

"If it's easier we can do this down the station," said the Sheriff. He walked to the back of his car and opened the door so I could climb in.

"He had a gun...I tried to get it away from him but it went off..." I said. "It was an accident but the store clerk, he got hit..."

"What store clerk?" asked the Sheriff.

"I don't remember his name!" I said. I could feel myself getting upset as I recalled the look on the old man's face when he noticed he'd been shot. I remember the look in his eyes as he went to say something to me. I wish I could remember his name.

"Get in the car, let's continue this conversation down the station," said the Sheriff.

I didn't argue with him. Not whilst he had that stern expression on his face and six-shooter in his holster. "I'll just close the cabin up," I said. The two officers stood and watched as I pulled the door to - as much as the broken hinges would let me. "I don't suppose you know someone who could fix this?" Neither of them answered me. "Well, maybe you'll be able to point me in the right direction after we've spoken down the station," I said. I walked over to the car and climbed into the back whereupon the Sheriff slammed the door shut. I put the seat-belt on and waited as the two officers climbed into the front of the car. The Sheriff started the engine. "You know, I think this is the first time I've ever been in a police car..." No one said anything. Not even a 'well done'.

The rest of the drive down the dirt track and through the pretty town of Brattleboro was done in relative silence, other than a strange whistling noise from the Sheriff's nose and a funny 'throat-clearing' noise he'd occasionally make. I didn't think anything of it other than he must be coming down with a cold, or something. I didn't feel the need to ask given how chatty both the officers had already proven to be.

"We conducting the interview tonight?" asked the Sheriff's partner.

"Not sure," the Sheriff replied. "Already got one in the holding cell. Could just wait until morning. I have things to do tonight."

"Sorry but can we do it tonight?" I asked having presumed they were talking about me. Nothing gets on my nerves more than being spoken about as though I'm not there; like I'm not worthy enough to talk to. "It's just my wife is expecting me." The officers didn't acknowledge that I had even spoken. "Well, if that's the case, can I at least call her when we get back to the station?" Again, they didn't give me an answer one way or another. "This is fucking ridiculous," I snapped. "I want to report a murder to you and..."

"Accident," said the Sheriff's partner.

"What?"

"You said, earlier, that it was an accident. A night in the cell might help you get your story right in your own head," he said. He twisted in his seat to look at me, as though he wanted to gauge my reaction. I tried my best not to show one.

"Look, I saw someone get shot today...The store clerk...He's dead and I saw it happen. I just want to tell you guys what happened and get back to my wife and children."

"And where are they now?" the Sheriff's partner asked.

"They've gone onto my mother-in-law's house. I didn't want the children involved with any of this..."

"If they were witness to a crime..."

"They didn't see anything. They were at the cabin. I had popped to the stores to get some cleaning products to try and sort out the mess...You did notice the graffiti, right?" The Sheriff's partner gave me a stern look. He obviously didn't like the tone of voice I was using despite it being their fault I had a tone in the first place. I tried to get it back to a more 'normal' tone. No sense getting angry with them, despite wanting to...Not whilst they're already being difficult. It'd only make things worse. "My wife and children waited at the cabin," I said. I didn't bother telling them Ava was in the truck while I went into the store; didn't want them deciding they have a need to question her too.

"So what happened at the store?" asked the Sheriff's partner. He was still twisted in his seat looking back at me.

I fired a quick glance to the Sheriff. He was staring dead ahead, at the road he was driving down, unblinking. Was he even listening?

"There was a group of kids there..."

"How old?"

"What?"

"How old were they? How many were there?"

"What? I don't know - late teens, I'd guess. Six or seven...I can't remember. They stopped me from going into the store. They blocked my path..."

"Why?"

"I don't know. Just having a laugh? They said some stuff to me, I said some stuff to them..."

"Like what?"

"I can't remember! I didn't think I'd be needing to recall the conversation later on...Anyway, it got heated..."

"How so?"

"They started squaring up to me. One of the teenagers was encouraging the older of the boys to hit me and that's when the store clerk came out. He had a shotgun and scared the group off before letting me into his store."

"And they just left?"

"They had a shotgun aimed at them. What were you expecting them to do?" my rhetorical question earned me another stern look from the Sheriff's partner. "I went into the store to get the cleaning stuff I wanted and that's when the oldest boy came back - this time with a gun."

"A gun? What sort of gun?"

"I don't know...The firing kind. He was waving it at the store clerk...saying how it wasn't nice to get a gun pointed in your face and then he turned to me. He wanted an apology from me. He wanted me to say sorry for how I'd spoken to him..."

"So why didn't you give him an apology?"

"I did! He had a gun in my face."

"So what happened next?"

"He wanted me to beg for my life."

"Did you?"

"No."

"What was the store clerk doing all this time."

"I had stepped between the two of them. He had picked up his shotgun. He told me to step aside. I didn't want to because I thought I could still talk the lad into putting the gun down. Had I stepped aside, the store clerk would have shot him. You know he would..."

"The store clerk was protecting his business and himself, maybe even you. The other was waving a gun around in a threatening manner. I know what I'd have done..."

"I didn't think anyone needed to die!"

"So what happened?"

"I went for the gun and we wrestled with it...It went off...I turned around and the store clerk had been hit. He just dropped to the floor..."

"And now who had the gun?"

"I did."

"So you shot him?"

"What? No. It was in the lad's hand when it went off...I then got it free from his grasp and turned it on him..."

The Sheriff's partner looked to the Sheriff to see his reaction but even he couldn't get one from him. He turned back to me, "So where's the boy now?"

"He knew I wasn't going to shoot him...I'm not a murderer...He went for the clerk's shotgun and I ran..."

"You ran?"

"Yes. I ran. I'm not in the business of shooting people. I didn't want to shoot a boy...A fucking child...So I did what felt right and ran to my truck... Got in and sped off. As I was driving away I noticed the boy, in the rear-view mirror, standing in the middle of the road with the shotgun in his hands."

"Did he fire?"

"No. He knew he wouldn't have been able to hit me. I wasn't exactly taking my time to drive away from there."

"And where's the gun now?"

"I left it in the cabin," I said. A genuine mistake. I didn't mean to leave it behind. I had meant to tell the officers where it was immediately so they could take it away and do whatever they had to.

You keeping it as a memento?" asked the Sheriff's partner.

"Look, this is all happening quite fast...I called you guys to tell you what happened and you're not exactly being the most warm and friendly, you know what I'm saying?"

"What do you do for a living?"

"What has that got to do with anything?" I realized he wanted the answer regardless, "I'm an author. I write books for a living..."

"So you're good at making up stories then?"

"You think I'm lying?" I asked. The officer smiled and turned to face forward, in his seat, again. "You think I walked to the store, shot the clerk and then left without taking the bits I needed or any of the money in the register? Why would I do that?!" Again, my question was ignored. "I want to call my lawyer," I said.

"You'll have your chance to make a phone call when we get back to the station," said the Sheriff, finally breaking his self-imposed silence.

Maybe Susan was right. Maybe we should have all just left and hoped for the best no one noticed and reported my truck leaving the scene.

Back at the station I was frog-marched through to the holding cells at the back of the building as though they had already decided I was the one who murdered the clerk. Once there, the Sheriff opened the cell door, and invited me to step inside with a helpful shove from his partner.

"What about my phone call?" I asked as they closed the cell door.

"You can have your phone call in the morning," said the Sheriff.

"This is ridiculous," I said, "you're treating me like a fucking criminal."

"No, we're treating you like a material witness," said the Sheriff. "This is for your own protection." The sly smile on his face suggested otherwise.

"Look, Sheriff..."

"Why do you keep calling me Sheriff? I'm not the Sheriff..."

"What are you talking about? It says it on your badge..."

"Oh, I know what it says on the badge, it's the reason I took it off his bloodied shirt. I thought it looked good."

"What?"

The man I thought was the Sheriff pointed over to a desk at the far end of the office. A foot clearly sticking out from behind it. "That's the Sheriff...

Well, it was the Sheriff anyway." He laughed, "I think it's fair to say the inmates are running the asylum now."

My heart skipped a beat as panic set in...

⅄

I opened my eyes with a jump. I was sat on one of the living room chairs. I don't even remember falling asleep; only that I sat down because the room had started to spin due to the stress of the situation, lack of proper food and general tiredness. At least, I presume it was because of those factors. I never intended to actually doze off. The longer I leave stepping forward, about the murder, the more suspicious it will be. What's the betting a store that size doesn't have any CCTV which actually works?

I stood up and walked over to the door, which I had blocked shut with the single seat before I had sat down on the other chair. I pulled the chair away and the door slowly swung open. It's getting dark outside.

I forgot how creepy the woods were, looking out from the cabin, when darkness fell. Years ago, I used to sit on the end of my bed and shine a torch out of the window into the darkness beyond just to check that nothing was out there that shouldn't be. I blame my father for scaring me with all the local ghost stories before I was supposed to go to sleep; they never did invite me towards a peaceful slumber. I don't believe in ghost stories and I don't believe in things that go bump in the night but, even so, I'd give my right arm for a torch right about now.

I reached into my pocket, for my cell phone. No sense putting the phone call off. The body has, no doubt, already been reported so they're probably already looking for me. I'm sure the Sheriff will believe what I have to say. After all, I have no priors. Never even had a speeding ticket or parking fine. Shit...I checked my other pocket. Nothing. Where the Hell's my phone? Don't say I dropped it back at the store when I went to call the Sheriff's department? I remember having it in my hand...I don't remember still having hold of it when I got to the truck, though. Or did I? I might have thrown it onto the passenger seat...Shit. I think I did.

I looked outside again. I don't fancy walking through the woods in blackness. It's about a two hour walk to get to the main road from here. Yet, when driving, it feels like no time at all. Still walking in the darkness, that's probably asking for trouble. Dammit. Why didn't I check I had my phone before Susan drove off?

I should walk in the morning. In the daylight, there's less chance of tripping on something and doing myself a mischief. Also less chance of stumbling into a predator. Not sure what's in these woods but I'm pretty sure there'll be some kind of nocturnal creature which will look upon me as a snack. I turned back into the cabin - shit everywhere. Kind of wish I had managed to grab some of the cleaning products before I left the store. Not quite sure where I really want to sit in here!

CHAPTER 6

I took refuge on the living room's chair having moved the single seater across the door again, blocking me in once more; for two reasons - the first was so it would keep the draught from blowing a gale through the wooden cabin and the second was because it looked eerie as Hell outside as a sudden fog seemed to have started to descend, weaving its way through the thick rows of overly tall trees.

I felt nauseous. I don't know whether I'm simply tired, hungry or nervous about what the morning will bring with the Sheriff. What if he doesn't believe me? Could I end up going to jail? What about my wife and kids? They'll have to carry on living their lives with people looking at them and judging them because of what I'd done. At least, what everyone else will presume I'd done if I do get sent down for it. I know I didn't do it. It was never my intention for someone to get killed.

Jesus, what was his name? That'll probably end up haunting me along with the look on his face when he realized he had been hit. I had a hand in a man dying and I can't remember his name.

I stood up and walked back over to the window, looking out into the eeriness beyond. I wished I still had my phone so I could call the Sheriff and get this over and done with. I had ages to wait before the sun would start to come up - enough, at least, to make it possible to see where I'd be treading outside. That's hours and hours worth of time to build it all up in my head and panic that everything is going to go extremely wrong when I do finally get to talk to them.

I started to wish that I had stayed at home instead of coming out here now. I should have sold this damned place when my father died. I should have known it stood a high risk of getting vandalized. I suppose I should be grateful there isn't anyone living in here. Mind you, having said that, if someone was living here then I wouldn't have had a reason to go back to the store and the clerk would still be alive.

I can't quite believe how my feelings for this place have changed so fast. At the start of the day I was actually excited about coming back here and seeing the cabin again. I liked the idea of looking around it and having memories of my dad pop into my mind once more but now, when I look around, those happy memories are tainted.

Outside the fog is getting heavier. Can barely make the trees out more than a few hundred yards away from the cabin. Never seen it so thick. It's probably a good thing that Jamie and Ava have gone with Susan, they'd both be freaking about now. My little ghost story, in the car earlier, wouldn't have helped with that. I might have had to tell them that I had made it up...Well, not made it up so much. Just added to it. The locals always used the story of the asylum's ghosts wandering around the area and the scream but I'm sure high stress levels and a poor diet were to blame for my dad's eventual heart attack a year later. The timing was nothing more than an unfortunate coincidence.

I heard my dad's voice in my head reminding me of the inmates, "They'd scream and scream, all night long in their tiny little rooms, banging their heads against the walls...For weeks their screams of terror, desperation and, of course, madness echoed through the corridors of the asylum driving the doctors to despair. Eventually, the doctors had had enough and they started performing procedures on the loudest of the patients whereby they'd cut down their necks and remove their vocal chords silencing them forever..." at the time my dad told me the story, he even demonstrated where the doctors would make the incision by running a pen down my neck. A move which would always make a cold shiver run down my spine. I remember my dad telling me what the locals had told him after he mentioned the ghostly foot-steps and the scream whilst on a shopping trip, the following day, "You'd never see the ghosts, not properly. You'd only catch a glimpse of their shapes out of the corner of your eye and you'd hear their stolen, vengeful scream; an ear-piercing shriek to steal the lives of anyone who heard it."

My dad always had a glint in his eye when he told that story and, when I grew up, I always wondered how much of his story was true to what the locals said and how much he had embellished. After all, being a writer, his imagination was more warped than that of the average man on the street and I'm sure he wouldn't have wanted to miss the chance of putting his own stamp on the story.

As I continued staring into the grey night outside, I couldn't help but feel a chill run through me as I remembered the stories my dad used to tell. The more I think back, the more I have to question whether this really was a father and son holiday time, as I used to believe, or just the chance to scare the living shit out of me without mum close-by, ready to shout at him for taking a story too far.

"A car broke down just along that dirt road," my old man had whispered once as I laid, as an eight year old boy, in bed with the duvet tucked around me, "the driver, a man in his forties, turned to his wife, a pretty lady in her late thirties, and told her to wait right there whilst he walked back to town to fetch help...She begged him not to go and leave her because it was dark outside, just as it is now, but he insisted. He said they couldn't spend the cold night sitting in the car hoping for someone to stumble upon them. He kissed her on the forehead, reminded her that the town was only about half an hours walk back in the direction they had come, and whispered that he wouldn't be long. Half an hour passed. An hour came and went...Two hours passed and still there was no sign of her husband. On the third hour there was a bang on the roof of her car... BANG! and then another... BANG! as though something heavy was being smacked against the car's metal roof. She froze with fear as the heavy thuds continued to rain down upon the car and felt a huge sigh of relief when she noticed oncoming headlights in front of her. As the car neared the thuds on the roof got louder and heavier and more constant...BANG! BANG! BANG! BANG! She didn't move, though. She desperately wanted to climb from the car and run towards what turned out to be the Sheriff's patrol car. BANG! BANG! BANG! BANG! on the roof. The Sheriff jumped from his car and called for the lady to get out of the vehicle and walk towards him...He told her, whatever she does...She mustn't look back..."

BANG!

Something heavy hit the wall of the cabin behind me and I jumped from my memories back to the present. I span around to where I thought it had hit. Whatever it was, it sounded so hard, I thought it could have come through the wall. What the Hell was that?

BANG!

I looked out of the front window again. It doesn't look windy out there. I thought, perhaps, it could have been a branch knocking against the wall. If anything, it looks stiller than I've ever seen it before.

BANG!

"Hello?" I called out. I waited...

BANG!

"Hello?"

BANG!

Curiosity got the better of me and I pulled the single-seater away from the cabin door and stepped outside into the darkness. This would probably be easier with a torch. I walked down the porch, which ran the entire length of the front of the cabin, and turned down the side of the building. From out here, I couldn't hear the banging anymore. Even so, I continued to the back of the building. Nothing there. Not even any trees close to the back wall which could have been knocking against it had there been a sudden gust of wind. Weird. I peered into the darkness to see if I could see anything but it was too dark and, even if it hadn't been, the fog was almost impenetrable.

"Hello?"

Nothing. Another chill ran down my back. A grown man and I'm getting creeped out by the woods and a little fog. My dad would be laughing in his grave if he knew the effect his stories were having on me. I about turned and hurried back to the cabin's living room. Once inside, I pushed the single-seater against the door again and took a step back.

BANG!

I jumped again. It came from the same place, on the back wall. I walked over to where I thought it came from and placed my hand on the wall. I jumped again when whatever it was banged against the wall once more. Whatever it is, it feels heavy. I bet, if I check in the morning, there's a mark against the wall. What could it be? I held my breath as I waited for another impact but there was nothing. A minute passed and still there was nothing.

BANG!

It came from the next room; the bedroom just off the living room. I ran through, stopped in the middle of the room, and waited. Come on, you son of a bitch. Where are you?

BANG!

Back in the living room. I hurried back through and pulled the single-seater away from the cabin's front door. Had I stopped to think about it I would have realized what a stupid idea it was, to try and catch whatever it was banging against the wall. For all I knew it could have been one of the inmates from the asylum...Don't be so stupid. Within seconds I was stood out the back once more but there was still nothing to see.

"Hello?"

Leaves rustling in the wind were the only thing to respond to my call out. Nothing else.

"I have a gun!" I shouted just in case there was something else, other than the dancing leaves, out there. I waited a moment longer than entirely necessary giving whatever it was plenty of time to reveal itself yet nothing came and nothing happened. Thinking of the gun, as much as I hate them, I'm kind of glad I have it. I returned back to the inside of the cabin and retrieved the gun, from the side where I had placed it earlier.

I pushed the door to but didn't block it with the seat this time. I want to be ready if the noise happens again. I don't want to give whatever it is any idea that I'm coming for it. I'll just run out there and squeeze a few rounds off into the darkness. Perhaps I should do that anyway without waiting for the noise to happen again. If there is something out there it will soon disappear if I start firing bullets. It would show I'm not afraid to use the gun and that's not a bad thing to reveal even if I don't really want to kill anything. A couple more minutes went by with nothing happening and I started to relax a little - well, as much as I could given the circumstances.

BANG!

It came from the kitchen area of the cabin. I ran out the front of the cabin and ran to that side of the building with the gun raised high in the air - pointing to the black sky.

"Fuck you!" I yelled. I pulled the trigger twice letting off two rounds into the foggy air. With the gun still raised I froze and waited, listening for the sounds of something running from me. Nothing. Either there really is nothing out there and I'm going mad, hearing things, or - whatever it is - it's not scared of bullets. If it's the latter, I really don't want to know what it is or what it wants. A few more silent seconds went by. I lowered the gun and walked backwards, towards the cabin's entrance, keeping my eyes on what I could see of the tree line.

Back in the cabin I moved the larger of the living room's seats in front of the broken door. I slid the single-seater across the room from where I had pulled the larger one. With that done I closed the curtains to the windows. Seeing outside was only fueling my childish thoughts of monsters in the fog. With everything done I dropped down in the single seat once more and rested the gun in my lap.

"You know there's nothing out there," my dad used to tell me on the nights where I was so scared I couldn't fall asleep because of his stories; the nights when he pushed it too far.

"There's nothing out there," I repeated his words out loud. "Nothing out there."

BANG!

It's been about twenty minutes or so and everything's gone quiet. Whatever it was, out there, must have got bored and wandered off. It was probably the people, or person, responsible for all of the graffiti and general damage. I expect they came back and saw me here...Probably tried to scare me off so they can take refuge in their den.

"See I told you everything was okay," my dad would say once he'd proven there was nothing outside waiting to get me as soon as I closed my eyes. I wish he was still here to reassure me - not that there's nothing outside, despite my over-active imagination, I know there's nothing outside. At least, nothing waiting to get me. I just wish he was here to reassure me that everything's going to be okay when I see the Sheriff tomorrow. I'd give anything to hear his voice. Anything.

Yesterday I couldn't wait to come to the cabin for some peace and quiet. Some isolation. Now I just want to disappear, though. The isolation paired with the guilt I'm feeling is killing me and reminding me more and more of memories I'd sooner keep buried. This cabin was supposed to remind me of the good times with my dad, as well as give me the peace needed to write, not drag up the shit I'd rather forget.

"How long have you been seeing her?" I had asked dad after I burst into his study; a small room where he used to sit and write his novels.

I remember how my dad swiveled around, in his chair, to look at me. He didn't even get up to talk. Just sat there and tilted his head down so he could peer at me over the top of his black-rimmed glasses. Already he had had a look of denial on his face but his eyes gave him away just as they always had when he was guilty of something or simply bending the truth to put himself in a more favorable light.

Mum had suspected for years that dad was seeing the other woman. Every year he'd get the Valentine's Day cards, penned in the same styled handwriting as the birthday cards he thought we never knew about; the secret cards he'd stash in his office despite putting all the others out on display in our front room. Why else would you hide something away other than to conceal a guilty conscience? What made it worse is that she wasn't even that special, this woman he chose over my own mother. Just a cheap tart who liked to dress herself up in high market clothes and designer jewelry to try and make herself look important. Even then, the jewelry was most likely paid for by my father. No matter how you paint a turd, though...A turd will always be just that.

I never told mum. I never told her how I found the notes between dad and this woman. Dad hadn't been around. He must have popped out to pick something up or run a chore and simply forgot to lock his study like he normally did. He often went out without locking it but would always remember it and come back to close it up as soon as he possibly could, even if it made him late for meetings. This time he wasn't there, though, and a constant ringing of the alarm was annoying me so, despite knowing he didn't like people going in his study when he wasn't there, I went in. There were notes scattered all over his desk. Most of them seemed to be about a new book he was working on but one in particular caught my eye. Obviously I was going to take a closer look. I'm only human. I wish I hadn't. If I had just ignored it I'd have never seen the messages backwards and forwards with this woman. This piece of shit friend of the family. The most two-faced human you could possibly imagine. Numerous messages where they declared their love for one another and called each other by their sick-inducing pet names.

Despite bursting in on my dad and confronting him, I never told him I had seen the notes. I wanted him to be man enough to admit to me that he was cheating on my mother. His wife. But he couldn't even do that. Not man enough. It's funny, I always thought he would have been given his dislike of anything less than 'honest'. Maybe it's the way I burst in on him? Maybe if I had handled it differently he would have responded truthfully? I was young, didn't have much control over my emotions back then. Especially when it came down to people, or things, hurting my mum.

I'd never forgive my dad for what he had been doing behind my mum's back but I'll always regret not being able to establish some form of relationship with him again before his heart attack. The last words we had were said in anger and it tears me apart inside. I sat back in the chair and wiped a tear from my eye. So much for reminiscing about the happier times.

I closed my eyes and tried to block it all out; the guilt from what I had been a part of earlier in the day, the deep feeling of regret at not being able to patch things up with my dad before his heart attack...I was even feeling guilty about how I had been treating Jamie this past year. She was obviously going through a difficult time, trying to discover who she really is, and I'd just take the piss out of her if I'd even comment on it in the first place. More often than not, I'd simply shut myself away in my own little study and work on my own pieces of fiction. With things feeling a little strained, from time to time, between Susan and I as well...Am I turning into my father? I hope not. I promised myself I'd never do that. I promised myself I'd be a better father and a better husband but at the moment it feels as though I'm failing on both accounts.

As soon as I see them again, I'll start to make amends.

Another promise to myself.

CHAPTER 7

A gentle knocking on the cabin's door stirred me from my unexpected sleep. There was no light coming through the cracks in the curtains so I couldn't have been asleep for long. Was there even a knocking or did I imagine it? I didn't move. I just stayed rooted to my seat with the gun still in my lap and my hand close by, ready to grab it should it be needed.

"Hello?" I said quietly. Deep down I hoped that, if there was someone out there, they wouldn't hear me and they'd leave. I've learnt from writing horror and watching films over the years, hell even watching the news on television...I've learnt that if someone is out walking in the woods, late at night, it's generally a good idea not to open the door to them should they come knocking. "Anyone there?" I asked again in a quieter tone than strictly necessary. I waited in silence desperately hoping no one would answer. With a general feeling of unease creeping over me I took up the gun in my writing hand and raised it towards the door. Part of me just wants to put two bullets through the door on the off-chance someone is out there but I hold back from firing. Good self-control. Guess I'm hearing things. Either that or I dreamt it in my shallow sleep.

A couple more seconds passed before I heard the familiar sounds of heavy footsteps walking the length of the cabin, away from the front door. My heart jumped in my throat as I recalled the sound from my childhood when it woke me from my sleep and I had gone running into my dad.

Someone was out there.

I leapt up from the chair, with the gun in hand, and dashed through to the bedroom, as quietly as I could, where the sounds of the footsteps were headed. With any luck they'd pass in front of the bedroom window and I'd be able to see who it was but by the time I crossed the bedroom, to the window, the footsteps had all but disappeared. Whoever it was had obviously stepped off the wooden porch, down onto the soft mud to mute the sounds of their unwelcome steps. Dammit. I peered out of the window but, again, could see nothing. Even less by the time my heavy breathing had misted the window panes up. I wiped them clear with my free hand and suddenly screamed, falling backwards onto my ass, when I saw the pale face of a young boy staring right back at me, inches away from my own face.

Whoever it was stepped back, into the blackness, out of view. I rushed over to the window again and peered out but they were gone.

I closed my eyes tight and tried desperately to remember his face in case I recognized him as being one of the youngsters hanging around outside the store earlier but all I could recall was a long scar running down his neck. Did I really see that or did my imagination paint that picture to fool me and make me feel even more nervous? I opened my eyes again and squinted into the eerie night-air.

BANG!

The thud echoed through the cabin causing my heart to miss a beat once more - a horrible feeling becoming all too familiar.

"Leave me alone!" I screamed at the top of my lungs. I didn't believe my yelling would help. If the sound of bullets flying through the air didn't scare off whoever was trying to mess with me then I'm sure my pathetic cries would do nothing apart from maybe encourage them to continue.

BANG!

I don't know why but I hurried back through to the living room, where the noise was coming from, and froze in the middle of the room as I nervously waited for the next bang.

KNOCK! KNOCK!

I span around, on the spot, to face the front door; someone's knocking again.

"Who is it?" I demanded. I raised the gun to what I thought would be head level for whoever was out there. "Who's there?" I watched, in terror, as the door handle started to slowly twist counter-clockwise. "I have a gun!" I warned them. The handle stopped moving. It seems, whoever it is, does have some common sense in them after all.

BANG!

I span back towards the wall behind me. How many people are here?

"Fuck off!" I yelled. Yelling is all I can do. I'm too afraid to move the seat out of the way of the door to run out and confront whoever it is. It's fair to say the image of someone standing at the window and old memories of what I had heard when I was here with my dad, all those years ago, have me more or less frozen with fear. Morning can't come quick enough.

KNOCK! KNOCK!

I looked down at my watch. It's only just turned midnight. There's at least five hours before the sun will start to come up, illuminating enough of the woods to allow me to walk into town.

BANG!

I can't take five hours of this. I turned my attention back to the door handle which had started to slowly turn again. I hesitated for a split second before raising the barrel of the gun back towards the door. I mentally gave whoever was out there a couple more seconds to stop moving the handle. One. Two. I squeezed the trigger and put a hole straight through the door. The handle stopped moving immediately. I lowered the gun and froze, waiting to hear if someone would cry out in pain or if I'd hear the sound of someone dropping to the floor like a dead weight. There was nothing. Did I even hit anyone?

"Hello?" I called out nervously. No one replied.

Suddenly, with no warning, a loud ear-piercing scream echoed through the house followed by loud banging noises from what felt to be all of the cabin's walls. I too screamed as I dropped to my knees, letting the gun fall to the floor beside me. I placed my hands over my ears to drown the racket out.

Before I knew it the only noise in the cabin was the sound of my own screaming. I stopped. My throat was sore from the strain I had put upon it. I nervously moved my hands away from my ears. Silence. Blissful silence. I wonder how long for, though? I didn't get up. I didn't move in case my movement triggered it all off again. I just stayed there, on my knees, in the middle of the living room.

This is stupid. I'm stupid. No. I'm being stupid. There's nothing out there. My dad told me so. There's no such thing as ghosts. Ghosts are nothing more than figments of a tired imagination or cruel tricks of the mind. It's probably just a group of teenagers mucking around. Probably the same people who caused all the damage to the cabin. I expect they came back to hang out in their den and were annoyed to see me here. They're probably just trying to scare me out; a logical reason to calm my shattered nerves.

My logical reason isn't helping much. I've fired three shots now; two outside and one through the door. How would that not have scared them off by now? Had the shoe been on the other foot, I would have run after the first shot had been fired. I certainly wouldn't have hung around to encourage more bullets to be shot towards me.

Slowly, and quietly, I pulled myself up from my knees and onto the seat. Once comfortable, I reached down and collected the gun from the floor. If the gunshots weren't enough to deter whoever is trying to scare me, maybe I'd be better off just leaving the cabin and letting them have it. I mean, if they want it that desperately they fear no bullets...Perhaps they deserve it?

"There's no one out there," dad had said after I'd woken him up to tell him about the footsteps I'd heard out the front. Dad seemed to be more annoyed by the fact I'd disturbed him than by the fact someone could be outside pacing up and down in front of his cabin. I'll never forget that. On the rare occasions when one of my girls had woken me up, in the past, to tell me something was wrong - I always checked out their story with no hint of my annoyance, no matter how tired I was. What if they had been right and someone was in their closet or someone was stood at the back window, looking in?

"There is someone out there," I had insisted as I tried to pull him from his bed.

"Just ignore them," he had replied, "they'll soon go away."

Is my subconscious serving up that memory as a way of telling me to simply ignore whoever is out there? Is that what I need to do? Just ignore them and they'll leave. Worry about them if and when they decide to try and walk through the front door. Why should I feel scared anyway? I'm the one with the gun after all. Perhaps they should be out there fearing me?

This is silly. They've gone quiet again. I'll do the same. I'll creep around here, until morning. I won't shout at them anymore. I won't go running out there or start screaming. Whatever they do, I'll just ignore it. I just need something to help distract my mind; I'm sure it's my own mind making this feel a lot worse than it actually is anyway. I'm tempted to try and go back to sleep but I know my body won't let me. I know I'll regret the lack of sleep in the morning, when I go to the Sheriff's department, but I have too much adrenalin flowing through my system at the moment. Besides, if I did doze off, whoever's outside will only give me a jolt awake again when they start their scaremongering once more. Fuck that. I won't give them the satisfaction. And I had best be on my guard on the off-chance they do happen to come in. I'm not saying they'll try anything, if they crossed the threshold but, even so, I'd rather be ready for anything. Sleep can wait. So much for trying to distract my mind from thinking of them. I think, since deciding that, I've actually thought about them more.

I shook my head and stood up as quietly as the creaking chair allowed me to. I wonder if any of my dad's old paperwork bits and pieces are still here? The last time I was here, I found some stashed in a drawer in the office. I had always promised myself to have a flick through, in case there were any notes or anything I could use for a new story, but I never got around to it. Despite wanting to do it - I never seemed to manage to find the time. Well, time is all I have now...

I crept through to my study, and my father's study before that, and sat down at the desk where we used to write. Where he used to scribble notes down, on various scraps of paper, at the desk - before using a typewriter - I used to just bring my laptop and do everything on that. It was much easier. Back in those days, though, I guess my father didn't have the luxury of computers. Even when he could have turned to them, towards the end of his writing career, he never bothered. He said he preferred the feel of using his typewriter. He wasn't superstitious with most things in life but he did always worry his words would never flow so well if he changed from using his trusty typewriter.

For a while, after his death, I tried to use his typewriter after my mother passed it down to me. I hated it. I guess I make too many mistakes to use a typewriter. It's much easier with a computer; the 'backspace' key in particular.

I sat at the desk, on the old wooden chair, once I had brushed the various bits of rubbish from the surface of both of them. The wooden table used to be a fine piece of furniture but now there's hardly an area which doesn't have some kind of childish etching scratched into it; whether it's some silly slang or some immature doodle.

BANG!

That's cool. Ignore it. They'll go away. Besides, it came from the living room and I'm not there anymore. They're not even near me. Forget about it. I pulled open the desk's drawer and was confronted by an old photograph of my father and I. My heart sank as I realized it had been drawn on. The young image of me was untouched but my father's image; his eyes had been crossed out and a line, with stitches, had been drawn down the length of his neck. Had my dad still been alive, it probably wouldn't have angered me as much. I took the photo from the drawer and placed it on the top of the table.

BANG!

I wet the bottom of my thumb, with my tongue, and ran it across the ink but it made no difference. I had hoped it would have wiped it clean off but no such luck.

"They said, if you hear the scream, you die a year later and your soul goes to haunt the very same woods where you originally heard the scream..." dad had told me. His face was so serious, why wouldn't I have believed him as he passed on what he was told by the locals. Twelve years old, I would never have believed he'd lie to me. I had no reason to doubt him. Not until just under a year later when I discovered the affair more or less detailed in the many notes. Part of me wonders why he had kept them. Surely, for a man who liked to keep his own business private, he'd have just burned them once he had read them and savored the words within. I'll never know for sure but maybe he was planning on publishing them; a cruel way to inform his wife, who read all of his work, that he was actually having an affair with this whore. I digress. Before I read those notes... I'd have never doubted him and so I never doubted what he said the locals had told him about the footsteps and the scream.

Although I still dreamt about hearing the footsteps, I more or less had forgotten about the story until dad's death. Practically a year, to the day, since the final night of our last happy holiday together. It was but a few months, from getting home from our cabin adventure, that I ventured into his empty office and read the truth about my father.

Now his story is at the forefront of my mind and I can't shake it out despite knowing, deep down, it's ridiculous.

"...your soul goes to haunt the very same woods where you originally heard the scream..." his words echoed through my mind as I tried to ignore the footsteps which were pacing the front of the cabin once more.

"It's just a story," I said to myself. "A story to scare kids from venturing into the woods by themselves. That's what all ghost stories are - simple, yet effective, storytelling methods to keep you from doing something stupid."

KNOCK! KNOCK!

"It's just kids out there. Nothing more, nothing less. They'll get bored eventually and they'll go home. Worst case scenario, they'll come in and then you can scare them away with your gun..." I whispered to myself. The sound of my own voice offered me little comfort.

Your gun? I'd rather not get used to referring to the gun as mine. It's not my gun. It's Josh's gun. It's the murder weapon. Don't refer to it as 'your gun' again.

KNOCK! KNOCK!

Why did I have to leave my cellphone in the car with Susan? This could have all been dealt with by now and I might have even been on the way to meeting her at her mum's. I picked the gun up, once more, and crept back through to the living room, where the knocking was coming from.

I'll wait. That's what I'll do. I'll wait until they go quiet again. And then I'll creep out of here, into the woods, where I can watch the cabin. I'd bet my last dime that, as soon as I'm out, they'll all come in and start their partying. It's just kids. It's just kids. It's just kids...I crept across to the chair, opposite the door, and quietly lowered myself into it before I placed the gun to my side. I'm just going to sit here until they go quiet and then I'll make my move.

'What if there's no one out there and no one runs in the cabin, after I vacate it?' a random thought asks in the back of my mind. I don't even want to think about it. If it's no one fucking with me then I'm going mad. There's no other explanation.

I'm just grateful Susan and the kids didn't stay here tonight. I'd have hated for them to have to sit through this too. I know it would petrify Susan and Jamie but Ava...She's too young to be exposed to these kind of mind games. She'd never sleep again. Not entirely sure I will yet.

KNOCK! KNOCK!

⋏

"Yes?" my dad had called out from his office door. He needn't have bothered. I would have gone in regardless as to whether he had invited me or not. I hadn't meant to knock on his door, when I went to confront him. It was force of habit. I had meant to just burst in and have it out with him.

I stormed over to his desk. So young and yet acting so old I demanded to know, "How long have you been seeing her?"

Dad span around, in his swivel chair, to look at me. He didn't even bother getting up. I remember, at the time, how it annoyed me; the way he dared to look at me as though it was I who was in the wrong and not the other way around. He tilted his head down and looked at me over the top of his black-rimmed glasses - couldn't even be bothered to take them off to address me properly.

"What are you talking about?" he had asked me.

"I know, dad, I know..."

"Know what?"

"Just tell me how long you've been seeing her?"

"What do you think you know, son? I have no idea what you're talking about."

"Don't lie to me!" I remember I shouted at him. The first time, and not the last, that I'd dare to stand up to him; dare to point out how he, Mr Perfect, was in the wrong.

"Look, I'm really busy at the moment. These books don't write themselves...What do you want?"

"I want to know how long you've been cheating on my mum!" I yelled.

Dad didn't say anything. I remember how he just looked at me as though I was muck on his shoe, like I was nothing more than an unpleasant inconvenience to him. I remember, at the time, wondering whether the previous times we'd spent together, laughing and generally being happy, were nothing more than a lie on his part. An act he'd put on to keep both my mother, and I, happy so as to give him a relatively easy life. It's amazing how one look from someone can ruin years and years of 'progress' with regards to a relationship.

"Son, I don't have time for this..." he had told me. It was at that point, in the conversation, he originally turned his back on me and, from that moment on, it felt as though he had his back to me for the rest of his life.

I've just realized that everything is quiet outside. They must be taking another break before they start again. Okay...This is it. Stick to the plan. Get out. Keep watch. And then it's my turn to scare the shit out of whoever comes in. I grabbed the gun, tucked it into my belt, and stood up. With the adrenalin back to pounding through my body, I stood up and made my way over to the seat which blocked my exit. Not quite sure how to do this...Do I do it quickly and risk making noise and making it obvious as to what I'm doing or do I try and keep it as quiet as possible? Noisy. Has to be noisy. I want them to know I'm vacating the property. Okay...Here we go...

"Leave me alone!" I yelled at the top of my lungs as I ran from the cabin, having unblocked the way to the front door. As I ran, as fast as I could, down the dirt track which I drove in on, I panicked that the gun was going to slip from where I had it hidden. The last thing I need, right now, is to drop that. I hoped that whoever would have been watching me run away would think I had left the gun inside - giving them more reason to go in; anything to get them to come out from the darkness they hid in.

As soon as I was out of view of the cabin I stopped running. I took a moment, bent forward, to catch my breath and turned back towards where I had just run. I felt that went well. I especially liked my acting abilities begging for them to leave me alone. Hopefully they bought it as I had intended them to.

I quickly walked over to the trees and stepped off the dirt track. If I'm careful, I'll be able to sneak through the woods until I can see the cabin again. From my new, hidden, vantage point, I'll hopefully be able to see them enter the cabin. As I crept through the undergrowth my heart was beating fast with the surge of adrenalin. Not because I'm scared. I'm not scared anymore. No. Now I'm excited. I'm looking forward to catching whoever it is and giving them a piece of my mind. If they're willing to go to such extremes to get me out of the cabin, you can bet it was them who trashed it in the first place. Little fuckers. I wondered what the chances were of getting some money out of them to cover the damage they had caused and the necessary clean-up operations. Chance would be a fine thing.

As I crept the last few hundred yards, towards the large oak tree I had my heart set on as my lookout post, I tried desperately hard not to tread on any of the many branches and sticks which littered the muddy floor. With every 'snap' and 'crunch' I accidentally caused I increased my chances of being seen, or heard at the very least.

For this to succeed I'm going to need the element of surprise and I really, really want this to work out.

Chapter 8

I'm not sure how long I've been waiting here now. The only two things I'm sure about are the following - it's damned cold out here and no one has gone into the cabin yet. Perhaps it would have been a good idea to check my watch before I got too carried away with spying on the door.

Come on, they must have seen me leave and even if they didn't see me, they surely must have heard me running and shouting as I left. What are they waiting for?

I heard something snap behind me and span around to see what it was. Nothing there. Could have been anything. I waited a few moments more to see if anything moved in the many shadows but it was dead out here. Had it not been for all the banging, footsteps and the scream earlier - I'd have believed I was completely alone. I wished I was. Actually, no, I wished my wife was with me. I wished my wife and my children. I wished the cabin was fine and I wished, more than anything, the whole incident in the store didn't happen. Seeing as I'm wishing for the impossible, I might as well wish for it all.

"Come on, come on, what are you waiting for?" I whispered.

They can't have been that desperate to get in there. Maybe they were more interested in seeing if they could scare me out and they didn't actually want the cabin for themselves? I looked at my watch in the limited light on offer. I'll give them another fifteen minutes. No. Twenty. I'll give them another twenty minutes, just in case they're watching the cabin to make sure I've definitely gone. I don't want to have done this for...

SNAP!

I span around again as another branch snapped behind me. I couldn't tell exactly where it came from other than to my rear and that it sounded close. I held my breath and laid perfectly still, amongst the dead leaves and fallen branches. Could just be an animal. Could be nothing. In my mind I see the face of the boy, with the scar running the length of his neck, staring at me but I'm quick to shake it off. Ghosts don't exist. Just an animal. I turned back to the cabin. First impressions show nothing has changed since the distraction behind me. The door is still half open, the lights are still on and, more importantly, I can't hear the cheering or laughter of any kids who've succeeded in what they set out to achieve. Where are you, you little fuckers? I know you're out there somewhere, hiding like the little cowards you are. Come on, show yourselves...

Suddenly the same haunting scream, from earlier in the night, filled my ears as though it was coming from close behind me. I span around to see if I could make out where it was coming from but was soon distracted by another scream coming from my right...And then another scream coming from my left. I jumped up and wasted no time in getting back to the dirt track. As soon as my feet touched the solid dirt of the track I started to run, as fast as I could, back towards the cabin - all the time the screams filled my ears. I pulled the gun from where I had it stashed, down my belt, and carried on running with it close to my side on the off chance anything jumped out on me.

It didn't take me long to reach the cabin's porch. I leapt up the two wooden steps and bounded over the porch and into the living room where I quickly span around and slammed the door shut. Seconds later the larger of the seats was across the door and I was standing at the window, peering out from behind the old, tatty curtain with my heart pounding in my throat. Seconds later, all of the screams stopped. Regardless of the silence, I stayed at the window in case I could...what the fuck...

I see it. Down in the dirt track where I had just come from. It looked like a young lad was just standing there watching the cabin. It was so dark out there it was hard to make anything else out, other than his size. I let the curtain fall back into place, blocking my view in the process, and stepped back shaking, violently, with fear.

I took a few deep breaths. I should go out there. Confront them. It's only a lad. One of many, probably. It's not a ghost. It's not a ghost. Just a lad. They only want to scare me. They succeeded.

I stepped forward, back to the window, and pulled the curtain across again. The dirt track was deserted. Whoever it was had disappeared into the night. I let the curtain drop to the side and pushed the chair away from the door again. I pulled the door open and stepped onto the porch.

"Who's out there?" I called out. "Come on, I saw you! What do you fucking want?! Money?! I have money! If that's what you want..." I stopped speaking and gave them a chance to answer but no one spoke out. "Come on, this is stupid. I'm sure there are places you'd rather be than out here, right? Hello? Anyone?" still no one answered. "What's the matter? You too chicken shit to face me?!" I yelled.

When it was apparent no one was going to step forward, I returned to the living room and pushed the door to. I didn't block it this time. Instead I'll simply sit opposite and wait for them to knock again. If there's nothing to stop the door from opening, the force of their hand, against the wooden door panel, will expose them to me.

"There's no one out there," my dad had said.

Time's have changed. There is someone out there and we're going to have words...I went to sit on the seat, opposite the door, when I noticed a piece of cloth, on the arm of it, which wasn't there earlier when I had been sitting there. I walked over and picked it up. On closer inspection it looked to be a piece of cloth torn from a shirt. Perhaps from a pocket you'd find on the chest area? Red ink in the corner where a pen could have leaked...I froze. I recognized the pattern on the cloth. It belonged to the store clerk's shirt. How the Hell did it get in here? I ran through and checked the other rooms to see if any of the windows were open. None of them were. They couldn't have come through the front door, though. They couldn't have! I was watching it the whole time.

Unless...

I only took my eyes off the door from a split second, when I heard the snapping sound from behind me. Could they have run in and out again in the time it took for me to make sure nothing was behind me? Surely I would have heard them? Everything else, out there, was so deathly quiet. It's practically impossible to walk on the cabin's wooden porch without your footsteps being audible. I should know, I used to try and do it years ago when I tried sneaking up on my dad.

"The screams would be of the dead, haunting the woods as they sought vengeance for what had happened to them when they were still breathing," my dad had told me years ago. The inmates were given jobs around the town to help with the rehabilitation program. What if the store clerk was previously one of the inmates and now his ghost had been added to the others which haunted the town? The cloth is a sign he's come for vengeance for what happened to him? No. That's stupid. Just my overactive, guilty imagination again poisoned with memories from my childhood. It's ridiculous. I know who it is. It's Josh.

Josh and his friends are probably trying to scare me out of the town completely so I don't go to the Sheriff. Another negative thought sprung to the forefront of my mind; what if he wants to do more than scare me? What if he wants to make sure I never say anything to anyone? What if he wants to silence me permanently? He's already shot one person and even though it was an accident, he didn't seem very remorseful. Even less guilty when he ran for the dead store clerk's shotgun...I'm even more grateful for having made Susan and the kids leave now. They don't need to be part of this. If that is the case, though...If he is here to silence me for good...How come he hasn't already done it then?

I glanced down to the gun in my hand. I don't want to have to use this other than to scare someone away but if it comes down to it...If it's between him and me...I'll do what needs to be done. All I can do is sit and wait him out...Him and his friends...Hopefully nothing more, other than noises, will happen before morning and I'll be able to get away from here and into town. Once I'm in the town I know I'll be okay. Even better when I'm sat opposite the Sheriff in his office.

I quickly walked through the cabin closing all of the doors. I figured if they tried to sneak in through one of the windows, to surprise me, I'd hear them come through the door and be able to act accordingly. Other than that, all I can do is sit on the living room's seat, again, and wait. If they're going to make a move, hopefully they'll do it sooner rather than later. I just want to get this over with. This whole nasty experience. I want it finished and as far out of my mind as someone's dead body resting on my conscience will allow.

I sat down on the chair, opposite the door, and mentally prepared myself for what I might have to do. I didn't have to wait very long.

BANG!

Ah, I wondered where they'd gone. It obviously took them some time to get back to behind the cabin, from after they'd surrounded me further down the dirt track. Come on, you son of a bitch, stop playing 'ghosts' and come say hi.

BANG!

The banging noises which bounced off the various cabin walls didn't even bother me now. They needed to learn some new tricks. Something I hadn't grown used to hearing in the darkness. A little part of me felt disappointed they hadn't yet started to moan, groan and rattle chains. Everyone knows that's what evil spirits are meant to be doing as they haunt the living.

Footsteps started to pace the front of the cabin. This is it, I thought. This is it. I raised the gun towards the door. Come on then, Josh, stick your head through the gap. I dare you. I double dare you. The footsteps didn't stop at the door, though. They continued past it towards the other side of the cabin. I tracked them, along the wall, with my eyes looking down the barrel of the gun. They stopped. They must have reached the far end of the porch. They didn't stop for long, though, before they about turned and walked along the wooden boards of the porch once more - following the path they had just walked down. Again I kept track of them down the gun's barrel. I had expected them to knock on the door this time but they didn't and I watched as a dark shadow passed between the slight gap caused by the door not being closed properly. I didn't even call out to them. I didn't invite them in. Although I'm not worried about doing what needs to be done...At the same time, I don't wish to invite it.

BANG!

Another thud on the wall behind me. Meanwhile whoever paced the front, of the cabin, turned and walked back down the length of the porch once more. Big, heavy footsteps. Either Josh knew some big lads who were in need of a diet or they were purposefully stamping their feet to make the steps sound louder in here. Regardless, they aren't coming in. They're just trying to mess with my mind. True to form a dark shadow passed between the gap as I had expected them to. Part of me was tempted to rugby tackle them to the floor when they walked on by but I didn't. I stayed rooted to the spot. No need for me to invite trouble.

BANG!

The more they do it, the more pathetic they're coming across. Surely they couldn't have honestly believed doing the same thing over and over again would be enough to get to me? Sure, to start off with, it was a little unpleasant but not now - now it's just laughable.

The footsteps out the front stopped just as sudden as they had started. Must be draining, stamping their feet like that. They probably need a little break. If that were me, out there, organizing things then I would have had a system set up which would see a few lads take it in turn to stamp their feet. That way they would get tired less quickly.

BANG!

But then maybe there aren't enough of them out there to make that a possibility. The footsteps started again. I tried not to laugh out loud. Okay, I guess they just needed a little more time to switch places. No doubt the one who had paced the front of the cabin a minute ago is now standing out the back ready to hit the wall with whatever it is they're using to cause such a thud and the youth who had been out the back...Well, now he is the one pacing.

Sure enough a shadow passed the gap in the doorway.

BANG!

I smiled. The other youth has now managed to take up his position at the back of the building. Absolutely pathetic. In fact, I've had enough of this. I stood up and dashed out of the front door with the gun raised.

"Okay, you little shit!" I yelled.

What the Hell? By my calculations the foot-stamping culprit should have been standing by the far bedroom window, the same window I had seen them through earlier, but there was no one there.

BANG!

They're still around the back of the cabin. I'll catch them there. I ran around to confront them but, again, by the time I got there - no one was to be seen.

"Okay, you're quick. I'll give you that..."

Slowly I backed up along the side of the building, towards the front, as I kept a watchful eye on the bushes which lined the back of the building. None of them were even swaying as they might have done had someone recently disturbed them. Everything was eerily still. Where the Hell do they run off to then?

"I know it's you, Josh...This is pointless. You might as well just come out here and face me. Let's deal with what you want..." I stopped moving and waited for a response. "I am going to the Sheriff in the morning...Now's your chance to come out here and talk about what happened at the store..." Still nothing. No movement. No laughter. Nothing. Just stillness. "I know it was an accident...Come on...We can talk about this...Talk about what we're going to tell the Sheriff...It was all just a big misunderstanding...What happened was an accident...They'll be able to see that. We didn't want anyone hurt. No one wanted anyone hurt. It just happened..." Still nothing. "Come on, talk to me...Show me you're not as stupid as you're making out..."

With no warning something hit the window next to me from the inside. I span around and yelled in terror as I saw the face of a young lad staring back at me in the brightness of the room. His skin was pale and I could make out tiny, blue veins all over his face, his eyes were cloudy-blue surrounded by red rings, hair greasy black, his teeth were stained yellow and his lips crusted over with dried skin caused, at a quick guess, by dehydration. Down the length of his neck was a long scar which looked as though it had been stitched shut in a hurry. He pointed a bony finger at me and his eyes went wide before I heard a god-awful scream. The loudest of the screams so far but it wasn't coming from his mouth. His mouth remained as closed as his bucked teeth allowed. It was as though it was only heard in my head. I yelled again, shut my eyes and dropped the gun, choosing to cover my ears with my hands instead of pulling the trigger. By the time I dared to open my eyes again, only after the screaming had stopped, the boy was gone from the window. I pulled my shaking hands away from my ears and grabbed the gun from where it had landed amongst the dead leaves and mud, all the time I refused to look away from the window in case the boy appeared again.

"Okay, very good," I yelled, "you got me..."

My voice was shaking, nearly as much as my hands, and my heart was beating harder and faster than it had ever beaten before. So hard, in fact, I thought it was going to burst out from my rib-cage. A quick check behind me to make sure nothing was there before I turned the corner of the cabin and talked myself into heading back in to catch whoever was in there. It was just make-up, I kept saying over and over again in my mind. Just make-up. There's no such thing as ghosts. The lad just took the opportunity to run into the room, whilst I was outside, to try and scare me. Little fucker succeeded.

"Come out, I know you're in here," I called into the cabin, from the doorway. I waited to hear the laughter of someone who's prank had just worked beautifully but there was nothing. No laughter. No gloating. Nothing. "Come on...You got me...Very good...Well done..." Still nothing. I raised the gun and stepped in. Weird, it feels colder inside than it does out. Forget about it. A quick look around the first room soon revealed it was empty. There aren't even any places someone could hide in here. Definitely rule this room out. I opened the living room door which led onto the rest of the cabin...All the other doors were still closed, from where I had closed them earlier.

Another feeling of unease spread through my body. No. Ignore the feeling. They're obviously good at whatever game they're playing. It wouldn't have been hard for them to close the doors behind them, even if they were in a hurry so as not to be spotted by me. They're trying to keep everything as authentic as possible, of course they would have closed the doors. They wouldn't go to all this effort just to ruin it there.

I opened the door to the bedroom where I had seen the boy. How old must he have been anyway? Hard to pin-point an exact age, given the make-up, but he didn't look a day over ten years old. I wonder if his mother knows he is out so late. "I know you're in here," I said. "You might as well come out...I'm not angry." Given what they've put me through, I'm pretty sure he wouldn't believe me but I felt it was worth a shot. I felt as though I've tried everything else.

Like the living room, there's not much in here for anyone to hide behind other than...No...Surely not...I dropped to my knees and rested my head on the wooden floorboard so I could get a good view under the bed. No-one is there. Not just that but, considering the state they had left the rest of the cabin, there was nothing under the bed at all; no rubbish, none of my old bits and pieces, not even any evidence of spiders. Who'd have thought it would be the cleanest part of the whole damned cabin?!

I sat upright and instantly felt the hairs on my neck stand to attention as the feeling of warm air was breathed against my skin by someone standing behind me.

"I know you're there," I whispered. "What do you want?"

I didn't dare turn around. I desperately wanted to just so we could finally finish everything but every part of my body refused to allow me to do it; too scared by the stories I grew up with and the night's weirdness.

"This is silly," I said. I tried to sound cool and collected but knew I failed miserably. I sounded as scared as I felt. "We can all be friends," I continued shakily, "we don't have to do this..."

Whoever it was didn't say anything. They just stood there. I could feel they were practically on top of me. Why weren't they saying anything? Why? All I could hear were strange gargled noises which sounded as though they were coming from the back of their throat.

"Why won't you talk to me? What's all this meant to achieve?" I tried to take control of the situation but was once again let down by my tone.

Nervously I turned my head to see who was behind me. I managed to twist my head halfway round before I froze with fear. Out of the corner of my eye I could see all I wanted to see.

"Please...Tell me what you want..." I begged. I felt my eyes begin to fill up as the fear became too much for me to handle. The sound of my own heart pumping was nearly drowning out the weird clicking noises from the back of his throat - perhaps forming where his vocal chords used to be.

With no warning he placed his hand on my shoulder and an ear-piercing scream filled the room.

Chapter 9

I opened my eyes. I was face down on the bedroom's wooden floorboards. I must have blacked out; the shock of what was happening too much for my body to take. As soon as I realized where I was I sat up and cast my eyes around the room. It's empty. I'm alone again. I must have been unconscious for some time as daylight is spilling in from the window on the side of the room. Thank God for that. I need to get out of here. It's over...

BANG!

No. It can't be. It came from the front of the cabin this time. What do they want? It's daylight now. They must know it's over. They must do. My dad used to tell me things only went bump in the night.

I heard footsteps across the front of the porch. Will they ever leave me alone? A knocking on the front door followed. No. I'm not having it. I'm not. I looked to the floor and spotted the gun. Without giving it any hesitation I grabbed it and aimed it at the door.

"I'm in here!" I called out. "Come and get me!"

Footsteps across the floorboards in the other room. The door opened and I pulled the trigger.

BANG!

I screamed and dropped the gun. It hit the floor before Ava's body did. My daughter. My beautiful daughter. She fell backwards with blood trickling from the front of her delicate face. What have I done? What have I done?

"Baby?!" I called out as I scrambled over to her lifeless body.

More footsteps from outside which sounded as though they were running towards where I was sat, cradling the body of my youngest. What had I done?

Susan screamed as she came through the cabin's front door.

"My baby!" she screamed. "What have you done?!"

I couldn't answer her. I didn't know how to. Jamie came in and stopped in the cabin's doorway. Her face was pale as she took in the scene before her eyes.

I screamed out as Susan pulled Ava's body away from me and cradled it in her own arms.

"Daddy?" said Jamie from the doorway where she'd just stopped in her tracks. Her voice was shaking.

"My baby! My baby! What have you done!" Susan kept wailing over and over again.

"I'm sorry," I wept with my head in my hands; tears flowing uncontrollably.

"Call someone!" Susan demanded. "Make it better! Make it better!" she screamed.

Jamie dropped to her knees and started to weep, her black mascara running down her pale face, as what happened slowly started to sink in.

"Don't just sit there!" screamed Susan. "Call someone!"

"I'm sorry," I cried as I tried to put a comforting arm around Susan.

"Don't fucking touch me!" she screamed. The anguish and hatred in her voice flowing through every syllable.

"I'm sorry," I repeated.

I stood up and staggered out of the cabin, into the bright daylight of the warm Saturday morning. I didn't even manage to get off the porch before I threw up over the side, into the foliage below. I've killed my daughter. I've killed my daughter. I desperately wanted to forget...Block out the pain...But the screams of Susan's pain and the whimpering of Jamie, from the doorway, refused me the luxury of forgetting and pretending it never happened. I need to call someone. I need to get help. I ran over to the car...I didn't even hear them pull up...It was an accident....Had I known it was them...I opened the car door, which must have banged shut when they climbed out, and reached into the passenger seat to grab my cellphone. I flipped it open and pressed '9' on the keypad. I stopped.

Who am I supposed to call? Who can make this all better? No one can. There's no one. No one can bring little Ava back to life. No one can erase the pain Susan, Jamie and I will feel for the rest of our lives. No one can take away the image of the bullet piercing the front of Ava's face and the look of shock in her eyes. No one can fix this. They'll never forgive me. I'll never forgive myself. Our lives will never be the same again. I've destroyed them for good. People won't believe what happened during the night to make me feel on edge. They won't. They'll just know I killed my daughter. And, if I did that, I must have killed the store clerk too. Josh wins. He'll get away with it. They probably won't even know he was even in the store when the gun went off. They'll pin it all on the city-man. I've lost everything. I've destroyed everything.

I'm not crying anymore. I'm in shock. Nothing can fix this. Where do we go from here? How do we move on? I sat for a moment with only the sounds of the girls screaming keeping me from being in complete silence.

"I'm sorry," I whispered.

Moments later I knew what needed to be done. I know how to take the pain away. It's the only way. I climbed from the car and walked back to the cabin. I passed Jamie who was still crying in the doorway and I tried to block the image of Susan cradling Ava as I stepped past them and across to the bedroom. With no hesitation I picked the gun up. This is the only way I know how to take their pain away. This is the only way. I'll have to be quick. I'll have to make it quick. They don't deserve any of this. The least I can do is make it so they don't know what happened.

"What did you do?!" Susan screamed from the other room.

I walked back to where she was huddled over Ava and apologized once more. I raised the gun to Jamie first and pulled the trigger. I shot her straight through the head; the force of the bullet sending her out of the cabin's doorway and onto the porch. Susan screamed.

"I'm sorry," I whispered. The shame oozing through the tone of my voice. "I'll always love you. I'm sorry." I turned the gun on Susan. Her final scream was cut short with the sound of a bang. She slumped over Ava's body. I just stood there, for a moment, as I took in my actions. Seconds later, without even realizing I had started, I was screaming at the top of my lungs.

This isn't my fault. This isn't my fault. It's whoever was tormenting me through the night. Whatever was tormenting me. If they had just left me alone, I'd have had no reason to have kept the gun so close to my side. Ava would have run into the room and into my loving arms. Susan and Jamie would have followed. Why did they even come back? Why? They weren't supposed to come back. They were supposed to wait for me to call them. Susan must have known I didn't have the numbers because my phone was on the seat. She must have come back to find me. She must have come back to make sure everything was okay. To make sure I was okay. Maybe her mum and dad weren't in and they had had no choice but to come back? I screamed again.

"Please forgive me...Please..."

I walked through to my dad's office and slumped down in his old chair. I looked down to the picture of my dad and me, for one final time. The picture had been changed again. My face had the eyes crossed out too, along with a scar drawn down my neck. I didn't care how or why? Not anymore. I was past caring. I raised the gun to my head. As well as the cold metal of the gun, against my temple, I felt the horrible feeling of warm breath against the back of my neck. I didn't care anymore. I was numb to it all.

"Please forgive me," I whispered.

I squeezed the trigger.

CLICK!

"NO! PLEASE! NO!"

I pulled the trigger again.

CLICK!

No. It can't be. It can't.

CLICK!

It's empty. It can't be. Please God no. Let me finish it. Please. I frantically started squeezing the trigger again and again and again on the off-chance there was, somewhere, one final bullet in the chamber. I know I hadn't fired them all. I know I didn't. There should have been one left. There should have been one left. I wept as I realized the gun couldn't have been fully loaded in the first place. Come on, keep squeezing the trigger. There must be one left. There has to be one left. Come on, please. Please don't do this to me. I've been through enough. Please...

CLICK!

CLICK!

CLICK!

I screamed as loud as I could.

~ FIN

PREVIOUSLY...

I opened my eyes. I was face down on the bedroom's wooden floorboards. I must have blacked out; the shock of what was happening too much for my body to take. As soon as I realized where I was I sat up and cast my eyes around the room. It's empty. I'm alone again. I must have been unconscious for some time as daylight is spilling in from the window on the side of the room. Thank God for that. I need to get out of here. It's over...

BANG!

No. It can't be. It came from the front of the cabin this time. What do they want? It's daylight now. They must know it's over. They must do. My dad used to tell me things only went bump in the night.

I heard footsteps across the front of the porch. Will they ever leave me alone? A knocking on the front door followed. No. I'm not having it. I'm not. I looked to the floor and spotted the gun. Without giving it any hesitation I grabbed it and aimed it at the door.

"I'm in here!" I called out. "Come and get me!"

Footsteps across the floorboards in the other room. The door opened and I pulled the trigger.

BANG!

I screamed and dropped the gun. It hit the floor before Ava's body did. My daughter. My beautiful daughter. She fell backwards with blood trickling from the front of her delicate face. What have I done? What have I done?

"Baby?!" I called out as I scrambled over to her lifeless body.

More footsteps from outside which sounded as though they were running towards where I was sat, cradling the body of my youngest. What had I done?

Susan screamed as she came through the cabin's front door.

"My baby!" she screamed. "What have you done?!"

I couldn't answer her. I didn't know how to. Jamie came in and stopped in the cabin's doorway. Her face was pale as she took in the scene before her eyes.

I screamed out as Susan pulled Ava's body away from me and cradled it in her own arms.

"Daddy?" said Jamie from the doorway where she'd just stopped in her tracks. Her voice was shaking.

"My baby! My baby! What have you done!" Susan kept wailing over and over again.

"I'm sorry," I wept with my head in my hands; tears flowing uncontrollably.

"Call someone!" Susan demanded. "Make it better! Make it better!" she screamed.

Jamie dropped to her knees and started to weep, her black mascara running down her pale face, as what happened slowly started to sink in.

"Don't just sit there!" screamed Susan. "Call someone!"

"I'm sorry," I cried as I tried to put a comforting arm around Susan.

"Don't fucking touch me!" she screamed. The anguish and hatred in her voice flowing through every syllable.

"I'm sorry," I repeated.

I stood up and staggered out of the cabin, into the bright daylight of the warm Saturday morning. I didn't even manage to get off the porch before I threw up over the side, into the foliage below. I've killed my daughter. I've killed my daughter. I desperately wanted to forget...Block out the pain...But the screams of Susan's pain and the whimpering of Jamie, from the doorway, refused me the luxury of forgetting and pretending it never happened. I need to call someone. I need to get help. I ran over to the car...I didn't even hear them pull up...It was an accident....Had I known it was them...I opened the car door, which must have banged shut when they climbed out, and reached into the passenger seat to grab my cellphone. I flipped it open and pressed '9' on the keypad. I stopped.

Who am I supposed to call? Who can make this all better? No one can. There's no one. No one can bring little Ava back to life. No one can erase the pain Susan, Jamie and I will feel for the rest of our lives. No one can take away the image of the bullet piercing the front of Ava's face and the look of shock in her eyes. No one can fix this. They'll never forgive me. I'll never forgive myself. Our lives will never be the same again. I've destroyed them for good. People won't believe what happened during the night to make me feel on edge. They won't. They'll just know I killed my daughter. And, if I did that, I must have killed the store clerk too. Josh wins. He'll get away with it. They probably won't even know he was even in the store when the gun went off. They'll pin it all on the city-man. I've lost everything. I've destroyed everything.

I'm not crying anymore. I'm in shock. Nothing can fix this. Where do we go from here? How do we move on? I sat for a moment with only the sounds of the girls screaming keeping me from being in complete silence.

"I'm sorry," I whispered.

Moments later I knew what needed to be done. I know how to take the pain away. It's the only way. I climbed from the car and walked back to the cabin. I passed Jamie who was still crying in the doorway and I tried to block the image of Susan cradling Ava as I stepped past them and across to the bedroom. With no hesitation I picked the gun up. This is the only way I know how to take their pain away. This is the only way. I'll have to be quick. I'll have to make it quick. They don't deserve any of this. The least I can do is make it so they don't know what happened.

"What did you do?!" Susan screamed from the other room.

I walked back to where she was huddled over Ava and apologized once more. I raised the gun to Jamie first and pulled the trigger. I shot her straight through the head; the force of the bullet sending her out of the cabin's doorway and onto the porch. Susan screamed.

"I'm sorry," I whispered. The shame oozing through the tone of my voice. "I'll always love you. I'm sorry." I turned the gun on Susan. Her final scream was cut short with the sound of a bang. She slumped over Ava's body. I just stood there, for a moment, as I took in my actions. Seconds later, without even realizing I had started, I was screaming at the top of my lungs.

This isn't my fault. This isn't my fault. It's whoever was tormenting me through the night. Whatever was tormenting me. If they had just left me alone, I'd have had no reason to have kept the gun so close to my side. Ava would have run into the room and into my loving arms. Susan and Jamie would have followed. Why did they even come back? Why? They weren't supposed to come back. They were supposed to wait for me to call them. Susan must have known I didn't have the numbers because my phone was on the seat. She must have come back to find me. She must have come back to make sure everything was okay. To make sure I was okay. Maybe her mum and dad weren't in and they had had no choice but to come back? I screamed again.

"Please forgive me...Please..."

I walked through to my dad's office and slumped down in his old chair. I looked down to the picture of my dad and me, for one final time. The picture had been changed again. My face had the eyes crossed out too, along with a scar drawn down my neck. I didn't care how or why. Not anymore. I was past caring. I raised the gun to my head. As well as the cold metal of the gun against my temple, I felt the horrible feeling of warm breath against the back of my neck. I didn't care anymore. I was numb to it all.

"Please forgive me," I whispered.

I squeezed the trigger.

CLICK!

"NO! PLEASE! NO!"

I pulled the trigger again.

CLICK!

No. It can't be. It can't.

CLICK!

It's empty. It can't be. Please God no. Let me finish it. Please. I frantically started squeezing the trigger again and again and again on the off-chance there was, somewhere, one final bullet in the chamber. I know I hadn't fired them all. I know I didn't. There should have been one left. There should have been one left. I wept as I realized the gun couldn't have been fully loaded in the first place. Come on, keep squeezing the trigger. There must be one left. There has to be one left. Come on, please. Please don't do this to me. I've been through enough. Please...

CLICK!

CLICK!

CLICK!

I screamed as loud as I could.

MATT SHAW'S

THE CABIN

II

'ASYLUM'

CHAPTER 1

"Daddy!" Ava's little voice whispered from somewhere in the back of my mind. I've missed her dulcet tones.

I only have myself to blame.

"Daddy!" she repeated.

Is this a dream? Or is she really here trying to wake me from my nightmarish slumber?

"Daddy! Wake up!"

She's here.

She has to be.

This isn't part of whatever dream I was having.

This is real.

I know it is.

I opened my eyes. Ava's voice - nothing more than a cruel trick of my imagination. She isn't here. No one is here other than me and the jet-black spider which has made the corner of the cell its home.

I sat up and rested my back against the soft padded wall. I wonder whether the padding on the wall is to stop me from hurting myself, as they had explained when I first got here, or to drown the sounds of my banging and screaming as I beg for them to let me out; not that they ever will.

They didn't even let me attend their funeral to give them a proper goodbye. They didn't permit me to stand at the gravestone and grieve for a couple of minutes by myself. There were no goodbyes. No peace of mind for me as my family got a proper send off. None of that. I'm destined to be stuck with images of them on the cabin floor - dead forever. It's all I see when I close my eyes.

Their dead bodies.

The pools of blood.

The smell of death, lingering in the air, as smoke filtered into the atmosphere from the barrel of the still-smoking gun.

"I don't want that in the house," Susan had told me when I brought it home from the shop where I purchased it. She hated guns. She always had. I told her she had nothing to worry about. It was for peace of mind, that was all. I told her to trust me. "You know I don't like them," she had continued.

"It's just for protection," I always reminded her.

Protection.

The word echoes through my mind as I remember what her brains looked like, splattered on the walls of the wooden cabin. Her body slumped next to our daughters'.

Protection.

I was awake now. I wished I wasn't. I wished I was dead. I should be dead. I should have died in the cabin, with my family. I didn't want to live. I didn't want to live and I don't want to be awake now. When you're awake... They come for you. Even if you pretend to sleep...They know. They always know.

I jumped as a small flap on the cell's door slid open. I closed my eyes regardless.

They always know.

I sensed a cold eye staring at me. They always looked through, at an angle, so you could only see the one beady eye. Not being able to see the rest of their faces...Only seeing the one eye which was watching you so intently...It always made it worse...Always made you feel even more uncomfortable than you already were. And these rooms, with their padded walls and lack of furniture...Even their lack of bedding...There's nowhere to hide from their gaze.

"I know you're awake," a voice whispered. "I heard you move around. We thought, perhaps, you might want to answer some more questions?"

I didn't answer him. No point. It wasn't a choice I was being offered.

A key audibly went into the door's lock. A little bit of fiddling and it clicked open. No handle on this side of the door, but I knew it wouldn't be long before the door would be open. Seconds. If that. Seconds to contemplate running. Seconds to contemplate fighting him. Seconds to remember they'd have help close-by if I didn't cooperate.

Seconds.

The door opened.

The doctor stood out of sight in the corridor, giving the illusion of no-one being past the open doorway; an illusion which tempted me further into making a run for it. I know he's there though. I know he is. They're always there. I have to keep telling myself not to run. It only makes it worse.

"Come now," he whispered from the corridor.

Slowly I stood up. I hesitated for a split second before stepping into the corridor. The harsh brightness of the lighting stung my eyes. A couple more seconds to adjust. I felt a hand grip my arm and turned to see one of the doctor's helpers. They always have helpers. Another reason not to run, or to try anything. Could I take the doctor down? Yes. He's stick thin. Old. Gaunt- looking. He wouldn't put up a fight against me. Not enough of one anyway. But his helper? His helper looked as though he belonged in one of the rooms. Probably broke out and forged a career as a helper instead of getting locked up again. Twice the man I am. Literally.

The doctor led the way down the long corridor, past all the other locked doors, towards the usual room in which he questioned me. The helper walked with me, his hand never releasing its tight, unforgiving grip on my arm.

"Please," I said, "I'm feeling better now..."

Both the doctor and the helper ignored me. They always do when I tell them I'm okay now...I promise to them I don't hear screaming anymore...I promise I don't see the boy...The boy with the scar down his neck...I tell them I know it was all in my mind...The stress of what had happened in the store with the teenager and the store clerk. I promise...

They never listen. When will they listen? A real prison must surely be better than this place...

I'm supposed to be here whilst they see if I'm fit enough to stand trial. I want to be fit enough. I want to stand trial. I'll plead guilty. I know what I have done. I was the one who pulled the trigger...Just let me out of here.

Let me out.

"Take a seat," the doctor said. He didn't need to. I knew the procedure and, even if I didn't, the helper was on hand to push me into the only seat opposite the doctor's table and chair.

I sat down.

"So..." the doctor continued. He leant forward and pressed a red button on a tape deck which rested on his desk. "From the top..." He sat back in his chair and waited for me to tell him my story. It was the same story I had told him on numerous other occasions.

The story that no one believed.

The story which led me to this hell-hole.

"I made a mistake," I said. My voice was shaking. They seem to know everything. Will they know I'm about to lie? If so - did they know before I did that I'd try it on?

"Go on," the doctor urged me. His face was expressionless. If he did know I was lying, he didn't let on. I looked at his helper - his face, also, expressionless.

"I think...I was tired. The drive here was long."

"I can imagine. The traffic can be quite heavy on that route..."

I shifted uneasily in my seat. They know I'm lying. I know they do. How long will they let me continue?

"And..." I stuttered. Damn. Pull yourself together. "And I was stressed from what happened..."

"At the store..."

"Yes..."

"The store clerk..."

"Yes...I was tired and stressed. I didn't sleep whilst I waited for morning to come round..."

"And why were you waiting for morning?"

"I was going to go to the Sheriff Department...Explain what happened."

"Of course. I remember now."

"I was going to..."

"And why didn't you just wait for the Sheriff, or go right there after the incident?"

My mind is blank.

I can't remember.

Why didn't I go straight there? I could have...

Wait.

My wife.

My kids...I wanted them to leave town. I didn't want them to be part of it. I didn't...

"Well?" the doctor pushed me for an answer.

"It was late. I had to walk back to town. I didn't want to walk through the woods in the darkness...Thought it best to wait until morning..."

The doctor made a funny noise in his throat. I'm not sure if he was just trying to clear some phlegm or whether it was a noise to show he understood what I meant...Perhaps he even agreed with my logic?

"Tell me about the boy. The one with the scar down his neck..."

I hesitated. I remember everything about the boy. I remember the way the stitches criss-crossed down the length of his neck, from some botched operation...I remember his dead eyes staring at me...The sound of the scream that filled my head despite seemingly not coming from his mouth. Even his smell. An earthy odour.

"I was saying, I made a mistake. I know he wasn't there. I know there was no boy."

"Oh?"

This was the first time I had denied his existence.

"It was my imagination."

"Imagination?"

"Yes. Caused, no doubt, by stress and tiredness."

"Quite an imagination you have," said the doctor. He still didn't give any indication as to whether he believed me or not. I'd rather know - one way or another - what his thoughts were.

"My dad used to tell me stories about the patients from here...They said the doctors would..." I went quiet. No point going into it. I don't want to upset him after all. The doctor raised an eyebrow. He looked down at a pad, on the desk near the tape recorder, and scribbled down a note with a plastic pen. I couldn't read it as much as I wanted to. Reading upside down wasn't a strength of mine.

"The stories featured a boy with a scar down his neck?"

I nodded.

"And a scream?"

I nodded again.

"You said, when you first got here, that you only had a year left to live. You explained that, if you heard the scream of one of the asylum's ghosts... You'd die in a year. Your notes..." the doctor opened a file, the last item on the desk, and cast his eye down the first sheet, "...You linked that little story to your father's heart attack, didn't you? You told my colleague that he heard the scream, when you didn't, and a year later he was dead."

I forgot I had told them that.

"Coincidence," I said after a slight pause.

"Hmmm."

The doctor scribbled something else down on the pad of paper. I wish I could see what it said. I might have been able to use it to my advantage.

Might have.

"The locals, around the town, they speak of similar stories..."

"I know," I said. "I remember one of them telling my dad."

"Emphasis on the word 'stories'. You know they are just that?"

I nodded. "Yes. I was confused."

"So now you're saying you didn't see any ghosts?"

I nodded again. Still no expression on the doctor's face. I still couldn't tell if he believed me or not.

"We have a test..." he looked up at the helper. I, in turn, shot him a glance. The helper didn't give anything away. He just stood perfectly still.

The doctor turned his attention back to me. "We have a test which tells us whether you're lying or not."

"A lie detector test?" I asked.

The doctor showed his yellow, nicotine-stained teeth as he smiled.

"Yes," he continued, "a lie detector test…"

"Okay…?"

"Would you be willing to cooperate with such a test?"

I hesitated for a second before nodding. I've heard there is a way of beating lie detector tests but I've never heard the exact method needed. I'll just have to try my best to convince the machine I'm telling the truth. The fact the doctor wants me to take the test…Surely he must think I'm telling the truth or else he wouldn't have volunteered the test. I just hope I have as much luck with the machine. If I can fool that, too, then I am one step closer to getting out of here. A real jail has to be better than this. It has to be.

"Well okay then," said the doctor. His eyes lit up brightly as though my cooperation gave him a sense of satisfaction. A feeling of unease creeps through my body.

To my side, the helper stepped over to the doctor and handed him something out of his shirt pocket. What was that? Whatever it was, the doctor cupped it closely, in the palm of his hand. I'm not sure whether he just doesn't want to drop whatever it is or whether he is actively trying to hide it from my sight.

Is this part of the test?

The helper stepped behind me and suddenly grabbed my arms.

"What is this?" I demanded. My heart was beating harder and faster than I had ever felt it before. Harder than when I first saw the boy, even.

No one answered me.

The helper pushed my arms forward so that my hands were on the doctor's table.

"Please try not to move," the doctor said, "and we'll begin the test."

He opened his clenched fist to reveal a small pile of pins.

"What are you doing?" I asked; the panic was clearly audible in my voice.

The doctor took one of the first pins and positioned it under the nail of my small finger, on my left hand. The other pins were positioned, in the same way, under my other nails as the he explained what he was doing.

"This is the test," he said. His voice was quiet and slow of speech as he concentrated on where best to stick the pins, "it will tell me if you're lying or not."

"What are you talking about? How so?" I turned back to the helper who kept my arms locked in position despite my best efforts to break free from his grip. "Get the fuck off of me..."

"Once the pins are in place..." the doctor continued, "...we then hit them with the edge of your folder..."

"You're insane..."

"You're the one seeing ghosts," the doctor bit back. "This is a tried and tested method for revealing liars...Are you a liar, Craig?" He looked up at me. His once bright eyes looked a darker shade of black now.

Don't admit you were lying.

Don't tell him you did see the boy.

Don't.

He's bluffing.

He's a professional.

He wouldn't do this.

He wouldn't.

"I was tired and confused," I insisted.

"Well then...We hit the pins with the edge of your folder..." He picked up the folder of notes, from the table, and positioned it against the pins. "If you scream...You're lying...If you're telling the truth...You will remain silent."

"You're insane," I said again. I could feel the sweat beading on my forehead but still refused to admit I was lying. I have to try everything to get out of here; everything to convince them I'm well enough to stand trial for what I did. Anything and everything.

With no more words the doctor swung the folder into the pins which, in turn pushed deep underneath my finger nails. As the agonizing pain tore through my body I couldn't help but scream...

CHAPTER 2

I was standing at the edge of the forest. The lake was in front of me, along with my family; two daughters and my loving wife. I couldn't see them. I could just hear their laughter as they enjoyed the last bit of sunshine the clear blue skies offered them, on our weekend vacation. Splashing noises, coming from somewhere at the edge of the lake's crystal blue waters, were audible between the infectious fits of giggles.

I couldn't help but smile despite knowing none of this was real. It was just a dream - one happy scenario of many that I had thought about since what had happened in the cabin. This is what the weekend should have been about; my wife and kids enjoying themselves whilst I worked on my book, back at the cabin, before joining them to share in with the fun, laughter and memories to cherish in the years to come.

I stepped into the clearing and headed towards the small bushes a little further down the banks of the lake. I couldn't see past the foliage but presumed my family must be playing just beyond them as there was nowhere else for them to be so hidden.

As I neared the bushes I was able to see over the top of them. There they were, playing on the edge of the water; my family.

"Hey!" I shouted. They didn't respond. "Room for one more?" I called out, a little louder, as I continued to move towards them.

Again, they didn't respond.

I got to the bushes. I didn't realise they were so thick. There must be a way around them. The kids may have crawled through them but not Susan. She'd have wanted to go around them; especially if she were the one lugging all the bags as I suspect she was.

"*Fuck it*," I whispered.

I dropped to my knees and started to crawl through the undergrowth.

Thankfully there are no brambles.

No bugs as of yet either.

Also a good thing.

As I got to the other end, I pushed through with my hands followed by my head. I could see the clearing but I couldn't see Susan, or my daughters, Ava and Jamie.

I could still hear them though; laughing and having fun. It's strange. When I'm awake I struggle to recall the sound of their voices, even their laughter. It's as though my memory is punishing me for what I had done by taking the sounds away from me. At least, in my dreams, I can still hear them. Even if they are short lived.

"Honey?!" I called out. I stood up and looked around. I could see them, playing in the water just off a wooden pier which ran from the bank of the lake. Ava was hanging onto the edge of a small rowing boat, her way of staying afloat - with the added aid of inflatables around her arms. She was kicking back with her legs causing large splashes to go over her mum and sister. She was in hysterics while they were screaming as more and more water soaked them. I couldn't help but laugh. I'll run up the pier and jump in next to them...I'll soak them all.

I removed my tee shirt and kicked my shoes off. I was only wearing shorts now and it didn't matter if they were to get wet. Besides, with this sun, they'll soon dry. With any luck they haven't seen me yet and I can surprise them all. I crept onto the pier's wooden floorboards, making sure to keep low, and dropped my shirt. By the time I looked back up my family were gone from view.

I looked around.

They've gone.

They couldn't have come out of the water.

I would have seen them!

"Susan?" I called out.

Nothing.

"Ava? Honey?"

Again, there was no reply.

"Ava!" I repeated louder this time.

Although they had disappeared, I was used to it. This always happened in my dreams. You'd think I'd learn from the many dreams I've had since that day, but I never do. I'll keep looking for them and I'll never find them. They're there one minute and gone the next. The strange thing about this dream, this time, though...There're no sounds other than the sound of my own breathing.

The trees were swaying gently indicating a breeze but I couldn't hear the wind rustling the many leaves. Even my footsteps on the wooden boards made no noise as I continued to walk to where my family had been playing. There was nothing. It was as though the world had been muted.

I came to the edge of the pier, next to where the boat had been tied. No sign of my family. The water wasn't clear anymore - it was a murky colour - hard to see anything under the surface. They wouldn't be down there. They wouldn't have gone under. I know they wouldn't have. One could have but not all three of them. Especially Jamie, the eldest daughter, she's a strong swimmer.

No.

They definitely aren't down there.

So why am I being drawn to the ripples dancing across the water?

Come on, I know they're not in there.

I know they're not struggling for air, out of sight, in the murky depths.

Walk away.

I called out for my wife again but no words managed to escape my mouth; not just the world that was on mute.

Mute?

I couldn't take my eyes away from the water.

What if they're under the water?

What if they're thrashing around, stuck in weeds?

What if they're screaming for my help but also on mute?

I know they're not.

I know it.

I know I'm going to jump into the water and find nothing.

I never find them once they vanish.

Yet...I have to go in there...

I jumped into the water and immediately ducked my head underneath the murky surface. Despite the water stinging my eyes, I did my best to keep them open on the off chance I could see anything which resembled the shapes of my family. I couldn't see anything though. Not because they weren't there, for sure...Just because it was too dark.

Running out of air.

I broke the surface of the lake, still in mute, and took a large gulp of air before ducking under again. Just once I wished I could find them. Just once I wished my dream would have a happy ending. It would have made sense for a happy ending considering the state of my life. I was always led to believe dreams worked in reverse; if you had a bad dream - in your waking life you'd have good fortune - and if you had a good dream...In the real world, you'd be in for a rough time. That being said, I was also told that if you lost your teeth in your dreams, it was supposed to mean you were soon to be losing some friends. Well I've had the 'teeth' dreams and I've never lost friends afterwards.

Back under the water, I still couldn't see anything. They can't be here though. I know they can't. It wouldn't have made sense for all of them to suddenly slip under without as much as a scream of alarm. I could understand if it were just Ava who was missing, what with her being the youngest - and weakest - of the three but...Not all of them.

I broke the surface again.

Damn dirty water is stinging my eyes. I shut them as tight as I could in a hope to cleanse them. Can't feel it working. A few more seconds of trying to force the water from my eyes and I slowly opened them once more - I half expected them to start stinging again.

As soon as my vision cleared I saw the boy directly in front of me. He looked just as he did in the cabin. The same dead look in his black eyes. The same scar down his throat. He opened his mouth...

The world was no longer in mute as his terrifying scream filled my head.

⋏

I woke with a start just as I always did. I don't know why. I should be used to it now; used to him appearing from out of nowhere. It's the same every night. Every dream.

Did my dad go through this, too, on the lead up to his death?

Do I have a year left like he did?

A year before a fateful heart attack steals my life?

A year being haunted by what I've done?

I'd rather die now.

"You okay?"

I jumped again at the sound of a female voice. I rolled onto my side, on the padded floor, and looked towards the door. A woman in her mid to late twenties was crouched in the doorway. Despite asking if I was okay she didn't look too concerned either way.

She asked again, "You okay?"

I sat up and leaned back against the wall, my favourite position in this little box room of mine.

"It looked like you were having a nightmare." She barely stopped for a breath, "They look sore," she continued. She was looking at my fingers.

They felt sore too.

"I've not seen you before," she said.

The gown she was wearing, the blank expression on her pretty face - a look achieved through a high dosage of medication - all signs she wasn't one of the many doctors who patrolled the area. Not a guarantee though. Some of the doctors here...The way they act...I often wonder if there's substances flowing through their sadistic veins.

"Are you coming out today?" she asked.

Every day we had the opportunity to leave our cell to go to the day room; a room filled with various tables and chairs, a television in the corner of the room which was hidden behind a cage to avoid being damaged if a fight ever broke out, board games - no doubt with pieces missing...A nurses' station in the corner of the room, which led onto a larger - and plusher - office in which they were able to relax. It was from this station that they issued the meds out at a certain time.

In a room full of crazy, I'd rather stay in my cell.

"There's a card game happening."

If she wanted to tempt me to leave the relative safety of my cell, she was going to have to do better than a card game.

"I heard you killed your family. That true?"

I shot her a look and tried my best not to react to what she said. It's one thing having to go over the same story again and again with the doctors. I didn't need to relive the experience with a crazy too.

She crept into the room and leaned against the wall opposite me. For the first time ever I wished they left the cell doors closed for the people who didn't want to leave them; the people who wanted to keep some privacy in their already ruined lives.

"Vicky."

I presumed that was her name.

I didn't respond with mine as I didn't plan on being here long enough to make any new friends. We both sat there, in silence, for what seemed to be an eternity. It reality it was probably a few seconds but everything here... Everything seems to go on for longer than what it actually is - including uncomfortable silences.

"Look, I'm sorry," I said when I could no longer take her impenetrable stare, "I'd like to be by myself," I finished.

"You want to convince them you're not broken?" She must have sensed my look of confusion as she went on to explain, "The doctors...If you want to convince them you're okay to leave, you need to act normal. Locking yourself away in a small room isn't what they'd consider normal," she said. "You do want to get out, don't you?"

I didn't answer her. It seemed as though she already had the answers; sometimes before she'd actually have the question.

"They say you want to leave. They say you don't belong here."

"They say a lot," I said - more or less to myself as I struggled to hide the fact this stranger was annoying me.

She smiled at me, "Come on, I'll show you around." She clambered to her feet and offered her hand to help me to my mine.

Maybe, leaving the room will help convince the doctors I'm okay to leave?

Whatever.

One thing it will show them is that I'm not scared of them.

Especially after last night.

I'm not scared of them.

I'm not.

"You should be," Vicky whispered in my ear.

Chapter 3

always envisioned places such as this asylum, to be clinical - with their white walls, white floors, various security points and reception desks - due to the nature of what they were about. Inoffensive colours so as not to antagonise the patients, everything white so it was easier to keep clean when the janitors passed through with their mops and buckets. Security points just in case of trouble breaking out. Reception desks to help the few, and far between, visitors when they came to see a loved one or near-forgotten friend...I just thought they might have stretched to a few paintings to make the place feel more homely and a little less clinical; something, I'm sure, which would help the patients settle in easier. Perhaps, even, paintings - or sculptures - made by some of the inmates here during one of the many arts and craft lessons I'd heard the doctors and nurses seemed to favour.

I was following Vicky as she led the way to the day care room; a room I had caught a glimpse of on the many walks to the doctors' rooms. A room I had never had the inclination to visit on my own. Vicky was relishing the opportunity to be the perfect tour guide; telling me about anything and everything as we passed what she believed to be points of interest - one of which was a dirty-looking drinking fountain in one of the many aged corridors. She informed me the water tasted funny from here. I didn't have the heart to tell her I wouldn't have sipped from it if I were dying of thirst and my miserable life counted on it.

We turned into the day room.

"And here we are."

It looked the same as when I had first caught a glimpse of it; various patients sat around at the tables - some playing games whilst others simply dribbled on themselves - nurses working at the station, behind the glass shield at the back of the room, a television - not switched on - in the far corner of the room, attached to the wall by a rusty looking mount and tucked behind a protective cage which would surely obscure most of the picture had it been showing anything.

"Did you want to play a game?" asked Vicky. "They have quite a good collection."

I shook my head.

"How did you kill them?"

"What?"

I wasn't sure whether Vicky even knew how blunt she was being. Her small, dilated pupils hinted she wouldn't care though, nor remember the following morning.

"They have Snakes and Ladders," she continued.

I shook my head again.

"You shot them, huh?"

"Daddy!" I heard a faint whisper from the doorway and turned to see Ava standing there, a trickle of blood running down the centre of her forehead. She didn't wait for an answer, she turned her back on me - the back of her head was a bloody mess. She whispered my name again and disappeared around the corner.

"What's wrong?" asked Vicky.

I didn't answer her. I stood up and walked towards the door where I had seen my daughter. Beyond the door was a corridor. It looked different compared to the way it had looked when Vicky and I just walked down it. Darker. Colder. So cold, in fact, that I could see my breath as I exhaled.

"Ava?" I called out.

One by one the overhead fluorescent lights switched off plunging me into near darkness. The only light was coming from the daycare room I had just left and the far end of the corridor, the only direction she could have gone in. The light, down there, was flickering on and off. One second darkness, the next it was light.

Darkness.

Light.

Darkness.

Light.

Am I asleep? I can't be. I never sleep during the day and I didn't feel tired. It's just the stress of the situation. The stress playing tricks on my already broken mind. It has to be that. None of this can be real. If it were then the others would have noticed it too - unless they're all too medicated.

Darkness.

Light.

Darkness.

Light...

"Ava?" I called out again and again. There was no answer. I turned back to the daycare room. I know I should go back in there. Go back and sit with Vicky. Ignore what is happening out here. If anyone sees me acting strangely, they'll keep me here longer and I desperately want to leave. I don't like it here.

I needn't worry about anyone noticing my odd behaviour. The quick glance I stole into the daycare room shows no one is looking. No one. I guess they're used to 'crazy' around here.

"Daddy..." another whisper. This time it came from around the corner where the light still flickered.

Darkness.

Light.

Darkness.

Light.

The pull of my daughter was too strong to ignore and I started walking down the poorly lit corridor towards the flickering light at the furthest point. I haven't even thought about what I'd do, or say, if I did bump into Ava.

I walked down the corridor and turned the corner. Another corridor. Again, all the lights were off except for the one at the other end; this one was on - not even flickering. A sign on the far wall pointed around the corner. A sign which read 'Morgue'.

None of this was here earlier when I came through with Vicky. Am I losing my mind? Is it already lost?

I froze about mid-way down the corridor. I don't want to see what Ava is leading me to. I don't. Not in the morgue. I turned back in the direction I came from only to see a sign on the wall I just passed pointing me to the morgue. What? That's not possible. That wasn't there. The daycare room is down there. Not the morgue.

"Daddy, please..." little Ava's voice sounded desperate and sent a chill down to the base of my aching spine. "Please, daddy..."

Please let her voice be in my head.

Don't let her be haunting me.

It's bad enough she's dead.

It's bad enough that I killed her.

I don't want her to be stuck.

I want her to be resting.

I want her to be at peace.

My heart sank. When do people like me get what we really want and not what we deserve?

"Ava?" I called out to her.

"Quick, daddy..." her voice was coming from around the corner in what must have been the morgue.

I can't not go.

I walked down the corridor with my heart beating hard and fast. I felt sick. What do I say to her?

The next corridor was shorter than the previous two. At the far end some double doors with a 'mortuary' sign; a window in each of the doors revealing bright light from the room beyond. It looked warmer through there. It looked deceptively inviting compared to these dark corridors.

"In here," whispered her delicate voice from behind the doors.

Slowly I walked towards them and stretched my hands out, ready to push the doors open. It'll be okay. I know it will. I know there'll be nothing in there. It'll probably be the daycare room. Yes, that'll be it. I would have walked in a big circle; my brain playing tricks on me. That girl...Vicky...She'll probably be sitting in there asking me where I went. What am I talking about? I doubt she's even noticed I've left.

I stopped next to the doors.

Okay.

This is it.

Deep breath.

I pushed the doors open.

Not the daycare room.

There were cold, metal tables lining the middle of the room. Three bodies, covered by white sheets, on the last of the tables. I swallowed hard. Harder when I noticed the trolley next to one of the tables; various sharp implements, coated in blood, laid across the top.

Slowly I walked across the room, towards the far tables. My hand was shaking - no doubt anticipating having to pull the sheets off; worried about what laid beneath.

Silly.

There's nothing to worry about. It won't be my family. They won't be here. They were buried. They had a funeral.

"Did they?" hissed a voice from behind me.

I twisted my head and saw the doctor standing in the shadows of the corner behind me, "You weren't there..." he reminded me. "Maybe we dug them up again as part of your ongoing treatment?"

"My ongoing treatment?"

"Clearly you're not well."

"I am. I told you. Everything about that night...I was stressed..."

"You were lying. You screamed. Remember? Unless..." the doctor looked to someone behind me. I turned around and saw his helper standing in the opposite corner of the room. He continued, "...Unless you want to retake the test?"

I shook my head.

"I'm supposed to be here for evaluation. You're supposed to be seeing if I'm fit enough to stand trial."

"You think you'll be leaving here?" the doctor laughed. "There's only one way you'll be leaving. You're here until we say you're mentally fit enough to leave..."

I turned my back on the doctor; my attention stolen by the three bodies lying on the tables. Would they really have dug them back up? I'm being haunted by Ava because her sleep was disturbed?

Sleep?

She's not asleep. She's dead. I killed her.

"Yes, you did..." the doctor agreed.

I turned back to him, "Why are you doing this?"

"Because people like you deserve it. To fix you, you must first realise the true nature of what you've done."

"You think I don't already know? My family is dead."

"And you need to be punished. You come here hoping for an easy path. You come here hoping you can avoid doing your time. You're mistaken. We all need to pay for our sins."

"Who is under the sheets?"

"I told you."

"You lie."

"Do I?"

"You wouldn't dig them up. There's no need."

"You need to understand what you've done."

"I do."

"You will."

"It's not them." I turned to the tables and slowly walked towards them. It won't be them under there. It'll probably be some of the other patients; people who have succumbed to madness or the various cruel tests performed on them by the just as mad doctors. I'll prove it's not them. I'll prove he's lying.

I was standing next to the tables now and the dirtied sheets - stained with blood, potentially caused by the wounds on the bodies. The smell is rancid. Whoever's underneath smells as though they've been under there for a while. I held my breath; not only to stop the smell invading my nostrils but also to try and hide my nerves from the doctor and his helper.

Need to be strong.

Need to be brave.

I just need to pull one of the sheets back.

Just one of them will reveal it's not my family underneath.

Just one.

"What are you waiting for? Take a look at what you've done." asked the doctor.

I closed my eyes and took a hold of the sheet with my left hand. A second later and I gave the sheet a sharp tug. Whoever was underneath was clearly visible now. All I had to do was open my eyes. Just one, even. A quick look and then I can close them again.

A quick look.

Five seconds.

I'll open my eyes in five seconds.

Four.

Three.

Two...

One.

I opened my eyes and screamed as I looked at the table; a loud scream which echoed around the room even after it had been cut short when I realised there was nothing on the table. No body. Nothing. Not even a sheet in my hand although I didn't recall letting go of it. I turned to the doctor only to notice he was no longer standing in the room. Neither was his helper. There was no one. I turned to the other tables - also empty.

"What the hell is going on?"

The tray of bloodied equipment wasn't even there anymore. There was nothing. The room was derelict. Even the paint, once white and clinical looking, was now peeling off the walls and looking aged.

I shut my eyes again.

This isn't happening.

This is impossible.

None of this is real.

"What are you doing?" Vicky asked.

Slowly I opened my eyes. I was standing in the mortuary still. The walls were once again coated in fresh white paint. The tables which lined the room were more or less empty with the exception of one of them - the one I was standing in front of. The body of a young boy laid open it. His eyes fixed to the ceiling, skin pale and puffy looking. A terrible scar running down the centre of his neck.

"What are you doing?" Vicky asked again. "You'll get in trouble if they find you in here. And put that back over him..." she nodded towards my hand - a sheet securely in its grip.

"Did you see the doctor?"

Vicky shook her head.

"He was just in here. I was just talking to him."

"I just followed you from the daycare room. He wasn't here. Look, we really can't be seen in here. We need to leave." I looked back to the boy. He was staring right at me - his eyes unblinking.

"Who is he?" I asked.

"I don't know. I've not seen him before," said Vicky. "I'm going. You should come with me."

I put the sheet over the boy - choosing to ignore his gaze - and stepped away.

"Am I losing my mind?" I asked her.

"If you're in here - you've already lost it."

Chapter 4

I was lying on the padded floor in my small cell trying to get my head around what had happened in the mortuary. I couldn't figure out how I even got there; the way back to the daycare room, led by Vicky, was completely different to the route I had taken to get to the mortuary in the first place. I looked around, on the way back, hoping to see the route Ava led me down earlier but I couldn't. There were no other obvious routes I could have come down. Nothing made any sense to me anymore. The only thing I knew for sure was what I had done and the mess I was in now.

Maybe I am insane like the doctors believe. Not just the doctors either. Other people must think I am too or else I wouldn't have been sent here. The Sheriff would have taken me straight to the courthouse.

"Why are you doing this to me?" I whispered.

I knew he was there. Not sure how he got in the room - now the door was closed, and locked, for the night - but, even so, I knew he was there; the faint wheezing noise coming from his mouth gave him away. I didn't look at him as I knew he'd only point at me and scream; he does it every time I catch his gaze.

"Why can't you leave me alone?" I felt my eyes start to well up, not that I wanted to cry in front of...him?

Does a ghost count as a 'him'?

Or an 'it'?

If I did start to weep would it leave me in peace?

Would it make this nightmare end?

I turned my back on it and closed my eyes as I felt a shift in the padded floor as it walked closer to me. Another shift in the padded floor. What's it doing? A cold hand went around my chest. Seconds later, a cold body snuggled in behind me.

"I'm scared, daddy. I don't like it here."

"Ava?"

I opened my eyes. The hand holding the front of my chest has painted nails - a pretty pink colour - Ava's favourite colour. I immediately rolled over to offer her comfort; reassure her that everything is going to be okay.

Not Ava.

A cruel trick.

The boy opened his mouth. His eyes went wide. His scream filled the small room; not even drowned out by my own scream. I closed my eyes - the best way to make him disappear. Seconds later I realised I was the only one screaming in the room. I opened my eyes. Alone again.

My heart skipped a beat - just as it was starting to settle once more - when the small flap on the door slid open. The doctor's beady little eye staring at me with a look of contempt.

"You'll wake the other patients," he hissed.

"I'm sorry," I stuttered. "I had a nightmare." He didn't need to know I saw the boy again. "I didn't mean to."

"Seeing as you're awake...What say we conduct another interview?"

"Please - I'm tired."

The privacy screen slid across, blocking the doctor from my view once more. I heard the lock click back into place just before the door opened. As usual the doctor hid out of view giving false hopes of a forbidden freedom.

I hesitated for a moment. If I stay here, will he just close the door again and lock me back in?

"Come now," the doctor hissed.

So much for being left alone. I reluctantly clambered up to my feet and left my cell. My cell? I wonder how long it will be my cell for. I fear it will be forever if these people have their way.

Nothing less than I deserve, I guess.

They think the same - the doctors - they think I deserve this.

I know they do.

I killed my family.

My daughters.

Ava was only six.

Six years old and, thanks to me, she'll never have another birthday.

None of them will.

Same room as the last time I had a proper sit down conversation with the doctor. My notes are still on the table as are the pins he had previously inserted underneath my finger nails. I wonder whether they're there to serve as a painful reminder to what he's capable of if he believes I'm lying.

"Why did you lie to me?" I asked the doctor. I wasn't sure if I was going to say anything knowing the lengths they're willing to go to make things uncomfortable for me but I couldn't leave it.

"I beg your pardon?"

"You said you had dug them up. In the mortuary. You said. My family. You said you dug them up. Why would you say that?"

The doctor didn't say anything. He just raised an eyebrow. After what seemed to be a lengthy pause he reminded me, "I'm asking the questions thank you."

I didn't know what to say back to him. Should I have argued? Would that have made me appear saner or would it simply have fueled their fears that I'm not fit enough to leave here?

An impossible situation.

"What have you been telling your new friend?" he asked; a stern look upon his face.

"My new friend?"

"A Miss Victoria Sheldon..."

My new friend? Is she my friend? Have I allowed myself to have a friend? She's certainly comforting to have around. There's something about her. She reminds me of my childhood. There was a person, back then, who I had nearly forgotten about. Even now I can only vaguely remember how they made me feel when I was scared; they made me feel as though everything was going to be okay. They made me feel like nothing could touch me. I'm not sure why, or how, but Vicky makes me feel the same way. She's a little silver lining in an otherwise grey world.

After she led me away from the mortuary we had gone back to the daycare room and, for some reason, I ended up telling her everything. I confessed my crimes, I told her about the boy - the ex-patient with the stolen scream - I even told her how I keep seeing him and hearing the scream in the real world and not just in my dreams. The same cursed scream my father heard. The scream, the locals said, which meant you only had a year left to live. She didn't laugh at me. She didn't even give an impression she thought I was mad, unlike the supposed professionals working here.

"Well?" the doctor demanded - the coldness in his harsh voice ripping me back to the present.

"I don't know what you're talking about," I said. I should just tell him. I know I should. I shouldn't play games with them. I should have learnt from yesterday. I should have learnt from the pins forced under my nails - which still feel tender.

"Some of the patients here are fragile people..." the doctor said, "...some of them are going through a strict rehabilitation program. Some of them," he continued, "are a lost cause. Regardless of their mental state..."

"I didn't say anything to her..." I pushed the lie further. Is my subconscious trying to get me punished?

"...They don't need you filling their impressionable minds with your far-fetched stories..."

"I didn't!" I protested again. Not really a lie. To me it wasn't a farfetched story. It was the truth. Just as, if she had wanted to tell me anything about herself, she wouldn't have been lying to me. To us the reasons we're in here are all very real.

"Would you be willing to take a lie detector test?"

I shook my head.

"You told her about the boy?"

I nodded.

"What did you say exactly?"

"I can't remember."

"There's a test we can perform to help you remember..."

"I just told her I had seen him. I told her about the scream. I said it was a ghost story the locals told my father one day. That's all..."

Nicotine-stained yellow teeth; the bottom row look a little browner today. The doctor leaned closed to me. His breath was as bad as you'd imagine it to be. An unpleasant pungency caused, no doubt, by a heavy diet of cigarettes, coffee and digestive biscuits. I tried my best not to react to it. "You understand how telling someone as sensitive as she is could be dangerous?" I nodded. I'm not sure whether it's more dangerous for me or whether it's more dangerous for her. "We can't have the inmates thinking there are ghosts floating through the corridors of their safe-haven."

I tried not to laugh. Safe-haven? There are war-zones, around the world, which would have a safer feel than this Hell-hole.

"I just hope you haven't caused her any lasting damage." He sat back on his chair and sighed deeply, "We've had a meeting about you today," the doctor continued - the tone in his voice changed. "It seemed only right considering that you're adamant that you're cured and ready to stand trial for your crimes...."

I foolishly raised my hopes. Could tonight be my final night here?

"We agree..." the doctor paused and shifted his yellow fingers through the files of notes they had compiled on me, "...you're not fit to stand trial. All this talk of ghosts, the fact you think you only have a year left to live... You seem more concerned about the supernatural than the fact that you butchered your own family...And the store clerk..."

"I didn't kill the store clerk." My heart sank.

"Regardless. It's obvious to my colleagues - and I agree - that you're not well and need to stay with us for the foreseeable future..."

I tried to hide my tears and frustration but am unsure on how best to react; should I get upset at the thought of staying here? Should I get angry? Is that how a sane person would react or an insane person? Should I start shouting that I'm fit enough to leave here and stand trial for my crimes? Should I...How does a sane person react to news like that and, more to the point, who's the one who decided, in the first place, the rules and regulations set apart for how sane, and insane, people react? What's to say the person who made the rules up was sane themselves? They could have been wrong.

"You don't think I feel bad for what I've done to my family? I wanted to die right there with them..."

"Ah yes, lack of bullets wasn't it?" the doctor said. I could tell from his tone of voice he was mocking me. Was he goading me into a fight with him?

"Fuck you. You don't think I feel bad? You don't think I see my family? You don't think I hear their voices...I do. Every day since it happened..."

"Well we can help with that," the doctor jumped upon what I said, "Because you're unwell. We can make all that go away. We can make you better and that's why you're going to stay with us for the foreseeable future... Until all traces of them are gone..."

"What if I don't want them gone? What if I want to keep seeing them... What if I want to keep hearing them?"

"And why would you want that?"

"Because I'd sooner not forget them and if that's the only way I can remember then so be it..."

"And you think that's normal behaviour, do you?"

A tear rolled down my cheek, "It doesn't matter what I think, does it? Whatever I say...Whatever I do...You'll always disagree."

"You sound ungrateful...You should be thankful..."

"I should?"

"We're going to fix you. We stopped you from having to go to jail for the rest of your life. Locked up with other murderers and criminals...At least here we want to help you...Now...We just have a few tests to perform and then you can go and get some sleep..."

The doctor took the pins up from the table.

ᛉ

I sat opposite Vicky in the daycare room; the table in the corner of the room away from prying eyes if there was such a place around here. They could still see us, I expect, and listen to what we had to say if they so desired. I'm sure of it. Be foolish to think otherwise.

"Have they spoken to you yet?" I whispered to her as I took my seat. I nervously glanced over my shoulder to see if anyone was coming to stop us from talking. No one seemed to care. "They spoke to me last night...Warned me not to talk to you anymore. I'm sorry if you got in trouble," I continued. I turned back to her, "did they say anything?"

She didn't respond; just sat there as though she didn't see me.

"Are you even listening to me?" I asked her.

It was then I saw it; a little trickle of blood matting her hair above her left ear.

"What's that?" I asked. "Are you okay?"

She still didn't respond. I leant forward in my chair and reached out to the side of her head where the blood was. She didn't even flinch or register I was there; she just stayed perfectly still. When I ran my finger through her hair, a clump of it came away between my fingers when I moved away.

"Vicky?"

More blood suddenly trickled from the top of her crown, near her hair-line.

"What the fuck?" I turned around and called for the one of the nurses, "We need some help! Someone! Anyone?"

No one looked up. A situation not helped by the fact that half of the people in the room had been reduced to nothing more than dribbling idiots. The other half were on minimum wage and simply didn't give a fuck.

"Come on, Vicky..." I urged her. I hurried to her side and took her arm. If they won't come to us, we'll go to them. I pulled her arm and tried to walk with her. I had hoped a tug would have pulled her to her feet and she'd have walked with me but it didn't quite go to plan. She slumped forward in her chair and I couldn't help but scream as the top of her cranium slipped off as though it were nothing more than a cheap wig. Underneath was a bloody mess but I could still make out her brain - a large chunk missing from either side. I jumped back in shock and couldn't help but throw up onto the white-tiled floor.

"What have they done?!" I screamed at the top of my lungs as soon as I had finished puking.

$$\lambda$$

I woke with a start, tucked into the corner of my padded little cell. Small traces of blood on the floor's soft fabric. Must have come from my nails - caked in brown, dried flakes of blood after the pins were inserted underneath them once more. Damn they're sore today. Can't take another night of it.

"You're awake!" Vicky's voice gave my heart another jump.

I sat up and did my best to hide my fingers from her. Seeing as she's okay...It's probably best not to tell her about what was said last night. I'll just have to try my best not to get her in any trouble.

No reason we can't be friends.

Friends?

It still feels strange to think of us as friends. I can't help but wonder whether I'd have woken up, feeling the same, if the doctor hadn't pointed it out to me last night. In his poorly hidden threat he pushed me closer to her.

Don't want to get her in trouble though. I'll be careful from now on. Just talk to her about mindless stuff to pass the time. Avoid the past. Avoid my crimes. Even avoid her crimes if she chooses to share.

"I was thinking about what you told me yesterday," she whispered.

So much for not talking about the past...

Chapter 5

I **was sitting** in the daycare room with Vicky. Rather disconcertingly I realised, soon after taking the seat, we were sitting at the same table which featured in my dream. I only hope it doesn't have the same ending.

"I was thinking about what you told me yesterday afternoon," she continued, "you know, about the boy..."

"It was the medication," I lied, "I didn't know what I was saying yesterday."

"You didn't take any medication yesterday."

And speaking of medication - there was something about Vicky today that was different; a spark in her eyes. A welcome glint of life. Clearly she had opted not to take any pills today too.

"Listen..." she went to continue.

I stopped her dead, "Maybe we should just drop it," I said.

"What?"

"I didn't see any ghosts..."

"What?" she looked confused.

"I made the story up."

"You didn't..."

"Yes, I did. It was some old story that my dad was told. Something I used..."

"No..."

"Yes...I told the authorities so they'd send me here instead of a real jail. I wouldn't last in a real jail amongst the general population. I killed my kids. You know what they'd do to someone like me in there?"

"You're lying."

Is there anyone in here who believes what I say without questioning it?

"No I'm not. I needed people to think I'm insane."

"You're lying," she repeated. "You're scared. That's all."

"No, I'm not."

"Listen..."

She won't let it drop. A chill ran down my back as though someone was watching us. A quick look over my left shoulder - the doctor was standing in the room's doorway. His eyes clearly fixed on us.

"...I know who it is," she continued. "I found out his name."

I turned back to Vicky. I'm curious to know what she thinks she knows but I understand the danger she...We...I know the danger we're in if she continues talking about it. For all I know my dream was a premonition of things to come; a dream I want to avoid for Vicky's state. I know I don't know her - and I don't have a reason to care - but I don't want her hurt. Enough people have been hurt because of me. I don't need to be adding to the list.

"I've got to go," I said. I stood up and turned around. The doctor was still watching us; his head shaking slowly from side to side as though warning me of my actions.

"Don't you want to know?" she called out after me.

"It wouldn't do any good," I told her with my back still to her, "it won't bring my family back."

I walked away, through the room of crazies, past the doctor and out the double doors he stood in front of. I wanted to ask him if he was happy. I wanted to tell him to go fuck himself. I said neither. No point in angering him, or his colleagues. Hopefully they'll soon tire of tormenting me...At least, that's the hope. Just as long as I don't rise to the bait.

As soon as I was standing in the corridor I stopped and leant against the wall. A few deep breaths to calm myself down. I wonder if outsiders know how patients are treated within these walls. I wonder - do they care?

"Dad!" Jamie's voice called out from the side of me. I turned my head and saw her standing at the far end of the corridor. She motioned, with her hand, for me to go over. I felt no fear. I'm used to seeing my family now. Grateful even, despite part of me wishing they could rest peacefully.

I checked behind me to make sure the doctor wasn't still watching. He wasn't. A quick look through the door's window and I can't see him at all. Probably for the best. I turned back to my daughter and walked towards her - my eyes fixed at the bloody hole between her eyes.

The hole my bullet caused.

Just as Ava did when I met her in the corridor, when I neared, Jamie disappeared out of sight. I turned the corner - half expecting to see her further down the next corridor - and jumped when I practically walked into her.

"Jamie..." I went to hold her in my arms but she stepped back, away from me.

"Talk to her..."

"What?"

"The lady. Talk to her."

"Vicky?"

Jamie nodded slowly, "Please...listen to what she has to say...Talk to her."

Jamie's eyes suddenly widened with fear as something behind me caught her eye. I turned to see what it was, half expecting to see the boy with the scar or the doctor, but there was nothing there. I turned back to Jamie. Her eyes were completely black now. She opened her mouth and screamed. A scream so loud it echoed throughout the corridor and straight through my splintered soul. I closed my eyes and covered my ears to drown it out.

I opened my eyes when the screaming ceased. Jamie was gone and I was back sitting opposite Vicky in the daycare room.

I looked around. She must have noted the confused look upon my face.

"What is it?" she asked with a genuine look of concern.

"How did I get back here?"

"What do you mean?"

"I left. I was sitting here with you. I left. And now I am back. How did I get back here?"

"I don't know what you mean. You didn't go anywhere."

"Yes. Yes I did..."

"We've only just sat down..."

I looked over my shoulder expecting to see the doctor watching us. He wasn't there.

"I was thinking..." Vicky continued.

"I know. You were thinking about the boy I told you about yesterday. We've had this conversation - well, part of it. I stopped you and walked out because I don't want to get you in trouble..."

"What are you talking about?"

"The doctor...The one who did this..." I showed her my fingers; a look of disgust on her face as she flinched away ever so slightly. "He told me, last night, that I shouldn't be talking to you about what happened...I shouldn't be talking to anyone...I think, if we carry on, they may do something to you."

Vicky didn't say anything to start off with. She fidgeted in her seat uncomfortably. Eventually she asked, "What do you think they'll do?"

I shook my head, "I don't know."

"They wouldn't do anything, they're just trying to scare you...What have you done to them to make them hate you so much?" she asked.

I raised my fingers again, "I don't know....Maybe because I killed my family? Maybe because they're sadistic sons of bitches? You heard the story, right? They pulled the child's vocal chords out because of his screams at night...The locals said he wasn't the only one..."

"His name was Anthony Ward."

"What?"

"The boy...I found out his name - Anthony Ward. I was talking about your story to one of my other friends... My friend was on the same ward as him...The boy...He had his vocal chords removed just as the boy you described...There's a whole ghost story centering around it..."

"You were talking about me?" I felt a surge of annoyance. I had told her something in confidence and she couldn't wait to gossip it to her crazy friends?

"His name...He'll have a file...We can find out what happened to him..."

"What good would that do?" I asked.

She didn't have an answer for me, unsurprisingly.

What, did she expect the curse to suddenly be lifted if the boy's story was revealed?

"This isn't a movie!" I told her.

I heard the double doors to the daycare room slam shut - loud enough to make me turn my head. The doctor was standing on the other side of them, staring through the glass straight in our direction.

"What is it?" asked Vicky.

I turned back to her, "We have to stop talking about this. I don't want them to do anything to you..."

"Who?" Vicky peered over my shoulder. "What were you looking at?"

I turned back to the doors; the doctor was gone.

"Nothing. I guess." I stood up and said, "I've got to go."

"Where are you going?" Vicky asked.

I didn't answer her. I didn't have anywhere in particular to go. I just wanted to back away from the unwelcome conversation and the possibility of angering the powers that be more than they're already angered.

If I have to stay here, I'd sooner have a quiet life.

I passed the other loonies and pushed the doors open to escape their random, barely audible, mutterings. I should never have bothered leaving my room in the first place. I was right - people like me don't deserve friends and a friendship between Vicky and I will never work...Even if I wanted it to. I can't trust her not to tell other people anything we talk about. And I don't want her hurt. She doesn't deserve it.

Just as my family didn't.

I'm the only one who deserves everything I get.

I turned right, when I left the daycare room, and headed down the long corridor - lined with the various colourful art projects I had seen so many times before - back towards my room.

I stopped.

A framed picture of a small hand-print, made with red paint, on the wall. There was a plaque next to it which read 'Anthony Ward - aged 6 months'. Another one next to that, slightly bigger, which read 'Anthony Ward - aged 1.5 years'...The next picture was a scribbled mess of various colours. 'Anthony Ward - aged 2 years'. The whole wall was like a private gallery to this little boy.

Aged six months? Who admits their child to a mental institute at six months? Surely it's impossible to diagnose someone, at that age, with mental illness. It's hard enough; I'm led to believe, to diagnose an adult - let alone a baby.

I hurried to the last picture on the wall; a picture of two people - an adult and a child - in front of what I presume to be the asylum. Is that one of the doctors?

'Anthony Ward - aged eight'.

The next, and final corridor before my room, was lined with artwork from an assortment of different patients.

There was nothing else from Anthony Ward.

CHAPTER 6

The doctor stopped inserting pins under my nails and looked me directly in the eyes as though shocked by what I had just asked.

"What did you say?" he asked. He sat back in his chair and put the remaining pins onto the table which separated us.

"I asked who Anthony Ward is."

"How'd you learn of that name?" the doctor asked. I couldn't read his mood. His face suggested, though, that I had awakened a long since dead memory.

"Who is he?" I pushed.

The doctor stood up; a flash of anger through his eyes. Unfortunately it's quite easy to read his mood now. Definitely angry. He yelled in my face, the first time I had heard him actually yell, "I told you! I'm the one who asks the questions!"

I screamed as he hit the single pin underneath my nail. I tried to move my hand away, to nurse it close to my chest, but the doctor's helper kept it firmly on the table.

The doctor moved closer. The stench of his breath was enough to distract me, momentarily, from the pain. "Do you understand me?"

"Who is he?" I asked again.

"You have no rights here!" he screamed. He stood to his full height and nodded towards the helper. The helper released my hands, from the table, allowing me to pull my hurting hand close to my chest to massage it better with the other. It helps a little but doesn't numb the sting entirely.

"He's the one I've been seeing..." I continued, ignoring the anger of the doctor.

"Just because a crazy person tells you a name - it doesn't make it true. You're simply dragging an innocent into your story to make it seem more real to yourself. The truth of the matter is, you're nothing more than a murderer..." the doctor spat.

"The ghost stories around the town...They center around this boy... There are paintings of his on the walls...I've seen them myself...Who is he?"

"He is an ex-patient..."

"What happened to him?" I shouted.

The doctor looked to the helper, once more, and gave him a nod. With no warning, the helper slogged me on the side of the head. A hit, so hard, it shook my brain.

The room was empty.

Derelict looking.

I was alone.

I shook the pain of the punch off.

The doctor was standing opposite me again with his helper to my side.

What the hell was that?

"Look at you...You're pathetic..."

"I'm not crazy and you know it," I argued back - still reeling from the pain of the helper's fist. "Others have heard of the story..."

"The story! Exactly that! The story. Just because of what happened to that poor boy...It doesn't mean he, or any other patients from here are living on as tormented spirits..."

"I've never been in trouble with the law. I wouldn't hurt anyone. What happened to my family was because of what I went through on that night..."

"I've had enough of this..." the doctor looked to the helper again.

Another fist to the side of the head.

✦

I'm not in the room anymore.

Not sure how.

I'm in the daycare room - unlike earlier it's near empty. The doctor is in the far corner of the room, standing over a nurse who was clutching a little baby. Both of them are smiling. The first happy scene I've witnessed since being in here.

I can't hear what's being said. The world is on mute once more, just as it has been in dreams prior to this one. I'm expecting to hear a scream any minute. That's what happens.

Suddenly the doctor and nurse looked in my direction. There's no anger in their eyes, though. They looked as though they were looking through me. I turned on my heel to see what had caught their attention.

I was in a different room.

Same decor as the daycare room.

It looked to be some kind of visitor's room; smaller tables than the ones found in the daycare room. Grey plastic chairs either side. The room was empty with the exception of a little boy and a man - a man who had his back to me. The boy looked genuinely happy to see him as the man slid a present across the table to him.

His father?

I stepped closer and noticed a birthday card on the table - a large number five was on the card.

"Am I coming home soon?" the boy asked.

The man shook his head from side to side. The little boy - Anthony I presume - bowed his head down in disappointment. The man tapped on the top of the nicely wrapped gift he had passed over - no doubt a gesture to encourage Anthony to open it.

Anthony duly opened it but he didn't look excited about it. If anything it looked as though he was doing it more to please his father as opposed to actually wanting to see what it was.

He held it up, once opened, allowing me to see it too - not that that was his intention. It couldn't have been. He didn't know I was here. I was nothing but an invisible witness to a scene gone by. It was a jigsaw. A picturesque scene of a cabin in the woods - brilliant sunlight spilling through the dense woodlands behind the wooden building.

Anthony dropped the box and ran from the room. I gave chase. I don't want to miss what happens. All these images, the messages from my family - someone is trying to tell me something and I need to know. I want to know.

Out in the corridor and Anthony had vanished. The doctor was at the far end with a man who had his back to me. They seemed to be in heated discussion.

"We can't keep him here forever."

The man passed over an envelope. The doctor opened it. I could see it was full of cash. The doctors didn't force the lad to stay here? The father paid them to? Why? The doctor slid the envelope into his white jackets inside pocket. He then shook his head and disappeared around the corner.

The man scratched the back of his head and then followed - a few steps behind.

"Wait!" I called out.

I ran down the corridor and turned into them - straight into Anthony.

We're in the daycare room.

Anthony is on the floor painting - the finishing touches to the painting I saw hanging on the corridor wall; a man and child standing outside of what must be the asylum. He looks older now. If memory serves correctly, from the plaque on the wall, he must be eight. He looked up, directly at me, and called out, "Dad! You came!"

I turned around and jumped when I came face to face with Anthony. He was practically standing on top of me. His skin was pale, his eyes clouded over, a messy scar running the length of his neck; he opened his mouth and his scream filled the room.

I stumbled backwards and screamed at him, "What are you trying to tell me?!"

He didn't answer me with anything other than his ear-piercing scream. I turned my back on him and was pleased to note his screaming stopped as soon as I did. The room had changed again too - I was back in my padded cell...Standing right slap bang in the middle of it.

I'm not sure how much more I can take of this time shifting. My head felt as though it were going to explode. I spun around, to make sure I was alone in there. Thankfully I was - other than the familiar spider nestled in the corner of the ceiling still.

I fell back against the wall and slid down until my arse was on the floor. I'm exhausted; physically and mentally. I closed my eyes. I could sleep for a decade at least.

"Are you okay?" asked Vicky.

My heart skipped a beat at the sound of her voice. I opened my eyes and saw her standing in the open doorway.

"You coming out today? I missed you yesterday, after you left..." she continued.

"You can't be here," I turned my head to the side in the hope that she'd disappear. Out of sight, out of mind. It was a trick which worked for the boy when he appeared to me.

The boy?

I struggle to think of him as Anthony.

The way he looks.

Inhuman.

"It's no wonder he is so angry," I said.

"Who?"

"Anthony," I told her. "Here all his life? Abandoned. If I had been left like that, I'd want to haunt those responsible too..."

Vicky walked over and took a seat, next to me, on the floor.

"I mean it, you can't be here. You shouldn't be here." I sighed, "None of us should be here...He shouldn't have been here."

"He isn't anymore," said Vicky. I knew she was trying to comfort me but I still fretted about what the doctors would do if they saw her with me. I shifted uneasily on the padded floor.

I want to talk to her.

I want to but I can't.

I daren't.

I need to talk to someone and it's obvious I can't discuss it with the doctors. It's weird; in the dreams I've been having...The vivid dreams...The doctor I've been seeing is completely different. Compassionate even. He looks as though he actually cared about the child.

"None of us are here anymore," Vicky continued. I looked in her eyes - didn't look as though she was on medication. She started to laugh, "You still don't get it, do you? You still can't see it?"

I didn't have the time for this. My head was banging from everything that had been happening - a pain only matched by the feelings coming from my tender finger tips.

"You really don't recognise me, do you?" asked Vicky.

She stood up and walked from the room.

"What?" I called out after her. "What?"

I clambered to my feet and hurried into the corridor, after her. She was gone. Impossible. The corridor stretched too far for her to have made it around the corner.

Recognise her? What was she talking about?

I ran down the corridor. Maybe she did make it round the corner.

I turned the corner and slid to a stop.

"You haven't got a hug for your old man?"

Dad?!

"What are you doing here?" I asked.

He didn't respond.

Footsteps behind me.

I turned around and saw Anthony running towards me. He ran straight past; I followed where he was going. He ran straight into the arms of my father. A tight hug. Warm. Loving. A pang of jealousy shot through me. What the fuck is this?

My dad scooped him up in his arms and held him tight.

"What have you been doing today?" he asked.

"Painting!" Anthony yelled - obvious excitement in his tone of voice.

They disappeared around the corner.

"No! Wait!" I called. I ran after them and around the next corner.

Mum and dad's old living room? What the hell? Dad was standing by the fireplace; a fire blazing across the logs. Mum was sitting on the sofa, her usual place in the room. She used to say it was comfier than the other seats. I'd argue with her that it wasn't and they were just the same but she'd never move.

"It's just for the weekend," dad was saying, "I'll be back before you know it."

"I just don't see why you can't do your writing here," mum replied.

"I told you - I can't concentrate. I just need to get away for a few days. Just a couple. I'll get the project finished, my agent will be happy...We might get some money which will help with the bills...Just a couple of days. Come on, I need your support. I can't do this if we're arguing..."

"I'm not arguing, I'm just disappointed. Where will you go?"

"There's a cabin out of town...It's peaceful there..."

"Can't Craig and I come with you? We wouldn't be any trouble. We'd go for walks and leave you to write..."

"Maybe next time," my father replied. "I love you," he said. He sounded genuine but knowing how the story ended - with dad and that woman all those years later - I found it hard to believe the sentiment behind the words.

"I love you too." Genuine.

Dad smiled at her and walked out of the room. Mum didn't get up and follow. She just sat there and stared into the fire as though crushed by disappointment that my father was going away again. He was always going away when I was growing up. I remember now.

I followed dad into the next room only to find myself back in the asylum's corridor. Dad was standing with the doctor - both of them talking in hushed voices.

"You can't keep him here forever," the doctor said.

"I just need time," my dad replied.

"Time? Time for what? The longer you leave it the worse it will be. You need to tell your wife you have another child."

Anthony's my brother?

"You don't understand. She'd never forgive me…"

"You should have thought about the consequences at the start," the doctor hissed - it was clear he and my father weren't the best of friends.

Dad pulled an envelope out of his pocket and thrust it against the doctor's chest, "There's more than enough in here…More than last month. Come on, I just need a little more time. Please. I'm begging you. It's not just my family at stake here…If word got out about any of this…About my affair… My reputation would be ruined too. Come on…Please…"

The doctor took a hold of the envelope and put it into his pocket.

"You have one more month," the doctor spat. He turned his back and walked away from my dad. The first time I had seen anyone turn their back on my father.

My dad sighed, "I'll come by again tomorrow…I've got a cabin just a short way from here…"

I felt sick.

Whoever was showing me all this…Whatever was making me see all this…

I'm not sure I can take anymore.

I closed my eyes and fell back against the wall.

Padded walls?

CHAPTER 7

I opened my eyes.

My cell again.

Did I ever leave?

Something's different.

The padding on the floor and walls isn't quite as white as it used to be. It looks as though it's been affected poorly by damp. Black mould growing in patches. I looked up to the corner of the ceiling. Plenty of webs but no spider. The cell door was wide open. The lights in the corridor, beyond my room, were off yet I could see the paint on the walls was peeling.

"Hello?" I called out. My voice was shaking. "Doctor?"

There was no response.

I stood up and walked into the corridor.

"Hello?" my voice echoed and bounced off the furthest point of the corridor. The place looked as though it had been empty for years. All of the cell doors were open. Slowly I walked down the corridor. I half expected something, or someone, to jump out on me but nothing did.

The next corridor was the same other than the fact I could see a little light coming from a room at the other end. I hurried towards it - thankful for the sign of life. Seconds later I could hear screaming - an angry child. I ran the last few steps to see what was happening.

As I turned the corner I realised I was back in the daycare room. A few people milling around, minding their own business or unsure of their business due to high levels of medication, and Anthony at a far table - sitting opposite him was my father. Anthony looked upset.

I approached them and noticed he was surrounded by his painting tools - the picture he was working on was the last one I had noticed on the wall earlier...A child and man standing in front of the asylum. Father and son?

"You promised! You promised!" Anthony was screaming at our father. "You said I could come home! You said I could!"

My dad didn't say anything. He just sat there - an angry expression on his face.

Anthony continued, "You said when I was eight you'd take me away with you...You promised! YOU PROMISED!""I can't. I told you...My wife...She doesn't know about you..."

"Tell her!"

"It's not as simple as that!"

"Why don't you love me?"

"I do!"

"I want to come home! I'll tell them!"

"Don't say that."

Anthony started to shout to everyone else in the room, "He's my dad! He's my dad! He's my dad!"

My dad suddenly lunged forward and grabbed Anthony by his throat - his tightening grip silenced him more or less immediately yet my dad didn't let go or loosen his grip. He just kept the same pressure. The same force...

Doctors and nurses were calling from across the room as they came running over - ordering dad to release his grip. It took two of the hospital staff to pull him clear. Anthony dropped to the floor as soon as dad let go but air still wasn't getting through as he continued to choke.

I looked at my father in horror. He fought the hospital staff off and stood up. Seeing what he had done he turned and ran from the room.

One of the nurses called out, "He can't breathe...He can't breathe...Do something!"

Another of the staff - a doctor - ordered her to, "Get a scalpel...quickly..."

I couldn't watch.

I turned and gave chase to my dad. I hurried into what should have been the corridor. Not the corridor. A small room - a doctor's office. Dad was sitting opposite the doctor.

"This is how you repay me?" the doctor was angry. "We went out on a limb for you. Took him in so your dirty little secret wouldn't come to light... So your family can live happily ever after..." The doctor shook his head. "You make me sick."

My dad didn't normally allow people to speak to him like that. It was the first time I had actually seen him tongue-tied.

"Is he going to be okay?" my dad asked eventually.

"There were complications. His vocal chords were damaged..."

"Damaged? Damaged how?"

"You nearly crushed his throat completely..."

Dad looked visibly upset, "Can I see him?"

"I'm not sure that's a good idea. In fact, I think it best if you just stay away. Either take him back to your happy little life or move on...Forget about him. You can't keep leading him on like this. It's not fair on him. It's not fair on the staff here. Some are getting attached to him. Some of us more so than others, for obvious reasons...So what's it to be?" he asked.

Dad hesitated, "My wife wouldn't understand..."

The doctor looked disappointed.

"I can't lose her."

"If my daughter had survived the birth...Would things have been different?"

Again, my dad didn't answer.

His daughter? My dad was having an affair with the doctor's daughter? How many affairs did he have?

"Perhaps you should just leave," the doctor continued.

"What should I tell him?"

"Just leave."

There was a pause. Dad stood up.

"I'll send money..."

"Don't bother. Go. Stop coming here. You're no longer welcome."

The doctor swiveled around, in his chair, so he didn't have to face my father. I can't say I blamed him. Had I been in the same position - I would have done the same. Dad should have come clean. He should have told mum. He should have told me I had a half-brother. Should have let us decide what to do about it. But he took it away from us.

He took away everything.

A sudden pain in the side of my head dropped me to my knees. I couldn't help but close my eyes; shut them tight hoping it would make the pain disappear. For once it worked. I opened my eyes and instantly recognised where I was.

My old bedroom. I was sitting on the floor, huddled up in a little ball; knees pulled close to my chest as though that would protect me from whatever was causing this fear I felt surge through my body.

"It's okay, they'll be home soon..." a voice behind me. "Come on...Come downstairs...We'll play a game...Before you know it, they'll be home..."

I felt some of the fear disappear from my body. Some of it. The person's voice...Comforting...I looked over my shoulder.

My babysitter.

Victoria.

I remember this day.

The first time we met.

Mum and dad had gone out for the night. I was about six years old; one of the earliest times I could remember them going out and leaving me with a stranger.

I was scared at first but Victoria...Vicky...Of course...I knew there was something familiar about her. She looked older now. Older in the asylum. What's she doing in there with me though?

She always had a way about her - a way of making me feel better. That hasn't changed.

Another blinding pain in the side of my head.

Eyes shut.

Wish the pain away.

I opened my eyes. Not in my bedroom anymore. Back in the office with the doctor and his helper. The doctor sitting there, opposite me, with that same sadistic smile on his face. The helper standing at my side with his fist clenched - ready to hit me again.

"Wait!" I shouted. "Wait!"

The doctor nodded to the helper, stopping him in his tracks. "Something you want to say?" he asked.

"I know."

"You know what?"

"You're his grandfather..."

"What?"

"You're his grandfather...My dad...Your daughter..."

The doctor froze. The sadistic smile, on his face, disappeared - replaced with a deep look of regret.

"What happened?" I asked. "You're punishing me because of what my dad did? At least tell me what happened..."

"You're punishing yourself," the doctor mumbled. He stood up and walked straight past me, with his helper, right out of the door.

"What? That's it? No...I need to know!" I stood up, unsteadily on my feet, and followed him out of the room but he wasn't there.

No one was.

The corridor, outside of his room was empty. Derelict. Looked like it had been for years.

I turned back to the room I had just come from. Same scenario. Peeling paint on the walls, dust and cobwebs...No table...No chairs...Nothing.

"Hello?" I called out - distinct panic in my voice. My voice echoed with no one answering it. "Anyone?"

I started to run down the corridors. A quick look in every room I ran past revealed the same as the last - empty. Derelict. Even doors which were once locked were now open for me.

When I was starting to think I was the only one here I heard the sound of a woman screaming in pain. It was coming from a door to my right. I wasted no time in opening it...Empty and yet the screams continued. Male voices urging whoever it was to push. Male voices promising it was nearly over and that they could see a head. The screaming stopped suddenly. Male voices in a state of panic. A baby crying. I backed out of the room and continued to run down the corridor I was previously running down.

Maybe all the doors are open?

Maybe I can get out of here.

Escape.

Just keep running.

To where I'm not sure.

More screaming from one of the doors on my right. I'm scared to look but can't stop myself. I pushed the door open unsure what to expect. The room was just as empty as the previous rooms.

A female was screaming. I recognised the doctor's voice barking orders at her - not in a stern fashion. A panicked fashion.

"Get it away from his neck! Get it away!"

"He isn't breathing!" the female voice screamed.

The sound of someone trying to resuscitate someone.

"Anthony! Anthony! Hold on!"

I backed out of the room. He killed himself? I don't need to hear that. Why am I hearing these things? Why am I seeing them? There's nothing I can do about it. Nothing.

"LEAVE ME ALONE!" I screamed down the empty corridor.

Empty.

This place.

It's always been empty.

I remember now.

I remember.

CHAPTER 8

I had broken the doors down. They were boarded up to stop people, such as myself, from getting in. But I didn't care. I had to get in here. I remember coming here, straight from the cabin. There was nowhere else to go. I remember running from the cabin. Running from what I had done. Running from their bodies.

Ava.

Jamie.

Susan.

I'm sorry.

Why am I being punished by Anthony though? I didn't have a choice about what happened to him. It was out of my hands. I never knew about him. I never knew. No one told me.

I remember walking to the abandoned reception desk, the same one I've reached now, and asking to check myself in. There was no one there. Yet, in my mind...I remember having the whole conversation. I remember signing that I understood what I was asking of them...To assess me. In my mind I was shakingly clutching a pen and scribbling my signature on a piece of paper. In reality - there was nothing in my hand and nothing in front of me.

My mind playing tricks on me. Making me believe they were there...

The doctor putting the pins under my nails?

I remember doing it to myself.

Torturing myself because I believed it was what I deserved.

A broken mind.

I remember crashing out in the nearest padded room I could find. The asylum's ghosts teaching me the truth whilst I was here? Are there even any ghosts? Was it Anthony showing me? Wanting me to know he was my brother...Wanting me to know I need to be punished just as my father had been punished...But why was my babysitter here? My mind desperately trying to offer me some comfort in my hour of need?

I need to get out of here.

I need to leave before I lose my mind completely.

"The door's open, sir. Will you be making a follow-up appointment?"

A nurse was standing behind the reception desk. The first person to smile at me for as long as I can remember.

"No. I don't think that will be entirely necessary," I said to no one.

There was no nurse there.

Broken mind.

Need to leave.

I turned and hurried towards the broken door. I could feel a breeze from beyond. My heart was racing as I pulled it open.

A scream filled my head. Anthony was standing directly behind me. I spun on the spot to see him. His mouth was wide open.

"Look," I said, "I'm sorry...For whatever happened...For everything...I'm sorry. I didn't know. I didn't! No one told me! I wish they had before it was too late. I wish they had! Everything could have been different!"

With no warning his scream intensified as he suddenly charged towards me.

I shut my eyes and braced myself for impact but nothing happened.

I opened my eyes slowly - thinking it was a trick.

I was in the cabin's bedroom. A gun in my hand.

Anthony was standing in front of me, by the bed. His eyes weren't cloudy. His skin looked a healthy pink colour. He smiled at me and disappeared.

I looked at the gun in my hand.

What the hell?

Footsteps outside, coming towards the front of the cabin.

We've been here before.

I ran through to the other room - close to the front door - and aimed the gun at the door. Whoever is out there...

The door opened fast and Ava came running in. I didn't pull the trigger. I raised the barrel of the gun into the air as quickly as I could so as not to frighten her.

"What the hell are you doing with that?" asked Susan when she walked in.

"You wouldn't believe the night I've had!" I said. I wanted to give them a hug. I wanted to give them both a hug but they'd wonder what I was up to.

"Night? We haven't been gone that long! Anyway, can you give Jamie a hand with the shopping..."

"Shopping?" I asked.

"The bits you asked us to get."

"Sure," I said. I thought I sent them to her parents? I thought...After the accident...After the store clerk got...

"Did you know the store clerk knew your father? They aren't happy with him!"

"They aren't?" I asked - still dumbstruck as to what was going on.

"Apparently he made a ghost story up about the old asylum...The store clerk was saying they're continually getting ghost hunters running around here, asking questions, trying to find out more." Susan laughed, "He was saying he enjoyed the extra business at first but, apparently, each year the tourists were getting freakier and freakier...One of the doctors was so upset by the story he's rumored to have jumped from the top of the tower you said the patients helped build..."

The grandfather, no doubt.

Jamie came in with the bags of shopping, "Where do you want the cleaning stuff?" she asked in her own grumpy way.

"Let's go and stay in a hotel instead," I suggested.

"What?" Susan said, "I thought you wanted to stay here to get your writing done?"

"It's not important. I was thinking...Hotel tonight...More driving tomorrow...Let's find a beach. It's only a few more hours of driving!"

Ava cheered.

"What about the cabin?" asked Susan.

I looked around the room. Still vandalised. Still a mess.

"Let it rot."

As we drove away from the cabin, I gave it a final look in the rear-view mirror. I could see Anthony standing in the doorway, looking at the floor. I'm not sure why he wanted me to know what had happened but part of me is glad I do know. Another part of me wishes I could forget everything.

All those years ago I remember my father telling me the story of the screaming ghost. The story he invented, not the locals. The woods weren't haunted by the ex-patients of the asylum. The locals weren't living in fear as to whether they heard a scream or not...

Only my dad was.

As I pressed my foot harder on the accelerator I just wanted to get away as fast as possible.

Get away from this nightmare.

Bury dad's secret with any remaining love I once had for him.

I hoped he burned in Hell for what he had done - not just to Anthony but the other lives his lies affected too.

I won't forget.

I won't forgive.

I won't allow myself.

I'll just treasure my own family more.

Don't let go.

THE END

THANK YOU FOR VISITING BRATTLEBORO
PLEASE COME BACK AND SEE US SOON!

THE 8TH

PROLOGUE

Just like every other day I was the last one into the classroom. It wasn't because I was late. Most days I was early as I opted to get the earlier bus to avoid the crowds and my fellow classmates. It was just easier that way - with regards to getting the earlier bus and being one of the last into the classroom.

With my heart pounding hard in my chest I stepped into the classroom just behind Mrs.. Price, the teacher, who paid me little attention as she briskly walked across to her desk, in her tight-fitting black pencil skirt and white blouse, in front of the pupils. I closed the door and pulled the window-blind down to stop people from being able to look in. This was something I didn't usually do. Normally I was happy for other teachers to poke their noses in - to make sure we were behaving while our teacher had her back to us as she scribbled on the blackboard. Today, though, I don't welcome their attention.

By the time I turned away from the heavy oak door, Mrs.. Price was staring at me with a look of contempt on her face; an expression she regularly adopted whilst looking at me through no fault of my own. I'm almost positive she's fairly pretty, with her curly shoulder length blonde hair, big blue eyes and full lips painted heavily in a seductive red lipstick...It's hard to be sure whether she is actually pretty or not...under that stern expression. It was fair to say she was one of the stricter teachers. I didn't move. Part of me wanted to go and take my usual seat in the front row of the classroom; as far away from Piers and his friends as I could possibly get without sitting in the teacher's lap. The other part of me wanted to carry on as I had planned.

Mrs.. Price folded her arms. You knew she was angry when she did this. First came the deathly stare which could penetrate the most hardened of souls and then came the folding of the arms. Next up she'll speak in a tone which would send most sane men running for the hills for fear of spontaneously combusting at the sound of her voice. I pity her husband. After a few warning words, which were normally laced with sarcasm, she'd suddenly flip a switch and start shouting.

A quick scan of my fellow classmates showed they were all looking at me. Some of them looked worried for me and others just sat there with a sadistic look of glee upon their faces as they waited to enjoy the floor show Mrs. Price and I were about to put on for them. All of them were thankful they weren't standing in my shoes at this precise moment. I'm starting to wish I had waited for my second class of the day to do this. Mr. Smart was a much friendlier teacher.

"Oh, I'm sorry, I wasn't aware you were teaching the class today," said Mrs. Price with just about the right level of sarcasm I was expecting. A few quiet sniggers from around the classroom. I didn't say anything. I just stood there, blocking the doorway whilst wondering whether this was the right thing to do. Had I really planned it through? It's too late now. There's no turning back. With my left hand shaking I reached into my rucksack, which was one-strapped over my right shoulder. I froze. I could feel it in my hand but part of me was still screaming that this wasn't the right thing to do; screaming there were better ways of dealing with things...

"Shut up!" I whispered under my breath to the part of me which was scared. I knew this was the right thing to do. It had been building for far too long. They had it coming. They all did. Everything that was to follow, when I pulled my hand from the rucksack, is deserved and I refuse to let the scared part of me, the quiet side of my personality, ruin the enjoyment I'm going to get.

"What did you say?" said Mrs. Price; a tone of voice I had never heard before. Neither had the rest of the class. A quick scan of my classmates showed they had all sunk back, ever so slightly, in their uncomfortable grey plastic chairs. The ones who previously had gleeful smiles upon their faces were now sat expressionless so as not to attract the attention of Mrs. Price. Their faces were white as they feared what they were about to witness. They have no idea. Today, it's not Mrs. Price they need to fear.

It's me.

I pulled my hand from my rucksack, my father's 9mm Glock gripped firmly in my palm with my index finger on the trigger and my other fingers around the handle. Everyone screamed, even Mrs. Price. Need to control them. Need to silence them. Don't want to attract any unwanted attention. I don't need this to be any worse than I already have planned.

"I said shut up!" I hissed. I pointed the gun at Mrs. Price first. She fell backwards onto the floor. I couldn't help but smile a little. All those years of her shouting the odds at us. All those years of her believing she was untouchable. It was nice to see her fall. I spun the gun around to point at my classmates; some of whom were cowering behind their hands, as though they had the power to stop a bullet should I choose to fire, whilst others were trying to get under their desks. The sadistic part of me was surprised no one tried to make a dash for me. No one tried to wrestle the gun away from me. No one tried to control the situation. I'm glad. I don't want the sound of gunfire. Not yet. That would have ruined everything I have planned. The fact they're all petrified, it should make controlling them that much easier...

CHAPTER 1

It was weird seeing Mrs. Price sitting in the front row, amongst the pupils who despised her so much. Not just because I was used to seeing her at the front of the class berating someone but...Her expression...Tears in her eyes, a pale complexion...Shaking...She's shaking. I've never seen that before. Not from a woman who presents herself as being so domineering. Speaking of 'domineering' I had often heard Piers talking to his little gang, discussing whether Mrs. Price would look good in skin-tight latex with a whip in her hand. The majority of the group said she would. Some of them even admitted to masturbating to the thought of her like that. One of the group said the bulge of her penis would ruin the overall look. Seeing her, sat here now...There's nothing manly about her. There's nothing domineering. She's a nothing. Maybe I should get her to stand up and prove to Piers and his gang that she doesn't have a cock hidden under her black pencil skirt. No. That's not fair. This isn't about belittling her despite what she puts us through on a day-to-day basis. At the end of the day she is just being strict to keep us in control. Outside of the school she's probably a human. Deep down. Somewhere.

"What are you doing?" she asked in a meek voice. I have to confess, she surprised me. Most of the time there was a little masculinity in her voice but not now. Now she sounded like a scared little girl. Had you not seen who it was speaking you could have been forgiven for thinking it was one of the school's many female pupils talking.

I didn't answer her. Instead I reached across to her pile of folders, which she had placed on the desk when she first came into the room, and picked up the one labelled as 'registration'. I flicked it open to the first page: a list of names of the boys and girls who should be sat in front of me for this lesson.

"When I call out your name," I said, "please say here." One by one I called out the various names from the list in front of me, not that I needed a list. I knew their names; my classmates. The people who had tormented me day in and day out for the past two years whether it was by name calling or physical abuse. I won't ever forget their names. And after today, people won't forget my name either. Minutes later and the roll call was done. No one was absent for a change. Good. I'd have hated for them to miss this.

I put the folder down and cast my eyes around the class. It's unfortunate some of them are here and have to witness this. In a class of twenty-five there are some who are like me. They don't deserve to be here. They don't deserve what's coming. I don't have a choice but to include them, though. If I let them go, they'll no doubt inform someone what is happening in here. If I were in their shoes I know I'd go and get help if I was let out. My gaze fixed upon Rebecca Clarke who was sitting in the middle of the classroom, towards one of the walls. Rebecca was one of the louder girls in the class. She was more centred upon sleeping with as many of the boys as she could as opposed to soaking up useful information. If the rumors are to be believed, and I have no reason to doubt them, she's swallowed more cum than I've had hot meals. Of course she doesn't struggle to attract the boys' attention looking the way she does: long dark hair down to her petite waist and large breasts enhanced further by a tight-fitting school shirt. Unlike a lot of the other girls who chose to wear trousers, she always opted for the skirt. She even took the time, in lunch-breaks, to roll it up a little to show off more leg. Sometimes she rolls it up so much you can't help but think of it as nothing more than a belt. Pregnant by eighteen, I reckon.

Rebecca had her mobile phone in her hand and was frantically pressing buttons. I picked the handgun off the table and pointed it directly at her, looking down the aiming sights. It's a little scary how easy it is to end her little life right about now. A simple squeeze of my trigger finger and her brains will be all over David Barlow who was sitting behind her. Poor David. He's one of the good ones. Whenever I wasn't feeling sorry for myself, I'd be feeling sorry for him. Unlike Rebecca, we both at least tried hard in class. We just struggled to 'get it' most of the time. Our stupidity was a great source of entertainment to the other classmates - some of whom were just as baffled as David and me by what we were being taught. The only difference was, they simply didn't care.

"Rebecca," I said. My voice was calm. No sense shouting. There's no need. Not all the time I have a gun. Rebecca looked up and froze when she realised she was staring down the barrel of a 9mm pistol, "Be a good girl and pass your mobile phone to me..."

"I wasn't doing anything..." she tried to tell me. How stupid does she think I am? Well, soon she'll realise I'm someone to be reckoned with. She realised her words were of no use and slowly stood up. "Please don't shoot..." she whimpered. She looks scared but it's hard to feel sorry for her. Every time I look at her I just remember that night; her hand on my leg, her breath against my ear, the words she whispered, the glint in her eye as she gave my crotch a squeeze...

"I said give me your phone."

She walked up to the front of the class and put her phone on the teacher's desk where I was sat. I didn't take my eyes off her. That night, the rare occasion I was actually invited to one of the many school parties, she thought it was a good idea to pretend to want me. Whispering sweet nothings into my ear she told me how she had always wanted to make love to me but was too scared to make a move. Part of me knew she was just winding me up but another part of me, the lonely part, wanted to believe her. I was stupid. Rebecca isn't the sort of girl who enjoys 'making love'. She just wants to fuck people. Trying to be clever, she got me aroused as Piers and his gang waited outside with their mobile phones at the ready...

"Is that everything?" she asked, her quivering voice pulled me back to the present. I shook my head. No, that's not everything. "You can see I didn't send any messages..." I pushed back on the chair to put some distance between myself and the table - enough of a gap to allow her through.

"Get under the table," I said.

"What?"

Rebecca's punishment was easy to think of. Ever since that night it's all I have really thought about. Forcing her to do what she teased. Now's a good a time as any. "Get under the table," I said.

"No..."

I stood up and walked over to her with the gun still raised. I pressed it against her skull and she made a funny whimpering noise. She sounded a little like a dog crying when you stand on its tail. "I said...Get...Under...The... Table..."

She nodded and stepped round me to get to the space under the table. As soon as she was under there I sat down on the chair again, and rolled myself closer to the desk. Underneath the table I had a leg either side of Rebecca. I could hear her crying but it didn't bother me.

"Please...This has gone far enough..." said Mrs. Price. I shot her a glare. I haven't started yet. She fell silent.

With my spare hand I unzipped my trousers, out of sight of the rest of the class although they knew what I was doing, and pulled my penis out. Semi-hard already. Not sure whether that's because of the control I have over everyone or because of what I'm about to get from Rebecca.

"Did you know," I said to Mrs. Price, "I went to a party once and Rebecca was there. She was telling me how much she liked me and had always wanted to make love to me. She was being so kind. I'd never felt that from someone before...Kindness to that extent. A feeling of worth, you know. She was saying all sorts of nice things. She was touching me. Kissing me. Stroking me through my trousers. I honestly thought all my birthdays had come at once when she started to unbutton me..." I could hear Rebecca crying from underneath the table saying how sorry she was but I didn't care, "...The next thing I know Piers and his little friends burst in on us... Laughing...Pointing their camera phones at me...Some of them videoing...I was just sat there exposed in more ways than one. I don't know how many people saw that video...The video they were even kind enough to email over to me...You know, that night when I got home I tied a noose round my neck and sat on the edge of my bed thinking it was the best thing to do...Hang myself...Only the thought of my mum and dad finding me swinging in the morning stopped me from actually doing it. You know how it feels to feel that low? Like you can't go on living?"

"Think of your mum and dad now," said Mrs. Price.

I shook my head. "I'll never be the son they want. I know that now. They want someone academically bright. They want someone who can make something of their lives. That isn't me. I'm a nothing. I'm a nobody. If it weren't for what's to come today, no one would remember me when I'm gone. No one. Rebecca...put it in your mouth. If I feel teeth, I'll shoot your friends."

"This isn't the way," said Mrs. Price, "we can suspend them all whilst we look into this. We can..."

"Rebecca...What are you waiting for?" I said interrupting Mrs. Price from her desperate flow. A thousand jolts of electricity shot through my body as I felt Rebecca's fingers brush against my hardening penis. Just as good as I had always imagined. I couldn't help but close my eyes for the briefest of seconds as I felt her warm mouth envelop my shaft, sliding down to the base. Feels so fucking good. I knew it would. Slightly flustered, I addressed the rest of the class, "One by one, I want you all to bring your mobile phones to the desk...Starting with you..." I pointed the gun in the direction of Craig Clemo, a dark haired lad with big brown eyes who sat on the far right of the classroom, against the wall. I didn't mind Craig. He's a bit of a nothing like me. When the bullies are out in force he just keeps his head down and doesn't get involved. I sometimes wonder how different my school days would have been if I had chosen his coping mechanisms too. Had I not stood up for David Barlow when Piers was picking on him would Piers ever have known of my existence or could I have just ghosted my way through his life?

Craig stood up and brought his phone to the front of the class. He put it on the desk and walked back to his seat.

"You," I said pointing the gun to Rachel, who sat behind him. She too stood up and dropped her phone onto the desk. When she sat down the next person brought their phone forward too without having to be asked. I smiled and sat back. Whilst they're doing that it affords me the time to enjoy what Rebecca is doing. A flicking sensation on the tip of my penis, with what feels to be her tongue. A gentle tickling around my scrotum. All those years of practising have most certainly paid off for her. I couldn't help but sigh as her mouth slipped down the shaft once more before sliding back up. Faster..Faster...Slower. Teasing. But nicely so. I wonder if the other girls in the class are as good as this. My eyes fix upon Mrs. Price. I wonder if she's as good...

A tingling sensation, not dissimilar to pins and needles, spreads through the tops of my legs. The pleasurable, familiar feeling of an orgasm about to hit. I tried my best not to show it in my face as I continued staring at Mrs. Price, wondering what it would be like to fuck her. I moved my spare hand under the table and held Rebecca's head in place. Just in time too. She tried to pull away from me as I ejaculated into her mouth. Hold her there. Listen how she chokes it down. Good girl. I released my grip on the back of her head and let her move away. I can hear that she's crying. Was it really that bad?

A feeling of guilt rushed through me as I suddenly became aware of everyone looking at me. Watching my every move. Watching me cum. I pushed my cock, coated in Rebecca's saliva, back into my trousers and zipped myself up. What have I done? What have I become? I don't recognise myself anymore.

Chapter 2

Another new school to find my way around. I love my dad but I don't love what he does for a living. Constantly moving house and taking Mum and me with him, leaving behind friends I've only just met...Having to start again from scratch. Catching up in classes I already struggle with because they've chosen different books to study from the last school I attended. I hate being the outsider. The one who can't find any friendly faces amongst the crowds. It's always the same. Go to school. Get lost looking for class. Arrive at class late, or with a teacher escort - which is far worse...Stand in front of the room and introduce yourself. Explain why you're new to the town. Sit in the only spare seat, in the front of the classroom, and feel the gaze of every pupil fix upon you for the rest of whatever lesson it is, awkwardly share books with someone who'd rather you had your own...A pile of homework to catch up on; mainly reading assignments you know you'll never be able to complete. Yes, I love my dad but I hate that we have to move around so much.

"Have a good day, honey," my mum called out. I turned back to her, when I got to the school gates, and saw her waving frantically. I should wave back but it's embarrassing enough that she just called me 'honey' in earshot of other people who may or may not be in my classroom. I gave her a faint smile and turned towards the school. Here we go again.

The first days are always the worst. At least by the end of the first day you have normally made one friend; someone to look out for on the second and third day whilst you establish new friendships. As I scanned the various faces in the crowd walking with me to the front door, I wondered whether any of them were likely to be my new friends. I have to say, on first impressions none of them look to be that friendly! Not even through the front door yet and I feel uncomfortable. Not the best of starts I think to myself as I hear the random mutterings of small groups that I pass, all wondering who the 'new kid' is and how 'weird' I look.

How they can say I look 'weird' is beyond me. Across the car park, in the corner, I saw a group all dressed in black. Even the boys had make-up on from what I could see. Another group, in the same car park, all wore matching clothes with their hair styled in various multi-coloured spikes...And here I am dressed in faded blue jeans, a black hooded top with the hood down and newish white trainers - which, admittedly, are a little on the bright side but I expect that'll change after a couple of days schooling here. My hair is the natural brown colour I was born with and I'm clean shaven. My eyes are the same dark brown colour as each other, unlike the girl I just walked by who seemed to have one blue eye and one green...Yet people are saying I'm the weird one. If anything, I reckon I'll blend in here. Unless, of course, I decide to take refuge in the car park at any moment. Definitely a place to avoid going to by what I've seen.

I pushed the large double doors open and stepped inside my new place of supposed learning. The familiar smell of 'school' hit me as soon as I stepped over the threshold. I don't know what it is about schools which make them all have the same old musty scent. Perhaps it's the old text books we're to work from? Perhaps it's those which smell of old-age and death and you just notice it more because there's so many littered around the building. Perhaps.

The corridor in front of me stretched as far as the eye could see. The walls were lined with tall wooden lockers with occasional gaps between the lockers where the doors were to the various classrooms. What's the betting this is like all the other schools I've been to and the classrooms aren't in any particular order despite being known, on the timetable, as 'class one', 'class two' etc etc? The last school I was in, a few towns away from where I am today, the first door I came across was labelled number twenty-four. Days later I found number one stuck in a different wing entirely and even then it wasn't by the main entrance. Instead it was tucked away on the top floor next to room sixty-five. The first time I noticed this - I can't even remember what school it was - I thought it was because some bored student had simply gone around swapping door plaques around to confuse people. With all the different schools I've been to, I know this isn't the case. Not unless the person responsible is in the same boat as me and doing it in every school he, or she, is visiting. I doubt it, though.

I stepped to the side of the corridor, to get out of the way of the never-ending sea of students, and reached into my pocket to find my timetable; a small piece of paper with my lessons and classrooms printed upon it which the school posted out to my house about a week ago.

"You new? Looking for somewhere in particular?" asked a quiet male voice from behind me. I turned around and saw a lad of similar age to myself. A mousey-blonde colour to his hair and freckles on his face. A cheeky smile with massive dimples on his cheeks. I couldn't help but wonder whether it was a smile to be trusted or a smile because he was about to send me in the completely wrong direction just because he could.

"Is that obvious?" I asked.

"Well for starters you're wearing your rucksack over both shoulders. No one does that in this school unless they're new. And secondly, you're looking at your timetable with a look of confusion on your face. You know...Putting two and two together..." he laughed. "Where you headed?"

I checked my timetable, "English with Mrs. Jones," I said.

He smiled wider. "Snap! You may as well follow me," he volunteered. I thanked him and slipped the timetable back into my pocket. "What's your name?" he asked after informing me his name was David.

ⴷ

David was looking at me, from his seat just behind Rebecca's, with a look in his eyes which suggested he had no idea who I was. As I listened to Rebecca's sobs as she took her seat, I couldn't help but wonder who I was too. I'm not this person. I'm not. I'm a good person. Normally. I'm like my friend David. I'm one of the good ones. Who I am today...This isn't me, usually. It's not. They made me. They turned me into this. Sadistic. Hateful. Vengeful. This is their fault.

I looked around the rest of the classroom. They're all looking at me with the same look as David. Mrs. Price is looking at Rebecca. I can see in her eyes that she desperately wants to go and comfort her. She suddenly turned to look at me, as though she could feel my glare burning into the side of her pretty face. I don't recognise the expression in her eyes. It's as though she's asking, 'what have you done?' without actually speaking the words. I forgot how much I hated myself, right now, to answer her with a look of my own. A look which told her - 'I did what she deserved and that was only the beginning'.

I stood up, behind the teacher's desk, to address the class. I feel as though I should say something. Whilst I am sure some of them know why I am here, I'm positive some of them don't have a clue. After all, some of my classmates...I've hardly spoken to them and, in turn, they've hardly spoken to me. It's only fair, given the circumstances, I give them a chance to understand what I'm doing here. And it's only fair to let them know, they'll come to no harm.

"If I call your name, I'd like you to stand up please...David Barlow..." the class went silent, "...Lindsey West..." One by one, when I called out the names, they stood up just as I had requested them to. Each of them looked just as nervous as the one who was called out before. They have nothing to be nervous about. Seven names in total - David, Lindsey, Elizabeth, Marcus, Samantha, Kate, Helen. Funny how it's mainly girl's names I'm calling out. I guess it's more in boys' nature to be cruel to one another. Not for much longer. Not by the time I'm done. And word of what's to come will soon spread around the town too; a harsh warning to others who may be making similar mistakes as made by Piers and his little friends.

I looked around the classroom at the pupils still sat down. One of them was Craig Clemo. I considered calling his name out too but...I recall him being involved in one of the incidents where I was under fire. He kept his head down. He didn't offer help or anything. Not even when the group left me alone and I was nursing a bloodied nose. He didn't ask if I was okay. He didn't offer to get help. Nothing. Just stood there watching me. He can stay sat down.

"If you're currently standing up, I'm sorry you're here. Had there been any other way, I would have taken it I can assure you. I don't want to hurt you. You've done nothing wrong to me or, as far as I know, anyone else. If you'd like to come forward...You can bring your chairs...You can sit to the side, near me; out of harm's way..." There was the briefest of pauses before each of the seven came to the front of the class as I had requested. The rest of the class just looked nervous and confused. "I know you won't but... Should any of you attempt anything funny...You'll have to join the rest of your classmates. Understood?"

They nodded. David looked as though he desperately wanted to say something but no words came from his quivering mouth.

Mrs. Price asked, "What about me? What have I done?"

I shot her a look, "It's what you didn't do..." I know I originally thought this wasn't about her but Mrs. Price is just as bad as some of the students who sit in front of me. The way she berated some of us, in front of the whole class, did nothing for self-esteem and embarrassed us. The more I see her, sitting there...The more I see her as another form of bully.

CHAPTER 3

David led the way to my first classroom. I have to say, it was a nice stroke of luck meeting him. I hate meeting new people; I always feel awkward... Never sure what to say to potential new friends. Normally I just hang around a large group and occasionally laugh at a joke one of them may say. Then, hopefully, one of them will start to include me in their conversations too. Of course, it doesn't always work like that. Sometimes you can just sit there and be completely ignored. That's never fun. It makes you feel worthless and insignificant. It was definitely a stroke of luck bumping into David now. I only but hope we share more than one class together.

"Here we are," said David. He stopped outside a classroom door. "You might not want to go in with me," he said.

Okay, I wasn't expecting that. "Don't want to be seen with the new guy, huh?" He didn't answer, just looked away with a sheepish expression on his face - the once cheeky smile now faded. I can't believe he actually looked worried about being seen with me. I know no one really likes to be seen with the new kid on the block but this was the most extreme I've seen it. "Fine, whatever."

I pushed past him and walked through the busy sounding classroom. The room, full of my new classmates, went quiet as soon as they saw me. I won't lie, it's not the most comfortable of welcomes. I felt like a stranger stumbling through a small town for the first time...A town where they aren't used to seeing a new face. They aren't used to it and nor do they welcome it.

"Hi," I said. Unsurprisingly no one answered. I turned back to the door hoping to see David's once friendly face. He wasn't there. Well...By myself then. "Okay then..." I muttered, more or less to myself, as I walked over to one of the spare seats at the front of the classroom. I always prefer sitting at the front of the class. I learned long ago that the teacher picks on you more if you choose to sit towards the back of the room as they think you're not paying any attention to what they're trying to teach you. I'm sure this teacher will be no different.

I started to root around in my rucksack. I wasn't looking for anything in particular; simply trying to distract myself from the whisperings coming from behind me. Little voices enquiring who I was and what I was doing here...One voice explaining how bent I looked. A friendly bunch then. In times like these, as sadly it's not the first time I've experienced this, I just have to keep telling myself that everything is going to be okay and they just need the chance to get to know me a little better. Day one is always awkward. By day two - you're yesterday's news. Just need to make it through to tomorrow.

"Faggot!" shouted a voice from behind me. I turned away from my rucksack and looked in the direction of the voice. One thing to whisper behind my back, it's another thing altogether to start name calling me...The insult came from a lad in the back of the class. Of course it was the back. A scruffy, stocky lad with messy blonde hair. He wasn't looking at me, though. Was the insult even meant for me? I followed his gaze to where David was stood in the doorway of the classroom. David looked anxious. Is this why he didn't want to come in with me? Worried the lads would pick on me because I was with him? Makes sense. I did think it was weird how he went from being so friendly to so cold. "I was starting to think you weren't coming in today," said the boy at the back of the class.

"Just took him longer to wank off Mr. Fitzpatrick this morning..." said a lad to the left of the one who started the insults. Laughter rippled through the classroom from most of the students. David didn't laugh. He simply walked over to an empty chair behind a pretty girl who was also laughing at him.

"Fuck," said the first lad, "why are you such a fucking faggot? Your mum and dad must be gutted to have you as a son. Oh wait, your mum's dead isn't she? Surprised I forgot that. After all, it was only last night I was skull fucking her corpse...Still...Your dad isn't dead. Probably just wishes he was. I reckon he's sat at home now wondering why his son is such a bender..."

"Maybe he's using you as his role model," I said. I couldn't help but speak up. David was visibly upset and this was obviously a daily occurrence. No sooner had the words escaped my mouth than the class fell silent. The lad looked at me; a look of hatred in his blue eyes.

"Fuck you say?"

"Well I too was wondering how he's as gay as he is...The way he so expertly sucks cocks...The only way I can see someone his age, being so great at swallowing spunk, is if he had a role model. I look around here and the only possibility is you and your bum-chum friends."

"Who the fuck are you anyway?"

"You don't recognise me? I'm the one who was fucking your mother late last night...Could have sworn I saw you hiding in the cupboard tugging yourself off at the sight of my fine ass and your mum's pert breasts."

The lad stood up and started to walk over to me. I think it's fair to say we're never likely to be friends even though most of the other classmates were finding me hysterical.

"Take your seats!" shouted a female voice from the front of the classroom. I looked around and saw a pretty female teacher. I think it's fair to say she couldn't have timed that better if she had tried.

I turned my back on the lad. He wasn't going to try anything with the teacher there. Who knows, maybe he'll have a chance to calm down during this lesson? Don't really care either way. Bullies like him...They're all talk. I've met his kind before. I shot David a quick look and smiled at him. He wasn't smiling back. He almost looked apologetic.

❧

I recalled seeing that expression on David's face the first day when I had stood up for him. He looked sorry for thinking he had got me involved in his troubles. I want to tell him this isn't his fault. I want to tell him that they had brought it upon themselves. I want to tell him but I don't.

I turned back to the rest of the class. They all look worried. No doubt they're wishing I had called their names out too. Give them a way out. Looking around at the remaining classmates, I didn't realise there were so many who had wronged me. I can't help but think it would have been better picking a double lesson to do this. Where to start? Where to start? Given the fact I might not get to everyone...Only one place to start really...

⅄

As another fist connected to my already bloodied nose, I couldn't help but think - through the intense pain flowing through my body - day two was already worse than day one.

I dropped to my knees, on the bathroom floor, and tried to focus my vision. I could hear David screaming from the far side of the room as he was receiving the same treatment. My blurred vision snapped back to the best focus it was able to...Just in time to see Piers, the lad who I had had a run in with on day one, spit at me.

"Not such a smart-arse now, are you?"

I wish I could come back with a witty retort but my brain is telling me I've taken enough of a beating for today. Another fist to the face floored me. I didn't move. I just lay there on the tiled floor, near the puddles of piss by the urinal, wishing for it to end. At least I think that's what I am thinking about. So many thoughts buzzing through my brain that it's hard to make sense of many of them. Another fist flew towards my face in a blurred motion. This will hurt...

By the time I could hear my thoughts clear enough to make sense of them, they were being drowned out by the sound of David's voice. He was crying. My eyes focused on my surroundings. Still on the toilet floor, the stench of stale urine filling one of my nostrils. My other nostril blocked with blood. Every part of me aches.

"I'm sorry," said David again. He helped me to my feet. He looked just as battered as I did although, I think it's fair to say, I took the brunt of it. Probably deserved after sticking up for him yesterday.

"You've got nothing to be sorry for," I said. Even my voice sounded broken. "Besides," I lied, "I quite enjoyed that." Not sure why I do that, trying to put a brave face on and all that. Not the first time I've used that as a defence mechanism for when I'm in agonising pain.

"If you hadn't stuck up for me yesterday," he started to say...

"I wouldn't have been much of a friend," I interrupted. Even had I known the beating I was to endure, I still would have spoken up yesterday. I hate bullies. They're nothing more than cowards hiding behind their little friends. Normally picking on the weaker people just to try and make themselves feel better about their own miserable lives. Fuck them. We both looked at ourselves in the mirror. "Remember..." I said, "...The first rule of Fight Club is...Don't talk about Fight Club." David laughed and suddenly grabbed his jaw as a bolt of pain shot through him.

Surely Day Three will be easier.

CHAPTER 4

I think I'd make a good teacher. I believe I have the voice for it. The right amount of authority in my tone.

"Piers," I said, using my teacher's tone, "step forward." If time is lacking, for my lesson, I'd best start with the main culprit. The one who has constantly been nasty. Seeing what I do to him...That might just be enough for the others to learn by, if I don't have the time to get to them. Piers didn't move from his seat; his usual place in the back of the classroom. Was he really going to make me repeat myself? "I'm sorry," I continued, "maybe you didn't hear me all the way back there." I turned to Mrs. Price, "Do you often struggle with students at the back not hearing you properly?" She didn't answer either. Can't help but think that's a little rude. It was a civil enough question, I feel. I'll come back to her later. I turned my attention back to Piers. Just looking at his face makes me feel sick. Memories of what he's put me through. I'm sure David must feel the same too. "Piers, don't make me ask again."

"Fuck you," he spat from the area he foolishly perceived as being 'safe' at the back of the room. Little boy obviously doesn't appreciate how far bullets can fly. The rest of the class, especially those who sat in close proximity, wasn't as foolish as a clear gap appeared between me and Piers. I took the gun up from where it rested, close to me, on the table and pointed it directly at Piers. "You won't shoot me," he said. Damn, he's clever. Shooting him will be too easy.

"You're right," I lowered the gun.

"You're a fucking pussy," Piers hissed. His voice so full of venom towards me. How did someone so young get so much hatred inside of them? I blame the parents. I stood up and walked down the aisle of wooden desks and chairs to where Piers sat.

"I forgot," I said, "you're the big man aren't you? You're the one people should be afraid of. You're the one who calls the shots and controls the classrooms and corridors...Those who don't like you, or follow you, you set about destroying...You and your little gang. You think you're something special... You really do, don't you?" He leaned back on his chair so that he was resting on the back two legs of the chair only; the front legs completely clear of the floor. A defiant expression on his face. I smiled at him. I have to say, had the situation been reversed...Had he been the one with the gun pointed at me, I'd have been trembling. I'd have done anything he asked to save myself from getting shot. Is he brave or mentally retarded? "Well, I guess we can come back to you...You know...When you're ready to come forward," I said.

"Long wait," he muttered. A cocky glance to his surrounding friends. Little show-off.

"Well - long enough for you to start feeling better," I said. His defiant expression turned to one of confusion. I flashed him a smile and then hit him in the face with the butt of the handgun. His nose cracked and split open as blood immediately gushed over the table he sat at. One of his friends, a dark haired jock to the left of me, made a move as though to take me on; a move which stopped when he came face to face with the barrel of the gun. "Be smart," I whispered. I backed away from them...Back towards the front of the class...Back to where I could see everyone.

"Please stop!" Mrs. Price begged.

I shook my head. "These people...They made my life miserable...They didn't stop. I asked them. David asked them. They never stopped. Even when we asked you for help...You turned us away. Remember that?"

"Had I known..."

"We tried telling you. You didn't listen!"

"I would have stopped it."

"Hindsight is a wonderful thing, isn't it?"

Thinking about hindsight I wonder whether I made things worse, for David and I, when I initially spoke up. Would things have turned out differently had I stayed quiet like Craig? David never said the general level of abuse had gotten worse because of me but he was the sort of person to keep that sort of thing to himself. Maybe it wasn't as frequent before I came? Could ask him. Doubt he'll answer.

"This isn't the way to put things right," Mrs. Price continued. You'd think she'd shut up but obviously it's against her nature. "They can get suspended...Expelled even..."

"You really think they care whether they're in school or not?"

The third, fourth and fifth days were easier. They were even quite pleasant. Mainly because the back row of our class was empty as Piers and his friends didn't show up. I'm not sure where they went and I don't really care. Their absence, probably due to the beating they gave David and I. No doubt they were scared to come in, expecting a one-to-one with the Headmaster; not that David and I told anyone what had happened. Sure, we were asked but... We figured...It's done. It's over. Move on. Hopefully Piers, and all, will move on too.

By the end of the third day, I was comfortable enough to make my own way around the school without needing David showing me everything but I still hung around with him. Definitely one of the good ones. Who knows, when I leave this school - as, no doubt, I will as soon as Dad says we're moving away maybe, just maybe, this is a friendship that will stick. Be nice. Normally, when I move on, friendships are quick to disappear. That's always disappointing.

"I'm sure they'll care," said Mrs. Price as she still tried to convince me that grassing the bullies up was still the right thing to do.

I shook my head again. "Do you know what they say about you?"

"I don't care..."

"You should. Half of them want to fuck you...Disrespectful to both you and your husband...The other half...They think you have a cock..."

"Playground stuff..."

"Not denying it..."

"What?"

"Show us."

"Don't be so ridiculous."

"I said show us...Prove they're lying," I pointed the gun at her.

"What have I ever done to you?"

My mind drifted back to the numerous occasions she made me, or one of my classmates, feel stupid in front of everyone else. We'd stand there, after she told us to stand, and not be able to do a damned thing to stop her from tearing us apart over the slightest thing. Talking in class, no homework, poor homework, not paying attention, not getting the required pass mark on one of her many surprise tests...Anything could set her off. Sometimes it was justified but most of the time the dressing-down we received was over the top and probably against the school's policies. I wonder if the school actually has any policies, thinking about it.

"Come on," I said. "We're waiting."

"What do you want?"

"What do I want? I want to make you feel as little as you make us feel..."

"I make you feel little?"

"You know you do and, more to the point, you know when you're doing it. You always have the same wry smile upon your face."

"If I've ever made you feel stupid, I'm sorry..." She looks as though she's about to cry but I don't care. She deserves this. I aimed the gun directly at her eye so she could see straight down the barrel. "Please don't make me do this..." I pulled the hammer back once more, having carefully released it earlier. She started to cry. I, on the other hand, started to get excited. The feeling of power I'm wielding, I could get used to this. "Okay..." she said. She stood up, with her legs shaking, and unzipped the back of her tight black skirt. She paused, perhaps hoping I was going to tell her I was joking and she didn't have to remove it. I'll be doing no such thing. I could feel myself harden. Is it wrong to ask Rebecca to come back over? Maybe I should test out Mrs. Price? Well, that is if she doesn't have a cock. Don't think I fancy a blow job from a woman with a prick.

"What are you waiting for?" I asked, a wry smile on my face. Her face reddens as she drops her skirt. I can't help but feel a little disappointed to note she isn't wearing stockings but rather tights instead. On the plus side, they're over the top of a white cotton thong. Not quite the PVC or latex we were expecting to see. Perhaps she saves that for the weekends and days where she works the detention hall? A further plus to the situation reveals no penis. Just a nice mound where her pubic bone is. I'd love to fuck her. I bet she fucks like a good 'un.

"Happy?" she asked, fighting back her tears.

"What do you think class?" A quick scan of my fellow classmates, of which I thought the lads would be grateful for this, revealed no one was looking at Mrs. Price. They were all looking directly at me. "Look at her!" I ordered and they did. I looked back at Mrs. Price, "Turn around...Let them see you..." Following instructions like a good little student, she turned on the spot. She looked at them...A look in her eyes suggesting she was hoping one of them would come and help her, perhaps give her a jacket or something to wrap herself in. "Bend over I ordered."

"Surely this is enough," she said.

I shook my head. "Not yet. Bend over." She wept as she bent over, facing me. "Now turn around," I said. She did as she was told until her sweet arse was facing me directly. I can see the outline of her pussy lips through the material of both the tights and the thong. It makes me wonder what it would taste like. Perhaps a step too far? I'll have a bet I'm not the only one thinking along those lines, though. Even Piers, through his bloodied face, must be fancying a taste too. I should have made him turn around. I didn't mean to give him such a delightful treat. I licked my lips at the thought of what her juices would taste like and shifted in my chair. I've heard people say it tastes of fish but I don't believe it. I hope it doesn't. I'm not a fan of fish. I'm hoping it tastes like chicken, like one of my other friends described. Maybe I'll be in this school long enough to make a relationship with a girl.

That'd be nice. But then...Maybe I could just pull Mrs. Price towards me now...Pull her towards me, rip her tights...Pull her knickers to one side and give her a lick. My mouth is watering. I'm tempted but I won't. Not because I don't really want to and not because she isn't attractive. It's just...She is older than me. Maybe too old? Maybe she is past her sell by date and her creamy juices are off? Perhaps that is when they taste of fish. All this picturing what it tastes like...Rebecca...I'm ready for round two...

Chapter 5

"She is fit, though," I said to David. He didn't answer. He just smiled as he tucked into his lunchtime sandwich. "I mean, how are we supposed to concentrate when faced with that every day? I definitely would..."

"I wouldn't," said David. He swallowed his mouthful and took a sip of his carton of orange.

"What?"

"I said I wouldn't."

"You wouldn't want to sleep with Mrs. Price?" I asked with a surprised tone of voice. David shook his head. "You're kidding me, right? I think you're the only person who doesn't want to sleep with her...I mean, as long as the rumours aren't true and she doesn't have a manhood growing down there."

"Not my cup of tea," said David. I looked at him again. It was hard to tell whether he was having a laugh or not.

"Not your cup of tea?"

"No...Well...Not unless the rumours are true..." he continued.

"Wait...What? You want to sleep with her if she does have a cock?"

He smiled.

"What? Are you gay?"

David looked me straight in the eye as he swallowed his next mouthful of cucumber sandwich, "Yes..."

"Oh..."

"Is that a problem?"

I shook my head, "No, not at all...Just...You know...When Piers and his friends were calling you gay...I just thought...Well, you know...I thought they were name calling. I didn't realise they were stating actual fact. Not really any of my business..." There was an awkward pause, "I'm not, by the way..."

David laughed, "It's okay, I'm not about to pounce on you. I kind of guessed you weren't going by conversations we've been having! But...I mean...How do you know if you've never tried it?" I looked at him with a worried look on my face. He gave me a wink and suddenly responded by bursting out with laughter, "I'm messing...Jesus, should have seen your face."

"Yeah, good one...Okay...You got me..." I started to laugh; a delayed reaction.

I didn't care whether David was straight or gay. His sexual preferences were of no concern to me. Just because he was homosexual, it didn't mean I couldn't have him as a good friend and, sitting here with him in my first week, I felt lucky to consider him a buddy.

"The story about you and Mr. Fitzpatrick?" I asked when he had stopped laughing long enough for me to get a word in edgeways.

"That is a lie," he said.

"Fair enough..."

"I just wish I had!" he started to laugh again. His infectious laughter set me off too. "I mean, his arse...To die for...Seriously..."

"Dude, please stop..." I said, still laughing.

"Oh, I see, it's okay for you to discuss Mrs. Price's arse but not okay for me to discuss his tight, round butt...Imagine those muscles squeezing around your cock as you try not to squirt deep inside him..."

"Dude! I'm not listening anymore..."

"And he'd be groaning, and moaning...Begging even, to have it deeper in him...Deeper and harder..."

I put my fingers in my ears, "I'm not listening...I can't hear your disgusting thoughts...La La Laaaaaaaa....."

David cracked up and, as a result, thankfully stopped.

"You're sick," I told him.

"What are you two laughing about?" asked a pretty girl from my class. I think her name was Rebecca; the girl who sat in front of David. As soon as she got our attention by speaking, David stopped laughing and fell silent.

"You don't want to know," I said. I didn't know her well enough to be sure she'd appreciate the comments between David and me. I had seen her hanging around with Piers and his narrow-minded friends so...

"Listen, I just wanted to say I think you two were really cool..." she went on.

"How so?" I asked.

"I'm not stupid. None of us are. We know who caused those bruises... You not grassing them up to the Head...That was cool..." She smiled at me, a flash in her beautiful eyes.

"Well...Thanks..." I said. I felt myself blush; an annoying habit whenever a pretty girl spoke to me. I wonder whether, in years to come, I'll be able to control that...Better yet, I wonder whether it will stop completely. That'd be nice.

"Some of us are having a party this Saturday...Be nice if you could both come. Show there are no hard feelings between anyone. You know, a fresh start..." she continued.

I looked at David, "Sounds good, what do you think?" He didn't answer, he just stared at Rebecca as though he were expecting a punch line to some amazing joke she was telling. "David?"

"I can't," he said. "Busy. Some gay thing."

"That's too bad," said Rebecca, "it would have been nice...And...I could have got to know you a little better too." Her eyes were fixed on me. It was everything I could do to keep focused on her and not her cleavage. "Look, if you change your mind..." she fished in her pocket and pulled out a small card with a phone number on it..."Just give me a call and I'll pass on my address... Be nice if one of you could make it at least."

I took the card off her and, just as suddenly as she had appeared, she vanished back into the crowds of pupils all milling about with their lunches.

I turned to David, "I knew they were hiding from us. Scared of whether we had gone to the teachers...It's good, isn't it? A fresh start she said. Might leave me alone from here on in...Us alone. Both of us. Come on, it will be a laugh..."

"Have you heard the term 'fuck-buddy'?" asked David.

"Of course I have..."

"Well she is fuck-buddies with most of the school but...I think her and Piers are more than that. She's a piece of shit."

"She seems nice enough to me," I said. I smelt the card in my hands, "Even her card smells like perfume...Come on, it will be a laugh," I said.

"You can go if you want but I don't want to. Wherever they are, I tend to avoid."

"You mind if I go?" I didn't want to upset David but at the same time I didn't want to miss the chance to put things right with everyone. It would be nice to come to school not wondering whether I'm going to get another hiding or not.

"You do what you want," said David. I could tell by his tone that he didn't think it was a good idea and, more to the point, he didn't really want me going but...Surely he wouldn't fall out with me just because I chose to try and put things right...The chance to have things easier for both of us. How great would that be?

⅄

I couldn't help but think how great this was, as Mrs. Price pulled her skirt back up and took her seat amongst my fellow classmates. Her face is still red and the tears, in her eyes, are nothing more than an added bonus. I have a feeling, if she survives this, she won't be so keen to belittle any of her students again. Hell, she might even quit. Never teach again. No loss to the education system, that's for sure.

Rebecca was still crying in her seat too. Two scarred, hopefully for life, and one battered. I'm just disappointed the bruises will heal.

"Well, Piers, you ready yet?" I hope he tells me to 'fuck off' or something similar from his lacking intelligence; give me another reason to smash him in the face. Normally I'm against violence. I don't think it solves any-thing. That's partly why I never fought back on the occasions they jumped me. I mean...Ignoring how big he is in comparison to my skinny frame any-way. Even if I had wanted to fight back, I wouldn't have gotten very far. I'd have covered even less metaphorical distance on the times his friends were helping to give me a hiding. I never understood why he had them help - it's not as though he needed a hand.

Piers tipped his head back so it was facing me. His nose was still bleed-ing. How satisfying. I'm loving this. It's nearly making me as hard as the sight of Mrs. Price's cunt and the feeling of Rebecca's tongue. With his hand away from his face, he raised his middle finger.

Oh, Happy Days...A sadistic smile spread across my mouth. Like I said, normally I'm against violence but, I won't lie, it's slowly starting to grow on me.

Chapter 6

"Are you going to want us to pick you up?" asked my mum. The problem with my mum is that she wasn't trying to be helpful. She was trying to be nosy. She just wanted to get a glimpse of my new friends. No doubt she wanted to thank them for taking me under their wings as I found my way around a new school. She was always the same. It was embarrassing. The friends I did make often asked whether my mum would be home before agreeing to come around for a night of gaming on the console. They said she freaked them out a little. I couldn't blame them. Her only son, she had a habit of treating me as though I was still a baby. Definitely embarrassing. When she first saw the bruises Piers and his friends inflicted, she wanted to frog march me back to school and demand the Headmaster expelled everyone immediately. I tried telling her it wasn't necessary. I tried telling her it would just make things worse for me but...You know how parents can be especially when they have a bee in their bonnet about something.

"I'm fine," I muttered as I pulled a clean, black shirt from my wardrobe.

"Don't you have anything brighter you can wear?" she asked. "You're always dressing in black...Colour suits you so well..."

"I want black. Black is cool," I said. I also perceived it was a power colour too. Mum once said she thought I was a Goth. I couldn't help but laugh. I'm hardly a Goth. It's not like I wear make-up and dress head to foot in black and go around listening to heavy metal whilst cutting myself...Mind you, I don't really know any Goths...Maybe they don't do that? Maybe it's just bad movies portraying them in a negative light.

"Well it's nice to see you settling so quickly," she continued. "Especially after what happened at the start of the week...Do you at least want a lift?"

"It's fine, Mum, really. I can make my own way."

"Well, if you're sure..."

I feel sorry for Mum really. I know why she is so keen to be part of my life. It's because she doesn't really have her own life. She gets moved around just as much as me, because of Dad. At least I have the chance to meet new friends and different people by going to school. She doesn't have to work. In fact, Dad said he didn't want her to. He wanted her to be at home...Keep the household together and meals on the table whilst he went out and provided. Old fashioned views, I guess. It did mean that Mum didn't get to socialise with people her own age, especially as she lacked the confidence to join local groups that would have opened the door to meeting new, like-minded people. She just stayed in the house and went a little more stir-crazy each day.

"Thank you, Mum. Really. But I'm sure."

She gave me a smile and said, "Well, I'll leave you to get ready then..." and, with that, she left the room.

I do love her though.

⋏

My heart was beating fast and hard as I pressed the doorbell button to Rebecca's house. I know this is all for the best; a fresh start. A chance to turn the hatred Piers and the others feel for me into something more positive. Doesn't make me any less nervous though. Not a good thing, being nervous. I have a bad habit of being ultra-sarcastic, without meaning to be, or extremely quiet. Neither are traits which make me any more endearing. I wish David had come with me. At least there'd have been someone here who definitely liked me.

Footsteps from beyond the door. Someone is coming. The door opened and Rebecca was stood there. A vision of beauty. She was dressed in a short black dress which looks as though it's barely covering her backside. I won't lie; she looks hot. Really hot. Her face was done up with heavy make-up. Normally I prefer 'subtle' but...It suits her.

"You came!" she exclaimed. She actually sounded as though she was pleased. "I was hoping you would!" She reached across to my hand and led me into the house.

I already feel as though I'm out of my depth. She took me through to the lounge where Piers and his friends were sitting. There were six of them altogether. The room fell silent when they saw me. I feel sick but I can't show it. Piers was the first to stand up and walk over.

"You didn't grass," he said, "I respect that...And look, we've both said and done some stupid things but...What do you say we start afresh?" he sounded sincere.

"I'd like that," I said.

"You're alright," he said. He turned away from me and joined his friends again. Seconds later they were back to whatever it was they were talking about before I walked in.

"See," said Rebecca, "a fresh start."

I smiled at her. Was that it? Was that all that was needed?

"Can I get you a drink?" she asked. She didn't wait for an answer. Still holding my hand she pulled me through to the large kitchen which was crammed full of various drinks - mainly of an 'alcopop' variety. "We pretty much have everything here," she said.

"That's a lot of alcohol," I said.

"Everyone chipped in." Whoops. Was I supposed to offer money too? A little bit of cash towards the alcohol pool? I don't have anything on me now other than the cash I need to get the taxi home. Could give her that. Could give Mum a call to come and collect me...No. Forget that. I don't need her seeing Rebecca. She'll jump to conclusions, no doubt, that we're a couple. Probably end up having the safe-sex speech and everything. Worse still, she'll invite Rebecca over for Sunday dinner...Although, that wouldn't be a bad thing...Ever since I first saw her I thought she looked nice. "Try that," she passed me a red drink. Not got a clue what it is and what it'll taste like but I don't want to appear uncool by asking or refusing it.

"Thanks," I said.

"David couldn't make it, huh?" she asked.

"No, he said he was busy..."

"A shame." Laughter boomed from the living room. "Did you want to go upstairs so we could talk? It's quieter..."

"Ummm, sure," I said. It was the first time I had had a girl inviting me upstairs. I desperately tried to sound relaxed and cool about it but I'm pretty sure I failed. She smiled and led me through the house, back towards the stairs. She went up the stairs first, leading the way. I always thought I was a gentleman but, as I stared at her tight little arse the whole way up...Well...I guess I'm not that much of a gentleman!

"It's just through there," she pointed to a door across the landing from the stairs, "I'll be right there - make yourself comfortable." She turned into what looked to be the bathroom and I crossed the landing to what turned out to be her room.

Weird. Everything is pink. I'm not sure what I expected but I'm pretty sure it wasn't a completely pink room. Pink walls, pink duvet...Even the carpet is a lighter shade of pink. Definitely a young girl's room. You wouldn't have guessed this was her room. I guess I half expected pictures of semi-naked pop stars hanging from the walls and make-up scattered around the place...Hell, I even thought I'd see different outfits dropped on the floor from where she was trying things on for her party. But, in this room, everything seems to have its own place. Speaking of which, dressed in black, I must really look out of place here!

"Sorry about that," she appeared in the doorway behind me. I turned to look at her. Was it just me or did her breasts suddenly appear to be...Well....larger? No complaints here. I tried to avert my eyes so as not to offend or come across as a creep. She simply smiled and walked past me, brushing my crotch with her hand. Was that a mistake? That smell...She smells even more so of the sweet perfume I caught a scent of when she first opened the door to me. I'm not sure what it is but I like it. She sat on the bed and patted the mattress next to her. An invitation for me to join her? Embarrassingly, I felt myself harden. I can only hope she didn't notice.

I crossed the room and sat next to her. I wonder if I looked as nervous as I felt. Come on, you're supposed to be a man. Act like one. "I have to say, I wasn't expecting your room to look like this," I said.

"No? What were you expecting?" She turned her body to face me and dropped her hand on my leg. I am now fully erect and feeling incredibly awkward. "You look good tonight."

"Thanks," I stuttered. Stupid. I should have told her she looked good too and not just tonight. She always looked good.

She laughed, "You feel tense...Relax..."

Before I could answer she leant forward and kissed me on the mouth. Seconds later and she was kissing me again with her tongue down my throat. Aggressive...Nice...

She pulled away slightly, "You're a good kisser."

I tried to answer but my mouth didn't want to work. Besides...I wasn't sure whether she was just saying that. Being kind. I wonder if she could tell it was my first kiss. She leant in again with her left hand on my cheek. As she continued to kiss me, her hand stroked down my cheek with her nails scratching me ever so gently. Lower it went...Down my neck...Down my chest...Until it rested on my crotch. She made a funny 'mmm' noise from her mouth and, using both hands, fussed around with my belt until it was un-done - allowing her access to do the same to my jeans. Is this really happening? I desperately wanted to touch her, like she was touching me. I wanted to feel the softness, and warmth, of her skin. I wanted to feel her breasts...I wanted to but didn't. I was just frozen to the spot; allowing her to do as she pleased.

"Ooh, big boy," she purred as she freed my erection from the confines of my boxer shorts. I feel like I should stop her. Perhaps get to know her a little first? I thought the correct order was a few dates, holding hands, couple more dates, a first kiss, more holding hands and then, eventually, some kind of sexual act. I didn't think it would be like this. "I have some condoms in the drawer over there..." she whispered in my ear. Fuck it. Holding hands is lame anyway.

"Sure," I stammered, my hands still frozen to the mattress.

She jumped off the bed and walked across the room, leaving me on the bed momentarily.

"Now!" she suddenly yelled. Within an instant, the bedroom door flew open and Piers burst in with a mobile phone in his hand and a huge, evil smile on his face.

"Gross! What are you doing! Having a wank in Rebecca's little sister's room? You know how fucked up that is? She's only eight. You fucking pervert!"

I didn't know what was going on nor did I hang around for an answer. I got up as quickly as I could, turning my back to the mobile phone, and adjusted myself to hide my erection. The sound of Rebecca laughing, from the corner of the room, echoing through my worried mind...

So much for a fresh start.

CHAPTER 7

If Piers had meant what he had said, that evening, about us having a fresh start...If Rebecca hadn't tricked me into making me look stupid...Right now, Mrs. Price would, no doubt, be shouting at one of us for handing in a below par homework assignment. As it is, she's just sat there, looking mortified at what she's just done. Rebecca is still sniffling away in the corner of the room and Piers is still bleeding as he deserves to.

"Have another little think," I said to Piers as I went back to the front of the classroom, "and we'll have another chat in a bit," I said. Back at the front of the class, I turned to Ben Griffin and Daniel Gordon. Two of Piers' closest friends. Unlike the physical violence Piers liked to dish out, these two were too weak to do much damage like that. Instead they preferred the tried and tested method of name calling. Whoever said 'sticks and stones may break my bones but words will never hurt me' clearly hasn't been on the receiving end of people who spend the vast majority of their time using hateful words. I've lost count of the amount of times, in my short time in this school, where I've been on the receiving end of a bout of name calling from these two narrow minded little pricks. It's stupid of me, and others, to get hurt by it but...You hear something enough times and you start to believe it. It wears you down. "Ben and Daniel, can you come to the front of the class please?" I'm not sure why I said 'please'. I don't need to say things like that anymore. I don't need to be polite. I'm the one in charge. It wasn't a friendly request. It was an order.

They looked at each other, unsure whether they should or not. A quick glance at Piers, who was barely conscious from the last pistol whipping he received, and the two of them stood up; neither of them wanting to be on the receiving end of that kind of brutality. I wonder, had they known what was coming their way...I wonder whether they'd still have chosen to stand up. I smiled. Slowly they came forward. Both of them were tall individuals. Both with dark hair. Both with dark brown eyes. Same size, width-wise, too. You'd be forgiven for thinking they were brothers.

"Do you remember when David told you about Ben and Daniel?" I asked Mrs. Price. She didn't answer. How rude. "Do you remember he reported that they kept calling him names? I remember. He told you how it upset him and how he didn't like it. He asked for your help and you told him not to be so silly. It was, after all, just name calling. Which, by the way, is still bullying. Do you remember?"

"Yes," she nodded.

"We were just playing around," said Ben.

"Oh, well, that's okay then...Please, take a seat..." I said. My sarcasm slipping out again. Ben, foolishly, went to move back to his seat at the back of the class, "Don't you fucking move," I hissed. He froze on the spot. Good lad. Not as stupid as he appears. "Tell me, what did you call David when you were playing around?" I asked. Neither of them answered. Maybe they've forgotten. "Faggot. Queer. Beaver-leaver. Homo. Gay. Gayboy. Rimmer... Just a few of the names..."

"We were just playing..."

"You knew it upset him. You knew he didn't see it as playing."

"We're sorry," said Daniel.

"Too late." I tried not to show glee as they both looked as though they were about to cry. "Well...I suppose...We could kiss and make up..." They didn't say anything. They just looked at one another hoping one of them would understand what I was talking about. They turned back to me with blank expressions on their faces. There was a pause. "Come on then, kiss and make up..."

After the video that Piers took on his mobile phone was emailed to - as it turned out - everyone who subscribed to the school's digital magazine, which was run by the students, it was Daniel and Ben who started the rumour that I was a paedophile. It was them who stated the whole video couldn't be shown because it showed Rebecca's younger sister dancing for me in her underwear. They admitted that was a lie when the police were involved but not so everyone could hear - only the officers, my mum and Rebecca's parents. Rebecca denied being in the room at the time; her denial helped by the fact that the sound was muted with dodgy 'porn' music edited over it. Ben and Daniel never did apologise for the trouble it landed me in. It didn't help that David was sulking with me too. He had warned me not to go and felt that I should have trusted what he said.

"I don't understand," said Daniel.

"Let me spell it out to you," I said. "I want you to kiss Ben."

Daniel looked down to the gun, in my hand, and then over to Piers at the back of the room. He turned to Ben and leant forward. After he closed his eyes he gave him a quick kiss on the cheek.

"Well," I said, "that was very sweet but...I think you can do better than that. Kiss him like you mean it. I want to see tongues. You know...Because I'm such a faggot."

"We didn't mean it!" said Ben; a look of panic on his face and his voice shaking. "Please...We didn't mean it. Okay?"

"Okay. Thanks. Means a lot to me. Now...Kiss. And look as though you're enjoying it."

⋏

The fallout from the leaked video footage was more or less over by the third week. At least, it was at school. At home Mum still wouldn't let me go out and she still wasn't entirely happy with what had happened. I kept telling her it wasn't my fault but she just kept saying how embarrassing it was for the family. For the family? What about me? I didn't ask to have the video shown everywhere. I didn't want people seeing it. I'm the one who has to go out and see the people who have seen the video. It's not like Mum bumps into the people who watched it. It's not as though Mum bumps into anyone.

"Your father is going to be so disappointed when he gets home," Mum kept reminding me.

"Who cares what he thinks? Who cares what anyone thinks? It's not like we'll be here for very long! We never are!"

"And then what did she say?" asked David. I was sat with him in the cafeteria. It was the first time we had spoken properly since the video leaked.

"She said I was ungrateful. Apparently Dad does all this for me…Moving around…The working…Apparently it's all for me but that's rubbish."

"How so?"

"If they wanted the best for me, they'd have left me in the same school. They wouldn't move me around. They'd want me to meet new people, make new friends and, more importantly, keep them!"

"Dad works because it's what he wants. He doesn't give a shit about me or Mum. Pretends he does but…He doesn't."

David didn't say anything. I guess he realised I just needed to vent.

"Well, I'm sorry for everything you went through," he said eventually.

"Thank you."

"But…"

"Don't say it."

"I told you so…"

I gave him a look which said 'thanks for that'. He simply smiled.

"Everything sorted now though?" he asked. "I mean, with regards to the police and Head?"

I nodded, "I nearly got expelled for it."

"I saw the film…" he smiled, "…impressive."

"Oh, fuck you."

David laughed.

"Look out…a new film in the making," said Daniel.

I spun around and saw Daniel and Ben on the table behind us. They were laughing, like they usually were when they were mocking someone or something. A real life version of Tweedle-Dee and Tweedle-Dum. David rolled his eyes.

"Who do you think will be the giver and who will be the taker?" asked Ben.

I didn't say anything. There was so much I could say but...There was no point. I had already learnt that smart arse comments don't make them go away. Today was all about trying something new; ignoring them. I looked at David and hoped he'd stay quiet too.

"Look...Look at the way they're looking at each other...They're going to kiss..."

⚔

"Look..." I said to my fellow classmates, "...Look, they're going to kiss..."

"Please," said Ben. "We've said we're sorry."

"And I appreciate it. Now kiss." I raised the gun up to his face. "I won't be asking again..."

Ben and Daniel looked at each other. A slight pause as they both processed what they were going to have to do.

"Wait!" I suddenly yelled. They pulled away from each other. "Wait..." There was relief on their faces. I took up a mobile phone, from the table on the teacher's table, and loaded up the camera. "Okay, now you can kiss." They knew I wasn't joking. "And...Action..."

There was a long pause as they just looked at each other. They turned to the camera. Off shot I waved the gun in the air. They looked back to one another. They knew what they had to do. The funny thing is, though, they don't know the half of what they have to do. Today, they are my performing monkeys and I'm going to make the most of it.

"Kiss him, faggot," I hissed.

Mrs. Jones shifted uneasily in her chair. Probably remembering her little show and tell for the class. I shot her a glance to keep her quiet. By the time I looked back to Ben and Daniel they were standing nose to nose. Be interesting to see who makes the first move. My money is on Ben. 'Bender Ben' has a certain ring to it. Daniel leaned forward and kissed Ben on the mouth. I'm glad I didn't put any real money on it. They stopped and turned to me. I hadn't moved. I was still pointing the camera at them. That wasn't a kiss.

Not a proper one. Not like lovers. I peered out from behind the phone's screen and gave them a stern look...A stern look they both understood. They turned back to each other. This time it was Ben to make the move. He stepped forward and tilted his head to the side with his mouth slightly opened. Daniel moved closer too, his mouth also open slightly. Soon their lips were interlocked in a passionate embrace. I could be wrong but...They look as though they're enjoying it. Certainly making for interesting footage. Wonder what the rest of the school will think of it when I email it to the same people Piers emailed when he made his little video?

Chapter 8

"Let's go," I said to David. I did my best to ignore the comments from Ben and Daniel; did my best to rise above it but they were starting to annoy me and I knew David would have been feeling the same.

"Aw, where are you going?" Daniel asked.

"Toilets, I expect," said Ben. "Probably want to have a little sausage for their pudding." They laughed. Other people, who were sat around them listening, also laughed. Very funny.

Ben and Daniel pulled away from their kiss. A little string of saliva was the last to snap away from their embrace.

"So how was that?" I asked. "I have to say, and I'm sure I'm not alone in saying this, it looked as though you both enjoyed it. Did you?" They didn't answer. First time ever they've both been silenced. Should have done this ages ago. "Remove your trousers." They both looked startled. No doubt they had hoped I was going to let them sit back down. They're wrong. I'm not done with them. I'm a way off being done. Daniel undid his trousers and dropped them to the floor. "Well, looks as though your efforts weren't up to his standard," I said to Ben. Ben didn't budge. "Your turn." Again, he didn't move. "Help him, Dan...You're his friend, aren't you? You'd hate for him to be hurt, right?"

Daniel turned to Ben, "Please...Just do as he says...Don't make me..."

Ben reluctantly lowered his trousers and I couldn't help but laugh when I noticed he was hard. "I guess Dan's the better kisser, huh?" Ben went bright red, as did Daniel. We're still not done yet, though. "I bet you could murder a little sausage right about now, huh? Some nice pudding..."

I stepped forward and pulled Ben's shorts down. His erection popped up, standing to attention for the whole class to see and be disgusted by. I don't want to look too closely but I bet it's covered in pre-cum.

"You talk about it all the time," I said to Daniel, "because I reckon it's what you want...YOU want to have a little sausage for pudding..."

"What? No. No..."

"I think you protest too much. Here's your chance...Put him in your mouth."

"Please, no...I'm not gay."

"Me neither but you two insisted on saying I was just because I was friends with someone who happened to choose that particular path in life. And that wasn't the worst that you said, let us not forget that...Now, put him in your fucking mouth and keep him there..." Daniel didn't move. I stormed over to him and swung the gun down to his kneecap, catching him on the side. He let out a squeal and dropped to his knees. "I said, put him in your fucking mouth..."

"Just do it," said Ben.

"See, he's begging for it. He wants you to...This little faggot here...Put him in your mouth."

Someone fidgeted in their seat behind me so I swung around with the gun and aimed it at them. They froze. I turned back to Daniel and pressed the gun against his temple.

"The lesson is almost over. You can nearly walk away from this...If you don't do this...If you refuse...You won't walk away."

Slowly he edged closer and closer to Ben's penis. He opened his mouth and let the shaft slide to the back of his throat. Ben moaned. Not sure if that was a groan of pleasure or one born from being uncomfortable.

"Doesn't that taste good?" I asked. "Now move back and forwards...You've seen how the ladies do it in the movies you have undoubtedly watched...Do it. Do it."

Daniel started to move back and forwards, just as I had told him to, and Ben's moans became more frequent. Every time Ben's penis hit the back of Daniel's mouth, Daniel couldn't help but gag.

"You like that?" I asked Ben. His eyes were shut. I'm not sure if he was picturing Daniel sucking him off or picturing, perhaps, Rebecca or Mrs. Price. Either way, this wasn't for him to be enjoying. With no warning, I turned to Daniel and kicked up, as hard as I could, between his legs. The sudden rush of pain caused his mouth to clamp shut...I was surprised at how far the blood spurted, from Ben, when Daniel moved away. Both of them dropped to the floor in agony.

"Who's next?" I asked the class.

John, one of the quieter members of the group, jumped up and made a dash for the door. I was unsure of his intentions. Maybe he wanted to get help for Ben. Maybe he wanted to escape his own lesson. Either way...Silly move considering I wasn't exactly so far away I wouldn't get to the door first. I thrust the gun in his face.

"Sit the fuck down."

I'm still amazed at how easy it is to control a small group with one hand-gun. Surely they must realise I don't have enough bullets for all of them? I guess none of them are willing to sacrifice themselves in order to save their friends. The cowards. All they need to do is rush me. I probably wouldn't even be able to empty the entire clip. It is, indeed, a selfish world we live in.

$$ \wedge $$

"I hate this place!" David exclaimed when we were away from Ben and Daniel's earshot. "There are all these anti-bullying posters around making it look as though the school actually gives a damn but they don't. They don't give a flying fuck about their pupils getting bullied." I didn't say anything. I just let him have his little rant. "I've been to the teachers before but they don't care. They don't want to know. If they do say anything to the people involved...It's half-hearted. It's not meant and certainly isn't enough to deter them. It makes me sick. Just shows you really are alone." He started to cry. Should I put my arm around him? Not sure. Would he get the wrong idea?

"All that talk about sticks and stones breaking bones but words never hurting...Broken bones heal. Bruises heal. Harsh words can have a long-lasting effect." I couldn't argue with him. He had a point. He looked to me, "You're not doing a very good job of making me feel any better."

"I'm sorry," I stammered. "Not really sure what to say."

"Anything!" he said.

After a slight pause, "There, there...Everything will be okay..." He couldn't help but laugh at how useless I was. Comforting people never really was my strong point. I guess I don't really have the family background to afford me that little life skill. Dad was always working and Mum would always over compensate which I found annoying. "So what do you want to do?"

"I just wish I could make them all suffer."

"Well, I'm sure that would be great but...I don't think it's very practical. Besides, I meant what do you want to do now?"

"I'm not going to class. Fancy going to the cinema or something?"

I nodded. Hopefully he'll be paying.

⚔

Daniel was on the floor, at the front of the class, crying with blood smeared around his mouth. I'm not sure if he is crying because he's just bitten his friend's penis off or crying because of the pain from being kicked. Maybe a little bit of both? Ben, on the other hand, is deathly quiet in his unconscious state. He looks pale. I wonder whether he'll eventually end up bleeding to death from his injury? Maybe. If he does, he brought it upon himself.

"Go back to your seat," I said to Daniel.

Slowly he stood up and walked down the middle aisle back to his seat - all of his classmates staring at him. I liked how everyone was looking at him. All staring...All judging for what he has just done. He won't be able to forget their looks. They'll be with him forever...Just as the taste of human flesh will haunt him.

I looked around the class. Who's next? My eyes settled on a girl at the front of the class. She immediately started to cry. She knows it is her turn.

"Please, I haven't done anything to you..." It's true. She hasn't done anything to me. It's only from hearing her call out, during the many registrations we have sat through, that I am aware of her name; Chloe. "Please..."

"I know you haven't," I said. "But this isn't all about me." I turned to look at the seven stood behind me: David, Lindsey, Elizabeth, Marcus, Samantha, Kate, Helen...They all look to be enjoying my little floor show. I turned back to Chloe...Sitting there, looking pretty with her short, dark hair and her big brown eyes, carefully applied make-up used to enhance her looks as opposed to hide them behind an unnecessary layer of slap. Looking into her eyes, she already looked as though she were going to start crying. Pathetic. You'd have thought people who were nasty to other people...You'd have thought it would have been harder to break them but this is proving fairly easy. "Come to the front of the class," I instructed her. "Let's have a chat."

Reluctantly Chloe stood up. She gave a glance in the direction of her friends. No doubt she was hoping one of them would step forward and offer her some assistance. Not a chance. They didn't want to get involved. They didn't want the spotlight turned onto them. Chloe stood a few feet away from me. I had never really noticed before how skinny she was. I wonder if she was naturally that skinny or whether she was one of these girls who'd eat a meal just to sick it back up in the toilet when they thought no one was looking?

"Lindsey..." All I did was say a girl's name and Chloe started to cry. She knew where this was going. "Do you want to tell the class what you did to Lindsey?" Chloe shook her head. "Oh, come on now...Don't be shy...Would you rather we asked Lindsey?"

"Please stop it."

They all say the same thing. It's getting tiresome. I'm not going to stop, just as they didn't either when they were asked. Fair is fair, after all.

"You look nervous. Don't be. We're all friends, aren't we? Here...I got you something..." I reached into my rucksack, which I had left by the table at the front of the class, and pulled out a Tupperware box. I pulled the lid off and showed Chloe the contents. "Chocolate cake..."

"I don't want any."

"Of course you do, don't be ungrateful. I got one for you and one for your friend Lindsey...You know she likes cakes."

"I'm sorry."

"For what? You've done nothing to be sorry for...Have you? Have I missed something?" I hadn't missed anything. I knew what Chloe had done. She would spend her time, with her friends from the year above, following Lindsey around taunting her because of her weight. Lindsey being one of the school's larger pupils. I'm not sure if it was because she over-ate or some genetic thing which made her so. It wasn't important. The consequences of their words always had the same ending; Lindsey would cry herself to sleep, sometimes cutting herself before she climbed into her bed.

"We need to get Ben some help," said Mrs. Price. She wasn't watching Chloe and me. Her eyes were fixed on Ben. He looked pale, there was no denying that. "He's dying..."

"I'm talking to my friend. Please don't interrupt me again," I said. I turned back to Chloe and handed her a cake. "Eat it."

"I'm not hungry."

"You can eat it willingly or I can feed you. I don't mind which."

She looked back to her friends. None of them made a move to help her. Slowly she took the cake from me and looked at it.

"It looks good, doesn't it?" I asked. "I made it myself."

"Please, I'm not hungry."

"Of course you are. Look at it! How can that not make you hungry?"

The cake did look good. Chocolate sponge covered in chocolate icing. I would have eaten it myself. Had I not put in the little extra ingredient. Chloe moved the cake closer to her mouth. Slowly her mouth opened. It must be watering in there. How could it not? The cake looks amazing. I should set up a little shop. Start selling them. I could make a fortune.

Chapter 9

was sitting with David, in the cinema, waiting for the film to start. He paid; some chick flick he had wanted to see. I should have known when he invited me to a film that it wouldn't have been a typical horror for boys to enjoy. Ah well, I couldn't grumble; it was still better than being in class, I suppose. Just.

"So how would you teach them a lesson?" I asked him.

"Not really thought about it."

"Really?"

"Okay, I'd make them kiss each other," he said, a split second later.

"What?"

"Piers and his friends...In front of the whole class...I'd make them kiss each other. That way they couldn't call me gay anymore."

"They couldn't?"

"Of course not..." The lights dimmed and the screen flickered into life. David whispered to me, "If everyone has seen them kiss...They'd hardly be in a position to carry on calling me gay!" I didn't answer him. I suppose, all being said and done, he had a point.

"How'd you make them kiss?" I asked.

He shrugged, "I don't know...Wave a gun in their face?"

I laughed, "You have thought about this, haven't you?"

"Lots," he answered immediately. "Want some of my popcorn?" He tipped his large tub of popcorn towards me.

I shook my head, "No thanks. Hate popcorn. It tastes like shit."

⚔

A smile spread across my face as fresh dog shit dribbled down Chloe's chin. I guess the little stint in the oven made it runny? Should have expected that, not that it's a problem. It was probably worse for her, to have it trickle down her face. She'll be tasting that for days. As soon as she realised what it was, she gagged and spat the cake onto the floor.

"No!" I shouted. "You must eat it all!" I grabbed the cake and shoved it into her mouth. My hand clamped across her face to stop her from spitting it out once more. She struggled, in my grasp, but I didn't release her until I felt her swallow some of it. "That's it...Good girl..." I couldn't help but think of Rebecca swallowing my own poison too. A smile spread across my face. As soon as I let go of Chloe, she threw up on the floor. It's starting to smell in here...What with the blood, puke, shit and stench of fear. Thank God the lesson is nearly over. It'll be nice to get some fresh air. "You can sit down now," I whispered to Chloe when she finished sicking up, what she had eaten, onto the floor. She stood up and made her way back to her seat, spitting as she went.

"You're going to burn in Hell for this," said Mrs. Price. "You know that, don't you?" She didn't look scared of me anymore. She looked angry. A familiar expression we, as a class, were used to. Maybe she knew I wasn't going to actually shoot anyone? "Your mum and dad will be known around the world for what you have done. You'll be rotting in prison, and then Hell, and they'll be having to live with the consequences of your actions."

"Then I guess, with all of us residing there, Hell will be full."

"Just let us go before you do something you'll regret."

"I'll regret nothing of today."

"You say that now but in years to come...You'll realise...This wasn't the way..."

I turned to David, behind me. The look on his face...The look of sorrow. Lindsey's face...Having just seen her tormentor eat dog shit...I won't regret anything about today.

"When you're quite finished," I said, "there's still much to do."

"You're a psycho," she continued.

"No, I'm not. I'm a product of my surroundings. You...All of you sitting here...You all made me."

"That's rubbish," said Mrs. Price. I knew I could count on her to ruin my buzz. "People are bullied every day. You don't see them holding their class to ransom."

"I'm not holding anyone to ransom! As soon as the bell goes, you're all free to leave."

"Let us go now!"

"Now you know you're not allowed to wander the corridors during lesson time. You can get sent to the Head's office. You can go as soon as the bell goes. Those aren't my rules. They're the schools..."

"They'd allow an exception..."

I glared at her, "Did you want to come to the front of the class again? Have you not learned your lesson?" She didn't say anything. "That's what I thought."

I turned back to the seven behind me. Lindsey seems satisfied how I dealt with Chloe. David seems to be quieter than usual. Funny, really, considering this was his plan initially. Five more students who need someone to fight their battles for them; Elizabeth, Marcus, Samantha, Kate, Helen. I'm not entirely sure I'll be able to help them all. Not entirely sure there is time enough to deal with each of their complaints. Never enough time.

⅄

"Where have you been?" asked Mum as soon as I stepped into the family home. I didn't answer her straight away. I wasn't expecting to be bombarded with her questions as soon as I walked in. Couldn't exactly tell her I had been at the cinema with David. She'd be mad that I hadn't gone to school. She might even be mad enough, after the video incident, to report it to Dad too - when he comes home from work...If he comes home from work. "I asked you a question - where have you been? Dinner is ruined." Dinner wouldn't have been ruined; I doubt she would have even cooked it yet.

"I was in the library with David," I lied. Stupid, really, as she knew it would be a lie. I can't remember the last time I went to a library.

"The school phoned."

"What?"

"They phoned. Apparently you didn't show up for registration after lunch. They wanted to know if everything was okay."

"They actually called?"

"Yes..."

"They do that?"

"So where were you?" Mum's face reddened. I knew she was mad. One of the signs she was angry was when her face went a bright shade of red; similar to if she were embarrassed. The thing with Mum, though, is that she'd only be angry because she wouldn't have known where I was... Because she would have been worried...Not because I didn't go to class. "Well?"

"I was at the cinema..."

"With David?"

"Yes, with David. We had some problems at lunchtime and couldn't face going back for the afternoon. We didn't think it would be a problem..."

"More like you didn't think the school would have called?"

"And that...Look, Mum, I don't like it there. The name-calling...The bullying..."

"They'll settle down, it's just because you're new."

"What? No. No it's not. It's because I am friends with a homosexual and I dared stick up for him. You saw what happened with the video. You saw that. The trouble I got into...It's going to carry on. God only knows what they'll do next. I don't want to go back..."

"You have to go back! I'm sure they'll soon get bored and move onto someone else."

"It's different to the way it was when you were at school, Mum...You know, when the world was in black and white and you didn't lock your front door at night..."

"Well you're going back tomorrow. If you want I can go in with you."

I couldn't help but laugh. I didn't mean to. "Thanks but I'm pretty sure that won't help!"

"Well just stand up to them then! Now promise me you won't bunk off again." I didn't say anything. "Promise me."

"Fine. I promise. Whatever." I pushed past her to head up the stairs to my room. I knew it was pointless telling her about what was happening at school but figured there was nothing to lose. Nothing to lose, at least, other than my patience. Once upstairs, and in my bedroom, I closed the door for some privacy. I don't know how David does it. He's been dealing with this for months now, I've only had it for a couple of weeks and it's getting to me. Perhaps it's because I am tired; tired of moving around from school to school...Home to home...Tired of the pressures of playing catch up with school work...Tired of having to meet new people and try and make new friends...Trying to pretend that everything is okay, at home, when really...I've had enough of my mum's constant smothering and the fact my old man is never there - always working for the Ministry of Defence...I'm even tired of not knowing, exactly, what he does for a living which causes us to move around so much. I'm just tired. I've had enough. And...I can't believe the school phoned home on my first missing afternoon. So much for escaping from time to time, to get some peace and quiet. I can't have them call home all the time. It'll only cause issues at home too. Then there'll be no escape.

The door opened and Mum came in, "Your friend David is downstairs. Is he okay? His face looks terrible..."

"What?" I jumped off the bed, where I had slumped, and hurried downstairs. David was standing at the foot of the stairs with his face all battered and bruised. "What happened?" I asked.

"I've had enough!" he said before I had even finished my sentence. "I've fucking had enough of it all..." David was getting more upset. It looked as though the only reason he wasn't already crying was because he was so angry. "All of them...I've had it...I'm not going back...That's it..."

"What happened?" I asked again. "Jesus Christ, David...Just tell me!"

"Piers...His friends...They happened. Outside my house, man. Outside my house."

"What about your parents? They didn't see what happened?"

"They're not home. They never get home until later in the evening. They fucking waited for me outside my house."

Mum appeared behind me, "Are you okay?" she asked David.

"No, of course he's not okay. Look at him!" I said. "This is what it's like at school. Those bullies...The ones you said would leave us alone...This is what they do..." I felt myself getting as angry as David. "Come on," I said to him, "you can get yourself cleaned up in the bathroom." I led the way for him whilst Mum just watched, a look on her face which suggested she still didn't get it. I couldn't help but wonder what it would take for her to understand.

CHAPTER 10

"**Y**ou okay now?" I asked David. We were standing outside his front door having been given a lift by Mum. She waited in the car whilst David and I chatted.

"I'm fine," he said. I didn't believe him. I was worried about him. He didn't really seem as though he was there; the lights were on but he wasn't home.

I looked towards the living room window. The lights were on so I guess one, or both, of his parents were home now. "Are you going to tell them what happened?"

"Don't think I can hide it..." His face did look a mess. "It won't make a difference, though. They'll still make me go back tomorrow."

"They don't care?"

"Dad said once that it was deserved."

"What? How?"

"Because..."

"You're gay?" I asked. David didn't say anything but I guessed that's why his dad felt as though he deserved a beating from time to time. There was a slight pause. "You going to be okay?"

He shrugged, "What's the alternative?"

"It'll get better," I said, not that I believed my own words. It has to get better. We don't actually deserve any of what we are being subjected to. David didn't react to what I said. "Well," I continued, "I best get back...I'll see you tomorrow. You never know, Piers and his friends might not show up again…Could be scared you'll get the teachers involved and they'll be suspended."

David shrugged. I turned to look at Mum who was still sitting in the car. I could tell she was getting impatient but hated leaving David like this. I guess everyone has a breaking point and this must have been his. I don't blame him. I haven't been here half as long as him and I'm already close to mine. I turned back to David to continue our conversation but he was already stepping in through his front door. Without so much of a goodbye he closed the door. Maybe he'll be back to normal tomorrow, after a good night's sleep?

I walked back to the car and climbed into the front seat, next to my mum.

"He seems quiet," she said. I shot her a look.

⅄

"What are you doing?" asked Mrs. Price. I was just standing there, in front of the class. My mind was elsewhere. Drifted off for a minute. Disappointed there isn't enough time to deal with them all individually. "We need to get Ben some help."

"He's dead," I said. I didn't even look at him. I could tell he was dead. His breathing was noisy earlier. Now I can't hear it at all.

"You're going to prison…" said Mrs. Price, "for a very long time."

"No, I'm not." I smiled at her and glanced at the gun.

"You killed someone!" she continued.

"So did Piers!" I yelled. "Chloe…" I pointed to where she was still weeping. "Murderer! Lynn…" I pointed to a girl sat towards the back near to where Piers was sitting, "Murderer! Robert…" one of Piers' friends, "…Murderer… John…" another lad close to Piers, "even Ben and Daniel…They're all murderers…The only difference is they didn't pull a trigger."

⅄

Lessons are about to start. The class is quieter than usual. David is doing his usual trick of leaving it until the last possible minute to come to class. There

649

are whisperings from the back row. I can't quite make them out. Something about David. I wonder, after last night, whether he's coming back to class or whether his mum and dad are finally pulling him out of here and sending him somewhere else?

I turned round to look at the back of the class. Piers and his friends are missing again. Same old story with them. They fight with someone and then disappear for a few days. A few days later they re-emerge from whatever hole they crawled into, as though nothing has happened. Pieces of shit. With the mood I'm in, it's probably a good thing they're missing. For what they did last night, I don't think I could keep my calm. It wouldn't be so bad if it were just Piers by himself but...Him and all of his gang? I would have just ended the same way as David did last night.

My attention turned to the back of the class, again, when the door opened. I half expected it to be David but it wasn't. Mrs. Price walked in; a solemn expression on her face. Well, this is new.

The class watched, in silence, as she put her bag by her desk. She looked as though she was taking a couple of minutes to collect her thoughts.

"We've just heard," she said after a few more minutes, "that last night David took his own life..."

⅄

"No one in this class is innocent!" I shouted. "No one!" I waved the gun around at each of the pupils. They tried their best to duck out of the way of the barrel. "Not you! Not you! Not you! No one! You all need to learn...You need to be taught a lesson. The only innocent ones are standing here..." I turned to see David, Lindsey, Elizabeth, Marcus, Samantha, Kate and Helen.

"There's no one there," said Mrs. Price.

"Just because you don't see them, it doesn't mean they aren't there but they're always here. Always walking the corridors where they were tormented for so long...What I'm doing...What I'm here for today. Someone should have done this a long time ago..."

"What you're doing...This doesn't make anything right. This doesn't change anything..."

"It will! Don't you see? People will hear of this. This story will spread across the world...Newspapers, television programmes...A warning to others who may be tormenting colleagues close to them..."

"It won't. You'll just go down in history as another psychopath killing innocent people in their school..."

"Just as David will be another suicide statistic?"

ᛪ

Mrs. Price's short words were all that was mentioned of David in the school - at least in front of the pupils. There were no speeches in the morning assembly, offering people in the same position as David any help. There was no advice for handling bullies. There was nothing. Even the local newspaper hardly went into any details about it when it landed on the doorstep three days after the event.

My mum felt bad for me, as I had lost a friend, but then went on to say she could see it coming. She could see it in his eyes that he was a troubled young boy; a damaged soul. Teachers didn't have much to say either. Apparently David had a history of depression which he brought to the school with him - documented in his file from his previous school. I told them about the bullying but it was, more or less, brushed under the carpet. Piers and his friends, of course, denied everything. What made it worse, with regards to Piers and his buddies, was that every time I looked at them - they were laughing. I'm not sure what about but...Did none of them feel any remorse? Did they honestly believe they weren't to blame for what happened to David?

"What are you doing in here?" Mum asked. I was sitting in Dad's office. An office which was normally out of bounds due to the sensitive documents he sometimes had with him. I could never help but wonder why, if they were so sensitive, he brought them home and, more importantly, what difference it made whether we were allowed in the study or not...It wasn't as though he left them on his desk. They were all locked away in his large wall safe. Speaking of which...I was frantically trying to guess the combination. "I asked you a question." The locking mechanism of the safe clicked open.

Success. Having tried his date of birth, Mum's date of birth, my date of birth...I was surprised when it clicked open on their wedding anniversary. In a world this shitty it was nice to see he still valued his marriage; more than can be said for some couples. Unless, of course, he just doesn't know how to change the combination code now that it is set. "Get away from there...Your father will kill you."

I doubt it. He's never here.

I pulled the door open. There it is. Just as I had hoped. I reached in and took hold of his handgun. His favourite piece to use whenever he is training new cadets. At least, that's what he tells me it's for. For all I know he could have purchased it from the black market just as a source of protection for the house. I wonder if Mum knew it was here? I only knew from when I had seen it over his shoulder.

"Put that down!" Mum said sternly as I pulled the gun from the safe.

"I can't. I need it."

"Need it? For what?"

I just looked at her. She knew what it was for. Did I really have to spell it out? I need it to teach them a lesson. All of them. Just as David wanted to do. I'm doing it for David...

"You're not leaving the house with it," Mum said. She blocked the doorway. I can only hope she isn't going to test me. "You're not taking that to school," she continued - proof that she knew exactly what I wanted it for.

"Yes, I am. I need to show them they can't push people around anymore. I need to show them there are consequences to their actions. They need to know I'm not afraid. They need to know..."

"You're not afraid? Then you don't need to take a gun to school..."

"I need to show them!" I shouted. I could feel my eyes start to well up. "Did you know David wasn't the first to kill himself at my school? There were others too...Others who were bullied like David. The first I have heard of this was yesterday...In the cafeteria...People talking about it...Remembering the others who had taken their lives as well because they were bullied..."

"So you go and hurt the one who bullied your friend?" said Mum. "There will just be another bully further down the line. No matter what is said and done, there will always be someone to take their place."

"There doesn't have to be. I can teach them. I can show them the error of their ways. I can show them. They won't hurt anyone again. They won't. And when news gets out about what I've done...When the news gets out - no one will want to hurt anyone again..."

"You're being silly," said Mum, "the world doesn't work like that."

"It can. No one has tried it yet."

"I'm sorry about your friend. You know I am. If you want to look at changing schools, I'll talk with your father when he calls..."

"What's the point? Every school is the same! I need to do this. Not just for me but people like David...."

"But..."

"Lindsey, Elizabeth, Marcus, Samantha, Kate...Helen...Now David. I found the newspaper reports on them on the school computer. They all killed themselves using various methods. All dead because of bullies..."

"You don't know that, it could have been because..."

"Of course it was to do with the bullies. There may have been something else in their life to upset them too but you know it would have been the likes of Piers who had tipped them over the edge. Every time I shut my eyes I see them standing there. Every time..."

I looked at David and the others. Time was running out. Too much taken up with arguing with Mrs. Price about what I was doing. How wrong I was. I'm not a psychopath. I'm not. I'm the innocent one. David and the other six students...We are the innocent ones...Backed into corners with no visible exit other than what I'm doing here or suicide. I need to do this. Just skip across to Piers. He is the main culprit, in my eyes. Teach him a lesson so harsh the others will learn from it.

This is it.

This is what I've been gearing towards.

Chapter 11

"Enough is enough," barked Mrs. Price, "give me the gun!"

Who does she think she is giving orders like that? She forgets, this is my class. I am the one in charge. She is right, though, enough is enough. I've already passed the point of no return. Now it's time to end it.

"Give me the gun!" she screamed.

I'd never heard my mum shout like that and it took me back a bit.

"Give me the gun!" she screamed again. I went to push past her but she grabbed for the gun. She was screaming for me to hand it over but I wouldn't. For a split second we both danced around the room, fighting over the gun, when suddenly a shot rang through the house - echoing in the small room we were in.

Mrs. Price looked startled as I looked at her down the barrel of the smoking gun. Blood immediately poured from the hole in her chest. She dropped to her knees without another word and then face-planted onto the hard floor. The rest of the class screamed and immediately jumped up from their desks. Someone would have heard that. Someone would be coming now.

It doesn't matter if the sound of the gunshot does attract people. I won't be here. I didn't mean for it to happen. I didn't mean for the gun to go off but I can't stay here regretting what's happened. As I looked down at Mum, who was lying face down in a pooling puddle of blood, I knew that none of this was my fault. I feel numb about what I've done. It's not my fault. None of it. This is their fault. The bullies. Piers. This is his fault. Lessons start in less than an hour. I need to be ready. I only hope I can get this finished before they come for me.

⚔

I didn't care that the class was in a panic. I didn't care that some of them had dared to make a rush for the door. They could go. It didn't matter anymore. All that matters is him...Piers. He is still in the back row of the class. I'm not sure whether he is still too stunned to make a run for it or too stupid. Either way I'm grateful. I didn't want to have to chase him through the school.

I stormed over to where Piers was sitting, smoking gun still in my hand, and grabbed him by his hair. He let out a funny little wail as I pulled him to his feet and marched him to the front of the classroom. By the time we get there, most of the class is empty. It's just me...Ben, Mrs. Price and Piers. Even Daniel managed to get out of the room - no doubt racing off home to brush his teeth and rinse out the flavour of cock with extra strong mouthwash. Fucking faggot.

"You did all this!" I screamed at Piers. "You!"

It didn't matter about being quiet now. I knew they were coming for me. Someone would have called the police by now...Someone would have run to the other teachers. Time is against me.

"Fuck you!" hissed Piers. I smashed him in the face with the butt of the gun and he let out a scream. His front two teeth cracked on impact with the hard metal. That's going to hurt in the morning.

"No! Fuck you! You did all this." I raised the butt of the gun back into the air and dropped it down onto his face once more. A loud crack. Was that his nose? He looked dazed. "Don't you fucking pass out..."

"Stop! What are you doing?" came a voice from the doorway.

I looked up to see the Head Teacher standing there with a look of horror on his face. I pointed the gun directly at him. He put his hands out in front of him as though they'd stop a bullet from flying towards him.

"Tell me about David," I shouted.

"What?"

"Tell me about David...What sort of person was he?"

There was a slight pause.

"He was a confused la...." he started.

I pulled the trigger and he dropped dead. David wasn't confused. David was a victim. We're all victims. "Because of people like you," I said to Piers - the final string of my thoughts coming out vocally.

"Please...Don't kill me..." he said. Have the beatings finally broken him down? Or was it the sight of the Head Teacher and Mrs. Price getting a bullet? This 'hard man' who gives off an image of someone who won't be controlled finally broken? I won't pretend not to be a little disappointed. I was looking forward to hitting him some more but, truth be told, it's probably for the best. I'm pretty sure I can already hear the sirens in the distance.

"I'm not going to kill you," I said to Piers. "I want you to live with this. I want you to live with the knowledge you killed Mrs. Price. You killed the Head. You killed my mum, you son of a bitch, and David. Even Ben's death is because of you. Everything that happened...Your fault. Say it..."

"It's my fault," he spluttered through broken teeth and bloody gums.

"Louder!" I ordered.

"It's my fault," he repeated.

"Shout it!"

"It's my fault!" he shouted at the top of his voice.

"Again!"

"IT'S MY FAULT!"

The sirens are outside now. They're here. That's it. Game over.

"Open your fucking mouth," I hissed. Piers was crying as he opened his mouth. "Wider!" I told him. Broken boy did as was instructed.

Doors are banging against walls in the corridors beyond the classroom. This is it. The lesson has come to an end. Seconds later there were officers standing in the doorway with guns pointed at me. I'm sure there are more, waiting for their turn to take a pop, in the corridor.

"DROP THE FUCKING GUN!" one of them shouted.

I put my head against Piers face so that my ear was level with his mouth. I swear, despite the shouting police, I could hear his fear coming from his body. And smell it. Broken boy wet himself? A smile spread across my face as I placed the gun against my other ear.

I hope the knowledge he is responsible for all these deaths...I hope it haunts Piers for as long as he lives. If he forgets, I hope the taste of my brains, in his mouth, serves as a distasteful reminder. As I ready myself to squeeze the trigger, I only hope the bullet doesn't go through my head, and his too. I can't promise it won't.

If it does, it's not the end of the world. Just his. I closed my eyes and readied myself. This is it. I wonder if it will hurt.

"I love you."

A friendly voice, louder in my head than the shouting police officers and sirens...I opened my eyes. David was standing slightly in front of me.

"I love you," he said again, "always have."

I smiled, "I love you too." All this time and I've only just come to realise I was living a lie. No previous girlfriend because, subconsciously, I didn't want it? I never realised. It doesn't matter now. "I love you too," I repeated. I couldn't help but laugh. All this time I was trying to teach everyone else a lesson. Trying to teach them something, for their lives, and it was me who ended up learning something.

The school, town even, were quick to forget the previous seven who had killed themselves. I bet they aren't as quick to forget the eighth.

I ignored the shouting from the doorway, and squeezed the trigger.

~ FIN

Enjoyed what you have read?
Follow Matt Shaw on Facebook to learn about future releases!
www.facebook.com/mattshawpublications

Printed in Great Britain
by Amazon

61822339R00379